Mortal Friends

Books by James Carroll

MADONNA RED
MORTAL FRIENDS

JAMES CARROLL

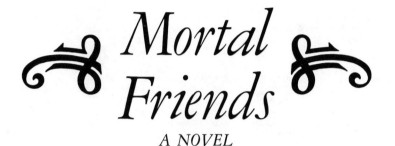

Mortal Friends

A NOVEL

LITTLE, BROWN AND COMPANY   BOSTON   TORONTO

FIRST EDITION

T04/78

Lines from the poem "Easter 1916" reprinted with permission of Macmillan Publishing Co., Inc.,
from *Collected Poems* by William Butler Yeats, copyright 1924 by Macmillan Publishing Co., Inc.,
renewed 1952 by Bertha Georgie Yeats.

LIBRARY OF CONGRESS CATALOGING IN PUBLICATION DATA

Carroll, James.
  Mortal friends.

  I. Title.
PZ4.C3194Mo   [PS3553.A764]   813'.5'4   78-1420
ISBN 0-316-13009-5

Designed by Susan Windheim
Published simultaneously in Canada
by Little, Brown & Company (Canada) Limited

PRINTED IN THE UNITED STATES OF AMERICA

For Lexa

ONE

WHEN HIS RIGHT ARM went to sleep Colman Brady woke up. He was lying on it. He rolled over, held it over his head and shook. The tingling in his hand intensified momentarily, then subsided. What now? he thought. It had taken half the night for him to fall asleep, and here he was awake again. He put his culprit arm under his head and stared at the gray seams of the ceiling.

Colman Brady was a twenty-two-year-old farmer in a small village half a day's horse ride from Clonmel, Tipperary. He never had trouble sleeping, but on this night he had his reason. He was getting married the next day to Nellie Deasy, and he was filled with an unsettling emotion he had never had before and which he could not identify. It was, he thought, the first phase either of panic or ecstasy.

"The hell with this," he muttered, flinging back the blanket. He got up, dressed and went into the snug room where his sister Bea, aged twelve, and his brother Conor, aged fifteen, were asleep.

"Conor," he whispered. "Conor!"

The lad rolled away from Colman.

"Conor! Come with me! Hey, old man! Wake up!"

"What, Colman?"

"I'm going up to the Dolmen. Come with!"

"Now?"

"We'll watch the sun come up like a pair of Druids!" Colman was shaking Conor, trying to infuse him with his eccentric energy. "Come on, chap!"

"Never! Never!" Conor pulled his blanket over his head. It was November. The night air would be cold and wet. They would wreck their feet against loose stones climbing in the dark. "Go away, Colman!" Conor whispered.

"Come, you fearful little Druid Jesuit!"

Colman picked up his brother, a lump of blanket, and slung him on his shoulder like a sack. Conor yelped, "Put me down!"

"You'll wake Bea! Shush!"

At that Bea woke, rubbed her eyes, asking, "What's wrong?"

"We're off, dearie, for a stroll," Colman said, stooping through the low door, holding onto his brother easily. Colman was a large and strong man. Conor was a stately lad, but small for his age.

"Now?" Bea was mystified. "Shall I be left then, alone?"

There was no one else in the house. Their mother had been dead twelve years, since Bea's birth. Their Pa was dead a year. Jim, the oldest of them, was two years dead in the war in France. Their oldest sister, Maeve, was living in the States.

Colman heard the worry in Bea's voice. It hadn't occurred to him that she should come. But why not? The three of them, the night before his wedding, an outing, a lark, their last without Nell.

Colman waved at her to follow. "Come along, love!" he cried. "Come along!"

Colman's excitement caught his brother and sister then, like wind catching leaves. Soon all three were dressed and outside. Typically, Colman had forced his brother and sister into his mood and had forced them to love it. They could barely keep up with him as he crashed across Moore's field and up the steep hill that rose, a tumulus, behind it.

The Dolmen was a great standing stone, an ancient and eerie marker that prehistoric pagans had noted time by and perhaps worshipped on and probably buried their dead under. It looked like an altar for giants, and it was a miracle of lifting and balance. A giant unhewn granite block rested upon two smaller ones, forming an opening beneath the table-stone through which a large man could pass only slightly crouching. Colman and Conor often went there in the summer, sometimes sleeping under it so they could see the sunrise from the highest point in the county.

When Bea hurt her foot on a stone halfway up the hill, Colman swept her up to his shoulder and carried her the rest of the way. She clung to him, her face in his bush of hair. She was delighted and happy.

"You're such a burden to me," he claimed gaily. "You make me old before my time." But it was far from true and Bea knew it. Colman could terrify her, and when he swatted her with his razor strop, Bea hated him and wished him dead. But when, as then, he was affectionate and playful, he was better than her Pa had been and she loved him more than anyone in the whole world.

As they approached the summit of the hill, the black outline of the megalith could be seen against the sky. It was an awesome and mysterious sight. It filled Bea with dread, but she didn't let on.

"We should have a procession," Colman announced. He lifted Bea, readjusting her on his shoulder so that her legs straddled his neck. "Conor, you be my acolyte and go in front." Conor dashed in front of him. "And, love, you be my tiara! Now chant with me!" And with that

Colman began to make a weird throaty noise of the sort monks make at their funerals.

Conor joined in, but Bea remained silent. They proceeded in a circle around the huge stone altar that was bigger than the poultry shed. Then Colman approached it. Bea, on his shoulders, could just see the top of it at the level of her eyes. Colman lifted her and set her on the stone.

"Introibo ad altare Dei," he said. "I will go up to the altar of God."

And Conor replied, *"Ad Deum qui laetificat juventutem meum."*

"The God," Colman translated, "who gives joy to your youth."

"You shouldn't!" Bea said urgently. "You shouldn't play the Mass."

"Ohh," groaned Conor contemptuously.

"It's not mocking, darling," Colman said while hoisting himself up onto the stone. He hauled Conor up in a swift jerk. Then the three adjusted themselves. They were like birds perching. They sat close together, their legs dangling. Colman put an arm around each of them and hugged them. Conor was all right, but Bea, Colman feared, was an intimidated girl. She was afraid of everything. Including the religion. Including the priest.

"It's not mockery to come watch the sunrise — God's masterpiece," he reassured her.

"I hate the dark," she said, snuggling into his shoulder.

"The dark is God's creature too."

She didn't reply.

"Eh?" He pressed for a response.

"Yes."

"Of course it is. Next summer, love, you'll sleep out here the whole night through with me and Conor. Right, Conor?"

"And Nellie too?" Bea asked.

Colman had forgotten Nell, had not imagined that she would be with them then. But of course she would.

"Aye, all of us! Praise God for that!" Colman laughed with his head back, a great roaring laugh that frightened Bea and made her think of the Druid giants who'd built the altar on which they sat.

When he stopped laughing Colman realized that his sister and brother could not understand the surge of feeling that made him brazen and eccentric. He hugged them closer to himself, wanting them to feel the promise his love was making: Nell would make things better for them, not worse. He himself would always be theirs; that is what he would have said if he'd known the words.

Conor thought Colman was going to break his collarbone. He freed himself from his brother's arm.

"Pax tecum," Colman said to Conor. "Peace be with thee, Kipper."

[5]

But Conor did not reply. He was feeling suddenly put upon by his brother and overwhelmed. He wished he'd let him sleep.

"Well?" Colman said. He wanted the Latin response.

"*Et cum spiritu tuo.*" Conor said it a bit broodingly. The joke had paled, but Colman just would not let it go.

Bea was squirming again.

Colman instantly sensed their uneasiness, and it irritated him. His prude of a sister, his mope of a brother.

"You're a moody pair," he said.

Bea felt a rush of misery. His rebuke was unfair. Her eyes filled tentatively.

"This place is beastly and I'm cold," Conor said sharply.

"But we always come here." Colman was shocked at his brother's mood.

"That was before."

"Before what?" Colman demanded.

"Before her."

"Who, Nell?"

Conor did not reply. Colman looked at Bea. "Is that why you're grousing?"

Still they said nothing.

Colman was determined to force it out of them. "What are you, bumps on a log? You can tell me. I want you to tell me."

Nothing.

"You're afraid Nellie will change things, aren't you? Well, she won't. I promise you. She won't."

"She already has," Bea said, and then burst into tears.

The scutter, Brady thought. Serves me right. The ingrates. Here I've been mother and father and feeder and friend!

"Damn right she has! Damn well right!" he exploded. "And about time!"

Bea wailed.

"And you, you calf-nun! Whimper! Whimper!"

Brady slammed his palms down on the stone perch, angry and hurt. His brother and sister, his vestige of family hobbling him with their pouting and brooding and on the night before his wedding! To hell with them!

"Off! Off! Both of you!"

Colman clipped them both with bright vicious blows to the backs of their heads, nearly knocking Bea from the megalith and stunning Conor. Colman took Conor by the scruff of his shirt and dropped him rudely to the ground. "Here. Take your pale-face sister!"

Only a little more gently, Colman handed Bea down to Conor.

"Get home! *Go* to sleep! Sorry to have disturbed you!"

They set off, stumbling loudly down the hill, Bea sobbing, Conor slamming the rocky earth with his boots.

"Druids!" Colman muttered after them. "Damn Druids!"

He had wanted only to sit with them through a night, only to be their benign maternal-paternal brother. But they were ragging spoiled children who were useless on the farm and who continually and repeatedly failed him.

Brady sat on the great balanced stone staring at the black place before him where he knew soon the first gray of dawn would appear.

The Neolithic inhabitants of Ireland occupied the hilltops above the bog and woodland where soil was nearly impossible to cultivate. But on the higher elevations they developed a formidable repertory of techniques not only in farming but in the making of tools and in the building of shrines. In the village below the hilltop on which Colman Brady sat, groups of farmers and herders had lived continually since the New Stone Age. In November of 1920 it was called Four Mile Water, Tipperary. It was four miles from the village to the water of the River Nire, and the land sloped the whole way down the hundreds of feet to the perfect crease of valley cut by the river. When the air was sharp and the day hard, a man could stand on the south portico of the village church and seem to reach past the Nire and touch the Kilworth Mountain Range in Cork, the next county west. To the south a quilt of fields fell away with hedges and the road to Ballymacarberry crossing it like seams. Some days smoke could be seen from the turf plant in Dungarvin, though that was all the way to Waterford. Four Mile Water commanded a view of three counties, seven roads, two rivers, and four little towns. With the priest's glass a man could count forty-seven thatched farmhouses, three churches, and seven cemeteries. If he knew where to look he could see the school and the weed-ridden manor house where Lord Barnes lived before he parceled his estate and returned to England.

On the east the Dolmen hill rose up behind the village, stern and gaunt like the giant Druid priest who'd found the place before the Great Flood. A black breast, ominous, empty. It was a rock shadow over the village, at once enchanting and threatening. Colman Brady was one of the few villagers who loved the place and went there often.

By dawn Brady was still sitting on the edge of the stone, and, though he was staring at the brisk sun, he barely felt the sting in his eyes. Watching the sun come was like watching a ship rise on the horizon, or so he imagined. He had never seen the ocean, but he considered himself an expert on the rising of the sun.

It was, at least on that day, as if it happened for him alone. Perhaps it did, he thought blithely; it was his wedding day, after all.

"In the pink!" he said aloud. "In the pink!"

And he slapped the stone with both hands and vaulted down from it. He stood with his arms open to the earth at its horizon, threw his head back and chanted, *"Ite; Missa est!* The Mass is ended! *Deo gratias!* Thank God!" And then he roared with laughter, glad there was no one there to think him blasphemous.

As he set off for home he felt a twinge of regret at his blows against the kippers. He'd wanted to reassure them that Nellie's coming into their family would only make things better. But instead he'd reinforced their fears. Was that because of his own fear that they were right? Why couldn't he be a bit more gentle with them? Why couldn't they . . . ? Christ! he thought, they're kids! They meant no harm, the pitiful buggers. *Oh, I can mine my feelings endlessly,* he chided himself, *for ways to take offense!*

He leapt and skipped down the dark hill and then kicked his way across Moore's field. He was aware of the morning chill for the first time, and his shoes and trousers were quickly soaked through with water off the autumn hay. Moore hadn't mowed his field yet. Brady snorted with satisfaction that he had already cut his entire twenty acres. He had some of the best land in the parish and he worked it hard. He was the youngest owner in the county, and he felt obliged to prove that he could manage, that he was a worthy heir of his father's land, that despite his years off at school, he was more farmer than clerk. And it was true. He had a good crop of barley and oats, and his dozen cows were in excellent shape. The County Council had asked him to judge livestock at the September Fair, and some of his neighbors were asking for his help, which he was proud and anxious to give.

He stopped at the cemetery and went in.

Colman Brady stood six feet, one inch, in height, but he looked taller there because the dozens of granite markers were squat or fallen. Several Celtic crosses and grand obelisks paid for by relations in the States were scattered in the yard and reached higher toward heaven than any of the local stones, but they too failed the level of Colman's chin. The graveyard always made him feel big and alive.

He made his way through the weeds toward the familiar corner, thinking the priest was a fool to forbid the goat to chew the grass there, as if grass was sacred, as if goats chewed corpses.

J. M. Brady, 1840–1918. The National Land League.

Colman's father had begun as a tenant farmer on the land of Lord

Barnes, whose family seat was in Berkshire, but who owned a large part of Tipperary. Jim Brady was one of twelve Four Milers who'd founded the county chapter of the Land League in 1879. Their purpose was to bring about a reduction of rackrents, to enable tenants to become owners of their holdings after paying a fair rent for a number of years, to promote organization among tenant farmers and to defend those who were threatened with eviction following a refusal to pay unjust rents. Brady himself was able to take title to his own place in 1890, thirty-two years after he had begun working it and just months after Lord Barnes began liquidating his holdings in Ireland for fear of Parnell's Home Rule movement. The purchase of his own land was the hailed moment in Jim Brady's life. The land had been precious to him before; from then on it was sacred.

Jim Brady was fifty-eight when Colman was born, having married very late, and the hard life of hillfarming had made him old even beyond that. But the man had confidence, brain, and temper, which made him formidable even in decline. Even though the village stories about his father always emphasized his youthful Land League days, when he and Davitt and Lyons wrested ownership of the hills from the English landlords, the great age of the man held something awesome for Colman.

The figure seated continually on an upended barrel by the barn had been that of a shaggy-bearded, deep-voiced patriarch who measured shoulder to shoulder several hands and who thundered out orders and instructions as if his sons together could not receive all that he knew. "I know everything!" he would proclaim. "I know everything!" As far as Colman cared or knew, he did.

But Colman's older brother, Jim Junior, seemed not to think so. He could be surly and mean. He and the old man fought viciously, at times bloodying each other. Yet Colman always considered that he himself alone had something to resent because the farm which he grew up worshipping as he never worshipped God was to be Jim's. Primogeniture. Colman was the servant of his own envy. Because his father believed that a man without land had better have schooling Colman was sent off to the Christian Brothers' College in Clonmel, where he studied for five years, mastered Latin, Irish history and the Greek lesson that some victories can be worse than defeat.

10438 Private J. Brady Jr. Irish Guards 2 June, 1918 Aged 22. And in the center of the stone not a cross but the round seal of the British regiment.

Jim was dead before his father.

He had gone off after a particularly terrible bout, in the course of which the old man hit him with an iron spike, thus loosing such rage that the son thought he would kill the father. Instead he joined Redmond's Volunteers, who were showing the King that not all Irishmen were revolutionaries and uprisers.

And then the Kaiser killed him in France.

And not a month later their father died.

Colman left school and took over the farm. He did not feel like an usurper. He felt genuine grief for his brother and his Pa, and he was afraid to be responsible for Bea and Conor. But there was also a justice in the turn things took, for he *did* love the land, and he would keep its trust.

Colman let his glance fall on his mother's tombstone. It was weathered and sinking. He should tend it, he thought. "Ma," he said out loud, "you'd love her. She's just like you."

But that was not so, as far as he knew. He barely remembered his mother. He'd been ten when she died birthing Bea. He guessed she had looked like Maeve. He suspected his mother would have a qualm or two about his marriage. She would want him single yet, alone until the edge was worn from his desire so that when he finally did marry it would be to his hazy memory of her.

Brady crossed himself, touching his thumbnail to his forehead, lips, and breast. "God, Mary, and Patrick bless you all," he muttered, turning. He walked out of the graveyard as away from duty done. But the mood was on him, heavy, sad.

He tried to dispel it, shoving his hands in his pockets, jauntily crossing the adjacent field and even beginning a tune. "A growing moon," he sang, "and a rising sun are good times to marry in."

Even if it was November. It is the deaths of those you love that make you a man. The babe in the bulrushes became Moses, man of stone.

Brady stopped at the edge of Peter Gavin's place. The road dog was barking at one of the Shetlands, who paid no attention. A goat nibbled on the stalks of dead honeysuckle at Gavin's door. In Gavin's yard three cows stood uneasily looking toward the door, waiting for Gavin to come out and milk them. It was obvious from their swollen pendant udders that the cows hadn't been milked in more than a day. Peter Gavin would be more careful of his cows, Brady thought, if they gave whiskey instead of milk.

Colman decided to relieve them.

He leapt the gate and grabbed a wooden pail and seized a pair of teats and began squirting them. Of what you don't want, there is more than man or beast can bear.

"What's this?" Gavin cried from within. After a moment the door burst open. The farmer stood bleary-eyed in a sleeveless rough fabric nightshirt that went to his calves.

"Morning, Peter," Colman said pleasantly from his haunches. He continued to milk the cow.

"What the damn hell is this, Brady?"

"Your cows need . . ."

"Blast you! Don't tell me what my cows need! You get out of here, go on! You choirboy!"

Colman stood and lifted the pail by its handle. He was not going to have a row on his wedding day, not even with Gavin.

"Why, Peter," he said innocently, "I assumed you were sick." Indeed. Sick with the dear, dear rotto. Brady prepared to pour the milk into the large metal jug near the door.

But Gavin lunged at him swinging.

Brady stepped inside Gavin, ducking, turning the other's momentum against him, sending him nose-first into the mud.

"Oh, Peter, did you fall?" Brady's sarcasm went harmlessly over Gavin, who was choking with mud. "Perhaps a pint or two to steady you," Colman said, laying it on cruelly. He poured the rich white milk on the filthy man. "Tend your cows, Peter Gavin," he said sternly. He tossed the pail aside.

Colman leapt the gate and went out across the field toward his own place to tend his own cows. Gavin was made for the mud as far as he was concerned, but he regretted the scene. One's wedding day, after all. But the melancholy that had come over him in the graveyard had blown away like loose ashes. Colman Brady felt properly begotten, and his trek toward home was not the sedate pace of a tired man or the hesitant step of a remorseful one. It was the rolling, jaunty walk of a perfect groom.

2

MAJOR PURCIVAL was brisk and absolute as he inspected the column shortly after reveille. Twenty men, each at attention, rigid and stern, stood in the rectangle between the Barracks buildings and the post wall. Each held a rifle at present-arms and each carried two revolvers — one strapped to each thigh — and two Mills bombs hung at the waist from each man's cartridge belt. Their uniforms were the blue of the Royal Irish Constabulary instead of the proper brown of the Crown military. But they wore the black berets of the Essex Regiment to distinguish them as the Auxiliary Division of the RIC. No Micks, these; no petty police; no motley hybrid; not colonials. They were the King's Own. They had destroyed the greatest military machine in the world. As Lloyd George himself promised, they would have Irish murder by the throat before spring.

They were crack strikers, but their officer was even more than that. Major Edmond Purcival was one of a group of sixteen distinguished veterans — the Cairo Group, as they were called — recently transferred to Ireland from the various colonial outposts to command the new British effort to smash the Irish rebellion once and for all. By November of 1920 the original leaders of the '16 Rising were all dead excepting Michael Collins, the elusive IRA general who escaped in 1917 and whose photograph hung on the walls of the duty rooms in every British barracks, and Eamon de Valera, the President of the Republic, who was in exile in America and, frankly, not expected to return. Collins's army was demoralized and split, while the English, fresh from their victory in Europe, were turning their full attention once more to the IRA.

In Purcival's opinion, the entire job had been botched in Ireland. That was why he would tolerate only professional soldiers in his group; no ex-prisoners, no disciplineless sadists. The Black and Tan motley had disgraced London and, understandably, outraged the local populace. Purcival wanted the sure, trained force of veterans of service against the Hun. Before the Armistice and his assignment to Cairo, Purcival himself had seen fire from the Loire to the Danube. He won the D.S.O. at the Somme and the M.C. at Château-Thierry, and a dozen other ribbons hung on his breast. He neither took his duty lightly nor pursued it carelessly.

Major Purcival nodded. He was a tall man, but he was so thin that he gave on first glance the impression of seeming altogether rather weak. But when he drew himself to his full height and locked himself into the perfect posture of his class and office, all hint of weakness dissolved at once.

"Mount!" the sergeant-major bellowed.

The men scrambled aboard the two armored lorries. Purcival slapped his thigh with his baton, turned about and took his seat to the right of and behind the NCO driver of the Crossley Tender.

He was leading his first sortie out of the RIC barracks at Clonmel, Tipperary. In addition to establishing and maintaining order in the region adjacent to Clonmel, Purcival was to secure the entire eastern half of the province of Munster, including the County of Cork, the East and West Riding, the City of Cork, the City of Limerick, and the County of Waterford as far as Dungarvan. He had spent the first week of his tour on the field drilling his men and at his map board calculating distances and elevations. If his first task was to tighten discipline in his own ranks, his second was to select the strategic sites on which to anchor his roving line of assault.

Beginning with the area around the River Nire he had decided to occupy permanently the pinnacle of the hill rising northward from the valley. From the maps Purcival surmised that a small village with a church and a tavern was on the very site he wanted. The lines and hues of the maps indicated that the village commanded a view across the Nire to the Kilworth Mountains. The main road south could likely be observed much of the way to Waterford. Though he had no military file on the place — it galled Purcival that intelligence was so shoddy, but he had learned in France to jerry-build his information — the civil census told him that the parish and public house were gathering points for no more than one hundred and thirty adjacent farmers. As to the political stripe of the place, he could reasonably expect an absence of revolutionary sympathy, since the Republicans, like European radicals, tended to be urban, educated, and — rhetoric aside — contemptuous of the peasantry. How to humanely and efficiently suppress Irish rebellion; how to humanely and efficiently secure the site for his first outpost — tin-school exercises both.

"Four Mile Water, Sergeant, double time!"

"Sir!"

At Four Mile Water everyone was in the church waiting for Nellie Deasy.

Nellie Deasy was in the room off the vestibule with her father and Deirdre Shea. Bea Brady was standing awkwardly in the corner, holding flowers. Nellie was studying herself in the window's reflection. Her long hair, red and soft, fell in two streams to her shoulders. Her skin was dark and rich-toned against the pure white of her veil.

Deirdre was fussing with the train of Nellie's dress, the dutiful handmaid. Deirdre was her best friend, and Nellie knew that her pinning and unpinning was an unconscious refusal to let things proceed. The great bond of their girlhood was about to be broken. Deirdre was sad.

Nellie was not. Certainly she felt no such sadness in relation to her family. Her father stood, impassive, detached, in the corner opposite Bea. His black suit made him look even more morose than usual. Nellie thought his customers at the butcher shop would not recognize him without his bloody apron, without the gross smell of whiskey. She hated working as a clerk in his shop where the meat was raw and fly-ridden. The smell of guts never left her. She hated life in his house, where it was all shut fists and silence. The silence was broken only by his drunken rages. Nellie's mother had not spoken to Deasy in nearly a year.

When Colman asked Nellie to be his wife she forgot the coy reply she had planned to make and leapt on him repeating, "Yes! Oh, Yes! Yes!" Later she confessed to Colman that she thought her motives were impure, that though she did feel an infinite fondness for him, she feared she was marrying him for another reason. But before she could say, "to get away from home," he broke in on her saying in scandalized triumph, "Simple lust! You want me for my manliness!" When she recovered from her surprise at his response she realized that he had dispelled her qualm with his irreverent thrust. They had laughed then and held each other.

"Ready," the sacristan said.

The pained old organ began forcing out a tune. It was unfamiliar to everyone, and they did not sing. St. Lawrence O'Toole's rafters had never bounced with the singing of its people, and it was no different then. The commotion of the congregation rising from its knees to greet the bride nearly drowned the organ out. Nellie and her father came together behind Bea and Deirdre, who proceeded down the aisle singly, gamely, and too quickly. Patrick Deasy dutifully offered his arm to his daughter, who dutifully took it. As soon as she crossed the threshold into the church proper she began looking for Colman.

He was just coming out of the room behind the Blessed Virgin, side by side with her own brother, Patty. Patty had been Colman's mate at the Christian Brothers' College, and it was through him they knew each other. Both of the young men looked spiffing. Colman was wearing his new suit, a gray pinstripe with waistcoat. His hair glistened and he seemed more strapping than ever, yet elegant with the high stiff collar that served as a shrine for his face.

He looked at her and it was as if he snapped his fingers in the air.

Nellie's father stalled at the head of the aisle. He didn't know how to relinquish his daughter. She was pressing the inside of his arm firmly and seemed unready to move away from him. She was still looking at Colman. Her father was looking at the priest. Colman Brady's eyes went from the priest to his brother Conor, the acolyte, to the butcher, to Nellie. And then he moved toward her, offering his arm. She left her father without kissing him, took Colman's arm, and stepped with him into the sanctuary. The priest made way for the couple, gestured them to the prie-dieu, turned his back on the people, bowed to the altar and began the Mass in Latin.

At the opening phrase, *"Introibo ad altare Dei,"* Colman found Conor's eye and winked. The boy stumbled over the Latin response, cherishing the secret joke he shared with Colman. But he reddened too, remembering the blow Colman had struck him and feeling the hurt of it again.

[14]

The congregation fell noisily to its knees. A bright mood hung tangibly over the people. They stroked the couple with a fond, satisfied gaze. Every wedding, like every birth, in such a small farming village in Ireland was a blow against its greatest fear — that it would end as a barren waste with no youth, no future. "Fewer Irishmen in Ireland," it was often said, "than Redmen in America!" This wedding was particularly special because of Colman Brady, a young man whom the fogies had foreseen gone. He had learning. He had a touch of rebel blood. He had energy and brain. Few expected him to return from the school in Clonmel. They were surprised at the brisk authority with which he had taken over the farm after old Jim's death, and soon they admired his efficient methods and some copied his checkerwork system of planting. Within the year he had been elected to a seat on the board of the Cow Traders Association, the youngest at twenty-one ever to hold the position. If there was a bit of the swagger about him, and if he was less than self-effacing toward his elders, well, the old croppies said, life is the great teacher. The important thing was that Jim Brady's best boy — a strong and not unwise lad — had thrown in for good with his own people. They rejoiced.

For November the day had turned soft and warm. The people milled about the churchyard after the ceremony. Some of the men had begun to drift toward Morrissey's, where the relatives of the bride and groom wouldn't be expected to pay for their first drinks. Some of the women were already in McClusky's house setting out the foods. Children were wrecking their clothes on the gate to Moore's field. The priest was walking through the crowd, black-robed and pleasant.

Villagers were greeting Nellie and Colman.

Boody Desmond, a toothless old goat, the town canker, shocked those who heard him when he offered polite, nearly gracious good wishes to the couple.

"God shield you, Colman, and your Missus."

"Thanks, Boody. Nell, this is Boody Desmond."

"Pleased to meet you," Nell said.

"Are you?" Desmond said suspiciously. "You'd be a stranger. We're not fond of strangers. Be you Jew or gentile, Greek or slave, or what the hell are you?"

"Her pa's the butcher on Wren Road, Boody."

"Where?" he snarled.

"In Clonmel."

"Clonmel, is it? There's a Jew for you!"

"Boody, go on with you. I'll stand you a drink."

"You will?"

"Indeed. Just tell Andrew; go on."

"Thanks, lad. God bless you both." Boody bowed and went off.

"He's our old Yahoo."

"Wait'll Pa hears he's Jewish!" Nellie said, squeezing off a laugh.

"Like Christ himself. And Mary his mother."

"Colman!" Nellie said, feigning shock.

"Tell me, Mary, how to woo thee," he sang.

Nell's mother approached them looking askance. She kissed them both awkwardly, then rushed into McClusky's to weep. Colman drew Nellie to him with his arm about her waist, silently supporting her.

"Brother Christopher!" Colman cried, seeing his old teacher coming out of the church.

"Well, the bridegroom cometh!" the stout cleric laughed as Brady leapt toward him to hug and pound him. "Introduce me! Introduce me!"

"You've met Nell, haven't you?"

"Never."

"Brother Christopher Reed, Nellie Deasy. Nellie is Pat's sister."

"So I understand. A union born of the college."

"By God, you're right! Something else I owe you!"

"Well," the brother said, "You won't be coming back now, I suppose."

"What?"

"For your diploma. Your last course . . ."

"How could I? Brother, you know I've . . ."

"I know it. It's a great regret to me that you couldn't finish. I thought you might live a spell in town and . . ."

"Not for me, Brother, as St. Peter said to the dead priest."

"Colman!" Nell said, squeezing him, reining him.

"I can see you've your hands full now," the brother said.

"Yes, I do," Brady replied earnestly, solemnly. "My duty lies clearly here, Brother . . . with my heart." Colman grasped Nellie again. He could hardly keep his hands away from her.

"Well, I wanted you to know. . . . Miss, your husband was my best Greek student once."

"I believe it, Brother." Nell smiled.

"She thinks it's Greek when I woo her."

"Hurrah for you, Brady," Brother Christopher sliced in, "if you can fool anyone with your Greek!"

"Even me," Nell said, but the brother missed her barb. She did not like the implication that his marriage to her marked the end of Colman's learning.

"*Hoi nebrakada,*" Colman announced, "*Heigh-ho! Heigh-ho!*"

"Indubitably," the brother said. Colman could always win him over. *"Tooraloom* to you both."

The three laughed.

"And this is my chum Eddy, Nell," Colman said, including a pimply-faced boy in their circle. "Eddy Donovan."

"Hello, miss."

"Eddy's my hired man on occasion, ain't you, Eddy?"

"Indeed, aye, Colman. Conor and me, Miss, took in the hay. Two-pence per day."

"Did you buy yourself that fine belt?" Nell asked, nodding at the leather strap that crossed his chest at an angle.

"No, Ma'am. My pa took my pennies. I bought a bun once."

"That's Eddy's Sam Browne, Nell."

"Your Sam Browne?"

"Yes, Mum, I'm in the IRA."

"Are you, then?" Nellie asked seriously. Colman withdrew a mite, holding his smile down. This one was all hers.

"Indeed, I am. Only sergeants and us officers wear the Sam Browne," Eddy said as if Nellie was one of his schoolmates.

"And how goes the Rising?"

"At the siege of Ross, Mum, did my father fall."

Nellie looked at Colman, who shook his head.

"Bad luck," said Nell.

"We've a barricade on Barnes Mount," Eddy said, drawing himself up.

"Good kipper," Colman said, mussing the boy's hair and leaning to whisper at Nellie, "Bockedy Ed. Our *young* Yahoo!"

But the exchange with Eddy was not so harmless or silly as it seemed. The boy, in calling to mind the Rising, had scratched his nails down the slate.

Four Mile Water had never been assaulted by the vicious Black and Tan. Despite an unspecified local sympathy with Irish nationalism, the conflict with the English was remote, especially so since the chief cause for resentment in the region had been removed with the Land Act, which enabled farmers to take over their acreage from Lord Barnes and other owners. Some Four Milers, responding to Redmond's call, had joined the King's Irish Guard at the very time — in '16 — when the Easter Rebellion was underway. Colman Brady, as a scholastic in Clonmel at the time, had harbored a thrill of support for the revolutionaries, but that faded when the Rising lost its momentum as the leaders were jailed or killed and their successors concentrated on the large cities. Then Jim Brady Junior had been killed in France in an English uniform and honored in burial by the King's Regiment. Colman's loyalties became subdued, if not confused. He had come to wonder if his own earlier worship of the heroes of the General Post Office was so different from Eddy Donovan's mindless Erin-huzzahs.

"Where's your rat-tat-tat, Eddy?" It was Peadar Kelley, asking from the edge of the circle around Colman and Nellie. Colman thought the tease cruel. He sent a blazing look at Kelley.

But Keogh, a boy just older than Eddy, picked up the taunt. "He left it in Cork City. Michael Collins is cleaning it for him."

"Lay off Cork!" Brady ordered. Keogh blushed to be rebuked so. Brady was saying "Lay off Eddy," but not only that. Cork was a sorely stretched city just then. Only weeks before, on October 25, 1920, Terence Mac-Swiney, the Lord Mayor of Cork, had died on hunger strike in Brixton Jail in England. MacSwiney's determination in fasting to death had the effect — as he intended — of drawing the notice of the world to the Republican cause. In Four Mile Water nearly everyone had attended the MacSwiney Memorial Mass at St. Lawrence's, and for the first time in several years, the attention and sympathy of the people had been caught and held. The events which followed on MacSwiney's death brought no lessening of worry. Indeed, ancient Irish embers had been stirred, for the news was very upsetting.

Three of MacSwiney's followers were executed without any sort of trial at Dublin Castle. When the IRA tried unsuccessfully to kill Lord Ames, the new commandant of the Cork Auxiliary Division recently assigned to Ireland from Cairo, reaction from the British came almost immediately. Lorry-loads of Auxiliaries drove up to Croke Park on the afternoon of November 12. There a large crowd was assembled to watch a Gaelic football match. The Auxies opened up point-blank, firing into the crowd of men, women, and children, killing fourteen, including one of the players, and wounding many others. Word of the incident had spread like fire all over Ireland, quickening the old anger. But there was no reaction from the IRA.

Colman Brady guessed accurately that the Republicans, after a long series of failures, were demoralized and bereft by the loss of MacSwiney, and by the new efficiency with which the English were prepared to work their terror. He had himself been stunned and enraged by Croke Park, but the orations of his neighbors in Morrissey's pub seemed blasphemous, so safely delivered, so cheaply.

"And leave Collins out!" Patty Deasy said to Keogh roughly. Deasy wouldn't have been more offended if Christ on His Cross had been made light of. Michael Collins was an object of reverence. Keogh was mortified.

"The hell!" a voice barked fiercely.

Everyone turned toward it. Peter Gavin was standing in the road with his fist raised at them. He had been at the juice already and it made him mean.

"Collins'll be off in America," he bellowed, "giving speeches while kids at football get their asses shot!"

"It's not Collins you should be blaming . . ."

"Where's the grand bastard now?" Gavin roared. "Where's the IRA?"

The crowd was silent.

Gavin seemed to snap out of his fit. He turned on his heel and made for Morrissey's.

Finally Nell spoke up. "Your politics were not invited to my wedding, fellows."

"Ah, said like a wife," Colman teased.

"It weren't politics, Nell," Peadar Kelley said, reaching to toss Eddy's hair. "The Sam Browne serves to hold in Eddy's stomach. Ain't that so, Eddy?"

The obvious affection of this tease relaxed the tension and there was laughter and an outburst of small talk.

Colman and Nellie separated, she moving to join the women at Mc-Clusky's house, and he to go off with Patty and Peadar Kelley to Morrissey's.

When they entered the low, dark room a dozen older men who were already crowded up to the small bar happily made room for the groom and his friends. The men had to squeeze their way into the pub, which in fact was the front room of the old Morrissey house, barely big enough for twelve, much less twice that number. But the pressing and crushing added to the charm of the moment, and the spirits of the men were high and light as they pushed toward Dick Morrissey, who had joined his father Andrew in pouring whiskey and drawing stout as fast as he could.

"A drop for the faeries, fellas!" someone shouted. All the glasses went up and tilted slightly, enough to splash a bit of the various liquids out, but in the press none of it hit the floor as tradition required, and the room resounded with laughter. It was the moment the men loved. Their easy and permanent fellowship was the core of life for all of them. The drudgery of tending small herds of moody cows and the bickering of wives and squealing of children cramped in the snugs of sheds, old lofts, and tiny cottages was all outside.

"Here's to you, Colman Brady," old Con Davitt offered. He was the best friend Colman's father ever had and a kind of village elder who commanded the respect of all those gathered. At his voice the talk and laughing subsided and an air of happy solemnity fell over the men as they prepared to join in the toasting of the groom. Since the groom in this case was Colman Brady there was a tangible fondness in the way they looked

[19]

toward him, raising their pints and tumblers. Those nearest Colman cleared a small circle around him, and he stood poised and smiling at his friends, one hand in his trousers pocket. He threw back his head to toss the falling lock of brown hair, and he grinned with delight and embarrassment as the men repeated after Davitt, almost in unison, "To Colman Brady!" And they drank.

"Land without rent to you forever!" cried Andrew Morrissey, the publican. And they drank again.

Colman lifted his pint and drank to that himself.

"A child every year to you, Colman!"

"Like yourself, Moran!" Colman replied, laughing. Kevin Moran had thirteen children and he wasn't forty yet. The men laughed, slapped Moran, and drank.

"Turf for your fire!" And they drank.

"Spite for your devils!" And they drank.

"And Colman —" The toaster now was Will McCauley. He stood with his glass poised, waiting for the attention of the group, which had grown boisterous with each downed glass. When he had the attention, Will said, more seriously than the others, "Here's to a death in Ireland!"

But Colman looked back at him with benign stubbornness. No one drank. They waited for Colman to speak, because his manner made it clear that he had something to say.

"No grief at a feast, Will," he said, grinning. "I'll not be drinking to death today. This is a wedding." There was an instant of silence in which the men were embarrassed for Will. He had meant nothing gloomy. It was a traditional toast. And he hadn't been outside when Gavin had meanly referred to Collins and called the troubles to mind. The jovial momentum of the toasting was broken. But still Colman was smiling broadly. He threw his hair off his eye and reached to McCauley to put an affectionate hand on his shoulder.

"To a *life* in Ireland!" he said and then downed his drink in one toss. An approving burst of murmurs and laughs followed then as the men drank to Colman Brady's improvement on the custom.

"To the woman of your heart, Colman!"

Colman raised his hand, calling for attention again. One of the fellows pushed a fresh jar into his other hand and he raised it to the very rafter of the ceiling.

"To Nellie Deasy!" he said happily. "To Nellie *Brady!*"

"Aye!" someone shouted and several cheered and all downed their drinks and turned to the bar for more. Brady had reversed the tradition — instead of receiving toasts, he gave them.

Dick Morrissey and his father poured out the Bushmills and the

Guinness as quickly as they could. The men began to resume their competing conversations in small groups of threes and fours. But before the amiable chaos had reestablished itself, Peter Gavin banged his glass on the bar repeatedly and then bellowed, "A final toast, fellas! A final toast!" A resisting murmur swept the room briefly, but the noise subsided, and everyone fixed his attention on Gavin. Those who'd been in the circle in the churchyard knew that he was still bristling with antagonism and they feared that he would stir the dust up again.

"A toast!" His glass was solemnly, if not steadily raised. There was nothing frivolous about him as he continued, "To His Royal Highness King George the Fifth!"

The men gasped as one person, and then a growl of disapproval rose from them. Just because they weren't revolutionaries didn't mean they were traitors to the Irish people. They knew Gavin was deliberately baiting them, but they didn't realize how cleverly until he completed his toast.

"And to the repose of the soul of his loyal subject, Private Jim Brady of the Irish Guard!"

The growling stopped. There was no gasping, but only an iron silence as the men stood under the weight of their dilemma, of the cruelty with which Gavin had rubbed their faces in it. They could never toast the King, but they could never think of Jim Brady with anything but love and grief.

"Get out!"

It was Colman.

All eyes were lowered. No one wanted to see the anger on Brady's face. They could hear it in his voice.

"Not until we drink to your brother's courage," Gavin said evenly. "He at least could choose a side."

Half a dozen men separated Gavin from Colman. They tried to move out of the space between them, but there was nowhere they could go.

"You'll not poison his memory with your spite, Gavin."

But Gavin raised the glass to his lips, saying, "Here's to him."

Before he could drink, Colman Brady had moved through the pressed bodies and had seized the glass away from Gavin's mouth, splashing his face. Brady didn't speak, letting his glare say it all.

Gavin wiped the porter from his face. He dropped his eyes and moved off, squeezing his way toward the door, mumbling, "No disrespect . . ."

He slammed the door behind him.

The silence in his wake lasted only for an instant, for Dick Morrissey hollered, "Here's to Michael Collins!"

"No!"

It was Brady again, and he was stiff with fury. No cheap toasting!

He handed his glass and Gavin's to the men at his side and pushed his way out of Morrissey's, leaving the group confused and miserable.

The sun had broken through the clouds, warming the day, making it more like April than November. The women took that as a sign of Mary's favor and had decided therefore to set the food on tables in the yard. Cloths were spread. The few pieces of Waterford in the village had been loaned and were out, filled with jams and preserves. Nellie's father had carried two whole yearling lambs and a suckling pig up from Clonmel in the back of his small truck, and they were on the spit by McClusky's wall. Nellie's mother was supervising their turning and basting. Other women retrieved from their houses the breads and cakes they had prepared. Everyone moved quickly, efficiently, yet with distinct care not to soil their good dresses. More than one wife wanted the food ready soon enough to draw her man out of Morrissey's before he had imbibed too much on an empty stomach.

Father Devine was sipping sherry from a teacup that Marie McClusky had provided him without comment. He was seated in a straight-backed chair to the left of the long table, just out of the way of the women who shuttled in and out of the houses. It was he who noticed Gavin storm out of the pub and away into Moore's field. When Colman came out, Father Devine waved to him.

"The groom himself," the priest said, raising his cup, a little toast of his own.

"A bit early for tea, I'd have thought, Father." Colman spoke with broad and affectionate irony. Everyone knew the priest had a fondness for sherry, but he kept it in bounds and loved to joke himself about his custom of drinking from a teacup. He would never drink at the bar in Morrissey's, but the men were thankful he wasn't an abstaining Pioneer like Father Curtin in Ballymacarberry.

"You know me, Colman. Tea anytime."

"Indeed, Father. It picks a body up."

"You were efficient enough with your own drink, I'd say."

"I thought I'd see if I could be of some use."

"The ladies . . ." Father Devine didn't finish, but only nodded toward the bustling women at the table. They didn't need any help at all. Certainly not from a man.

"Yes," Colman said, taking in the scene. Mrs. Deasy put a platter of fresh sliced lamb on the table, and Colman helped himself to a morsel of it, drawing a rebuke from his new mother-in-law.

"Not yet, Colman Brady. You'll be called."

But Colman had it and retreated, licking his finger as he sat on the wall near the priest's chair.

"What happened?" Father Devine tossed his head toward Morrissey's. "With Peter Gavin?"

"You'll have to ask him, Father."

"I'm asking you."

"I know you are." Colman smiled, dispelling the hint of haughtiness in the priest's manner. Colman was not going to tell him. Once that became clear, they relaxed. Father Devine knew that Colman Brady paid him proper if minimal respect, but he was not one of those who squirmed before priests or who laid resentment thick with piety.

"The weather turned out nice, eh?" the priest said.

"Indeed. Lovely. A grand day for a wedding."

"Nellie's people seem nice enough."

Colman hesitated. "Her pa's a butcher."

"I gather."

"Did you meet Brother Christopher?"

"Aye. He's inside. Says you were an exceptional student."

"Between you and me, Father, I squirmed myself raw in his Greek class."

"You never learned your Latin, did you?"

"I did. *Ad Deum qui laetificat juventutem meum.*"

"But do you know Caesar's *Wars?*"

"A pagan, Father?"

"The Church permits it, Colman, as you well know, for the purpose of developing the mind."

"Well, in that case, I'll take Boccaccio."

"You know he's forbidden."

"But he was a Catholic."

"A filthy, perverted Italian."

"And Caesar?"

"A noble general, Colman." Here the priest paused, found Brady's eye and held it. "Like our Collins."

"Caesar is dead, Father."

"But 'honored in his death,' as Shakespeare has it."

"Perhaps," said Brady, but he was thinking that was Brutus, not Caesar.

" '*It is more worthy to leap in ourselves than tarry till they push us.*' " The priest sipped at his teacup, satisfied with himself. Then he lit a cigarette.

"A justification for suicide, as I recall, Father."

"I was wondering what you thought of Collins, Colman."

" '*This was a man!*' "

[23]

"Was?"

"Well, I admire his eluding the Brits. But to tell you the truth, Father, I'm afraid it's lost as far as the army goes. There's little enough honor in defeat. None that I see in pursued futility."

"Futility, thy name is Ireland."

"Talk is cheaper than ale, Father. That's what I think. I'm inclined to hold my tongue on the subject."

"I've noticed."

"We're not serfs here. We shouldn't seek to be whipped like them."

"So you're a Tory?"

"Come, Father. You know the Bradys. It's only that I believe more in victory than I do in tragedy. Force against force only when you've a chance."

The priest considered Colman silently.

"A penny for your thoughts," Colman said after some moments.

"My thoughts are for Michael Collins. I pray for him daily." The priest knocked an ash from his cigarette and faced Brady. "You know, Colman, the likes of Collins are given to the human race only rarely. Ireland has had its share of heroes, but mostly because they were dead. Collins is alive. He worships his men, which is why they do him. He embodies the hope of Ireland. Don't you see the symbol of it, son? Collins eluding the Brits is like Ireland after four centuries still refusing the English yoke. Futility? What's futile is England's effort to enslave us. And that's what a free and living Michael Collins demonstrates, which makes them want him all the more."

Colman Brady was surprised when the priest stopped talking because his words had seemed so earnestly delivered, so deeply felt, like the beginning of a sermon. "It's a little soon for hagiography, isn't it, Father? Where Collins is concerned?"

"You're not as indifferent to the man or his cause as you pretend."

It was true. The legend of Collins, especially when evoked in its mythical shrouds, had an enormous effect on Brady. Michael Collins was large in just the way that all the other men Brady knew were small. Brady already wanted one thing above all else — not to be small like them.

"You're not indifferent," the priest said, "to Croke Park."

That also was true. The slaughter enraged Brady and revealed to him the depth of his own hatred of British terror. But he resisted that emotion, would not admit it to himself, much less to others. "No, Father. I'm not indifferent to Croke Park, nor to the Rock of Cashel nor the bog of Allen. It's all green Guinness, Father. I don't think of it. And I don't think of Saint Michael with the price on his head. My thoughts are for twenty acres and twelve cows and Four Mile Water and two kin and one wife."

The priest snapped the butt of his cigarette away. He put his teacup down and faced Brady. "I've been meaning to say something to you, Colman. You've influence in this village beyond your years. If we had a mayor it'd be you soon enough."

"We needn't a mayor, Father, as long as we've a priest."

"If your pa were here, lad, your streak of rudeness would be less broad."

"If my pa were here, you'd be getting less butter for your fish. What did you want to say to me, Father?"

"A word about the love of your country . . ."

"You'd like us going off to war bearing palms and harps and swords and olive crowns singing *Gloriae* ahead of you beneath a canopy of gold cloth woven over with *Erin go Bragh.* It's mean and bloody scut, Reverend. Don't wish it on your parish in the name of your nation."

"That'll do now, mister. If you'll not be subject to the spiritual authority of the Church even on the day of your sacrament, don't blaspheme your martyred countrymen by such puffery."

"I mean no disrespect, certainly not to them. But there's a green fog over the whole subject. I didn't want to hear pub-talk from you."

"You won't, son, believe me." The priest drew himself up. "Sorry I presumed to talk to you at all." He turned like a rock off a pole and made for his house across the way. Colman watched him go, not understanding how their banter had become bitter so suddenly.

The bile of this war; the island will sink in it.

Brady strode across the dusty yard to McClusky's house, looking for his wife.

"Nellie!"

"Hold that fellow!" she called from the tiny pantry off the kitchen. She came out to him. Her long white dress was protected by a full checked apron.

"Why aren't you having your toasting?" she asked.

"We had it."

"Already?"

"I married you, not them."

"What's wrong?"

"My corns!" he said pettishly. "I must sit somewhere."

"Corns! What corns?"

Colman threw his head in the direction of the pub. "Barleycorns. Your new neighbors."

"I like the ladies well enough," Nell said cheerily. The little house was abustle with women.

"Can we sit?"

"Upstairs?" She lifted her eyes to the ceiling.

"Why not?"

"Babies, I think."

"Better them than the biddies."

She untied her apron and dropped it on a chair. Taking Colman's hand, she led him to the narrow staircase in the parlor corner.

They trod the stairs lightly and went into the bigger room, McClusky's bedroom. Two bassinets were crowded between the large bed and the far wall. Colman sat on the near edge of the bed. Nellie peered at the sleeping infants.

"Moran's kipper," Colman said.

"Aye. And Cunningham's."

"You learn fast."

"You think?" she said, pleased. She sat by him and lifted his trouser leg a bit. "Do you really have corns?"

"No." He unfastened his waistcoat. "Corns on the humor perhaps."

"Meaning?"

"My curt neighbors pinch me."

"Oh, and you . . . ?"

"Pinch back."

"Leaving marks, I reckon," she said, pinching him on the flesh at his ribs, showing him her tongue.

"Hey! Be careful of that!" He pulled away.

"Lower your voice. The babies!"

"Let's go off. Let's go home, Nell."

"We can't."

"Pity. Irish beekeepers below."

"What's bothering you, Colman?"

"*At the siege of Ross my father did fall.*"

"You're being vague and irascible."

"Am I now?" he said, offended. "To be less vague I'd have to raise my voice."

"Colman, was it that Gavin from outside?"

"Yes. And I tackled Father Devine."

"Why?"

"He's a disappointed bishop."

"He regards you fondly. I can see it. So do the others."

"Gavin hates me."

"He hates your youth and your success. He envies you the respect of your neighbors."

Colman eyed her with a suspicious glare. "You think I'm daft, don't you?"

"I think you're a man who has his reactions. Which is why you're a gallop to keep up with."

"I'm not running from you."

"That's what makes me special, I think."

"It is."

"That and . . . this." She put her mouth on his in a lush, exotic kiss, while he felt with his hands for the cut of her breast beneath the white silk.

"You're beautiful," he said.

"And you've interesting prospects."

"Indeed, I do!" He played with the hooks along her spine. "Very interesting!"

"You are the pulse of my heart, Colman."

"*Cuisle mo croí.*"

"And in Greek?"

"Heigh-ho! Heigh-ho!"

Nellie covered her face, laughing. Colman stood and drew her up after him. "We must be . . ." He gestured with his head. "The biddies."

"The beekeepers," she said, composing herself.

"The honey," he said, stroking her hair, pushing her gently through the door.

3

MAJOR PURCIVAL ordered his party to halt.

He stood, pulling himself up over the edge of the windscreen. He put his binoculars to his eyes, brought them into focus, and stared at the great tumulus that rose up from the summit of the highest hill across the valley.

Perhaps a mile, he thought.

He focused on the large stone formation on the pinnacle.

"I wasn't briefed on that, Sergeant. What is it?"

"Pagan antiquity, Major. The region's full of them."

Second-rate Stonehenge, he thought.

Purcival lowered his binoculars to find the tower of the church. A stand of trees prevented his seeing the base of the building or the handful of cottages that he knew were nestled in its shadow. The only movement was the stirring of the trees' gaunt branches. By November all the leaves had fallen, but the cluster of trunks was enough to obscure the village. He let his glass drift across the ridge. There was an orchard of fruit trees, bleak, sterile, to the south of the tower.

He could just make out the peak of a thatched roof. A chestnut tree stood alone below the orchard, its branches supplicant. A road wound its way down the hill between hedges leading to a low farmhouse. Purcival could see a naked trellis by its door, but there was no movement.

He raised his glass to the ridge again and slowly retraced his way back up to the megalith. He saw a slab of stone on two uprights. The structure resembled a large square-cornered mushroom, but with an aperture under its crown. It was the highest point in the region, and it stood starkly black against the sky. Eerie. It would make the perfect site for his first outpost. The surrounding geography was just as he'd anticipated. Even with inferior maps, he'd mastered the scope of it.

The major was well prepared and, now, satisfied.

He continued his surveillance.

To the north of the church tower and down the hill slightly was a point where three distinct fields met. A dozen cows were grazing. Perhaps two dozen. At the near side of the largest field was a farmhouse. It too appeared deserted. Purcival was surprised that he could see no people. There should have been people in sight. He lowered his glass and considered that.

Then he raised his glass for a last look at the Druid stone. Eerie.

He steadied himself against the windscreen and, without looking at the driver, said, "Move!"

The small convoy wound its way slowly toward the summit of the hill. The soldiers were relaxed, lounging against the wooden slats of their lorries. The major in the lead car couldn't see them and they could risk dispensing with the rigid, nervous, and somewhat false alertness he insisted on. The soldiers knew, if the major didn't, that the Irish in the area were intimidated and subdued. After patrolling the terrifying roads of the Continent in the war, duty in Ireland was like a holiday. Though a man could die of tedium at times, it surpassed the other alternative, a return to civilian life and unemployment lines at home.

The children were the first to see them. The coming of an automobile of any kind was an event of importance in their lives. When Patrick McClusky, aged seven, ran past the bend in the road by the chestnut to retrieve a ball, he was transfixed by what he saw. The Crossley Tender looked like a monster to him. It was the color of mud and a vertical pipe was spewing out black smoke. The low roar coming from it made him think of an angry bull. He was joined by several other lads, who stood there with him, stunned, watching the thing come closer. Then they turned and ran as fast as they could. Patrick slipped and fell and got up, giving not a thought to the damage he had just inflicted on his Sunday pair of pants.

"Ma! Ma!" he screamed, crashing by the food-laden tables and into the house. "Soldiers! Soldiers!"

The bustle ceased. The women froze.

Everyone had the same thought: Black and Tan! They drew their beige shawls tightly around themselves, hiked their heavy homespun skirts, and moved tentatively to the window, where they crowded to see and to comfort each other with nearness.

Dick Morrissey, breathless and flushed, came to the door. "It's true!" he said, "They are coming here!"

"Black and Tan?"

Four Mile Water had been exempt, but all knew the verse and rhyme of a dozen horrors inflicted on like villages all over the south by the ex-criminal sadists and brutes of the English special squads. The McCluskys had cousins whose village, Ballynoe, had been plundered. There had been raping, though no one spoke of that openly.

"Black and Tan?"

"No," Morrissey said, going off, "blue. RIC."

"Thank God! Thanks be to God!"

The women began filing through the door into the yard to see. The Crossley was just pulling up in the little square in front of St. Lawrence's. The men had poured out of Morrissey's and hovered back of the tables in the yard.

Colman Brady went to one of the tables and took a mug and dipped it into a pail of milk, scooping up a portion. "Easy," he said in a low voice to those around him, "easy." He took a piece of cut cake from the table and handed it to Will Moran. "Eat," he said. "Here!" He picked up the plate and passed it around. The men took slices of cake. Brady took a drink from his mug, leaving himself a white moustache. "Just be easy," he kept repeating. "Don't quake."

Father Devine was standing by the church hedge. Two lorries had rolled up behind the armored car, from which the officer, standing, was speaking in a loud voice.

". . . Auxiliary Regiment," he was saying, "of the Royal Irish Constabulary."

Auxiliaries! Croke Park!

The officer wore a holster with a weapon in it. He was holding a baton under his arm. The troops in the lorries were standing, rifles at ready.

Brady, still holding his mug, made his way through the crowd to a place by Father Devine from which he could nearly touch the officer's vehicle. Nellie joined him there, took his hand. The scene seemed liturgical with her formal white dress, Brady's high-collared waistcoated suit, the priest's cassock, the officer's uniform, the rapt congregation.

"In the name of King George the Fifth, Sovereign Ruler of Britain, Scotland, Ireland, and Wales, be it hereby proclaimed that the hamlet known as Four Mile Water, Ballymacarberry, County Tipperary, Greenwich coordinates eight point three four seven by five two point eight one aught, the Royal Ordnance Survey of nineteen seventeen, is forthwith requisitioned for the uses of His Majesty the King."

The man stopped speaking. Very few of those who'd heard him understood what he'd said. The words were unfamiliar and his accent was strange. When the silence made it clear that he was not going to continue speaking, there was a nervous shifting in the group and some cast sidelong glances toward Father Devine.

Finally the priest spoke. "Begging your pardon, sir, but what you just said, what would be the meaning of it?" Father Devine had been one of the few to understand the announcement, but he could not believe it.

"Good-day, Reverend," the major said. He assumed an altogether different air then. While not nearly informal, it was considerably less terse than the proclamation had been. "I am Major Edmond Purcival."

The priest nodded, but did not speak.

"You are . . . ?" The Englishman let the question hang.

"Raymond Devine, Parish Priest."

The people sensed that Father Devine was nervous, perhaps intimidated. They were not accustomed to hearing him questioned.

"I wish I could say it was a pleasure to meet you, Reverend, but I am afraid the circumstances of my visit are not happy ones. Four Mile Water — an enchanting name, I might say — together with the adjacent four hundred acres of land, has been designated a military security zone."

"By whom?"

"By myself."

"Why?"

"That is an inappropriate question."

The major stood square against the authority of the priest. The people were astonished, and they began to be afraid. Most of them had never seen an Englishman up close before. This one frightened them.

"I presume, Reverend, that you . . ." Purcival hesitated, choosing his words, ". . . are the person in authority here."

"I am."

"Then it is your duty to see to the evacuation of the village and the adjacent properties, which must be vacated in three days, at which time they will be occupied by forces of the Crown."

"You mean . . . move?" The priest was incredulous.

"Exactly."

"Everyone?"

"Yes. And the livestock. And personal property."

"But this is our home. These people . . ."

"You will be allowed to return when the area is redesignated for civilian population. In the meantime, I assure you, all property will be respected and maintained."

"For how long?" Father Devine asked.

"That is an inappropriate question."

"But . . ."

"You are in authority, Reverend. You will be responsible for the evacuation of this area by noon on November seventeen, three days from today."

Colman Brady released Nell and stepped a pace forward. His right hand was in the pocket of his trousers. In his left hand he held the milk mug. "The priest has charge of our souls, Major. But not of our land."

"Who are you?"

"Colman Brady, farmer."

Purcival nodded toward the driver, who withdrew a pad and pencil from the flapped breast pocket of his tunic. Colman noticed, stepped close enough to touch the Tender, and leaned toward the NCO.

"B-R-A-D-Y," he spelled.

The driver wrote, looked up at Colman, then at the major.

"We have charge of our own land here," Colman said. He spoke pleasantly, as if he assumed there'd been some mistake in the King's paperwork. "Indeed, it is so by order of the Crown itself, whose Land Reform Act of aught six makes us responsible to remain here. It would be derelict of us to leave."

"You misunderstand, Brady. I am not here to debate with you. I have come to give you seventy-two-hour notice of land and property requisition as required by the martial code."

"You trying to say we have to leave Four Mile!?" Dick Morrissey shouted from the crowd. There was a murmurous second to the question.

"Who asked, please?" The major was polite, ominously so.

"I'm asking!" Will McCauley shouted defiantly.

"And you are . . . ?"

McCauley looked at the driver, whose pencil was ready to note his name. He did not answer.

"Are you burning our houses?" It was Marie McClusky. *Croke Park!* was in her voice. *Black and Tan!* was in her voice. The rape of her cousin was in her voice. Panic coursed out from her and set young Patrick to sobbing into her apron. Other children began crying audibly.

"Your property," the major said, "will be respected. However, if the village and all fourteen farms within the boundaries of St. Lawrence O'Toole's parish are not voluntarily evacuated by the appointed time they will be forcibly so evacuated. In that circumstance there will undoubtedly be consequences for property and for persons. Do you think your parish understands me, Reverend?"

Father Devine's eyes were cast down. He glanced at Brady. The priest did not speak. Taking a hint from the clergyman's look, Major Purcival said, "You, Mr. Brady. Do you understand me?"

"I do." Colman stared at Purcival, showing him nothing.

"Then I can assume your neighbors do."

"I'll never move!" Will McCauley shouted. "You go to hell!"

"Seize him!"

At the major's command one of the two lorries emptied of soldiers. Eight men encircled McCauley, while two grabbed him from either side. The ten troopers in the other truck all had their weapons trained on the crowd. Major Purcival glared at Brady.

"What is his name?"

"Ask him," Brady answered.

"I'm asking you."

"I know you are."

Major Purcival snapped open his holster and leveled his pistol at Colman. There was an audible gasp from the crowd, which, as if one person, retreated a step. Eddy Donovan tried to hide behind Dick Morrissey, aching with fear that the soldiers would notice his Sam Browne.

Because the major was standing up in the Crossley, the gun barrel came to the level of Brady's eyes, but the Irishman continued to stare at the officer's face.

"My name is William McCauley!" a voice cried out.

Purcival looked toward Will.

"McCauley?" The Englishman returned his pistol to its holster.

"Aye."

Major Purcival turned slightly to his right and raised his arm, pointing to a farmhouse on the edge of a small field a hundred yards past the cemetery. "That is your house, is it not?" A test of what his maps had told him.

"Aye. And my father's before me and my son's after me. We're not moving!"

McCauley's resistance, even in the grip of the soldiers, stirred the crowd. A few men nodded and muttered their approval.

"Burn it!"

The second lorry, still holding its contingent, shot into gear and past the Crossley, down the road and over the worn cowpath that led to McCauley's house. The lorry jerked to a stop and the soldiers swarmed out of it into and around the house. Jerry cans of white liquid were splashed about and then, before the villagers could comprehend what had happened, McCauley's house was aflame in a burst and the soldiers had retreated to their lorry, which roared back up the hill to its place by the Tender.

Will McCauley was limp with shock between the Tommies as he stared at his burning house. The thatched roof sent a torch of red fire and black smoke into the sky, and the odor of burning straw filled the air. There were squeals of livestock running in all directions. The same animal panic had the children, who screamed and hid by their fathers and mothers. But the men and women of Four Mile Water were silent. All of them were staring at McCauley's, except Father Devine, Colman, and Nellie, who had come to his side. The three of them were staring at Purcival; Nellie with horror, the priest with disgust, and Colman with an open effort to see weakness in the man.

"Wednesday at noon, then," the major said. With the barest nod he ordered the soldiers around McCauley to remount. McCauley slumped to the ground when they released him; he wept in defeat. The major slapped his baton against his thigh, commanding the driver to move. But then he held his hand up, and the driver waited in gear.

Major Purcival looked down at the priest. "You may resume your . . . *fête champêtre*. What is the occasion, if I may ask?"

"A wedding," Father Devine said.

Purcival looked at Colman and Nellie, who were holding on to each other. He nodded at them, touching his baton to the edge of his beret. "Congratulations."

"Thank you, Major," Colman said evenly. "Same to you."

Purcival led his convoy off.

Within an hour of the departure of the Auxiliary force most of the Four Mile men had retreated to Morrissey's and were desperately drinking. They had been unable to douse the flames on Will McCauley's house and it had burned to a shell. McCauley himself had regained his composure and, with his wife, was trying to comfort his children. A group of women had gone with Father Devine into the church to pray the rosary. Brother Christopher was shepherding the contingent of lads he had brought up from the school into the wagon. He wanted to get them back to their dormers safely.

Patrick Deasy had his daughter firmly by the arm and was screaming at her. He was trying to haul her into his truck.

"You'll do as I say. You're returning to Clonmel with me, your ma, and your brother."

"I'm not," Nellie retorted. "Let go of me!"

"Don't you pull away from me, girl!"

"You're hurting me!"

"You're not staying here!"

"I am!"

Brady was coming up slowly from McCauley's when he saw the butcher strike Nellie.

"Deasy!" Colman shouted, breaking into a run. But Nellie's father ignored him and struck the girl again, knocking her against the wooden wheel of a wagon. Colman hurled himself against the older man, sending him sprawling into a hedge.

"You son of a bitch!" Colman cried. "You've done that for the last time!"

"She's coming with me and her brother!" Deasy said, recovering.

"She's mine now! You leave without her."

"The soldier said . . ."

"Damn the soldier! She stays."

"None of you can stay!"

"That's a decision for us to make. You're welcome to leave."

Patrick Deasy brushed himself off, glaring at Colman. Nellie stood alone, apart from both of them, unable to distill the rage from her humiliation. They made her feel like one of their animals, as if the butcher were fighting the farmer over a side of beef.

Mrs. Deasy was sitting in her place on the bench of the truck, stoic and patient as the machine itself. She had been endlessly through it all. She refused to take in the fact that her daughter, still able to generate such fierce emotion in Deasy, had defeated the man in exactly the way that he, years before, had defeated her.

Deasy focused his glare on his son Patty.

"Get in," he barked.

"I'm staying. They need me."

"Damn you to hell, get in that truck!"

"No!"

Deasy went at his son. Colman stepped back, knowing that this at least was not his.

Patty Deasy stood his ground before his father. His fists were raised and he was ready to strike the man. He felt an immense calm that it had finally come to this. Perhaps that is what the elder Deasy saw, for suddenly he stopped. He lowered his arms and unclenched his fists. A look of pure amazement crossed his face.

"Well," he said, "King bloody George is welcome to you." His glance swept to his daughter and Brady. "The lot of you! Don't come looking in Clonmel for a cozy roof and a warm fire. The devil take you! And the English!"

The villagers who witnessed the terrible scene watched as Patrick Deasy drove his modest lorry furiously down the hill, past McCauley's smoldering ruin, around the first curve, and away. Brother Christopher led his dray out of the shade by McClusky's barn. It was filled with schoolboys and the shopgirls who'd come to dance. They were all grave and unhappy, oblivious to their stained clothing. They were boys and girls on opposite sides of the wagon as if the nun had been there. It was a rare chance to rub up against each other's bodies, as if by accident, but they would miss it.

Brother Christopher looked mournfully down at Colman from his perch.

"Listen, what he said about Clonmel, that isn't . . ."

"I know, Brother." Colman said.

"We can put up thirty, maybe forty, at the school. And there's the parish hall."

"Thanks, Brother. We have to talk it over here. We'll let you know."

"Colman," the brother said, instructing him suddenly, warning him, "those Brits . . ."

"Yes?" There was respect in Brady's voice. He gave the brother profound attention, partly from habit, partly from the certainty that he was the smartest man in the county.

"They're Auxies, Colman. They're Auxiliaries."

"I know."

"They're not like the others. They're the honest-to-God real thing."

"I know, Brother."

Brother Christopher nodded. He snapped the rein at the pair of horses, jerking them into motion. As the wagon went by the church, Father Devine and three women were just coming out. They waved to the young people and watched them go.

Colman turned to Nellie, who still stood apart from him. She was shivering.

"Well," Colman said tentatively, "Mrs. Brady."

"Yes . . ." She dropped her eyes. "Thank God."

He would have gone to her, but the priest interrupted.

"Colman, I want a word with you."

"Father," Colman said. He touched a forefinger to his forehead, a hint of deference. "Can it wait a bit? I was just about to lead my bride to her new home, before she had to leave it."

"It's about that I wanted a word."

Colman tugged on his waistcoat. "Father, this is . . ."

"It won't wait, no. Come with me."

The priest turned abruptly and strode into the church, a cavalcade of one.

Brady was startled by the priest's command. It cut through him, through the numb shock that he shared with all the others.

"I'll be just a minute, Nell," he said quietly and followed the priest in.

"Well?" It was all the priest said. He waited for Colman to speak.

Colman shrugged. "God help us."

"That's not what I expected to hear from you."

"Oh? You expected a battle cry? *Fuit Ilium?* Coriolanus? Charge of the bloody Light Brigade?"

"I expected your anger to be at them, not at me."

"My anger, Father, is not at you. It's at the lambs we are. We have no choice but to go off meekly, while we can. We're lucky the bastard gave us a warning."

"You don't really feel that way!"

"Of course I don't!" Brady said, raising his voice, slamming the back of a pew. "Of course I don't! But what can we . . ."

"We can stay."

"That is the most bloody stupid thing I ever heard. Forgive me, Father, but it is."

"I forgive you."

"Suppose you tell me what you think then."

"We have three days."

"And about that many weapons — including my brother's Hun Luger — and a group of terrified ragtag farmers."

"I'm going to Cork, Colman, to stay the night with Father Anthony Rowe."

"Yes?" Back to the bird nest, these priests.

"He is the chaplain to the West Cork IRA. He knows Collins and Barry, is in touch with them both."

Brady did not reply. Father Devine obviously was not having happy-hunting-ground fantasies.

When it became clear the priest was waiting again for him to speak, Brady asked, "Why are you telling me?"

"Because I think someone should convene the vigilance committee. And you're a member."

"The vigilance committee! That's to keep mad dogs off the sheep."

"Well?"

Brady looked at him carefully, aware of the incongruities. The priest was sixty years old at least, a small fragile-looking man whom the ladies catered to and the men avoided. He combined an obsequious fawning manner with officiousness in the way peculiar to clergy. But when his back was up he could stare down the statues in his church.

Brady felt a tremor in his hands, a gap in his stomach.

"What could Collins or Barry do?" he asked, but his mind was turning, considering possibilities. A thin line of perspiration had broken out above his brow. He withdrew his handkerchief and wiped it away carefully.

"I don't know, Colman."

"I'll tell you what we'd need, Father. We'd need backup. Perhaps we could risk something straight on, a shocker Wednesday. But we'd need a way to get by Thursday and Friday, with what came next. Alone, we'd have no chance of keeping them off our hill, but if there was . . ."

"I'll tell them that."

"You tell them there are men here who would gladly take the bastards on. I would. But we'd need a glimmer of a chance. The Brits have left us be to now. Maybe we could give them reason to leave us be a while longer. Quench their bloodthirst somewhere else."

"Else than Ireland!"

"No, Father Devine. Else than Four Mile Water. The hell with Ireland."

"You've peculiar loyalties."

"I'm loyal to what and who I can see and touch. If Collins can help us stay on our land, I say, 'Up the IRA!' If not, the hell with him too."

"You've cold blood in your veins, lad."

"Which is why you asked me in here, no?"

"It's your pa's blood, that's for certain. Brady brains and Brady stomach have held us hostage before. This place is all the Ireland either of us need worry over now."

"My point, Father, exactly."

"You'll wait then, before leaving?"

"Yes."

"And gather the boys?"

"No point to it until you return. There's nothing to discuss without word from Collins or Barry."

"But keep them from leaving."

"Can you return by noon tomorrow?"

"Say two."

"All right. We'll meet them. Whoever's game."

"You must ask them yourself. If they hear it from you they'll know it's not frivolous."

"From a cynic like me."

"That's not what I meant. Don't buckle so, Colman, beneath my report of their respect."

"Theirs?"

"Are you so starved a man that you need me to say it too?"

Colman did not answer. Parish clerk, he thought, dropping his eyes.

"Colman?"

"If there was a hair's chance of stopping them and surviving to celebrate for more than an afternoon, I'd be ready."

"Will McCauley was right," the priest said.

"He was right and he was stupid."

"Yes. That's why I asked you in here. We want your brains."

"I said 'if.' I for one will not offer myself, my family, or my home in a blaze of defiance for poetry's sake."

"Yours but to reason why."

"Among other things, yes."

"*That* is why I asked you."

"Alas for me."

"Time will tell. Meanwhile, we're agreed about tomorrow?"

"Yes."

"Good. I'll be off, then. Good luck here."

"Good luck *there*. Tell them we want assurance, solemnly vowed support, and a sensible plan if they expect fight from us."

"I will. I agree."

Father Devine offered his hand to Brady. They shook, both aware of their new and urgent partnership.

Outside, Nellie was staring across the valley toward the Kilworth Mountains. She wore a heavy wool cape. Colman approached her quietly.

"As we were saying . . . ," he began.

She faced him. "Not many brides are left waiting at the church *after* the wedding."

He laughed, but she, more aware of the rue in her statement than the wit, did not.

"Not many brides have the enemy as guests either," he said. He felt unfairly put on the defensive.

"That will do, Mr. Brady," she said. "Take me home."

"All right, Nell," he said quietly. He took her arm and turned her. They walked together up the road.

In front of Morrissey's pub Peadar Kelley came out and stopped them. "Colman!"

"How goes it, Peadar?"

"A sea of drink. Whiskey speeches. Defiant today, gone tomorrow."

"Who can blame them?"

"Will you come in?"

"No." Brady still held Nellie's arm. She was staring at the dirt. "We'll talk later."

Kelley eyed them. He picked up on their mood, the tangible sadness. It was their wedding day the Brits had ruined. He had forgotten.

"And Peadar . . ."

"Yes?"

"Leave the stuff alone."

"I know."

"And get Dick and Patty and Moran. Tell them to save their thirst for the thunderstorm."

He turned with Nell and walked the road out of the village toward his farm and, now, hers.

4

FATHER DEVINE made his report the next day immediately upon his return. He tugged continually at the folds in his soutane, and his eyes darted around the small room at Con Davitt, in whose cottage they were meeting, at Peadar Kelley, Richard Morrissey, Colman Brady, John Moran, Jack McClusky, Will McCauley, his brother Tom, Francis X. Landers and Terence Murphy.

"I met with Barry himself and with Riordan," the priest said. Tom Barry was commander of the Cork Flying Brigade. Sean Riordan was executive officer to General Collins himself. "And they said Purcival's coming here was providential."

"For Purcival or for us?" Moran said.

"Let him talk, John," Landers said.

"For Ireland," the priest replied firmly. "They said they've been waiting for just such a turn as this. The Volunteers have been laying back for an opportunity to hit the Brits in force, and they think this is it."

"They're coming here?" Jack McClusky asked. There was relief in his voice, the hope that the IRA would defend the village.

"No," Father Devine said, "they plan to attack the Barracks in Clonmel while Purcival is up here. I'm afraid the first volley is ours."

"We hit Purcival," Colman Brady said, "and they hit the Barracks. Then what?"

"Then the Brits in Cork move to Clonmel to reinforce, and they hit them. Collins himself will lead the attack on the Cork Division."

"How do you know that?" Brady asked.

"I talked to him."

"What, to Collins?"

"Yes. On the telephone. Barry rang him up in Dublin. General Collins devised the plan." The priest stopped. The men were as impressed to hear it as he was to say it. "He told me that all Ireland was looking to Four Mile Water. He told me to tell you that we — the men of this village — have his admiration and his esteem."

Francis Landers exhaled audibly. The sound expressed the feelings of the group. They were amazed and flattered. For a moment no one spoke.

Then Colman Brady said, "Admiration and esteem aren't what we were asking for, Father."

"I know, Colman. I told him. I told him we wouldn't make a move without the assurance of support."

"Well?"

"He gave me his oath. General Collins gave me his oath." The priest paused to let the weight of that settle. "He said the British would be too busy defending their camps in Clonmel and Cork to give a further thought to us. We'd be off the hook."

"All we have to do is take on that Purcival?" McCauley said. His voice snapped with hatred, and the men remembered his home in flames.

There was another silence.

"We'd be choked," Landers said at last.

"Not if Tom Barry was here and his boys," Morrissey said.

"Barry won't come up till after the ambush," the priest explained again. "The first row needs be ours. The Volunteers will cover us in Clonmel."

"What about weapons?" Moran asked.

[40]

"You'd be on your own," Father Devine explained. "Half the IRA uses broom handles for guns."

"I've a shotgun," Peadar Kelley put in, "and so do half a dozen other fellows."

"Shotguns are useless past ten yards," Moran said. Contempt, despair, fear could be heard in what he said.

"So," Colman Brady said, pausing, harvesting their attention, "we'd have to get that close to them."

"Are you in favor of it, Colman?"

"I think we could stop them. Once."

"Riordan and Barry say that's all they'd need."

"And then the bastards would leave us alone," Moran said, nodding. There were murmurs, approving and hopeful.

Colman Brady was sucking on his blackthorn pipe. He took it from between his teeth and exhaled a cloud and turned to the old man in the chair next to him. "What do you think, Con?"

"I wish your Pa was here, Colman. He'd know what to do . . ."

Con Davitt had been one of the leaders of the land reform movement at the turn of the century. He had had his taste of victory over the English. He had been the chairman of the vigilance committee for years.

"But I reckon . . ." His voice went flat. "You'll have to do for yourselves."

Several men dropped their eyes. Davitt himself turned his attention to the small fire at his feet. The turf logs were burning smartly.

Colman touched him. "It's all of us together in this, Con," he said quietly, "or no one."

"I'm afeard of them, Colman." The old eyes brimmed. A line of spittle fell down his chin.

"Good!" Colman said boldly. "We all should be afraid of them. It's harps against the Empire. Any man who is not sick to his heels with fear right now is of no use to us."

"If I was you," Davitt said, "I'd go to the States or Australia. If I was young."

"Would my pa go, too?"

"No. Your pa . . ." — Con looked up at Colman fiercely — ". . . would make them work for it!"

Colman nodded.

"He'd hit them before they got here Wednesday!"

Colman nodded.

Con Davitt looked around the room. It was hushed. No one had yet ventured to describe what they might actually do.

"He'd hit them on the road someplace!"

"We'd need a good plan," Francis Landers said.

"We'd need to organize ourselves better, I think," John Moran said. He was a large red-bearded man and he spoke with authority.

Father Devine nodded. "Tom Barry said we should have an elected leader."

"Who'll it be?" Moran asked. "No offense to you, Con."

Con Davitt smiled and some of the men laughed nervously.

No one spoke.

It seemed to some that Moran himself was waiting to be nominated. But no one looked at him. He was a man you could trust to drink too much. When he drank too much he turned moist and soft as kidney pie.

"It should be Colman Brady," the priest said.

"Aye," Dick Morrissey put in instantly. He'd been about to say so himself.

The men looked at Colman.

Colman shook his head. "You wouldn't want it the way I'd have it. The only way."

"How's that?"

"Absolutely. This committee would be disbanded. I would devise the plan and make assignments as I saw fit. No one would participate who was unwilling to submit to me in everything having to do with the defense of Four Mile Water. Anyone who agreed to participate under this condition and who then disobeyed during the course of the action — I would kill him."

Colman paused, waiting for a shudder to come over him. Even as he spoke with crisp, sure authority, the words shocked him. He had no idea where they had come from, but he knew that they were absolutely necessary and exactly right. He did not shudder.

"That's a harsh way to put it, Brady," Moran said.

"It's harsh business."

"We should keep the committee," Francis Landers said.

"You think the Brits run it by committee?" Colman asked.

The men were silent. The inexorable logic of Brady's proposal sank in on them.

"You feel up to it, Colman?" Moran was obviously looking for an opening for himself.

" 'Up to it'?"

"You might be . . . a bit young . . . for the others."

"I don't relish the job. Indeed, I don't want it. I'm simply willing to go by the judgment of this group. But if it *is* me, this group must then go by mine."

"Or you'll kill us."

"In point of fact, John, it won't matter whether I do it or the Brits do it."

"Colman's right," Peadar Kelley said. "If we can't match them in discipline, we can't match them."

The group was silent again.

"So?" Colman said at last.

"Yes," Peadar said.

Several men nodded.

"I say yes."

"Aye," said John Moran.

Relief crossed the group like wind grain.

"Yes, Colman," the priest said, settling it.

"All right, Peadar, you have your pencil?"

"Yes."

"Make a list. These men, as well as Tom Gallagher, Joseph Sheehan, O'Brien, Malloy, your cousin Teo, Manning, and Ed Donovan."

"Eddy?"

"No. His pa. Eddy's a boy. But we could use his Sam Browne."

Some thought Brady was joking, and they laughed.

"You can't exempt the boys," Moran said. He had three adolescent sons himself and thought they would serve well.

"No exemptions, John. There'll be something for the lads. But the heart of it is ours, and the men I've named. For now speak to no one else."

"What about Peter Gavin?"

"No. Gavin will be with the lads, if at all." Colman remembered their exchange the day before and added, wanting the men to understand it was not personal, "Gavin is even more of a lush than . . . Father Devine."

The men roared with laughter and the priest blushed furiously.

When the laughter subsided, the tension was tangibly lessened.

"Walter Lyons will want in, Colman," Con Davitt said.

"He's too old, Con. He's seventy-four."

"He's a better man still than half you named, Brady! He was worthy of your pa's respect. He's worthy of yours!" Con checked himself and lowered his voice. "Besides . . . he's younger than me . . . and I want in."

The function of the silence was clear; Davitt was waiting for Brady to accept him.

"All right, Con. That's it. Who can get Will Reilley's shotgun?"

A man raised his hand.

"And Burke's?"

Another.

"And Dougal's?"

And a third.

"All right. We'll meet on Sander's Hill at sunset. We've two days to become what we aren't and don't want to be and must for God's sake become. Now if you'll all stand, perhaps Father Devine would be good enough to lead us in making our vow of strict silence . . . and yours of obedience."

Nearly sixty hours later, shortly after one o'clock Wednesday morning, Major Purcival was reading the intelligence report on Four Mile Water. The village had been totally vacated by sunset the day before. His spotters had observed the two-day trickle of herds and wagons down from the hill into the valley. Most of the people had put up with farm neighbors in the parish of Ballymacarberry. Some had gone as far away as Dungarvan, and a few had been taken in by citizens of Clonmel. The priest was reported to be en route to the bishop's house in Kilkenny. The potential troublemakers, McCauley and Brady, were both reported to have transferred their livestock across the Nire at the Mission Ford.

Just as Purcival had anticipated, the operation was proceeding in order. He knew the routine well, having supervised the evacuation of eleven comparable villages in Flanders and Normandy. The methodical, exact procedures of the military code always accomplished their purpose if carried out with firmness. The random terror of Black and Tan hooligans stiffened resistance. Proper operations with a precise but deadly minimum of force preempted it. The regular military would not only be more humane in putting down Irish rebellion, but more effective.

Major Purcival decided to alter procedure to a minor extent.

Since the rush of pleasure that came with command-in-action would not subside that night, he decided to lead the occupying party up to Four Mile Water himself. Ordinarily the brigade lieutenant would do so, but he would indulge his restlessness this once, even though the operation would be uneventful.

Purcival decided to try to sleep again. He switched off the light in his office and returned to his quarters. An hour or two was all he needed.

Meanwhile, Colman Brady's breathing was steady and slow, but Nellie knew he wasn't asleep. Her ear was against his breast just above his heart. She could hear it beating out of pace with itself. They were lying together on a bed of hay in the loft of Tomas Macken's barn. It had been after midnight when Colman had finally arrived. She hadn't seen him since they had left Four Mile Water by separate roads Monday afternoon after he had returned from Con Davitt's place. She knew without his telling her what he had been doing, but she felt her first great disappointment in him that

[44]

he had not confided in her. She knew he would be leaving her again before dawn. She didn't know what else to do than hold him with all her strength.

Colman's mind would not stop. He knew he needed sleep, and he was trying to force it to come. He had not slept in two nights, but the images kept flashing before him. He saw the road again, the place just south of the bridge over the Nire. It was eerie country, where the heather grew sparsely in bogland that sloped down to the river. The only cover was provided by outcrops of gaunt rock. At a distance there was a low ridge marking the boundaries of the area. He wondered for the hundredth time if he had chosen the right place. He saw the faces of the men looking strained and frightened as he pushed them through the drill for the tenth time. Everything hinged on timing: on the gate falling at exactly the moment, on each man knowing his part and sticking to it.

But no; everything hinged now on fortune, on the Brits halting at the precise spot, on there being only two lorries full, on their surprise, on *their* loss if only for an instant of composure and poise. Colman had lied to the men, telling them the troops were green, boys, easy to scare off. He had lied, saying the plan could not fail, no one would die. But now he found it impossible to lie to himself. The plan was more reckless than bold, more desperate than daring. It was insane; a few farmers, old men, shepherds with bird-guns, shovels, axes, and blackthorn sticks taking on veteran soldiers. It was insane; their leader a terrified newlywed whose meager knowledge of the tactics of ambush derived from rabbit hunting — a little bait, a big trap, swiftness was all. Brady saw the face of Major Purcival, a battle-hardened, certain, decisive officer who knew exactly what to expect from the worthiest military foe. But Colman's every instinct told him that was the British weak point, the Irish hope. A few jittery farmers in backwash country couldn't have been less military, less worthy. Purcival knew they would have to be insane to defy him, senseless to attack him. And *that,* Colman assured himself for the thousandth time, was why the plan was so sane, so sensible.

"Colman?"

"Yes?"

"Are you all right?"

"Yes."

Nellie Brady knew that if she was to be the perfect Irish wife she would never ask questions of her man directly, never voice her doubts openly. But she did not want to go so easily into resentment. She did not want the silence between them to become a weapon.

"Are you going to tell me?"

"What's to be gained?"

"What's to be lost if you don't."

"It's better you not know."

"It's better you tell me facts, Colman. Otherwise I'm a victim of my dreams. I'm thinking the worst."

"The worst is true."

"You're going soon, aren't you?"

"We meet at four."

"How many?"

"All the men."

"And Patty also?" The only two men she loved, her husband and her brother.

"Yes. And Conor."

The image of the eerie place on the road flashed before him then and he saw dozens of boys and old men standing on the ridge and on the gaunt outcroppings of rock, each holding a stick made to look like a rifle, each back from the road far enough not to be seen closely, far enough to have a chance if things went wrong.

Nellie tightened her hold on Colman. Her heart was matching his in pounding.

Neither spoke again until she said, "I saw the gun."

He stiffened. "You opened my sack."

"Yes. Where did you get it?"

"It was wrapped in the tunic of Jim's uniform with his helmet; souvenirs that came home with his corpse from France."

Nellie had never heard him speak with such subdued bitterness. It was more like him to rant. His tight, suppressed emotion frightened her. He was coiled like rope, like wire.

"There were no bullets," he said, "but for the one in his heart, of course."

"Oh, God, Colman," she cried into his breast, "I hate it."

"You shouldn't have looked in my sack."

"You were telling me nothing."

"Now you've pecked it out of me, are you pleased?"

"I still don't understand. You can't possibly think . . ."

"Do you think I've coal for brains? The main assault will be in Clonmel. An IRA attack. We're just picking off the scouts." When he put it that way, it didn't seem so insane. Don't make it worse than it is! "By noon, it'll all be over. I'll come back here for you and Bea and we'll be home by night."

"I don't believe it."

"Would I lie to an Irish faerie?" He pressed her, hoping to dispel her mood.

[46]

"No. But you wouldn't take one into account if she wasn't of interest to you at the moment. It's as if we never married."

"I did not arrange this circumstance, woman!"

"But you chose right enough what's important to you."

Colman shot up out of the straw. The hole he left in it swallowed Nell up so that he couldn't see her.

"I chose none of it!" He hissed at her. "It chose me!" He clawed the straw away from her and grabbed her high on the shoulders, near the neck, and shook her, swallowed himself by anger.

"Choke me, you bastard! Choke me!" she urged.

He slapped her face.

They both froze. It was his first blow against her. She eyed him coldly. She had been through this before, if not with him. Her first large step toward that infinity of passive wifely scorn had not been so difficult to take, after all.

"Nell, I'm sorry."

"Yes. Aren't you."

He rolled back down into the straw beside her. They lay still, not touching, each waiting for the other to sleep. Then it was time for him to go. Her eyes were closed and she was not moving. Her breathing was steady. He left quietly, gratefully pretending that her pretense at sleep had fooled him.

So that day began with two acts of counterfeit. There would be more.

One occurred shortly after dawn. The last thing Purcival expected to see on the road was one of his own men. As his open car came around the first bend south of the Nire, he saw a private soldier, not an RIC Auxiliary, but an honest to God Tommy with a trench helmet and regular army tunic and Sam Browne belt. The major ordered his driver to slow down as they approached the uniformed figure. He stood in the road just past a gate that was overgrown with heather. Purcival was alert, squinting at the man intently through the haze of first light. The sun had not broken through the mists of daybreak. It was the sort of sight one had learned to expect in France as straggling, fleeing, or misplaced soldiers had dotted the roads throughout the campaign.

But this was Ireland.

It was like an apparition.

Purcival unsnapped his holster and let his hand rest on the butt of his pistol as the Lancia touring car came to a halt by the soldier. The Tommy had a cigarette between his teeth and was slouching with his hands hooked loosely behind his back. No bearing. No pride. He reminded Purcival of all the deserters he had shot.

"Good day, sir," the soldier said, not removing the cigarette, not saluting, stepping toward the car.

The first lorry was screeching to a halt directly behind and the sound of it set off the alarm in Purcival's mind: don't let the convoy stop! But before the major could order the driver, and even before he could draw his pistol, the man wearing the army tunic was on the running board and the snout of a German Luger was pressing against the flesh of Purcival's left cheek.

"Move and you're dead!"

Purcival froze.

The driver froze.

As the man reached across him to take his pistol from its holster, the major saw the insigne of the Irish Guard on the breast pocket of the tunic, and below it a Flanders ribbon and below that a bullet hole. He saw that the man's helmet was rusted and knew it for the war souvenir it was. Then he saw that the man's face was familiar. It was the farmer, the groom, Brady.

The lieutenant in the first lorry had seen what was happening, and he blew his whistle furiously. The ten soldiers in the truck flung back the canvas flaps and began leaping over the slatted sides. As they did so, the timber gate overgrown with heather five yards directly behind the lorry crashed to the ground. Two ranks of men, four kneeling in front, five standing immediately arear, pulled the triggers on their shotguns, and the blast slammed the leaping soldiers back against the truck. From the opposite side of the road half a dozen men armed with pitchforks and axes swarmed around the lorry, hacking at the soldiers, seizing their rifles and hurling them into the ditches.

The second lorry had come only a little way around the first bend before it had stopped. The Auxies leapt out, led by their officer, and sprawled on the ground, firing away. By then several of the attackers began to return their fire, using the soldiers' own weapons. Brady's shotgun section, each of whom had carried his second shell between his teeth, was reloading and firing toward the second lorry one at a time, according to the plan. The noise of the shooting was such that it was impossible to tell from the road that the dozens of figures who then appeared on the rocks and the ridge beyond were aiming sticks, not rifles.

Colman Brady had the major's own pistol against his cheekbone now.

"Surrender!" he screamed. "Surrender!"

"Yes," Purcival said, terrified. "We surrender!"

Purcival stood, pulling himself up at Brady's direction, turned back toward the awful scene and blew his whistle sharply three times, the signal for cease-fire. The gunshots died down, and all was silence except for the terrible moaning of the wounded. Everyone was crouched, seeking what cover he could find. Only Brady and Major Purcival remained exposed.

"Tell them!" Brady hissed.

"We surrender!" the major yelled.

Some of the Auxiliaries threw away their rifles. The section of four men, carrying shotguns, who had been drilled to do so, began moving among the sprawling soldiers, hurling their weapons to the others in the ditches.

Colman saw a figure coming down from the ridge, running in a crouch. At first he felt fury that anyone from that section should approach the road. Then, when he saw it was Eddy Donovan, he felt panic.

"Eddy! No!" he ordered.

But the boy ran onto the road. One of the soldiers who had hurled away his rifle raised his revolver and aimed at Eddy. Colman tried to get off a shot with his own gun, but it was too late. Eddy's face was red and destroyed, and the firing began again. Two of Brady's men fell in the road. One of them, he saw, was Patty Deasy.

Major Purcival seized the rifle that lay between the driver and the shift handle, but before he could aim, Brady had turned back. He shot the officer through the forehead with his own pistol and then the driver through the trunk of his body.

"Fire! Fire!" he yelled, furious.

The men stood firing the weapons they had seized until they advanced to within ten yards of the Auxiliaries.

"There are no good shots or bad at ten yards," Brady had told them repeatedly. It was so.

The enemy, most of whom were mercilessly exposed as they sprawled on the open road, began to shout again, "We surrender!"

Brady saw them writhing with their hands outstretched toward him. The soldiers cried, "We surrender, we surrender!" and were pleading with their eyes. They were pleading with him. That was what seized Brady. They were beseeching him, waiting for *his* mercy, *his* compassion, *his* restraint. But he had none to give them. An omnipotent fury unleashed itself as if from another man's breast, not his. Colman Brady shouted, "Keep firing on them! Keep firing, Number Two Section! Fire! Fire! Fire!"

And the boys did.

Brady's command triggered a spasm of killing. He watched the bodies of the Tommies jump with the force of bullets from their own weapons.

"Fire!" he yelled, the fever of it on him. The British Empire was at his feet and he had nothing for it but an appalling and — to him —

startling act of punishment. He would never be the same and he had the mad feeling that neither would Britannia. Finally there was no movement from the Auxiliaries, and Brady at last called, "Cease-fire!"

There was an uncanny silence as the sound of the last shot died away. No one was moaning.

Colman ran the short distance to where he had seen his men fall. Con Davitt lay in his own blood, dead. Patty Deasy was next to him, also dead. In the ditch, Richard Morrissey lay, eyes open, mouth agape, face as though fixed on the low clouds. He was dead. Farther down the road, Eddy Donovan's body was tangled with the bodies of several Brits.

"Section One!" Brady shouted. "By the drill!" The men who'd borne the shotguns began rapidly collecting the arms of the dead soldiers.

"Section Two!" he ordered, and two teams of four men began dousing the lorries with paraffin to make them ready for burning. The men had been standing amid the carnage dazed, too shocked to move. They responded to Brady's orders gratefully, as if released from a trance.

Old Walter Lyons approached the body of Con Davitt and he began to weep audibly.

Colman put his hand on the old man's shoulder. He couldn't allow this open expression of grief, not then. "Walt," he said softly, "do you feel up to going for the priest?"

"Yes, Colman, yes." Lyons straightened himself and stumbled off as quickly as he could toward Sander's Hill.

By then the ridge section with their painted sticks had moved timidly down to the road. Some of them walked as if asleep, hypnotized by what they saw. The strain was too much for one lad, who ran off screaming. Ed Donovan was on his knees, trying to free his son's body from the English corpses it was entangled with. He let out a loud screeching wail when he saw the red pulp where Eddy's face had been. He crushed his son against his chest, groaning loudly, rocking with grief. His collapse set off several others. Boys and men were weeping openly.

"Form your lines!" Brady barked. He would not allow them to crack. He learned instantly the military lesson; he could not allow them to feel the horror of what they had done. They would go mad. He had to make them feel the *order* of it, the rightness of it. He would offer them the refuge of discipline. He took for himself the refuge of power.

"Form your lines!"

The men fell into three columns. Brady hauled Ed Donovan away from his son's body. He ran up to Peadar Kelley, who was weeping uncontrollably, and slapped him fiercely.

"Your line, Kelley!"

Peadar moved dumbly into his section.

"Count off!"

The men began reciting their numbers, but Brady yelled, "Louder!" and they began again. When they came to the dead men's numbers, Brady called them out himself so that the rhythm wouldn't break.

When the counting was finished Colman harshly reprimanded the men, stalking about, ordering them to correct their posture and straighten their lines. Then he commenced to drill them, forcing them to march up and down the road.

The lorries were now ablaze. Like two huge torches they lit up the dull countryside and the corpse-strewn bloody road. The sun had not broken through the gray mist and the night seemed to linger.

Colman Brady could not look at the men as he marched them up and down endlessly, waiting for the discipline to grip. Conor was among them, but Colman showed no sign that he was his brother, who, for his part, marched the drill sternly, not seeking out Colman's eyes, not wanting to see what was there.

IN THE DAYS following the ambush the people of Four Mile Water found themselves bound together by the cause of their survival.

They were isolated from neighboring villages whose people were shocked and frightened by what they had done. Everyone assumed that the English retaliation would be swift and brutal.

The IRA was nowhere to be seen. The IRA promise had not been kept. The barracks in Clonmel had not been attacked, and the British force was at full strength, less the two squadrons slain in the ambush.

Wednesday passed and the English did not come.

Thursday passed.

By dawn Friday the tension in the Nire valley was unbearable.

The people were organized in groups to be ready for the raid and they expected it constantly. There were three sections of riflemen alternating guard, each composed of twenty men, most of whom had never fired such a weapon. In practice they could only mime the act of shooting because the captured ammunition was so precious. There were four sections of scouts, mainly boys and girls, commanded by the teenagers who had participated in the ambush. They roamed the countryside in a quilt of patterns that made it impossible for the English to approach the Nire in force without being seen. Sections of women headquartered in McClusky's sewed sacks morning, noon, and night, which were then filled with dirt and hauled up to the main lookout at the Druid altar and to the barricades in the village center between Morrissey's and the church. The pub itself was locked; the church was always open.

At dawn on Friday everyone but the sentry teams filed into St. Lawrence's to attend Father Devine's Mass.

Before the service started Colman Brady slipped into the sacristy and watched silently as the priest donned his vestments.

"Father," he said finally, drawing close to him, "we must have a word."

"About the dead?"

"No. That's settled. No funeral until . . . We can't risk the . . ."

"What then?"

"Where the hell are your IRA Volunteers?" he whispered fiercely. "The Barracks wasn't hit last night."

"Colman, I don't know. Is there any word from Cork? Was there a battle there?"

"Who knows? We're lucky to have word from Clonmel."

"The people are getting anxious."

"Indeed they might. They're sitting ducks. They had *your* word that they were not alone."

"I had Collins's."

"Well, if this war was fought with solemn oaths instead of the blood of boys we'd win it hands down, wouldn't we?"

"Don't raise your voice in here."

"You may get your bevy of martyrs yet, Father."

"You sound like a man about to lose himself, Colman Brady. You should consider your words and your actions very carefully. Don't be indulging the luxury of your indignation now."

Brady felt the rebuke's effect. The priest was right.

"Well, Father, we'd better pray that our lads get here before theirs do."

The priest picked up his chalice and covered it with the silk veil. He faced Brady, who was standing squarely in his path. "Indeed," he said. "Let that be our intention for this Mass. Now, get out of my way."

By midday a gloomy stillness settled over the Nire Valley. The anticipation of an IRA assault on the British outposts had been replaced by a fatalistic expectation of an English reprisal.

The alarm went up at one o'clock.

Teresa Dunn saw a pair of men on horseback coming up the road from Ballymacarberry. No one she knew owned such fine horses as they rode, and she could tell from a distance they were strangers. One of them wore a white dustcoat, the tails of which flapped along behind.

"The Brits!" she screamed at her brother. "The Brits!"

Hugh Dunn ran from his post all the way up the hill to the village.

By the time the horsemen pulled their mounts up outside the dirt-sack barricade, there were twelve rifles and three shotguns trained on them.

"Good day to you, friends!" the one in the dustcoat cried.

No one appeared. No one answered.

"Is there a public house here where a fellow could wet his beak?"

Colman Brady stepped out from behind the McCluskys' wall. He was holding a shotgun, ready with it. He spoke sternly: "Move on. The pub's closed."

"Could it be opened for a grand Irish thirst?"

"You are either very ignorant or very foolish. Move on!"

"You're Brady then?"

"Who are you?"

"Mick is my name. Mick Collins."

Brady did not move. He channeled his effort into discerning the emotions he felt at that moment — a sudden sweeping awe, an uncertainty, a rage. He held himself perfectly still as if the first motion would unleash what he was feeling. Heads of villagers appeared at windows and from behind the hedges. He studied the man in the dustcoat. He had a striking physical appearance — huge in the saddle, burly, blond-haired. His stare was a match for Brady's. There was an air of perfect confidence about him.

"Collins, I said."

"I heard you."

"This is Sean Riordan," Collins said, gesturing to his companion. "My exec."

Father Devine appeared from behind the shrub by the church. He nodded.

More people showed themselves. They gawked at Collins, Michael Collins! He did exist! He was in their village!

"Put your gun up, Brady."

Brady was refusing to admit his own awe, his own surprise. "Your orders are about two days late, General."

"My orders are never too late. Put your weapon up." Collins gunned him with his stare.

Colman recognized the iron in Collins's command. It was the same iron with which he, Colman, had spoken that week. Perhaps Collins had more of it. Perhaps Brady was too new at it. He broke the barrel.

"Now," Collins said, "for that pint."

"I told you," Brady said. "The pub is closed."

Collins exchanged a look with Riordan, then asked, "Who closed it?"

"I did. There's no drinking here until this business is resolved."

"At last," Collins said to his exec, "the real thing."

"Don't take more satisfaction than you should, Commandant," Brady said. "The publican was killed Wednesday because he was fool enough to believe in your solemn oath."

Father Devine took a step toward them. The people shuddered and averted their eyes. How could Brady say such a thing to Michael Collins?

Collins stared at Brady for a moment, then he looked around at the people. "Resume your watch!" he ordered. The villagers immediately responded, moving off, but letting their gaze linger on the commandant. Relief showed in their faces. With Collins there they were safe. Collins said to Riordan, "Talk to the priest." Riordan nodded. Collins flipped his leg over the horn of his saddle and slid to the ground, drawing off his wide-cuffed leather gloves. He walked up to Brady. He was taller by an inch. "I want your report," he said. "Take me somewhere." Authority was still crisp in his voice.

Brady was aware of the respect Collins had for him, and he was not unmoved by it. He had more reverence for Collins, despite himself, than he wanted.

Brady handed his gun to Will McCauley and led Collins out of the village, across Moore's field, and up the hill to the megalith. They did not speak until they had climbed the tumulus.

"How many did you lose?"

"Four. Six wounded."

"For twenty-seven of them." Collins exhaled through gritted teeth.

Brady turned his back to Collins and slammed his open hand against the huge stone.

Collins ignored the emotion of which that blow was a hint. "What is this thing?"

"Druid shrine. An altar. A burial place, appropriately." Brady refused to look at him.

Collins turned and stared out over the valley. "That smoke, is that Dungarvan?"

"Yes. The foundry."

Collins whistled. "No wonder Purcival moved. This'd be just the place for a bird's-eye. That the road from Clonmel?"

"Yes." Brady turned. "Do you see that dip? We hit them there." Suddenly Brady exploded. "Where the hell was your support? You betrayed us!"

"Did I? How?"

"You were going to hit Clonmel and Cork."

"No, I wasn't. I told you that because I knew you needed to hear it."

"You lied to us!"

Collins did not reply.

"And now the bastards will destroy us, like they did my wife's brother and a slightly touched boy and my pa's best friend and the man who ran the pub. All into the crowded halls of Irish martyrdom, murdered less by the Brits than by your false guarantee."

Collins refused to acknowledge Brady's rage. "Everyone wants a guarantee from me. You'd think I dealt in horses."

"You set us up! The Brits will cream us!"

"No, they won't."

The certainty with which Collins said this stopped Brady. "Give me that again?"

"I said they won't."

"How do you know?"

Collins took a newspaper clipping out of his pocket and handed it to Brady. "The *Times* of London," he said.

Brady read the headline. "Major Purcival, hero of Château-Thierry, killed in Ireland." The first sentence read, "A superior force of IRA revolutionaries ambushed Major Edmond Purcival's party while it was assisting in the resettlement of Irish refugees made homeless by the terror tactics of the rebels." He skipped down the clipping to a circled paragraph. "The Irish question was the subject of furious debate again in Parliament. Winston Churchill called for massive reinforcements to deal with the IRA terror once and for all, but Lord Derby, citing Dublin sources and a news story in the Cork *Examiner,* argued that the Auxiliaries had been done in by civilians and that a mass popular uprising was imminent. The military report from Dublin Castle and the Executive's Report from the Customs House supported Lord Derby's view and emphasized that the Irish population was increasingly restive. Lloyd George, reporting that the King was very upset, announced a major investigation into the incident."

Brady looked up.

"The Brits are under orders to sit," Collins said. "The American Ambassador is asking for briefings. The last thing London wants is the blood of your neighbors. If I hit Clonmel or Cork or stationed my lads here, I'd be giving the Auxies just the excuse they want. As it is, Brady, you live for now in the safest village in all of Ireland."

"Holy Mother of God," Brady said. But his sudden relief gave way to a new wave of anger. "You were counting on this, weren't you?"

"Yes."

"You make damn bold with other people's lives, Commandant!"

"Cut it, Brady." Collins would have no more of this farmer's pique.

Brady turned back to the stone, letting his relief wash over him again. They would not die this week, after all. He had been sure they would. He looked down at the clipping again. So Purcival had been a war hero. London took solemn note of his death. London took note, without knowing it, of Colman Brady.

Collins observed Brady's interest in the news story. "It seems that your grasp exceeds your reach, Mr. Brady, to reverse a phrase. The British are thunderstruck by what you did. The effect of your action has been to give the soft-liners in London a card to play, a face card, a king. The game is changed now. What do you think of that?" Collins was aware of the pleasure, the prideful pleasure, Brady was taking in his words. There is nothing — as Collins knew — to compare with the discovery that one's own act has effects on a grand scale. "Eh?" he pressed.

Brady could make no response. He was not prepared for this.

"Give us a cig, will you?" Collins said.

Brady produced a pack, then lit the commandant's cigarette. Collins puffed it calmly, looking off toward the Kilworth.

"It may surprise you, all this," Collins said. "To tell you the truth, it surprised us, what you pulled off. An extraordinary coincidence of timing, a not unremarkable measure of nerve." Collins drew on the cigarette. "Was Purcival the first man you killed?"

"Yes."

"How do you feel about it?"

"How did you?"

Collins answered him carefully. "There is nothing like an adventure of successful killing to fill a man with a sense of omnipotence. It can be exhilarating." Collins watched Brady carefully, as if describing what he saw.

"You didn't answer me."

"About the men I've killed?"

"Yes."

"I've never done it."

Brady was surprised. "You and Buffalo Bill, eh?"

"Right." Collins laughed. "He had hack novelists telling his lies. Me! I've the entire Irish theater and a squad of Gaelic poets. But *you* didn't answer me."

Brady lifted his shoulders. "I regret the man's death. I regret all their deaths."

Collins decided he was telling the truth. "Good," he said.

Brady handed the clipping back to Collins. "We can ease off, then, since your poker hand has its face card."

"Not at all. *Au contraire!* We must press them more than ever. We must help the people to be heard. The people are the aces in the deck."

"The people, Commandant, don't give a rat's fart."

"I'm here because *you* are the people."

"As the poster has it, eh? If we are 'the people,' you are in trouble because our commitment to this cause goes as far as the county line. What the English do in Ulster, or Dublin or Cork, for that matter, is of little concern to us. That's someone else's fight."

"No, Colman, you're wrong. What they do in the Customs House in Dublin, see, they do here. A push there is a shove here. A trigger, a slug, see? Like it or not, the Brits have us all in the same corner. That's why what you did this week rings even now like damn cathedral bells everywhere in Ireland. You stopped them cold. No one — not even Barry in Cork — has done that. We've been hit-and-run snipers up to now. We made a tactic of defeat. You've changed that. They know it in London. They know it in the farthest parish on Dingle. And you did it for exactly the right reason; not for the thrill of it or the glory. You did it to save yourselves."

"Damn, sir, if you don't sound just like Michael Collins!"

"I've a reason for talking to you like this." He knew what had been unleashed in Brady and he was playing to it.

"I'm sure you do."

"I want you with me."

Brady smashed his cigarette against the stone and said cockily, "But then I'd be 'the army,' not 'the people.' What good would I be to you then?"

"I don't think you appreciate that you've become something larger than life . . ."

"The only thing larger than life is balloons."

". . . and there are people who'd listen to you."

"Why? Because I killed a man?"

"Because you killed Purcival."

"Mr. Collins, you misjudge me if you think I'd use the carcass of a man as a platform from which to make speeches. Besides, you wouldn't like what I'd say to them."

"I'm listening."

"I'd tell them to look out for their own arses and to love their shingles and their acre and those people close enough to holler to in the evening. And the hell with noble Irish rebellion."

[57]

"Amen to that. It sounds to me like you know exactly what this fight is for."

"You don't think like a martial genius without your Australian bush hat."

"I never wear it but to my photo sessions."

Both fell silent for a moment. Brady wondered if their discussion was finished. Collins was thinking of another way to speak of it.

"Tell me, Colman," he said, "do you know the word *conscription?*"

"From the Latin, General; 'to write together.' Refers to the practice in dictatorships of enslaving men in the service of the state against their will."

"There is a dictatorship of events. One can be conscripted against his will by things that happen in his presence. I did not come up here to ask you to join me. I came to tell you that many who never heard of Four Mile Water are standing in your presence now and they are asking you to help them keep their land and their children. They are announcing your conscription."

"I'm not a warrior."

"No one is. They conscripted me, too, from my farm the other side of Cork. I did not want it either, Colman."

"And now?"

Collins shrugged. "Now I understand that, all things being equal, it's better to be in the center of the cup than on the rim. Know what I mean?"

"No."

"I think you do."

Brady looked away from Collins, grazing his eyes on the distant scene, on the acres he had sought to protect. From the Dolmen the land had always seemed huge to him, limitless. But now the Kilworth range fell like a fence, a limit. The valley seemed small.

Collins read him. "Live large, *amico*. I'm asking you to live large."

"Why?"

"Because Ireland needs you."

"I was made for this place, for these people."

Collins shrugged. "All right." He put the cigarette to his lips and inhaled, then flicked it away. "It pains me to see a man short-sell himself. Let's go."

"Wait."

"Well?"

Brady made an effort to turn his thoughts all to the same angle. He *did* love his land. He had been content, hadn't he, to take life's measure from the boundaries of the Nire? But Michael Collins had given words to another longing. Michael Collins, larger, surer, more a man than even perhaps his pa had been. And London had heard of what he had done. Could he forget that? Leave it be? Pretend indifference? Events *were* conscripting him. The presence of Michael Collins conscripted him.

"I'd have to talk to my wife, General."

"Not true, *amico*. You don't have to talk to anyone."

The certainty with which Collins said that shocked Brady. His marriage had changed nothing. Collins was exactly right, and Colman knew it, and he knew enough to be ashamed.

"I want you with me, Brady." At last, a clear, straightforward command.

Brady nodded. "Still, Commandant, I will talk to my wife."

"And then join me. I'll be in Dublin."

"I will. Yes."

"Good." Collins slapped his shoulder. "Now lead me back down to earth, would you?"

They descended the hill in silence. Colman could think of nothing to say. Banter or mere conversation was out of the question. Now that he had agreed to join Collins, Brady felt more than ever the power of the man. Brady was honored to have joined him and ready to do whatever he asked.

Riordan was waiting with the horses. Collins mounted, waved to the onlookers, and cried, "All Ireland loves you. Praise God for Four Mile Water!" And the villagers cheered him and waved as he and his exec rode off. Brady expected Collins to look him in the eye one last time before putting the spur to his horse, but he didn't. So Brady stood there on the edge of the small crowd staring after the flapping white tails of the commandant's dustcoat. They watched for a long time until the pair of horsemen dropped below a rise into the pit of the valley.

Colman guessed that Nell would be angry when he told her, and he dreaded it.

But he was wrong.

Her reaction that night was worse than anger. She greeted his announcement with weighty resignation.

"I suppose that your duty is clear. Your country needs you."

The line stung Brady. Was she being sarcastic?

They were sitting together before the turf fire in the front room of the Brady house. Bea and Conor were staying at McClusky's inside the barricades. It was only the second night Colman and Nellie had had a place to themselves.

Nellie, wrapped in a linen gown and an ancient quilt against the chill, sat on a low stool by Colman, who sat in the old rocker. He was holding a teacup, which had long since been empty.

"It's been a hell of a beginning to a marriage, hasn't it?" he said.

"I'm not complaining."

Colman let his hand wind through her downpouring hair. In the light of the fire it was all colors.

He rocked back in the chair and remembered his father presiding in it over the fire, over the family. While his father was alive no one dared sit in the rocker. It had been the old man's the way the tabernacle was Christ's, as years before the rocker had been his mother's, the way Christ was Mary's. Rocking gently back and forth, Colman tried to remember being held; *Rock me, Ma. Rock me.* But he could not. His mother was long gone. The vaguest ache in his breast was all that remained of her. He looked down at Nell and felt the same ache.

"Ow! Colman! You're pulling my hair!"

"Sorry, darling." He untangled his fingers, released her. He wanted to hold on somewhere. "Did I hurt you?"

"It's all right." Nell spoke with such long-suffering that Colman had to pinch off a wave of resentment before it formed. He could not prevent a gentle melancholy from rising in him and rolling over his determination to be cheerful and kindly. He felt how useless it was to struggle against the disappointment he was to her. He felt guilty and sad.

The bells of St. Lawrence's began counting the hour. They listened. Eleven.

"It's late," Colman said. He wanted to say more but shyness held him back. The thing to do, he decided, is to put on your best face and push on through whatever would pull you down.

"Shall we go to bed together, Nell?"

She blushed as if they weren't man and wife, and he used that as his opening. Raking her hair again he said, "To *bed,* darling, not the Moulin Rouge."

Nellie laughed in a way that said, *It's all the same to me.*

Colman formed two words with his lips, their old joke: "Hot stuff!"

She lowered her eyes, which he misread as "the immorality of it!" He squeezed her shoulder as if to say, *Come with me to Paris, Fifi!*

That was when she turned on him. "Colman, don't!" She nearly screamed.

He was shocked. "We're married. That means, Mrs. Brady, we go to bed together."

"Don't cheapen it or me by pretending nothing else is happening."

"Good Christ, they're right! Once you're married you're done for!"

"I'm not discussing it." She stood, gathering the quilt around her, blocking the fire.

"The hell you're not, woman. You either come with me now or explain why not!" He put his cup down and stood too.

"Because you're itching to be gone from me. Everything about you cries regret and fear that you've married me. Everything but your sly lust." She turned away from him and stood utterly still.

"I won't justify my actions to you." He forced her around to face him. "Or my lust." He kissed her, but she remained stiff and wooden. He held her at arm's length, a look of horrible realization on his face. "Dear God, I'm married to your mother!"

So surprised was she by that statement — and by the truth of it — that Nellie exploded with laughter, self-mocking, self-punishing laughter. "Oh, Colman," she said through her fingers. "I was just thinking that *I* was married to my Da!"

"God help us both."

She went into his arms and they held on to each other tightly. Their recognition was absurdly liberating, and it cauterized the bitterness they had been feeling.

"I'm married to you, Nell. And you to me. No one else."

"Not even Ireland?"

"Good Christ, woman, if I'm leaving you it ain't for Ireland. It's for your brother. And Con. And . . ." he lifted her face ". . . our kids."

A wave, responsive, sudden, urgent curled through her body. He felt it with his hands at her waist, and its energy flowed into him. He drew his hands up over the blades of her back. He had not seen her body fully naked. The times they had come together since their wedding had been hurried, nervous, in the dark, awkward fumblings through coarse linen and nightclothes. In Macken's barn they had lain in damp filthy straw. Each time he had wondered if she had been disappointed, having been disappointed himself.

She pulled away from him. "When will you go?"

"Tomorrow."

"So we have tonight." She dropped the quilt and pulled a string at her throat. Her gown fell to the floor. Colman saw her without moving his eyes from her face.

After a moment in which they were both utterly still she whispered, "Undress yourself, Colman Brady." And then she smiled.

Two nights later Colman Brady found himself, as ordered, before the frosted glass window of the door off the main corridor of the second floor of the building at 10 Exchequer Street in Dublin. It was lettered,

"George Doyle, Insurance Agent." He knocked on the door. A man he had never seen before opened it. Behind him were the littered desks and bureaus of a thriving business and, even at midnight, lit by a single gooseneck lamp, the room seemed to ripple with life and energy.

Half a dozen men wearing suits and ties were standing around the illuminated desk, on which a map of the southwest of Ireland was spread.

"Colman Brady!" Michael Collins said, crossing to greet him and taking his hand firmly. "Fellows, this is my new ADC, Colman Brady." Collins introduced him to the others, who welcomed him warmly. Sean Riordan was there, together with the senior staff of the Volunteer Army.

"I was a bit surprised to find you around the corner from the Customs House," Brady said. The Customs House headquartered the British administration in Ireland. Brady made his comment lightly, disguising his nerves.

"If you can't avoid kicking a bull altogether, *amico*," Collins said, "you should do so from as close in as possible."

Brady smiled. Collins's great confidence reassured him.

"Go on with your report, Tom," Collins ordered.

The men resumed their places around the map. Brady stood in the gap between Collins and Tom Barry, but back a step.

Barry was commander of the Cork operation. He leaned forward and said, "MacReady has orders from Whitehall to keep his men in barracks and out of sight of the population, but the Auxies, especially Napier's boys in Cork City, are aching for reprisal." Barry looked up at Brady. "They seem to take what you did to Purcival as a personal insult." Barry grinned in a way that seemed macabre and inappropriate to Brady. "If we're going to have trouble, it'll be in Cork."

"MacReady wants new orders," one of the others said.

"He won't get them," Collins said.

"It's on Napier now," Barry asserted. "He was with Purcival in Cairo, and a good number of his lads were in the trenches. They worshipped Purcival. Napier may have a mutiny on his hands, or he may lead one."

As Brady listened to the officers in their cool, unemotional exchanges, he understood that the consequences of his ambush were as large as the feelings it had loosed in him. But there was something foreign in the deliberations of these men. They were not responding to pure instinct, primitive and hot, as he had. They were not discussing a rabbit trap. These men were at the formal business of war and they betrayed no self-consciousness about it. Brady felt uneasy and out of place.

"Well," Collins said at last, ending the discussion, "we have to wait and see. Tom, you get down to Cork and get ready. If you're right we have to get the ball up fast. I want all other brigades on alert. Be prepared to move south. Any questions?"

No one spoke.

"You, Brady?"

Brady was startled. He hadn't expected to be addressed. He had to ask something. It had to be intelligent. The men were looking at him. He had no idea what to say. When he opened his mouth it was to ask the only question he had.

"Who's MacReady?"

"General Sir Nevil MacReady," Collins answered, no hint of condescension in his voice. "Son of the famous actor, C-in-C of Crown forces in Ireland, our neighbor at Dublin Castle, former governor of Bengal, chief of the Allies in Flanders, wartime commissioner of police in London, a hell of a soldier. Any other questions?"

"No," Brady said. He was relieved to have been taken seriously.

The meeting adjourned.

Tom Barry's instinct proved accurate, for, a week later, MacReady decided to remove the Auxiliaries from their posts in urban centers. He was convinced that their mutiny would not be postponed, and he wanted their terror confined to rural areas, where it would be less notorious. But that decision was a miscalculation.

When the officers and men of the Cork Military Barracks under Brigadier Oliver Napier received the order to leave the city and establish a new deployment in Kinsale on the coast fifteen miles south, they did so. But on the way out of Cork they went on a rampage. They burned the central city, including the Municipal Buildings on Patrick Street, to the ground. They sacked offices and stores. They fired their weapons indiscriminately on the street. Civilians were kicked and beaten severely. One contingent of Auxies broke into a church during Mass and, at gunpoint, forced the congregation to sing "God Save The King." At Dillon's Cross eighteen Irish people, including three children, were shot to death. With blood from their bodies one of the soldiers wrote in the street the words "For Major Edmond Purcival."

In all their raging, none of the British soldiers was killed or wounded or rebuked by an officer.

That night Michael Collins and Colman Brady met with Tom Barry and other members of the IRA West Cork Flying Brigade. They were demoralized and afraid after the burning of the city, and it had been months since their last action. But the arrival of Collins stirred them. When they met Brady they knew his name; their spirits lifted when they realized that the man who had led the attack on Purcival's column was with them.

Collins spent the next twenty hours developing a plan and drilling the Cork men in it. Brady served as the commandant's aide, and all of the Cork men, even Barry, deferred to him.

The next night, December 2, they moved against Kinsale at two o'clock sharp under the bottom of darkness. Eighteen riflemen under Ted O'Sullivan were ordered to occupy ambush positions at Browns Mills covering the brigade's broad flanks. Ten were sent to hold the Cork-Kinsale road. When time sufficient for these parties to take their positions had lapsed, thirty-two men moved on to Kinsale to attack the Auxiliary Barrack. The post stood away from the village's main street. It was a ramshackle compound of tents and requisitioned cottages surrounded by unstrung rolls of barbed wire. In the center of the post was the old RIC Barrack, which served as the officers' quarters. In all eighty men and nineteen officers of the Auxiliary Division were deployed on the compound.

Three small parties of four riflemen took up positions covering the sides and rear of the post. The remaining twenty men were divided into two sections. Ten of these were armed with revolvers, and they were to rush the compound after the gate was blown. The other section consisted of eight men carrying jerry cans of gasoline and two carrying sticks wrapped at one end with paraffin-soaked rags. These sections halted thirty yards from the wire and waited.

Michael Collins lit the fuse to the mine. It was a point of IRA honor that commanders placed the mines. It was the most dangerous part of the operation. Such explosive devices were unreliable, and the IRA were far from expert in building them. Tom Barry and his second-in-command prepared to pick up the mine. But Collins shook his head, ordering them back. He looked at Brady, who stood pushing the lock of dank hair away from his eyes. Then, without speaking, the two of them took the mine and quietly walked out into the open space in front of the post. The fuse sizzled. It would have a run of sixty seconds. Both men resisted the urge to hurry with the dangerous box, indeed to throw it against the gate before it blew them to small pieces. Instead they walked calmly and placed the mine gently and methodically in its proper place against the gate. They tiptoed back to where the storming party waited, all flattened against the ground, ears covered.

The mine exploded.

The riflemen at their stations held their fire.

The British camp came alive. There were shouts. A sentry whistle was shrilly blowing. Lanterns were lit. Windows opened in the two-story RIC Barrack.

The section of IRA men bearing pistols rushed through the blown gate. The first Auxies to appear at their tent flaps were shot. The men bearing gasoline stormed into the camp and splashed the liquid onto the canvas tents. The men with torches followed and dashed about igniting them.

Colman Brady, Tom Barry, and Michael Collins, each armed with two pistols, had taken up positions directly opposite the entrance to the officers' quarters. As the British officers rushed out of the building, cocking their pistols, barking orders, the three Irishmen picked them off. There were no good shots or bad within ten yards.

When the tents were completely ablaze the entire party withdrew. The attack took less than two minutes. Seventeen Auxiliaries died, including six officers. Thirty-two Auxiliaries were badly burned. Nine were wounded by gunfire. There were no Irish casualties.

"Commandant," Brady said. It was later. He and Collins were alone in the kitchen of the safe house. The small window, brighter than the room that was lit only by a flickering faint lantern, showed the first signs of the sun's coming. They had been sitting alone, not speaking, since the others had gone into the next room to sleep. It seemed to Brady that the general had lapsed into stupefied brooding. But he wasn't sure. It could have been exhaustion.

"Commandant . . . ," Colman repeated. Collins seemed hardly aware of his presence.

"Yes?" he said finally, as from a distance.

"I don't know . . ." Brady hesitated. ". . . how to speak of what I feel."

"Then leave it unspoken. It's better. They were *my* first. Not yours."

"I'm a farmer. Till now, it's been my business to enliven things, not kill them."

"I'm a farmer, Brady. Don't hint about at remorse now for those bastards. A farmer, you say. Did you never slaughter swine?"

"Aye, I did." Brady stopped. Collins's mood devastated him. He had wanted only . . . what? Colman thought of Nellie.

Collins began to speak. It seemed to Brady that the turns of his speech were softer than before. "After chores, I'd go about the fields hunting birds' nests. I collected them. That is, I noted them. Never touched them. Never disturbed them. Never showed them even to my closest pal. Not even to Hannie, my sister. I feared that all of them, or any of them, might steal the eggs."

Brady looked at Collins as he fell silent. He saw for the first time the infinite loneliness of the man. He was a man without a fireside of his own. Perhaps he always had been. Brady understood better what there was in the man that drew others to him, an aching vulnerability that cried out for solace. It made Brady want to hold him.

[65]

Collins lifted his head, took his eyes off the untouched glass of sherry they had fixed on. He looked at Brady.

"What were you going to say to me, old son?"

"Why do you call me 'old son'?" Brady asked, thinking, *Why not call me friend?*

"I don't know. You're older than your years."

"But I am not your son."

Collins laughed, more to himself, and said cynically, "All Ireland is my son."

"Ireland . . ." Brady was thinking of the tales of Cathleen ni Hoolihan. He was thinking Collins had a streak at once self-pitying and pompous. ". . . is a frail old lady."

Collins slammed his fist on the table, bouncing the glasses. "What the hell do you know about Ireland?"

"More than you know about manners!" said Brady, startled. He looked toward the other room where the men were sleeping.

"You're right," Collins whispered, suddenly sheepish. He wanted to say something too. But he didn't know what it was.

The two men sat opposite each other in the ferocious grip of their common inarticulateness.

Then Collins said dreamily, " 'If I exist as I am, that is enough./ If no other in the world be aware I sit content./ And if each and all be aware I sit content.' Walt Whitman, *Leaves of Grass*."

Brady knew suddenly that where Collins stored his stoic solitude, he himself carried love for a woman.

"Just like the Irish, Commandant," Brady said lightly, trying to diffuse the tension he felt, "to depend on poets to say what we mean when we're tired."

"Right, *amico*!" Collins said, tossing down the sherry. He hit the table with the glass and looked toward the bright window. It was morning. "Oscar Wilde points out," he said, standing, shaking himself, "that only dull people are brilliant at breakfast."

6

ON DECEMBER 22, 1920, Eamon de Valera, president of the illegal Provisional Government, returned secretly from eighteen months in

America. His exile had not cost him his thin, grim demeanor. He still looked more like the National School teacher he had been than a revolutionary hero. Bespectacled and gangling, he gave all the appearances of a classroom master who was meek with townspeople and stern with pupils. In a way, the image fit. To those outside the Republican movement he *was* mannered and shy. But to the men and women rebels over whom he had authority, he was forthright, stubborn, and at times as ruthless with them as he habitually was with himself.

De Valera came home as events on both the war and peace fronts were breaking in Ireland's favor for the first time. He knew from his own experience how shocked the American public had been by the burning of Cork and the killing of civilians. The British ambassador had been publicly summoned to the White House to explain. The British at first took the line that irresponsible citizens of "Rebel Cork" had burned their own city from pure fecklessness. But no one was misled by that. Even members of Parliament denounced the government's lie, and less diffident Auxies all over Ireland wore burned wine-corks in their glengarries instead of campaign ribbons. But civilian opinion everywhere, even in London, was against them. The Irish population was increasingly vocal in its resentments of England, and there were public celebrations when the reprisal against the Auxies at Kinsale was carried out.

De Valera knew that the two great goals of the Republican effort were finally being achieved; international pressure on London to come to terms with the Irish was intense and mounting, and the Irish people in great numbers were openly supporting the rebels.

During the course of his first briefing from Collins, the president ordered that Colman Brady be brought to the safe house in Monkton, outside Dublin. He wanted to meet the man who had struck the flint that kindled these good fires.

On the morning of Christmas Eve Michael Collins ushered Brady into De Valera's office, a small room that had formerly been the rear parlor of the modest house that served as the rebel executive mansion. Collins made the introductions, then he and De Valera chatted cordially about several matters, including funds from New York and the status of the National Loan.

It was clear to Brady that the two men were close friends. They were among the few leaders who had survived the initial Post Office seizure on Easter Monday, 1916. Brady recalled the great story of Collins's daring rescue of De Valera from Lincoln Jail in England itself. The two shared the obvious intimacy of men who had saved each other's lives.

After five minutes Collins left, and the president turned to Colman Brady.

"Please sit, Brady."

"Thank you, sir." He took the upright wooden chair by the table. De Valera sat in the upholstered chair by the fire.

"What rank do you hold?"

"I am not in the army, Mr. de Valera."

"I assumed Mick had commissioned you."

"No, sir."

"Why not?"

Brady shrugged. "I'm not in it like that. I'm doing what's necessary. That's all. I'm a farmer. I've a wife."

"So I gather. You had uninvited guests at your wedding."

"Yes."

"That's what began it?"

"Yes."

"Tell me about it."

For two and a half hours the president questioned and listened. His manner made Brady perfectly at ease. He took in with interest the most minute details of Brady's story. He was generous in his praises and he looked unhappy and troubled only when told of those who died. As Brady talked, revealing more and more of himself, he had the feeling that he was having the intimate talk with his father that he'd longed for and never had.

Finally Eamon de Valera said, "I don't suppose you know why I've asked you here."

"I assumed, sir, it was for this talk."

"Yes, Colman. That was the first part. And now, since I've had confirmed for myself what Collins told me, the second part." He stopped.

Brady looked at De Valera intently.

The president continued. "We're very nearly home, Brady. The English need be pressed only the smallest bit more and the war can be over."

"I understand that."

"Well, listen carefully. For the sake of our political position after the truce, it is urgent that we are perceived now as at the peak of our strength. England will try to make the peace look like our surrender. If she succeeds she will concede nothing to us beyond Home Rule. We will not surrender, nor will we seem to surrender. We will have nothing less than national independence."

"What has that to do with me?"

"We have decided to establish a special unit. We're calling it the Active Service Unit for now. I want you to head it up."

"What will be its function?"

"L'audace et toujours l'audace!"

"I don't speak French."

De Valera smiled. He regretted his own display as much as he did Brady's ignorance. He felt like a teacher. "As I said," he went on with the barest hint of condescension, "to assure that the world and the English and the Irish people understand that we enter negotiations from strength, not weakness."

"A military unit."

"Yes. Small, mobile, and deadly. With one eye fixed on the political impact of its action."

"Action?"

"Yes. I want you to destroy the Customs House."

The Customs House! The center of the English executive in Ireland. The boldness of it stunned Brady. But the place was massive, crowded with clerks and bureaucrats. The images of all their faces flashed before Brady.

"Mr. de Valera, I am not a killer."

"That is why I want you. I want you to arrange to destroy the building with a minimum of deaths. We are strong. We are humane. That will be our twofold message to the world."

"But . . ."

"I refuse to debate the matter with you, Brady. I want an answer. Yes or No." Now the sternness. Now the bark.

"I must know what it requires."

"It requires your total effort for as long as it takes. The timing will be a matter for me to set. Some months at the outside, I would say. And it requires your oath of silence. The unit will be composed of men like yourself from outside the army, who are known neither to the Volunteers nor to the British. And you will have nothing to do with anyone but Collins and me."

"I must tell my wife."

"No."

"I can't, then."

"All right. Get out."

"Wait."

"No, Brady. Get out of my sight."

The swiftness of his dismissal, the extremity of De Valera's judgment, the absolute rejection: these were what shocked Brady into changing his mind.

"Agreed. I'll do it."

"Your oath!" De Valera demanded.

"I swear. I swear to Jesus Christ to do as you say."

"Report to Collins after Christmas."

[69]

"Yes, sir."

"You should go home today. How long have you been away?"

"Nearly a month."

"Have you a way to travel?"

"I'll go by train."

"Take my car, Colman. Come back Friday."

Brady nodded, stood and started for the door. De Valera remained seated, in the grip of a sudden mood. He halted him.

"Your wife, son," he began mournfully, "do you love her very much?"

"Yes, I do. Despite myself."

"Tell her *that*. It matters more." Even as he expressed the nearly gentle sentiment, the president did so harshly. He was still stern and brusque in manner. Colman understood that the initial politeness of their conversation had depended on his being an outsider. But he was not an outsider anymore. In the peculiar way of the upside-down world of the revolution, it was an honor to Brady that Eamon de Valera should speak to him so rudely.

Outside De Valera's house Colman panicked. An aide had shown him to the automobile. Brady stood looking at it, a large, closed sedan with four doors. It was nothing like the open, carriage-like truck that Nellie's father owned. That was the only auto he had ever driven. He knew that in order to start the butcher's truck, and for that matter the touring car that Collins used, one inserted a handle into the hole beneath the bonnet and cranked rapidly. He walked completely around the president's car, looking for the hole. The aide seemed to be glaring at him.

"Where do you crank?" Brady asked pitifully, brushing his hand through his hair.

"You don't." The man pushed by him into the car. He leaned over the driver's wheel. There was a chugging, a bang, and suddenly the engine caught.

"See?" the aide asked, leaning back, indicating the button on the panel. He obviously felt very superior about it all.

"Yes. Thanks."

The aide hopped out of the car.

Colman stepped aboard, grasped the wheel firmly with both hands and tried to remember how the procedure went. Awkwardly and with much grinding and stuttering the machine finally began to move. The aide continued to glare as Colman coaxed the thing down the road.

Even after he was out of sight of De Valera's house he did not relax. Suddenly he felt entirely incompetent. The two great leaders of Ireland were putting an immense trust in him. He was afraid it was misplaced. If De Valera knew he had only driven twice before he would never have given him the car. If Collins and De Valera had any idea how frightened and worried he was they would not count on him for messages, much less the Customs House. The Customs House! Good Christ! What had he agreed to do?

Brady turned on the Monkton road away from Dublin. The car stalled twice. After going toward Naas for some miles he turned onto the road for Carlow. By the time he reached that town his nervousness had eased off some, and he was driving the president's car quite well.

Four Mile Water was beautiful on Christmas Day. The sky above the open country was pink and silver. The bark of the great chestnut was dark red. Its last few leaves glowed like copper. The Nire in the valley was a streak of glass, a winding mirror flashing the sun back at itself. The clouds moved in procession above the Druid monument like the Wise Men coming. The earth, turned under everywhere but for Moore's field, which was given over to winter wheat, seemed to burn against the cold air. On rainy, foggy days the same scene was dead and eccentric. But in the brisk, crystal light, what could be seen from the hill was like a faint premonition of the first Christmas, or the last one.

Nellie kept her hand on his knee. Colman steered the big car around the narrow little road, laughing with the thrill of it. He was going a little too fast, but they loved it. Conor and Bea were holding onto each other in the back seat. Each time the car swept down around a blind curve they squealed together. Conor had intended to be sophisticated during his first auto ride, but the spell that turned twelve-year-old Bea into a clutch of giggles had its effect on him too. It was the most exciting thing either of them had ever experienced. It was better even than going fast on Mc-Clusky's horse.

Nellie was thinking that she had never been as happy in her life as she was then, huddling next to Colman, crushing his leg with her hand, having him back, hearing him laugh, laughing with him and repeatedly surviving the curves in the road where she thought they were going to crash. It did not feel dangerous to her at all. Although she knew it was, very.

Colman was enchanted by the fit of the machine to the road, by the harmony of the double serpentine. He loved the order of it. Even as the heavy car hurled itself down the steep hill, all one had to do was trace one's way along what had already been set, ordained even. That was why the risk of it did not frighten but delight. The faster they went the more Brady felt the power of his own reflexes. All he had to do was react to the road. No initiative required, no thought, no real responsibility. Only the counterfeit boldness of speed. *"L'audace!"*

When the pitch of the road leveled and the turns were fewer and less abrupt, they knew they were coming out into the plain. The river was just ahead and across the bridge, the village of Ballymacarberry.

"Who's for an ice?" Colman asked cheerfully.

"Me, Colman, me!" Bea yelled.

"It's Christmas, man," Nellie said, rebuking him lightly. No shops would be open on the Holy Day.

Colman slapped himself in mock repentance, but he pulled the car over in the village anyway. His brother and sister ran off to find the McCauliff children, who were staying with their aunt. Colman and Nellie decided to stroll a way down the Nire.

The path running along the river was trim and neat, and the banks at that point were at right angles to the water about three feet high. The river had an aged dignity about it there, not like the youthful breaks above the village or the lazy marsh a few miles down. They walked toward the crumbling Norman keep, half a mile downstream. They held each other's hands.

"I could enjoy the River Nire," Nellie proclaimed, "and the love of you forever!"

"Could you now?"

"I could."

"In that order?"

"Oh, the cruelty of such a question. Would you ask me to rank two of God's masterpieces?"

He laughed as she wanted him to. They walked along, arms swinging between them, sharing an impression of boundless joy. Colman kept looking at her; she was tall, slim, full-breasted, more beautiful than the women he'd seen in Dublin.

He told her so.

She turned red, the color of her hair, and when she told him that he was only flattering her, she thought that was exactly the case. She was sure that in Dublin she would appear old-fashioned and faded. But she could not hide the delight she felt anyway for his saying it.

Colman had told Nellie all about Dublin and about Kilkenny and Wicklow and Wexford and Youghal and other places he had gone with Collins. He had described streets and coastline and marvelous buildings. He had talked about automobiles and lorries, huge ones. He had seen an aeroplane in Bandon. But he had told her nothing about what he had been doing, who he had been with, what would happen now. Since his return she had not allowed herself to feel even minutely the immense pain this silence and mystery caused her.

Not until he asked her that awful question.

They were standing in the shadow of the watchtower that had stood guard by the river since the Normans had conquered Ireland in the eleventh century.

"Nellie," he began, slipping his arms around her waist, "what of our son?"

She would have laughed at him if the question hadn't come like a blow to her stomach. She pulled away from him, hurling herself half over the stone wall of the little bridge that cut the water at the Keep. She made fists. Was he that naïve, that innocent? Did he really think it was automatic, that babies came, willy-nilly, the first month? If it was naïveté, why did she hear his question like a charge? An accusation? *Was* she sterile? Would she be barren? Why *wasn't* she pregnant?

"What's wrong?" He was stunned by her rejection.

What's wrong! The question roared inside her head. Did he think to implant me and call it quits? Give me a baby and go off to war? Was that why he had come home, for his *son?* Had it not been for *her* at all? If he cared for her he would stay. He wouldn't so willingly go off to fight or even die for Ireland. *Die for Ireland!* Was that why he wanted her pregnant? Die? Was she losing him already?

"What's wrong?" she repeated dully, not to him at all. Her quiet resignation was all the hint he needed of the storm that was raging inside her. "What's wrong, Colman? You tell me."

"Nothing's wrong, Nellie. It's Christmas."

"And you were hoping for the coming of the baby, no doubt. In a manger if possible. Well, I'll tell you what's wrong, Colman Brady . . ." She drew herself erect, her voice rose, anger poured from her cleanly. "I'm not the Blessed Virgin Mary. Maybe she could do it without a man, but I can't! If you mean to be a father, you'll have to be a husband first!"

Brady blushed furiously.

"But we . . ." he started.

She cut him off mercilessly. "Yes, we did, didn't we? A total of six — no, six *and a half* — times!"

"Nellie . . ."

He had felt her anger before, but never her cruelty.

He thought of her father, how he withered before her blasts until finally driven to strike her. Her father's mistake had been to try to outdo her in abuse. It could easily become his.

Colman forced calm down like a bitter draft. Her reference to his inability the second night to complete the act only strengthened his resolve not to match her emotion with his own.

"Nellie, stop it. I won't have you talking to me that way. I'm not your pa."

That cut short her savagery. Colman expected her to burst into tears, but she didn't. She spoke firmly, purposefully, rationally. "It's only that I miss you," she said, "and I fear for your safety."

"You shouldn't."

"Why shouldn't I? I'd be happy to hear. For all I know you're leading assaults on the stars, husband. You could be leaping off the Cliffs of Moher with umbrellas or swimming beneath the sea with German submarines."

"Neither," he laughed. "It's nothing like that."

"What's it like, darling?" Surrender was palpable in her voice.

"I've met De Valera."

"I'm not surprised."

"It's his auto we're joyriding in. I must return tomorrow."

"I knew the machine meant that when I first laid eyes on it. I knew you'd leave instantly."

"I don't want to go back." The way he said this filled her with sadness. She didn't dare look at him. She knew that he was afraid and that, whatever it was, it was very dangerous.

"Don't."

"I must." His gloom, profound, bottomless, was what drew her out. She began by looking at him, ended by stroking his hair and his face. He let his hand rest on her hip.

"Tell me," she said softly. She said it no longer for herself, for her own need to know everything, but for his evident need to speak of it.

"I don't want to worry you."

She laughed. She was a mountain of worry already. He could be so thick. "I'm here to be worried."

"I took an oath, Nell. Of silence."

"Against me?"

"Against all."

"I thought . . ." Well, they did stick together, those fellows, didn't they? Now she was feeling the pity for herself again. The anger. Damn De Valera! ". . . it would be different than this."

"It will be, darling."

"When we have a son?" The bitterness with which she said this devastated him.

When Colman drove away from the farm the next morning at dawn, it seemed to him that just below the surface of everything was a welter of mistakes. He had made a mess of Christmas. Nell was angry and hurt. His brother and sister, ever sensitive to the emotional weather, were depressed and moody. The house itself seemed to him a stranger's place, not his. The livestock hardly knew him, the old cow kicked while he milked her. He felt guilty about leaving the animals in the care of Conor, who was too young still, too green. The field was gone to hay, lacking the perfect tending he'd given it since it was his. He should get back soon to turn the earth. The barn sagged southward over the warping, slipping wall. The entire place cried out for him, but it didn't feel like his. His land had filled him that morning frankly with sadness. Much as he hated leaving Nell, though, there was something about the place he was glad to be rid of. Was it just that once you've been to Dublin . . . ? It was a season for other things than farming.

He got the auto going, waved at Nell, who stood in the door, and headed up the hill toward the village. He stopped at St. Lawrence's to pay a visit, feeling like an old man returning to scenes of his youth. No one was about, it still being early.

In the church he knelt at the Virgin's statue, trying to see Nellie, wanting her forgiveness. But it was not Nellie. It was not even his mother. It was just a plaster image, nothing really. He lit a candle.

"Good morning, Colman."

"Father!"

The priest had appeared out of nowhere, startling Brady.

"Sorry for your fright."

"How are you? I meant to greet you yesterday, but the Mass was so crowded and . . ."

"Yes. A pleasant Christmas, I hope."

"Yes, Father."

They were walking down the aisle to the entrance. They were under the same compulsion to talk, but they could not do so comfortably in the church. Their movement to exit was automatic and shared. But when they stood on the steps in the dank chill outside, they both fell silent. They had so much to say. Neither knew why they could say nothing.

The road dog was barking at one of the shetlands. The Morrisseys' goat nibbled on the stalks of dead honeysuckle at Gavin's door. In Gavin's yard three cows stood uneasily looking toward the door waiting for Gavin to come out and milk them. Brady, at least, left his women in charge of his cows.

"Some things never change, Father. Peter Gavin still neglects his cows."

"Oh, they do change, though, Colman. He's gone."

"To where?"

"Clonmel. He's joined a contingent of Volunteers. Real IRA, they say."

"And he was the one to toast the King!" Brady did not stifle his bitterness. From Irish treason to IRA glory, the fickle bastard. *Beneath the surface of everything was a welter of mistakes.*

"If I could read your thoughts now, Colman, I think I'd be scandalized."

"Not likely, Father. Just worried."

"Worried for Ireland?"

"No. For Gavin's cows."

❦ 7 ❦

THE CUSTOMS HOUSE sat in Georgian majesty on a small bend in the River Liffey at Beresford Place. Like the old Parliament Building and the Four Courts and Leinster House and the great halls of Trinity College, its splendor was the work of the old Anglo-Irish Ascendancy, who were firmly ensconced in Dublin by the late eighteenth century. They enshrined their power over the Irish Catholic population and their increasing importance in the Empire itself in these stone structures from which the political, cultural, and economic domination of the English was administered. When the Customs House was built in 1791 Dublin was just coming into its own as the Second City of the Empire, and its importance was reflected in the size, design, and innovative structure of its grandest building. The great Ascendancy architect James Gandon is credited with the design of the mammoth capitol, and it was considered his masterpiece. John Wilkenson of Shropshire, the ironmaster, supervised the construction of the soaring dome, two hundred and seventy feet high, the first of its kind in the world. Flanking the dome were two sprawling wings, three stories high, to accommodate the scores of civil servants who were to tend the softly purring machinery of rule and commerce between Britain and her most ancient colony. But the Act of Union in 1800 destroyed Dublin's significance as a capital, and the city gradually declined, being increasingly taken over through the nineteenth century by Irish Catholic peasant refugees. The Customs House, however, maintained its grace and fulfilled its purpose as the symbolic and real center of the English administration of Ireland. It remained the grandest building in all of Ireland. And the most British.

The Customs House burned on May 25, 1921. The bureaucratic systems essential for British control of Irish life were thrown into chaos. The most visible sign of the Crown's authority went up in smoke.

The two wings of the Customs House were gutted, yet there were no injuries to the four hundred and seventy-two persons employed there. The fire broke out simultaneously in nine places at exactly noon, while the bulk of the office workers were lunching on the sunny banks of the River Liffey. Those employees still in the building were efficiently escorted outside by masked men who carried rifles. The grand dome itself, made of Wilkenson's iron, was scorched but not destroyed. Nevertheless the fire warden for Dublin said it was the most efficient and massive act of arson in the history of Great Britain. Allowing for professional hyperbole, the man had been fire commissioner for London and a chief before that in New Delhi, and was therefore in a position to fairly offer an opinion.

The next day, May 26, two things of political importance occurred. The American consul in Dublin, Mr. Dumont, wrote a secret memorandum to Lord Derby, the Secretary of State. "It is beyond argument now, Sir," the memo read in part, "that the Irish people will not yield to any but the massive force the King would not consider and my government would not support. His Majesty's policy toward Ireland is for His Majesty to determine. But the United States of America cannot appear by its silence to approve the further denial of the clear and determined popular will of a people against whom she has no grievance and toward whom she can have only gratitude for the gift of so many sons and daughters. Further communication to follow from Washington."

On the same day, Eamon de Valera sent a message to Lloyd George, the Prime Minister, indicating his willingness to meet with him to discuss "their respective points of view on the future of Ireland." Lloyd George did not reply. But De Valera could wait.

When the Customs House burned on his order, he was ready. Instantly he replaced the sabotaged machinery of the British government with appointments of his own, which had been in preparation over a year. The Dail Eireann, which up to then had been a secret shadow parliament of illegally elected representatives, was convened openly for the first time at the Mansion House on Dawson Street. All over Ireland, the governmental functions of courts, police, and even postal service were taken over by the Sinn Fein. Great Britain was no longer dealing with an outlaw band of revolutionaries but with a functioning, sovereign government. For the first time since before the Norman invasion the Irish people were being governed by their own. The effect of the takeover was instant and stunning. Ireland was proud and dignified. America was attentive and respectful. England was silent.

In the paneled wardrooms of Whitehall long and unsatisfactory discussions were taking place. General Macready and Sir Hamar Greenwood, the Chief Secretary for Ireland, urged the cabinet to place the damned island under complete martial law. Winston Churchill supported them and advocated the immediate dispatching of two hundred thousand troops to occupy the place. He hastened to add that such a mobilization would simultaneously relieve the massive unemployment crisis that had beset Britain since the end of the European War. "It's time to settle the infernal Irish matter once and for all!" he stormed. Lord Derby and most of the cabinet agreed that intensive military operations under new emergency laws were exactly what the situation demanded. But Lloyd George demurred. He still felt there was a better way to accomplish their shared goal, and he alone appreciated fully that without huge forthcoming American monies, the British economy would never recover from its Pyrrhic victory over the Germans. The Prime Minister wanted a way to restore the hegemony over Ireland without ruffling Yank feathers.

On June 22 King George V went to Belfast to open the royally constituted Parliament of Northern Ireland. He stunned his listeners when, in his formal speech, he issued a call for peace to all Irishmen. Committing his own government to a policy of conciliation and forbearance, he appealed to the people: "Let us forgive and forget," he said grandly, obviously speaking to the southern Irish. "Let us join in making for *your* land a new era of peace, contentment, and goodwill." British — indeed, Commonwealth — opinion crystallized around the King's speech. Though couched in vague terms, the royal will was clearly tilted toward a negotiated, not military, settlement.

As the world hailed this "breakthrough in statesmanship," De Valera and Collins and the leaders of the Dail waited. The next step was patently with Lloyd George, and he took it. Availing himself of the atmosphere of tolerance that had resulted from the King's speech, he sent a personal letter to De Valera inviting a meeting in London between them to see whether a way to peace could be found.

Despite the suspicions of some Irish leaders about the lack of specific terms in the offer, De Valera knew their moment had come. In his reply to the Prime Minister he graciously accepted the invitation, but pointedly stated that he did so as the elected leader of a free people. The truce ending hostilities between England and Ireland was signed on July 9, 1921, and both sides began to convene delegations that would conduct the negotiations in London.

In Dublin the sun was nearing the lips of the Liberties chimneys. Two men were walking on the bright side of St. Stephen's Green, Colman Brady and Michael Collins.

"Shouldn't have dressed in black, Mick," Brady said, squinting at the sun. "It's going to be a scorcher."

"You don't call on the president of the new Republic in mufti, Brady, even if it is earnest old Dev."

"Ah, forgive me my gombeen origins. I forgot I'm strolling with the Minister himself."

"Bureaucrat, you mean." Collins was in a dark mood. He had a great distrust of good weather.

"Statesman," Brady cajoled. *Don't give in to a soldier's self-pity at the end of a war,* he added to himself.

"Functionary." Collins seemed unaware that Brady was having him on.

"And a retired general to boot, at the age of thirty-two. If you don't like being Minister of Finance, you could become a museum and charge admission to yourself."

"Sarcasm ill becomes the feebleminded, Brady." Collins had caught on. He smiled and slapped his companion on the shoulder.

"Aye. As resignation does the victorious notorious."

"Have I been so blatant?"

"To me you have."

"Well," Collins said carefully, "I would be with you. You don't see much of the army's 'merry big fellow,' do you?"

"I'd rather see you as you are. You don't have to put on the act for me."

"To keep your morale up?"

"My morale couldn't be higher. I'm going home."

"Ah, yes, your fabled bucolia. Tell me," Collins said a bit edgily, "how did you manage to cling to that? Men like us never go home."

"Men like what?" Was there nothing more to their friendship than the cause?

"Would you like to hear a horrible admission? Well, would you?"

"If you chose to make one."

"I miss the bloody war."

Brady could think of nothing to say.

"As I said, Colman, horrible."

"Human. We had a blue hell of a year."

"By God, we did!" Collins slapped Brady's shoulder again.

"We beat the buggers, Mick!"

But Collins's caution was in-built and deep. "Maybe. Maybe."

"What do you mean?"

"If Dev and his crew fail at the negotiations, it'll be Cromwell all over again. The Brits will shrug at the world and say, 'We tried,' and then they'll throw two armies at us."

"Dev'll bring the bacon home."

"Ah, home, home, home! You're a man of few metaphors. Who would you be fooling? Yourself? Or me?"

"What do you mean?"

"Jesus Christ, man, you've been at the heart of it! One — Purcival! Two — the Customs House! Three — the Truce! Ireland owes a small measure of its recent luck to you."

Brady took offense instantly at the modesty of Collins's assessment. A small measure? Didn't Ireland owe him more than that? He had set the great events in motion. He had brought them to their climax. A small measure? But just as instantly, Brady rebuked himself for his conceit. He was one of many. If he had made his contribution, he was one of the nameless. He was not a hero. He was not Michael Collins.

"It's good of you to say so, Mick." Brady still had to force the graceful sentence. He wanted praise from Collins, overblown, abundant praise. He wanted, he knew, Ireland itself to say its thanks. "But whatever role I've played, I can't help but think it's over. There's nothing for me to do."

"Stay with me."

For what, he thought almost bitterly, *to straighten your desk? To be your clerk?* Colman Brady was not raised in Four Mile Water and had not left it to be an assistant functionary. "You don't need me."

"Is it Nell?"

Only partly. "Yes."

"Make your home here."

"You know I can't."

"Move Nell up. She'd love it."

"I've a brother and a sister too."

"Ah, the children in the streets of Dublin."

"You can't eat the streets of Dublin, Mick. I'm a farmer." The simple statement seemed true even as Brady thought of all it disguised. If he stayed with Collins it would be forever as his lackey. The man threw too vast a shadow. Better the sun in a small place. "You once said to me, stay off the rim of the cup. I'd be living on the rim of Dublin if I stayed." Dublin belonged to Collins. It was his cup.

"Stay till Dev returns. I'm to be in charge of the cabinet while he's in London."

"I guessed as much."

"Will you?"

"No, Mick. I won't."

Collins stopped walking. "You've never refused me."

That's because, Brady thought, it took a while for me to learn from you how strong I am. "You know what you are, Mick?" he said, but uneasily.

He wanted him to think it *was* Nell. "You're a loveless, landless, womanless bull-spinster. How long are you going to be a ten-shilling-a-night boardinghouse lodger?"

"For as long as my damn country needs me to be!" Collins was suddenly furious. He wanted loyalty and self-sacrifice from this pup in the same degree that he himself gave it to Ireland. But with this difference; Collins wanted to be Brady's Ireland.

"Don't steam up now. I'm just telling you there's more than that. You can't sleep with the love of your country. There's a variety of ways to waste oneself."

Collins forced a steely calm into his voice. "You've some cheek talking to me like that."

And Brady, for his part, forced himself to finish what he'd begun. If he was stepping out of the man's shadow he would do so cleanly. "Just don't be thinking we should all live the way you do. And don't assume the sowing of seed is of less import than the buzzing of Mansion House drones."

At that Collins quickened his pace, turning left toward the street. "If you don't know the difference, mister, between busting sod in Tipperary while having at your lovely wife on the reeds before your cozy fire and the building of a sovereign Celtic nation, I'll not be telling you! Ireland can do without you." He broke into traffic and crossed to Dawson Street. "And so can Michael Collins!"

By the time Collins was shown into De Valera's office at the Mansion House a few minutes later, he had outwardly taken hold of himself again and made his entrance cool, reserved, official.

The Mansion House, a gaudy ostentation, all white and pink, had been built by Lord Dawson in the peak of the Anglo-Irish Ascendancy. The residence wing was serving as the executive office for the Provisional Government of the Republic. Another wing, a huge rotunda which Dawson's grandson had built in 1901 as a reception hall for the coronation visit of H.M. Edward VII, served as the congressional chamber for the Dail Eireann.

"Sit down, Mick."

De Valera looked morose and unhappy. He was weary after the months of long-distance cat-and-mouse with Lloyd George. The president did not thrive on the slow pressure of politicians; he endured it. Collins saw the tension in his face and felt a stab of worry for him. De Valera *had* to hold up. Everything was riding on him.

"How are you, Dev?"

"I'm all right, Mick."

But he seemed far from all right. Collins's own preoccupation — his rage at Brady's impudence — evaporated.

"Here's the latest. . . ." The president shoved a cable across the elaborate Jacobean desk. De Valera, thin, ascetic to the point of looking wasted, couldn't have been more out of place in the flamboyant room, behind the showy desk. A reed in opulence.

Collins took the long message and scanned it; the P.M.'s final statement on the subject of the conference agenda. ". . . to ascertain how the association of Ireland with the Community of Nations known as the British Empire can best be reconciled with Irish national aspirations."

"This is what I sent back," De Valera said, shoving another message at him. It was short, succinct, terse. "The Irish Republic will be glad to discuss these questions with the Community of Nations known as the British Empire."

"Community!" De Valera exclaimed. "They're not going to yield, Mick! I know it! I can see it clear!"

"How do you know without . . ."

"For months they haven't once acknowledged that this is more than a squabble between headquarters and an outpost. They will insist on an oath of allegiance. They'll have us kneeling to the King yet."

"We just won't do it, Dev."

"And then what? What then, Mick? A terrible, terrible war. They will . . ." His voice trailed off. He slumped over, head on his hands, silent.

Collins had never seen him so wrecked, so weak, so shaken. The general sat very still, not knowing what to say.

After several moments the president raised his head. He looked intently at Collins. His eyes were black, buried in hollows of weariness and despair.

"Mick, I'm not going."

"What?"

"I'm not going to London."

"But, Dev, Christ . . . !"

"Griffith is going to head the delegation."

"Griffith! You can't mean it!"

"I do. I can't go."

"Why?"

"Do you want my pragmatic political reasons? Or the real one?"

Collins didn't answer. He knew the real. De Valera had nothing left.

"But Dev, no one in the group carries your weight. Lloyd George and Churchill will demolish them."

"I know it."

"Well . . . ?"

"That's why you must go, Mick."

"Me!"

"Yes. You just gave the perfect explanation for it yourself. We can't allow them to bully us."

"I'm a soldier, Dev. I'm not a politician. I'd make a mess of it."

"You're the Minister of Finance. You have the confidence of the people. You're the only one the army will obey. *That's* why you must go."

"What do you mean?"

"We're negotiating for something different than what we fought for. They'll never yield on total independence. The negotiation must find some kind of middle ground. At the end the King must feel he still has us — and we must feel we're free."

"That's nonsense, Eamon, and you know it."

"Yes. The exact business of politicians. Michael, you must find that middle ground, and then when you come home you must convince the people to stand on it with you. And the army. You're the only one to sell them less than total victory."

"I'm for total victory myself, Dev."

"Well, after a few tumbles on the mat with devious George, you'll have forgotten the meaning of either of those words."

"I won't forget the ancient longing of our people."

"It's been for freedom, Mick. Whatever fancy name or political designation you want to give it. Will you go then?"

"You're certain about yourself?"

"Dead."

"Then I must go, mustn't I?"

"Good, Mick, good."

"But I need . . ." Collins paused. He had to make his statement very carefully. " . . . an assurance, Dev. If what you say is true, it would take both of us to sell a compromise to Ireland now. I want your oath."

"My oath, Mick? I'd have thought my word would do."

"You will support whatever we bring back?"

"Well, I can't say that, can I? How can I endorse what I haven't read? That's irrelevant. It's you I endorse. We'll push it through together. The state rides on our friendship. You've my word, Mick. Is there anything else you need?"

Collins did not reply at once. It seemed to him the wicket had fallen to the wind while he was looking for the pitch. He shrugged. "Yes, there is something else. There is still the matter of ten thousand pounds riding on my head."

"You'll be exempt, of course, from arrest."

"As long as the truce holds. But beyond the police, there's the average limey thug who'd prefer to bag Wyatt Earp, but . . ."

"You're right. You should take security."

"I want Brady. He can double as general factotum, an aide, and so on."

"Done. I'll tell Griffith myself."

"In that case, Dev, excuse me for a moment, would you? Brady was just leaving."

"Yes. I want to summon Lynch down here, anyway. You must be briefed thoroughly on all the traffic to date. We'll meet after lunch."

Collins dashed out of De Valera's office. He was certain that Brady was en route to the railway depot at Beresford Place. If he hurried he could catch him.

But Brady was sitting on the steps of the Mansion House and Michael Collins nearly fell over him.

"You're here!" Collins said.

"If we left it at that . . ." — Brady shrugged and raised his brows — "I knew you'd want a chance to apologize."

Collins remained standing, which made it awkward for Brady, who remained seated. He had to crane his neck to see Collins.

"Well, you're lucky I didn't step on you."

"As England said to Ireland."

"Don't provoke me, *amico*." Collins grinned. "I'm no Quaker."

"And I'm no bug to be squashed. Sit down, General."

Collins leaned on Brady, settled himself and sighed. "No, Colman," he said. "It's 'Excellency.' "

"Since when is the Minister of Finance 'Excellency'?"

"Since he became Envoy Plenipotentiary."

"What?"

"Oh, boy! Penitentiary! I'm going to London."

"You can't be serious!" Colman's face was lit with alarm.

"I am. I'm taking Dev's place."

"I don't get it. How can the president possibly forgo the trip?"

"One look at him would answer your question. They've worn him down. He's afraid of what he'll concede. Terrified of it. He's whipped."

"But what will he say?"

"That he's too strongly identified with the extreme position to negotiate in good faith."

"And you're not? Damn it, Mick, you're the one that's got criminal charges, not him. They'll hang you."

"I'm a free man for as long as the truce holds."

"And fair game for every Brit bantam, castoff soldier, fusilier, grenadier that sees a place at Westminster for the man that kills Michael Collins. You can't go!"

"Not alone."

"Not at all."

"If Dev doesn't go, I must. That's clear. Tweedledum or Tweedledee."

"Mick, please . . ."

"No, Colman!" Collins fixed his gaze across Dawson Street on a man who was shoveling up the horse dung from the curbside. He would sell it to housewives for garden fertilizer. Collins let a beat fall before he said, simply and softly, "*You* please."

"Did you arrange this to keep me . . . ?"

Collins cut him off with his stare, which said, *Don't you dare!*

This was not their earlier argument at all, thought Brady. This was Mick putting his neck in the noose. What could Colman do? Stand aside and say *Ecce homo?*

"I'm with you, Commandant. You know that."

"Thanks, *amico.*"

"But De Valera. He wouldn't duck the glory of peacemaking unless . . ."

"There's to be no glory."

"Exactly. I don't trust the position you're in."

"You don't trust Dev?" Collins thought of the fallen wicket. The pitch he never saw.

"You don't trust Dev?" he repeated.

"I didn't say that, Mick."

"We get paid to suspect bloody London," Collins said. "If we can't trust Dublin, well, it's eyes front, present arms, forward march, and shoot yourself."

And so Michael Collins, accompanied by Colman Brady, joined the Irish negotiating group.

The Articles of Agreement that the entire Irish delegation would sign were, as De Valera anticipated, a terrible compromise. The British refused to yield on the partition between Northern Ireland and the South. They tried to soften that stand by guaranteeing that, as soon as Protestant citizens were either reassured or resettled, the "essential union" would be accomplished. The British insisted on their right to maintain a naval base in the harbor at Cobh, south of Cork. When they agreed at last to make annual payments for the use of the port facility the Irish chose to take that as the token of obeisance they sought. But the most explosive issue of all had to do with continued Irish allegiance to the Crown. The British insisted repeatedly that they required it. But even on that issue a compromise was achieved. When the Irish proposed that they swear "allegiance" to their own constitution and "faithfulness" to the King, the British accepted the formula.

Collins himself would never have signed the Articles — he was the first to do so — but for a private meeting he had with Lloyd George at 10

Downing Street. Collins brought Brady with him to take notes on the conversation. The Prime Minister's Chancellor, Lord Birkenhead, was also present.

"You are the man, General, the only one who has it in his power now to avert the horrors of immediate and terrible war." When Lloyd George imparted this ultimatum, the bones of his jaw seemed to click. He was a man of the sort children draw when they draw prime ministers, tall, thin, perfect. He seemed naked without his top hat. When he said the word *war* he laid into it, extending it by six *r*'s and letting the bass reverberations of his voice conjure up for his listeners all of those "horrors" he was promising. And it seemed, as he looked toward Collins, more a promise than a threat.

Collins was unmoved. He knew the horrors of war better than Lloyd George did. He did not need histrionics to make him understand what was at stake.

"Mr. Prime Minister," Collins said coolly, "our subject is not war. Yet. Our subject is the treaty. It is my responsibility to refuse to sign it until . . ."

"England has given away everything!" Lloyd George broke in, "I tell you, man!"

"No! Listen to me! Until I am convinced that the treaty in its actual terms and its implications offers all that Ireland can gain at this time and at least enough to be accepted by her people."

"Well, what is the problem, then?"

"I want the word *Republic*."

"And I want the word *Dominion*. So where are we?"

"Right. Frankly, I don't care what it's called, but I want guarantees in writing, in the document, of freedom. The extent to which you clear out of Ireland is the extent to which we shall be free."

"Let me ask you something, General. In your opinion, is Canada free?"

"Yes."

"Well, that is exactly the arrangement we propose for Ireland."

"Why not say so then in the treaty? 'Free like Canada'?"

"I can't. The Parliament would reject it."

"The Parliament wants us 'free like Scotland. Like Wales.' "

"Yes. We must finesse them. I need your help."

"I want it in writing."

"There is a fog around the language of the treaty. *Allegiance. Faithfulness. Republic. Dominion. External Association. Community of Nations.* No one knows what any of it means. And *that* is how you and I want it. You and I know that Ireland, by virtue of this treaty, will be free to become whatever nation she chooses to be. That is as it should be. England concedes, General! But don't force her to grovel! She will not! Take this treaty and go through the door it opens. That is all it is: a door into a new room. Don't ask us or yourselves to define in advance the room's dimensions."

Lloyd George was speaking with formidable passion. He had not spoken of the treaty in such a way before. In public he played a very tight hand. Collins was impressed. Perhaps they *had* conceded everything. Perhaps the difficulties over words and phrases were insignificant. That the treaty opened the door to freedom was true, even if it did not articulate all that a free state would be. But Lloyd George had just conceded more than ever before; Ireland like Canada. A simple comparison. Canada could do whatever it chose. Ireland's immunity could never be challenged without challenging the immunity of Canada. That was a security not to be lightly rejected, and certainly not in favor of "terrible and immediate war."

Brady was watching Collins, reading his mind. Ireland like Canada, yes. But Colman Brady didn't like it. Canada had three thousand miles of ocean as a guarantor of its status. All Ireland would have would be the words and phrases of this treaty. "Be careful, Mick!" Brady signaled.

Collins said sternly, "The Irish people must have proof that the treaty really means something. I want the release of all interned Irish prisoners."

"Done," Lloyd George said.

"Including Sean McGrath." McGrath was in for murder without political status.

"Done."

Collins turned and looked at Brady. "What can we do now," he seemed to ask with a shrug, "but exercise our new habit and trust the bastards?"

And so they did.

At two-twenty on the morning of Tuesday, December sixth, the Articles of Agreement between Great Britain and Ireland were signed. As Michael Collins put his hand to the treaty he said to Lord Birkenhead, "I have signed my own death warrant." The Chancellor thought the man's grim joke inappropriate and thought again how relieved he was that these dreary and mean Irishmen were going home at last.

Collins and Brady went to Mass together at five o'clock that morning. Neither of them had ever felt so religiously committed, so *Catholic,* as since they'd come to London. The weight of worry and responsibility was giving way to gratitude. Perhaps Ireland's long night *was* over. The prisoners would be released, the English soldiers withdrawn, the government completely Irish. By the time the Mass was over the two friends had released the brakes on their nerves, their emotions, their joy. It was done! Ireland would be free! They were suddenly jubilant leaving the church, and they danced their way into the street, holding each other.

COLMAN LAUGHED out loud, laughed with delight.

"What?" Nellie asked, pulling the blanket over her bare shoulder.

"George M. Cohan." He whistled a tune.

"Sing it," she begged.

"How you gonna keep 'em down on the farm —" he sang pathetically, but she loved it "— after they've seen Paree?"

"Once they've seen the farm, you mean."

"Just show 'em London. They'll be back." He hugged her.

"Briefly."

"I beg your pardon. I've been home more than a month, with no plans to leave."

"But you wake up singing 'Paree.' "

"It's a long way to Tipperary . . . ," he sang.

"You haven't seemed to fit the place. You work without . . ."

"The slow horse reaches the mill."

"You weren't slow before."

"Hard churning makes bad butter."

"And a good beginning is half the work. Don't be quoting proverbs to me."

"You've a sharp eye for my discontent, woman."

"A blunt eye would do as well. I suppose you're too important for farm labor now."

"Perhaps I am."

"There's more dignity, I presume, in carrying Michael Collins's suitcase."

"Nellie Brady!"

"I'm sorry."

"No, you're not. You'll take a crack at me for every day I was gone." He hugged her, and she pushed her head up under his chin, inviting him to stroke her with it. He did. He touched her softly and repeatedly, then lifted her face so that he could look at her.

"The point of a rush," he said, "would draw blood from your cheek."

"One of your whiskers will do."

He rubbed her lightly with his chin again.

But suddenly she rolled away from him, showing her back.

"Nellie, what's wrong? Tell me."

"It's too soon," she said into the pillow she crushed at her mouth.

"What's too soon? What do you mean?"

"To be certain . . ." She turned back, showing him her burning eyes. "I've a feeling I'm . . ." She crushed herself against him, weeping.

"Pregnant?"

"Yes."

"But why the tears?" He wiped her cheeks. "That would be wonderful."

"It makes me feel all the more . . ." She could barely bring herself to say it. "Alone."

"Nellie, I'm home. For keeps."

"Colman, what's horrible and devastating — I don't believe you. You've left so often. It's so . . ."

"I swear it, Nell. The same oath I gave to them I give to you. The very same." He waited for that to have its effect on her.

It did. "I won't hold you to it," she said, sniffing, "if I'm not . . ."

"Don't be a fool. I'm home for you. Not for your belly. Whether it's empty or full." He ran his hand down over her navel. She raised her mouth to him and he kissed her.

"When will you know?"

"Very soon. Very." She pressed his hand down on herself and they kissed again.

The day that Nellie knew for certain she was pregnant was the same day the terrible news came from London.

The *Irish Independent* for Wednesday, January 2, carried the blatant headline "P.M. Says Ireland Capitulates!" The news story described a speech Lloyd George had made to the House of Commons on the occasion of the start of the Irish Dail's official consideration of the treaty. Lloyd George declared, "The representatives of Dublin yielded on every point of the English agenda, including and especially so, the Oath of Allegiance. Every Irishman's representative in the Dail must swear it, and the King collects his due each time over."

"The son of a bitch!" Brady cried, slamming the paper down on the table. "The lying son of a bitch! It was 'faithfulness,' not 'allegiance'! Bloody goddamn 'faithfulness'!"

"What's the difference?" Nellie asked in all innocence.

Colman turned on her. "What do you *mean* 'What's the difference?' The difference is we negotiated in good faith, which that bastard is going to exploit to assure the humiliation of Ireland." Colman opened the paper again to reread the article. Shaking his head, engrossed, gone from her, he said out loud but to himself, "They'll *kill* Mick and Dev with this. They'll kill them!"

Brady was half right.

Lloyd George's gloating convinced those who called themselves separatists that with acceptance of the treaty all hope of gaining the full measure of Irish freedom would be forfeit. They denounced the English concessions as bribes to defer the real freedom — a declaration of independence *entire* from the United Kingdom *and* the Commonwealth. They had taken an oath to the Republic, and if war was the only alternative to the Republic, then it must be faced. Those who sought to put that war away from Ireland were traitors.

"De Valera Denounces Treaty!" the headline blared a week later.

Brady couldn't believe it. He read the story in shock and rage. In his speeches before the Dail De Valera sided with the separatists against Collins, who was cast in the role of appeaser and sellout. Something clicked in Colman. Betrayal from Lloyd George was one thing. But De Valera! "Eyes front," Mick had said, "present arms, forward march, and shoot yourself!"

"Nellie," he said, "they're killing Mick. They're killing him."

Colman was white as bleached bone, flat up against the wall in the kitchen. The mid-January freeze was on and he was shivering. She would have gone to him and held him. But she heard him clearly. She knew before he did what he was saying. She felt like wrung rags. She knew she should eat something. But the thought of food stirred the bile in her throat.

Colman's eyes were fixed on the beam in the ceiling. She saw the paper spread on the table.

"I don't understand," she said wearily, taking a seat. She pushed the paper away.

"Nor do I. The President lied."

"Some lies go farther than the truth."

"What the hell does that mean?" he asked, looking at her sharply.

"You're going." She was resignation itself.

"You bloody martyr! I hate it when you whine!"

"You swore you wouldn't go!"

"I haven't even broached the subject!"

"But you're going. It's written all over you."

"You'll be crushed if I don't. What wound would you lick? What pussy sore would you rub in my face? You bitch, goddamn it!" He slammed his fist on the table in front of her with such force that the wood cracked. A teacup fell to the floor and broke into pieces.

They stared at each other in silence.

Finally Nellie said, "He probably needs you more than I do."

"I imagine he does, Nellie," Colman said with a bitter nod. "I'll say this; he never invited me to leave."

"You don't want a martyr. Neither do I. Go."

She infuriated him. His anger prepared him to go, but he could not. If he went, he knew, it would be only to spite her.

There would be no winners in Dublin. The Dail would eat itself. It was more crucial than ever to stay out of it. Collins could stay afloat all right. What could Brady possibly do there? "I made my oath to you. It's not martyrdom to keep it. There are splintered words enough in this country without my adding to the pile."

"I don't care."

"Well, I do. This is *my* home, *my* farm. You have *my* oath. You carry *my* child. I'm here for myself, not merely for you."

"Merely." Nellie rose, wrapped her shawl around her shoulders and walked with as much dignity as she could muster through the door and out into the freezing yard. She went into the jakes, where, amid the stench of waste, mold, and lime, she vomited and wept.

Brady went to his barn and shoveled feed at his cows.

From that day on he was slower at his chores even than before. He habitually bundled himself in his slicker, for the air was always some degree of wet, and made across the hills, wandering pointlessly. When his neighbors greeted him he would stop for a chat but, soon restless, would move on quickly. He ended his daily meanderings at Morrissey's, hoping for the papers up from Clonmel.

"Hey, Peadar," he said to Kelley coming in one day. It was a week after his fight with Nell, and he sought a refuge from her silence as much as his pint. Kelley was leaning on the rail. Andrew Morrissey, who'd lost his son Richard in the Purcival ambush, was craning over a paper, the *Independent*.

"The treaty won," Kelley said. "Mick Collins's side won."

"Mother of God!" Colman said, crossing to see. "Dail Approves Treaty," he read, "64- 57." When he looked up he saw that Morrissey was weeping as he read. Brady resumed reading. An ache he had ignored flared up in him. He *did* want to be there. "When the Clerk to the Dail, Mr. Diarmud Hegarty, declared the result of the vote, Mr. de Valera rose slowly to his full height and declared, 'It will be my duty to resign my office as Chief of the Executive.' He was interrupted by loud cries of 'No! No!' which he silenced by raising his hand palm outward. 'The people established the Republic and only they can disestablish it. This vote changes nothing!' Then Mr. de Valera sat. There was applause throughout the Chamber.

"Mr. Collins then rose and, looking at Mr. de Valera, said, 'I don't regard the passing of this thing as establishing or disestablishing anything. Many things have been said against me, but I say this here and now. We are still one nation! And I have just as high a regard for those opposite as I have always had. The President knows how I tried to do my best for him and he is exactly in the same position in my heart now as always.' Mr. Collins paused emotionally before adding, 'What I propose is a joint committee of the two sides to arrive at . . .'

"Before he finished, Mr. de Valera stood again and interrupted, saying, 'A Joint Committee at this time would be frivolous. Faithful Republicans should henceforth convene in separate caucus.'

"Mr. Collins cried, 'Dev! Dev! Don't say that! Our common love of Ireland allows us the right to differ!'

"Mr. de Valera removed his glasses and said, 'Before we leave I should like to have a last word as your honored President. Up to this we have had a glorious record of four years of magnificent discipline in our nation. The world is looking at us now . . .'

"He got no further. Overcome by emotion he broke down, resumed his chair and sat for a moment with his face buried in his hands. He made one attempt to stand again, but failed, collapsing. His shoulders shook. The painful silence was soon broken in every part of the Chamber as men on both sides of the issue, including this reporter, sobbed and wept like children."

Brady looked up at Andrew Morrissey, whose face was wet with tears. He looked older than ever. He seemed unable to focus his eyes. Colman looked at the paper again. They love it, he thought, this misery, they bleeding love it!

"What do you think, Colman?" Kelley asked.

"I think, Peadar, the curse of God sits on us. Snap out of it, Andrew. I need my pint."

Morrissey drew him a Guinness. Brady raised it to the two of them. "Here's to a life in Ireland, fellows." And then he downed the drink, thinking for the first time in his life that the only Irish with real brains and real nerve were in Australia or the States.

"No, I mean," Kelley pressed, "what do you think of Collins? What'll he do now?"

Brady shrugged. "What he did before. The country'll survive the loss of Dev. Mick won the vote, thank God." Maybe now Brady's guilt at having left him would evaporate.

"But Dev's got an army."

"Don't be a fool, Peadar. The government is Mick's now. De Valera's gang will gripe for a month and then come along. They have no choice."

"Not after last night."

Brady glared at Kelley. "Last night? What of it?"

"I just come up from Clonmel. Dev's boys hit the barracks armory, got themselves the whole Brit arsenal: Sterling rifles, Brownings, machine guns, Colts, Welbys, and bullets to go with."

"That's not possible! The Auxies would have smashed them like bugs."

"The Auxies left yesterday. The Brits have been pulling out all week, since the treaty's passed and signed."

"But they wouldn't leave behind their weapons!" Brady was incredulous and afraid. If the malcontents were armed, then by God, Collins *was* in dutch.

"They did," Kelley asserted. "Fellow at the GPO told me it was the same everywhere. The Brits left their stockpile behind, a little fare-thee-well, and passed the word on to Dev, so as to . . ." Kelley drank.

Brady stopped listening to him. Of course! Just like the English bastards to give Ireland not only a measure of freedom, but also a civil war! And Dev played right into it! How Mick must be tormented, Brady thought. But Mick would hold his turf, he assured himself. Mick would be all right. Brady accepted another pint from Andrew and drank.

"And you know what else?" Kelley tugged at Brady's sleeve, bringing him back. "The foray into the Brit barracks in Clonmel, guess who led it. Guess who was one of the first to declare his eternal loyalty to De Valera and enmity to Mick and the Free State traitors. Guess."

"No, Peadar," Brady said evenly. "Tell me."

"Gavin, the son of a bitch. Peter goddamn Gavin."

Brady made no comment. He shook his head, finished his pint and left the pub, out into the soft January drizzle. *Australia?* he wondered. *Should it be Australia or the States?*

But it would be neither, and he knew it. Irishmen with land did not leave. There was treason enough in that country without his adding to it. So, after that, Colman Brady forced himself to concentrate on the winter chores. Over the next months he shored up the sagging beams of the barn and built a new shed adjoining it. He repaired harnesses and sharpened tools and brought up new seed from Dungarvan. He was determined to make the spring crop the best yet, and he continually forced thoughts of Collins and the worsening civil war from his mind. He even began avoiding Morrissey's, where the talk was of little else. He and Nell arrived at a cool truce of their own. She was having a hard time of it with the child and spent most of the winter in bed. Conor and Bea spent as much time as they could at the school and with their mates. They hated the mood of the house, which, though free of outbursts, seemed grimly uneasy to them.

One morning in May Colman was digging a ditch to drain the bog at the southeast corner of his field. The spring rains had soaked the earth. No more water could be absorbed. If he didn't find a way to spill off the pools, a third of his barley seed would rot before it sprouted. While he was at work the moving speck of an auto on the road from Ballymacarberry caught his eye. He ignored it at first. More and more motor traffic could be seen in the Nire, but this one headed west at the fork instead of north toward Clonmel. That was when Brady began to watch it between spades full of muck.

He stopped shoveling altogether when the auto halted at the point in the road nearest his field a quarter of a mile away. He thought at first it was stuck in the mud, but then he saw a figure walking away from the car and into Landers's pasture. It was a man, a large man. A thought crossed Brady's mind, but he dismissed it. It was impossible. It could not be Collins.

But it was.

Brady began digging again, channeling his sudden overwhelming emotion into the act. How could Collins be here? What did he want? How could he ever face the commandant now? He pretended not to know that Mick was drawing up behind him.

"Colman Brady."

Colman straightened and turned and feigned surprise with an unnatural smile. "Commandant," he said heartily. But he was shocked by Collins's appearance. He looked tired, dangerously exhausted. His eyes were sunk in dark hollows and the skin on his face was pale, nearly the white of chalk. He was wearing city clothes, and their loose fit betrayed the enormous loss of weight. How different was this arrival from that other time! Collins's shoes were ruined and mud was spattered on his serge trousers.

"Colman Brady," Collins said again.

"Hello, Mick."

The silence hung stubbornly between them.

Collins coughed. He bent momentarily with the force of it, and when he straightened his eyes were glazed. "You recognize me," he said.

"You look unwell."

"I meant it's been so long." Collins coughed again.

The sound of it went through Brady. The last question he wanted to ask was the only one he could think of. "How goes it, Mick?"

[94]

Collins smiled morosely. "Splendidly. We've a stout roaring war going. The glamor of bearing arms for one's principles is irresistible. The young prefer it to clerking at the post office. We've thousands of recruits. So does Dev. Lads who couldn't see their way to join us against England are leaping in for a crack at their cousins. Patriots all, enthusiasts, unfettered by common sense. I hate them." Collins started to cough.

Do you hate me, Mick? Brady wanted to ask. Instead he said, "And the campaign?"

"Dev's boys took the Four Courts."

"I heard." The Republicans had seized the huge judicial building in Dublin at the end of April.

"Oh?" Collins said. "Did you hear about Hunt?" Ginger Hunt was second-in-command to Collins, his chief of staff.

"No."

"He's been kidnapped and they've got him at the Courts. They're holding him hostage. Dev swears to kill him if I attack."

"Mick . . ." Colman wanted to ask Collins not to tell him more, but the general went on. He was using his own agony as a blade.

"Churchill says if I don't attack, he'll take 'full liberty of action.' I'm fighting against Irishmen to appease Englishmen."

Brady did his best to ignore the despair in Collins, but Collins had indulged it as much as he would that day. He corrected his posture and altered his tone. "And you, old friend, how are you?"

"Well, Mick, thank you. Up to my knees in cow dung, as you can see."

The general laughed. "Same as me, only yours has the manners to be the real thing. I've thought about you, Colman. How's Nell?"

"She's having it hard with the kipper."

Genuine concern showed in Collins's eyes. His face softened and he seemed about to step toward Brady. "God, Colman, I hope she's all right."

Brady was not prepared for a taste of Mick's love. He felt a jolt of emotion, a fresh dose of guilt at having failed both this man and his wife. He felt an acutely physical desire for the old camaraderie he'd had with him and a like desire, simultaneously, for the unstilted fondness he'd had for Nell. Brady tried to smile, but his face cracked like wax. He had been holding himself rigid — against such feelings — for months. He was afraid now of being overwhelmed by them. "She's a strong lass, Mick," he said. "She'll weather it."

"I envy you your love, *amico*. You were right about me."

Oh, if you knew, Brady thought. But he said, "Yes. I've been blessed," and hated himself instantly for the sentimental falsehood. What if he simply told Collins the truth? That he was a moody solitary man unworthy of anyone's love, much less Nell's, much less Mick's. That he hated the farm and the dull, mean narrowness of bucolic life. That he longed for a board on which to stand with his lever from which to move — as he knew he could! — the damned earth itself! *That* was the truth! The arrogant, prideful evil of it. It terrified him and left him nothing but this grim, resigned detachment. Colman Brady was tasting suddenly his own despair, the ashes of it.

Michael Collins saw none of that, not because his faculty for reading men failed him, but because he chose to see none of it. He had come to Four Mile Water because he needed, however vaguely, a blast of Brady's strength. He was surrounded in his command by desperate failures. Brady's very distance from the war had come to represent his wisdom, his capacity for deeper loyalties than those which had driven Ireland to its orgy of fratricide. Collins turned and looked up at the megalith that dominated the hill. "It's still here," he said as if amazed.

"Aye. After two thousand years, *that's* dependable."

Collins grinned at him. "You've a stone like that in you somewhere, you bloody Druid."

"I've *that* stone in me, Mick."

Collins nodded.

"What brought you here?" Brady asked.

"I've been feeling . . . very done up. Colman, I need you."

Brady thought Collins was going to collapse right there in the mud. For his part, he *did* feel that ancient stone, its strength, its chill. "Mick, what could I do?"

"You could take Hunt's place at my side."

"You know I can't. I can't leave Nell."

Anger welled up in Collins, not aimed at Brady exactly, for his further refusal, but at the irony; what Collins needed in Brady was the very thing that made his refusal inevitable. If Brady said yes and came, Collins knew, he would soon be a walking carcass like the rest of them and therefore useless. But still Collins pressed, "But what of Ireland, *amico?*"

"What of it?"

"You ask the question coldly, friend. Have you no feeling for your country at a time when she's on the cross?"

"My only feeling in the matter, Commandant, is for you."

"Stop, Brady!" The general felt the truth of Brady's statement. He knew it and he could not bear it. "Stop," he repeated weakly. "This island is afloat on lies." Then he gave in to a new fit of coughing.

Colman stepped toward him to touch him, but Collins raised his arm. "No," he said. "That's the point, isn't it?"

Brady did not answer.

The general turned and stumbled away from him, lurching across the field. Colman shuddered to think that that was how he would have to remember Michael Collins.

Two days later, the first shell was fired under Collins's orders from a British artillery piece. He knew that if the new state were going to survive, much of Dublin would have to be destroyed. Later, after the Free State bombardment ceased, the Four Courts with its garrison of rebel Irishmen had been blown sky-high. O'Connell Street north of Nelson's Pillar was irrevocably ablaze. The Gresham and the Hammar were destroyed. Ginger Hunt had been executed as promised, and dozens of Collins's old comrades were dead. The rebels were driven out of Dublin.

On June third Collins received a telegram from Winston Churchill. "If I refrain from congratulations," it said, "it is only because I do not wish to embarrass you."

Collins carried the assault then to the country outside Dublin, and he mustered from himself and from his men renewed energies that came from the desperation to bring the war to an end. His own brush with physical collapse had frightened him terribly, and, if he recovered from it, it was because he willed to. He wanted, among other things, to spite Brady for his pity. By the end of spring he was fit again and rolling.

The Republicans had the initial advantage of holding a large proportion of the barracks in the regions of Munster and Connaught vacated by the British. Macready had enabled that. The land from Waterford to Limerick and most of the country to the south was in their hands. But the killing of the Four Courts leaders had resulted in confusion. De Valera was in hiding. The National Army under Collins was superbly led, and its summer campaign was coordinated and brilliant.

Four Mile Water was in territory more or less controlled by the Republicans, but it was far removed from the fighting. The army barracks in Clonmel, which had once quartered Purcival's men, were now occupied by De Valera's. But they were a motley group, inexperienced boys mainly, and their isolated offensives in the area were pointless and ineffective.

Once Peter Gavin, who was one of them, went home for a visit. He was an officer, a captain, and that alone, in the opinion of his neighbors, was reason enough to think the Republicans would lose.

He'd been drinking in Morrissey's all afternoon when Colman Brady arrived for his pint before dinner.

"You," Gavin said drunkenly, staring at Brady.

"Hello, Peter," Colman said, and then to Dick Morrissey behind the bar, "half, Richard, if you please." Brady reached past Gavin to get his glass of stout.

The others gave them room, drawing back the way leaves turn over before thunder.

"You heard this one, Colman Brady?" And with that Gavin threw his head back and began to sing. He had a good voice, and he sang with a drunk's energy, eyeing Brady all the while.

"England blew the bugle/And threw the gauntlet down/And Michael sent the boys in green/to level Dublin town."

"Don't sing that song in here, Peter," Brady said quietly.

"Why not?"

"Because I said not to, Peter."

"Do I detect an implication of condescension in your voice, Brady?"

"It's not an implication, Peter."

"Your problem, Brady, is your cowardly indifference to your country."

Brady drank his glass off and then faced Gavin. "That's not my problem, Peter. It's my solution." Brady winked and smiled.

Gavin drunkenly took a swing at him, but Colman easily seized his forearm before the blow landed. He held it firmly.

"Peter, you get out of here."

"You're hurting my arm."

"Don't darken these roads with your shadow until this shit is ended!"

Gavin left Four Mile Water then, but with an oath to himself and to God that he would return.

NELLIE CLENCHED her teeth, dug her fists half through the straw mattress, slammed her left knee up against the wall repeatedly and, at an angle, pressed her right leg against the bureau. The bedclothes were soaked through with her sweat and bunched behind her head. She was panting, groaning, grunting, pressing, pressing, pressing. The child would not come.

Marie McClusky went into the other room, wiping her hands on her huge apron. Bea stayed with Nellie, mopping her face.

"How is it?" Colman asked, frantic.

"To tell you the truth, it's a difficult one."

"What's wrong?" Oh, God, what was wrong?

"Not a matter of 'wrong,' Colman. A large child. A slim woman. She could do with a bit more hip."

"Should I go to Clonmel? Perhaps the doctor . . ."

"It'll be done by then. Get out of my way."

She pushed by him into the bedroom again, carrying a fresh load of clean towels.

"Oh, Christ," Colman repeated to himself. He and Conor looked at each other helplessly, miserably.

And Nellie stiffened her knees and pushed one more time, groaning with the effort and then screaming with the new pain, the ultimate pain, as the child's head slipped closer home.

The scream brought Colman into the forbidden room. He pushed his sister aside and slipped behind the bed, caressing Nellie's face. It was twisted in agony and effort. She looked awful. The sockets of her eyes were deep and full of water. She looked as if she were dying. She grabbed him with her arms over her head, pressed into him until he felt the pain too, a hint of it. She pressed and pressed and pressed, screaming, until the head of a child dropped from her womb.

"Push, darling!" Marie yelled. "Push! Push!"

Colman had his cheek on hers. "Nellie, Nellie, Nellie," he repeated. She was dying. The certainty of that is what unleashed in him an overwhelming love. For once he was not more conscious of his reaction to her than he was of Nellie herself. He held her from behind, his hands a vise locked on her ribs, pressing, pressing, pressing, trying to hold the life in her, to keep it. He wanted to forbid that life to leave. He did not close his eyes to see her face the way it was when they met, all loveliness, asparkle with youth. He kept his eyes open, seeing from an inch away her fear and pain, and seeing the iron set that was so familiar, so mean. It was not the soft, pink, youthful face he loved. He loved her fixed determination, that iron, that effort to survive. She had turned that grim face to him often, having determined often that *he* was what she must survive. Now it was turned against death. What he had thought he hated in her, he loved. He was free suddenly of every desire save one; he wanted his wife to live. "Please, Jesus, let her live!" he prayed. He prayed it over and over again, not realizing he was saying it aloud and into her ear.

"A boy!" Marie McClusky proclaimed. "You've a fine son!"

Colman didn't hear her and remained unaware that the child had been born. He was pressing his face against his wife's. It was she who knew, who released the tension in her arms as the tension had been released in her body. She softened her hold on Colman, ran a hand around his neck, lifted his face from her shoulders.

"Look," she said.

"Are you all right?" he asked.

"Sure."

"I thought you were dying."

"I am. So are you. But another time, not now."

"Oh, Nell . . ."

"Why, man, look at your son!"

Later they sat together motionless until she took the little form away from her breast, asleep. The dearest possession life could give. They listened to its breath, a curious whispering. Colman could feel the shudder passing through Nellie, running from her shoulder into his arm and down his back. A shudder of awe and gratefulness.

"Thank God for you, Nellie Brady."

"And for this boy."

They sat in silence, praying.

Finally, she said, "Have you a name yet?"

"No. Not a suspicion of one. You?"

"Yes."

"What?"

"Colman Brady, Junior."

"No."

"What then?"

"I don't know, Nellie. Maybe Jim?" He thought of his father, of his brother, the Irish Guards, the grave, the British seal on the stone.

After a long time during which they both watched the baby sleeping, Nellie said, "Did you think I'd not notice the torment in your eye?"

"It was for you. I was scared, girl."

"No, I mean the torment of these months."

"I'm sorry I've been so . . ."

"I'm not indifferent to your pain, Colman, anymore than you were just now to mine."

"I know it."

"You've never spoken of it to me."

"I've a . . ." — he thought of what Collins had said — ". . . stone inside me."

"I've touched it, when I thought I was touching you."

"Perhaps you *were* touching me."

"Hard-hearted Brady."

"That hurt," he mocked, holding his side.

"Because I hit you in your self-pity."

"Listen to her! Such recovery!"

"I am recovered, Colman. I felt a birth and a rebirth."

"I love you, Nellie."

"It was thick of me to be so long in knowing it."

"I didn't know how to tell you."

"Well, you found a way."

"While you were giving birth to the kiddo, I was giving birth to something too." Brady paused. He was not a man to accuse himself, but he was chastened, changed. He had withheld himself from the Irish war because he felt it unworthy of him. He had abandoned Collins because he felt himself too large for another man's shadow. He had been restless about the farm because the mowing of hay was too menial. He had the habit of thinking he was born for something special, but now he knew the one talent he lacked was the only one he wanted. He wanted to say he was giving birth to love, but he couldn't bring himself to it. He leaned over her and kissed her and said again, "I love you."

She joined her arms behind his neck and held him. Their son slept on by her side.

He was nearly overcome with relief. All that time he had longed for a way of living that was worthy of him. He had wanted action on a grand scale, significance, power, nobility. He had wanted to move the earth. Well, he was doing it. Not by adventures of war or politics, but by loving this woman. Colman Brady had given birth to the knowledge that the most value-laden human act is the simple, faithful act of commitment to one person.

"And do you know something, Mr. Brady?"

"Tell me."

"I love *you*."

"Oh, Nell," he crushed his face into the hollow of her neck. She knew about him what she knew, and still she loved him. For the first time in his life, Colman Brady felt unworthy.

They lay together like that for a long time, his heart on hers, one beating.

Finally she said, "Colman?"

He did not reply. He did not want to end the moment. He did not want to disturb its peace. He felt calm and whole.

"Colman?"

"Yes?" he said, but her flesh muffled it.

"What about Michael?"

"Who?" He didn't budge. He wasn't sure he'd heard her.

"Michael Collins."

After a moment Colman said, "What about him?"

"He'd want to know about your son."

Colman adjusted his face in her neck to speak clearly. "No, he wouldn't. He thinks I've forgotten him."

"But you haven't."

"No."

"He'd want to know because . . ." Nell inhaled deeply. ". . . he loves you too."

Colman did not reply.

"He came here, didn't he?" Nell pressed.

"And I refused him."

"No. You refused his war, not him. Colman, speaking as an expert on the matter, you must find a way to tell the man you love *him*. He needs that — like we all do."

Colman raised himself and looked at their son sleeping in the well her left side made. Brady was filled with joy, a rush of it, as the realization hit him: their son! "Yes, Nell," he said. "I will tell him."

On the night of August twenty-first Brady found Michael Collins in the second-floor lounge of the Imperial Hotel in Cork.

"Hello, Commandant."

Collins looked up from his paper. He was holding a glass of sherry. He did not speak.

"I went to Dublin first," Brady explained, "then came down here after you."

Collins still wasn't speaking. A mask, indifferent, bored, covered his face. Brady longed for the familiar grin.

He went on awkwardly. "I'm surprised to find you in Cork, out in the open."

"Why?" Collins asked. Was there scorn in his voice?

"Because Cork is Republican through and through." Brady felt like an officer briefing his senior.

"Cork is my home county. These people . . . worship me."

"They fight you."

"Well, at least . . ." Collins shrugged.

They were silent. Colman remained standing. He ignored Collins's gesture toward a chair.

"What brings you here?" Collins asked.

"I came to tell you something."

"What?"

Brady felt a surge of panic. How could he tell him everything? How could he tell him anything? Afraid of his own silence he said, "I've had a child."

"Colman, when?" There was a hint of warmth.

"Two days ago. I came to tell you."

"Good, Colman. Good for you! How's Nell?"

"Fine. Strong."

"And the kid?"

"A boy."

"Great! An inch of lad beats a foot of girl!"

"I'd have taken anything, Mick!" Colman laughed. "It didn't have to be a boy."

"A soldier. Like his pa."

Brady was wounded by that until he realized from Collins's face that he wasn't thrusting at him. "Like you, Mick." Colman blushed, dropping his eyes. He felt like a schoolboy.

After a long silence, Collins stood and with easy grace draped his arm over Colman's shoulder and turned him toward the bar, surreptitiously hugging him firmly.

"Champagne, waiter! Champagne!" he cried grandly.

"Mick," Colman hissed, "don't attract attention to yourself."

"What do you mean? I've a godson, don't I? Well, don't I?"

"Yes, of course. But, Mick, your . . ."

"Brady, you're my friend. You're not my exec. Right? Right?"

"Yes."

"Then leave the army shit to me. All right? All right?"

"All right, Mick."

"Let's toast your son. Let's toast him good."

It was four in the morning before they went to bed. They were both pleasantly and morosely drunk by then.

But at ten past six the cars of the commandant's convoy were brought around to the front of the hotel.

Collins appeared, wearing his green uniform, tunic, and broad leather gloves and peaked hat. All for show. He was making a tour of captured outposts and his purpose was to boost the morale of his own men and shake the rebels by defying them in their own country. He barked orders to the soldiers as they were loading the cars. The convoy consisted of a motor-cyclist scout, a Crossley Tender with a complement of two officers, eight riflemen, and two machine-gunners, Collins's car, a Leyland Thomas, and, bringing up the rear, a Rolls Royce armored car with two drivers.

Just as Collins was climbing into his touring car, Brady appeared in the canopied hotel entrance.

"So! You *do* want a lift!" Collins greeted.

"As far as Clonakilty, yes. You said you'd wake me."

"I figured you'd get up if you wanted it."

"I can get a train."

"Come on! Get in! We stop in Bandon first. Then Clonakilty."

Brady sat beside Collins in the rear of the Leyland. The driver and Major General Dalton were in front.

"Still think I'm careless, Colman?" Collins asked, jerking his thumb at the machine guns ahead.

"Your car's open."

"Of course it's open, *amico*! My entire purpose is to be seen!"

"But not shot."

"You're full of common sense, aren't you? *Some* of us must expose ourselves to *some*thing if Ireland . . ."

"*Touché*! *Touché*! I'll keep my martial opinions to myself."

"Like a good farmer. Would you prefer to ride inside the Rolls?" Collins slapped Brady on the shoulder in almost total jest.

"No, Mick," Brady said quietly. He refused the bait.

"All right!" Collins shouted to the cyclist. "Let's move!"

At Bandon, Collins admonished a large contingent of troops to hold onto what they had captured. He spent an hour in discussion with the garrison commander. From Bandon the convoy proceeded toward Clonakilty.

"What do you think?" Collins asked Brady on the way out of Bandon.

"They *do* worship you."

"That's because they don't know me."

"True."

"And the other side of their worship is the rebel hate."

"I'm glad you recognize it," Brady said.

"Righto."

The first hint of the trouble occurred a mile from Clonakilty. The road was blocked by newly felled trees. The men in the convoy would either have to clear them away or detour over the mountainous roads to Sam's Cross and then back around.

The road was deserted and Collins did not want his men dismounting there. For all his bravado and show, he relied absolutely on his inbuilt caution. Newly felled trees, the cover of brush and hedges, the isolation of the place all pointed to ambush. He ordered the detour.

But Brady had an opposite and equally urgent instinct. He said so. "Let's clear the trees away, Mick. It'll only take an hour."

"No. We don't dismount here."

"But maybe they want you to take the other way."

"Ah, yes. You made your reputation on the tactic of ambush, didn't you? And now you're back from retirement."

"Mick, come on." Brady hopped out of the car and made for the trees. He desperately wanted to remove the blockade.

"Come about!" Collins ordered the driver. "Move!"

The cars were completing their turns.

Collins glared down at Brady. His look said simply, *I don't need you anymore.*

Colman felt that terrible blast of guilt and regret. He *had* failed this man, and he was not forgiven.

The Leyland left Colman behind, so he leapt aboard the Rolls and rode on the left rear fender, exposed.

The summer day's noon light beat down mercilessly as the convoy wound east along the deserted road toward Sam's Cross, where it would bear north again. The road ran down into a bleak valley. It was a deadly looking place, and Brady hated it. It offered no cover and the road was too narrow to turn around and flee. The place seemed all too familiar. He had looked for just such terrain when he had prepared to take on Purcival. The bottom of Brady's stomach shifted constantly in the tide of the rocking car.

At a blind curve in the road, a spot noted on the map as Beal na mBlath, the motorcyclist nearly crashed into an old four-wheeled brewer's dray, which lay lopsided across the road with one front and one rear wheel removed. The cart was loaded with cases and bottles, and immediately in front of it the road was strewn with broken glass.

Everyone knew instantly what was happening. Collins lifted his rifle from its customary place by his feet. Before he could give an order, machine-gun fire commenced, coming from behind the single clump of shrubs and alder.

"Drive like hell!" Brady was screaming. But from their places in the vehicles ahead of him no one heard. Collins gave the order to stop and return the fire of the ambushers.

Collins's men sought what cover they could. Dalton ran back past the armored car and crouched behind a low bank, where Colman Brady joined him.

"Where's Mick?"

Dalton didn't answer. He fired his side arm wildly at the hillside.

When Brady finally identified Collins's form he was in the road, kneeling upon one knee and firing his rifle. He was dangerously exposed. But before Colman could react, a shot found Collins and he fell over.

"The C-in-C is hit!" Dalton cried. "Fire! Fire!" They kept up a heavy barrage while Colman raced out into the road and dragged Collins into the shadow of the Rolls. The general's head was a mass of blood and wet hair.

Colman put his mouth against the man's ear and recited in a loud voice the words of the Act of Contrition. And then he kept praying over and over, "Let him live! Let him live!" But Colman Brady knew from the weight of the body in his arms that Mick Collins was dead.

While the others returned the fire of the ambushers, Dalton and Brady, with the general's body slung between them, made off across the fields.

There is nothing like carrying his corpse for two hours to bring home the merciless fact of a man's death. Colman Brady, long thinking that he was immune to the epic myth of Michael Collins, had deceived himself. Michael Collins dead? It had been inconceivable. That perhaps was why he and Dalton carried Collins upright with his arms slung over their shoulders across the fields and up and down hills. When Dalton suggested they haul the body horizontally by the legs and arms, Brady refused. If they carried him as though he was only wounded perhaps he would be. In his exhaustion Brady periodically closed his eyes and stumbled blindly on. The huge weight of Collins made him think once, strangely, that they were not bearing the commandant at all, but instead the table-stone of the Dolmen from the tumulus behind Four Mile Water. Nothing existed but the burden and the goal — to get Collins the measure of safety and comfort he needed to be revived. Brady knew that this test would be the one against which he would compare all others.

They succeeded in stealing a farmer's small truck. Dalton drove. Brady rode under a tarp in back with the body. By the time they arrived at the post in Bandon, it was inconceivable that the bloodied, wrecked, gross-smelling form in Sam Browne and tunic had ever been alive.

Dalton went immediately in to confer with the local commander and to try to reach Dublin.

While the soldiers looked on, stunned, some weeping openly, Brady carried Collins in his arms into the chapel. He laid him on the stone before the sanctuary. While the priest went through the futile rites, Brady knelt, trying, just as futilely, to pray. After the priest departed, Dalton arrived with a cloth and a basin of water. "I must leave," he apologized, as if he and Brady had been ordained together to prepare the body. "This will unleash a terrible reaction. I must get to Dublin." Brady nodded and took the cloth and water. "They will bring him on," Dalton said, "in the morning." Brady nodded again, and Dalton left.

Brady washed Collins from head to foot, slowly, with a detached precision. As darkness fell he lit candles and sat watching their dance. He knew enough to clamp the old vise on his emotions. If he went with them he would never, he was certain, return.

The next morning, a heavily armored convoy arrived from Dublin to take Collins back. The trip required secrecy and caution because the news of the killing had already spread. In some places his troops, out of anger and grief, had defied their officers and gone on rampages against Republicans and their sympathizers. Republicans, in turn, were already retaliating. Brady watched as Collins's body was placed inside a small lorry. He wanted to say a word of farewell, but could not. He raised his right hand, timidly waving, as the truck pulled off behind the Crossley.

Brady asked the post commander for a horse and was given it. He drove the unlucky animal brutally all day. He ached to be with Nell. Only with Nell could he dare allow himself to feel the bottomless sorrow. Halfway home, well after midday, the horse showed signs of giving out. At a town beyond Fermoy Colman slipped into the firehouse stable and traded his mount for a fresh one, and then pressed on through evening and into night.

Less than half a mile from his own village an army lorry roared out of the darkness at him. He had seen others on the road that day, barreling to or from some raid in the spiraling, violent madness that blasphemed the one whose death had begun it. As he'd done repeatedly, he ran the horse off the road and behind the hedge, but now he was trying to imagine what troops of either side would be doing in Four Mile Water. When the lorry crashed by Brady's hedge he saw Peter Gavin along with several others clinging pathetically to the wagon slats, and that is what set off the alarm. When the lorry had passed, he whipped the horse mercilessly.

The fire the raiders set was just reaching the thatched roof when Brady arrived. The stone walls of the house had retarded the flames, but now they were about to engulf the house. He could not enter by the main door; the blaze licked out of it like flags in wind. But the window of his bedroom was dark yet. He climbed through it and instantly heard the wailing of the baby. He crawled toward the sound and found himself hands and knees over Nellie's body, which was inert and leaden. The baby was under her, all but his little head, which protruded, screaming, from between her legs as if being born a second time. Colman cradled him in his left arm and began pulling Nellie with his right. But he could not lift her to the level of the window. He went through with the baby, but before he could return for Nell or to find Bea and Conor the entire straw roof collapsed, a torch which flashed like powder against the dead night sky.

Neighbors arrived with buckets, and a brigade was formed, the line reaching from the well behind the barn to the house. They worked furiously, but their effort was meager compared to the fire, which devoured the perfect fuel of the roof.

"It's a miracle, a miracle!" Marie McClusky kept repeating. She was holding the baby and, apparently, referring to its survival. Colman took the baby back when there was nothing to do but watch the fire burn out.

"Marie," he said, "I'd like to use the filly."

"Sure, Colman. Now?"

"In a bit. I've something to do in Clonmel."

Marie was frightened by the dull choke of his voice.

"But I must know first . . .," he said.

"Colman, you shouldn't look . . ." Marie gestured to her husband, who came over. "Jack, Colman shouldn't go in there now."

"I'll take care of it, Colman. Go to our house."

"Nellie's in the back room, Jack," Colman said.

"All right."

"I must know about Bea and Conor."

"All right. Go to our house now."

"No. I'll be back in a bit."

With his son in his arms, Brady walked up the tumulus behind the village. Though it was a dark, moonless night he followed the path without stumbling or hesitating.

The megalith, even in the pitch black, stood out against the sky starkly. Colman looked across the countryside. Lights from farmhouses dotted it. There was a near glow from Ballymacarberry and a distant one from Clonmel. At the foot of the hill the cinders from what remained of his house sent up a red flush.

Brady put the baby down in the soft grass. He turned and leaned against the huge stone, his forehead just touching it. He closed his eyes. He was aware of his own breathing, of the pulse in his ear. A faint, ill-defined emotion, beginning in the hollows behind his knees, surged through him, growing less faint as it moved upward through his body, so that by the time he clenched his fists and began to slam them against the stone he was in the grip of an infinite rage. An animal wail came out of his throat, a roar which rose and fell with each blow he struck with the heels of his fists. It was only the pain shooting up through his arms that stopped him striking. He opened his hands and pressed against the stone, flat out, pushing, pushing, pushing, trying to topple the primeval rock, trying to hurl it down from its mountain, trying to have for once some effect on the goddamned thing which after all those years of his coming there and bringing Nellie and bringing Mick and bringing Conor and bringing Bea — still the bedeviling stone ignored him, showed him nothing, was unmoved and indifferent and cold and ignorant and blood-thirsty to devour its victims, his loves, his only loves, whom the stone, an altar, claimed now as sacrificial due, and that was why he was pushing, pushing, pushing, pushing — roaring all the while like God the day He cut His hand off to drown the earth in blood.

It did not budge.

Its age and weight mocked him.

Its silence accused him. He was the one, after all, who had failed them. He was the one who had abandoned Nell for Collins and abandoned Collins for Nell and then Nell again for Collins and through it all had never given himself to either. Brady pushed and pushed and pushed, only now against the twin guilts. Nell and Mick were dead and he had done it and it mattered not a tinker's dam that he wanted it some other way. Why could he not have loved them? Loved them? Loved them? He was pushing against himself, wanting to have some effect on that pitiful acorn of a heart he had. Why could he not have loved them? His love would have kept them living, kept them well, kept them warm, made them happy. Like God's. His love like God's. But that was it: like God's! How could he squander what was so sacred? And so he pushed and pushed against the consequences of his hoarding, the consequences of such pride. He would not feel them.

And as for the stone itself, the hell with it. He stopped pushing and stepped back and stared at it. *I want something that will move! I want something that knows when I've touched it! I want something that will take its shape from my hands! The hell with the stone!*

He looked down at his son, who had fallen asleep in the grass. He picked him up and held him toward the stone at the level of his eyes and in a loud deliberate voice, he said to the stone, "Him you will not have! You will not have my son!"

And then he returned to the charred remains of his house.

"I found them, Colman," Jack McClusky said. "All three."

Brady said, "I told Marie, Jack, I want the filly. Will you take the kid?" Colman handed the baby over. "Give him to Marie."

It was not dawn yet, when he reached the barracks and the camp was not stirring. Brady walked up to the adolescent sentry as if he were De Valera himself.

"Good morning, Private."

"Morning, sir."

Brady went by without hesitation. He walked into the officers' building. At the notice board inside the door he unclipped the billet roster, found Gavin's name, and went down the corridor to Quarters Seven.

Gavin was fully dressed, passed out on his bed, asleep in his own vomit. He smelled of the fire. His pistol was on the floor.

Brady picked it up, muffled it with a pillow and kicked Gavin until he awoke.

Gavin looked up, dried vomit flaking from his beard, with a misery and self-loathing that Brady recognized.

"Who are they?" Brady demanded.

Gavin only looked at him sickly. He did not fully appreciate his position until Brady exposed the gun, dropping the pillow and forcing the barrel into Gavin's mouth.

"Who are they!"

He held the billet roster in front of Gavin who desperately pointed his finger at each of six names. Then Gavin looked up at Brady. There was nothing in the man that could deceive or resist. He barely had enough left to beg for his life.

"Please, Colman," he sobbed when Brady took the gun out of his mouth.

But Brady did not waste a thought or a moment. He muffled the gun again and shot Gavin through the eye.

Then, consulting the roster, he slipped down the corridor to Room Four. The door was ajar and it was empty. He looked at the roster and crossed to Quarters One. Three men, unconscious and ruined, were sprawled in the small room. The stale smell of fire rose off them. They bore smears of blood.

That was evidence enough for Brady, but he wanted them all.

"Wake up," he said, kicking.

Finally one opened his eyes and stared drunkenly up at Brady.

"Yes, sir?" he slurred.

"What's your name?"

"My name? Uh, McCue."

"And him?"

"That's Pepper."

"Pepper what?"

"Pepper Dea."

"And him."

"O'B."

"O'Brien?"

"Yea, O'B."

Colman shot them through their pillows, the conscious man first. Slaughter pigs.

Two of the others were passed out in the next room. He shot them without waking them. He found the sixth man in the latrine, hunched over the trough in a seizure of dry heaves. Brady had nothing to muffle the shot with but he fired anyway.

The gun clicked impotently. The chamber was empty. Brady struck the man square on the skull with the butt end of the weapon. He struck him again.

He left the barracks the way he entered.

His love like God's, and his vengeance.

That morning he buried what was left of Bea, Conor, and Nell, and he listened in silence while Father Devine and the McCluskys prayed the rosary for them in the church.

Colman lit a candle at the feet of God's Mother and held his hand over the flame to see if he could feel it.

"Colman, are you . . . ?" The priest touched his shoulder.

"Father, I want you to baptize the boy."

"What, now?"

"Yes. Baptize the boy."

The priest knew a command when he heard it. He led Colman and Marie and Jack to the marble stool with its stained basin. Marie was still weeping.

"What's his name?"

"His name is Michael Collins Deasy Brady, and he's coming with me to America."

TWO

1

WHEN THE PHONE RANG on Curley's desk the dust flew. His office was like an open-air stall at Haymarket, a chaos of tables, jars, old cane chairs, boxes of books and papers, stacks of handbills, and fallen piles of folders. A gaudy velour shamrock, framed in gold, hung on one of the dark paneled walls. Old campaign posters with torn corners covered panels on another. An old whale-oil lamp which had been electrified stood on a corner of the desk next to the phone. It rang again.

James Michael Curley seemed not to hear it. He was standing at the high bay window, dressed in faded black broadcloth trousers and a defeated white shirt with frayed cuffs. His face was thick and slightly pitted. His hair was a mat of fine brown curls, parted sharply on the left side of his head. It was August of 1927. He was fifty-two.

Curley was the president of the South Boston Democratic Club when, as now, he was not the mayor of Boston. His office was on the second floor of a musty Victorian relic that sat like an aging clerk across from the big new courthouse on Dorchester Heights. His window opened on the slope of Southie as it ran down to the Fort Point Channel and the harbor and across to downtown. It seemed to Curley that he spent hours at that window. He refreshed his gaze continuously on its vista. That he was temporarily out of city office — he had been defeated narrowly for his third term the year before — meant that he surveyed his domain from this window instead of from the one on School Street. The view from the Heights was spectacular, and, though he was counting the days until the next election, in some ways he preferred it.

The phone's bell was cut short in the middle of its third ring. That would be Alice Mahon, his secretary, answering from the small anteroom where she worked the typewriter. She would put him off, whoever it was, and Curley was relieved. The day had bloomed into crisp August perfection, and he wanted to look at his city sparkling there.

The Irish were concentrated in three sections of Boston: Charlestown, East Boston, and South Boston. But the latter was their stronghold. A mile-wide peninsula reaching four miles out into the harbor, it had been laid out a hundred years before as a summer retreat for wealthy Bostonians, but it fell by default to the droves of famine Irish who had no place else to go. By the end of the nineteenth century it was a booming phenomenon of tenements, wharves, ships, churches, graveyards, and factories. The mass production of cheap nails and the development of balloon-framing enabled the construction of hundreds of three-deckers which just kept pace with the influx of immigrants.

At its Broadway Station end, South Boston was a rough and merciless district where tenement flats with lamplight and cellar toilets rented for two dollars a week. There were howling families next to rowdy boarding-houses filled with the micks who were digging the city's subway tunnels. The buildings there were dilapidated. Warehouses and stables made the streets dark and dirty, fearsome at night. In daylight there was noise and dust from the truck and cart traffic in and out of Gillette's razor factory and between downtown and the wharves lining the north shore of the peninsula. That end of South Boston, closest to the city proper, was ugly, weighed down by poverty and crime. Outsiders took it to be typical of the entire ward; Southie was an Irish slum.

But the farther half of the peninsula, from Dorchester Heights out, was not like that at all. On East Broadway were the grand bowfront mansions the old families had built before the Irish came. Now they were the neatly divided dwellings of self-respecting working people who paid, typically, fourteen dollars a month for five rooms with all improvements: kitchen stove, penny heater, inside toilet, and gas piped in for lighting. Having avoided the "shanty," they mocked their own relative affluence by referring to themselves as "Steam-heat-and-nothing-to-eat Irish." Their section of Southie was called City Point, and in 1927 it was home to ten thousand people, all of whom knew that they had the choicest part of Boston. Their parents and grandparents had abandoned the crowded and crumbling North End to the Italian eel-eaters. Back Bay and Beacon Hill, where the Brahmins lived, were regarded as sterile, eerie places for their lack of children playing and their lack of old men watching from the corners. South Boston was the farthest thing from a slum to those who lived there. It was, as Curley himself always said, the citadel of a people who had come into their own.

The door to his office opened behind him.

"Mayor?" Alice Mahon said timidly. She was not supposed to disturb him until noon.

Though he was irritated, Curley cracked his face into a merry grin. "Yes, dearie, what is it?"

"It's Chief McGrath calling from Precinct One. An emergency, he says."

Curley nodded and Alice left.

He crossed to his desk in two lanky steps, picked up the phone, and put its pieces to his mouth and ear.

"Hello, Brian!" he said grandly. "What's up?" Curley had engineered McGrath's appointment himself.

"Mayor, I knew you'd want to know. We're going to clear out those anarchists today."

"From in front of the State House?"

"Yes, sir. Their leaders are bringing in Reds from New York and Chicago and all over. The judge said picketing's to be allowed, but not a demonstration."

"What's the difference?"

"Sixty. Judge Thayer says sixty makes a demonstration. We know a bus of thirty will be pulling in shortly. There's already forty or fifty of them up there. At sixty we move. I got the mounted unit behind the Senate wing and then the stick squads will cuff them."

"When do you expect to go?"

"An hour. The boys would sure appreciate it, Mayor, if you could be there. These anarchists are a tough lot and, well, the boys would like to see you there. You never know."

"Sure, Brian, sure. I'll come right over."

"Thanks, Mayor. I knew we could count on you. This Peters fellow don't give a rat's fart about the boys."

"Forget Peters, Brian. I'm your mayor, no matter what the *Transcript* says."

"Damn right, Mayor. I'll be glad when this is over. Wish they'd plug those two dagos right now and get done with it."

"Just a few days, Brian. The execution's set for Tuesday, eh? You can hold."

"Not if the Bolshies come up from Charlestown at the jail. If the whole crowd marches on Fuller's office we'll need the Marines."

"You *are* the Marines, Chief," Curley said. "You'll have those runts on the first boat to Moscow by supper. I'll see you in an hour. Don't do anything till I get there."

"Thanks a lot, Mayor."

Curley clicked the phone together and put it down with a bang. "Alice," he hollered; "Alice!"

Alice Mahon opened the door.

"Get Brady in here!"

Colman Brady was the treasurer of the South Boston Democratic Club and an associate in Curley's insurance business. He had started out as a foreman on the Castle Island landfill four years before, a city project which had Curley's special interest, and he had impressed the mayor with his energy and easy way with the men. Brady was bright and quick and Curley had liked him instantly. During the campaign the year before, Curley had made good use of Brady's brogue, and he made him treasurer afterward because he wanted him locked into the next campaign as well. Brady was great with the Irish and Curley was too smart to take them for granted. The cops loved the big Mick. He'd be just the fellow to have along if there was trouble.

While he waited for Brady to come down from the fourth floor, Curley went back to the window. He had to imagine the lines of Beacon Hill and the State House dome on its pinnacle because it was obscured by the large commercial buildings just west of South Station. But Curley had no trouble picturing the Bulfinch masterpiece or the rows of Federal mansions below it. It was turf he was very familiar with, but it was not his own. He was familiar with it the way a soldier is familiar with the terrain of his enemy.

Brady knocked politely on the door and waited for the loud grunt. It came. He went in.

"Well, Colman, me lad of gold, how goes it?" The emphatic intimacy of his greeting had its effect on Brady despite his knowing that the warm grin and open affection were chief tools of the man's trade. Curley could endear himself instantly to his own kind.

"Hello, Jim."

"Oh, laddo, am I glad to see you! We got a hot potato. They expect big trouble from the Sacco-Vanzetti crowd. The boys are going to round them up and I want you to come with me."

"To Charlestown, the jail?"

"No, Beacon Hill. Come on."

"Wait a minute, Mayor. I don't get it. That Sacco-Vanzetti stuff is dynamite. You want to keep your distance. It's Fuller's problem. And Peters's. Not yours."

"Fuller and Peters ain't going to be on that street this afternoon with a bunch of looney-bin Bolsheviks. McGrath just called. The boys need me, and by God, whatever the peril, political or otherwise, they'll have me. Come on."

The former mayor grabbed his tired black coat from the back of a chair and strode out of the office. Brady put both hands in the pockets of his trousers and stared after him for a moment. He understood exactly what was happening. Curley loved a crowd. He would play it the way musicians played their instruments. And, even better, he would play it in front of the State House, in front of the Brahmin Temple, in front of Mayor Peters, who had defeated him, in front of Governor Alvan T. Fuller. With their mealy-mouth ambivalent foot-dragging on the case —

for six years they had put up with these anarchist protests — they had invited the notoriety and chaos and worldwide attention that was on them now as they prepared to put the two Italians to death. Curley wanted to gloat. The mob was theirs. The Boston police were his.

Colman had to hurry to keep up with Curley. It never occurred to the mayor to take a car to Beacon Hill. It would take them three quarters of an hour to walk it, but that was no problem. McGrath had said an hour. The promenade was one of the best-used routines in Curley's kit, and this one would display the mayor's urgent response to the call of his people. The two men cruised down Broadway. Brady frankly admired Curley's knack for moving quickly while still greeting shoppers and storekeepers and mothers at their carriages. When Curley waved at you and called your name and remembered your sick aunt or your brother's lost job, by God that was something! That James Michael, what a fellow!

Brady waved and greeted friends too, but not so grandly. He was a step behind Curley, and that was exactly where he wanted to be. Curley was the master and Brady was his best student. In the five years since he'd left Ireland, he had mustered sufficient nerve and luck to win a place in the snug of Curley's shadow. After Michael Collins, Brady had considered himself a connoisseur of shadows, and he knew the mayor's was a worthy one. Brady had come to understand Curley's genius as if it was his own. No one had ever embodied the yearnings of a people better than the mayor did those of his own. But Brady saw clearly too that what made Curley a giant on his own turf made him a midget, a circus figure, off it. Colman Brady was learning what to do and what not to do from James Michael Curley. Curley's end would be Brady's beginning. Brady was going to be mayor and more, and with a difference. In the way that Southie was Curley's, the whole city would be Brady's. His people would be the harp immigrants among whom he already moved so easily, but not only them. His people would be the North End Italians too, and the South Cove Chinese and the Roslindale Greeks. And more. His people, before he was through, would be the Beacon Hill Brahmin elite, whom Brady intended to defeat finally, as if they were British, by forcing them to love him. And once he had them all as his own, then he would do wonderful things for them. There was nothing simply self-interested about his ambition. He wanted to be of great and lasting service to Boston. At twenty-nine Colman Brady was a man who wanted everything.

And he dressed like it. He wore a fashionable white linen suit and sported a bright red tie. He flourished a thin cigar at his friends and knew that, when he passed, people feasted on the sight of him. Brady was not cocky, exactly, but he believed in posture and he walked as if he brushed his sand-colored bushy hair against the sky itself.

Terry Griffen, who pumped gas at the Socony on D Street, fell into step with the mayor. "Thanks, Your Honor, for coming to Amy's wake."

"Sorry for your troubles, Terence." Curley let his arm drape the man, who was stooped and red-faced.

"Honest to Pete, Mayor, Ma nearly died when you showed up."

"Now, Terence, we can't have folks dying at funerals. Give a bad name to the Irish wake."

Brady watched Terry Griffen drift off, shaking his head, delighted — that Curley was a card! — anxious to repeat the mayor's crack to the boys. He slid into the speakeasy at Miller's flower shop.

Curley turned to Brady. "Laddo, it startles me at times, how little they want. Just a mere hint or two of your friendship."

"It's more than a hint, Jim, when you help them bury their dead."

Brady's remark pleased Curley, as it was intended to. Brady knew where to touch him, as Curley did them. Curley nodded. It was a sad thought, which was why he loved it.

They crossed the Broadway bridge into downtown, where the lunch-time crowds swirled in and out of stores and foodstands. Curley waved to these strangers as if they were his neighbors too. Everybody was his crony. His large, full figure, that endearing grin — how could they not notice? His loud, glad "Hallooo!" — how could they not like him?

Through all this, they were making good time. They crossed through South Cove, by the movie houses on Washington, and past the musical instrument stores on Boylston. They entered the Common, cut by the Parkman Bandstand, in the shade of which salesgirls and clerks were eating their sandwiches, and onto the paved path which cut diagonally across the park up to the State House.

The first pickets they came upon were milling at the foot of the Shaw Memorial stairs at the State House edge of the Common and below Beacon Street.

"They Shall Not Die," a placard read.

Curley and Brady brushed past the picketers, up the stairs and onto the street. A large line of fifty or more protesters moved slowly in their oval on the sidewalk.

"Ladies Full Fashioned Hosiery Workers," another sign read. "Support Sacco and Vanzetti."

A squad of red-faced Boston policemen stood with folded arms on the lowest of the grand stairs that swept up from Beacon Street to the Capitol, the golden dome of which flashed the August sun back at itself. The police eyed the oval line.

Curley crossed to them, pressed their shoulders, pinched their forearms, let everybody see that they were his. Brady hung back. His instinct was a bit different from the mayor's at that point. The police were about to make themselves some real enemies — and not just the Reds and the *artistes* who were going to get it.

Gusts of shouting from the picketers greeted the arrivals of new protesters, little dark men with eyeglasses and seamstresses with their long braids piled on top of their heads. A pair of women in summer dresses and big hats arrived in a large Packard, which drove off without them. Brady remembered that well-heeled Yankee matrons and Harvard professors as well as Communist agitators and Italian peddlers were outraged at the impending execution. Brady was afraid that Curley was seeing the thing a bit too simply. The cops would make many enemies, he was sure.

"Please, Governor, Pardon Them!" read a sign. "The World Waits!" It was carried by a small old man whose hair was white as paper and whose skin had the moist sticky look of paste. He looked unwell, but he walked his line with a determination that made others clear the way for him.

Automobile traffic passed slowly by, drivers staring. A Ford coupe honked — whether in protest or support — before turning down Park Street. State House workers began coming outside in pairs and threes to eat their bag lunches on the Common.

"Join us! Join us!" the picketers chanted.

The girl secretaries giggled and hurried down the Memorial Stairs into the park. But an old lady, a civil service veteran who had rubber thimbles on her forefingers — even at lunchtime — sneered at the marchers.

Curley spotted Chief McGrath standing between the pillars of the State House portico. The mayor took the stairs casually, greeting cops as he went. Brady saw and hurried after him; he wanted the scoop too. He didn't understand why McGrath should be so worried. The picketers were numerous, and a few of them had the fanatic's eye, but mainly they were orderly and quiet, not a particularly threatening lot. As he followed Curley up the stairs Brady reflected again that he himself had no position on the heated question of the two anarchists. Maybe they were guilty. Maybe they were victims of the bias against foreigners — he had felt blasts of that himself in Boston. But the debate seemed futile to Brady. He was certain the men would be put to death. The Lowell Commission had sealed that sentence.

Abbott Lawrence Lowell, president of Harvard, had chaired a special committee appointed by Fuller to review the trial, its verdict, and Judge Webster Thayer's sentence. Lowell found no reason to recommend any leniency whatsoever. Some had argued that Lowell's refusal represented the final proof that Sacco and Vanzetti were classic victims of Beacon Hill bigotry. But it wasn't that simple to Brady. Their lawyer had been Arthur Dehon Hill, a leading member of the bar Establishment. Their great defender in print had been Felix Frankfurter of the Harvard Law School. Brady'd never heard of any harp having free legal weight like that. If Harvard couldn't get them off nobody could. They were probably guilty.

But as far as Brady was concerned there was no point in expressing an opinion on the matter. The affair was poison from start to finish. Everyone who touched it would be infected. There would only be losers in this one. That was why Brady was sorry to see Curley rushing into it. It seemed he wanted to make a fool of himself too, just because Peters, Fuller, Lowell, Hill, Frankfurter, Thayer, and all the others had.

"So how goes it, Chief?" Curley asked loudly. He wanted everyone to hear him. If Fuller was in his State House watching, he'd be furious to see the former mayor's strut.

"A problem, Mayor, a problem. Mayor Peters is in with the governor right now. Peters wants to give them a permit for the demonstration."

"What's that all about?" Curley asked. "Peters can't want this riffraff out here any more than we do."

"It's Mr. Lowell, Mayor. He's asking for the permit himself."

"Lowell? What the hell does he have to do with it?"

"He says they have a right to peaceable assembly. He says this is not Spain or Russia." McGrath smirked as he said this.

"Hell, it was his gang said they're guilty. It's time to stop this lollygagging about."

"That's what I told him, which is why the mayor told me to wait outside."

"The mayor?" Curley asked. He scored the point with McGrath silently; James Michael Curley was the Mayor.

Brady sensed the drive of Curley's arrogance and wanted, for Curley's own sake, to deflect it. He turned and looked down on the picket line. Three young skylarking toughs in tweed caps and knickers were attempting to join it, but a young woman was standing them off.

"You can't walk here with that sign," she said loudly. Several pickets joined her.

One of the boys carried a placard which read, "Two Fried Wops Coming Right Up."

Brady nudged Curley and pointed to it.

Curley strained to read the sign.

The toughs started dancing on the edge of the oval line and chanting. The boy with the "Fried Wops" sign led them, waving his placard rhythmically.

"There, Brian," Curley said. "Look at that. There's a scuffle brewing for sure. Your boys still behind the Senate?"

"Yes, sir. All mounted up and ready."

"Well," Curley said, "I'd sure hate to see you wait too long." Curley was staring at the sign and the shoving that was going on around it.

"What can I do, Mayor?"

"You're the chief of police, McGrath. You uphold the Law. Have they got a permit to demonstrate like that?"

"Not yet, no sir."

"There must be a hundred and fifty of them."

"Mr. Lowell said that . . ."

"Don't you worry about Lowell, Chief. I'll take care of Lowell."

Brady read Curley; he'd love a head-to-head with Lowell right there on the street. He seemed to expect it. But Brady understood the difference between Curley and Lowell. Curley loved the display of power. He was desperate for signs of everybody's deference. Lowell exercised his power almost invisibly. He wanted deference so total that there were no hints of it. Curley take care of Lowell? Not likely. Curley would never see him.

The boy with the sign inserted himself between two pickets. They seized the sign, broke its stick and ripped the cardboard. They shoved the boy to the ground.

His companions jumped on the pickets and flailed away.

Curley had McGrath by the elbow and was yelling, "Stop them! Stop them!"

McGrath blew his whistle sharply three times.

Horses' hoofs clattered on the street.

Bystanders screamed and fled down the stairs into the Common. The picketers tried to link arms, some of them going limp and falling with covered heads as they'd been trained. The police swarmed over them, swinging their clubs, which whacked down viciously.

Bars of the "Internationale" rose and broke off as the cops honed in on the singers.

Patrol wagons with their eerie sirens could be heard coming up from the stationhouse on lower Joy Street.

One protester, bleeding badly from the head, was singing, "Mine eyes have seen the glory of the coming of the Lord."

A mounted policeman ran his horse up the stairs halfway to the State House entrance to club down a bespectacled radical who had been screaming, "Comrades! Comrades!"

Curley was not pleased by the scene, though he'd goaded McGrath into it. He loved his city, and the quick brutal chaos of the police swarming down on the pickets besmirched it. Still, the Law had to be upheld.

Brady thought the whole business unnecessary and he was shocked by it, if not openly. People were being banged about and bloodied more for the sake of Curley's vanity than for the peace of the city. Brady lit a cigar and backed into the shade of the portico. He watched the melee alone. It seemed to him a kind of contest. The horsemen were too aggressive and, by not allowing an orderly retreat, they were forcing the protesters to resist, and some were determined fighters. Stones were hurled. At least two policemen were pulled from their horses and pummeled with their own nightsticks. But most of the pickets were writhing in the street in panic and anger. Horses stepped on some, tearing open red wounds.

At the sight of the tumbled policemen, McGrath ran down the stairs to bark orders at his men, and Curley followed. Brady stayed where he was. There was nothing to be done.

He watched as demonstrators were hauled roughly into paddy wagons, but after a moment he noticed a man coming up the broad stairs and he had, unaccountably, the feeling the man was coming to him.

He was right. The man, dressed in a black serge suit that must have been suffocating, walked into the shaded portico and took up a position right next to Brady. He turned and looked down on the melee. It seemed at first as if he was going to say nothing.

He was Sergio Capelli, a North End second-stringer who worked a small corner of the home-brewed wine business. Brady recognized him as one of Gennaro Anselmo's boys.

"Mr. Brady," Capelli said, but without looking at him. Both men stared down at the street.

Brady said nothing. It was unusual for the likes of Capelli to be on the Hill and extraordinary for him to be near such a massive police action. The North End hoodlums were invisible people. It occurred to Brady that perhaps it was sympathy for the two anarchists. Was Capelli part of the demonstration? Not a chance. North Enders had mastered a remarkable stoicism about Sacco and Vanzetti. The public protests were more the work of Jewish lefties and Brahmin do-gooders than of Italians.

"What brings you out of the old neighborhood, *amico?*" Brady asked. He drew on his cigar and smiled at Capelli.

Capelli replied, "You," and stared at him.

"Me?" Brady laughed. "I don't get it."

"I would like you to come with me." Capelli spoke without a strong accent, but, as the son of immigrants, he had a formal, stilted cadence in his manner of speech. He was about twenty-five.

Brady knew that Capelli himself had nothing for him. He had to be on somebody else's errand. Whose? The answer was obvious. Anselmo. Gennaro Anselmo was a North End comer who ran a large garbage collection business which had started out carting residue from the home stills and which now had a city contract to clean up Haymarket every Sunday.

Brady had obtained the contract for Anselmo from Curley, having first met him when he hired his trucks for the Castle Island land fill. Curley had not wanted to hire an Italian outfit for the land fill job since it was in Southie, but Brady'd insisted. He needed the trucks. For Anselmo, that job had provided exactly what he was looking for — a connection outside the North End and a foot inside the door of city contracts. It wasn't that Anselmo needed the trucking business, but that he wanted the cover for his efforts to start a bootleg distribution system outside the Italian neighborhood. He was a ground-breaker. He was the first North End hood to work in tandem with the Irish.

"Why should I go with you, *amico*? For what?"

"A friend wants to see you."

"My friends speak for themselves. Why'd he send you?"

Capelli shrugged. He did not know. Anselmo was a discreet man. Capelli waited.

Brady had to go with Capelli and he knew it. One of the key factors in Curley's loss to Peters the year before had been the Democrats' failure to get the North End vote out. Curley had little use for Italians, and that was one of his mistakes. Any politician who expected to carry and keep more than his own yard had to have a hand inside the Italian district. Anselmo was far from being one of the North End powers, but he was young. He was first-generation and appreciated the value of cooperation with other ethnic elements. And he was damned ambitious. One could do worse, Brady thought, than tie his tail to that kite. If Gennaro Anselmo wanted to see Colman Brady, then he would. Brady knew what it was to be used and to use.

He dropped his cigar and stepped on it. He looked down at the street and saw Curley heading off to the precinct house with McGrath. Nothing else was going to happen there. "All right," he said. "Lead on, friend."

The North End was the oldest residential section of the city and looked it. The streets were crooked and narrow, following the contours of the land abutting the old wharves. Men clustered on corners and argued. Women with bundles pushed by on the narrow walks. The cobbled streets were jammed with trucks, pushcarts, the ranting hawkers of figs on strings and the day's fish catch. The old brick buildings were tall; their height prevented sunlight from falling anywhere but in the middle of the streets. Old people, elbows on pillows, watched everything like eagles from their windows, and below them slain rabbits and yearling lambs hung from the hooks of butcher shops dripping blood into gutters. Fire escapes slashed down the sides of buildings like wrought lightning, but the landings held mattresses, where the men slept on the summer nights.

Along Hanover Street all of the signs on the doors and store windows were in Italian, and Brady felt even more the foreigner than he did on Beacon Hill. At Fleet Street, Capelli turned east and, though the difference was lost on Brady, by the time they walked two blocks, all of the signs were in Sicilian.

Capelli stopped at the corner of Fleet and North streets.

"If you wait here," he said, and then he was gone.

Brady lit a cigarette, using the business of it to stifle his uneasiness. He had rarely been in the North End, and never alone. It felt more like Italy than Boston.

"Hello, Brady."

The voice from behind startled Brady. He turned quickly. Gennaro Anselmo was there, a short, stocky man with a delicate face that seemed the foil to his powerful body. He looked at Brady intently, displaying confidence and purpose in his steady, strong gaze.

"Hello, Gennaro. Fancy meeting you here. I was waiting for a friend." Brady cracked his face into a grin and held out his hand, a politician's offer.

Anselmo shook Brady's hand firmly. He had known that Brady would come. Didn't every outsider long to be invited in? Anselmo trusted his intuitions absolutely. He thought he understood exactly what was stirring in the Irishman and he was prepared to risk nearly everything that he was right. That was not unusual. Anselmo continually gambled on his own intuitions. What made this different was that he was about to gamble that Brady's intelligence and ambition were as large as his instinct told him they were.

"North Street!" Brady said. "Did you know that Honey Fitz was born here? On North Street!"

"Who?"

"Never mind."

"One of my sisters was born . . ." — Anselmo pointed to a building halfway down the block — ". . . there."

"Used to be Irish over here, they say." Brady could not conceal the faint disgust he felt at the cramped, smelly, steamy neighborhood. "*Dearo,* they called it. Dear Old North End. And before the Irish, the Yankees. Paul Revere, right?" Brady was thinking the Italians got what the Irish didn't want who got what old Boston didn't want.

"I want to talk to you about something else, not the neighborhood." Anselmo studied Brady carefully.

Brady inhaled smoke and said, "Curley's out of office, you know. I'm not sure what we can do for you."

"It is not business I had in mind." Anselmo paused. His eyes flicked up and down the street. "This is not a good place. Come with me."

"You have to give a clue first. What's up?"

"You were at the demonstration?"

"Yes."

"About that."

"The anarchists?"

"They did not kill those men."

Anselmo turned on his heel and walked halfway down the block and stopped in front of a low door.

Brady stared after him. What the hell was this? Every damn leftie in America had been hollering that for six years. But Anselmo was no leftie. There was not a frivolous cell in him. He was serious and he wanted Colman Brady's ear. Brady followed him down the sidewalk and through the door.

Anselmo closed it and faced Brady. They were in a cramped, shadowy vestibule.

"I want to ask your help," Anselmo said. He spoke with a weighty deliberation that communicated his dead seriousness to Brady.

"Lots of people claim they didn't do it," Brady said. "Mainly girls and college kids."

Anselmo didn't reply to that, and Brady wondered if he'd offended him. "So tell me."

"I will prove to you that the two are innocent, and then you must go to the governor."

"Fuller? He hates my guts."

"He hates Curley, not you. You represent Curley to him. You have met with him twice in the last month."

"On a couple of things left over from last year. But you do know your civics, don't you? You studying to be a citizen?"

Anselmo smiled faintly. He had been born in Worcester. Brady's gibe was at the fact that even first-generation Italians were foreigners to old Boston, more foreign even than recently-over Irish like Brady. "I know what you do, Brady," Anselmo said. "You carry the mayor's discreet messages to the governor. Both men talk to you."

"How do you know that?" Brady asked.

Anselmo nodded as if Brady had confirmed what he said. And then he stated a new fact. "The city of Boston bought two hundred heavy trucks from Fuller before he was governor. You brought the bid to Curley."

"Don't make me laugh!" Brady began to move away. "I didn't handle deals like that."

"Fuller paid you one thousand dollars in cash. Discreet."

Brady halted again and slammed Anselmo with a look. "You wouldn't be implying that I was bribed?"

"No. I say these things only to show I appreciate your position. You are a man of great ambition, I think."

"Do you now?"

"If you were to be the source of the much-sought evidence . . . ." Anselmo let the sentence hang. It was true. The execution of the two Italians was to take place on August 22, barely a week away. There were reporters from all over the world in Boston. Fuller, squirming in his position as hangman, had practically begged the Lowell Commission to give him reason to commute the sentences to life. Lowell, Samuel Stratton, head of the Massachusetts Institute of Technology, and Robert Grant, a blue-blooded judge of probate court, had not done so. But new evidence might.

"What do you know?" Brady asked.

"I know who hit that payroll."

"Who did it?"

"It is not for me to say."

Brady studied him. Anselmo was totally serious. And he was right. If there was evidence, if Brady could get it, if he could be the source of it — that would be the first rung up on his ambition. He had to play this very carefully. "All right," he said. "But listen, one doesn't just walk into the governor's office and say the two geeks didn't do it, honor bright! What do you have?"

"I need your word first. Your solemn word." Anselmo fixed his stare more inside Brady than on him. He was making a fresh and last assessment before going further. Could he trust him? Were his intuitions reliable? If he was wrong on this one, Anselmo knew, he was dead. "Your oath that you will not mention my name in connection with this to anyone."

Brady nodded immediately. He caught the menace of Anselmo's request. The man lived by the subtlety of his threats. "You have it, my word. But that won't be enough for Fuller."

Anselmo turned and led the way down a dark narrow corridor that wound around a front room to a curving staircase. Brady stifled a wave of nausea at the rancid smell rising from the cellar. It was the odor of boiling wine, and it was piercing and indelible like vinegar. The home brewing of wine had become, with Prohibition, the most ubiquitous and profitable business in the North End.

The staircase seemed to rise forever. At every turn Colman tried to avoid touching anything with his white suit, but there was no light and he kept bumping the walls.

Finally they went through a low door and out onto the roof of the building. Laundry hung from lines strung between chimneys. The adjacent buildings were taller, and so the only view was of brick walls. Anselmo ducked under a line of bedclothes. When Brady found him he was halfway up a filthy rickety ladder that led to the rooftop of the next building.

"Jesus, Anselmo! Where now?"

But Anselmo ignored him and, with considerable agility, climbed to the top of the ladder, vaulted over a high ledge, and disappeared again.

Brady followed, ruining his suit.

When he came over the ledge he was shocked and thrilled.

There, on the next rooftop, was an elegant, manicured garden. It was evident at once that someone had taken infinite pains to haul soil bit by bit up to the roof and to cultivate fruit trees and flowers with great skill. As Brady brushed dirt from his sleeve, he stared at the garden. It was practically an orchard, full-blown, running the entire length of the roof, thirty yards at least, and across by ten. There were fig trees, orange trees, and a lemon tree with a ready crop of five or six lemons. Brady walked into their midst, touching the leaves and smelling the fruit.

"How wonderful!" he said aloud. "How wonderful!"

An old man appeared suddenly from behind a shrub. He was tiny and stooped. His skin was the color of olives, but wrinkled as stewed figs. He was smiling at the tall Irishman.

"You have a wonderful garden," Brady said formally.

Anselmo stepped to the old man's elbow and spoke to him in Sicilian. The old man smiled again at Brady and nodded like a drinking bird. "*Grazie, grazie.*" And then he said something which Brady did not understand. Brady looked at Anselmo, who said, "He bids you welcome to his house."

"Thank you," Brady said. "I never heard of a garden on a roof like this. I used to be a farmer myself."

Anselmo translated.

The old man nodded and smiled. Most of his teeth were gone.

After an awkward silence, Brady said, "All right, Anselmo, what's the story?"

Anselmo touched the old man gently on the elbow and spoke confidentially to him. Brady watched as the old man's expression changed. Suddenly he stepped closer to Brady and seized his lapels and began speaking rapidly and urgently. His eyes brimmed and he rushed through whatever he was saying with such great feeling that Brady felt himself drawn to the man and moved. When he finished speaking he did not release his grip on Brady's suit, but lowered his head until it nearly touched Brady's chest. The man seemed exhausted and ashamed.

"It is not Gennaro Anselmo who says this," Anselmo began; "it is Giuseppe Tucci."

"What does he say?"

"He says it was not the two who robbed the factory in Braintree. It was a group of seven men from this neighborhood, including Enrico Zorelli."

"Zorelli!" Brady knew the name and showed it. Enrico Zorelli was the head of the Unione Siciliana, the disciplined North End organization that controlled the tenement district and the citywide marketing of its bootleg wine. Zorelli was known to Brady because he had been competing with Jerry MacCurtain from South Boston for control of whiskey smuggling on the waterfront. Zorelli was a typical Old World don; he was ruthless, devious and contemptuous of outsiders. He had, above all, refused to put his organization to work for Curley during the election the year before.

"Including Enrico Zorelli," Anselmo repeated, "and his own son, Antonio Tucci."

"His own son?" Brady stared at the old man.

"Yes."

Brady lifted the old man's face and looked at him. Tears were streaming down his cheeks but he made no sound.

"Sacco?" Brady asked.

The man shook his head: No!

"Vanzetti?"

Again, no!

"Antonio Tucci?" Brady asked.

The man nodded. *Mi figlio.*

"I have a son too," Brady said gravely, feeling older than he was, feeling like a father.

Brady looked at Anselmo.

"His son is at Concord prison. He asked his father to make it possible for him to tell the truth."

"Why is he there?"

"A bank robbery in Lynn."

"And he's willing to admit murder?"

"He wants to arrange . . ."

"You need a lawyer, not me. I sell insurance."

"He's willing to tell how it was Zorelli's soldiers who did that, not Sacco. Not the other one. He was there. He has nothing to hide."

"Zorelli will kill him."

[*130*]

Anselmo did not respond to that.

Brady studied him carefully. "I would have guessed that you're in the Unione yourself, Anselmo."

Again Anselmo did not reply. Brady understood then how bold a stroke this was. Anselmo was delivering himself into Brady's hands. It seemed a rash and careless move, a foolish one unless the bet was for the entire house. Brady guessed what Anselmo's moves were aimed at, but he pressed him. "What's your interest in this? Justice for your compatriots?" Brady smiled and thought, *Here you tell me I'm ambitious.* He wanted not to be Curley's lackey for longer than he needed to be, that was true. But it seemed to Brady that his ambition paled by comparison to Anselmo's, who wanted nothing less, Brady saw, than to bring down Zorelli. "I admire your nerve," he said.

Anselmo shrugged. "What Tucci says is the truth." Anselmo looked at the old man, who stood there as if *he* were guilty. "Many of our people know the truth. That's why the picket lines are of bohemians and college boys, not Italians. We know and we are afraid, most of us."

Brady could not take his eyes from the old man. He put his hand on his shoulder and pressed it with warmth and fondness, almost forgiveness.

"If you arrange for the governor to see him, young Tucci will provide details of the holdup that only a participant could know. He will provide names of others who can be persuaded to support him. Sacco and Vanzetti are innocent."

Anselmo paused. Brady took his arm away from the old man, who had withdrawn into his own sadness; his body had gone wooden.

"You can be the one to save them," Anselmo said.

Brady nodded. He was thinking, *Nice for me and nice for the two bastards. If they're innocent they should get off, even if they are Reds.*

"The discussion is ended now," Anselmo said. He took old Tucci by the arm and led him away between the fruit trees. It took the Irishman some moments to realize that neither of them was coming back. He made his way off the roof, down to the street, and out of the North End the way he'd come.

Colman Brady walked down Atlantic Avenue, across the pier, up Summer Street, and into South Boston. On the hill at Dorchester Heights he went into the Democratic Club. At the entrance an old porter sat at his table with a row of dominoes.

"Mr. Nagle, good day!" Brady said cheerfully. "Is himself back yet?"

"Hello, Mr. Brady. Indeed he is. I just brought up the paper."

Brady took the winding wooden stairs two at a time and went to Curley's office. Alice Mahon was not at her desk, so he knocked quickly and breezed in. "Hello, Mayor!"

"Colman, damn it!" Curley ranted. "They're crucifying me!"

"Who?"

"Goddamn *Transcript!*" Curley slammed his hand down on the newspaper open on his desk. "This afternoon's, just out! Listen to this! 'With the former mayor himself standing by, the troops assaulted the picketers without provocation. The reaction of the police was extreme and irresponsible, even allowing for the fact that the former mayor — disregarding the City Charter and the will of the people — was himself directing the operation.' " Curley looked up. "Goddamn *Transcript!* Goddamn Prescott! They ought to make up their minds. Are they for these Reds or not? It's Fuller, I tell you, trying to drain this Sacco-Vanzetti pus off on me!"

"That's what I wanted to talk to you about."

"Oh, Christ, never mind. I don't want to talk about it. Let's go to Fenway. The Sox are playing the Yanks."

"No. Jim, I must talk to you."

"Goddamn Yankees, all of them."

"I've come across something important."

"What, are the Reds going to march again?"

"No . . ."

"I can hear your heart thumping from here. What is it?"

"Do you recall meeting a fellow name of Gennaro Anselmo?"

"Garbage trucks, right? He bootlegs that terrible dago hooch."

"Right. He does the Haymarket and worked for us on the land fill at the Island."

"For *you,* not me. I told you not to hire him. Wops building the Irish Riviera! What does he want now? Another city contract?"

"No." Brady paused, letting the weight of his silence draw Curley's attention. "He says they didn't do it. Sacco and Vanzetti."

"Oh, Jesus H. Christ, Brady! Not you too! I don't care *who* did it! I just want the goddamn thing over with. Reds from all over the damn world swarming down on Boston like maggots. You think those State House coachmen have to deal with this crap? You think that ass Peters will? No! It's *my* boys on the line! My city!"

"Jim . . ."

"Don't you 'Jim' me. I'm going to the ballgame."

Curley grabbed his suit coat from a chair, fuming, "That wop don't know a bee from a bull's balls!"

Brady grabbed Curley's arm. "Maybe not, but I do!"

Curley's sail fell and he stopped. He stood looking at Brady, waiting. He was on the verge of an explosion and Brady knew it.

"I don't care who did it either, Jim." Brady's face wasn't six inches from the mayor's. He would out-cynic him. "I don't care any more about 'justice' than you do. I'm talking about a stick of dynamite with names on it — Alvan T. Fuller. J. J. Peters. How would you like to blow them out of the water? And not only them, but a fellow name of Enrico Zorelli?"

"I'm listening."

"Here's the scene. Sit down, Mayor." Curley sat. Brady went on melodramatically. He was going to use Curley's method against him; he was going to talk to him as if he were a crowd. "Here's the scene. For Sacco and Vanzetti, it's two minutes to midnight. Boston, America — no, the world — is holding its breath waiting for the switch to be thrown by Governor Alvan T. Fuller of Massachusetts, who regrets he has no choice under law but to send ten thousand volts of electricity into the emaciated bodies of two misguided immigrant slobs who couldn't even spell the word *anarchist*! When suddenly, the former mayor of the great city of Boston announces that what the U.S. Department of Justice and the entire court system of the Commonwealth and a team of blue-ribbon lawyers and even the commission chaired by the president of Harvard University itself could not do, he — out of his own modest zeal for justice and love of the little guy — *has done*! On his own! Without government funds! Namely, uncovered the true culprits and produced one of them to confess and name the others!"

"I'm still listening."

Brady smiled. "I can hear you listening — with your heartbeat."

"So go on."

"That's it. I go to Fuller, present the evidence, and get him to issue the executive order for stay. Then I alert you, and before the news breaks you call the boys in and take credit for it."

"But what . . . ?"

"Jim, Anselmo's fingered the bird for us. He's at Concord right now, waiting to sing. *He* did the payroll job in Braintree. *He was there.* And guess who else was?"

"Zorelli."

"Your North End nemesis."

"Oh, my God, Colman. Oh my God!" Curley pulled away from Brady and walked around behind his desk to sit. "Do you know what this is?" Curley was allowing himself the faintest grin. "This is the luck of the goddamn Irish! Peters, Fuller, *and* Zorelli! Oh my God! I'd save the good name of Boston!"

"Anselmo's given us a wedge, all right, but we have to hit it square on."

Curley sat forward. "What if it's a put-up job?"

"It could be. Anselmo's out to get Zorelli. He wants the Unione for himself. It's the young kicking up against the old, same as everywhere.

[*133*]

But it won't matter. If the mate in Concord is willing to swear *to his own part in it,* the public will buy it. What better proof of a man's truthfulness than the willingness to incriminate himself? Fuller would have to pardon S. and V. after that, and the world would thank *you!*"

"And you too, of course." Curley's glance was knowing, not disrespectful. "What's the bird's name?"

"Tucci. I talked to his father."

"Why would he do it?"

"I don't know. Anselmo has a hand in his bowels. Hell, maybe the guy wants to tell the truth."

"Not likely. But you're right. It doesn't matter as long as the last couplet rhymes."

"Anselmo wants no part of the whistle. In fact he asked me not to mention him to anyone, including you, for obvious reasons. I gave him my word on that."

Curley nodded. He knew that Brady wouldn't break his word lightly, but also that Brady would never keep a secret from him. "It's better for us that way. We can take the credit."

"And Anselmo gets the north corner on poteen for the rest of Prohibition."

"Fair enough," Curley said. "Jerry MacCurtain can work with him. Zorelli won't even talk to Neapolitans, much less the Irish mob. Oh, it'll just kill Fuller and Peters and Lowell and the goddamn *Transcript.* We can make it look like a Brahmin cabal!"

Brady shook his head. "Not so. The Brahmin split on this one. The *Transcript*'s been out front for S. and V. all along, and don't forget Hill and Frankfurter and Gardner Jackson. They've been solidly behind them."

"Tokens! Tokens! It *has* been a Brahmin plot, by God. They just hate foreigners!"

"So do you."

"Not if they'll vote for me! I'll *love* 'em! I'll love the goddamn *Reds* if they'll vote for me!"

"After this they will."

"After this they'll get a chance. You're looking at the first four-term mayor this city ever had."

"Four! You're not in your third yet."

"You got to think big, Colman. You got to think big."

"You're right, Jim." But Colman was thinking, not for the first time, that the mayor thought too small.

2

WHEN COLMAN BRADY returned to the State House on Beacon Hill, the secretaries and office workers were in full flight, as if the end of another day of running the Commonwealth was occasion for a panicked rush home.

He stood on the curb of the street and watched them swarm down the great stairs, mostly women, mostly young. He saw Mary Ellen Shields, a typewriter girl, with whom he had kept company for a time in the spring. He noticed her legs, slim and white, kicking out from her skirts. It was the bold fashion among young women not to wear stockings in the summer. She walked toward him confidently, showing her Connaught rearing.

"Hello, your ladyship," Colman said, bowing slightly.

"Why, Colman Brady! I didn't recognize you with that clean suit on."

He looked down at himself. The elbows and one shoulder of his suit were filthy. He blushed.

"Are you working on the docks again?"

"Oh, stop, woman, for God's sake! Can't you give a man a civil greeting?"

"If *he's* civil, yes." She walked by him haughtily.

"Mary Ellen Shields!" he bawled after her. "And you wonder why . . ."

But apparently she didn't. She was gone.

"Got me," Brady said to himself, "which makes us even." He brushed at his suit. He'd have gone home to change, but he had to get to Fuller before he took off for the day.

He waited outside the governor's office for ten minutes before the councilor, Arthur Symons, came out. Symons nodded to the receptionist, ignored Brady, and left.

The office of the governor was furnished entirely with antiques. A large pewter inkwell with a quill sat on the mammoth desk, which was actually a monastic refectory table. The governor's chair was from a medieval taproom, and his wastebasket was a colonial butter churn. Art from France and Spain hung on the broad white walls. Though the governor had spent a considerable amount of his own money and his staff's energy on the collection, none of the art pieces and none of the antiques was especially noteworthy. Alvan T. Fuller was a newly rich man who had made his fortune selling cars and trucks, and who had become the latest political front man for the established Boston families, who, having all too often lost control of City Hall to the motley immigrants, intended to maintain their hold on the State House. There had never been a governor of Massachusetts who did not owe them his position, and there never would be if the Hill had its way. But Colman Brady knew Fuller well enough to sense the Brahmin chagrin; Yankee blood does not the manner make. Political office and bad art can be purchased cheaply. Admittance to the class itself costs much more.

"Thank you for seeing me, Governor."

"Not at all, Mr. Brady." Governor Fuller was a huge man. He sat expansively back in his chair. It was possible to imagine him decked out in leather doublet and demanding a chalice of mead from the tavern wench. "What can I do for you?"

"It's what I can do for you."

"I beg your pardon."

"I can give you a way out of the Sacco and Vanzetti tangle."

Fuller sat up. "What?"

"Surely you're not looking forward to pulling that switch on them this week."

"Don't you tease me, Brady. What are you saying?"

"I'm saying you are the most observed politician in the world right now. If you listen to me you can come out of the Republican convention in Chicago next year as your party's nominee for the office of President of the United States."

"You have my full attention."

"I'm sure I do. If you don't listen to me, Governor, you become the most famous executioner in the world and you're finished in public life."

"Brady, you've already crossed the line into impudence. I'm fully aware of the dimensions of my situation. Suppose you tell me what you have in mind."

"I can prove that Sacco and Vanzetti had nothing to do with the Braintree holdup."

Fuller did not reply for a moment. He looked at his hands, clasped them and unclasped them. "Half the country makes that claim."

"I am prepared to come through on it."

"Does Curley have anything to do with this?"

"Nothing. He does not know about it. You are the first person to whom I have come with the fruit of my investigation."

"I don't believe you."

"Governor, I am an ambitious man. Curley is a general in an army of privates. He can't help me. You can."

"How can you prove they're innocent?"

"First things first. What I am about to tell you is the result of a lonely and long effort I have taken on my own part and at my own expense."

"How much?"

"Two thousand dollars, cash."

"Jesus, Brady!"

"Half now, half when it's all public and you're off the hook. I trust you. And you can destroy me. So?"

Fuller shook his head slightly, but he stood and walked to the wall behind the desk. He swung a Cranach reproduction aside and dialed the combination to the safe it concealed. He opened it and withdrew a single banded stack of bills. He sat again and flipped the money across the desk at Brady.

Brady counted it.

"A man named Antonio Tucci is a prisoner at Concord right now. He is four years into twenty for a bank robbery at Lynn. He is a member of an Italian gang that operates out of the North End. He is prepared to testify that he and six others held up the shoe factory and that they — not Sacco and not Vanzetti — shot and killed the paymaster and his guard. The detail of his testimony will prove that he is telling the truth."

Fuller did not respond. He was trying to think of the way that Brady was deceiving him.

"That can't be true," he said.

"Why?"

"Because . . ." — Fuller shook his head dramatically — ". . . it's too simple. You make it sound like a rabbit out of a hat."

"I think perhaps a pigeon."

Fuller grunted.

"Begging your pardon, Governor, but I thought a rabbit out of the hat was what you were hoping for."

"No. Believe it or not, Brady, all I want is the truth. And what I want to do is the right thing."

"Don't tell me you've become blind to your own interest. Just because it'll make you a bigger hero than Lindbergh doesn't mean it isn't also right. But, well, if you'd rather, I can take my information to the *Herald*."

"Bigger than Lindbergh, Jesus! But I can't believe some sucker is sitting in a cell waiting to confess to this thing."

"He was hoping he wouldn't have to. He thought, like you and every-body else, that the Lowell Commission would recommend clemency."

"How I hoped they would!"

"Sure. You have your conscience. Tucci has his."

"You've talked to him?"

"No."

"Well, shit-a-damn, Brady? How do you know all this?"

"I have my sources. I found his father today and he broke down in my arms and wept. A little Italian fellow who doesn't even speak English. And he confirmed everything."

"You speak Italian?"

"Enough. Sicilian, actually. Not all of us Irish are illiterates, you know."

"Well, if you haven't spoken to the man himself . . ."

"I couldn't do that now, Governor, could I? Not until I'd spoken to you. I have to give the man assurances, first of all that you'll hear him out and, secondly, that you'll protect him from the retribution of gang mem-bers, and, thirdly, that he can look forward to a bit of clemency of his own when he's brought to trial on these charges."

"Is that all?"

"He's not asking for money. All the man wants, I tell you, is an easy conscience."

"That's right. You're the money man."

"I can live with my conscience, Governor. I take great satisfaction in knowing that I am the instrument of justice in this case."

"Yes. Well, when are you going to see him?"

"Right now. You'll have to call the warden to get me through, and I'll need a car."

"I want Webster Thayer to go with you."

"Thayer! Christ, you can't be serious! He's the judge!"

"He's the one we have to convince."

"No, Governor," Brady stood. "*You* are. Leave Thayer out of it. He's determined to see those two fry. His job is over. It's up to you now. You're the governor!"

"All right. I'll leave Thayer out. But I'll go with you myself."

"Fair enough. Let's go."

They rode to Concord in the governor's black twelve-cylinder Olds. It was after seven o'clock when they arrived at the large iron gate that was itself dwarfed by huge gaunt trees. The sun was just down, and the loom-ing brick prison was dark and morose-looking. Brady had never seen the place.

The guard stooped down to the car window, but before he spoke Fuller ordered, "Call the warden. Tell him Governor Alvan T. Fuller is here. I'll wait."

As the light faded and his memory stirred, Brady was aware that an old emotion gnawed at the accommodations he had made with himself. What had he become? A two-bit pol, flashing about other people's corridors, waiting for his break? No. Not even at his most morose was Brady that cynical about himself. He was simply looking for a place on which to stand with his lever, to help his people and to help his family and to help himself. But being with Fuller made him nervous. What was Fuller, for all his twelve cylinders and governor's chair and wall safe? A codfish coachman. And Curley, for all his bluster, was still their vassal with his fief. A man can be emasculated and not know it — that's what Brady thought. By God, if he was going to trade on his soul, it would be for *real* power. His lever was for the earth itself. It was Brady's hunch that a man is damned not for selling his soul, but for selling it cheap.

He gazed out of the car window on the cheerless evening landscape. The grim prison with its cathedral-like windows and gothic arched portals and chivalric turrets seemed to mock the bucolic countryside with its vulgarity. It was impossible to imagine that human beings were confined indefinitely within that false and obstinate building.

He thought of Mary Ellen Shields. They had first met when, in late winter, they had been two solitary walkers on the promenade along the harbor at Marine Park. It had been a cold and gloomy day. As he had drawn near her, about to pass, she had startled him by turning and saying suddenly, "Empty beaches are so sad." He took the remark as an invitation and joined her. They walked along together and, though he was known as a Southie gay blade, he was more awkward in their talk than she was. The pictures of her face that day — the defiant note of her gaze — and of those wintry beaches were fixed permanently in his memory. The sight of the prison building called them to mind. He did not know why.

"Governor! Good evening!" A wrinkled face with huge sweeping moustaches appeared in the window. The man still held his dinner napkin. Brady imagined him choking on his greasy cabbage when told the governor had come. His breath issued irregularly with a wheezing sound.

"Lennon!" Fuller barked, "It's about time!"

"I had no idea, Governor, you were . . ."

Fuller was a man who knew what it was to be humiliated and badgered. He required his underlings to be obsequious and servile, as he supposed his superiors required him to be.

He got out of the car on one side as Brady did on the other.

"What's his name?" Fuller asked.

"Tucci," Brady said, "Antonio Tucci."

"*Anthony* Tucci," the warden corrected. "We don't let them use foreign names here."

"Take us to him," Fuller ordered.

"Wouldn't you like to use my office, Governor?"

"Yes. All right." Fuller looked at Brady, who nodded. "Yes. Take us to your office."

From one window of the warden's office they could look into the inner yard of the prison, a shadowy, empty dirt lot. From the other window they could gaze along a shallow river that ran down through a small valley. The institution sat on a small rise and commanded a modest view of the surrounding farmland. The valley was dotted here and there with the glowing spots of lamps as the twilight became night. The feeling that had first jogged Brady's memory had lodged itself in his stomach. He lit a cigar with his customary flourish, which he now intended to override the strange nervousness that had him. He looked out on the gray gleaming river. It was a small and predictable matter, given his mood, for him to see the river Nire and the hills of Four Mile Water.

He recalled standing with his back to the Druid dolmen and looking out over that valley and seeing it, fresh, limitless, forever green, as an image of his own interior geography. Those hills, he thought now, were innocent. Innocent; he let his mind stall at the word. Who hadn't been? Brady thought he was unusual in his ability to remember exactly when his innocence had ended. Major Edmond Purcival had intruded upon it sure as any serpent upon the ancient landscape. Innocent? We are all innocent in hindsight, he thought, which means nothing, as Sacco and Vanzetti would tell anyone. What means something is whether they plug those electrodes into your skull or not. The thought of the two Italians brought him back. Just as well; Colman Brady hated himself for brooding.

"Ever been in prison, Governor?"

"Yes, in point of fact." He smiled. "I dedicated the new wing at Walpole. Let me have one of those cigars, will you?"

Brady gave a cigar to Fuller, then held a match for him.

The governor's hands shook badly. "Little nervous, I guess."

"Understandably. This could do big things for you."

"I've been thinking about that convention." Fuller was perspiring freely. He took a deep drag on the cigar. "I've been thinking about Lindbergh. I'll tell you something, Brady. I won't forget this. I could use a man like you."

"Thank you, Governor. I appreciate that." Brady smiled ingratiatingly.

It was then they heard the sounds of rapid footsteps. The office door burst open and the warden still clinging to his napkin, which by now was wrung and knotted, breathlessly cried, "Oh, my God, Governor! Oh my God!"

"What?" Fuller demanded.

"He's dead! Somebody cut his throat!"

Brady drew on his cigar, trying to stifle and disguise his shock. He understood immediately that he was involved himself in the man's death. Innocence? Guilt? It made no difference now. Suddenly Brady was nearly overcome with the thought that it made no difference ever. *That* is the knowledge of evil — the righteous and the sinner alike get it in the neck. The man's throat was cut. What kind of bargain had he struck for *his* soul? Well, he was finding out now, wasn't he? A fear of quick turns gnawed at Brady. He had not expected Tucci to get killed. Obviously, he should have.

He turned away from the governor, went to the warden's desk, picked up the phone, and called his sister.

"Hello, Maeve, it's me," he said when she answered. He cradled the mouthpiece of the phone in the crook of his arm and stood looking out the warden's window at the dark river. Fuller was on the opposite side of the room looking into the prison yard. "I won't be home till late. Put the kiddo to bed without me, would you?" Brady listened for a moment and then said patiently, "Sister, your little brother can take care of himself. I'm not in a brothel." He laughed. "I'm in a prison. I'll tell you later. Cheerio."

He hung up and turned back to Fuller.

Fuller pulled away from the window almost reluctantly and led the way out to his car. He and Brady were silent most of the way back to Boston. Finally the governor said, "It's a kind of proof, isn't it?"

"A kind of, yes."

"I couldn't defend a commutation in terms of it."

"I know it."

"Not on my own. Maybe if we talked to Thayer."

"He'd laugh at you."

Fuller fell silent, let his gaze follow the dark country road. Brady stared at the back of the chauffeur's neck.

"I know!" Fuller slapped his knee and turned to face Brady. "Lowell! If Lowell knew about this. . . !"

Brady nodded slowly. "You're right. He could do it."

"Hell's bells, then. Let's . . ."

"You set it up, Governor. I'll get Tucci's father and see you there."

"Now?"

"Yes, Governor. Now."

[*141*]

The North End that night was in the jolly throes of celebration. It was the Feast of the Assumption, and the streets were packed with dressed people. Lights were strung from opposite windows and a great old-country band played opera music in the square in front of St. Leonard's.

Brady had to fight his way through the crowd. He nearly kicked over a tin pan of chestnuts, and the old man who was roasting them cursed him cheerfully. At the corner of Salem and Hanover, Brady had to wait while the parade passed. The statue of the Virgin Mary behind which a throng marched was bedecked with dollar bills, and even tens and twenties. Brady slapped his hand against his breast to feel the bulge of the money Fuller had given him.

At Salem and North he went into the building Anselmo had led him into before. It seemed to Brady weeks had passed since he had been repulsed by the smell of wine dregs and the other stale odors of the narrow winding stairs. But it was only hours.

On the rooftop the laundry was gone, but the rickety ladder was there. Brady climbed it and remembered his effort to keep his suit clean.

He half expected that the rooftop orchard would not be there, that he had imagined it, or that the trees had been collected and stored like the laundry. But it was there and the pungent smell of citrus filled his nostrils as he went over the low wall. The sounds of the band music drifted up from the street. A soprano was struggling through an aria that was an ocean beyond her. Brady walked among the trees unsteadily while his pupils asserted themselves in the strange light. The garden was dark and discreet, isolated utterly from the surroundings of brick and stone like a secret from the city.

Brady tripped over a bundle and nearly fell. He nearly ran. He wanted to be out of that garden, out of the North End, out of the whole business, because he knew a corpse when he kicked one. It was his first corpse since Ireland, and he did not want to see it or touch it again or smell it.

It was old Tucci. His throat had been cut, and the blood collar was black and thick. He had been dead for hours. The sight and stench attacked Brady's stomach and his nerves. He thought for a moment he might vomit, but he didn't. He couldn't take his eyes away from the old guy who was looking up at the sky past the lemons under which he had died. It was as if he were staring wistfully at the moon. It was as if he were alive.

Brady slowly knelt by him. He did not stifle the uncharacteristic impulse he had to pray. He began reciting the words of the Act of Contrition. He remembered doing that for Michael Collins. Priests said you could never be sure when the soul left the body. He would make the old man's confession of sorrow for him. But Brady knew it was his own. He was involved in this death too, and he was sorry for that. What was happening? What was he doing? Was he doing *this?* After killing Gavin and the other murderers he had resolved never to touch another's blood again. He had left Ireland for Boston to be clean of that killing. And now he couldn't even keep his suit clean.

Looking down at Tucci and thinking of the old man's murdered son, a picture of his own son forced itself on Brady's mind: his boy with fine, immobile features, sleeping so, face upward. But he had left Ireland above all to keep Collins clean. He was never to see such a sight as this, or to smell it, or to touch it. Brady reached down and closed the old man's eyes.

A voice said, "I'm sorry."

Brady jumped with shock and whipped around.

Gennaro Anselmo stood against a brick wall a few yards away. He had been there the whole time.

"I'm sorry," he repeated, putting his hand up palm outward, a gesture of reassurance. Brady stood ready to defend his own throat.

Anselmo shook his head. "I'm sorry to have introduced you to this."

Brady let his nerve drain a bit. "Ugly," he said, glancing back down at the corpse. "Ugly damn business."

"Yes." Anselmo stood with his hands shoved in the pockets of an old overcoat. Looking at him bundled so, Brady realized for the first time that there was a cold edge to the night. The band music still played below and the fiesta lights shone up from the street eerily.

"This is not all of it," Brady said. "I've been to Concord." Brady slowly raised and lowered his shoulders.

"I assumed. The same?" Anselmo touched his throat.

Brady nodded.

"It is a death worse for those who must see it than for those who undergo it." Anselmo spoke formally and rigidly.

"I wonder what either Tucci would say about that. I'd prefer to see it myself, thank you. You've a vicious set of friends, Gennaro."

Anselmo seemed not to hear Brady. He looked toward the street. The Virgin's parade was passing below, and voices were raised in a rousing Marian hymn which drowned out the band music.

"I'd have more expected you to get it than him," Brady said. "You overreached yourself."

"This time." Anselmo knew that Zorelli's men were looking for him at that very moment. Anselmo was in deep trouble. He and Brady both knew it.

"Tell me something, Gennaro. Did you start this or did Tucci?"

"Antonio. You won't believe me, but it's true anyway. He cared about justice."

"Justice," Brady said absently. He looked down at the corpse and felt once more a kind of unwelcome contrition. Do things go wrong because you are not worthy of their going right? No. This went wrong for reasons he did not anticipate. It was that simple. He was not responsible, and that was what frightened him, really frightened him. Two men were dead. For what? That two others might live?

Goddamnit, Brady thought, though the limits of his own interest had been reached, he knew he could not walk out of this web, not yet. Old Tucci had touched him. "Anselmo, would you come with me to talk to Lowell?"

Anselmo had only a brutal stare for him.

"You're as good as dead anyway, *amico*. Why not make something of your last act?"

"It doesn't matter now."

"Perhaps not to you."

"The anarchists have their reward. Their deaths are worth less now than the songs about them."

"But there's his death to consider." Brady looked down at the corpse. "And his son's."

Anselmo said nothing. Brady looked at him and was surprised to see not a resigned, emotionally rigid fatalist, but a determined, willful and still-powerful man. A chill shook through Brady. Anselmo clearly did not consider himself a dead man. He had a set of clamps on his life; he would dare Zorelli to undo them. Clamps like that Brady wanted, but he did not know yet if he could bear their pressure himself. Brady thought he could learn from Anselmo if he could keep from being afraid of him.

Anselmo remained motionless against the wall, pressing his arms against his sides, looking off toward the sounds of the Virgin's hymn, which was fading in the distance.

Brady left him alone in the strange garden with the old man's body. He was thinking as he wound down the steep unpleasant staircase that such a garden in such a place was wrong. It was like having a perfect dream in daylight.

President Lowell lived in Quincy House at Harvard, but lately he had been the target of demonstrations there. Since it was summer vacation in any case, he had been staying in his longtime residence on Marlborough Street in the heart of the Back Bay. Compared to the North End only a few minutes away, the streets beyond the Public Garden were silent as a graveyard and, to Brady, as eerie. He found Lowell's number easily, pulled on the bell, and waited.

Lowell opened the door. He was a tall man. His brown eyes surprised Brady because they were soft and weary. "Mr. Brady?" he said, offering his hand. Though it was nearly midnight he was still dressed formally in black coat, striped trousers, stiff collar, and tie.

He led Brady into a room just inside the entrance foyer. It was the president's study, a dark, book-lined room with mahogany cabinets and heavy chairs and a large desk which was cluttered with papers, a pipe rack, a miniature bust of Ralph Waldo Emerson, a tobacco canister, and a quarter of the antler of a deer. Fuller was standing in front of a brass-studded leather chair that looked Spanish. Behind the chair was another bust; Brady guessed it was Plotinus, but it could have been Marcus Aurelius. On the wall beyond that was an ornately framed oil of the Madonna. It was a Renaissance original, Italian, and Brady sensed its age, venerability, and the anomaly of its presence in Lowell's study.

"This is Colman Brady, Mr. President," Fuller said nervously.

"We met," Lowell said.

It dawned on Brady that he was probably the first foreign-born Irishman to enter Lowell's house by the front door. Certainly he was the first to be received in Lowell's library at midnight.

"Where's the man's father?" Fuller demanded. He was literally quaking with agitation.

Brady did not reply at once, and Lowell, with a broad courtly gesture, said, "Please sit."

Lowell pulled an armed windsor chair with a Harvard seal away from the bookcase for Brady.

When the three of them were seated Brady looked at Lowell and said, "He's dead."

"No, no!" Fuller cried. "I told him about that! Where's his *father?*"

Brady looked at Fuller. "Tucci's father is dead. His throat was cut tonight."

"Oh, God. Oh dear God." Fuller grasped his chest with both hands.

Lowell looked calmly at Brady, waiting.

Brady said, "Clearly, Mr. Lowell, the people whom Tucci was prepared to implicate killed him. And his father."

"How very tragic." Lowell shook his head slowly. He had a high, thoughtful brow which was bent forward slightly in a scholar's stoop.

"Tell the president, Brady, what he said."

"Don't!" Lowell held up his hand. "Don't tell me. There is no point."

"But, Mr. President," Fuller said, "surely these killings indicate . . ."

"Nothing for us, Governor."

"Mr. Lowell," Brady began.

But Lowell cut him off. "Mr. Brady, do you have personal, firsthand knowledge about the robbery of the Morrill shoe factory?"

"No, but I'm . . ."

"I'm not interested. I'm sorry. I do not mean to be rude, but anything you would offer at this point would be hearsay. That is not acceptable. It is not relevant."

"Wait a minute," Brady protested.

"No. There is nothing to discuss." Lowell stood up.

Fuller begged. "Please, Mr. Lowell . . ."

But Brady put his hand on the governor's sleeve. "You can't eat sawdust without butter, Governor."

"I'm sorry," Lowell said, but without a hint of apology. "I am bound by the rules of evidence."

"Bound and gagged, I'd say, Mr. Lowell." Brady stood.

"Perhaps, Mr. Brady . . ." — Lowell's politeness was exquisite — ". . . when you've been in our country a little longer you will understand that there are reasons for such rigid procedure. What seems to you now inhumane and lacking in compassion will someday . . ."

"I take my civics class at the Lyceum in South Boston, Mr. Lowell."

"Yes, I'm sure you do."

The president and Brady stood squared against each other for a moment. Brady felt as though he knew the man, had been in his presence before. He recognized the thin smile, the pressed hands, the ingratiating condescension; they belonged to General Sir Nevil MacReady, to Lloyd George, to Churchill. They had belonged to Major Edmond Purcival.

Lowell eyed Brady carefully. He was accustomed to the deep-seated anger of the Irish, their envy and resentment. But in this man those were combined with a controlled resolution that was unusual. As long as the Irish obeyed like Fitzgerald, as long as they ranted like Curley, nothing would change. But Lowell recognized something in Brady that he associated vaguely with himself, and that was what impressed him and made him uneasy.

"Well, Mr. President," Fuller said, rising belatedly, "We're grateful . . ."

"No, Governor," Brady interrupted, "we're not. Mr. Lowell, I would like to make a comment, if you don't mind."

Lowell nodded. He was attentive.

"Inertia in a matter of this kind for the sake of form and procedure is not high-minded conservatism, as you would have it. It is only vulgarity. It is *your* vulgarity."

"That is your opinion, Mr. Brady."

"Yes. I'm sure it is." Brady offered his hand to the president, who took it. Fuller watched the two men shake hands firmly and he felt to his own surprise utterly outside the acute antagonism that bound them together.

On Marlborough Street Fuller said, "About that thousand, Brady . . ."

"I won't require it from you, Governor, in the light of . . ."

"Not the *second* thousand. I'm talking about the first."

"Would you like a receipt?"

Fuller stared at Brady.

"No? Well then," Brady said, turning away from him, "good night. Enjoy your week."

The next morning Colman Brady, Jerry MacCurtain, and James Michael Curley met in the latter's office.

"Fuller wouldn't budge without a nod from Abbott Lawrence Lowell."

"What?" Curley cracked, "from all three of them?"

"So I'm afraid there's nothing to be done from here either," Brady said. He had not laughed.

"The hell!" the mayor stormed. "We'll use it anyway!"

"You'd be a laughing stock, Jim. You can't prove it."

"We'll get Anselmo to back us," Curley said.

Brady shook his head. "You'd never find him. Anselmo's on the lam. He'll be dead as soon as Zorelli catches up with him."

"Don't count on it, Colman," MacCurtain put in. "Anselmo has his own people, who are loyal to him. He's a survivor, if you ask me. He'll hole up somewhere until Zorelli cools off and remembers who he's dealing with. Anselmo's the only wop over there who speaks-a da English, if you get me. As long as the booze joints in this town are run by the Irish, Zorelli needs Anselmo." Jerry MacCurtain was a beefy longshoreman, whose appearance belied his cleverness. He stood leaning against a wall with his shoulder softly jarring a framed needlepoint that read, "Boston — where the Caseys speak only to Curleys and the Curleys speak only to whom they damn well please!"

"Well, to me," Curley said, "a dago's a dago."

Brady studied his nails. He knew Curley was speaking for effect. He was not dumb. He knew the difference between Anselmo and Zorelli, and when he needed to sidle into it he would.

MacCurtain thought he still needed to make his point. "Anselmo was born here, Mayor. He'll work with somebody besides his own. We'll need his kind, especially after Prohibition."

"Come on, Mac," Curley said, "one thing at a time. What about this week?"

"Don't play your ace on your king, that's all, Mayor."

"It's over, Jim," Brady said. "Sacco and Vanzetti are dead."

"But hell," Curley said, "I'd still like to try it."

"Without evidence, without something, you'd be just another Red sympathizer. You want that?"

"No, but damn! We had them. I hate to let that son of a bitch Fuller off."

"He dies when they do. Lowell already treats him like a leper. I'll tell you what I think, Jim. The stink from this thing could drive the Republicans right off the Hill. You could be governor!"

Curley gave Brady a malevolent look, and when he spoke his voice came out hissing. "Colman Brady, don't you ever presume to tell me what I *could* be! Don't you dare give me advice about *my* prospects!"

"Sorry, Mayor," Brady said unhesitatingly.

Curley turned to MacCurtain. "See what happens, Jer? Bring a lad up from the minors a little too soon, he throws his arm out."

When Curley turned back to Brady there was nothing apologetic or morose in either of them. They had both done what was required. Curley reached over and slapped his aide's shoulder. "Come on! Colman! Me among them chowderheads! The codfish aristocracy! The term's an insult to the fish. Besides, first things first. I have to win Boston again."

"You're right, Mayor," Brady said. He would play it however Curley wanted it played. Obviously, the mayor was not ready for the slight shove Brady was giving him. Brady had to be patient, and he reminded himself of that. His shot at the mayor's chair depended totally on Curley's successful run for governor. Once Brady had his own base he could get his distance from Curley and keep it. Until then, Curley would be right every time.

The mayor squeezed his aide's shoulder. "You know something, Colman," he began. He had assessed Brady's mood and was going to dispel it with a blast of his best stuff. "I like you."

Brady blushed despite himself. In addition to the exasperation and impatience and, at times, contempt that he felt for Curley, he had an unabashed affection for the coot that was part admiration and part Irish pride and part simple awe at a man-writ-large. Curley was like Michael Collins in the way he drew out of Brady that mixture of envy, respect, and, even, love. Curley was finally as much Brady's master as he was Southie's.

"So, laddo," the Mayor went on, shifting back to his previous tone, "where's that leave us on Sacco and what's-his-name?" He wanted a summary and a conclusion.

"Nowhere," Brady said. "They're dead."

"I knew it! I should have gone to the ball game!" Curley dismissed them with a disgusted wave of his hand.

Jerry MacCurtain and Colman Brady left the Democratic Club and walked together down Broadway toward O'Houlihan's speakeasy.

"The old man's got a hair on, eh?" MacCurtain said as they crossed Dorchester Street.

"I'm afraid I jacked his hopes up, Jer. He's going quite mad sitting on his duff on the edge of things. He'd have been unbeatable if we'd pulled it off."

"He'll waltz back in, Colman. You watch."

"To the mayor's office, maybe. But he can't do that for another three years. He could run for governor next year."

"He'd rather be mayor."

"Don't shit yourself, Jer. Curley won't rest until he's had it all." Brady looked at MacCurtain and repeated with emphasis, "I mean all." He looked away. "But he wants a sure thing. That's his trouble. That's what makes him like Fuller and Lowell. Everybody plays the second bounce in this town, Jerry."

"I haven't noticed you waiting back."

"Well, start noticing. Nothing happens on my turf until Curley gets in again. Three years. Damn."

"I was thinking you might like to occupy yourself with something else meanwhile."

They were outside O'Houlihan's Hardware on Flood Square. The tavern was in the back room behind a wall of rakes and venetian blinds in all sizes. The two men remained talking on the street for a moment.

"Jerry, I've thought of it. Your corner shows real promise, I must say. Especially if you can force Zorelli off the waterfront. And keep him off, which I've no doubt you can. But to tell you the truth, it's not for me."

"What? Trading in hooch bothers you?"

"Not particularly. But it has a limited potential. It's a bit marginal, you know."

"Your phony insurance company is what's marginal, Brady."

"I learned in Ireland, Jer, that insurance covers a multitude of sins. Michael Collins was an insurance broker."

"Who?"

"Never mind. The point is nobody knows what an insurance business is. That's why Curley claims it as his profession."

"Second-class shyster, if you ask me."

"What's a poor uneducated Druid to do, begorra begam?"

"You're fast on your feet for a mick, Colman."

"For what I have in mind I have to be."

"You want Curley in the State House so that you can have Boston."

"For a start, Jerry. Exactly. Do you think it's an offense against pride?" Brady slapped his friend's shoulder and laughed.

"I think politics is for lightweights, Colman."

"Maybe you're right, Jer," Brady said, steering MacCurtain into O'Houlihan's. "You know what Sean O'Casey said, don't you? 'A man should always be drunk, Minnie, when he talks politics. It's the only way in which to make them important.' "

JACKIE MCSHANE was eight years old in September of 1927 and on the Nativity of Mary he, along with all the other third graders, made his First Communion at St. Eulalia's. He was dressed in a neat white suit with short pants. His hair was slicked off a part in the middle of his head. After the Mass he stood with his new prayerbook on the walk outside of church between his Uncle Colman and his mother. They were proud of him and he knew it. He loved his uncle, but he worshipped his mother. He could tell, from the way she kept looking down at him, that she was having the happiest day in her life.

Maeve McShane was fifteen years old when she announced in 1908 that she was going to America. Her father had forbidden it, but her mother knew the sense of it. Four Mile Water had nothing for Maeve; better a life full of promise in the States than harbored disappointments close to home. The girl had arranged her own passage through a representative of a Cork firm that recruited colleens to work as domestics for well-to-do Yanks. After seven years as a maid for a doctor's family on Bay State Road in the Back Bay, Maeve's passage debt was paid and she had her nest egg. She quit.

She found a husband, Larry McShane, a steamfitter who worked for the city. They had five years together and three children before he disappeared. After that her friends treated Maeve like a widow, but she knew the bastard had gone off at last with his one true love — bootleg whiskey. The hell with him and good riddance, she'd thought. She determined to make more of her children without the bum than with.

When Colman arrived in Boston Maeve was overjoyed. Her brother's coming meant she would have a man in the house again, and, with little

Collins, a second son. Maeve was a strong-willed woman and, though Colman had not intended to stay with her, she'd insisted.

"I'm so glad you've come, Colman," she said a few hours after he'd disembarked from the Cunard steamship. They stayed up late telling their stories to each other, she with energy and fiery emotion; he with a subdued detachment that frightened her.

"You're good to put us up, Maeve." He paused. "The kiddo loves you already."

"What do you mean, 'put you up'? You're home. You're staying."

The flat, the top floor of a Southie three-decker, was large enough. A room in the back was empty. But Colman was reluctant.

"No. As soon as . . ."

"As you like," she cut in. "You may want your own place. You may find you want to move on altogether. Whatever. But you can stay here if you want to. For good if you want. That's all."

"Thanks, Maeve. If I did I'd take over the rent."

"Rent! God, didn't I tell you?"

"What?"

She got up from the sofa and crossed the room to a lowboy that stood in front of a six-foot-high mahogany-framed mirror. She opened a drawer and took out a cigarette and inserted it into a long gleaming holder, which she flourished as she struck a match. Leaning against the table, she faced her brother and smiled. She was a large, strong, handsome woman and proud of it.

"I own the place."

"You *own* the place!"

"Yes. This ain't the ould sod, brother. I bought it last year. Well, of course it's mortgaged. But it's mine. The Wills and the Reilleys downstairs pay me. You're looking at a landlady, Colman."

She leaned back, laughing at the idea of herself. The crown of her head touched its own image in the mirror behind her.

"By God, Maeve," Colman said. "You've done all right for yourself. You're still a Brady."

"Indeed."

"And a suffragette, no doubt."

"In my own fashion, Colman, in my own fashion. You see, I want you to stay, but I don't need you to. I don't need any man. Except my son."

"How did you do it?"

"I saved every penny for ten years. Used to steal McShane's change, who never knew the difference, passed out he was from drink. After he went — I had just birthed Jackie — I got the widow's dole from Curley."

"Who?"

"The mayor. He was ward boss then. When a city worker dies . . ."

"But he didn't die."

"Your first lesson in the meaning of America. Curley comes from M Street two blocks over from here. He knows the varieties of Irish widowhood. He takes care of his people, Colman." She paused, took a deep drag on the cigarette. "He'll take care of you."

"I don't need anyone to take care of me, Maeve."

"Aren't you the proud mick?"

"Not particularly, no."

"Well," Maeve said, smashing out her cigarette, "you should meet Curley anyway. He could be useful to you."

Colman looked stonily back at his sister.

"And perhaps you could be to him."

Who could have predicted how Maeve's advice would pay off? By the time of Jackie's First Communion everybody knew that Colman was the mayor's righthand man. That was why — Maeve was certain of it — Curley had come to the Communion Mass, to honor Jackie.

When Curley approached them from the church, Maeve pushed the boy forward to shake with him. "Ain't he a grand-looking sight, Mayor?" she asked. She shone with satisfaction.

"What a dapper fellow!" Curley said, "Just like his uncle!" Curley picked the lad up and, though it strained him to do so, flamboyantly flew him over his head like a flag lettered "James Michael Curley is here!"

"What do you say, Colman? Is your nephew going to grow up to be a loyal Democrat?"

"No, Mayor," Jackie said proudly. "I'm going to be a priest!"

"A priest!" Curley exclaimed. "And not a Democrat! Why, that's the bishop!"

The crowd circling the mayor and Brady's family on Broadway outside the church laughed. *That James Michael is a card!* Jackie beamed down at the mayor, loving the attention. His proclamation of intention to become a priest always had the magic effect of drawing praise from strangers and immense waves of love and pride from his mother.

"I'd have been a priest myself, young fellow," Curley went on earnestly and for effect of his own, "but I wasn't worthy."

That James Michael is quite a fellow!

Colman was standing off to the side. His own son, Collins, five years old and looking younger, stood next to him clinging to his hand. Collins was mystified by the focus that had centered on Jackie, and he couldn't understand why he didn't get to wear a white suit and why he couldn't be in the eye of the circle too.

Jackie was such a bright little youngster. Collins was very bashful.

Maeve never tired of saying how far ahead Jackie was of all the children in his class. Though Maeve scrupulously attended to Colman's boy and would have died rather than have him feel neglected, Collins knew that Jackie was far ahead of *him* too. Now and then Maeve saw a peculiar look in her nephew's eyes that revealed a depth the dimensions of which she had no idea. But most often there was so little movement in him, especially compared to her own son, that she gave less and less thought to what might be the matter. Collins favored his father, that was all. And it was natural that he did so.

"Come here and meet the mayor, Collins," Maeve said, reaching her hand out toward him. The boy only retreated behind his father. Colman winked at Maeve and held snugly to his son in his shadow, leaving him be.

But Curley didn't. He made a show of circling Brady, stooping over and slapping his mouth in war-dance fashion, singing on one note, "Woo-woo-woo-woo-woo."

Collins Brady, full of fear at what seemed so strange to him and mortified to be so singled out, buried his face in his pa's body. Colman drew him around to press him against his side. He put a hand on Curley's shoulder.

"No, Mayor, please."

"Ah, come on, Colman!" Curley was still hopping about. "Shouldn't pamper the kid. We got to break that shell!"

"No, we don't, Mayor." Brady's voice cut through the prancing mood. He was serious, and his tone jolted Curley and the standers-by who heard.

"You'll spoil him. You'll make him a sissy." Curley took off in a weaving circle again, crying, "In and out the window, in and out the window, in and out the window . . ."

Brady did not speak. Finally the mayor skipped away toward another family. He had lots of contacts to make, anyhow.

Maeve and Jackie went back into the church to get the priest to bless the boy's new white rosary.

When Collins took his face away from Colman's waist and looked up, his father was looking down at him. The boy desperately tried to read his pa's face for shame, but at first he read nothing.

Then Colman Brady grinned and said, "Thanks for holding on to me, *amico*. I need you near me for luck."

Collins looked at him with relief.

"Brady!" It was Curley again, but now he had his homburg on and was about to go. The people had begun to drift down Broadway to their various family parties and communion breakfasts. The former mayor wore an expression that said, *The show's over.*

"Yes, Mayor?"

Curley postponed what he was going to say when he noticed the kid and said instead, "I'd be honored to meet your son."

"Collins," Brady said, but without nudging him forward, "this is your pa's boss. His name is Jim. Can you say, 'Hello, Jim'?"

"Hello, Jim," the boy said, extending his hand.

"This is Michael Collins Brady, Mayor."

Curley took the small hand and, without a hint of condescension, said, "You've a proud name, son. I'm proud to meet you." Then Curley straightened up and looked at Brady. "I'm sorry for making a prop of him back then."

Colman nodded.

The two men began to walk up Broadway toward the park at N Street, the boy between them.

"Why 'Collins'?" Curley asked.

"I admired him."

"Didn't take you for the sort to swoon over Irish martyrdom."

"Michael Collins was a friend of mine. I'm a man of strong loyalties, Jim."

"Speaking of which, you gave me a bum steer on Sacco and what's-his-name."

"No, I didn't."

"I would have made a fool of myself. Fuller's a hero now that they're dead. And Peters is basking in his light."

"A hero to some."

"If there were elections today, they'd both walk in again. We got our work cut out for us."

"Fuller won't run again, Jim. They've written him off, I'm certain of it. They'll run Ely."

"That milk-bottle robber! But no matter the State House is their playpen. We've got three years to get our railings up around the city again. I'm starting up the citizen-classes at the club."

"You can't count on the croppies now, not the way they've run the new quotas through. Immigration is over, Jim."

"Not if the Democrats take Washington next year."

"They won't if it's Smith."

"Who gave you the eyes of God? It's time for one of us."

"There'll be a mick on Beacon Hill before there's one in the White House. And remember who said so."

"Either way, it don't solve our problem. I can't rebuild a base on a bunch of well-fed clerks and trolley drivers. Short damn memories, these people have. I'm the one that replaced the pauper's dole in this town with civil service and public works and jobs for everybody. By the time I need their vote they'll all be wearing striped pants and having two last names."

"Well, speaking as a dumb harp immigrant, I'd say Beantown hasn't heard the last of James Michael Curley."

"Name your next kid after me."

"Only if you're martyred. And then only if it's a girl with Orphan Annie hair."

"Ha! Curly! Anyway, you'd need a woman first, and who'd have you?"

"A lot can happen in three years, Jim."

"A lot better happen."

The first signals of what would happen in those years began coming in very soon. They were subtle and easy to miss at first, but by the following summer a traumatic event in South Boston foreshadowed the disaster that would nearly destroy America and would bring James Michael Curley to the peak of his power. In August of 1928 one hundred and twelve of the workers at the Gillette plant near Andrew Square were temporarily laid off. Little was made of that outside Southie, where they lived, but at the Democratic Club on Broadway, to which a trickle of hard-pressed men went immediately for help, the Gillette layoffs had the effect of a blast from a starter's gun. By the middle of autumn Curley had established and publicized the Democratic Employment Assistance program, which consisted, in effect, of his use of his contacts at the telephone company and other public utilities to provide jobs for the slowly increasing stream of jobless from private industry. But he could smell the coming catastrophe, and he lost no time in preparing to exploit it.

"A chicken in the White House," the poster behind Brady's desk read, "and two in Massachusetts."

Colman Brady was managing the day-to-day effort to find work for Curley's constituents. His office was in the left rear of the second floor of the old Victorian mansion on Dorchester Heights. A steady line of men filed into Curley's office, where the mayor would listen to the monotonous recitations of fears and worries as if, in each case, for the first time. In a few moments Curley could impress each supplicant with his own deep and abiding concern for the man's plight and that of his family. If Curley knew the man well or owed him the favor, he would personally place the calls to find the man a job. More often the man would be referred to the office in the back, where Brady would see what could be done.

"I'm a steamfitter, sir," the claimant said nervously.

"Don't 'sir' me, *amico*! My brother-in-law was a steamfitter."

"Name of what?"

"McShane. Never met the fellow."

"Me neither."

"You'd be about forty."

"Forty-seven."

"Call it forty-two."

"Yes, sir. Forty-two."

"That means you were born in eighty-six."

"Yes, sir. Eighty-six."

"Just a minute." Brady put the phone pieces to his mouth and ear, banged the lever several times, said a number, then waited. "Maeve? It's me. Indeed. Listen, love, what was McShane's boss's name? Downtown." He listened. "No, I'm trying to help a fellow here, a steamfitter like your own lost throb. Aye. What plant? And he's the super? Righto. Thanks, dearie."

Brady clicked off. "How'd you like to work the icehouse on Lewis Wharf?"

"Anyplace, Mr. Brady. Anyplace."

"Okie doke. Let's take a swing."

Brady called the supervisor at the Municipal Ice Works, who thought he might — since it was the mayor himself asking — be able to find a place for the fellow. Brady thanked him, promised him Curley's note, and hung up.

"Remember," Brady said as the steamfitter got up to leave, "forty-two."

"Yes, sir."

"And eighty-six."

"Indeed, sir. Eighty-six." The man grinned at Brady gratefully. "Thanks."

"Don't thank me. It's Curley you owe this one to."

"I won't forget."

"Neither will he." Brady winked.

The man shuffled out of the office. There was an uneasy rustling out in the narrow corridor as those who waited shifted their positions in the line of high-backed chairs along one wall of the hallway; each moved one seat closer to Brady's office like patients at the public clinic.

"Who's next?" Brady cried, but he was looking down at his desk where several lined forms waited to be completed. Brady routinely filled out the civil service forms for men who could not read or write. One of the applications on his desk was for the job of letter-carrier, and it was just dawning on him that an illiterate mailman would have his troubles.

"I am," a woman said.

Colman looked up sharply. The last thing he expected to hear was a woman's voice. His surprise doubled when he saw that it was Mary Ellen Shields standing in his doorway.

Brady stood.

Mary Ellen Shields crossed to the high-backed caned chair that was placed alongside Brady's desk. Her skirts came to mid-calf and revealed a perfectly turned leg. A certain taste came to Colman's mouth as he suddenly remembered running his tongue all along that leg. That very leg.

A thin blue scarf trailed from her shoulder, and her hair, light brown and very short, was just visible under the navy blue cloche. After she sat down, Mary Ellen unwound the scarf from her neck and removed her hat. She sat with her knees together and slightly to the side. She was not wearing stockings.

Brady sat down.

He waited but she would not look at him. She busied herself folding the scarf. He tried to decide whether she was wearing a touch of lipstick and rouge, or whether she was blushing. He wanted her to look at him so he could see her eyes.

"It's good to see you, lass."

"I had no choice," she said sharply. She raised her head to look at him. Her eyes were like a pair of moons, the color of slate. They revealed the fright and desperation that had brought her to Brady. "My father was cashiered. There's not enough food."

"What happened?"

"He's gone blotto completely. We haven't seen him sober in weeks. He takes all that I earn and drinks it. The wee ones, Timmy and Brian, are sick. I'm afraid they're very sick. My ma has taken to hanging around the docks waiting for the spoiled veggies to be discarded and then she fights the rats for it. It's worse than . . ."

She could not continue.

She broke into the most miserable sobbing and dropped her face into her hands, crushing it against her hat.

Brady sat watching her.

When she looked up at him she said, "I came to see the mayor. I didn't know it would be you."

"I'm helping him out a bit. Maybe I can help you."

"It's not me!"

"I understand."

"What can I do?"

"For one thing, you're entitled to the money you earn. For a start, we must keep the old coot from stealing your pay. How many brothers and sisters?"

[157]

"Eleven."

"You're the oldest."

"Yes. We're all still at home. Even with my salary it won't be enough."

"One thing at a time, Mary Ellen. Hush now for a minute."

Brady smiled at her. She lowered her eyes and exhaled once, a grand sigh. Her breathing slowed and her agitated and panicked air slowly evaporated.

Why hadn't he married her? Brady winced with the memory. They had been sitting on the beach at L Street and she was voluptuous in her swimming suit.

"I'm in no hurry, Mary Ellen," he had said. "I don't fancy tying myself up to one woman yet. I have some things to do before I put my head in that sack again."

"You no-good cad!" She had screamed at him. "Sack, is it? You've made a harlot of me, Colman Brady!" She leapt up, seizing her towel by a corner, and started to run off.

He grabbed her by the ankle and forced her to stop.

She glared down at him fiercely. She trembled like a leaf, angry and hurt. But the cold composure of her eyes was what struck him. They repelled him and irritated him. Even as she defied him in her rage, it seemed to him that her eyes were empty of passion and rapture. What she wanted was the security of a man and a home. Any man, it seemed to Brady. Any home. Seductive and lithe as her body was, and her manner, there was nothing voluptuous about her most intense longing. He knew why he hadn't married her.

"Do you think I've aged, Mary Ellen?" he asked. He let his hand run through the hair over his ear where the first faint gray streaks were. He asked the question to draw her out and to get her mind on something else than her father. "A little gray on the sides, what?"

She smiled at him as he hoped she would.

"I'm pushing thirty," he said whimsically. "I'd always hoped to die a young man. Now I guess I won't."

"Your first failure." She cracked her bluish eyes at him. She was pretty and prim.

"Do you mind if I smoke?" He produced his cigar case.

She shook her head.

He lit a cigar and puffed at it in silence. He turned to gaze out the window, which opened on a view of Boston. The Customs House tower pierced up through a gentle autumn haze that drifted in from the harbor. He watched the still scene and thought of the untidy old men who were moving through the alleys by the waterfront, decrepit women and scavenging children; Mary Ellen's mother collecting swill. Something mean was happening to Boston.

"Mary Ellen, you mustn't let it beat you."

"Colman, even with my earnings . . ."

"Your brother Peter, how old is he?"

"Thirteen."

"He should be working. What of Kate?"

"Sixteen."

"Could your mother work?"

"She's near dead with the defeat of it. He beats her terribly."

"We have to move him out. I'll get him in Pine Street."

"He won't go."

"Yes, he will. Send Kate and Peter down here tomorrow. I'll have something for both of them. Where does your pa drink?"

"Houlihan's. He's probably there now."

"All right." He stood up and took his suitcoat from the back of his chair. "You should have your check going to the bank."

"They say that banks are not reliable."

"Don't believe them. Do you want to control your money or not?"

"Yes. But, Colman, he'll never go."

"If I ask him nice he will. And I'll send a basket over."

"My mother will be mortified."

"Isn't she already?"

"But she goes at night and the neighbors don't know."

"Don't kid yourself. Look, pick the groceries up at my house. Folks on your block will think you're coming from the I.G.A. on Fourth Street."

"Colman." She stopped him from opening the door just yet. "Thank you."

He looked down at her and felt a gentle melancholy. She was so lovely. She was so nice. *Don't let it beat you,* he said to himself. And then to her he said — not realizing until afterwards how cruel it was — "Don't thank me. Thank the mayor."

It was during that winter that the mayor began to hit the stump in earnest, and almost always Brady was with him.

At meetings and rallies he railed against the twenties myth of universal prosperity as the first shadows of the Depression fell on the neighborhoods of the people he expected to elect him. Brady watched Curley demonstrate his huge talent, which, in that season, was perfectly honed. "What?" he would cry. "You say business is better? You mean Hoover died? Speaking of Hoover, he asked Andrew Mellon for a nickel to call a friend. Mellon gave him a dime and said, 'Here, call both of them.' And speaking of

Secretary Mellon, anybody can be a financial genius with a hundred million dollars. The real financial genius, my friends, is the Irish mother who keeps her family clean and decent on twelve hundred dollars a year!"

Curley carried a scrawny lamb chop in his vest pocket to pull out and holler, "This cost forty cents right here in South Boston! Now what working man's wife can afford to pay forty cents for a poor measly beaten piece of meat like this? Now I know for a fact that the poor sheepherder that raised the little lamb that gave this chop got paid a nickel a pound for his slave labor. And you and I pay seventy cents a pound for this same meat. Now that's sixty-five cents that got lost somewhere, and I'll tell you where you can find most of it — in the pockets of those sharpies on State Street and Beacon Hill. And the rest you'll find on the gold plate at Trinity Church! Well, if you'll pull out your pockets over here" — at this point in his speech Curley would turn his empty pockets inside out — "what you'll have is Hoover flags, Ely flags, Lawrence and Lowell flags!" The inside-out pocket became the mark of Curley's campaign for mayor.

Curley embodied an insurgency of the Irish in Boston that was born of resentment. Their frustration was made the worse because of the economic sterility that had been peculiar to New England. Few of the Irish understood, as Brady did, why their hatred of the old elite was as appropriate as it was inarticulate. Yankee money had not been invested in the national economic boom of the 1920s, but had gone into the privileged exile of family trust funds. Even during the sudden prosperity after World War I, the unemployment rate in Boston hovered consistently at thirteen percent. Brady had learned about that the hard way for several months after arriving from Ireland. Those days job-hunting had begun his wondering why the Irish in Boston were still worse off than their cousins in other American cities. By 1929 there were no more positions available in the crevices of civil service, teaching, or the fire and police departments, and the prospect of massive unemployment loomed inexorably over South Boston, Roxbury, the West and North Ends, East Boston, and Charlestown. Brady thought that Curley's protest lacked clear content and could have benefited from doses of facts and statistics, but he knew it embodied and exploited the vague sentiment that the Yankees, ensconced in their strongholds of State Street, Beacon Hill, and Harvard, were responsible for the hard times that were befalling everyone else.

Curley's ability to personalize the old conflict between the achieved and cultured upper class and the rest of workaday Boston was no quirk or accident, and Brady knew it. Curley's stature was itself an achievement, itself the product of a profound understanding of culture. James Michael Curley at his best was ingenious, and it was a thrill to work for him. The more he flexed his well-built ego in pummeling the Brahmins, the more the people fell in behind him, the more they cheered him, the more they loved him. And the more that happened, the more he needed Brady.

"I'm going to take it right to them, Brady! Right into the den of the thieves! Set up a rally for me at Louisburg Square!"

Brady did not reply. He was standing in front of Curley's desk. It was the first week of September in 1930. The election was a week away. All indications were that Curley would walk in. His instincts had been exactly right throughout the campaign and, though Brady had occasionally sought to downplay the unscrupulous and ruthless character of his attacks, still he rarely disagreed with what Curley had in mind.

But a rally in Louisburg Square posed problems. A four-acre plot in the dead center of Beacon Hill, bounded on the south by Mt. Vernon Street and on the north by Pinckney, and surrounded by dozens of Federalist period mansions, homes of the best families in Boston, the square was private property. Very private. It had been since the Proprietors of Louisburg Square had bound over this part of John Singleton Copley's pasture in 1844 to their own use and that of their neighbors. The property was as mercilessly restricted a hundred years later, but it was also a gem of a park, with statues dating to 1850 under a canopy of massive elms. It was the most elegant square of land in Boston and would continue to be so, its proprietors habitually pointed out to each other, because it *was* private.

"How about the Common, Mayor, instead? You'd have more room, be a better . . ."

"You heard me, goddamn it! Louisburg Square! Are you deaf or what?"

"No, I'm not deaf. Nor dumb. You'll give them just what they've been looking for. They can prevent a rally there, and you know it."

"Let them try! Who'll they get to do their police work, tell me that?"

"Now, Jim, take it easy . . ."

"I told you not to call me that!" He banged his fist down. During the last months of the campaign Curley had made a point — fanatically so — of referring to himself as "the mayor." A ploy, he called it, to underscore his experience. He forbade any use of his Christian name. His insistence bordered on the bizarre, and Brady found it wearisome.

"It seems unwise to me, Mayor," Brady said, stifling his pique, "to put the police in the position of having to choose between you and the law."

"It's a damnable law! That's city property every bit as much as Scollay Square or Copley."

"We might wish it so, but it isn't. If they choose they can evict you with private police."

"That, Mr. Brady, would be wonderful." Curley leaned back in his swivel chair and put his hands behind his head. A look of pure delight settled on his face. "Exactly what we need — a dramatic eviction of Boston citizenry from their own damn land! Exactly!" Curley winked. "And so," he said slyly, "we want lots of babies and carriages and old ladies to be there. And a cripple or two, if you can arrange it."

Brady stood looking down on Curley stonily. He was thinking that, for all his genius, there was a depth of vulgarity in the man that exceeded what he had guessed was there.

"Is there fur on your tongue, Brady, or what?"

"No, Mayor. No fur."

"Well, what do you say? I get the impression of a little queasiness in you, eh what?"

"Not queasiness. I was just thinking of what has to be done to arrange the rally."

"Good. I hope your little qualm there stays swallowed. I wouldn't want you spitting it up and choking on it."

"No blooming fear of that, Mayor." Brady knew what to do when he found himself in check.

"Good, my boy. Good. Then get to it. Louisburg Square; the bowels of the beast!"

Brady decided to walk. He wanted to see the square again before he did anything to arrange the rally. By the time he reached the Hill — it took forty minutes to walk from the pinnacle of Southie at Dorchester Heights — it was nearly sunset. From the crest of Pinckney Street was a view of the Charles River and Cambridge beyond, but what struck Brady first was the tawny gold of a great mountain of clouds that rose above the twinkling river and the distant towers of Cambridge. Brady thought the sky never seemed so lovely from Dorchester Heights. The view from the crest of Broadway in Southie had its charm, but it never affected Brady, never made him want to stop and lean against a lamppost, as he did then to watch evening invade the city. The twilight hush ambushed Brady, filled him with a contentment for which he was not prepared. He had not observed such a beautiful evening since watching the sun drop behind the Kilworth Range beyond the Nire from the Druid tumulus. The thought of home set off a fast sequence of powerful recollections: the thatched farmhouses across the valley; the coned stacks of golden hay dotting the landscape, filling it with the peculiar odor of autumn; the granite stones of the village cemetery, his mother's grave; the small church of St. Lawrence O'Toole with Father Divine waving from the portico; the boys at Morrissey's, spilling their Guinness and laughing. Brady thought of his own modest farmhouse, of Bea and Conor, of Nell. Suddenly, for an instant, he recalled that feeling he'd had when his house had become hers too. How he had longed at first to spend all his days there with her! The memory of that hope filled him with pain, yet he savored it, clung to it, wanted it to last. The terrible sense of loss was better than the numb forgetfulness which had eased it. The things he had expected from his life! A permanent home, love forever, a perfection of pleasure at turning the soil, an unshakable meaning to everything. How far short he had fallen of all of it! How far from home had he come!

He saw the red sun sparkling off the surface of the Charles, and that sight set off in him a rage of feeling in excess of what had gone before. The sun was still showering the earth with its warmth and loveliness. There was still beauty in the world. Colman Brady was still capable of achieving his deepest desire. He was not imprisoned by the past, by its losses and griefs. He could claim a place in the world as his own in which to raise his son and from which to do what the sun does for his people. He wanted to give them warmth and loveliness. He could. He could. There was the huge future laid out before him exactly like that vista of a river and its valley. What had happened to him in Ireland, the loss of his land, his loves and his innocence, had led exactly to what he was doing in Boston — though without land, without loves, without innocence. Was he simply trying to find them again? Yes, he said to himself, and he would.

He pushed away from the lamppost and walked down the hill the half-block to Louisburg Square. His footsteps clacked along the cobblestones. It was the dinner hour and he was a solitary walker on the street. At the point where public property ended and the proprietorship began there was a difference in the look and feel of the street. The stones suddenly took on the air of a gentle disrepair more triumphant than vagrant, rather like the dishevelment of an aging but proper gentleman. At the corner of the square and Pinckney, the sun flashed off a door knocker and the flash caught Brady unaware. He thought the mood, nostalgic and acute, was passing, but he was plunged into it again, more deeply. Now his senses seemed alerted less to memories than to what was before him. The door knocker, a simple brass curve ending in a knob, absorbed his attention. The door knocker itself was beautiful, set on an ebony door and framed by two panels of leaded glass. The door handle was gleaming brass, as was a modest, rectangular name plate. The door was set back in an alcove, which was also paneled in sharp black wood, and down from it to the brick sidewalk ran four granite stairs. Brady studied the house, a four-story red brick Federal with a width to accommodate three large windows, each bordered with black shutters. The small hardware of the shutters must also have been brass, for it too shone in the sun. It was as if that house were there to display the subtle glory of which the failing sun was capable each evening.

Brady's eye was drawn from that house to its neighbor and up a chimney line to the next and across a rooftop to the next. The row of houses on the east side of Louisburg Square overwhelmed Brady with the perfection of its details. Doors, knockers, knobs, windows, shutters, curtains lifting in the breeze, the gracefully proportioned curves of bowfronts and bay windows, the special reflection of glass tooled to match the curving lines of the windows, the carved lintels and beveled sills, the wrought-iron grillwork — the effect of it all was to stun him. He had been there before, but he had never *seen* it. He had never seen the order of it.

As Brady turned and examined each quarter of Louisburg Square he felt an enormous and inexplicable relief, as if he were seeing something for which he had been desperately searching. The harmony of construction, purpose, use, history was what moved him. This was a world in which all conflicts — architectural, cultural, esthetic — had been resolved in the perfect tension of the classic. Brady saw it as an image of his own hope for himself; the conflicts set loose by loss and loneliness and betrayal and even, once, murder, can be, if not resolved, held in an order and simplicity like what he beheld. That hope in the human capacity for balancing polarities and thus banishing chaos is what built cities in the first place. Brady, once a farmer who knew the curse of rustic loneliness, understood why the city itself was the greatest achievement of culture, and Louisburg Square was having its effect on him because it was the polished, exquisite gem of his city. Nothing in London or Edinburgh or Dublin or Rome or Paris would surpass it for simple ordered beauty. Louisburg Square was an example of what Anglo-Saxon culture at its best could achieve, and Brady, for the first time in years, felt absolutely at home. He was part of what wanted such a place. He was part, he insisted to himself, of what had produced it.

How far it was from South Boston. Brady could understand why a vast gulf separated the Irish from the Brahmin. Louisburg Square was a place in which excellence was a habit of daily effort. Louisburg Square, some would say, was "almost" like the park on Broadway at M Street in City Point. And, Brady knew, it was, with its lawn, trees, bowfront buildings. But the difference enshrined in that word *almost* was all the difference in the world. Human beings exist to close the gap, that narrow gap, between what is ordinary and what is excellent. Louisburg Square was civilization par excellence. Brady did not need to demean his own people to acknowledge that, but he felt the uneasiness of the disloyal when he admitted to himself that he could feel far more at home in the Brahmin preserve than he ever had or would in Southie.

But it was an illusion. Brady chastised himself for indulging such feelings. Louisburg Square was not his home, would never be, could never be. It was precisely an Anglo-Saxon achievement. Not Celtic. It was English. Not Irish. He left the corner of Pinckney Street to enter the square itself. He walked into a deep shade in which night, owing to the tall buildings on the park's west edge, had a head start. An old sign read, "Private Property. Public Access At The Discretion Of The Residents." Brady read the sign without seeming to as he strolled by it, hands in his pockets. He smiled to himself. He had never been farther from his own element. How could that place have offered him such solace, if only momentarily? It was gone, that solace, and in its place was a cold blast of that old loneliness. He felt utterly alien, not only to the square but to Southie and to the places of fond memory and to the places yet to come. The perfect beauty of Beacon Hill had done him in by not being his.

He stopped and leaned forward against the high black wrought-iron fence that enclosed the lawn, the huge trees, and dozens of tailored shrubs. The lawn was entirely enclosed by the fence, and surrounding the fence was a broad promenade paved with the ill-tended cobblestones. Brady squinted at a statue that stood like an eastern guard inside the spikes. Christopher Columbus; Brady laughed to think an Italian would preside in such a setting. But of course in America Columbus was a Yankee, even to Italians.

The thought reminded him of Curley. It was the sort of crack he would make. Brady realized suddenly why he had resisted Curley's plan to have a rally there. It was not that Curley's campaign would be damaged. Curley was right on that, as usual. The rally would be a master stroke of political nerve, making dramatic and explicit the conflict he was exploiting. No. What Brady had feared and only now understood was that Curley, his mentor, his sponsor, his friend, would come to Louisburg Square and defile it.

Brady shook his head; the ironies of his life!

He leaned against the iron spikes of the fence to examine the enclosed park. Its grass was manicured, the shrubbery perfectly tended. There were no paths, no bare patches in the lawn, no benches. At the far end was another statue, and though he stared at it, he could not identify it. He walked along the fence to Mt. Vernon and drew as close to the statue as the fence would let him. Brady focused on it. Made of limestone, the figure was badly weathered. The features of its face were mutilated. It was a man wearing a sort of Greek toga.

"Aristides," a voice said.

Brady turned to find President Abbott Lawrence Lowell of Harvard standing behind him.

"I'd have guessed Aristotle," Brady said.

[165]

"You'd have been close."

"Off by a hundred and forty years, I'd also guess. Good evening, Mr. Lowell."

"Hello, Mr. Brady. A second very good guess." Lowell smiled at him without any hint of condescension.

Brady thought Lowell had quite a nice smile and he found himself disarmed. "I've just been admiring Louisburg Square," he said.

Lowell noted that Brady, like most visitors, had mispronounced the name. It was *Lewis*burg, but Lowell wouldn't think of correcting him. He remembered Brady from their one encounter and had found himself on occasion thinking of him. He remembered liking the fellow's spirit. "Oh, it's a lovely park, Mr. Brady," Lowell said. "I often stroll around it of an evening after supper with Phantom here." Phantom was a cocker spaniel whose unclipped tail plumed up behind him, brushing at Lowell's leg.

Brady studied Lowell with some of the acute attention he had lavished on the square. The old man wore an unremarkable blue serge suit and a high stiff collar which, though starched, displayed the early signs of fraying. He carried a white panama hat in one hand and a tall, rough wooden staff in the other. He held himself erect and seemed vigorous and exceptionally alert. Brady understood something of what the man's life had been, its achievement, its substance, its constant service of the extraordinary. But there was nothing flamboyant about him, clearly had never been. There was nothing mammoth or grand or oversized. It was impossible to imagine him making huge gestures. He knew nothing, Brady guessed, of flourish. Yet there clung to him an aura of power that surpassed by far the champion rhetorician of them all, Curley. Both men were brilliant and confident and enormously successful, yet in the gap between Abbott Lawrence Lowell and James Michael Curley the British Isles and the Free State of Ireland could be buried. It was not that Brady preferred Lowell over Curley, but that he recognized in Lowell something that he had chosen for himself long before.

"I was wondering," Brady said, "how you get through the fence to go into the park."

"One doesn't," Lowell said easily. "One doesn't go in, so that it will always be as perfect as it is now."

"How does the gardener get in to tend the shrubs and so on?"

"Presumably, he climbs in." President Lowell said this as if the question never occurred to him.

No matter, thought Brady, since the gardener was surely Italian or Greek, like the statues. He forced himself to think cynically before Lowell. It was the only way he could defend himself from the powerful and perhaps treasonous attraction he was feeling.

"Well, it's a shame . . ." — Brady turned back to peer through the iron — ". . . not to have the privilege of strolling amid such loveliness, as well as about it."

"A commonplace sacrifice, Mr. Brady, that is made for the sake of something larger."

If the price of depriving the common people was to deprive themselves, by God they would!

"Indeed, Mr. Lowell. I was just thinking it's a shame you couldn't keep the weather out too, for the sake of Aristides. The poor noseless fellow looks like a leper in there, don't you think?"

"It hadn't occurred to me, frankly." The president put his hat on, touched the brim of it with the handle of his cane, and resumed his walk. He was a benign old man who seemed incapable of malevolence.

Brady watched him go. And he realized for the first time since Ireland exactly how the Anglo aristocracy always made him feel.

Election Day was the second Tuesday in September.

The rally for Curley at Louisburg Square was set for Sunday afternoon.

Brady had made arrangements that satisfied him. Hoping to avoid any incident, he had secured permission from Chief McGrath to close the streets adjoining Louisburg Square. A small platform was set up at the intersection of Willow and Mt. Vernon. Part of the crowd could thus be kept on the closed-off public street, and Curley himself would address them from city property. With any luck, Brady told himself when it was all arranged, by Sunday afternoon it would be raining.

But Indian summer came that day. The gold warm air descended upon the city and blew softly through its streets, waking up the bright, crisp leaves that kicked over, stretched, made ready to fall. A gaily colored crowd swarmed across Boston Common from the subways at Park Street and Arlington. There were women merrily pushing baby buggies and men, walking in clumps, dressed for the occasion in dark suits and ties and soft tweed hats. Some men had their pockets turned inside out. As they came down from Joy or came up Mt. Vernon from Charles, moving evenly, like balls in their slots into the Beacon Hill reserve, they gave off a certain tangible trepidation, mingled with pride and eagerness. Boston policemen funneled the crowd into the Willow Street intersection as far as the platform. The people cheerfully greeted the police, who returned their salutations merrily. There seemed to be no inclination to invade the precincts of the square itself.

Brady was standing on Mt. Vernon Street up the hill several dozen yards, nearly in front of the Otis mansion, with Chief McGrath.

"So far so good, Chief, eh?"

"This takes the biscuit, Brady, if you ask me. Of course nobody asks me, damn fool thing to do."

"Well, with luck we'll keep them where they are and it'll be a grand picnic of a finale for the mayor."

"A finale for me if we *don't* keep them there."

"Aw, Chief, what's the harm?" Brady had resigned himself. He had the capacity to draw his feelings smartly up behind his self-interest. He was drawing easily on a long thin cigar. He was wearing his white linen suit. The ends of his tie made a perfect equation halfway down his shirt.

"The harm is they'll get bashed, and *then* watch."

"Restraint, Chief. We must all exercise great restraint."

"I got to work this precinct, don't forget. I'm not worth a plugged nickel up here if these people think I won't protect them."

"I don't see any signs of them. Where the hell are they? They must have all gone to Gloucester for the weekend."

"Wouldn't you? But don't kid yourself. They're watching every move, right now."

Brady scanned the windows of the houses opposite. There were no signs of life in them. He turned toward the square. A third-floor curtain fluttered and caught his eye. He saw a hand withdraw and disappear.

The nineteenth-century houses were stony and mute, but they seemed to be staring down their bay windows — like noses — on the gathering throng indifferently.

"Just hope to high heavens," the officer said, "they keep their Pinkertons out."

"That's your job."

"No, it ain't, Brady. They've the right. Unless I get a warrant, they can have *me* thrown off that square. Just hope James Michael keeps his hat on, that's all."

Curley seemed oblivious to the fact that the rally was not occurring quite on the exact turf of Louisburg Square. He was buoyed by the tremendous cheer the crowd gave him when he arrived, and he walked happily through their midst, squeezing hundreds of hands as he went. The people roared at the sight of him. He cut a grand figure in his velvet-collared Chesterfield coat and striped pants. He mounted the platform and, with his back to the empty Louisburg Square, he raised his megaphone to the crowd who were pressed together along the entire length of Willow Street and up and down Mt. Vernon. He began speaking through the cone, but dropped it and went on with his rich, sonorous voice at its loudest. The people were attentive, even rapt.

"Here we are gathered in the very center of the power and the glory that was in the beginning, is now and — after Tuesday — never shall be again!"

The crowd roared.

"This is the center of the descendancy of those citizens who came over on the Mayflower to *de*-flower the New World! Well, their bloom has faded and we have come to pluck them! I am the vinedresser and *they* are the vine, and I say it's time to cut them down!"

Jets of approval and laughter followed one another out of the convulsed crowd.

"The Massachusetts of the Puritan is dead! Dead as Caesar! Dead as ancient Rome! But there is no need to mourn the fact, because their successors are here! Their successors are the Irish!"

"Hurray for Curley!" someone called, *"Erin go bragh!"*

"And the Irish," he hollered, "are not cowed by the phony finery of Blue-blood Hill! The Irish had letters and learning and culture and high civilization when the ancestors of the Puritans were savages running half-naked through the forests of Britain and relieving themselves squatting over lice-infested logs!"

The assembly interrupted him again, bellowing and clapping.

"It has taken the Irish to make Massachusetts a fit place to live in and it will take the Irish to make Boston a decent and honorable city at last. For never forget — as history will never forget — that the wealth and comfort surrounding us here was stolen by scoundrels who got rich selling opium to the Chinese and rum to the Indians and guns to the Kaiser and slaves to the plutocrats down south!"

At that Curley turned half away from the crowd and raised his fist to the upper stories of the great Bulfinch mansion of the Otis family, and he hollered, "You're nothing but a pack of second-story workers, milkbottle robbers, and doormat thieves! I'll be elected mayor of Boston and you don't like it! Well, here I am! Does any one of you bums want to step down here and make anything of it?"

As the gathering egged him on with its cheering, Curley slowly turned in a semicircle as if looking for a taker to his challenge. That was how his gaze came to fall on Louisburg Square.

"And look at that!" He pointed to the enclosed park. "Their little game reserve!" He leaned forward and with great show read the nearby sign in a voice booming with contempt. " 'Private Property. Public access at the discretion of the residents.' Well, the hell with that! Come on!"

Curley leapt down off the platform and led a swarm across Mt. Vernon Street. The high iron spikes deterred the first arrivals from entering the park itself, but when several boys scampered up and over the fence and down onto the lawn, there was a momentary gasp as if a sacred space had been violated. But quickly they were followed by dozens of others, who were over the hurdle and into the forbidden precinct. A squad of large men carefully raised Curley himself to the level of the fence top and handed him over so that he too had gone in. The crowd was delirious.

Curley raised his hands for quiet.

With great drama, his chin thrust high, his chest out, his fist raised, he announced, "We claim this land for the people of the city of Boston!" He paused. The crowd was absolutely still. He glared up at the grand houses and cried, "What are you going to do about it?"

The question hung in the silence.

Not a curtain stirred in the windows. There was not a sign that anyone had noticed that Louisburg Square had been violated. The great residences stood mute and detached. Soon the silence itself began to dissipate the effect of Curley's challenge.

He knew it, and rather than let the impact of the silence grow, he hollered again, "Well? What are you going to do about it?"

Nothing.

Only the leaves of the huge elms moved. The crowd was transfixed as if suddenly witness to a great spectacle. But it was the opposite of spectacle.

Curley had thrust his hand into the bowels of the sleeping beast, but the beast did not wince. As far as anyone could tell, all of the residents of Louisburg Square were still snug in their late Sunday naps.

"Perfect," Brady muttered to himself; "perfect." He stifled an admiring smile and chastised himself again for disloyalty. But they were so much better at it. They responded to Curley's demagoguery with nothing, with nothingness itself. Perfect. Curley would be elected easily Tuesday, and he would be approaching the peak of his power. But he had just been defeated again. Drastically defeated. Brady wondered if he knew it.

A bell began to toll, a church bell, and almost simultaneously, the door to the large mansion at the end of the square opened and six full-habited nuns walked out in single file, each clasping a prayer book. They walked single file down the hill past the rally as if no one were there. The people were Catholics nearly to a person, and they stared slack-jawed at the line of nuns. The nearest Catholic church was St. Joseph's in the West End. What were nuns doing on Beacon Hill?

Brady leaned into Chief McGrath and said in a low voice, "What the hell are they doing up here among the Freemasons?"

"That's their convent right there," McGrath said, pointing to the mansion. "St. Margaret's."

Sure enough, there was a yard-high cross engraved over the lintel. Why hadn't Brady noticed it before? "Convent?" Brady was shocked. Nothing he knew of Boston made sense if there was a convent of nuns on Louisburg Square. "A convent of Catholic nuns?"

McGrath laughed. He enjoyed the joke of it before Brady understood. "They're Protestants," the chief said. "They're going down to the Advent Church for evensong."

Brady was stunned. Whoever heard of Protestant nuns? The Advent — the Church of England?

Its bell still tolled.

Then Brady got it. Curley's crowd was silent, mystified, totally confused. The nuns ignored them absolutely, as if no one were there.

"Perfect," Brady said again. This time he smiled.

4

IN THE BASEMENT of a large slouching red brick building near the waterfront in the North End a lone light bulb strung from a cord snapped on. An echo of footsteps filled the caverns as half a dozen men dressed darkly made their ways singly to the large central room, the walls of which were lined with a hundred and seventy-four barrels of prewar bonded Kentucky bourbon.

Gennaro Anselmo was the last to enter. He hung back in the shadow of the arched, tunnel-like corridor while the others pulled chairs together in a semicircle around the thin man in the broad fedora who had to stoop to keep his hat from brushing the chalky ceiling.

When all of the men were seated Anselmo stepped before them and, facing the thin man in the center, said, "Don Enrico, it's my report."

Anselmo was always formal and cautious with Zorelli. He knew the don did not trust him, and he knew that the others were envious of him and suspicious. Anselmo played things with nerve and finesse. Zorelli and his henchmen had no choice but to deal with Anselmo because Anselmo still had the only lively connections with the Irish gangsters whom Zorelli hated but needed more than ever. Their speakeasies were making him rich beyond his dreams. That was why Zorelli had ignored what Anselmo had tried to pull with Tucci four years before. Zorelli could wait. Until now he had needed Anselmo's contacts more than he needed vengeance.

"I am listening," Zorelli said through his hand. A slight harelip, not nearly so serious as Zorelli fancied, marred the lean and ascetic look of his face. He habitually covered it with his hand. Once he had had a doctor operate on it and, when the bandages were removed and he saw that the lip was still twisted and scarred, he had taken a knife of his own and cut the doctor's mouth.

"It was a loss," Anselmo reported, "of eleven thousand dollars. Three full trucks — one of Canadian, two of Nassau rum. Already they have been taken to Newark and Philadelphia."

"Who did it?"

"O'Dwyer."

"Only O'Dwyer?"

"Probably using some MacCurtain men. And they moved it through Providence with Dever."

"What is the total?"

"In three years, twelve trucks to O'Dwyer of good whiskey or rum; seventeen of beer or wine."

"And MacCurtain?"

"I do not think he did the . . ."

"We know it was MacCurtain!" one of the others said sternly.

"It could have been Oweny," Anselmo replied in a low, clipped tone. "He wants to keep the Unione out of the clubs. It would be more like him to torch us than MacCurtain. MacCurtain is strictly a trader. The most he would defend is drugstores. He does not . . ."

"MacCurtain killed Mangio!" the other man protested.

"Mangio," Anselmo said slowly, "moved across the harbor against the don's wishes. He was asking to be killed by the Irish. There are the rules of territory."

Zorelli raised his hand. "No talk of vendetta. This is not Chicago."

The man making the argument with Anselmo stood up. "Don Enrico, respectfully."

"Yes?"

Francis Cosolimo ruled the North End docks and, increasingly, the produce markets. Most of the fish brought into Boston went through his dockside nets, and he was just completing the expansion of his influence to include the marketing of vegetables. He was infuriated that Anselmo would dare to instruct him on broadening operations beyond liquor. Cosolimo had prepared for the transition that Repeal would bring, and he was not inclined to conciliate the Irishmen, as Anselmo wanted, until his grip on the street merchants and truck farmers was even tighter.

"The taking of these shipments is not insignificant," Cosolimo said pompously, "but more important is the affront to the Unione Siciliana. These Irish must be discouraged from repeated assaults against us."

"But, friend Cosolimo," Anselmo said benignly, "there are natural divisions. We have the rum and Canadian. We have the wines. They have brewing interests. They have the sections of the city for their people."

"But *they* steal our trucks, no?"

"O'Dwyer, yes. Not all of them."

"And MacCurtain, you say."

"Some of his men, perhaps. But the urge for guns is senseless. Especially now. It is not the time for wars. Repeal is coming, and we must improve our Unione and make alliances."

"Not alliances, Gennaro, conquests!"

"That is a fool speaking, Don Enrico," Anselmo said, pointing to Cosolimo. "When *vino* is made legal, everything we have turns to dust unless we expand the gambling and move out of the family neighborhood. None of the Irish are in gambling like us. We should make agreements with them now. We should give them concessions in liquor for concessions in betting. The liquor will mean nothing soon. We must move quickly to extend our control."

"Better to kill them," Cosolimo said.

"And then what?" Anselmo asked. "Will you go into South Boston to peddle numbers and wine? You with your funny talk. Your pointed hat? Sell your fish and artichokes from a pushcart? You think Boston will give its silver to dagos?"

"So, we should be their servants?"

"No. We should buy them before they know they are for sale. They will come cheaply. They have no choice. We have defeated them with the efficiency of our system. We defeated MacCurtain for control of the shipping. Already, you see, they work for us. They drink what we sell. We must expand on that."

The don spoke then. "I do not deal with Irish."

"Don Enrico," Anselmo said respectfully, "you already *do* deal with Irish. They work for you."

"They steal my trucks."

"Yes. And they come into your territory. And they burn your club. They would do none of these things if they understood they need you more than you need them. You must give them reasons to respect you. Especially when Prohibition ends."

"What do you propose?"

"A meeting. Between the Unione Siciliana and the Irish leaders. A meeting *here* in the North End. They come to you. And you tell them the limits of territory. And the new contract for Repeal; you will forbid them to compete. You will invite them to cooperate. You would meet them in the old tradition of the dons who used Sicilian diplomacy to solve a problem."

Zorelli gently rubbed his forefinger over his misshapen lip, considering. His eyes shifted once from Anselmo to Cosolimo and back. The other three men, all old-country elders, sat still in their chairs. They thought what Don Enrico thought.

"Sicilian diplomacy, yes," he said finally. "Friend Gennaro, you invite them. And we will talk. And you invite O'Dwyer, and you invite Mac-Curtain. And we will talk."

On the evening of May 21, 1931, Jerry MacCurtain was at Colman Brady's house on Fourth Street drinking tea in the front parlor with Colman and Maeve. The room had a cluttered gentility about it. Glass shelves hung in the bay window and displayed pieces of Waterford and Cavan. Two old easy chairs that had been newly reupholstered sat opposite the stubby brown gas heater, framing it as if it were a fireplace. On the end tables at the arms of the sofa stood an army of dainty figurines.

MacCurtain picked up a Royal Doulton ballerina and fondled it. "How do you ever keep this stuff away from the wee ones?"

"The kiddos don't come in here, Jeremiah," Colman said.

"Not while you're looking, anyways."

"No . . ." — Colman winked at Maeve — ". . . or any other time. Maeve has a thought or two about how to run a house. Don't you, sister?"

"You run it, or it runs you," she said.

"Like a lot of things," MacCurtain said. The weight of his voice silenced them.

Maeve shifted awkwardly. "I'll go up. You two can talk."

"No, darling," Colman said, "finish your tea."

She raised her teacup to her mouth and sipped.

"It's about time you folks thought of moving to a new house, ain't it? Jamaica Plain or someplace fancy, like the mayor. Can't have the mayor's number one back in Southie."

Brady ignored the sarcastic edge in MacCurtain's comment. How the Irish resented each other! "I can't pull out of the old neighborhood until I've won my spurs. You know damn well my crack at mayor starts here. Southie and I are stuck with each other."

"You'll be gone, same as Jim."

Brady shrugged. "There are some differences between him and me, you know. He has shamrocks carved into his shutters. Hell, Jamaica Plain is just South Boston with steeper mortgages." Brady smiled. "Besides, you ought to ask Maeve about moving, Jer. The house is her place. I just rent."

"What do you charge your brother, Maeve?"

"Three good moods a week, Jer. He's several months arrear, believe me."

"I do. I do. Who wouldn't be glum working for a mackerel-snapper who'd betray his people by coming out for a Protestant patrician over one of his own?"

"You mean Curley backing Roosevelt?" Maeve asked.

"Aye. Over Smith. Did you ever think you'd live to see that? That's what comes of moving out of Southie."

"Don't be so sure, Jer," Maeve said, sharing his disgust. She jerked her thumb toward Colman. "Himself here is the one who put Curley up to it, God have mercy on him."

"Smith is a fool," Brady said.

"He's a Catholic!" Maeve protested.

"Also true. The two characteristics have been known to coincide before." Brady sipped his tea and then went one further. "But worse than either of those two issues, the man is a loser."

Maeve flushed. This discussion was making her angry again. "Well, it seems to me the mayor should remember who his people are."

"He does, Maeve, exactly. Al Smith is a tool of Wall Street. *He's* the one who's forgotten his people. It's not a matter of being Irish Catholic *simply*. Are we raising Jackie and Collins and the girls to be fisheaters or to be . . . ?" Brady paused. He couldn't articulate his ambition for them as sharply as he felt it. The word he wanted wouldn't come.

Maeve supplied it: "Winners. Yes. Why can't they be both? Like the mayor. Like Jeremiah here?"

Brady exchanged a look with MacCurtain that asked a question; was it that she really didn't know or that she so needed to maintain the pretense that he was the dockside labor chief and nothing else?

"I suppose they could be," Brady said, and he saw the pathetic shudder in MacCurtain, who knew that no son of Colman Brady's was going to grow up into such a seedy vicious world as his.

The silence imposed its weight on them again.

Maeve put her teacup down and stood.

"I'm glad you came by, Jer. You should stop by more often."

MacCurtain stood up. Maeve McShane still attracted him tremendously. He had made his overtures repeatedly. But she was a damned woman of the Church; as far as she knew, her husband was still alive, and therefore, for as long as that was so, the best part of her was dead.

"I would like to," the dock boss said.

"Good. Whenever Colman's home I'm sure he'd love to have you."

"See what I mean, Jerry," Colman said from his place in the sofa corner. "She runs my damn life. Might as well be married."

Maeve walked out of the parlor in a counterfeit huff.

MacCurtain stood looking after her.

"Forget it, Jer."

"I know." He sat. "I know. But she's a good woman."

"She can be a regular bitch sometimes, believe me."

"She really own this place?"

Brady nodded. "When I first came over I lived in the back room up-stairs. We used to rent out this as a flat, and downstairs where my office is was another flat. I *do* pay rent to her."

"She's some woman."

"Is that why you came over tonight?"

"Not exactly."

Brady held his teacup to his lips, though it was empty.

MacCurtain walked around the sofa to the large sliding doors which opened onto the dining room. He closed them softly and returned to his seat.

Brady put his teacup down.

"I want you to know about something," MacCurtain said. His voice was hushed, not so much from fear of being overheard but to achieve the shift in their talk.

"I'm not sure I want to know, Jer. You know how I play it."

"You're in the insurance business, right?"

"When the boss is out of office, yeah."

"Well, it's sort of for insurance I'm here. There's a big meeting in the North End. Me and the boys are going."

"Zorelli?"

"Yes."

"It's about time, Jer. We'd all be better off if you guys settled up your turf. But I'm surprised Zorelli would agree to meet."

"He called the powwow."

"You're kidding."

"No, I'm not. You remember that guy Anselmo?"

"Yes, I do."

"He came down to the pier. He's the one behind it."

"That figures. He's still after Zorelli's chair probably."

"What I don't figure, Colman, is the old guy going along with him."

"You sound worried."

"I am a little."

"Don't go, then."

"We got to go. Zorelli owns the spigot. We got to work a contract with him. I'm on my way now down to Houlie's. I just wanted you to know about it."

"Jer, I think if Anselmo's behind it, you can trust it. He knows how things have to be played now. You'd be smart to back him however you can. Zorelli and his thugs make the whole scene nastier than it needs to be. Anselmo's still after him. Back Anselmo."

"I know."

"Who's going?"

"Everybody. The Townies and Highland Ave gang too."

"O'Dwyer?"

"Yeah."

"Too bad. He's nuts."

"Yeah, but bigger than ever. Nothing moves around him now."

"He's the one to watch, Jer."

"You're telling me."

"Look, Jer, I don't want to know the details of it, but I want to hear how it goes, OK? You come by on your way home later?"

MacCurtain nodded.

"Good." Brady stood and pressed MacCurtain's shoulder affectionately. MacCurtain had given Colman his first job, and had introduced him to Curley. "Good men must not obey the laws too well." Brady did not cite Emerson because it would have seemed pompous.

"The laws are crazy, some of them," MacCurtain said, rising, covering his head with his tweed cap.

"That's true, Jer. That's true."

By the time MacCurtain reached O'Houlihan's on Broadway behind the hardware store, the other Irish toughs were waiting for him. They were a glum and moody bunch, the leaders of gangs from the Irish neighborhoods on both sides of the Charles. None of them wanted to go to the North End meeting, but none dared not to. Zorelli, mainly by virtue of his superior contacts with massive smuggling and bootlegging operations in New York and farther west, had firmly established the supremacy of his organization. All Canadian whiskey and rum and most Scotch came into New England through him, and his North End distilleries were by far the largest source of wine. The fourteen Irishmen presided over a network of suppliers and speakeasies that involved over two thousand illicit liquor outlets. Zorelli's monopoly on big-time smuggling made him the bootleg kingpin. If he called a meeting, no one who expected to continue in the business could absent himself. The Irishman knew that the agenda would include the problems posed for the liquor underworld by Repeal, and they were all anxious to stake claims in new lucrative income sources.

The Irish toughs included Frenchy Devine, who had begun as a speakeasy bartender in Charlestown and who had ultimately taken over the wholesale trade in needle beer. Several of his beer drops had been raided by Zorelli's mobsters and he was aching for vengeance. But, pressed by MacCurtain, he agreed to come peaceably to the meeting. By the time he arrived at O'Houlihan's he was wary and edgy.

Jack Demarra was a gang leader from Somerville. A huge man with a great barrel chest, he was tough and aggressive, the survivor of four separate attempts on his life. He had been indicted and tried two years earlier for kidnapping an uncooperative cider hauler, but had been declared innocent.

Mad Mick Murray, the Beer Baron of Roxbury, owned the giant Whitney Brewery, which by 1931 was the last major illegal beer operation in Boston. Volstead agents and police, especially under Mayor Peters before Curley's election, had systematically closed down all of Murray's competition. The crackdown never reached his huge brewery behind the arena on St. Botolph Street, and it was said that he had more judges and police captains on his payroll than German brewers. In fact, he earmarked three hundred and fifty thousand dollars per year to maintain his good relations with civic figures.

Dion O'Dwyer was a dapper blond thirty-year-old who manned the gambling traps and carriage-trade speakeasies in the South End which were patronized by college students, flappers, and rich adventurers who thought of his places not so much as bars but as clubs. O'Dwyer was an advocate of the new-style oasis in which women were welcome — in fact, in which more than one kind of woman was welcome. O'Dwyer already had a corner on the flesh-for-trade market, and he was getting ready to shift the emphasis in his watering places from liquor to pickups. Some of his Irish colleagues were offended by his crass and blatant promotion of organized prostitution, and he for his part had to swallow his disgust even to show up at O'Houlihan's, much less to drink there. He hated the traditional, males-only, dingy saloon where the specialty of the house was a home-cooked poteen that the old Druids called Irish gold. O'Dwyer never drank anything but imported whiskey and he stocked his places with the best Canadian and Jamaican, even if he had on discreet occasion to hijack it.

"Out!" MacCurtain barked when he arrived. He was talking to the half dozen or so patrons who were not to be part of the meeting. "Out! Get out! Place is closed for an hour!"

"Aw, come on, Jer," Den O'Coole whined. He had just bought a beer and a shot of corn. He liked to throw down the beer and nurse the poteen.

"Out!"

MacCurtain stood at the door waiting. O'Coole chugged his beer and his shot and slammed the glass down and left. MacCurtain closed the door behind him. "All right, sit down."

The thirteen sat at their tables. Ned O'Houlihan remained at his place behind the bar. MacCurtain stayed by the door.

"Here's the plan. We'll go over in three cars, separate routes. Joey, you go Atlantic Ave. I'll go Albany. Mick, you cut around by the Garden. Cantina Reale on Hanover Street, everybody know it? Go upstairs. Now nothing happens till we're all there, right? And somebody should do the main talking for our side. That'll be me."

"Wait a minute," Dion O'Dwyer said. He was leaning far back on his chair's two legs. "Who says you're the mouthpiece?"

"I do."

"Nothing personal, MacCurtain," O'Dwyer said, "but I ain't so sure you can represent my interests."

"You mean your twelve-year-old whores, or what?"

O'Dwyer smiled and dropped his head enough to sniff the carnation in his lapel. "I hold thirty thousand dollars in IOU's from the Valero brothers. I figure this is a good time to collect."

Jack Demarra stood up. "Listen, Mac, that Cosolimo's been selling that home-cooked stuff for three dollars a gallon all over Somerville. How can I get my six if he's doing that?"

"That's what we're going over there to settle, Jack. I couldn't agree with you more. Now one other thing." MacCurtain paused. "The heat stays here."

"What are you talking about? Bullshit!" Murray said.

"No bullshit, Mick. I ain't getting my ass blown off because you're stupid. You won't get near Zorelli with a rod anyways. Better to leave them here than have an issue."

"What are you going to do, Murray?" Frenchy Devine asked. "Shoot your way out of the whole fucking North End?"

"MacCurtain's right," Demarra said. He took a gun from his belt and tossed it to O'Houlihan. "Here, Ned. On ice."

MacCurtain opened his coat to show that he was not armed. "If it was one or two of us maybe we should worry. But as long as we're together, what can they do? We're the whole goddamn city."

"I don't like it," Murray said.

"Then stay home, Mick," MacCurtain replied. "Nobody says you got to be there."

"Shit, you guys'd cut me right out."

"It's up to you." MacCurtain waited. Murray and several others placed their handguns on the bar.

"No big deal," Demarra said, "a bunch of nodding little dons in long coats and big hats."

O'Dwyer did not move. He was still leaning back grandly in his chair.

"What about it, O'D.?" MacCurtain said finally.

"You know me, Mac. I never carry iron. This ain't Chicago."

"So I've heard. You wouldn't mind opening your coat, would you?"

"Of course not." O'Dwyer stood and lifted the flaps of his pin-striped blue suit. There was no sign of a holster or a gun. He was wearing a vest. His gold watch chain flashed as he turned slowly so that all the men could see.

"All right," MacCurtain said to the group. "Anything else?"

No one spoke.

"Let's go, then."

The Cantina Reale was a neighborhood restaurant on the corner of Hanover and Fleet streets which ordinarily handled a small clientele. But that night a wedding party had booked the place and it was jammed. An old-country band was blaring out *musica festiva* and the sidewalk outside was crowded with smoking men who preferred the balmy spring evening to the sweet musty air of the restaurant.

When MacCurtain pulled up in front of the Cantina Reale, he left the engine of his Chevrolet sedan running, having decided to wait until all three cars arrived before going in.

"Hey, you can't sit there!" one of the bridegroom's friends yelled from the sidewalk. He wanted the street clear so that the bride and groom could make a proper exit when it was time.

MacCurtain ignored him.

"Hey, you hear me?" The young man swaggered over to the car.

MacCurtain continued to ignore him.

The young man felt a hand slide easily between his arm and his ribs. Two fingers pressed into the space between his third and fourth ribs. The young man suddenly felt sick. He turned to find Gennaro Anselmo's face not six inches from his own.

Anselmo spoke to the young man in Sicilian, and he went meekly into the restaurant.

"You can leave your car there," Anselmo said.

"We're waiting for the others."

"As you wish."

Anselmo stepped back into the shadow of the building, in the frame of a door that was some yards removed from the Cantina Reale entrance.

MacCurtain sat watching the mirror. Finally Mick Murray's long green Marmon turned the corner, slipped smoothly in behind MacCurtain's car, and killed its lights. In another moment, Joey Donelley's Ford arrived. He parked in front of the Chevrolet. The Irishmen got out.

Anselmo led them through the door and up a staircase. The noise from the restaurant, the blaring band, filled the building. The smell of garlic hung in the place and offended the Irishmen to a man. More than one of them was thinking as he climbed the stairs that the building itself smelled like an Italian.

At the top of the staircase on a broad landing two men waited for them. Anselmo stepped between them and turned around to wait. Mac-Curtain started to cross between them, but they stopped him and, without speaking, ran their hands down the contours of his body. MacCurtain stood still but otherwise ignored them. When they stepped away from him, he moved to Anselmo's side in front of a large ornate door. Each of the Irishmen was searched in the same way. Then Anselmo led them through the door.

Don Enrico Zorelli was seated at a wooden table at the far side of a small auditorium. Three older Sicilians sat on either side of him. Directly behind them was a brown velvet curtain closing off a low stage. In the left corner were stacked flats and properties; the auditorium was home to the Salerno Opera Society.

Zorelli took his finger away from his harelip, raised it and beckoned to Anselmo, who was still standing at MacCurtain's side. The Irishmen had formed a casual line that mirrored the slight semicircle in which the Sicilians' chairs were arranged. As Anselmo crossed the room to approach Zorelli, MacCurtain was thinking the damn band downstairs would be too loud for them to talk. Dion O'Dwyer was wondering where they were going to sit. Mick Murray thought he saw the curtain move.

Anselmo bent over Zorelli, putting his ear to the don's mouth. Zorelli grabbed him by the neck and pulled him down.

The curtain opened.

Four men, including Frank Cosolimo, opened fire with their machine guns.

About dawn Colman Brady left his house on Fourth Street. He walked toward Flood Square. He had fallen asleep in the parlor and was surprised, when he awoke, that morning had come before MacCurtain.

Broadway at that hour was eerie, empty and glistening with a light dew. Its strangeness contributed to Brady's vague uneasiness. He imagined finding MacCurtain drunk at Houlie's.

Colman stared up the block as he walked, trying to see if Jer's car was in front of the hardware store. It wasn't. He resisted an urge to walk faster. There was no reason for his heart to be trotting.

Suddenly the tune of an old ballad ran through his mind and, before he could close it off, the lyric, "At the siege of Ross did my father fall."

The hardware store was closed tight. Brady banged on the door but nothing happened. There was no sign of life anywhere in the block.

Brady banged on the door repeatedly.

Finally Den O'Coole, worm-eyed and griping, opened it. "Jesus, Mary, and Joseph! Oh, Brady."

"Morning, Den. How goes it?"

"Terrible. Terrible. I'm sick."

"Who's inside?" Colman stepped past the little man and walked by the shovels, rakes, and squares of tin roofing to the back room.

No one was there.

"Where's O'Houlihan?" Brady asked O'Coole.

"In bed, I guess. I don't know."

"What do you want, Colman?" Ned O'Houlihan came through the door behind the bar. He wore a shabby nightshirt.

"Did Jer and the boys come back?"

"No."

"You know where the meeting was?"

"Cantina something."

"Cantina what? There are a dozen cantinas over there."

"Royal."

"Reale?"

"Yeah. Cantina Reale. You don't think. . . ?"

"I want to borrow your car, Ned."

"It's out back. Let me get you the key." O'Houlihan found the key in the cash drawer by the mirror and gave it to Brady. Brady strode to the corner door that opened on the alley.

Den O'Coole sat at a table, gray and sick.

When Brady stepped into the alley he saw the three cars in a line with the corpses piled inside, a cavalcade of blood and spilled brains. Someone's jaunty tan shoe sat on the sill of the rear window of the nearest car. MacCurtain's Chevrolet was at the head of the little line. The driver's door was open over a pool of red which marked the broken concrete of the alley. Mick Murray stared goggle-eyed from the seat.

Brady approached MacCurtain's car.

He saw O'Dwyer, Demarra, Casey. MacCurtain was not there. But then Brady understood that there was no reason for him to have returned from the North End in his own auto.

"Saints above!" O'Houlihan kept muttering. "Saints above!"

O'Coole stood gape-mouthed in the doorway until he rushed back into the dark room trying for the jakes. He fell over a chair and vomited.

Brady had the ballad in his head again. O'Houlihan kept looking away from the carnage and over to Brady, trying for his eyes, wanting very much to share a reaction with him. But Brady was staring at the scene and standing absolutely still before it. "At the siege of Ross," ran the ballad in his ears, "my father did fall." It was being sung by a boy, the pitch of whose voice grew higher and higher until the lyric was obliterated by a piercing steady scream. Brady wanted to clap his ears to stop the pain. The gray and red goo of brain and blood and twisted limbs was the most horrible sight he had ever seen. He thought of a ransacked butcher shop. Nellie's father had been a butcher and Colman had hated the smell of the man. The boy singing, the boy screaming, was Eddie Donovan whose face was blown off. Colman closed his eyes for a moment but the gray-red mess was there inside his head. He smelled the stench of the corpses. He thought of making for the jakes himself. But he sealed over his nausea and, to defy it, opened his eyes and took a step nearer the auto. He strained to see MacCurtain amid the bodies. Jerry MacCurtain was as close as he had to a friend. He had sent him off to his death. Brady felt suddenly that he should have anticipated this. You don't trust those frigging wops with anything, he thought; certainly not with the closest thing you have to a friend. He touched MacCurtain's Chevrolet, the fender of it, staring at O'Dwyer, Demarra, and Casey. They were obscenely, grotesquely cut, twisted, broken, and bloodied. Brady went to the Ford. Under McGahern's legs he saw Jer's head. He hadn't been shot in the face. Brady reached in to touch him, but his hand would not obey him and stopped inches from MacCurtain's brow. Brady withdrew his hand and suddenly, in a rage of feeling, clasped it with his other one and slammed them down in a fist on top of the car, denting it. He did it again and again, banging the car, trying to pound it down into the earth. Once he had tried to push the Druid stone off its base. It was the same kind of moment and led to the same release; he was going to kill someone for this.

O'Houlihan was as frightened by Brady's fit as by the carnage. When Brady gained control of himself, O'Houlihan said, "What do we do, Colman?"

"Do?" Colman waited for a wind to fill a sail. "Call the precinct, Ned."

"Jesus, Colman, I don't know. They'll think I had something to do with it."

"No, they won't. Call them."

O'Houlihan turned to go in.

Brady stayed where he was, staring at the dead. But he was not thinking about them. He was making his plan.

Gennaro Anselmo meanwhile was hiding on the rooftop of a building adjacent to the Cantina Reale. He had gone there immediately in the flurry of panic and confusion after the shooting had ceased. He knew that Zorelli was going to kill him. He was damned lucky he hadn't done it in the same moment he'd killed the Irishmen. For once Anselmo was grateful for the narrow margins of Old World loyalties. Zorelli could not kill one of his own in the massacre of foreigners. He would kill Anselmo now, separately, for two reasons. With the Irish eliminated from the bootleg scene — like that — Anselmo had no further usefulness. And since Zorelli had betrayed Anselmo and besmirched his honor, he knew that Anselmo would have to vindicate himself. The Irishmen had come to the meeting because they received Anselmo's word with respect. The Irish had more respect for his word than Zorelli did. Zorelli had to kill Anselmo or be killed by him and he knew it.

Anselmo had his own reason. The Unione was sure to be divided and uncertain after such a mad stroke as the massacre. The old method had been carried to an extreme which many would not support. Anselmo's instinct told him that the time had come. Zorelli had made a bad mistake. The Unione could be taken.

He waited for dawn and then lay quietly for another hour. Before he killed Zorelli he had to get Cosolimo. He got up at last and climbed over the low walls that separated the row houses. The sun was up and beaming brightly. It was a perfect spring morning. Four buildings over from his own, he crouched in the shadow of a chimney and took a pair of clippers out of his pocket and cut through the telephone wire where it ran out from the wall and up to a pole like a laundry line. He pocketed the clippers and entered the rooftop door and went down two flights to the fourth floor flat.

Cosolimo lived with his mother. Anselmo expected that she would still be at the early Mass at St. Leonard's. He tried the door. It was locked. He pushed against it and was calculating how much noise it would make if he kicked it in when he heard a voice from inside.

"Mama?"

Anselmo had expected Cosolimo to be asleep.

"Mama?"

Anselmo took a step back from the door, withdrew a pistol from his belt and fired twice through the wood. He could hear the thump of a body falling to the floor. There was a groan and a sound like an unhappy sigh. Anselmo knew it was the last of Cosolimo's breath leaving his body.

He raised his foot to the level of the knob and kicked once. The door cracked open a few inches, but a chain lock held it. He kicked again, but the chain showed no sign of giving. Cosolimo's body was on the floor against the door.

Anselmo froze when he heard the sound of the street door opening. He did not want to have to kill the old woman. He had to be certain Cosolimo was dead. He fired a third time through the door, aiming at the spot where the corpse was. Anselmo would not know it until later, but that shot, like the other two, had not killed Cosolimo. He put his gun in his belt and took a knife from his coat and snapped it open. He leaned down and reached through the cracked door and pulled Cosolimo's inert arm out from under his body. He cut Cosolimo's index finger off at the joint. He wrapped it in a rag, put it in his pocket, and left.

Zorelli lived over a bakery at the Sicilian end of Hanover Street.

A guard was posted at the street entrance. It was Lombardi, a dull-witted brute whom Anselmo decided to try and finesse.

"The Irish are coming!" Anselmo whispered to him urgently. "Wake your brothers!" The guard entered the building and hurried down the stairs to the basement where seven soldiers were sleeping.

Anselmo went up the stairs, taking his gun out as he went, and crying loudly in Sicilian, "Alert! Alert!"

The guard at the door to Zorelli's apartment rushed forward, but in the dark he could not make out his features to know it was Anselmo. "What? What?"

"The Irish downstairs! They've come! They've come! Hold them off!"

The guard crouched quickly and took aim between the banisters at the empty staircase. He heard the commotion of the soldiers rushing up from the basement, and he assumed it was the Irish gang coming.

Anselmo burst into Zorelli's apartment.

Two old ladies in black were seated at an open window. Anselmo heard the sounds of sirens in the street outside, but he was committed now.

Zorelli appeared at the door of his bedroom. He was wearing long underwear. His old man's paunch was evident and violated the tall, lean image Anselmo had of him. Zorelli had one hand at his mouth, and with the other hand he carried a large pistol.

Anselmo had to force down a clumsy delicacy he felt suddenly for the vulnerable old man. But the vulnerable old man was raising his gun.

Anselmo shot him twice.

The don fell across the easy chair just inside the door. One of its legs broke with the awkward jolt of his weight and he bounced to the floor. Anselmo shot the don once more through the head.

Anselmo took Zorelli's gun and turned to face the door. He would have to brazen it out with the don's soldiers, whom he expected to crash into the rooms momentarily. Everything rode now on Anselmo's ability to make his authority instantly felt.

The women at the window were no longer screaming. They clung to each other in terror.

There was no sound coming from the street. That should have warned Anselmo.

When the door crashed open, it was not Zorelli's soldiers. It was the Boston police, and with them Colman Brady.

Anselmo dropped his guns.

Captain Laughlin was violating procedure. Without informing the precinct on Hanover Street, he had, with four cars full of men, rushed immediately over from South Boston. Jerry MacCurtain and Mick Murray were friends of his. He wanted Zorelli himself. Brady wanted Anselmo.

While the police swarmed into the room, Anselmo said nothing, nor did he flinch when the captain rushed at him with his pistol raised like a club. Laughlin was going to slap him with the barrel.

Brady stopped Laughlin, grabbing him from behind. "He's mine, Pete!" Brady said, pushing Laughlin aside and approaching Anselmo. "You bastard!" he said, and he punched him in the face, jamming the bone of his nose against his brain. Anselmo staggered back but did not fall.

Brady's eyes fell to Zorelli, who was bleeding from holes in his chest and forehead. "Who killed the fuck?" he asked, but he could see that Anselmo had.

Anselmo said nothing. He pulled a rag bundle out of his pocket and tossed it to Brady.

Brady opened it. "Jesus Christ!" he said.

"What is it?" Laughlin asked.

Brady held the severed finger out to the policeman.

"It is," Anselmo said at last, "the instrument of their murders. Your friends are avenged."

5

A LIGHT FRINGE of snow lay like a nubby spread on the wrinkled farmland; the first snow of the year, tentative and dry. It was Wednesday,

December 6, 1933. Colman Brady and his son were driving along a winding back road well north of Boston. It was their day to find a Christmas tree, the third year they had gone off alone without the cousins. Collins Brady was eleven years old.

He was running his finger along the cold pane of the window, making spiderwebs in the fog. Some days were made completely of pleasure, of good smells and tastes and wonderful sounds like footfalls in the snow. Collins watched the fields. He was waiting for the orchards; after the apple trees came the pine forests. He wanted the woods to hurry and arrive. But also he wanted the day to slow down. It was already going by too fast.

Without Jackie there, Collins didn't have to worry about his father barking at him, "Behave!" There was no one to jostle elbows with.

"You're off in another country, *Micko*." Brady's nickname for the boy played on the combining of *Mick* and *amico,* and was pronounced *meeko*.

Collins loved it when his father called him that.

"Yes, sir."

"I mean what are you thinking about?"

Collins looked quickly at his father. It took him an instant to see that he was not being put upon.

"Apple trees."

"Apple trees! Well, you're in luck! Look there!"

Ahead on the left was a large orchard. The trees were bare and spindly.

"You've a terrific memory, Micko. I'd forgotten all about the apple trees up here."

"First the apple trees. Then the pine trees. Like the A & P."

Brady laughed. The kid was bright and quick. He reached over and hit him lightly, as if brushing snow from the boy's shoulder.

"How many trees make an orchard, Dad?"

"How many apples make a tree?"

"About a thousand. How many berries make a bush?"

"Oh, maybe a million. How many Tootsie Rolls make a tummyache?"

"No such thing," the boy laughed.

"How many Tom Mixes equal one Hoot Gibson?"

Collins began to quickly move his lips as if calculating. But he could not suppress his delight long enough to contrive a serious answer.

"Come on," Brady urged, "how many?"

"I don't know. That's too hard. But four Tom Mixes equal seven Buck Joneses."

"How do you figure that?"

"Well, one Buck Jones is the same as two Jack Hoxies, right?"

"That's true."

[*187*]

"And everybody knows that four Jack Hoxies equals two Tom Mixes."

"On the nose, *amico*! On the nose!" Brady thrashed at the boy with fondness, and Collins leaned toward him. Brady wondered if the boy had calculated something.

Brady slowed the car by the edge of pine woods, and pulled off the road onto a little turn-around. He shut the engine off. The layer of snow enhanced the silence of the place.

"OK, *amico*," Brady said, climbing out. He grabbed the ax from the back seat and slammed the door. Collins had his own hatchet.

"Boy, Dad . . ." He fell into step with his father. "We better walk like Indians. Listen." He ran ahead, placing his feet carefully. "Not a sound."

"You're right, Micko. Wouldn't do to get caught, would it?"

"Whose land is this, anyway?"

They had already left the road behind and were following a faint path. Inside the woods there was little snow on the ground.

"Who knows? But the trees belong to everybody."

Brady's son gave him a quick look which told him he didn't believe *that*. Private land equals private trees; the kid knew that much. But his look also said that if it was OK with his father, it was OK with him.

They mirrored each other, walking side by side, Collins a smaller version of Brady — thin, lively, self-confident, taller than average. Each carried his blade over his outside shoulder. Their inside hands swung along in synchrony.

"Look at that!" Brady pointed to sunlight streaming in rays down through the trees.

"Like a miracle," Collins said, "like a saint coming down."

Every once in a while the boy displayed a sort of nunnish sensibility. The Sisters at St. Eulalia's School were forever fussing over Collins, though it was Jackie who continually celebrated his vocation to the priesthood. Jackie, curiously enough, was the troublemaker and the misbehaver. Collins could look at a ray of sunlight and think of saints coming down.

After going a way in silence — a time during which Collins was thinking that silence outdoors was easier than silence indoors — Brady said, "Tell you what. Suppose you pick it this year."

"The Christmas tree?"

"No, your nose. Of course the Christmas tree."

"OK," Collins said manfully. "Let's see . . ." He started to eye the various trees as he moved by them.

"Too big, too big, too little, too big. That's a good one but for the bad branch."

They kept moving.

Collins thought there was something wrong with every tree he saw.

"This is like being up at bat, Dad."

"Any tree's a hit, Micko. How about that one?" Brady pointed his ax easily. "Or that?"

They stopped walking.

"Yeah, those are good ones." But he was trying to decide which one. He wanted it to be perfect. He walked all the way around a small tree, glancing up at his father as he did so. "How about this one?" He asked it with an enormous tentativeness.

"Gorgeous."

"That's good too, though."

"Yup. Either one, son."

"Really?"

"It's up to you."

"That one then."

"Perfect. Best tree in the woods."

"You think?"

"Go to it."

The boy stooped down and, with a large intake of breath, swung his hatchet at the trunk of the tree just above the ground.

He swung again and again. Not much seemed to happen. The tree shook off its coat of snow dust, but the wood of the trunk resisted the dull blade of Collins's old hatchet.

"Here, son." Brady held out the ax. The boy took it solemnly. His father hadn't insulted him by saying "Be careful."

He gripped the ax the way an ax is meant to be gripped, let it pendulum back and forth, collecting momentum and mood, and then he let loose with a mighty chop. The *thunk* of it soaked through the air and transformed Michael Collins Brady into the magnificent lumberjack of the north woods.

"What the hell do you think you're doing?"

The woman's voice startled them both.

Collins almost left the ground with shock. "Caught!" he thought. Suddenly the slice in the trunk of the small pine looked to him like a vicious open wound, and here he was nabbed with his hand in it.

The last thing Colman Brady expected to see in the woods was a beautiful woman on horseback. Apparently the trail they'd been following was a bridle path. The woman wore a brown canvas bush jacket with broad pockets and shoulder flaps that were partly obscured by her long blond hair.

"I know," Colman said, "Edwina Booth, *Trader Horn!*"

The woman smiled in spite of herself. The Australian jackets had been the fashion a couple of years before, when the film had come out. She'd forgotten.

When she smiled her face cracked into lines, and Brady was disappointed to realize she was older than he was, thirty-five at least. Her brows were pencil-thin and the lids of her eyes were dark and heavy. Her makeup had the peculiar and opposite effect, given the setting, of dispelling the woman's glamour. She seemed like a rancher's wife or a pioneer lady.

"This is private property, mister." Her voice was raspy and deep.

"Is it? Aren't we in the reservoir?"

"What reservoir? This is Pride's Crossing. You're trespassing."

"Is it someone's estate?"

"Mine."

"It's very nice. Lovely woods."

"So you thought you'd help yourself to some of it, eh?"

Colman shrugged. "Well, you know . . ." He winked, half at Collins, half at the woman. "It's Christmas."

"Oh my God!" she said. "A Christmas tree!"

"Indeed."

"Of course," she said, looking at the wounded pine. "A Christmas tree. God, it's December already?" She paused. "You've an accent," she said.

"I was just thinking the same about you."

They both laughed.

"I'm from Ireland. This is my son, Michael Collins Brady. He's from the States." Brady draped his arm over the boy's shoulder.

"The Irish," she recited, "are a fair people. They never speak well of one another."

"Samuel Johnson," Colman said.

"Yes. To Boswell."

"Who else?"

They nodded at each other, a mutual bare acknowledgement.

"I am Madeline Gardner Thomson. No *i* and no *p*."

"Sorry?"

"There are the blind Gardners and the one-eyed Gardiners. I am blind. That is to say, there is no *i* in my father's name. In like manner, there are the peeless Thomsons and the peed."

"I get it. No *p* in your husband's name."

"Peeless the peerless." She laughed in what Brady thought was a most charming way.

Collins was blushing, mystified by the talk of eyes and urine even while intrigued by the obvious game of it.

Brady stepped toward the woman's horse, a large chestnut thorough-bred, and ran his hand along the horse's withers. "You've a beautiful horse. Come here, Micko."

Collins joined his father in stroking the horse, which responded with a set of three broad shudders. Collins forced himself to keep stroking the animal, although, truthfully, it frightened him.

"Was your horse like this, Dad?"

"Not nearly so fine, son. Though there was a mare in the village . . ." Brady thought of McClusky's mare and then of Jack and Marie — his first thought of them in years. ". . . A fine horse, Mrs. Thomson."

"Do you ride, Mr. Brady?"

"I did." Brady laughed when he realized they were not talking about the same thing. "Not for the sport of it, though. Simply to go from one end of the field to the other. We used the 'hang-on-tight-and-you're-all-right' method of horsemanship, if you know what I mean."

"Perhaps I do." She watched Collins stroking and was pleased to see him growing less tentative about it.

"I'll tell you what, Mrs. Thomson. If you're agreeable, I'll pay you for the tree, since we already cut it half through."

"Nonsense. I'd forgotten about Christmas. Feel free."

"I insist." Brady handed her a five-dollar bill.

"Well, I can't accept that, can I? Five dollars, goodness! You'd pay no more than one for that tree at the market."

"Call it five. It's all I've got."

"I'll tell *you* what. I'll take *one* dollar for it. Which means you have to come up to the house while I get change."

"Don't be silly."

"And perhaps your son would like to ride Freddy." She swung off the saddle and down.

"Wow! Could I?"

"Well, Collins, we . . ."

"It's perfectly safe, Mr. Brady. Freddy accommodates children quite nicely."

Collins winced at that — children! — having begun already to think of himself as Tom Mix.

Brady picked the boy up and hoisted him onto the saddle. Mrs. Thomson kept the reins and led the horse along the path, clucking as she went.

Collins looked back at his father, excitement and pride in his eyes. But he displayed also the nagging discomfort that came with the knowledge that his father had not quite fully approved of this adventure.

Brady was watching the woman. She was tall and full-bodied. The belt of the bush jacket gave accent to her figure. She wore knee-length leather boots, which made her seem even taller. She led the horse off with easy authority. Brady could see why the animal would follow her.

He picked up the ax, swiped twice at the base of the pine, and took the tree down. He put it on his shoulder and followed his son on the horse, which followed Madeline Thomson.

The bridle path soon became broader and more beaten, wide enough to accommodate a motor car. The pine woods thinned and gradually opened out onto a rolling white field. On top of a knoll, dominating the scene, was a mock-Tudor mansion. Several small outbuildings stood between the threesome and the house itself; they were approaching from the rear.

Though it was just midafternoon, the sky was already thickening up with signs of evening.

"More snow, Mr. Brady?" the woman asked over her shoulder.

"It's a fat sky, I'd say."

"I love the snow."

Brady increased his pace and drew even with her. The horse's head was between them, just to the rear.

"It makes me feel like singing," she said.

"I know what you mean."

"What shall we sing, then?"

"Something for Christmas!" Collins put in from the horse.

"My God, yes! Look at us!" Madeline Thomson stopped and surveyed the boy on the horse and man with ax and tree. "Currier and Ives! All we need are the bells!"

"Hey!" Collins cried suddenly, "my hatchet! I left my hatchet!"

"Oh, damn, Micko! All the way back there!"

They had just drawn even with the house.

"I'm sorry, Dad, but I . . ."

"Forget it," Brady said a bit edgily. "We have to go back that way."

"Where's your car?" Madeline asked.

"On the road from Beverly."

"That's just over there. You needn't go all the way back through." She lifted the reins over the horse's head and gave them to the boy. "Here, Michael, take Freddy back for your hatchet."

"Oh, I don't . . . !"

"Are you afraid?"

"No! No! But . . ." He looked at Brady, who dramatically rolled his eyes to heaven.

"All right, Tom Mix," Brady said. "Hang on tight and you're all right."

"Thanks, Dad. Thanks, ma'am. But what do I say if he . . . ?"

"Just hold the reins tightly, dear, as your father says. That's it. How's that feel?"

"Good."

"Go along then." She turned the horse for him and stepped back.

Freddy sauntered down into the field again, already back on his customary trail.

"You're very kind, Mrs. Thomson, which, I must admit, wasn't my first impression."

"Well, you startled me. How was I to know you were Father Christmas and Joy Noel? Come inside. I'll get you your change."

She entered the house. Brady leaned his ax and the tree outside the door and followed her into a large warm kitchen. A black woman was peeling potatoes in a corner.

"Hello, Maybell."

" 'Day, Miz Thomson. How you?"

"This is Mr. Brady, Maybell."

" 'Day, Mr. Brady."

"Good day," he said.

"Oh, the *Transcript* came." Mrs. Thomson peeled her gloves while crossing to a big stainless steel counter in the middle of the room.

"Yes, ma'am. Henry, he just left."

"Oh, my God! Look at this!" Madeline picked up the paper and walked back toward Brady, reading.

Brady saw the huge print beneath the masthead of the *Boston Evening Transcript*.

It read, "Prohibition Repeal Is Ratified. Roosevelt Asks Nation to Bar the Saloon. Boston Celebrates with Quiet Restraint."

Smaller print under the banner read, "City Toasts New Era. Legal Liquor Is Scarce. FDR Sees End to Big-Time Crime."

"What do you think of that?" Madeline asked.

Brady cracked noncommittally, "Better to bar the saloon than grill the tavern, I say."

"Well, this calls for a toast! Good for Utah!" Madeline led the way down a parquet corridor. "Come along, Mr. Brady. Don't make me drink my first legal drink alone."

Brady followed, feeling somewhat like Collins on the horse.

They entered a large room that was dark and stale; the low-beamed ceiling hung on it like a weight. There were paneled walls and bookcases, a baronial fireplace, and several arrangements of stuffed furniture. Mrs. Thomson went directly to a window and slashed the blinds open. The field they had crossed lay before them, sloping down to the pine forest.

Light poured in, but succeeded only in heightening the mustiness of the room. Its use in daytime was apparently rare and somehow inappropriate.

"What will you have?"

"Is that a bottle of Bushmills I see there?"

"It is."

"May I?"

She poured an inch of the whiskey into a plain glass and handed it to him. She poured her own drink from another bottle.

Her hand shook slightly as she poured, the only hint that her composure was not complete and real.

"Here's to Utah," she said, raising her glass. "Isn't it strange the Mormons should be the ones to give it back?"

"John Barleycorn. Here's to him." Brady sipped the whiskey, savored it, the first Bushmills he'd had since coming to the States.

Madeline Thomson tossed her drink down without flourish. "No," she said, "they didn't give us back the liquor, just good citizenship. Another?" She poured her own.

"Doesn't taste nearly so well, does it? When it's legal."

"Oh, I don't know." She sipped at her glass. She was not downing the second. She leaned back against a solid oak table, on which a dozen bottles and glasses were spread.

The idea of the woman's accessibility was clutching at Brady, and it made him nervous.

When he was younger the habits of work and his driving compulsion to pull together a career with possibilities had withstood not only the periodic catastrophe of a short-lived painful affair, but also the increasing infrequency with which his affairs occurred. He was still nominally an assistant to the mayor, but access to Curley was impossible without going through Brady. The Depression, which had given absolute national power to Roosevelt, gave a similar local power to Curley, but its exercise depended on Colman Brady. Its exercise had consumed Colman Brady.

And now here was this woman looking at him with frankly parted lips, with defiant, self-assured allure. Clearly there was something jaded about her. Her brightness had waned the way the lights of the city wane after two in the morning. Brady saw the woman before him suddenly as an aging flapper. She had the modish slouch. She had the contrived extroversion. She had the pagan eye. Brady pictured her reading contraband James Joyce by flashlight under a blanket at some fancy college. He could see her snapping a string of pearls for the hell of it, spreading out her arms and saying she wanted to live, live, live! She took lovers at will and discarded them without qualms. She had wiggled through the Charleston on table tops. She passed out night after night from booze. She burned her candle at both ends; it shed such lovely light. She believed in salvation by fun alone. The world that self-expression made would be a better one.

But that was the world they were living with now; and it revolved on full-blown, institutionalized despair. Brady was accustomed to feeling the defeat and malaise of his neighbors in South Boston, nearly all of whom were unemployed and therefore hopeless. It struck him as curious and remarkable that he should suddenly find himself in a lavish house with a cozy socialite behind whose languorous gaze he detected the familiar vacuous ennui. It seemed to Brady that the woman was not quite able to carry it off as sleek sophistication anymore. World-weariness is attractive and seductive, like many things, only on the young.

"Have a cigarette?" She offered him the silver tray.

"Thank you. I will."

She unbuttoned the bush jacket and let the flaps of the belt hang. She wore a checkered man's shirt under it. The ample cloth obscured her breasts.

"How ludicrous of Roosevelt!" she exclaimed, "Bar the saloon, imagine! Is it Repeal or isn't it?"

"He has to say as much."

"He's a liar, don't you agree?"

"Of course he is. Isn't everyone? Take me; I steal Christmas trees."

"You have the grace to admit it. Speaking of which, here." She handed him his five-dollar bill.

"You were going to give me change."

"I just did. A change of mind."

Brady dropped the bill on the table.

"No!" she said, picking it up and stuffing it into his breast pocket. "I insist!"

He stared at her. She had moved close to him, close enough that her perfume filled his senses. He could easily have encircled her without moving.

"Thank you," he said, placing his drink on the table. He crushed his cigarette, and prepared to make a move either away from her or toward. His impulse was strong and building, but it had not articulated itself. He looked at her. Her lily-like drooping delicacy impudently on display as she met his look was almost too much for him. He had never seen such rough-toned rowdy showiness in a woman. The pearly chasteness of Irish lasses, however counterfeit, was soothing and easy in comparison, which was probably why Madeline Thomson exercised such power over him. She held herself at that moment like a flare hung in the sky, having just achieved its apogee.

How silent the house had grown, as if it were suspended until their choice had made itself. And how cold it was, as if some virtue, the warmth of it, had gone from that house forever.

You can drink your booze legally now, lass, Colman thought. *You can even read* Ulysses.

He was going to do it, to step even closer, bend slightly, listen, listen and kiss her forehead. Was it marble? Indomitable woman; unbreakable, tireless. His eye went to the wrinkles at hers. They crept cheekward carelessly. Her dark eyes gave him not a quiver.

"Oh, my God!" he cried. His look had suddenly been wrenched from the woman. He stared for an instant across her shoulder, and then turned and bolted out of the room.

Madeline Thomson shivered as if a creepy silent wind had entered the room and turned it cold. As cold as it would be if her husband had walked in and cast his customary frigid look on her, his well-loved enemy. She dragged on her cigarette, drained her glass, and turned to the window just as Freddy galloped out of view, riderless.

She mashed her cigarette out, but in doing so dropped her glass. It broke into pieces. She turned and ran out of the room, down the parquet corridor, and through the kitchen.

Brady was in a near panic in the yard. The horse had returned without Collins and was poking its nose down onto the thin sheet of ice that covered the water in a low trough.

Brady was running his hand under the horse's left foreleg, checking for perspiration. He had first to know if the animal had bolted and run, and how far.

"What's the matter? Where's the boy?" Madeline asked. She felt a merciful numbness coming over her.

Brady did not answer.

"Maybell!" she cried.

But before the servant responded, Brady ran down into the field toward the woods. Mrs. Thomson followed him, struggling with the flaps of the belt of her jacket as she ran. The day had turned very cold indeed. It was nearly over.

"Micko!" Brady yelled. "Micko! Micko!"

The sound of his voice carried back to Madeline Thomson, who felt a surge of terror spilling up through cracks in the numbing ice. Her own son, her only child, had fallen overboard the liner *Excalibur* on a trip to Italy three years before. He had been nine years old. His disappearance — she could not think of it as death; there had been no body — had ruined everything.

Brady felt as though he were in a vicious fistfight with an enormous opponent. The effort of running across the snowy field was like struggling to get out of the suffocating grip of the giant.

"Micko! Micko!" He darted into the woods. He hadn't run like that in years. Once the terrain changed and the ground was solid underfoot, the rush downhill, for all the fear of it, was exhilarating. If he'd gone any faster he'd have flown.

While running he admitted to himself that he always expected it would end like this.

"I thought you were dying, Nellie."

"I am. So are you. But another time. Not now."

Now! Micko would be dead! Colman could see him with the spike of a sapling stump sticking through his chest. The horse would have thrown him and he would have flown and landed on the thin knife of the cut tree. Good God! Was it the stump of the pine that *he* had cut that killed his son? His breathing failed to keep pace with the frantic pounding; was it in his ears, his heart? Was the pounding on the earth, his feet? His head ached and the trees he was passing tilted this way and that.

"Micko! Micko!"

He should never have let him ride the horse. He should never have let him go back to the woods alone. He knew that the woman was behind him. He knew without seeing her or hearing her.

"Micko! Micko!"

Brady had wondered about their women: Lloyd George's, Lawrence Lowell's, Jack Gardner's. Blind, peeless. She'd practically asked him for it.

"Son!" he screamed. "Son!" But the woods were dark and empty. He had trouble following the path, but ran it headlong, crashing branches and sending snow off like spray off breakers. This was the day, he was sure, it would happen. It would have happened already.

An intuition impressed itself calmly on Brady below the surface agitation, an intuition about his stakes in the death of his son. He had never adverted to it before, but his fatherhood of that boy had been the one clear, direct, unmediated experience since coming to America. Michael Collins Brady was Colman's link with Nellie and that one love, with Mick Collins and that, with damn, goddamned Ireland, which still owned Brady, as he knew every time he felt the piercing ache of not belonging to the world he had chosen. It had not chosen him. Not yet.

"Micko! Micko!"

The child was dead.

"Hi, Dad."

He was standing in the middle of the path. His hatchet was at his side, hooked in his belt. On his face he wore a great smile, which faded instantly when he took in the pale, frightened look of his father.

The boy's question — what's wrong? — was stifled by his father's body as Colman swooped down on him and closed him in his embrace with his mouth buried in the hollow of his son's shoulder.

"Jesus, Mary, and Joseph!" The words burst from Colman's throat, and their desperation caused an ache in the pit of Collins's belly. He thought his ribs would crack.

Colman's fear that the boy was dead was replaced suddenly by an opposite anger. "Goddamn you!" he railed, drawing back and slapping the boy square across the face. Even as he struck, Brady knew what an unjust blow it was, but he could not help himself. He loved the kid so much, and for an instant he had lost him and his entire life was ruined. He struck his blow not so much against Collins as against the very structures of a world in which parents *do* lose their children, if not sooner, later; if not to death, then to indifference. The venom of the attack more than the sting of the blow brought tears immediately to Collins's eyes. He thought he would faint. His father was looking at him with the fiercest rage, which the boy mistook for hatred. He had no defense. He had no idea of the accusation.

"Don't you ever do that again!" Brady commanded.

Collins managed to squeak out "What?" before he began to sob.

"Stop that!" Brady ordered. He shook the kid.

"*You* stop it!" Madeline Thomson screamed from behind him. She was seeing her own son and this brute torturing him. Didn't he know the boy was drowning? "You're mad!" she screamed. "You're mad!"

She was weeping and out of breath, with an excruciating ache in her side, on the verge of hysteria. She stood over Brady, who was on one knee.

Colman Brady had no idea what was happening.

He looked at Madeline Thomson. Her wrecked face — *there* was where the madness was — stunned him. What had this woman to do with Collins? With him?

He turned back to the boy.

He was alive.

That was it! That was the fact before which he was kneeling! The kid was alive! Relief and gratitude surged through Brady. But the boy was wretched. He was bereft of his habitual dignity and poise. There was also an abundant hint of anger in him.

"Ah, Collins!" Colman murmured pitifully, his own lips quivering minutely, his strong hands kneading his shoulders. "Ah, Collins, ah Collins!"

He bent over and kissed him warmly, and his son's great brown eyes, agleam with self-pity, closed slowly and his head sank down onto his father's breast, the hard old pillow.

Madeline Thomson could not bear to watch them. She turned and ran up the path, sinking her teeth into the fingers of her left hand. She was afraid if her weeping got the better of her this time, she would never stop again.

"The horse, son . . . ," Colman said after a moment, ". . . when it came back without you . . ."

"Dad, I'm sorry. I had to get off it to get my hatchet. It was on the ground. Then I couldn't get back on. It was too big. I didn't know how. . . ." The boy started to cry again. He felt like a miserable failure. He knew he would break his father's heart. Every time.

Brady nearly laughed, it was so obvious.

If he hadn't let the woman snag him in her little web, he'd have realized that of course the kid could not mount again.

Where *was* the woman? Brady turned. She was gone.

"Is the horse all right?"

"Sure it is! Are you?"

"Yea." The boy turned brave. "I'm fine."

"I'm sorry I hit you, son."

"OK, Dad."

"Let's go." They stood. Brady draped his arm over the kid's shoulder and they started for the road.

"Wait a minute!" Collins said. "What about the tree? What about the ax?"

"Forget it, son. You've got your hatchet. Forget the ax."

Driving along the winding road through the woods and fields of Pride's Crossing, Ipswich, and Beverly, making for Route One, neither Colman nor the boy spoke. The consciousness of disappointment and frustration persisted. Collins was relieved that his father's rage had dissolved, and he had successfully transformed his own anger into bottomless melancholy.

Brady was trying to think about other things than what had just occurred.

The Repeal of Prohibition, for example. It would change things, certainly. But Roosevelt's prediction that it would do away with big-time crime was laughable. Brady thought about Anselmo again. He'd been in Norfolk prison over two years. The Sicilian mobsters, having eliminated their Irish competition in the MacCurtain Massacre, had changed the face of the underworld in New England overnight. Now everything began and ended in the North End. Frank Cosolimo, whose finger Anselmo had sent to Brady, was running the Unione in Zorelli's place. But he was ruthless and stupid, and now that Repeal was on, his organization would be in trouble. Nobody outside the North End would deal with Cosolimo if he didn't have to. Now that liquor would be available legally, Cosolimo would be shortsheeted. But that would mean simply a major power struggle in the Italian underworld, not the end of it.

Brady reminded himself to check on Anselmo. He had arranged for two special guards to be with him at all times. He might have to make further provisions for Anselmo's security now. Cosolimo wanted Anselmo dead desperately. Brady would continue to protect him because Anselmo had earned it. When Zorelli killed Jer MacCurtain, he might as well have killed Brady himself; that was how intensely he felt the hurt and rage. Anselmo had avenged MacCurtain. More than that, because Anselmo had killed Zorelli, Brady did not have to, and he didn't have to kill Anselmo. He was grateful for that, immeasurably so, not only because such an act would have been the end of his ambition for himself and for his family, but because Brady revolted at the thought of killing a man. He was older. He was old enough even to regret his own acts of killing in Ireland, that they had been necessary. So Brady was determined to see that Anselmo did not die in jail. It was the least he could do. And — owing to the fact that the Superior Court was a Yankee stronghold and well beyond Curley's influence and therefore Brady's — it was also the most he could do.

Curley had been talking about having a great bash for party workers when Repeal came through. Brady hoped the mayor hadn't done anything about it, and certainly not for that night. Who'd have guessed the Mormons in Utah would have put Repeal over? Brady hated to be caught unaware, and if Curley threw a party that got out of hand it would be one more embarrassment. A public display of drunkenness by Curley and his crew would give the State House biddies just the opening they wanted and needed. There was a self-destruction about Curley, and at times . . .

"Jesus!" Brady said, swerving the car onto the road's shoulder as a huge yellow Packard with flamboyant chrome fixtures roared down on him from behind. He had seen a like car that afternoon in that yard on the hill by the mock-Tudor house.

Madeline Thomson! Blind and peed! Rushing after him, to hurl his ax at him, to force the pathetic tree on him, to flash her outrage at him. Tough shit, Lady! Morning wears to evening and hearts break. Leaves of grass and all that. All things doomed to die touch the heart. Including the first lust of winter. Go home to your husband! Celebrate Repeal! Get blasted! Read Joyce! Rejoice.

"Hoompa! Hoompa!" went the horn of the Packard as it careened wildly past Brady's Ford. Brady prepared to overwhelm her with a burst of curses, but the Packard did not, as he thought it would, cut him off and force him to stop. The yellow roadster flung itself around the next curve. There were three or four people waving bottles at each other and the world.

"Hoompa! Hoompa!" the horn went, celebrating legal liver disease.

Not Madeline Thomson.

He'd seen the last of her. What did it matter? He looked over at Collins, who was frightened by their close call with the other car. He loved the kid. Why did the world feel empty?

6

IT SEEMED as if no one could get a drink in Boston. Trucks and drays loaded with freshly distilled liquor and recently imported wines and brandies had been held in the huge warehouses on the waterfront in preparation for the moment they could legally be delivered to hotels and clubs. But their cheerful shipment had been delayed by mysterious accidents. Truck tires had been flattened. Warehouse locks had been changed and no one seemed able to open them. Several teams of draft horses had been cruelly slaughtered. As word spread through the city that the Twenty-first Amendment had been ratified at last, liquor entrepreneurs were clamoring for supplies.

Frank Cosolimo had been preparing his bold stroke for weeks. The warehouse men, the dock bosses, the teamsters, and even the customs agents who had observed the unloading of the liquor were all his. The hundreds of newly licensed retailers would have to deal with him if they wanted stock on their shelves. Though most of them had already paid for their orders, when they arrived on the waterfront to take delivery they were informed that, through strange coincidences, the only shipments available were those of holders of long-term contracts with a new firm, Rosa Imports.

The Rosa Imports office in the old Seaman's Building on Atlantic Avenue could process such contracts in a matter of moments. Some retailers objected and tried to bypass Cosolimo's agents. Theirs were the trucks sabotaged and horses slain. At least one tavern owner, an Irishman from Charlestown, was beaten badly. By the early evening of the day that Repeal took effect, Rosa Imports had contracted to be the exclusive supplier of spirits and wines for over two hundred hotels and clubs.

Curley's crowd gathered at the Parker House, up the street from City Hall. Hundreds of revelers squeezed into the cellar Grill Room, anxious to toast John Barleycorn. For them the occasion was the Irish-American equivalent of Bastille Day. The Puritan Wave had been turned back. Never again would the grim Roundhead morality of the Reformation impose itself on the merry conviviality of Desmonds, Reillys, and O'Connors. America was theirs at last, and fully.

"Do you know why Protestants are forbidden to make love standing up?" A young red-faced drunk asked the gang.

His circle of companions listened expectantly.

"Because people might think they're dancing!"

Everyone laughed.

"Where the hell is the champagne?" someone yelled at the bartender.

"Not here yet," the stout dispenser replied. He was handing over mugs full of the same old bootleg beer that speakeasies had been serving for years.

"I hate this swill!" another cried, as he poured his beer on the floor.

Someone offered him a silver flask. "Try this."

"Has it been tested?"

"Sure. On my thumb," the benefactor replied, holding up his hand. The thumbnail test; pour it on your thumb. If the nail doesn't come off, the stuff is safe to drink.

Curley and Brady were down the corridor from the bistro in the hotel barbershop, where they had repaired for a sudden meeting with Pete Malloy, the bar manager, who had just come up from the waterfront. Curley's frame was draped like a barber's sheet across a reclining chair.

"That wop bastard has the whole place tied up," Malloy concluded. "That's why we haven't had the champagne or the imported stuff."

"The boys out front won't settle for the near-beer much longer," Curley said.

"That's beside the point, Jim," Brady said. "We can't let Cosolimo pull this off."

"What do *you* propose?" Malloy asked, exasperated and angry. "He already *did* pull it off. Everybody signed with him."

"Not you?"

"Of course, I did, Brady! Shit! I can't wait weeks or months for the stuff. What am I supposed to do? Serve grain alcohol with juniper drops? They want champagne!"

"Well," Brady said, "they'll get it now, won't they?"

"Damn right! No thanks to you or to you, Mayor. It's legal now, for Christ's sake! Why don't you do something about that bastard?"

"Presumably, Pete," Curley said, "his contracts are legal now too. You already *did* something."

"Oh, Christ!" Malloy stormed out of the barbershop.

Curley and Brady stared after him.

Finally the mayor said, "I want a brilliant idea from you, Brady."

"I'm not a tidy-minded man, Mayor. You won't like what I'm thinking."

"Where's Jerry MacCurtain now that I need him? All my best fellows are gone." Curley paused. It occurred to Brady that the mayor had a grander past than future. For once the man looked old. He was almost sixty and sounded it, sighing, "We're all so damned white-collar respectable we can only wring our hands while that murderer plucks Boston like a fruit from a tree. Tell me what you're thinking."

"It's a fool's thought. If we iced Cosolimo he'd only be replaced by another one. You have to find a way to work with him."

"Not after what he did. Never."

"Anselmo."

"We can't touch him. You know that."

"We can keep him alive. A little patience is what we need."

Curley reached down below the armrest of the barber's chair and unhooked the leather strap and slapped it viciously across his own lap. Its sharp report startled Brady. The sudden pain through his legs purged the mayor of his emotion.

"The swine!" he said, "The dago swine!"

Brady said nothing.

Curley fondled the strop and let his eyes drift along the shelf below the smart mirror which held dozens of long-necked bottles of tonic and cologne.

"You know, Colman, I've always thought a barbershop is the most evil-smelling place in the world."

Brady laughed. He was aware of his own image in the mirror when he said, "Getting your hair cut's like going to confession. A messy business, but you feel clean as a penny after."

"I wouldn't let them priests at me with a razor, I'll tell you."

"Why, Mayor!" Brady loved Curley's faint irreverence.

Curley reclined like a Roman senator, lifted his shoes slightly to study them. "You know what I need?"

A queasy feeling unfolded itself in Brady.

"I need a shine, that's what."

It was typical of Curley — so vast his need for victories — that when faced with an intractable opponent he turned on his nearest ally. James

Michael Curley fed on the defeat of others. He preferred to defeat his enemies; he would settle for the humiliation of his friends. Brady knew this was no mere impulse of egomania. It was the mayor's carefully nurtured technique for maintaining his massive, solitary preeminence. His protégés and pretenders and potential successors were systematically skewered on his cruel wit.

Brady knew that once the mayor perceived him as a future rival he was finished. He had developed a technique of his own, a counterfeit subservience combined with a steady resourcefulness that made him too valuable to discard. Brady's effort was continually to show Curley how useful he was, but Brady knew that his position was safest when the mayor felt enormously threatened by his great enemy, the old Boston Protestant. When Curley was riding high, unthreatened, he was dangerous to Brady.

The mayor was turning his shoes this way and that.

Brady was thinking that what he needed was a new draft of the old bitterness for Curley to drink. Booze would do for starters.

"Let's have a drink with the boys, Jim."

"Damn, I need a shine."

"Would you like me to shine your shoes for you, Mayor?" Brady was jovial and direct. By so raising the bet on Curley, by articulating and accepting the taunt, he defused it.

Curley could only treat Brady's offer like a joke. Finally, it would demean him to have a shoeshiner for an aide. He laughed, flung himself out of the chair, and slapped Brady on the shoulder. "I couldn't afford your price, Colman! Let's make some whoopee! What do you say?"

In the Grill Room everything was yells and grunts of pleasure. The ransomed champagne had arrived and was being splashed around the room in small silvery fountains as the bottles were gaily emptied. When Curley and Brady entered the room they were cheered and hailed. Quickened by that spirit, the mayor grabbed a magnum and started to pour, instantly dominating the scene as if he himself had promulgated Repeal. When the bottle was empty Colman Brady put a glass in Curley's hand which he drank convulsively, carelessly spilling the stuff with great show. Then Brady replaced it with a fresh glass and watched him throw it down to the cheers of delirious men and women. Brady waited the way one waits at the pump for the priming to catch. When the mayor had the fiery, gleaming look, Brady knew the intoxicant was having its effect — not the champagne, the crowd.

Brady made his way to a corner of the bar.

He lit one of his thin cigars and held the flame of the match for a moment before blowing it out. He recalled a trick of street Gypsies in Dublin who, on summer evenings, went up and down O'Connell Street spewing petrol out of their mouths over hand-held torches which ignited the liquid spray and made them seem to be spitting great sheets of fire. Then they collected ha'pennies from the wonderstruck. Brady remembered thinking they would be dead soon, not from the fire, but from the gas they swallowed. Danger is often other than what it seems to be. He blew out the match with a lungful of smoke.

"How about it, Colman?" Pete Malloy said from his place behind the bar. He was holding a bottle over a glass.

"Indeed, Peter! Indeed! *Merci!*"

Colman took the glass, toasted Malloy with a glad eye, and sipped.

Though the room was packed, people kept arriving, and the pitch of the celebration rose steadily. Den O'Coole forced his way to the bar and joined Colman. He was already blasted. A two-day growth of beard gave his face a mildewed pallor. He wore a cap cockeyed and carried an empty fifth. He clapped Colman on the back.

"The Great God is good and just, Colman; the Great God is good and just!"

Brady, assuming a bleary drunkenness, embraced O'Coole. "Aw, it's a grand, grand day, Den, ain't it?"

"Oh, Colman, my friend!"

"O'Coole, my buggering battledog!"

"Colman! Colman!" O'Coole hissed in a great, thick-lipped whisper. "We've Ol' Man Prohibition hung in effigy over at the hall."

"What, an effigy?"

"Indeed! Strung him right up, we did! Me and Houlie!"

"Oh, Den, you shouldn't of done that!"

"Why not?" Offense and anger flashed in the drunk.

"You should have *drowned* him! *Drowned* him! Been more fitting!"

"Christ, you're right! Drowning, oh . . ." Oh, they'd made a mistake. ". . . but . . ." He looked mystified. "Where could we have drowned him?"

"Why, where he was born! Beacon Street! At the lake in the Garden ."

The Public Gardens at the far end of the Boston Common was a privately endowed park with an elegant swan lake and perfect lawns and shrubbery that were tended by a score of gardeners. Bordered by Beacon Street and Arlington, it was the preserve of Beacon Hill and the Back Bay, whose ladies regarded it as their own.

"By God, Colman, you're right! We should of drowned the old bastard there!"

"It's never too late, Den! Never too late! Why the mayor himself would love to put the old coot under with his own hands, I'll bet you!"

"I could go get it!"

"Good idea! We'll have a parade!"

"Oh, a parade! With everybody! Don't go away! I'll go get it!"

"Absolutely!"

O'Coole staggered under a sudden dizziness as he pushed away from the bar. "Ooh! The spirit is willing, but the flesh is weak."

"You can do it, Den." Brady supported him for a minute.

"Ooooh. I don't feel . . ." O'Coole shook himself, and with a practiced act of will stiffened his legs and assumed a rigid posture. He looked at Colman, slightly penitent. "I'm partially drunk, you know." He hadn't expected to carry the weight of such responsibility that night.

"I know you are, Den. All the better. You can do it."

"I can indeed! I'll be back!"

He took a dramatic breath and pushed his way through the bodies toward the door. Brady watched him go and then let his gaze linger on the crowd. He was calculating its potential for rowdiness. A man in a purple shirt with his tie askew was standing on a table and trying to negotiate a tune out of a banjo. Jack Lynch was squatting cross-legged on top of the piano in the corner, having failed miserably at the cossack dance, and now trying only to maintain his balance. A bald fellow was waving an empty bottle at Berkie Clyde, the piano player — a conductor's wand with which he beat time much too slowly. Kitty Regan, with peacock feathers in her hair, sat on the edge of the mantelpiece over the huge fireplace swinging her leg while staring at herself in a hand-held mirror. A couple whose heads came to the level of Kitty's knees necked ineptly. A girl in a burnished silk gown that displayed her breasts was dancing with her champagne glass. A man on a chair was pouring wine on all the heads he could reach. The mayor was surrounded by a coterie of men who were laughing uproariously. Curley's potential for rowdiness was, as usual, enormous. Good, Brady thought.

He turned back to his champagne and leaned over the bar to sip it. When he brought his eyes up they went automatically to the gilt mirror behind the bar in which they met, as if by appointment, the eyes of Mary Ellen Shields. He hadn't seen her in his survey of the Grill Room because she was at the bar too, separated from him by half a dozen revelers.

They stared at each other.

Brady thought of Madeline Thomson, and the afternoon's surge of desire came back to him. It seemed like years, not hours, since he had stood opposite her in the mansion on the hill. He raised his glass at Mary Ellen in the mirror. She returned the gesture. He studied her. She was smoking a cigarette, flamboyantly. He imagined her practicing her flourish with it in her room. She wore a knee-length silver satin frock that clung to her figure like lacquer and gave her a frank beauty that he had not seen before. Against the smoky tumult of rough and ugly characters, she seemed enormously delicate. There was a dangling vulnerability in the way she was looking at him.

The question was who would move toward whom.

He hesitated.

She dropped her eyes.

Was she with someone? Of course she was, but whom? Ben Ricketts probably. Brady saw him several yards past Mary Ellen. He was waggling a forefinger at his opponent in an argument.

Brady slid through the clinking drinkers to join her.

"You've cut your hair," he said. She was wearing it extremely short like some film star.

"Enter the ghost," she said, a little drunkenly.

"Not without an invitation." He raised his glass, repeating the gesture they had made to each other in the mirror.

"Still a proper gentleman, Mr. Brady, I see."

"Don't you know." He bowed slightly.

"What? I can't hear you."

Brady smiled at her. Something lusty and desirous in him showed itself.

Mary Ellen put her cigarette out in a dish on the bar. In doing so she stained her fingers with ash. She put her fingertips to her mouth and licked them. Brady watched the spittle bead on her lips.

"You seem," he said, "lean and sad." He could tell she was not wearing underwear.

"And you seem sober."

"I am."

"Then you've not the excuse I have."

"What excuse?"

"For going off with you. Tonight."

She drained her glass and reached for another at her elbow. It was half full and someone else's.

"Hey, dearie," the bloke behind her said; "no, you don't." He retrieved his drink with one hand and with the other circled her waist. He moved in on her neck with an amorous tongue.

Mary Ellen pulled away from him and hit him just below the eye with her fist, a manly blow which so stunned the fellow that he simply turned his back on her and drunkenly complained to his companions.

Brady had never seen such winsome fierceness in her. She turned to him with a whore's cockiness. "Well?"

"Well . . . love absorbs my ardent soul."

"Oh, you bastard." She dropped her head onto her hands. "You're mocking me."

"No, I'm not, Mary Ellen. I'm mocking myself."

"*Dreck!*"

He knew she was right. She was ahead of him. Madeline Thomson had been ahead of him. He was too sober. He could see the scene in the morning, how he'd hate waking up with her in the bed, how she'd look at him with hard insistence, stabbing at him with her falcon eyes. She would accuse him of having taken advantage of her drunken state. Well, what the hell.

He put his hand inside his vest, posing. "Mary Ellen, it's just that I haven't forgotten what we had. I didn't want to make light of it."

"It is fate, Colman. Not you or me. Fate." She was posing too.

Well, what the hell.

"Here's to fate, then." He sipped and then handed his glass to her. She downed it.

When she put the glass down, she was suddenly unsteady. Her eyes were watery. "I have to go to the jakes." She looked awkwardly around the room.

"It's over there, through those doors."

"Oh," she said, a note of panic. She moved away from him, steering through the bar like a wounded bird through trees.

A few minutes later a great commotion could be heard from the stairs up to the street. A roaring voice babbled like an animal, a moose calling a mate or something. It took Brady a moment to realize it was Den O'Coole.

So Curley wanted Colman Brady to shine his shoes, did he? The hell with that! Brady was startled at his sudden pique. The bastard had hurt him in the barbershop by taunting him exactly where he felt vulnerable. Ever since Michael Collins had coaxed him out of Four Mile Water, Brady's dread had been to wake up old having spent his life carrying somebody else's bags, shining — exactly! — somebody else's shoes. Brady's love for Curley, his devotion to him, was familiar. What he was beginning to discover was his hate. Shine the bastard's shoes? Not by a long shot. Brady would be wearing them before Curley knew they were gone.

But first things first. If Curley was at the head of a drunken outrageous mob, old Boston would go after him again. And Curley would not be riding quite so high. Certainly not high enough to ride on Brady.

He cut through the crowd, which by now was a swaying and staggering mass, crossed to the piano, and leaned over Berkie Clyde. He told him to play a bouncy tune as loud as he could, and then he grabbed the hands of those nearest and began to lead them in a dancing circle. Quickly others wanted to join, and as they broke in, Brady led the circle out of itself and into a kind of snake dance. Glasses were dropped and broken, chairs shoved aside, and tables rocked as men and women locked hands and kicked their feet to the music.

Brady steered the line to Curley, who grabbed on and, like that, was leading the dance. By then the knot at the door were chanting, "Drown him! Drown him! Drown the old bastard! Drown him! Drown him! Drown the old bastard!" Den O'Coole and two others held up a pathetic scarecrow. A sign pinned to its chest read "Prohibition." The dancers picked up the chant, and the piano reinforced it. "Drown him! Drown the old bastard!" The snake wound around and around the Grill Room, bouncing and twisting like a giant boa.

"Drown him! Drown him! Drown him in the Gardens! Drown him! Drown him! Drown the old bastard! Drown him! Drown him! Drown him in the Garden!"

Soon the snake was out on Tremont Street headed for the Common. A light snow was falling. Revelers in cars honked goodnaturedly for a block, but then the streets were quiet except for the chanters as they moved toward Park Street, where everything was still.

At the corner of Park and Tremont the snake dancers let out wild hoots at the Park Street Church, the steeple of which stabbed at God, and the pastor of which, the Reverend Horace Miffleton, was a great defender of Prohibition and a fierce attacker of what he labeled the "excesses of our poor immigrants." Someone threw a rock through one of the church's large smoked windows, but the building remained silent, dark, and, apparently, indifferent to the affront.

"Where did everybody go?" Mary Ellen Shields said. She had come out of the bathroom to find the Grill Room empty and wrecked. Someone was passed out by the fireplace. Malloy, the bartender, was dragging another drunk toward the door. Colman Brady was alone at the bar, smoking and sipping his drink. He had assumed she was gone. She was standing across the room, touching a table with her fingertips, steadying herself.

"They went to drown the old Yankee."

"What?"

"They're dancing in the streets."

"Oh."

"You could catch up with them."

She shook her head and crossed the room. She concentrated on her walking; left foot down, right foot. Left. Right. Passing tables, she touched them. When she drew alongside Brady, she held her figure with proud erectness, but the expression on her face was pure misery.

"I'll never drink again," she said. She reached for a stale glass of champagne. She sipped it.

He smiled at her.

"Never," she repeated.

"Every pleasure has its price."

"Colman," she said, "I love you."

"I know it, Mary Ellen."

He took her in his arms and held her for a long time before they separated enough to find each other's lips.

"Shall we stay together?" he asked when they separated again.

"Yes. Where?"

"Here. Upstairs. I'll get a room."

"All right."

"Are you sober?"

"Of course not. Do you think I'd open myself again to this if I was?"

"No."

"Colman, sobriety like yours is a luxury some of us can't afford."

"I pay for the way I am, darling."

"So do I, darling. For the way you are."

By the time Brady and Mary Ellen Shields left the Grill Room, Curley's crowd nearly had their keg tapped. They had woven an arabesque up the middle of Park Street past the State House and down Beacon. They went along weaving and unweaving, twirling each other, passing bottles, singing "There is a tavern in the town," chanting, "Drown him! Drown him! Drown the old bastard!"

The drunken mob stormed past the darkened row houses — the Union Club, the Parkman house, the Cabot house, then, across Joy Street, the Women's City Club, the Somerset Club, the third Harrison Gray Otis mansion, the King's Chapel Church House and Rectory, the Thayer house, and the Sears mansion. The revelers danced into the Public Garden and across the snow-brushed lawns and through the shrubbery and in and out of the flower beds, which had been elaborately mulched and covered for the winter.

James Michael Curley presided over the execution of "Prohibition." From the center of the footbridge that crossed the swan lake, he delivered his eulogy. "What the Good Lord gave," he declared, "they tried to take away! In this great country of ours you deny the inalienable rights of the people at your peril. They tried to keep our stomachs empty, and with

FDR's New Deal we've put an end to that! They tried to keep our throats dry and we've put an end to that!"

The crowd cheered.

Curley seized the effigy of Old Man Prohibition from O'Coole and held it up high overhead and out from the railing of the bridge. In his loudest voice he declared, "Faretheewell, you old bastard, for we must leave *thee!* There *is* a tavern in old Beantown!"

With that Curley hurled the scarecrow in a high arch off the bridge.

The people started to cheer.

But suddenly they stopped.

The dummy hit the surface of the pond, but it was solid. The water was frozen and the ice held. Old Man Prohibition sprawled disjointedly below them.

Was it an omen?

Prohibition refused to go under.

Curley gawked down at the scarecrow, not quite grasping what had happened. His head was fogging up. He had spent the last of his sobriety on the eulogy. He waited dumbly with the others for something to happen.

Steve Mulligan broke the ice. He hurled himself from the bridge to do it, and landed squarely on top of the old man.

The cheers went up. Steve's girl, Florry Joyce, hoisted herself carefully over the railing and then dropped the ten feet into the water. The ice gave under her, but she banged her buttocks on the bottom of the pond. The water was less than four feet deep.

When the boys saw the girl go in, they all knew it was either follow her or slink away in shame. And so two dozen giddy if not quite eager lads jumped into the pond. The shock of the water had a similar effect on all of them. They were instantly panting and choking with horror at the cold, with which they coped by jumping on each other and frantically dancing about in the water, smashing the remaining ice and splashing taunts up at the observers on the bridge.

More young women followed. Soon thirty-two men and seven women were cavorting about in the freezing water. In the jumping and tugging and splashing and hugging the girl who wore the burnished silk gown lost it. She was nude only for the moment or two it took a gentleman to cover her with his soaked coat, but later the city would believe that she and others had danced about the pond and Public Garden unclothed for hours. As if it were summer. As if they were not Catholics.

A cry went up for His Honor. The aqua-dancers wanted him to join them. How gloriously they would have received him!

But the mayor was gone. He was not so drunk that he didn't understand what had happened and what it would mean.

Shortly after the mayor left, the police arrived. With the police came photographers.

The next morning Mary Ellen woke before Colman did. He was in the crease of her arms. His cheek rested on the swell of her breast. She watched him.

She wondered what time it was. Their room opened on an airshaft, and it was impossible to tell whether the sun was high in the sky yet or not. She had to be at her typewriter by eight-thirty, and she had to go home to change first. Her mother would want to know where she'd been. She'd say church. The hell with her mother.

She could smell the hotel kitchen. The odor of bread. Parker House rolls.

Colman opened his eyes.

She nodded down to kiss him on the brow. "You know what you are?" she asked softly.

He looked toward her, trying to find the focus. It crossed Mary Ellen's mind that he might not remember her name. She would die.

"You are my Parker House roll."

He crushed his eyes closed and groaned.

Mary Ellen tugged the top sheet free, covered herself, and modestly eased off the edge of the bed.

"Oh," she groaned, "I'm bloody sick, Colman."

"Well you might be. You took a kick in the knackers."

"The price of pleasure." She found his waistcoat on the floor at the foot of the bed, picked it up and found his watch. "It's only seven o'clock."

"Is the thing running?"

"Yes." She hopped back in the bed and fought him for the blanket. When he opened it to her she went easily into his arms. They kissed and then held onto each other.

"I have to go home and change," she said.

"I'll drive you."

"No!"

"I can drop you around the corner. For Christ's sake, Mary Ellen, your mother won't know."

"It's not my mother! It's not the nuns! It's all of South Boston! I'll be the sap of the year if it gets out that I've gone back for more from you. 'There goes Mary Shields mooning over Brady again.' You can drive me to South Station. I'll catch the bus."

"Whatever you say."

They were still holding each other, but stiffly. All the warmth had gone out of their bodies.

Brady opened his arms and suspended them while he waited for her to roll away from him.

She didn't move.

"Well?" he said.

"You know . . ." — she ran her finger in small circles on his chest — ". . . if we stayed this way forever, that'd be some hotel bill."

But they were both past joking.

Mary Ellen accomplished a horizontal shrug and then, keeping the sheet about her, rolled away from him and out of the bed. She picked up her dress and stockings and went into the bathroom to dress.

A few minutes later they went down to the hotel lobby, but separately. As Colman was walking away from the desk, having paid the bill, he saw the stack of morning *Herald*s outside the grilled-over tobacconist's. He crossed to the stack and took one, leaving a nickel in its place.

A photograph of Den O'Coole holding his fifth and with a girl hugging him, both up to their thighs in water, dominated the front page. In the background of the photo could be seen the crowd of revelers.

"Curley 'Drowns Prohibition'; Friends Arrested," the headline read.

7

"Shit on Otis!" Curley exclaimed. "He can't do it! He can't do it!"

"He already has," Brady said, gesturing with the folder he held. It was a copy of the bill. The week after Curley's gang drowned Prohibition, Wysten Waverly Otis, Speaker of the House, brought a bill out of the Commonwealth Committee to revise the Boston Charter. The new law would make it illegal for anyone to succeed himself as mayor two times running. Curley's antics in the Public Gardens had given Otis just the occasion he needed to overcome the qualms of the few State House partisans who were reluctant to alter institutions to get at one particular politician. Brady was standing in front of Curley's desk. The mayor was holding his head, pressing its sides in exasperated fury.

"It'll never pass. They wouldn't dare!"

Brady knew it would pass. "Listen, Mayor . . ."

"No! You listen to me! This is *my* city! The people won't stand for it. They've got the whole rest of the state, those chowderheads! What do they want?"

"They want you, Jim. They want you dead. Politically dead."

Curley submitted to the realization. A new charter. A new law. He would *not* be mayor forever.

Brady watched his obstinacy evaporate. Curley slumped back in his chair looking old and defeated. Brady's own skepticism about the man, his detached private feelings of disdain for him — these evaporated too. The bill that he held in his hand loosed the more permanent feeling; an enemy was doing this to us.

"Shit on Otis!" Curley repeated, but without fire. "Who are the sponsors?"

"Bacon, of course. And Cabot."

"That old coot."

"No, the young one. And Governor Ely has called it 'a much needed reform.' "

"*That* thief."

There was a moment's silence. Then Curley said, "I got a hint or two from Washington, you know."

"I know."

Curley, who had backed Roosevelt over Smith the year before, had been mentioned for a variety of third-level federal appointments.

"He offered me London, you know."

Brady knew that Roosevelt had done no such thing. The thought of Curley in the Court of St. James was laughable, even to Brady. It was well known that Curley had been offered the post of Ambassador to Poland. "If it's such an important job, Mr. President," the affronted mayor had said in response to Roosevelt's slick pitch, "*you* take it!"

Still it was true that Curley had his seat on the Roosevelt Express, which by the end of 1933 had its steam.

Brady thought about that.

It was also true that Massachusetts was in the lowest circle of the Depression. The largest industry in the state was charity. Hundreds of thousands of workers were unemployed and on relief.

Brady thought about that.

"What are you thinking about?" Curley asked.

"I'm thinking . . ." Brady paused. This was the moment he'd been waiting for. Brady had his own purposes for the suggestion he was making, but they would coincide, finally, with Curley's. ". . . you ought to run for governor."

Curley looked at Brady impassively, showing nothing. The State House was the Brahmin stronghold. For an Irishman like Curley it would be the ultimate windmill. That he should run for governor was unthinkable. It was one thing to dominate a city of immigrants like Boston. The reaches of the state were populated by conservative nativists, weren't they? Besides, Democrats outside Boston had gone for Al Smith three to one in the statewide primaries. They regarded Curley's support of Roosevelt as a betrayal to Irish Catholic aspirations, didn't they?

But still. But still. Roosevelt's power and prestige were enormous after the Hundred Days.

"I could run on the New Deal," Curley said tentatively.

Brady had to stifle the tremor he felt. He knew that Curley was going to bite. Colman Brady had learned that James Michael Curley was a sucker for the show of power. He would, to spite Otis and to glorify his own huge ego, trade in the mayor's job without fighting for it to make a dash for governor just when the NRA welfare giveaways were going to make the mayor's office the most powerful in the state. But that was Curley; better the appearance than the substance. Brady wondered if it was an Irish flaw. Michael Collins had risked his life to display a power he didn't have. And the display had killed him. Colman Brady wanted in this regard to be more like Lowell, more like Anselmo. He would take the substance any day. He would take the mayor's chair happily.

"Righto," Brady said. "And you know who the Republicans are running."

"Bacon." Brady nodded and smiled. They were onto something.

Gaspar Griswold Bacon epitomized the Brahmin aristocracy, who owned the banks and who were terrified by what they regarded as the deadly socialism of Roosevelt.

"I've never won outside the old neighborhoods."

"You won in Puerto Rico."

Curley snorted. When Massachusetts Democrats went for Smith in 1931, he had arranged to attend the National Convention as an alternate for Roosevelt from Puerto Rico. He had introduced himself to the throng as Jaime Miguel Curleo. They had loved him. Roosevelt had embraced him on the platform.

"Besides," Brady went on, "the old neighborhoods are everywhere now."

"Goddamn it, Colman, you're right!" Curley slammed an open palm down on his desk. "Shit on Otis! We'll do it!"

The moment Otis's law was enacted, Curley called the press into his office and made his announcement.

The General Court rocked with laughter.

Editorial writers and pundits advised him to retire with dignity.

Curley's own constituency in the city of Boston were surprised and skeptical.

But James Michael Curley had an infallible instinct for the plight of the unemployed, and his ability to articulate their experience and to offer them hope did not fail him. Curley found, as Brady'd expected he would, that he had an enormous statewide base in the disenfranchised — the unemployment rate hovered at twenty-two percent through 1933 and 1934 — and he exploited it expertly with the simple slogan of his campaign: "Work and wages for all."

He threw himself into the fray with a fierceness that was rough-edged and merciless even for him. He took full advantage of the fact that, under Roosevelt, his own long-held philosophy of positive government that provided tangible benefits for voters, particularly jobs, was being vindicated. As a spokesman and advocate for the recently created Federal Emergency Relief and Civil Works administrations, he could legitimately claim credit for Roosevelt's early victories over unemployment, and he could convincingly promise the voters that with him as governor, Massachusetts would be a favored beneficiary of federal programs. Brady supported him in that conviction, though privately he doubted it.

On the stump he was magnificent, striking great poses that would have seemed pompous and conceited on anyone else. He habitually referred to himself in the third person, as if he were himself a detached arbiter in the momentous conflict between "the people's champion" and the established powers of the Commonwealth. He said, typically, "The Republican hatchet men referring to Curley said, 'A leopard never changes its spots.' Well, let Curley say to that that where he found a mud flat, there he left a playground! Where he found rotten pilings there he left a great harbor and the largest pier in America! Where he found dilapidated tenements, there he left a housing project. Where he found disease and dying children, there he left health clinics and the free Boston City Hospital. These, *these* are his leopard spots, and no! He will not change them, but *multiply* them!"

They heard him and they loved him. In Lowell, in Lawrence, New Bedford, Maynard, Fitchburg, Housatonic, Fall River — the milltowns whose industry had deserted for cheap labor elsewhere. In Haverhill, Lynn, Brockton, Newbury, Norwood — the shoe centers whose bosses had beaten back the unions and were exploiting the Depression cruelly. In Pittsfield, Worcester, and Springfield, where enormous factories seven or eight stories high and covering three or four blocks and with great unsmoking chimneys dominated everyone's consciousness by their very idleness.

Signs on vacant stores read, "For Rent — at your own price."

In 1934 even breadlines were going out of business. Soup kitchens were serving dark water. Desolate streets lined with weathered old wooden houses, unoccupied, uncared for, their windows broken, cut through every faded industry town in the state. Barbershops were closed; their cane poles were flaked and washed out because people cut their hair at home. Everywhere shabby men with paper in shoes which had no heels, in frayed overcoats split in the back, wearing old shirts for scarfs, leaned against walls and lampposts. They would wince and walk jerkily away if someone offered to help.

The winter of 1934 was the most viciously cold anyone could remember. There were no coins for the gas heaters.

The pathetic men on the corners swung their arms for warmth and for something to do.

These were James Michael Curley's people. He could walk among them and, where others saw only zombies, men worn out and utterly lacking in personality or human force; where others saw the living dead, Curley saw a last spark of life — it was anger — and could flame it.

"You are not the shiftless, the ne'er-do-wells, the immoral ones," he preached, knowing they felt otherwise. "The greed for higher and higher profits by the Lawrences and the Lowells and the Cabots and the Bacons — *that* is shiftless! *That* is immorality!"

When the despaired, stooped men said to Curley, "You don't know what it means to have a wife and kids and no work and no money and be in debt," his eyes would fill and he would pipe, "But I do! I do! I've been there too!" They knew he was lying and yet they believed him.

There were vast numbers of them. Four years of Depression had conquered the savings, the scruples, and the self-respect of hundreds of thousands of Commonwealth citizens. They were "on relief." They and all their relations and most of their neighbors would vote for Curley for governor. "Work and wages for all!" He knew what they needed if they were to live. He and Roosevelt would save them.

Brady suspected that among the reasons Franklin D. Roosevelt had for wanting Curley in the State House was the knowledge that there Curley would be removed from direct and unchecked access to the vast federal monies that were beginning to pour into cities, towns, and counties — and less into states themselves. Brady was sure that like the patricians of Massachusetts, the President regarded Curley as a petty thief.

If the office of governor was lacking in fiscal power when compared to the offices of big-city mayors in the New Deal era, still its cultural and mythic power in the Commonwealth of Massachusetts was enormous, and that was what Brady had counted on. The trappings of the office would draw Curley as the siren draws heroes.

For most of Harvard's history, for example, the governor of the Commonwealth had been an *ex officio* member of the Harvard Board of Overseers. That was no longer the case, but the governor still occupied places of honor in the inner circles of many of Boston's most prestigious institutions. He was automatically a member of the Board of Overseers of the Union Club. He was a trustee of the University of Massachusetts, the Lowell Institute, the Athenaeum, the Gardner Museum, the Symphony Orchestra, and the Massachusetts Society for the Preservation of Antiquities. The governor of the Commonwealth, since the seventeenth century, was an *officialis* at the annual commencement at Harvard College, and those governors not already holding the L.L.D. from Harvard were traditionally awarded an honorary degree. And in 1936 the governor of Massachusetts could expect to play a central role in the Tercentenary Celebration of the college.

Beginning on November 13, 1934, the governor-elect of Massachusetts was James Michael Curley.

On November 14, the Union Club's Board of Overseers, including the outgoing governor, Joseph B. Ely, met and unanimously adopted a new charter. It was to take effect on January 1, 1935, the date the new governor would take office. He would do so without benefit of membership in the Union Club. No one was surprised.

But on January 2 everyone was surprised because on that day Curley announced his first appointments, and three of the most important jobs in the Commonwealth went to aristocratic Republican reformers. Only a short time later would it be understood what Curley had done.

A governor in Massachusetts served only a two-year term, but the major policymakers, the so-called Governor's Council, served five- or seven-year terms. "A relic of royalty," Curley called it. And in fact the council was a carryover from the colonial system and a deliberate check on the governor's power. An independently elected body, it had the power to approve or deny all appointments, pardons, and Commonwealth contracts. When he took office Curley discovered that the council was solidly aligned against him by a seven-to-two Republican majority.

The three Republicans appointed to major positions were among that seven. Only after they had resigned their seats on the council did it become clear that Curley intended to take advantage of an obscure provision in the constitution to bypass new council elections and fill the vacancies by executive order. Immediately Curley reversed the majority on the council to five-to-four in his own favor. There was a predictable uproar from Republicans and the press. The Speaker of the House, Wysten Waverly Otis, denounced Curley and accused him of having "destroyed the people's barrier."

Curley said in the hearing of reporters, "Shit on Otis!" and he laughed raucously.

Among the appointed executive councilors was Colman Brady.

He accepted the state office with the understanding that he would represent Curley to Boston. As Curley's term got under way and the novelty of his being governor faded, Brady worked diligently at establishing his own network of loyal pols. He was determined that his performance in his first public office would be of high quality. By the end of the first year he had a reputation as a tough, fair-minded, and vigorous advocate of the city's interests before the General Court.

During the second year of the term, while Curley's fortunes entered an apparent decline, Brady, it seemed, was coming into his own. The press watched him carefully and increasingly sought out his views on a range of policy questions. The Republicans thought him more consistent and able than his mentor, and for that reason they were more wary of him. The Irish in the know thought of him, along with a handful of others, as one of Boston's comers.

"I know what you are, Brady," said Jack Hurley. They were seated alone at the large conference table in the ornate Council Chambers in the State House. Hurley was one of the other two Curley appointees, a weary party worker of Curley's generation, about sixty, a man widely regarded as a small-time political hack. Brady liked Hurley, but was always made uneasy by the air of disappointed ambition that clung to him. It was a Tuesday morning in April, 1936. They were the first two council members to arrive for the weekly meeting.

"What am I, Jack?" Brady had his thumbs hooked in his vest. His feet were on the table. He lit a cigar.

"You're the bloody dark horse."

"Am I?"

"I think you are. The mayor's getting old."

"The mayor's the governor, Jack."

"Right."

Brady had what by then had become a familiar thought: Curley's administration had been a great disappointment. The legislature had fought him tooth and nail on the great social welfare programs he'd proposed and had succeeded in paralyzing the state government at just the point when it needed to be vigorous. There had been some improvement in the statewide employment curve, but Brady knew that was due to initiatives from Washington, not Beacon Hill. The first year of Curley's term had been anticlimactic after the raucous heated campaign. Even his coup on the Executive Council had turned out to be less significant than expected. Curley had exercised total control over appointments and contracts, favoring his cronies and, as always, accepting gifts from the companies doing business with the Commonwealth. But the reform of the tax structure, the revision of property codes and the establishment of serious state relief systems — reforms for which Brady had worked vigorously — had all been thwarted by the Yankee opposition down the hall. It was significant to Brady that Curley was still "the mayor," even to his friends. That no one thought of him as "the governor" embodied his defeat.

"Even a dark horse . . ." — Brady drew on his cigar, studied its smoke — ". . . needs a track to run on."

"You've got your pick of tracks."

"What are you saying, Jack?"

"I'm saying I'll support you. I think you should run."

"For?"

"Mayor. And don't raise your eyebrows."

"What about Tobin?"

Hurley shrugged noncommittally, but then said, "I'd rather see you. So would Kane. The boys would rather you."

"Well, Jack," Brady said carefully, "I appreciate that. I do indeed."

"But?"

"I've time. I'm thirty-eight. I signed on with Curley. I'm willing to see that through."

"He's finished. He'll never get reelected governor."

"I know that." Brady pulled his feet down from the table and leaned toward Hurley. "And that's my problem. He may want to run for mayor again. He can, you know. It's only *successive* terms he's forbidden."

"Colman, he won't."

"How can you be sure?"

"Because — this is between us — he's going to run for the Senate."

"Washington?"

"Yup. The U.S. Senate."

Brady was shocked. Curley running for the Senate? Why didn't he know that? Why was he hearing this crucial news from a hack pol? Brady was suddenly filled with uneasiness. What did it mean that Curley had kept this from him? What was Curley up to? Brady knew instantly that he could not wait any longer. If Curley had his hand on the rug under Brady's feet, he had to step off. It was time to move. No matter what Curley did, he would run for mayor in the fall. Brady resolved to be very careful.

It was important that Hurley not detect his uneasiness. He forced a laugh. "The Senate? Curley? They'll kill him."

"Maybe." Hurley shrugged again. "Depends on Roosevelt."

"But Lodge is running. Henry Cabot Lodge."

"He's very young."

"He's my age, Jack. And he's one of *them*."

Hurley shrugged. "So was Bacon." Brady shrugged back at him.

"The point is, Colman, you've a place on the rail for mayor if you want it."

"I want it," Brady said simply.

"Good."

"But there's another problem."

"What?"

"I'm not certain Curley would . . ." He let it hang.

"What are you talking about? He worships you."

"But he *owns* Tobin. You should understand something about me, Jack. If I'm in Curley's shadow now it's because I choose to be. When I step out of it, it will not be into someone else's shadow. The reins on me are in *my* hands. Not his. Not yours. Not the boys'. See, the mayor understands that."

"The governor."

"Right. The point is, I'm not innocent. He might go with Tobin."

"And he might go with me."

They both had the same thought again. Curley had never gone with Hurley. That was the source of his subdued bitterness. Brady stared at him, knowing there was a lesson in the man for him.

"I'm glad you brought it up, Jack. And I'd welcome your support."

"If it comes to that."

"Righto, *amico*!" Brady smiled, leaned back in his chair, and put his feet back up on the table again.

Hurley turned his attention to the sheaf of papers in his folder. He made a show of reviewing the agenda for the council meeting.

After some moments Brady rose and crossed to the high windows and stood looking out at the Common, Beacon Street, Park Street, the Union Club, the Ticknor mansion, the first leaves of spring.

Don't squander your time, he thought. *Don't squander it, that's all. Enough of this remoteness. Enough of other men's shadows.* It was not that the glamour of office held any charm for Brady by then, nor that the ebullient agitation that convinced Curley of his existence held anything for him, nor that he needed the millions to tell him he was alive. Brady was aloof finally from the collective political ecstasies of his own people, and that was exactly why they needed him as their new political leader. Brady was in the prime of his life. His base was solid. His personal qualities — confidence, brain, diligence — were honed and well known. He was ready. He was fresh out of patience.

"Don't squander your time," he repeated to himself. He had served, if anything too long, as Curley's strolling sage and had promulgated his own image as a faithful and discerning aide. And he was. He had been loyalty itself. Brady owed nothing to Curley. The truth was, Curley owed a debt to Brady, though Brady knew full well he felt none. The intimacy Brady had achieved with Curley made its contradiction inevitable. Curley's sense of his own power would require Brady's humiliation. Brady had known that for a long time. Curley's omnivorous hunger, unappeased by the idolatry of strangers, fed on the faithfulness of his friends. But Brady had learned how to survive Curley. As he stood there then, looking out on the Common, he realized that he was no longer in Curley's orbit. He *was* his own man. It was possible that Curley would not support him for mayor, but Brady was sure he could cross-ruff him. What else did Hurley's ass-kissing mean? It was even possible that Curley would try to undo him, but Curley had nothing left with which to get him.

Brady felt a special pity for Curley, who had thought — it was the Irish dream — that conquering Beacon Hill was a way of conquering Mayfair and Knightsbridge, since the English plutocrats in their Brahmin incarnation were so untouched by the office of mayor and its prerogatives. But when Curley stormed the State House, Brady saw the great drawbridge going up. Curley was left with a form of power, but it was only power over allies, not enemies. But Brady's pity was tempered by his contempt for the rule Curley devised in response to his own emasculation: when the enemy is invisible and absent and indifferent, use your weapons on your friends.

That Brady understood this made him invulnerable. How queerly it plays, he thought. Curley was accused of habitual fraud and it was true. His great fraud was his power. The only difference between old Hurley and Curley was a pair of initials and the fact that the governor's suit fit. The Irish achievement was what they said it was, a mere agility in swindling. But they did not swindle banks or property owners or investors or contractors — or not only. They swindled themselves, an achievement of deceit, self-deceit. But there was no self-deceit in Colman Brady, and he knew it. He was going to be a very different leader, a man who embodied the best, not the worst, of the Irish in Boston.

Brady was staring at the top-floor dining room windows of the Union Club on Park Street, the old Lawrence and Lowell townhouses combined. If you didn't know it was there you'd never notice it. He recalled hearing that that dining room had been the maids' rooms of both the grandmothers of Abbott Lawrence Lowell. Real power goes unobserved and is held by simple men who have no need to show themselves. That was why Brady thought that the office of mayor would be the beginning of his power, not the limit of it.

"Colman?" Hurley piped wheezily through his nostrils. His voice was up in pitch. There was concern in it.

Brady turned to face him. He brushed the lock of hair off his forehead.

"What's this pardon business?" Hurley was staring at a page in his hands.

"Gennaro Anselmo. We owe him one."

"He's one of those gangsters, North End hoodlums."

"Small stuff, Jack."

"Says murder here."

"Self-defense. Third degree."

"But why the pardon?"

"He's done good time."

"Well, if it's third degree he can get paroled."

"He won't be eligible till Curley's out."

"But we usually leave this kind alone. I don't get it."

"Go on, Jack. We've pardoned third degree before. It's old hat. Besides, I told you. We owe him one." Brady wanted Anselmo out of prison for two reasons, one slightly sentimental and one totally pragmatic. Anselmo had avenged Jerry MacCurtain, but much more importantly, with luck and methods Brady wanted not to know about, Anselmo could replace Cosolimo as head of the Sicilian mob, which was more powerful than ever. If Brady was going to win Boston his first time out, he'd need the North End. Anselmo in power would deliver it for him.

"Risky, Colman, if you ask me." Hurley waited for Brady to turn around. "But obviously you don't."

"Don't what, Jack?" Brady continued to give him his back.

"Ask me."

"Ask you what?"

Hurley shrugged.

Edward Howard entered the chamber, one of the Republicans. He nodded toward Hurley without looking at him. He did not acknowledge Brady at the window. Howard was seventy-two years old, a retired banker, a musty man whose manner expressed patience and pessimism. He sat down at his customary chair and opened his valise and withdrew his folder. He started reviewing the papers, mirroring Hurley. He was followed shortly by Dr. Gregory and William Sargent, two more Republicans. Dr. Gregory, a short bald man, eccentric in his seersucker coat, displayed a studied courtesy. He shook hands with Howard and Hurley, then approached Brady, who snapped out of his reverie and greeted the doctor with a counterfeit politeness of his own. Within a few minutes the entire council was assembled. Hurley left the room to notify Curley. While he was gone no one spoke. Brady took his seat.

James Michael Curley entered the room like the *Queen Mary* entering Boston Harbor. The place suddenly seemed too small to contain not him but what he gave off. Hurley slipped in behind him, subtle, subservient, folding into his chair the way little waves fold out of the wake of a ship.

"Gentlemen," Curley said, acknowledging them when they rose. At his nod they sat. He dropped a pile of books, Commonwealth statutes, and papers on the table before him.

"The council is in order." He nodded at the stenographer, who had slipped into the room behind Hurley. She sat at her own small table by the door.

The governor put his reading glasses on, and they threw trembling flashes of sunlight about the room.

"As to the minutes . . . ," he said. There was a rustling of papers as members withdrew their copies from their folders.

The meeting proceeded according to the agenda, which, compared to most, was innocuous and lacking in controversy. Pro-forma budget matters, an in-house state police appointment, a maintenance program for the reservoirs, and the like. No judgeships, no fat contracts, no replacements of Republicans in the Bulfinch bureaucracy — none of the issues which drew automatic if futile fire from the outgunned minority. Curley expected the meeting to go smoothly.

He did not expect the protest from Howard about the pardon.

"Governor, I object," Howard said, just as Curley was about to move the question.

Curley glared at him.

"I received my copy of this proposal only this morning."

"Yes?" Curley often sprang things on them at the last minute.

"I'd have liked to make an inquiry of my own."

"Mr. Brady has prepared a thorough brief for the council. All the information needed, Councilor, is there." Curley flicked the corners of pages in his own folder. "The recommendations of the warden, and of the district attorney, and of the sheriff of Middlesex County — all of whom agree the man in question has been an exemplary prisoner. His records are there for you."

"But there's nothing from the judge. Who tried the case?"

"Daniel Bell."

"But he's dead."

"Quite so, God rest him."

Howard collected himself, pausing visibly to summon his patience. He was funereal and odd as he sat stoop-shouldered over the folder, examining it. He could on occasion ravage meetings with his ire, but clearly he did not feel strongly about this matter. He was simply whining. Curley was indulging him. It was not a big deal.

"But Governor, there's nothing here about his deed. Murder, it says."

"Yes. Third degree."

"But murder! Whom did he murder?"

"Zorelli."

Howard shook his head. "That's what I mean. I can't be expected to vote on this matter. I never heard of any of this."

"You never heard of Zorelli?"

"Never." Howard met Curley's glare with equanimity.

"Why, Mr. Councilor! Did you never hear of Al Capone? Did you never hear of Dillinger? Did you never hear of Judas Iscariot? What would you say if somebody did one of them in?"

"I would say, 'Thou shalt not kill.' "

"Jesus H. Christ!" Curley slapped his forehead. Then, visibly, he changed his tactic. "Anyway, I'm granting this pardon because of my belief that the man is innocent."

"You mean he did *not* kill this Zorelli?"

"No," he lied.

"I would like to review the evidence."

"So would I," said Dr. Gregory.

The others sat stonily, quiet, staring down at their papers.

"Move to table," Howard said.

"Second," said the doctor.

"All in favor," intoned Curley.

"Aye," the Republicans said.

"Opposed?"

"Nay," said the Democrats.

"Settled. Now on the motion."

"Nay," the Republicans said.

"Aye," said the Democrats.

"Carried."

Curley withdrew a formal-looking document from his folder. It was the official proclamation of pardon.

"As required of me." He adjusted his glasses and withdrew his pen from his pocket. "I will sign this order in your presence." He read the document silently, moving his lips. He looked up at Colman Brady and said, "Who's the petitioner?"

"What?"

" 'Identify the petitioner,' it says."

"That'll be Anselmo's wife. The petition is brought in his behalf by her."

"No."

"What?" Brady sat forward. What was Curley thinking?

"You're the petitioner."

"No, I'm not." Brady felt a sudden bulging behind his left eye. What in hell was Curley talking about?

"You are. You're the one who talked to all these people. You got their recommendations. You endorsed them. You did the checking."

"Yes. Of course. On your behalf. So that you could respond to Mrs. Anselmo's petition responsibly."

"Come here and sign this, Mr. Brady." Curley held the pen toward him.

Brady rose, walked behind Hurley to the head of the table, took the governor's pen and signed the proclamation without flourish. Then, also without flourish, Curley signed it.

Then the moment was past.

And the council moved on to other business.

The next day Gennaro Anselmo was released from the Norfolk prison colony without fanfare or publicity.

His wife was unable to pick him up at the prison, which was twenty-five miles outside the city. Though she'd been able to borrow her cousin's car, she didn't know how to drive it, and none of the men she asked were free to go with her. But she couldn't get a message to her husband to say she wouldn't be there.

Anselmo waited at the prison gate for fifteen minutes. He sat impassively on the weathered bench below the guard's turret, smoking. He wore a felt hat, a baggy serge suit, new, and carried his belongings — a few books, some underwear, his toiletry — in a cardboard box wrapped with twine.

When his wife failed to show, he guessed what had happened. No one would dare accompany her. That seemed reasonable to him.

He hitched a ride with a prison supply truck into the town of Walpole, and then walked to the bus station. The next bus to Boston would not depart for fifty minutes.

He crossed to the common and sat on the ground under a large elm. The ground was damp. The tree formed a fragile green-yellow canopy. He noticed for the first time that it was spring.

"Hey, Gennaro! Gennaro!"

A large black car cruised slowly along the edge of the park, and Sergio Capelli was leaning out of the driver's window, waving at him. Capelli had been running the garbage business while Anselmo was at Norfolk. He had visited Anselmo half a dozen times, and it was he whom Anselmo expected to accompany his wife.

But she was not in the car.

Two men rode in the back seat, not waving.

Anselmo picked up his bundle and walked across the grass to the corner where Capelli had stopped.

One of the men got out and held the door for him. Anselmo did not recognize him.

He got in. The man got in next to him, pushing in close, wedging him up against the other man, who was also unknown to Anselmo. They dwarfed him.

Anselmo had expected them to move against him before he'd had a chance to arm himself. Here it was.

"Hey, Gennaro! Gennaro! Great to see you!" Capelli ranted nervously, putting the car in gear and sliding around the corner into traffic.

The man on Anselmo's left had his gun drawn. He nestled it in his lap, the barrel pointed at Anselmo's groin. The man who'd followed him into the car was still pressing, trying to pin his arm.

Before the car was in second gear, and before the two had settled themselves, Anselmo struck.

He whipped both of his fists in opposite directions in a rapid flapping motion away from his stomach. His fists held steel dinner knives, which had been sharpened to stiletto points. The knives had been sheathed loosely in his sleeves and now plunged into the chests of the two men. He released the knives immediately and grabbed their gun hands, which he held until the wounds did their work. Both had gasped audibly, and then, almost instantly, almost simultaneously, had slumped slightly against the seats. Capelli continued his nervous chatter, slapping his gaze against the rearview mirror. Anselmo was staring at him. It was Anselmo's eyes that told Capelli what had happened.

Capelli nearly wrecked the auto when he turned to look. The sight of Anselmo, stony, impassive between the two inert hulks with red breasts plunged into Capelli like a blade.

"Oh, Christ!" he said. "Oh, Christ!"

The car veered toward a wall. Capelli caught it just in time, and then had the thought that he'd have done better to drive into it.

"Oh, Christ," he muttered again, staring straight ahead, aiming for a bus, trying not to look into the mirror again.

He passed the bus.

He brushed the mirror. Anselmo was still staring at him, a trancelike, rigid anarchy in his eyes. Capelli looked away and tried to concentrate on his driving. He would not look in the mirror again.

"Don't kill me, Gennaro. Please don't kill me."

Anselmo said nothing.

"They made me. They made me."

Anselmo still did not comment. He did not move. He continued to hold the wrists of the two, although death's grip already had them.

When Capelli understood that Anselmo was going neither to speak to nor kill him then, he put all his effort into driving. He neither spoke nor lost control of his glance again until they were nearly at Dedham.

"Turn here," Anselmo said.

Capelli turned onto a dirt road that seemed likely to lead to a farm.

"Stop."

Capelli stopped the car. There were woods on both sides of the road. Capelli felt himself overwhelmed by a giant terror. He was going to die and it was his bad luck to know it.

Anselmo took the gun and then leaned across the corpses to open one door and then the other. He pushed the bodies out of the car and that was all.

An enormous relief that threatened to take the form of giddiness filled Capelli. He put the car in reverse and squealed back out onto the main road. He was as high-strung and anguished as the overworked gear that screeched in protest at the way he gunned the car toward Boston.

As they crossed Jamaica Plain on the new WPA highway Anselmo said, "Cosolimo."

"Oh, Christ, Gennaro, don't make me drive you there."

Anselmo said nothing.

Capelli had trouble negotiating the fast curves of the Jamaicaway because his hands were soaked with perspiration and they slid futilely on the wheel. The harder he gripped the more his palms sweated.

The noontime bustle was just ebbing at Haymarket when Capelli wound his way past the pushcarts and vegetable stands that spilled spoiled artichokes and melons out into the street. He felt as though he were the pilot of a phantom ship. He expected everyone to be staring at them as he headed into Hanover Street, but no one seemed to notice the lumbering auto. Anselmo had pulled the brim of his felt hat down over the bridge of his nose and was snug against the brown cloth panel behind the rear side window.

Capelli pulled the car up in front of the Cantina Reale, and put it into neutral. He was afraid to turn the engine off.

"Go tell Cosolimo I am here."

Capelli looked in the mirror for the first time since Walpole, but he could not see Anselmo because he was in the corner. He turned half around to give him his most pleading look, but Anselmo's eyes gunned him.

Capelli pulled the brake up and got out. He went into the Cantina Reale.

Capelli knew they'd never let him in to see Cosolimo. Two bodyguards were sitting in wooden chairs on the cramped landing at the top of the stairs.

"He's here! Anselmo is here! Downstairs! Out front!"

The two guards both went into the office. Capelli pressed himself into the dark corner opposite the door. The guards came out again, followed by two others. They made Capelli lead them down.

The car seemed to be empty. The guards approached it cautiously.

Just as one of them whipped open the back door they heard the gunshot from the office. And then a second.

They looked at each other. No one wanted to lead the rush upstairs.

Capelli said frantically, "I didn't know! I didn't know!"

One of the guards looked down the alley. The rear door to the building flapped in the breeze.

The men continued to hesitate. Anselmo had the ability to murder. He had an ability that Cosolimo could not match. They knew it. If they were reluctant to rush the office it was not simply out of fear. It was also that the prize of power in the Unione belonged to the one who took it.

⟦8⟧

GREETING: It having pleased GOD to inspire the love of learning amongst the first settlers of the Colony of Massachusetts Bay and, in the infancy of their community, to direct their labors towards the well-being of Church and State through the establishment of foundations for the increase of knowledge and the education of youth, it is meet and proper that this Society of Scholars, founded in the Year of Our Lord one thousand six hundred and thirty-six, by Act of a Great and General Court of the Company of Massachusetts Bay convened in Boston the 8th/18th of September of that year, should celebrate in the company of friends and benefactors the THREE HUNDREDTH ANNIVERSARY of its foundation.

It was an iron fall morning, threatening rain.

Colman Brady could not have been more ill at ease.

He read the invitation again.

Then he looked across the coach at His Excellency the Governor, who was dressed — also — in morning attire and silk hat. They were riding in an old landau drawn by four horses, preceded by a company of red-coated cavalrymen on horseback and a small military band blaring trumpets. They had approached Harvard Square from Cambridge Street and were now on Peabody, the short angle-street between two segments of Massachusetts Avenue. They were drawing up to the Johnston Gate, an elaborate wrought-iron arch anchored on brick pillars. The arch was a tangle of wreaths and vines; in its center was a black cross over the numbers 1889. On both pillars were mounted molded scrolls with Latin pronouncements. The governor of the Commonwealth was traditionally a dominant figure at the Harvard commencement, but Curley had resurrected the old custom of the coach-and-four for the occasion of the Tercentenary. No governor had arrived at Harvard with such pomp since the nineteenth century.

Curley was like an excited child. To occupy the place of honor at Harvard! To receive an honorary degree, as every governor had before him! This was a day toward which the energy of his entire political life had aimed. James Michael Curley was arriving. They could not ignore him or defeat him this time.

Brady thought they were making fools of themselves.

Bystanders gawked and waved.

Brady dropped his eyes to read the invitation again.

Curley was leaning forward in the window, grasping the strap with one hand, waving with the other.

"It's a great day for the Irish, Colman! A great day for our people!"

"You won't see many of our people inside those walls, Governor."

"But that's over, son. Curley's here! You mark my word. I sit in the big carved chair in the middle of the damn stage! I get my degree! Me! Who hardly finished St. Eulalia's! A Doctor of Laws from Harvard! Ha! Ha!" Curley reached across to slap Brady's shoulder. The wonder of it! The delight! But the coach lurched sideways suddenly, throwing him off balance. One of the wheels had wedged itself in the streetcar tracks.

"Hey, Al!" he cried, and banged on the panel behind his head. "You watch it up there! And you," he said to Brady, "don't look so goddamn glum. This time next year I'll be the senator from this state! You'll be the mayor of Boston! And we'll have one of our own boys as governor! And degrees from Harvard for everybody! By God! By Curley!"

Brady knew that in some way he was right. Things had changed. He was about to be the preeminent government figure at the most solemn celebration in Harvard's history. In all likelihood he *was* about to receive the degree, though Harvard's custom was to keep secret the list of recipients. Much as it would gall them to honor Curley, Brady knew they were capable of conferring the degree on his office while ignoring him. Harvard would not change a custom of three centuries just because, for once, it involved an Irishman.

Brady was relieved when they pulled up to the gate. Curley would go to join the dignitaries in mustering for the solemn procession. Brady, having provided Curley with his preliminary company and having served as audience for his raucous agitation, would be free to wander about the Yard and take in the spectacle. It all held enormous fascination for Brady, and he was prepared to enjoy the great irony of Curley's participation. He wondered how they would deal with him. Brady expected that they would match Curley's exuberant ego with restraint and perfect manner. They would honor the governor while disdaining James Michael Curley, who wouldn't know the difference.

Curley hopped out of the coach when a gold-braided officer opened the door. The officer saluted formally. Curley, having mustered restraint of his own, nodded and doffed his silk hat. Brady got down from the coach, relieved. He looked up at the sky, half-hoping for rain. He chided himself instantly for the pettiness of the thought. Let them have their celebration in peace and dry weather.

A cluster of marshals, all bedecked in silk hats and cutaways, greeted Curley politely under the iron arch. One of them handed him a program and offered to show him to the staging area.

Curley opened the program as he started to follow the marshal and then stopped. Brady heard him say, pointing to the order of ceremony, "Is this where I give my speech?"

"Your speech, sir?"

"Yes. 'Greetings from His Excellency the Governor of the Commonwealth.' "

"Yes, sir. 'Greetings.' We have prepared the text for you."

"What do you mean?"

"The Chief Marshal will provide the text of your greetings, sir. If you will follow me."

The man turned and walked down the lane between the great elms which opened on the quadrangle where some of the earliest buildings of the College sat in cultivated simplicity.

Curley gave the man one of his fierce glares, but it was lost on him and the others as they strode away. Curley cast a look at Brady, who recognized its mix of anger and insecurity. "I'll see you later," his eyes said, and, "I wish you could come with me." Brady raised a hand, reassuring with a brash wave. Then Curley followed the marshals, whose obstinate gait embodied the capacity to be rude without being gauche. They strode between Harvard Hall and Massachusetts Hall, both of which predated the revolution, toward University Hall and its seated bronze of John Harvard, who brooded over the quadrangle.

Brady stood under the arch, taking in the scene. He noted the Latin inscriptions on the pillars and the cross of iron above his head; both seemed strangely religious, strangely un-Protestant. The acres within the gate were alive with intense activity. Great class banners and flags waving from poles located various contingents of alumni, faculty, undergraduates, and guests who were preparing for the solemn procession into the Tercentenary Theatre, which occupied the great expanse of the Yard that was on the far side of University Hall. The crackling of an electrical speaker system, still being tested, filled the air. There was a swirl of costume — the academic vestments with all their tassels and folds and brilliant colored hoods — which made Brady feel, even in his cutaway and top hat, inconspicuous and commonplace. Despite himself, he was filled with a kind of reverence as he strolled, hands in his pockets, past Harvard Hall into the center of the brisk scene. He walked casually past groups of men in clusters around their class flags, overhearing the clipped Brahmin accent. Waving from white poles were prominent heraldic banners of the college houses. He sauntered in and out of the groups, noting the arched eyes of the celebrants. Many of the participants seemed, with their thin, lanky postures, their fine jaws, their neatly trimmed moustaches, to have been stamped from one mold.

An alien mold. At communion breakfasts or picnics or rallies in South Boston, the faces were a little too thick, the necks fleshy and bulging uncomfortably over hard white collars, the legs shorter and slightly bowed, the backs curved, the skin flushed. But in Southie the eyes were brighter and there would be laughter. In the quadrangle, despite the noise, a mute, dull murmured introversion circled over the heads of the people in contrast to the gaiety of clothing and the glad-trappings.

Brady went by University Hall into the contiguous part of the Yard, which was a frozen sea of wooden chairs, thousands of them, all lined perfectly to face the huge platform springing from the steps of the College Church. Here and there groups of men and women — though mostly men — filed into sections of the seats. Above the theater was a canopy of elm and oak foliage which was punctured by the needle of the white church steeple. Compared to the chaos of the quadrangle and the trample of Cambridge, the Tercentenary Theatre achieved a seclusion and dignity that approached the monastic.

A passing student handed Brady a program. He took it and thanked the boy, thinking how young he seemed — not much older, he thought, than Micko. Brady suddenly felt old. He looked at the cover of the brochure. A paragraph in fine italics caught his eye.

I went to the College Jubilee on the 8th instant. A noble and well-thought of anniversary. Cambridge at any time is full of ghosts; but on that day the annointed eye saw the crowd of spirits that mingled with the procession in the vacant spaces, year by year, as the classes proceeded; and then the far longer train of ghosts that followed the company, of the men that wore before us the college honors and the laurels of the State — the long, winding train reaching back into eternity.

— Emerson: Journals, September 13, 1836

Brady stared at the brochure and mulled over Emerson's words. Even a hundred years ago, Harvard had a sense of itself as having spawned a long train of men who had embodied an excellence of mind and spirit. The idea, however pompous, surprised Brady by touching him. He envied that line of ghosts and knew that he could have been at home among them.

Brady looked up at the large platform at the head of the theater, the steeple stabbing skyward. The platform's score of chairs were empty and that seemed eerie suddenly. It was dominated by a podium in its center. Behind the podium was a single row of elaborately carved medieval chairs; in the middle of the row, on a level slightly higher than the others was a thronelike chair, the place of honor, the focal point of the entire scene. All at once Brady realized that that chair, that throne, would be occupied by James Michael Curley, Saint Eulalia's Class of '92. Brady laughed out loud. Emerson would shoot himself.

He felt a drop of rain hit his shoulder and looked up. The clouds glowered down.

Brady turned and surveyed the letters on the poles at various points. He withdrew the invitation from his inside pocket. The attached ticket had the bold inscription D8-221. The guidon of the section where he stood was marked with a bold *A*. He craned back and saw the letter *C* in the far corner of the Yard. Section D would be even farther off, on the rearmost fringe of the assembly. Typical. The Irish section, no doubt, he thought with sharp bitterness. He'd be seated with the gardeners and the maids.

Opposite the Memorial Church, forming an imposing rear boundary to the open-air theater, was the enormous Widener Library with its great sweeping staircase, solemn and pyramid-like. At the top of the stairs huge pillars supported the overreaching portico, which made the library itself seem a forbidden cloister. From the portico one could see everything in the Yard, and, if the rains fell mercilessly, one could stay dry. Brady crossed to the steps and ascended them two at a time.

He was thinking of the climb up the hill behind Four Mile Water to the ancient Druid monolith, the places where *his* long winding train began. Ireland at any time is full of ghosts. The anointed eye sees crowds of spirits. Brady thought that his eye and Emerson's were not so different. Others would have laughed to know that Colman Brady was recognizing alien Harvard as his own terrain.

He took up a position well away from the massive doors of the library, between two pillars, as close to the edge of the portico as he could get. Guides and marshals bustled about, and a staff of caterers hurried into the library. The reception for dignitaries would be held there after the ceremony.

A tall, dark, raven-haired man edged close to him, saying, softly out of the corner of his mouth, "Beg pardon, sir, but this area is . . ."

"Quite right, my man," Brady said in a false accent. "Do keep this area clear, would you?"

"Yes, sir." The man bowed slightly and moved off.

Brady took his case out of his pocket, withdrew a thin cigar and prepared to light it, feeling slightly mischievous as he did so. *The more outrageous I am,* he thought, *the more comfortable they'd feel if they knew who I was.* It was a thought worthy of Curley. Brady changed his mind and put the cigar back in its case, the case back in his pocket. He had no need to feign that reverence. He felt it.

"Hello."

Brady turned. Standing next to him was a tall blond woman with pencil-thin brows, a large hat brimming down over one eye. She wore a mannish black suit, but the tan ruffled blouse dispelled any air of masculinity. At the corner of her mouth was a twist of mischief, not quite a smile. Her forearms were crossed below her bosom as if to display it. Her skin was extremely white. Her face was slightly tilted toward Brady, as if she were offering him her uncovered eye, a patch of her marble forehead.

"I know," he said, "Edwina Booth. *Trader Horn.*"

"Right," she said, showing nothing.

"And you've come to tell me this is private property."

Her face broke into a full smile, which she held as if it were an achievement.

"How are you, Mrs. Thomson?"

"Aside from the fact that I can't remember your name, I'm fine."

"It's Brady."

"Of course."

[234]

"That was three years ago." He was thinking she looked younger, not older.

"The day of Repeal."

"Right."

"How's your son?"

"Fine, thank you."

"He must be . . ."

"Fourteen last month."

"How wonderful." A pause. "I must admit, I didn't expect to see you again."

"Nor I you."

"And certainly not here." As soon as she said this she realized the rudeness of it, given, well . . . "I meant," she began, "That is, I . . ."

"Are there no places for thieves at Harvard?"

"Only important ones." Her hand went automatically to her mouth; she had done it again. Was she trying to offend him?

But he laughed, relieving her anxiety before it built.

"Are you here to convey the greetings of Trinity College?" she asked.

"Hardly. Trinity is English."

"It's in Dublin, I thought."

He shrugged. The ignorance of Americans could still surprise him.

"And you?" he asked. "You're hardly a son of Fair Harvard."

"No. The unfair wife of one. My husband's on the Board of Overseers. He's going to be in the parade." She gestured toward the amphitheater. "It's going to rain."

A fitful wind was crossing the Yard, lifting the banners and wafting the leaves.

"Do you know the story of Widener Library, Mr. Brady?" She continued to stare over the expanse of chairs. More people had taken their places.

"No, I don't."

"Harry Elkins Widener was on board the *Titanic*."

"Is that so?" Brady said, genuinely affected. But somehow it seemed inevitable as soon as she said it. There were always events of drama and curiosity behind the most minor details of upper class life. Of course. The *Titanic*! The aristocrat of tragedies. What else for Harvard? A kick in the head from a horse?

"His mother gave the library in his honor."

The palpable sadness with which Madeline Gardner Thomson said this reminded Brady of her fury at him when he struck Micko. If she'd told him that her own child had been lost overboard at sea, he would not have been surprised.

Brady studied her.

She was perfectly still without being rigid. She gazed off across the Yard as if she could see Emerson's ghosts, the phantom ship of the tossing trees. She was looking out on her native land. To Brady for an instant she was a full-length oil painting, revealed in the subtlest way. He was aware of the nuance of light and shadow on her skin, the hint of darkness below her cheekbone, the desolate half-moon below her eye. He was drawn to her. He wondered what she loved.

A peal of bells erupted from the conical loudspeaker at the foot of Widener steps. Brady raised his eyes to the belfry of the Memorial Church; the sound was not coming from there. The bells crackled and reverberated, but there was a tinny, artificial quality to the sound that seemed wrong.

"Oh, listen!" Mrs. Thomson said.

Why would they have a falsely amplified carillon? All over Harvard there were bell towers; why weren't they all ringing to announce the procession?

"Listen!" she repeated, "All the way from England! At this very moment!" Her voice vibrated with the wonder of it. All the way from England!

The irony of it struck him; Trinity was Irish, but Harvard was English. The pealing bells, tinny and false, ringing from wires, not towers, seemed a proof to him. Of what he wasn't sure, but a proof, powerful and damning.

From behind University Hall came the blue uniformed figure of the sheriff of Middlesex County, pounding his sword-in-scabbard in rhythm with his walk. Behind him there fluttered a huge narrow crimson banner emblazoned with a silver *H*. And then the winding procession entered the Yard. Brady recognized Abbott Lawrence Lowell in the front rank.

"That's Former President Lowell," Mrs. Thomson said, pointing. Brady had last seen him at Louisburg Square before the Curley rally.

"And with him, that's President Conant," she said.

Brady saw the slender, frail man, James Bryant Conant, the world-renowned young chemist who had succeeded President Lowell in 1933. "There are the students," she said, as if it wasn't obvious what the entering ranks of black-robed boys were. Then came contingents of alumni behind marshals carrying class flags, members of the Board of Overseers, deans, faculty, and delegates from universities all over the world. They bobbed in two-by-two under threatening skies. In their billowing gowns and hoods and eccentric caps of all hues and fashions; in their showing of reds and greens and blues and yellows; in their display of feathered plumes and ermine and velvet stoles; in their slow, somber pomp, Brady

[236]

thought they looked like nothing so much as the species of the world filing into the Ark just ahead of the great storm.

"Alfred North Whitehead," Mrs. Thomson said, pointing to a short figure in Cambridge scarlet.

"They all have three names, don't they?"

"What?"

"Nothing."

At the end of the great train came the presiding officers. Madeline Thomson craned forward and tugged Brady's arm. "Look, there's Professor Morison, the historian."

Brady saw the erect, confident scholar.

"That's Bishop Lawrence ahead of him," Madeline said, "but I don't know who's beside him."

"James Michael Curley," Brady said.

Despite his top hat and formal dress, Curley's figure was drab and dull compared to the brilliantly robed bishop and academics.

"Oh. The governor."

"Yes. His Excellency."

She smiled at Brady. "He has three names, I notice."

"And two faces," Brady joked. He felt instantly disloyal, which prompted him to brag, "He's the presiding officer."

"No, he's not." There was an Are-you-kidding? aspect to Mrs. Thomson's voice. "*He* is," she said, pointing to the platform.

The dignitaries at the head of the procession were just mounting it, and the audience was rustling in observation as Franklin D. Roosevelt, '04, was unobtrusively being transferred by two large men from his wheelchair to the great throne behind the podium. He was dressed in silk hat. Light flashed off his spectacles.

"Oh, Christ!" Brady's heart sank. His eyes dropped down the aisle to Curley. He wondered if he knew.

"That wasn't announced, was it?" Brady asked.

"No. Even my husband was unsure whether he would come. He hasn't been well, they say."

It would kill Curley. Just kill him. At once Brady understood that Curley could not know; he'd have backed out. He wouldn't have let them do this to him. Not only the insult of superseded political preeminence, but the grating confrontation with Roosevelt, who had as yet refused to support Curley's bid for the Senate seat, and who had humiliated Curley by implying he couldn't be trusted with public funds. It would kill him, just kill him.

Brady stared at Curley's figure as the end of the procession arrived at the platform. While the throng of people were taking their chairs, few noticed the governor's awkward stumble, which occurred when Conant cut in front of him to greet Roosevelt — when the President greeted Mr. Roosevelt, as the Harvard wags would put it. Both Bishop Lawrence and President Conant stood with their backs to Curley, who stalled like a blindered horse, not knowing where to go. For a brief moment he cut a sad, pathetic figure. Curley had arrived, Brady thought. And they ignored him. Brilliant. Only the honorary degree would redeem the indignity of it.

With a show of courtesy, President Conant ushered Curley to one of the line of wooden chairs, seating him between a pair of foreign dignitaries. Bishop Lawrence sat next to Roosevelt.

The sheriff of Middlesex County approached the podium, banged his sword-in-scabbard three times on the platform and commanded, "The meeting *will* be in order!"

And then the rain began to fall.

Umbrellas sprouted all over the acreage of the Yard like mushrooms. They began a slow steady undulation, giving the entire gathering, when seen from above, the aspect of a black sea. The platform floated over it like the Ark. Its dignitaries ignored the rain with splendid disdain, aristocrats all.

Someone began speaking in Latin: "*Salvete omnes!*"

Brady wondered why they were dead set against Latin in church if they'd use it here. He looked at his program as if it held the answer. One more speaker would precede Curley.

Professor Samuel Eliot Morison's address was a long-winded description of how Harvard came to be established. It concluded, "From the small college here planted '*in sylvestribus et incultis locis*,' on the verge of the Western Wilderness, Harvard University has grown, and higher education in the United States is largely derived. So we are gathered here to commemorate our founders and early benefactors; to thank God for the faith, overriding all prudent objections and practical difficulties, that sustained them through poverty and struggle, in so ambitious and so excellent an enterprise."

Then the Tercentenary Chorus, lined against the rear wall of the platform, began to sing Gabrieli's "In Deo Salutari Meo."

"I'm struck by the irony, Mrs. Thomson . . ."

"Of the rain?"

"No. Of the Latin. The language of the Church."

"Latin serves the Church and Harvard equally well, Mr. Brady, since it's a dead language."

He couldn't help registering surprise at her caustic tone.

"Are you shocked?" she asked. "Doesn't it all seem like spectacle and pomp, much ado about nothing?"

"Frankly, it doesn't to me." The opening rites of the liturgy — it was as liturgy that it struck him — were affecting Brady. He was enthralled and he wished it were his the way it was hers.

"My husband worships Harvard. He's a fool."

"Well, only the possessors of privilege ever see through it, Mrs. Thomson."

"I'd say God sees through it. Lots of silk hats going to be ruined today. Be careful of yours."

"It's rented."

She gave him a look that said, "How quaint!"

"What are you doing here anyway?" she asked.

"I'm the gardener. With an *e*."

"You remembered." She smiled warmly.

"Blind and peeless." They both laughed.

The chorus had finished.

James Michael Curley was approaching the podium. He showed no sign of nervousness or embarrassment.

In his slow, enchanting voice he read the greetings that had been prepared for him. "As the Governor of the Commonwealth of Massachusetts I take special pride in bringing greetings to Harvard University on the occasion of its Tercentenary. Massachusetts men from the beginning have identified themselves with Harvard and Harvard men have endowed the Commonwealth with the riches of learning and *veritas*. Therefore, in behalf of the citizens of Massachusetts, I beseech God's Providence, which has watched over Harvard since its first home had to be fenced in to keep out the wolves, to continue to bless it, adorned as it is now with magnificent buildings and celebrated throughout the world as a great center of learning and as the proudest achievement of the Commonwealth of Massachusetts."

He stopped reading and raised his eyes. Brady thought Curley had achieved a dignity that made him almost venerable. Clearly he had come to the end of the text, and Brady sensed the enormous struggle in him. Brady knew how much he had wanted to make his own speech, and it seemed for a moment that he would. The crowd was hushed and attentive as Curley stared at them. What would he do?

He turned abruptly and strode back to his seat.

The audience stirred, umbrellas swirled slightly this way and that. They did not applaud. They were more intent on noting that the rain was stopping.

John Masefield, Poet Laureate of England, then read the poem he had composed for the occasion.

"When Custom presses on the souls apart,
Who seeks a God not worshipped by the herd . . ."

And so on, Brady thought.

Abbott Lawrence Lowell came forward then and, having to stoop slightly to the microphone, said, "The next speaker it would be impertinent for me to introduce to you or to any American audience. He is the fourth graduate of Harvard College to hold the office of Chief Magistrate in our nation — two of them named Adams, and two Roosevelt. Gentlemen, The President of the United States!"

The audience stood up and applauded, its first demonstration.

Roosevelt addressed them from his chair. "I am here today . . . as the President of the United States . . . as a son of Harvard who gladly returns to the spot where men have sought truth for three hundred years. . . . One hundred years ago . . . many of the alumni of Harvard were sorely troubled concerning the state of the nation. Andrew Jackson was President. On the two hundred and fiftieth anniversary of the founding of Harvard College, alumni were again sorely troubled. . . . Now, on the three hundredth anniversary, I am President."

The audience rose to its feet again and applauded wildly. As Brady watched them he realized they were not cheering the President. They were cheering themselves.

Harvard! Harvard! Harvard!

And Brady got it. Despite himself, he caught their spirit. Even as an outsider he understood in a sudden wave of feeling why they would stand and celebrate themselves. For three hundred years they had been commissioning the best men in America to America's service. Roosevelt was only the latest, and he had saved the nation from despair and, probably, from collapse. Brady understood that it was not arrogance or smugness he was witnessing. These men simply had the capacity to rejoice in the gifts they'd been given and what they were making of them.

After Roosevelt's speech, President Conant delivered an oration, "The University Tradition in America — Yesterday and Today," the point of which seemed to be that the university tradition in America had mainly limited itself to Cambridge. "He who enters a university," Conant said, "walks on hallowed ground." Brady recalled feeling as he passed under the wrought=iron cross at the Peabody Street gate that he was entering church.

When the speeches were given, the chorus rendered a song by Handel.

Mrs. Thomson touched Brady's sleeve. "Now the degrees. My husband is on the committee."

Brady looked at her. She had no idea that the bestowal of the degree on Curley could have the meaning it had not only for the governor and not only for Brady but for many people who had never been inside Harvard Yard.

"This is what I came for," Brady said.

"It'll be a bore. There are sixty-two of them."

"You're kidding." Brady had expected only a handful of men to be honored. Would Curley's mean less if the degrees were squandered?

There was a mechanical precision to the conferring of the degrees. President Conant read each citation, handed the diploma to one of four top-hatted aides — "That's my husband," Madeline said, pointing to one of them. The aide conveyed the diploma to the recipient, who rose from his seat in a flash of color, received it, bowed, and sat down amid applause.

As the names were read man after man rose and bowed and was applauded. Eddington, Svedberg, Fischer, Jung, Hopkins, Spemann, Krogh, Bergius, Maunier, Koussevitzky, Hu Shih, Wenger.

Brady had heard of the conductor, of the astronomer Eddington, of Jung, of course. But most of the scholars were unknown to him.

When Etienne Gilson was announced, Brady leaned to Mrs. Thomson and said, "Tell your husband he let a Catholic slip in when he didn't have to."

Mrs. Thomson did not understand the remark, as her blank look showed.

As the roll went on and on, Brady was aware that his vague uneasiness was crystallizing, as if around a grain of sand.

Curley's name was not being called.

It seemed every dignitary on the platform was being honored. Landsteiner, Rostovtzeff, Mitchell, Dent.

But no Curley.

Brady watched the governor carefully, but his rigid pose, arms locked onto his chair, displayed nothing.

Finally, Conant's voice fell silent.

Brady prayed that the silence was prelude to the special announcement which would cite the ancient tradition which had the new meaning of peace between Harvard and the sons of Boston. But Conant's silence had the purpose of conclusion, not prelude. He gathered his papers and turned from the podium.

Brady looked at Curley, half expecting him to rise and grab the little man by the scapular.

But it was Bishop Lawrence who stood. He strode to the microphone and intoned the benediction.

And then the audience was on its feet singing, "Oh God, Our Help in Ages Past."

At the conclusion of the hymn the dignitaries began to file two by two off the platform. The audience, still standing, broke into a second rousing hymn.

> *"Fair Harvard! Thy sons to thy jubilee throng,*
> *And with blessings surrender thee o'er,*
> *By these festival rites, from the age that is past*
> *To the age that is waiting before.*
> *O relic and type of our ancestors' worth,*
> *That has long kept their memory warm,*
> *First flower of their wilderness! Star of their night!*
> *Calm rising through change and storm!"*

"Well," Mrs. Thomson said, adjusting her white gloves, "the storm is over."

"Perhaps," Brady muttered, "perhaps."

"What a cryptic murmur. Whatever do you mean?"

Brady turned to look her fully in the face. She did not know what her husband and his friends had just done, but they bloody well did.

The procession of plutocrats was mounting the staircase to Widener like a great serpent entering a sanctuary.

Brady was alert for Curley's eye, but the governor passed stonily, impassive, still rigid. His partner was Bishop Lawrence, and they were studiously ignoring each other.

At the top of the staircase the procession broke as the robed dignitaries entered Widener, where, in the great hall beneath the massive dome, "comforting nectar" was being served.

Brady slipped into step with Curley and said, "Come on, Jim, let's get out of here."

"The hell with you," Curley hissed; "I'm getting a drink!"

Brady watched Curley make a beeline for the linen-draped tables. He could have predicted what followed.

"What do you mean 'punch'?" Curley roared at the serving girl. "I want a drink."

The girl stood helpless and mute before him.

"What's in it?" he demanded.

"Champagne, sir," she stammered, "or, in this one there's ginger ale . . ."

"All right! All right!" He accepted a cup-shaped glass, which he downed in a single gulp and held out again.

Brady drew up to him again. "Come on, Jim."

"Get away from me, you!"

Brady had witnessed the humiliation; that made him an enemy.

Curley downed three cups of punch in succession. Despite his trembling anger, no one seemed to notice his rudeness, aside from the waitress and Brady and a beefy young, formally dressed marshal, who approached the governor deferentially and murmured, "May I help you, sir?"

"You're damn right! Where's the bourbon?"

"I'll be glad to get you a highball, sir. It'll take just a moment."

"Who said highball? Just bourbon. About this much." Curley spaced his thumb and forefinger.

"Thank you," Brady said to the marshal, who slipped off into the crowd.

"I don't need you doing my thanking, Brady!" Curley was furious.

"Now, Governor . . ."

"You think I've the manners of a croppie, don't you!"

"I'm not talking to you like this, not here." Brady deliberately walked behind a marble pillar into a small alcove off the hall. The governor followed him; if they were going to tilt, at least they could do it out of sight of Harvard.

"Don't you walk away from me!"

"Look, Governor, you're upset. And I understand . . ."

"You understand! Shit! You're the reason I didn't get that degree."

"What are you talking about?"

"It's Howard's report. They've read it. They think they'll nail me with it. That's why Roosevelt won't back me."

Brady had no idea what Curley was referring to.

"What report? Edward Howard?"

"Bribery. He claims I was bribed, by your friend Anselmo! He bribed me and so I pardoned him! Howard has affidavits. He's going to the attorney general with it."

Brady knew of no report, and his ignorance set off alarms in him. Curley had probably stolen it from Howard's office, but he had not confided in Brady. Brady knew if he wasn't to be Curley's ally in this, he would be his patsy.

"That's impossible, Jim. Howard's shooting from the hip. It's not true."

"You're damn right it's not! *You* were the one who wanted that pardon, not me. *You* sponsored it! You signed it. *You* took the bribe, not me, and I can prove it."

Brady did not reply for a moment. He turned the governor's statement in his mind the way a survivor turns over the carcass of a victim.

"How?" Brady asked icily.

"An affidavit of my own. Jack Hurley's. You told him about it."

"That's a lie."

"We'll see, Brady. We'll see. We'll see who they impeach. Your plot has backfired."

"Governor, you're talking nonsense. If there's a plot it comes from Howard, not me. Don't let them . . ."

"They already have!" Curley said pathetically. Suddenly his eyes were filled with tears. Brady thought he was going to cry. But he held himself in check, if barely, only swaying slightly as he stared. His stung countenance said it all: "I know, Brady, that you think I'm vulgar, that I embarrass you, that you can't wait to shunt me aside. You are even worse than they are. You want to be one of them!"

Yes, Brady thought. The irony of it sliced through him. Brady, who regarded his own people with a caustic eye, would never betray them. He wanted to be like the Brahmin, yes. But not so much that he would finally repudiate the Irish. Curley, on the other hand, embodied the Irish and loved them, but he would do anything in his pursuit of power, even hand over his own to Beacon Hill Brit bloodhounds.

"This is not the time, Governor."

"Yes it is. I'm through with you. You're finished."

"No, I'm not. I'll fight you on this."

"Go ahead. I'm going to Howard."

"To offer him me."

"Yes."

"And a Republican on the council to take my place after it votes me out."

"Yes."

Brady considered it. Howard would accept. Such a deal would give them back the majority for the rest of Curley's term and, more importantly, for the new governor's term as well.

"Hurley," Brady said. "You'll back him for governor?"

"Yes."

"I'm beginning to get the picture. Hurley would swear to anything for a time at bat. But what happened? This morning you were backing me for mayor."

Curley said nothing.

"You were going to fight Howard on the bribe flimflam all the way, weren't you? Until they did their number on you here at Fair Harvard.

[244]

And now you can't wait to cut and run and cover yourself. You've let them get to you, Jim."

"No, Colman. Only to you."

"I could take you out with me. I could hang the real thing on you, and you know it."

"But you won't. For the same reason you won't let me make a fool of myself out there."

Brady smiled faintly, containing his rage and hurt inside his manners. The old bastard knew him inside and out. The English were still the English. His own were still his own. Curley was right.

"I know the difference, Colman, between your loyalty and your embarrassment."

"I doubt it, Governor." Colman was in fact surprised by his own loyalty, as he was surprised by Curley's total lack of it. Colman had, for all his planning, been careless, very careless. It was difficult for him to admit that, but it would have been worse to think that such a turn as this one could come from nowhere. Brady would rather be a cause of his own downfall than a mere witness to it.

"You remind me of someone, Governor."

"Who?"

"Eamon de Valera."

"Why thank you. The President of Ireland."

"Indeed. And a traitor and a murderer of his own." Brady struggled to keep the tremor from his voice. He did not want, even now, to give Curley a scene with which to shock Harvard. Brady would not let his own pain be a prop in another of Curley's displays.

Curley shrugged. "I don't know about that."

"I think you do."

They stared at each other for a long moment.

The beefy young marshal interrupted them, coming from around the pillar and into the alcove. "Here's your bourbon, Governor."

"Why, thank you, son. Thank you." Curley took the glass with a bow, then raised it.

Brady walked away from them, hearing the governor say as he did, "Here's to your health, son, and that of Fair Harvard."

Brady was making his way across the rotunda toward the door, through the rainbow of gowns and hoods, when Madeline Gardner Thomson caught his sleeve.

"I found out who you are."

"Who am I?" Brady smiled charmingly. There was a lead cover on his emotions.

"You're on the governor's council."

"I have been, but I won't be for long."

"Why?"

"Wait a week. Then ask your husband."

"You're a very cryptic man."

"I'm a Druid, Mrs. Thomson."

"Oh." She paused. "Well, I'm sorry you're not a gardener."

"Why?"

"Because you left your ax at my house that time. I thought you might need it. I was going to invite you to come and pick it up."

"To tell you the truth, I may need it after all."

"Do come for it, then. We could finish that drink."

"I'd love to."

"Good. Call me before you come."

"All right."

Their coy exchange was another lie. Brady knew that he would not call her or see her or accept her invitation.

They held each other's eyes for a moment, then Brady turned and continued across the hall. As he slipped between two robed figures, one of them turned around, his face nearly touching Brady's. It was Abbott Lawrence Lowell. He nodded at Brady and might have spoken to him, but Brady, fearing that he was going to break, pressed by Lowell and made for the great doorway. He left Widener without looking back and he channeled his emotion into his plunge down the long stairs, which he took two at a time. The ambition he had nurtured and fed on since coming to Boston had just been destroyed. His own career, his own crack at real power was over before it began. And not only that, to have been done in by Curley who owed him so much and who had seemed so nearly impotent! To have been done in at Harvard in one of its alcoves! Brady was ravaged. Each time his foot struck the stone, his weight jammed down and sent a shock to his brain. The series of jolts punished him like the slaps of a parent. Why was he not weeping? If he didn't then, he knew he never would. He babbled inside, ranting and accusing not Curley, but himself, thus assuming that his defeat, unlike all the others, was total and in some way permanent. To think he had expected a life not wasted —the nerve of him! A life not alone — what a fool he was! His great mistake had been in not preparing for the worst. Was he Irish for nothing? Colman Brady was too Irish and not Irish enough.

Two weeks to the day later, Colman Brady was formally impeached by unanimous vote of the governor's council for willful impropriety in the matter of the pardon of one Gennaro Anselmo. Brady denied the charge but did not defend himself.

Anselmo's pardon stood.

Three days after his impeachment, Colman Brady was approached by Gennaro Anselmo.

Rosa Imports and various other of the Sicilian's enterprises were bringing in more capital than the North End operations could profitably recirculate. Anselmo needed a discreet, trustworthy and non-Italian associate to invest such monies in legal sectors of business. He asked Brady if he would help him in this way.

Brady said he would.

A week later, Colman Brady bought a large colonial house in Brookline, and a week after that, over their vehement protests, he moved Micko, Maeve, and her kids, Jackie, Maureen, and Deirdre, out of the three-decker on Fourth Street in South Boston.

THREE

❧ 1 ❧

"WHAT I WANT TO KNOW," Jack McShane said, "is why you dress to the nines to go to the fights?" He replaced his cup on its saucer.

The three McShanes, Jack, Maureen, and Deirdre, were just finishing dinner. They were at the oval table in the breakfast room where they took their meals when the entire family wasn't eating. It was a low-ceilinged room with a great black Carpenter stove against one wall. The mild chill of an early spring evening blew through the open window.

"You're from B.C.," Colman answered from the doorway. "You wouldn't understand." Brady sipped at his bourbon, leaned against the wall and laughed. He hooked a thumb in the cummerbund of his tuxedo and felt its pressure against his waist, which was, for the first time in his life, thicker than he wanted. He was forty-two years old.

"At B.C., Unc, we wouldn't dignify boxing like that. Only Harvard could think up Fight Night."

"Have you expressed your views to your beloved cousin?"

"Joe Louis? Do I look like Arturo Godoy? He'd kill me."

"No, he wouldn't, Jack," Maureen put in. She was the oldest and at twenty-three was, in the midst of her first bloom, pretty and bright. She worked as a stenographer in one of her uncle's offices. "You shouldn't make light of Micko. Not tonight. He could get hurt."

"He won't get hurt, darling," Colman said.

"I agree with Jack," Deirdre said, waving her napkin. A fair, soft girl of twenty-two, a bit overheavy, with fattish Irish features, she was a nursing student at Newton College of the Sacred Heart. "He *could* get hurt. You shouldn't allow it, Uncle Colman."

"He's a big boy."

"He's a Harvard man!" Jack said, forefinger raised.

"I don't boss you blokes around. Why should I Micko?" Brady sipped his drink. "Besides . . ."

"Boxing is manly!" Jack said. There was more than a hint of bitterness in the remark. Jack was a senior at Boston College, a short, intense young man who had already decided to enter the seminary after graduation.

[251]

"Feeling pretty pugnacious, aren't you, kiddo?" Colman wasn't going to be drawn into *that* tangle again. Jack's resentment of his cousin was habitual, palpable and enormous.

Collins was at Harvard. Already, in his sophomore year, he was a class officer, an honor student, and a finalist in the collegiate boxing tournament.

" 'Scuse me, Mr. Brady." Clara, the cook, a black woman of fifty, pressed by Brady into the small dining room. She carried a tray with three dishes of ice cream and a plate of cookies on it.

Brady made way for her, raising his glass high so that she could pass under it, a broad maternal barge under a Mississippi bridge.

"Clara, we should have eaten here; I'm certain of it."

"What they gonna serve, Mr. Brady?"

"Watercress and baby crackers." When he smiled his face displayed the only places where age was touching him mischievously. Stringy lines encased his eyes.

Colman planted his drink hand in the upper right corner of the door frame, anchoring the bridge. He spread his stance across the threshold and pressed his strength against the wood. In that posture he could feel his house solid beneath him and permanent over him. A snug, safe feeling; he loved it. The house was a stately nineteenth-century mansion of thirteen rooms, including Clara's on the fourth floor, in the Brookline quarter known as Cottage Farm. The other houses on Prescott Street were equally large and graceful. Directly behind Brady's was the massive Tudor manor house in which Lawrences had lived, summers, eighty years before. Brady would have liked more land; his corner lot was less than half an acre. In good weather he cared for the modest lawn himself as if to fancy farming still. Like a farmer he still needed to love what surrounded him. In that house he did; the crafted, proud things, the high rooms, the molded angles, the diamond panes of the windows, the fireplaces. Brady loved his own room, in which he had his desk, his chair, his hearth, his bed, his books, the simple things enclosed there which pleased him enormously. In the house on Prescott Street Brady had found rooms that could hold his solitude *and* his love. The house was a guarantor that all was well with him and his family. Shelter. He pictured them asleep and vulnerable. Safe.

He sipped his drink.

What the hell, he thought. The kids were all grown up. Even Micko.

Maureen was touching a spoonful of ice cream with her tongue. Brady noted her fine ripeness again, proudly. Jack was fastidious with his dessert, seeming to ponder each bite as if it held a secret.

Deirdre said, "Mom's late."

[252]

Brady looked at his watch. It was true.

"She doesn't want to go," Deirdre announced.

Jack and Maureen ate ice cream.

"Of course she does," Brady said.

"No, she doesn't. She told me."

"In confidence, no doubt," Jack lobbed.

"She hates boxing," Deirdre explained.

"This is a very big night for Micko. Your mother appreciates that. She wouldn't miss it for anything."

"She also hates dressing up." Deirdre was irked and vengeful. She had a streak of pettiness in her that Colman disliked. He determined not to be baited.

"Why are you saying these things to me, Dee?"

"Will you please not call me 'Dee'?"

"Deirdre."

"Because you should not let Collins fight. He'll get hurt."

"Strange, darling, but I was getting the feeling of more from you than love of your brother."

"My cousin."

Brady stared his niece down.

"The thing is, anyway," Maureen began ingenuously, "college boxers don't hurt each other. Only the professionals . . ." Her statement hung in the air, incomplete, unnecessary. It was a pointless discussion.

It occurred to Brady that they were miffed because they couldn't go to the match, which was open only to members — the Harvard Club was for alumni, faculty, and officers of the university — and to the parents of the athletes.

"Anyway, we'll all celebrate together later, eh? If the laddo wins?"

"What do you mean *if* he wins?" Jack said gamely. "Of course he'll win! What can they have in Cambridge to compare with a tough mick from Southie? Tell the punk good luck, Unc!"

"I will, Jack."

Clara entered to clear the table, but before she had picked up a plate, there came from the stairs the rustle of cloth they had been waiting for.

Maeve made her entrance with a floating stiffness. She achieved, quite unpurposefully, a shy dignity. Her dress was black and shiny, silk, yet modest, demure. She was very large in it, since her upper arms were bare and therefore too prominent. Their bland flesh, loads of it, was not her best feature. She was forty-seven and still handsome in an unsexual way. A forthright, plain-featured woman, whose humor and character gave her a soft shine like a figure lit from behind. But she should not have displayed her upper arms.

"A cigarette! I need a cigarette!" she said, dispelling the embarrassment she felt at being tricked out in gauds. Her son offered her one and lit it.

"Well?" She turned around for them. Though her entrance had preempted their response, she was hurt that no one had complimented her.

"Beautiful, Mother!" Maureen said, and set about straightening a rear pleat in the ankle-length gown.

Maeve was looking at her son. "Beautiful! Gorgeous!" he said, smoking.

Colman touched her elbow. "The best, darling. The best!"

"A knockout, eh?" Maeve turned again. "A knockout for Fight Night at . . . What's this place called?"

"It ain't B.C.," Jack piped.

"Bully for B.C.," Maeve said. "Think of it that way: us against them!" She made a fist and mimed a punch. "Come on, Micko! Land one for our side!"

"That's the trouble, Mom," Jack said. "When they're both from Harvard, which side is our side?"

"You and your metaphysics. Did you all eat? Did you give them the lamb, Clara?"

"Yes'm. 'Bout half of it."

"Wrap what's left. Maybe we'll have it tomorrow."

"Yes'm."

"We should go, Maeve."

"I'm ready. What was the large discussion about down here?"

No one answered.

"I guess it was mice at each other that I overheard."

"No one was 'at each other,' Maeve," Colman said. He put his glass down on the oval table and went out for his sister's coat.

Maeve was staring hard at Deirdre. "Did you tell him what I said?"

Deirdre toyed with her spoon miserably.

Maeve gave her daughter a devastating look and moved her lips silently around the words, "Jesus, Mary, and Joseph."

Colman returned with her coat, which he held for her. She stepped into it a side at a time.

"Now, the threesome of you," she said briskly, "I want you to do the kitchen." She turned and called, "Clara, your night off, no?"

"Never mind me, Miss McShane, you just . . ."

"*You* never mind. Get out of that kitchen. All right, you three, something decent for a change . . ."

"Let's go, girls!" Jack said, hopping to.

Each one kissed Maeve on the cheek.

Colman stood in the short hall that held the telephone and led to the entrance foyer. When Maeve joined him they went out together to the garage. Colman held open the door to the big black Packard. Maeve paused, shivering still with indignation.

"A young woman to whom God has been unkind, Colman, how savage she can be! She knew I didn't want her to tell you that."

"Maeve, God has been far from unkind to Dee."

"Don't tell me she's done that to herself. She resents beauty and charm." She got in the car.

Colman slid in on his side. "No wonder she's so difficult with you, then."

"You dragoon!" She smiled at him.

When they were out of the driveway and headed for Commonwealth Avenue, she added weightily, "Resentment is a poor prop for anyone to lean on."

Colman shrugged. Deirdre wasn't his problem.

At Commonwealth he turned east toward town instead of west toward Cambridge.

"Why are you going this way, Colman? Harvard is . . ."

"The Harvard *Club,* dearie. It's next to the Eliot. It's one of their secrets. They have their places everywhere."

The house of the Harvard Club of Boston was an imposing classical building of granite and brick. Its entrance was just muted enough to be overlooked in a block that was bookended by two grand hotels, the Somerset and the Eliot, and otherwise dominated by several private ostentations which blatantly violated the understatement of the Back Bay. The Harvard edifice, built in 1913, lifting nearly a hundred feet, achieved a symmetry of Doric windows at three levels. In its center directly over the first floor balcony was the seal of the College — *Ve-ri-tas* — in marble, and below that the crimson flag fluttered, announcing a club function.

Colman and Maeve left their car with the valet and joined the line of gowned women and tuxedoed men filing into the house. The interior was dark, with wood panels on the walls and ceilings. Skillfully carved dentils and scrolls, not the mimicry of plaster, elaborated the pillars and lintels, but the effect of the lobby was somber with its low ceiling. Colman took his sister's coat and handed it to the young woman at the cloakroom. Then they joined the line moving slowly toward Harvard Hall at the far side of the lobby. A man at a desk received each couple, checked their tickets and handed them a program. Brady's tickets were marked "Guests," but the man did not bat.

"A Formal Evening of Boxing," read the program. The lettering was in simple red ink. Colman opened his and found, on the evening's list of bouts, the one he wanted; "For the Collegiate Championship, Phelps Otis ('41) *vs.* M. Collins Brady ('42).

"There it is, look."

Maeve nodded, though she did not see her nephew's name. There were five bouts listed.

At the entrance to Harvard Hall they waited for the maitre d' to return from seating the couple ahead of them. The hall was a stunning contradiction, a cavernous expanse reaching up three stories lit by three huge chandeliers, from the center one of which shone down spotlights on a raised square canvas-covered platform, which was bordered by three lengths of rope. Around the boxing ring were arranged dozens of tables elegantly set with linen, silver, and crystal. Maeve could not imagine nearly naked men standing in the midst of such opulence hitting each other. She resisted a sudden queasy sickness by finding Colman's hand and sliding her own into it.

The maitre d' seated them at a table for four at the far west side of the room by a large fireplace.

"Bad seats," Colman muttered.

But Maeve was relieved.

No sooner had they placed their napkins in their laps than the maitre d' appeared again, ushering another couple to their table. Colman stood.

"Hello there!" the man said with a great affability. "I guess you're stuck with us!" He was an old man, bent slightly over a cane, with a swarthy head of tousled white hair. He wore his tuxedo inelegantly; his tie was askew. His eyebrows, huge cotton bridges, made impossible demands on the rest of his face.

"Not at all," Brady said. "Delighted." He held a chair ready, and the old man stepped aside for his wife.

"Deborah, this is my wife, Deborah."

She smiled a bit shyly. She was younger than her husband, perhaps sixty, and wearing a slightly too youthful green velvet dress with a high-throated collar.

"I'm Fritz Amory."

"Good evening, Mr. Amory. I am Colman Brady. This is my sister, Mrs. McShane."

"Well, isn't that great! Brother and sister! Aren't you two the pair! I'm Class of Eighty-one."

"Indeed." Colman let it pass and resumed his chair.

"Well," Fritz Amory said, "how about you? What year?"

"I'm not an alumnus, Mr. Amory," Brady said through the smoke of his thin cigar. "We're here to see my son box."

"Is that right?" The old man was impressed. "Which one?"

Colman pointed to Collins's name in Amory's program.

"Well, I'll be! The championship! That's stupendous! Look here, Deborah. 'M. Collins Brady.' Isn't that marvelous? Well, Mr. Brady, it's an honor to be at your table."

"Thank you, sir. And at yours."

The waiter slid dishes of steaming consommé madrilène in front of each, and each began serenely to spoon at the warmth.

"It's a wonderful event, Fight Night," Amory announced. "Deborah and I have been coming for years. Wouldn't miss it. We love it, don't we, peaches?"

Mrs. Amory looked at Maeve, who construed her glance, rightly, to mean she hated it. "Fritz says it builds character."

"That's what my brother says." The two women smiled knowingly at each other.

"Well it does! I boxed in college! Did you, Mr. Brady?"

"No. I was a hurler."

"A what?"

"Hurling. A sort of Gaelic field hockey."

"Aha! Gaelic! You're Irish."

"I am."

Fritz Amory reached over the table to put his hand on Colman's arm. "I admire your country, Mr. Brady. It's been a great struggle, hasn't it? The Independence."

"I think of this as my country, Mr. Amory."

"Of course you do. I meant . . ."

"You're right. It has been a struggle there. A terrible beauty."

"Yeats."

"Yes."

"I'm a writer myself."

"Are you, Mr. Amory?" Maeve asked. "What sort of writing do you do?"

"Plays, Mrs. McShane. I'm a playwright. Broadway plays, that sort of thing."

"Well, *that's* marvelous! Have I heard of your work?"

"No, I suspect not, ma'am. I had a show at the Theatre de Lys once, but it had, shall we say, an economical run."

Maeve was toying with the lemon slice in her soup when she said, "They say it's awfully difficult to make a living as a writer these days."

Colman touched his napkin to his lips. Clearly Amory's main occupation, however he described himself, had been watching over the family fund.

"Oh, it is, yes. It is. Writing is a damnable profession. I despise it. What do you do, Mr. Brady?"

"Insurance, Mr. Amory."

"Oh? What firm?"

"My own. Monument Municipal, it's called."

"I don't know it, but that doesn't mean anything. I admire business. Great excitement in business these days. I've been thinking about doing a play about it. What do you think?"

Brady laughed. "Actually, I should call my company 'Monotonous.' Not much seems to happen. You should write plays about ships, like O'Neill."

"I already have a ship play. I call it *The Fog People!*"

"Or a play about boxing," Maeve said.

"Now *there's* an idea! Isn't that a good idea, peaches? We must pay close attention tonight."

"You could draw on your own experience, sir."

"By Jove, Mr. Brady, you're right! And I could meet your son, perhaps?"

"Of course."

"I never had a son. Always wanted one."

Peaches dropped her eyes. Maeve wanted to touch her.

"Would have gone to the College," Amory went on, oblivious. "You must be pleased."

"I am, sir. Harvard is a fine school."

"More than that! More than that!" The old man thumped the table, glistened, having left his grief behind. "I'll tell you, Mr. Brady, it's embarrassing, but I'll tell you anyway. After all these years — and it's too damn many — I look back on the College and, well, that was *it* for me. Absolutely the peak. I loved it. I was a boxer. And the Pudding. I love these things, reunions. Wouldn't miss it." Amory paused, looked at his wife, and had a new thought. "Well, not the absolute peak. That was my wife. Meeting her."

The palpable love passing silently between the old couple moved Brady.

"Of course," Amory said. "Peaches wasn't even born when I was at Harvard. Were you, dear?"

"Would you believe it? There was a time when I wasn't born." Mrs. Amory laughed.

Brady studied them, thinking of decay. His mind flicked from the fact of theirs to that of his own. He dispelled the sudden grim mood by leaning away from the consommé and taking out his case.

"Do you mind if I smoke?" It was gauche to smoke between courses.

"Of course not."

Brady lit a cigarette and flipped the match into the center of the modest fire that burned in the large hearth a few feet away from them.

"Can you read that?" Amory asked. He pointed to a Latin verse inscribed on the hearthstone. Before Brady could reply, Amory was translating haltingly. *"Dissolve!* Dissolve the winter cold. *Super Foco Large,* with large — or, better, plenteous — logs laid on the hearth, O Thaliarchus. Not bad, eh?"

"Very good," Brady cheered. The old man laughed delightedly. Brady urged him to continue.

"And draw from — *deprome* — the cask — *benignius* — benignly, no, generously! *Quadrimum Sabina.* I can't imagine what that is. The fourth Sabine. What the blazes?"

"Perhaps," Brady said tentatively, snapping his ash toward the fire, "the four-year-old Sabine wine."

"Do you suppose . . . ?" Amory studied the stone like a puzzle.

"Yes. Certainly. You know the Sabine wine in Horace."

"Horace? Is that Horace?"

"It is."

"I'll be damned." Amory raised his wineglass to toast Brady.

Brady raised his own glass and said, "To the hearthstone which is an altar of the safe and grateful warmth which nourishes hospitality, good fellowship, and friendship."

"Indeed so, Mr. Brady. Indeed so." He leaned over to his wife and made a show of whispering, "Isn't he splendid?"

During the several courses that followed — sautéed sweetbreads, duck, vegetables, and cheeses — the Amorys and Colman and Maeve carried on like good friends. There was an ease between them that no one could have anticipated.

All Fritz Amory knew was that for once at a damn reunion he wasn't being made to feel defensive by some doctor or lawyer about how he'd spent his life.

A bell was ringing.

The cordials had been served. Darts of fire from the tips of cigars flitted about the hall when the lights were lowered, all but the spots on the boxing ring beneath the huge center chandelier.

"Ladies and gentlemen," a man with a shining bald pate said from the microphone at ringside, "welcome to the Harvard Club's Evening of Boxing! Tonight's referee is George Kimball, Twenty-seven. I refer you to your program. The evening's first bout is the Harry Anderson Memorial Competition."

Two boys climbed into the ring, not even of college age. After further announcements and introductions, the bells rang and the boys came out fighting. That is, they came out for long periods of malevolent stalking, punctuated by instants of wild flailing that seemed mutually calculated to be as brief and painless as possible.

"They're children," Maeve whispered. Horrified as she was, she could not take her eyes off the ring. She was feeling giddy from the wine. She was smoking, but many of the women were.

"It's the Golden Gloves, Maeve. Boys' Clubs, that sort of thing."

"I hate it."

Several bouts followed, each one longer than the other. After the Golden Gloves fight there were two semiprofessional bouts between bantams, who fought with a fierceness at once brutal and detached, as though the fifty-dollar prize were everything and nothing. But the bouts of the night were between the Harvard men. The fourth event was the Harvard Club Consolation between the boxers who'd been eliminated in the tournament semifinals. Theirs was a sluggish, boring fight. Both men had already been beaten and their defeat was palpable. Who has ever fought heartfully for the consolation?

By the time the bald man announced the final bout — "Ladies and gentlemen, for the Championship of Harvard College!" — the four hundred and twenty ladies and gentlemen were ready for it. They had been mellow and subdued through the early contests, rewarding well-landed punches with applause, but not shouting particularly or leaving their chairs. The preliminary bouts had been just that. But the fight for the title of Harvard College — that was a contest for huzzahs. In the ironic tradition of Harvard athletics, Fight Night always achieved two things at once: a spirited and self-mocking satire as well as a damned fine match between excellent athletes.

"In the white boxing trunks, Class of Forty-one, and first runner-up in nineteen thirty-nine, from Peabody, Massachusetts, Phelps Otis."

A broad young man of average height with dark black hair trimmed short bounced down the aisle from the lobby to the ring. He wore a crimson robe. The people applauded vigorously.

"You know who he is, don't you?" Mr. Amory said.

"No."

"That's Wave Otis's nephew."

"The Speaker?" Brady asked. Wysten Waverly Otis had house-managed the bill against Curley in 1933. He had retired when Curley was governor.

"And," the announcer blared, "in the dark trunks, Class of Forty-two, from Brookline, Massachusetts, M. Collins Brady!"

The applause was equally vigorous.

Brady stood up to see his son.

A very tall young man with bushy brown hair and a huge smile, wearing a robe like Otis's, walked slowly into the hall and up to the ring. He did not hurry or jog. The poise with which he entered made his father think, despite himself, that by God the kid looked like a champion. Upon entering the ring Collins nodded at the crowd and then at Otis as if they were friends. And then, while listening to the referee drone the usual rules, young Brady's eyes began to cross the crowd. He could not see past the first few rows of tables, but Colman saw him looking and, knowing, began to wave wildly.

"Sit down, Colman," Maeve said, tugging at his sleeve. "He can't see you way back here."

"He's got the other bloke on size, doesn't he?"

"He does," Amory said. "Your boy looks the stronger. My money's on him."

"Smart money, Mr. Amory," Colman winked and sat.

"Call me Fritz now, won't you?"

Collins was still trying to pick his father out of the crowd when he returned to his corner to await the bell. He leaned against the ropes, barely listening to what his second was telling him. His second was a short young man who wore a white sweater with the red "H" on its breast.

The bell rang. A modest roar of interest went up from the crowd.

Otis and Brady approached each other similarly; circling in small, gliding steps, each moving opposite his opponent's crooked left arm, each one's left elbow down in front of his left ribs, each one's left hand extended shoulder-high a foot, each one's right hand cocked back below his right cheek ready to attack or defend.

Otis had his chin pressed down on his chest bone. Brady's chin was thrust forward. His father was instantly aware of this flaw in his stance and alarmed by it. Bad coaching. The chin must always be down. Like Otis's.

Otis saw the easy target too and moved in on it. Unlike Brady's, Otis's head had no singular action of its own, did not bob or weave, but worked along with his entire body. A shorter man, more solid than lean, he crouched forward in what Colman saw even from the rear of the room was a left feint before a hook.

Colman was on his feet. "Get your chin down!" he wanted to yell. "Get your chin down!"

Otis stepped inside Brady and exploded upward, leading with his left hand in a skillful, perfectly timed attack against Collins's chin, which hung in the air like a clay pigeon. Collins looked inept and vulnerable, Otis smart and quick.

Otis's glove smashed in on its target. The force of the blow could have jarred Brady to the point of finishing him.

But the left hook missed. Brady's chin was gone. He had drawn it in at the last possible instant and Otis's punch went harmlessly by.

While everyone was watching the hook to Brady's chin, Brady was driving a low right cross into Otis's midsection. His blow landed. He buried his glove in his opponent's stomach and the crowd could hear Otis's grotesque intake of breath.

Brady had given Otis the false lead of his chin. Otis had taken it. Brady had scored, a brilliant move, a great opening.

The crowd applauded.

Colman cheered, remaining on his feet.

Otis backed off.

Brady, with his chin firmly on his chest, moved in on him, leading with his left, jabbing and stepping back; jabbing and stepping back again — a classic tactic against a shorter opponent. It allowed Brady the full advantage of his superior height and reach. Jab and step back. Forward, jab, and back. An elegant sequence of moves; this Brady was a boxer.

The bell rang. The three minutes had seemed like seconds. The boxers retreated to their corners.

Colman Brady sat down and reached for the last of his wine. He was hoarse.

"By Jove, Brady!" Amory said. "What a boxer! Splendid boxer!"

"Isn't he great?"

Colman looked at Maeve, who was nervously lighting a cigarette. Her weak eyes told him she had nothing to say. But she spoke nonetheless.

"How many rounds?"

"Seven more."

"Jesus, Mary, and Joseph!"

"He'll be fine."

"What about the other fellow? Are we supposed to pray Micko kills him?"

"Now, Maeve, stop it."

"Don't 'now' me! This entire thing is perverse. Your son is their gladiator."

The bell rang.

The boxers engaged immediately. Otis drew Brady's left lead as the latter attempted to resume his tactic of jabbing and stepping back. But that was a mistake on Brady's part, too predictable. Now Otis was ready for it and, having drawn the lead, he slipped inside it, crouching forward and bringing both hands upward in sharp short blows to Brady's body. Brady should have gone into a clinch at once, but he tried to back off, allowing Otis to continue his rapid hitting in close pursuit. Otis had employed the classic infight tactic against an opponent who is taller. By the time Brady slid his gloves around Otis's waist to end the assault it was an act more of desperation than skill.

The bell rang.

Round two to Otis. The applause was vigorous and sustained as the men went back to their corners.

No one at the table spoke. The Amorys were embarrassed by Maeve's outburst. Maeve was trying to decide whether to leave altogether or wait for her brother in the lobby.

Colman was worried about the fight. Micko had blown the round badly, not out of lack of skill or strength, but out of cockiness. Otis had landed solid, damaging punches to the boy's body. And now Micko was sitting on his stool visibly stunned and, instead of listening to his second or concentrating on Otis across the ring, he was looking out at the crowd, still trying to find his father. Colman recognized the look in his eye — it was born of the old pathetic fear that his father was displeased. "Don't think about me, kiddo!" Colman wanted to yell. "Think about him!"

The bell rang.

Collins Brady was slower coming out this time. Otis carried the fight to him.

Now more and more of the crowd was on its feet. At a table near ring-side someone knocked a wine bottle to the floor and its crash was audible above the fight noises. An elderly man at a table near Brady was yelling, "Smash him, Phelps! Smash him, Phelps!"

Otis lunged forward toward Brady's chin, which was exposed again. Only this time it remained exposed to Otis's strongest and best blow, a straight right, which he threw with all he had, leaving himself wide open if this was another Brady feint. But it was not. All of Otis's weight was on his forward left foot, his right foot having twisted high into the air behind him. When the punch landed, Brady's two feet left the floor as he crashed down backward, slamming the canvas with his tailbone and then his head.

The bell rang.

"Stop it!" Maeve screamed at Colman over the noise.

"I can't. I can't."

"He's only up there because of you!"

"That's not true." It was true.

"They'll kill him! They'll kill him!"

"He's only fighting *one* man, Maeve!" But he knew what she was saying. The crowd was entirely mad now with its desire for Otis's victory. Blood was in the air.

"Dear God, it's your son!"

"I know who it is! Don't you tell me who it is!"

"Stop it, Colman!"

"Woman, *you* stop it! I can't!"

Maeve hurled her wrung napkin at him and stood and bolted from the table.

Brady stared down into his brandy.

Fritz Amory whispered to his wife, "Isn't that the saddest thing you ever saw? I could just weep for them."

Maeve made her way as quickly as she could to the women's lounge. As she pushed the door open she heard the bell clang and she groaned aloud. In the lounge another woman was seated in a low chair at the great mirror, hunched over. She had long blond hair and wore an amber velvet dress with a deep scoop down the back that made her appear slightly too naked, altogether vulnerable. Maeve was so struck by her that, for a moment she forgot herself and her nephew. The woman raised her head, displaying in the mirror the wreckage of her mascara. She had been weeping. Her brows, pencil thin, were smeared down into the dark pools of her lids. Her face was etched.

"Isn't it awful?" she said to Maeve. Her voice was raspy and deep.

Maeve nodded, barely controlling herself, and took the settee next to her.

"I know that boy," the woman said.

Maeve looked at her sharply. "Which one?"

"The Irish boy. Brady."

"You *know* him?"

"Yes."

"They're killing him."

"I know it. I know it."

"I've never seen such vicious evil people, never," said Maeve.

The woman turned away from the mirror to look at Maeve in the flesh. "I can't help noticing your accent. You're Irish."

Maeve nodded.

The bell rang.

And it rang again. Instead of stopping after its first sharp report, it continued to clang for some seconds. The roar of the crowd was louder than ever.

The two women went into the lobby and listened.

"The winner, by technical knockout, in two minutes, eleven seconds of the fourth round, Phelps Otis!"

Everyone in Harvard Hall was on his feet applauding.

Suddenly Collins Brady, his shoulders draped with the crimson robe and supported by the sweatered youth who'd been in his corner, burst into the lobby from the hall. He walked briskly toward the stairs that led down to the squash courts and locker rooms. There was blood on his face and his hair was matted, obscuring his eyes, but he seemed all right.

He walked within ten feet of Maeve. It was not clear whether he did not see her or was ignoring her.

"Oh, dear God," Maeve said after he had passed. Tears came into her eyes. The woman with her pressed her arm reassuringly.

Phelps Otis, waving and smiling, came out of the hall. The applause and whistling were deafening. As he crossed the lobby to the stairs, accompanied by his second and followed by the referee, he waved at the two women.

They only stared at him.

Colman Brady was the first one out after the boxers. He nearly bumped into Maeve on his way across the lobby. He was going after Collins.

"Maeve!"

She had rarely seen him so agitated.

When Brady saw the woman Maeve was with his jaw dropped. "Mrs. Thomson!"

"Mr. Brady."

Maeve removed Madeline Thomson's hand from her arm.

"You've met?" Colman asked.

"Met?" Madeline was as confused as he was. She looked at Maeve, whose glare was fixed on Brady. "Are you with him?" Madeline asked.

"Yes." Maeve did not look at her.

"Oh, God," Madeline said, closing her eyes, bridging her forehead with her thumb and finger, a dramatic, affected gesture. "I apologize, Mrs. Brady . . ."

"Not Mrs. Brady," Maeve said. "The boy is my nephew, though his father is no brother of mine." With that, Maeve turned abruptly and headed against the crowd into the hall to retrieve her purse.

Colman and Madeline stood facing each other as the swirl of fans made its way in eddies past them.

"You came with your husband."

"Yes."

"You remembered my son."

She nodded and looked at him directly. She did not look away in an instant as women usually did. There was nothing coy in her at that moment.

"Your son is all right."

"I know."

"I saw him looking for you. I knew you'd be here."

Colman shrugged.

"Is your wife with you?"

"My wife is dead."

Madeline Thomson did not reply to that.

"She's been dead for eighteen years."

"You must have been very young."

Brady nodded.

Perhaps it was the rare explicit reference to Nellie that did it. He found himself drawn inextricably into Mrs. Thomson's gaze. Her ruined eyes held him. He realized she had been weeping. For Micko?

She lowered her eyes. He dropped his, allowing them to fall along the lines of her body. The amber dress showed her breasts. Her figure was alluring, youthful. He guessed she was forty, but she looked younger, much younger. He had thought of her once as an aging flapper. Now she reminded him of Nell.

"I told you I would visit you. For my ax."

"I believed you. I wanted you to come."

"There's never enough time. It passes quickly."

"Doesn't it?" She raised her chin at him, leading with it, recalling Micko's feint, Micko's error. She had a wonderful chin, a perfect tight neck. The wrinkles of her face and throat were too fine to add anything but texture to her skin.

"Do you still live in Beverly?" He could feel his caution evaporating.

"Pride's Crossing."

"Might I . . . ?" He let the question hang. Would she require a more circuitous approach? Apparently not, because she nodded, then said softly, "Please do."

She turned and retreated into the women's lounge.

He forced his way through the crowd to the stairs leading down to the lockers.

He found his son seated on a low bench, his head back, face up to an attendant who was applying Merthiolate to a one-inch cut inside his mouth. His left eye was swollen purple. Otis had finished him off with a series of sharp blows to the face that so bloodied him the referee had intervened.

His eyes were closed.

Colman put his hand on the back of his son's neck and pressed gently.

The boy opened his eyes.

"Oh, Dad. I'm sorry. I'm so sorry."

Colman leaned down to kiss him on the brow, "Son, you showed real courage. That's what counts."

The boy's eyes were overflowing, which only made his self-loathing sharper.

Colman stroked the flesh in back of his son's neck. "I was proud of you, *amico.*"

❦ 2 ❦

ON THE TIP of Eastern Point in Gloucester there was a modest weathered pavilion to which the residents of the peninsula went in summer for band concerts. In early April the large houses on the rocky coast were still vacant. An eeriness hung over the place, twin to the fog which clung to the glistening low shrubbery.

Colman Brady waited for Madeline Gardner Thomson to appear. He leaned with his back to the ocean against a slatted bench and watched the road. The only movements were the undulations of the gray sea, of which he was only vaguely aware, and the sharp darting of wet gulls, which made periodic demands on his attention. The gulls were feeding on crabs left behind helpless by the tide. Once they chewed the legs away from the body they lifted the impenetrable shell to a height of fifty or seventy feet and dropped it, swooping down afterward to see if the fall had given them the crack they needed. The ingenuity of hunger.

Time seemed to Brady like a shell that refused to split. He refused to look at his watch, but still saw the slow, silent sweep that, over and over, traced its pattern precisely, achieving in her absence an exquisite futility.

They had arranged their rendezvous when he called the day after the fight. Madeline did not want to receive him at her home after all. He proposed the pavilion. She knew the place. Meeting there meant a plunge directly into the surreptitious, and her willingness excited him and made him anxious.

"When shall we meet then?" he had asked, thinking, *Perhaps this afternoon.*

"A week from Thursday," she'd said, crushing him.

And now no sign of her.

[267]

What woman could charm him away from that incomprehensible world in which he lived? Why had he allowed the impassioned hope of his youth to bubble up again, leaving him motionless and disengaged, gazing at a figure in his mind, hers, and thinking perhaps there are oases after all?

The week and a half since she'd given her promise had been filled with a happiness. He had been thinking continually, *I will be with her.* As long as she did not come he had the pleasure of his own highly concentrated anticipation. Even as he stared down the misty road it seemed to him his watching was of such an intensity that her coming would be somehow deflating. He was absorbed. In such a state of mind, satisfaction and resolution were not to be hoped for — only the prolongation of this new feeling. He had harbored nothing like it before, not even with Nellie, unless the haze across his memory misled him. With Nellie there had been desire and anticipation — he could summon those still by picturing her naked on the floor before the fire — but never this unsettling, paralyzing expectation which invests everything in the future, thereby destroying the present and, peculiarly, thereby making the present more intensely felt than ever.

What woman? What woman could charm him away from that incomprehensible world in which he lived? Perhaps this one. Why? Her modish slouch, the way her body wore its despair. The world-weariness of the young getting old. An aging woman in a gorgeous body. Her bronze and marble skin. Her confidence and brain.

Brady recalled standing with her on the steps of Widener overlooking the Tercentenary. It made him think of standing with Nellie before the altar stone of the Druid tumulus looking out over the Nire Valley. Was it that Madeline and he had seen the same thing when they looked at Harvard? Brady had seen a world of achievement and excellence which he admired but suspected, and in which he could never be at home. Though it was the world into which Madeline had been born, it was, he guessed, as alien to her as it was to him. She saw through its smug arrogance even more than he did. Brady recalled then standing alone in Louisburg Square overwhelmed by the perfection of it. He admitted to himself that he was attracted to this woman in exactly the way he'd been attracted to that place. But he was meeting her because of the ways they were like each other, not different. He had been of Ireland and South Boston, and he had with an enormous unforgotten pain left them both behind. She was of Pride's Crossing and Beacon Hill and she had — with like pain? — left them behind. Colman guessed that they had both transcended boundaries and limits, which accounted for that strength they shared and for that bottomless loneliness in the way she aimed its trembling at him, omnivorously, as if it would eat its object, him. He wondered if she knew of his loneliness.

He lit a cigarette and watched a gull wheeling grandly overhead.

In the shade of a clump of nearby bushes someone had planted fuchsias.

He savored the image of Madeline Thomson standing before him in the lobby of the Harvard Club, looking pained and vulnerable. How little she seemed to change. The same radiant forehead he remembered. The same untrusting eyes. Her amber gown that night had been exactly of the season's fashion, but still her body had kept the lines that had set her generation apart years before. It was not only that she looked young, but that she had looked young in that defiant, alluring way for years. Disturbingly unchanged, her presence that night had had the effect of delivering Brady bound at the ankles to his own past.

It was his past that bothered him because it was the one thing in his life about which he could do nothing. When he'd first met Madeline years before, he'd been laying down his planks, preparing to launch himself on Boston. He'd been holding in check that certain expectation of influence and power, that enormous ambition that had made him young. When next he'd seen her at the Tercentenary, that ambition had just been exploded, but inside him. Curley, the bastard, had only moments before hit him from behind, teaching him that what really matters are the things you don't expect. But he hadn't expected Madeline Thomson again either. She had taken her place by accident, by a kind of usurpation, among Brady's shuffling litany of ghosts. He seemed incapable of severing relations with the great foils of his past — Collins, Nellie, Purcival, Gavin, now Curley — whom he carried around inside him as if *he* were a megalith in which the dead were buried. His ghosts were what kept Brady permanently disappointed. But Madeline was alive, no ghost, and she filled him with an acute anticipation.

Perhaps she wasn't coming. A seagull abandoned a shell at Brady's feet. It seemed whole. Perhaps the thing had held out, refused to crack, survived with its meat. Brady flicked at the shell with his toe, turning it over. There was no underside to it. The gull had feasted. No, she wasn't coming, he was sure of it. She would have arrived by then. She was much too late. She was punishing him for never having called her. Why hadn't he? Furious and sad.

He walked around to the front of the bench and started to sit, but thought better of it. The slats were beaded with moisture. A foghorn sounded. Brady stepped across the puddle in front of the bench; water had collected in the depression that years of feet had made in the earth. As he stepped across it he caught a glimpse of himself in the reflection and turned back to it.

He was forty-two. Staring at his face in the pool, he insisted that his years had not yet etched their marks on him. Or not, at least, on his body.

"Good morning, Narcissus."

She was standing behind him.

He straightened to face her.

"Good morning," he said. He felt almost no embarrassment that she should have witnessed his display of vanity.

The top part of her face was obscured by a brown Robin Hood hat which left visible only her nose, chin and, as from within a cavern, the glint of her eye. She wore a cotton trenchcoat with an abundance of flaps and belts. The belt at her waist was fastened tightly. She wore brown leather gloves.

She's forty-four, he thought. *She must be.*

What did it matter? Nothing. Happiness and youth have almost nothing to do with one another.

"I'm happy to see you," he said.

"I'm glad. I'm sorry to be late. I got lost. I looked all over Gloucester proper for the gazebo."

"Eastern Point."

"I didn't know what they call it out here. We always just said Gloucester. And, of course, I never drove myself . . ."

"Strange," he teased, "but you give the impression of being quite a competent woman."

"I am. I hate being lost. I hate being late. I will not take kindly to being joshed about it."

"Noted." Brady smiled.

She took her hat off. Her eyes were large and tranquil. He had expected agitation. Her hair was short, freshly cropped. She shook it out.

"You've cut your hair."

"Yes. I always do in spring."

She crushed her hat and put it in the trenchcoat pocket, leaving her hand there. She arranged her hair briefly, roughly, with her other hand, which she then put in the other pocket.

Brady saw hints of gray amid the dark blond mass. The shorter hair fell off her forehead differently and made it larger. He was comparing the look of her to the image he'd been savoring. She was even better in the flesh.

"I'd suggest we sit, but . . ." He gestured to the bench, its beads of water.

"I'd rather walk anyway. Do you mind?"

"Not at all. I'd love a walk."

"Where shall we go? It's all private property."

"Well, you're with the right fellow. Stick close to me for a lesson in the fine art of trespassing."

He put his hand briefly on her shoulder and turned her toward the road. It was the first time he'd touched her. He could feel the blood moving under her skin, even through her clothes.

"No," she said, pulling away from him. "The ocean. We're at the ocean! Let's walk by the ocean!" She led the way across the grass to the boulders and ledges that lined the shore like cockeyed stairs.

Brady followed, slightly piqued, thinking if she knew where she wanted to walk why did she ask. He wasn't dressed to go dancing on slippery rocks. His street shoes, suit, and Aquascutum imposed a kind of timidity on him as he stepped from the sodden earth to the first great stone.

"The center cannot hold!" she hollered back at him, throwing her arms open to the waves which rolled in. "*I* am loosed upon the world!" The wind feathered her hair while she received, formally, the sullen water.

Brady had not noticed how rough the sea was. As long as one stood with one's back to the ocean — as he had, waiting — it did not exist. When one faced it, nothing else existed.

Brady had to stop looking at the sea to watch where he put his feet.

"It finds its own level, doesn't it?" Madeline Thomson said, sweeping the ocean with her left arm.

"Don't we all?"

She gave him a sharp look. He smiled a bit helplessly, steadying himself against the wind.

"Think of the stones as clouds," she said, "and of the spaces between as holes through which we see the earth."

"And the ocean is what?"

"The sky with green dye thrown in so that we can see the currents of the wind."

He knew her whimsy for the counterfeit it was — she had drawn it over her tension like a silk scarf — but still he was charmed.

"It is useless to argue about the ocean," she went on. "You have either sailed across it or you haven't." She gave him a salty look. "You and I have sailed."

He watched her. She moved nimbly, youthfully, skillfully across the boulders. When he followed it was as her wake. He checked himself, remaining back. She was alone; he was alone. That required that they move singly across the scape, each with his own footing, each with his own set of choices, each — he felt it suddenly — with his own burden.

He put the thought away. Grim romance. Young Werther.

"Stop!" he said, catching her. "Let's sit."

They leaned back against a rock and faced the sea. He continued to hold her arm, could feel a slight shiver coursing through it.

"Who are you, anyway?" he asked.

"I am, as you know, Madeline Gardner, born in Boston of approved parents, well bred and round in the rump, sure prey of the slow virus of quick madness that breeds in the quarries of middle age."

"Oh."

"And you are Colman O'Murphy from over there." She nodded toward Portugal.

"Aye. Born in winter at the right time for hearing stories by the fire. Which is why I know the difference between dreams and lies."

"And which would this be?"

"Neither, yet."

She laughed. "Do you drink too much?"

"No. I don't do anything too much."

"Too bad."

"I've always thought so."

"You don't seem Irish. You hold your fancy in check."

"Unlike yourself."

"I owe it all to my analyst."

When she said this it was as if a gull wheeled down too close to him and then flew away.

"But I am Irish, nonetheless."

"How is your son?"

"Recovered. A triumph of pride."

"You shouldn't allow him to fight."

"It's the sport of kings."

"That's racing, I thought."

"No matter. The sport is in watching someone lose. Anyone. At anything."

"It should reassure us, I suppose. But you wanted him to win, didn't you? You really wanted him to win."

"You mean: is my son the vicar of my own ambition?"

Madeline shrugged.

"You have no children?"

"None. My husband is impotent."

"That's a bit private."

"It's not true, anyway. I'm sterile."

"That's private too. And also untrue, I suppose."

"Why would I say it?"

"The love of grand agonies."

"Nothing grand about that piano, I'll tell you. Anyway, you're right. Nothing I've said is true. I had a son. He died, years ago."

"How?"

She nodded at the ocean again. "Like that. Overboard a ship. For you and for everybody, that is just the sea. For me . . ." She stopped, then added, "At first I regularly threw flowers into it. Then I stopped coming." She faced him. "This is the first time I've come to the shore in years."

"I wouldn't have suggested if I'd known."

"Don't be silly." She gave him her smile. "I'm glad to be here."

Brady kissed her.

"Me, too," he said.

"It took you long enough."

He looked at his watch. "About fifteen minutes."

"About eight years."

"I wasn't ready for a grand agony."

"Oh, Jesus!" She set her face in a mocking pout with her lower lip pressing up against her nose. She had a perfect profile, and her distortion of it only drew attention to its perfection.

Colman offered her a cigarette. She shook her head. He took one for himself. He retrieved his arm from the crook of her elbow and cupped a match. But the wind extinguished it. He tried another, then another. He placed the cigarette back in its pack.

"What was your boy like?" Colman asked. He was touching her sleeve, very gently.

Madeline was moved. No one had ever asked her that. When she announced the fact of her son's death, people habitually steered away from the subject. Here was a man asking her to share it with him. She felt the old emotion rising, as from its sleep inside her. "He was just a boy, Colman. Like any other." She was afraid if she said how wonderful he was she would weep. "But let me ask you a question. What do you do?"

"I sell insurance. I used to be in politics, but I was at the wrong place at the wrong time."

"I know. I read about it."

Colman was not going to steer toward that. He attempted a shrug. "I had a great future. I decided to get out when I realized it was behind me."

Madeline laughed. "How self-serving of you."

"Of course. Self-service — it's the coming thing."

She laughed again, but with an eccentric quality that made too much of his crack. Colman's cynicism was accustomed to its solitude. The thought that she was like himself in that way disturbed him.

She stopped laughing, and he said nothing. They were silent for a moment, then she said, "So where are we?"

"In the next parish over from Dunquin. Which is the westernmost village in Ireland, for your information."

"I guessed." She raised her arms dramatically. "Ireland wrecks itself on our shores, these rocks."

He stood, facing her. "Let's walk, Madeline."

"No." She was staring at the ocean, seeing it for the grave it was. Without taking her eyes from it, she reached up to him, touching his sleeve. "Please, let's stay a bit."

Brady felt that there was no more to say. Idly, he turned and skipped down several rocks and stood, shoulders hunched, hands in his pockets, pressing himself.

The tide was going out. Already a line of pebbles lay exposed and, with each wash, they scurried back and forth. He listened to them, trying to separate the sound of their rolling from the sounds of the wind and water. He heard a casual improvisation. Nothing false troubled the peace of the water at the land. Suddenly what had seemed ominous and grim was soothing.

Perhaps five minutes passed while they remained apart, separate complacencies. Then Madeline stood and joined him. She slid her arm inside his.

"It's good, isn't it?" she said.

He nodded.

"I can feel its power in my feet."

"Its loveliness."

She rested against him, finding his shoulder with her head. He put his arm around her waist. They were silent and still again for some moments.

"If you look long enough," she asked, "can you see Ireland?"

"I can always see it, Madeline. I left the best of myself behind." It was a thought he had never expressed before, and therefore never felt.

She wanted to tell him that she understood that. The best of her was out there, too.

She looked up at his face and saw the country in its contours, his strong brow, his sharp chin, his lips' thin sadness.

She went up on her toes to kiss him. He turned and covered her with his arms and kissed her in return, a strong, determined kiss. When their mouths parted, Madeline stuffed her face into the hollow of Colman's neck. She mumbled something, then raised herself and said, "Oh I didn't want all that talk. I didn't plan to talk to you at all."

"It's seemed like mostly silence to me."

"That's what I mean by talk." She stuffed her face into his shoulder again. "But you haven't told me!" she said. "The one thing I wanted to know. Your wife. What happened?"

"I could not begin to tell you, Madeline."

"You must!" She struck his breast with her face. "You must!"

His silence said he couldn't.

"You never married again?"

"No."

She pulled away to arm's length and cracked her face at him. He took it for a smile. "That's what makes you irresistible," she said.

"I don't know."

"It is. It is. Don't ever marry! You're irresistible." She was reasserting a coy playfulness and he was relieved. "That's why," she went on, "I shall never divorce Thornton. Don't you think I'm ever so much more attractive as someone's wife?"

"I don't know about that either."

"Oh, come now! Adultery is so much more . . ." — she winked and rubbed her body against his — ". . . than mere fornication."

"Don't be ribald about it."

"Oh, a streak of moralism!"

She turned away from him. He grabbed her shoulder and spun her back, more roughly than he intended. "Don't be so goddamned cynical! At least not about this."

"But about the rest I can be."

"I don't care about the rest."

"We're not children. We know what we're about. After seven years, eight, we can hardly be said to have been swept off our feet."

"Nevertheless," he said icily, "I am not a frivolous man. There is nothing frivolous about my being here."

"Then I don't understand it. Perhaps it's a mistake."

"Perhaps."

They fell silent.

"Are you leaving?" she asked at last with her lily-like drooping delicacy.

"No."

"Then shall we, as you suggested before, walk on?"

They did. As they hopscotched the rocks they talked in rising and falling voices.

"Has it been seven or eight?" he asked.

"December six, nineteen thirty-three."

"That's quite a memory."

"It was the day of Repeal."

"Ah, of course."

"And the day the court said *Ulysses* is not obscene."

"A lot they know."

"A lot *you* know."

They wandered along the broad shore's back, the rocks like the knobs of its spine. It was turning into one of those days on which the sun, not hot, showed itself through clenched openings in the clouds. Winter was over.

Madeline led the way up the ledge to a gaunt outcropping of earth. She climbed it and then faced back briefly to wave at Brady. He was having trouble making the climb. His shoes kept slipping on the stone. By the time he achieved the pinnacle she was gone. A path led into a thicket of brambles and the low scrub pine that thrives in the sandy soil by the ocean in New England. He followed it. The fog had entirely lifted and the last mist was burned away. There were little globules of moisture on the branches and small leaves of the undergrowth, but one could almost see them evaporating.

"Madeline!"

She did not answer. She had to have gone this way, he thought, and so continued along the path. It wound past a high chicken-wire fence that was nearly grown over. Brady stopped to examine it and discerned in the brambles and shrubs the ruins of a tennis court.

"I used to play here."

He heard her voice before he saw her.

She was standing inside the viny fence in the middle of the overgrown court.

"The baseline would have been here." She toed the dirt. "And the net . . ." She looked wistfully around.

"Whose place is it?"

"Phillipses'. The Sanford Phillipses. Friends of my parents. I'd forgotten their place was here."

"It seems ancient." Like the ruins of Pompeii. But a tennis court can return to the wild in a matter of years.

"It *is* ancient. That was years ago. I feel very old suddenly." She made her way toward him, drew very close, but they were separated by the chicken-wire.

"The mortality of playgrounds . . . ," Colman said absently.

"Colman, I . . . need . . . some reassurance."

They stared at each other through the fence, not moving. Then, as if on cue, they began going along the opposite sides of the fence, gaining momentum as they went, slapping brush and branches out of the way. Soon they were practically running, side by side, the wire between them.

They embraced in the gate.

Madeline was weeping.

As Brady looked over her shoulder onto the old tennis court, he suddenly saw the scene as it had been twenty-five years before. Young people, beautiful, tan, perfect in their whites, the two boys in flannel trousers, the two girls in pleats. They were playing a vigorous match. Madeline Gardner was serving.

Thwapp! Her racquet drove the ball deep into the service box, forcing the young man to skip backward and flick weakly at the ball, which arched back across the net. But Madeline was there for it and, with a graceful lunge, she smashed it back at him. He never had a chance.

"Game!" one hollered. "Set!"

"Great!" Madeline approached the net. She kissed her opponent on the mouth. Her lips were wet. "Let's go get loaded!"

Her partner threw his arm around her shoulders as they headed off the court, toweling themselves. Madeline let her right hand rest casually on his buttocks, her thumb hooked in his trousers pocket.

Brady felt her hand on his own buttocks. She was pressing, kneading, exciting him immeasurably.

"I know a place," she said.

Brady nodded and let her take him by the hand. They walked in silence along an overgrown path.

"There," Madeline Thomson said, pointing to a great stone mansion on a spit of land. The ocean crashed around it on two sides. "The Phillips house. Just for us."

The mansion struck no roots in the sand, sat there on its thorny peninsula just shy of the great rock ledges that guarded against the breakers.

A precarious place, Colman thought, *all too exposed.*

"Perhaps there's someone there," he cautioned.

"No. Not yet."

She set out across the high grass, still pulling him. It was the simplicity of her stride he envied; she had no thought that *she* trespassed. He watched the windows on the second and third floors, expecting curtains to be parted, but there was no movement.

The windows on the first floor were covered with cracked rectangles of wood the color of seaweed. The building itself was a compound of stones and beams. They entered a modest courtyard, formed on one side by a row of garages, on another by a detached cottage, and on the third by the house itself. Brady's initial impression of the fragility of the place held despite its massive stateliness. Little mortar was discernible between the large, random-shaped rocks, and the mansion seemed to be an achievement more of balance than construction.

"The servants' house," Madeline said, nodding at the cottage, but otherwise ignoring it. She fixed her attention on the main entrance, which she approached confidently. She tried to open it.

"Damn! Locked!"

"Of course, it's locked." Should the proprietor have left the place open all winter for the sake of their early spring tryst?

"My parents never locked their house at Vineyard Haven."

"Times were different then, dearie. And Vineyard Haven isn't Gloucester."

Madeline slammed her fist against the door which, solid oak, barely registered the blow. "Oh, damn!" She turned and slumped against the lintel and looked at Brady. She seemed a petulant, defied child, her mouth fixed in a showy pout.

Brady leaned both his hands on the wood by her ears. "You give the appearance of being a very competent person."

She gave him a look of such unfettered trust that he felt a pang, as if he were misreading it or unworthy of it.

"I'm not," she said. "I'm not."

He kissed her, brushing her teeth with his tongue.

"Let's see what we can do," he said. He took her hand and led the way back to the courtyard. He approached the servants' cottage. Now the determined self-assurance was in his stride, not hers.

The cottage window was not boarded over. Brady cupped his free hand and peered in. There was a chaos of furniture which seemed to have been brought in from some porch, wicker chairs, a chaise longue upended with its green cushion showing stains. It looked like an attic.

The door was locked, but flimsily so. It rattled when he shook it. Colman dropped Madeline's hand and stepped back. He threw his shoulder against the door, bursting it open.

Light sliced into the room like a butcher's knife. The stale air, thick and wet, made Brady aware of the dried taste buds in his nostrils. He listened for the sounds of rats scurrying. There were none. The only movement was of the dust particles that slid into the room on the blade of sunlight.

"It's a bit damp," he said.

"I can smell my youth." Madeline was standing next to him, pressing his arm.

Brady ignored her pressure and stepped out of the light. He stumbled against a large basket, pushed it aside and began moving chairs from their pile. He cleared an aisle and crossed to a door. He opened it and stood still for a moment, waiting for his eyes to adjust to the dark.

He was in his own cottage on the farm, listening to Nellie. "I thought you were dying."

"I am, darling. So are you. But another time. Not now."

Slowly what should have been Nellie's face turned itself to him, a room blank and bitter around a single sagging bed.

"We cannot do this, Madeline," he said. The sight of the miserable, dirty room unleashed an unexpected reluctance in him. This was not a woman with whom to satisfy an itch of the flesh. He had a clear instinct that to go a step with her would be to go a long way. He was accustomed to going his distances alone.

She blocked his way. "We must do it. I want you terribly." She put her arms around him and kissed him, forcing her tongue into his mouth, pressing herself against him until she could feel his erection.

He pulled away from her. "When I close my eyes I see this ending badly between us."

"Don't close your eyes," she ordered.

What he saw when he closed his eyes was the fire in which Nell died. He hadn't felt grief for her in years. Why was he feeling it now? He wanted to tell Madeline, but the only way he could think of doing that was to ask about her grief. "How old was your son when he died?"

"Nine. I never close my eyes."

"You're lying. Your eyes are closed now." Why did he say that? She was looking at him sternly. "It is wrong," he said, "our being here."

"Christ," she said and turned away from him.

"It would come to nothing," he insisted.

She shrugged, showing her weariness.

"You, Madeline, are the one who said we are not children. That's not your youth you smell. It's bat shit."

"The bats have their business. I have mine. You're vulgar."

Brady accepted her contempt and used it on himself. He had been avoiding this woman's overtures for years, as if he were some schoolboy. He admitted it; there was something in her that frightened him. Or something in himself that she drew out. He could hardly breathe.

She was standing with her back to him. He was aware that her shoulders were moving, and he guessed she was weeping, which surprised him. Perhaps she was like him after all. Perhaps their coming together had loosed inextricably a flow of her sadness too. He lifted his hand and touched her neck. The feel of her flesh stung him. He found the roots of her hair above the collar of her trench coat and traced them down behind her ear and onto her shoulder. He pressed her shoulder and pulled her toward him.

Madeline turned slowly. The movement he had seen and assumed to be weeping had not been that. She was dry-eyed when she faced him and she looked at him without shyness. She had been opening her clothes, untying the belt of her trench coat and undoing its buttons and unfastening the ties of her dress, a blue satin chemise, which hung open, showing her completely from her throat down. With a graceful quick motion she shrugged her clothing off, all but her bra and white silk underpants. She stepped toward Colman, put one arm around him, and kissed his cheeks and his throat in a flurry. At the same time with her other hand she was reaching down to his erection and pressing it through his trousers.

Brady thought he would ejaculate before he got his clothes off. He had never had a woman approach him so wantonly. She was rubbing his penis through his trousers even while undoing his fly, and then she had it out and was stroking it rapidly. He had to push her hand away to get his trousers off. She unsnapped her bra and offered him her breasts, which were large and taut. Her nipples were erect, and he bent to touch one with his tongue. Her flesh, to him, was like warm milk.

He let his hand glide down her body and into her panties. She moaned more loudly than before and began to move her hips against him. He turned her toward the bed. He said, "This bed was made for one."

"Wonderful," she said, lying down and taking him on top of her. She cupped his penis with both her hands and urged it into her. With a cry he began his motion. With her legs and arms she clamped him to her and then saved him for a time, despite himself, from the ache of his sterile worship.

⚜ 3 ⚜

"Good evening, ladies and gentlemen, this is Lowell Thomas. General Sir Arthur Jamison, Commander of the British Expeditionary Force, announced today the withdrawal of the last units of his army from the city of Rouen, leaving behind a panicked population, a scattered and disorganized French force, and an apparently unimpeded Nazi armored wedge, which by this hour, presumably, has taken control . . ."

"Turn it off," Brady said.

"I always listen to . . ." Madeline stopped to hear what Thomas was saying.

"Jamison denied that his army was in final retreat to the sea, but it seems clear to observers that the battle for France, ladies and gentlemen, is nearly over. Soon begins the battle for England."

"Please, Madeline."

"Colman, we must hear this."

"Alf M. Landon, former governor of Kansas and nineteen thirty-six GOP presidential candidate, replied to the President's recent fireside chat and called . . ."

She turned the radio off and slid back up to the head of the large canopied bed and fitted her naked body against the back of Brady's the way spoons slip together in their drawer. They were in her bedroom in the house at Pride's Crossing. Their affair was less than two months old. It was the last week of May. Though Lowell Thomas's evening news program meant it was seven o'clock, the day was still bright outside and the light in the bedroom was gold and sharp, streaming in through a haze of lace curtains.

"I should be going," Colman said quietly. He was facing away from her, curled inside her form in a snugness of safety, as if he had crawled into a white cave. Retreat. He did not want to think about the fleeing British soldiers, but he did.

"No. Stay. We never spend the night."

"I hate sneaking past your servants in the morning."

"They know, anyway. They could care less. Thornton mistreats them horribly."

"I doubt that. I'm sure he's perfectly fair."

"Perfectly."

"And if he returned to pluck me from the fire of your embrace, what then?"

"You know he's in Washington. He can't leave now."

"Of course not. England would follow France before the tide but for Thornton Thomson's finger in the Foggy Bottom dike. Which finger does he use?"

"It's hardly funny, what's happening."

"Oh? Do I seem amused?"

"You seem indifferent."

"I am."

"I don't like that in you."

Brady stiffened and she felt it. He did not reply to her. He clutched inwardly as though a bone had broken in the body they made together. He was always on the alert for signs of her condescension. Finally he ventured a hand back beyond his own hip to hers, to stroke the ingenious curve without seeing it.

"I thought we were friends," she said.

"I'm sure we are. I just can't stand you."

She found the blatant irony of his statement endearing. "May one ask why?"

Brady did not reply. The opposite was the case, and that was as obvious to her as it was to him. Since he had been seeing her, his life had changed. It was as if everything that had gone before had been a preparation for Madeline Thomson. Her presence cheered him. When he was not with her he could close his eyes and clearly see a woman's face again. Hers.

But still, that fear that had clutched at him in the servants' cottage their first day in Gloucester had not evaporated. Brady was a man who learned his lessons. The future would be like the past. All that had gone before, weighed in the scales of his pain, seemed to Brady a preparation for worse pain yet. He did not want it. He did not want her.

"Madeline," he said softly, not turning toward her, "I should go."

She studied him in the half-light, feeling the power of his sadness. She had the sense that she made him continually unhappy. He was touching the sharp edge of his upper teeth to his lip; she watched the red flesh there carefully, expecting blood. Somewhere among the dark aisles of their feelings for each other they kept getting lost.

"Colman, may I say something?" Her voice was just above a whisper.

He did not move. His body was dark against the window. His body was her dark source, immobile, huge. He seemed to her the strongest man she had ever known. That she could sense his fear and his weakness only made her think him the stronger. No other man had ever shown her enough of himself that she could think of him as someone like her, as someone who might not hurt her even if she, for once, made it possible for him to do so.

She watched his face muscles for a sign of effort. None. She watched his fingers not twitching. There was only the soft rising and falling of his form, which was bent over two folds of flesh at his stomach.

"Colman, I love you."

She waited for him to acknowledge what she had said. She'd been wanting to say it to him for weeks. She knew what a feeble expression it was, and how dangerous. They were the words that had jinxed her marriage and every subsequent affair.

Brady bent his face down to his fingers. Her words hung in the half-darkness between them. He was trying to assess his reaction. It occurred to him that she was deliberately introducing the one aspect their relationship could not sustain, trying to destroy it. But that was farfetched and he knew it. His trouble with her words was that they'd come so easily to her, as if she said them to every man who scratched her surface. He saw suddenly how she differed from him. For her the profession of love was a means toward it; for him it was an expression of what had already been established. He had not said those words to any woman since Nellie. He was not going to say them now. He felt cornered and unsure. He cursed himself for his silence and for the hopelessness it displayed. He never expected to use those words again.

Madeline felt her anger welling up. He was not going to acknowledge what she'd said. He was not going to reply. He was going, sensible bastard that he was, to gather up his clothes, dress, and go straight the hell away. Who cares?

She rolled away from him to her own edge of the bed. Still he did not move or look at her. She reached across the two-foot gap to the lowboy that held a lamp and a crystal decanter half-empty of Scotch whisky and two tumblers. With one hand she covered her breasts, hating the way they hung udder-like when she arched forward, and with the other she poured a drink. The noise of glass on glass betrayed her trembling. She tried to control the shaking of her hand; only people with alcoholic tendencies staccato the bottle off the glass while pouring. One thing for certain, she was not an alcoholic.

Colman turned to face her. "A thousand years ago," he said, "when I was a lonely kiddo living in a tiny space with a huge crowd, I'd go to the top of a hill and lie down if it was summer and now summer's all I remember. And I would lie there with the clover under me, a million leaves of clover, and the stars over me too many to count, and I would say to God, why is it with all this clover and with all these stars and the abundance of the earth, I have no ma?"

Madeline gulped her whisky.

"Do you know what God said to me?"

She shook her head.

"He said, 'No reason.' " Brady paused. " 'No reason.' "

"That's the only answer there is, Colman, for anything."

"No, love. It's the *best* answer. 'No reason.' "

"When did your mother die?"

"One night when the supper dishes were done, but before the sun had gone all the way down. I was very young."

"Were you nine?"

"No. Why?"

"No reason." Madeline tried to imagine him a boy, dying. She could not. She looked at him hard. He was telling her how alone he felt. She was thinking that if only she had died, like Colman's mother, then her son would have grown up to be like him. He was as alone as she was and it was not killing him. Why was it killing her? "Why won't you say you love me?"

"Why would you feel better if I did?"

Because, she thought, *then you would be like all those others and I could stop worrying that this was different.* She carried in her mind, like snapshots, images of those moments when she'd professed her love to men and they'd wiggled their feeble echoes back at her. "I love you too, darling," they'd say so easily, and then everything would be safe again because she had said it first. She could get her men to do anything, and she could leave them when she chose. But Colman would not say it, and that was terrifying to her. She had to defend herself, not from him, from her fear. "Do you think," she asked seriously, "that you are capable of love?"

Brady did not hesitate. "I love my son."

"Why? Because you can boast about him? That isn't love. It's blood cells."

That stung Brady, not that it was true, but that it was not precisely false. "It's like your kind, Madeline, to equate the object of loving with the object of boasting. The two activities have nothing to do with each other."

"What the hell do you mean by 'my kind'? I resent you." She poured more Scotch into her glass.

"You've a quake in your hand," he said.

"And you've a sneer in your eye."

"No, I don't. Anyway, if I did you couldn't see it." The room was much darker, and the canopy of the four-poster reduced Madeline and Colman to shadowy forms.

"Do you want a drink?" she asked.

"No."

"Bastard."

"Why 'bastard'?"

"For what you're thinking."

"What am I thinking?"

"That I'm a drunk."

"Well, you are."

"I guess I am." She reached over to the lowboy to put her glass down. "Anyway, I have to go to the bathroom."

She slid out of bed, taking a blanket with her, covering herself. Brady was always struck by her shyness outside of bed. Lying with him she could flaunt her nakedness, use it, display it, sell it to him for his glances. But standing, walking around the room, her nakedness mortified her. Though to Brady the sight of her at a distance, leaning over to pick up a dress or sliding a garter up her leg, was exceedingly pleasurable. His mistake was in thinking that her body was as new to her as it was to him. She thought the body of a woman her age had to be embarrassing.

He could hear her noises from the bathroom. He got out of bed and crossed to the chair onto which he had folded his clothes. He put on his trousers, socks, and shoes. When he straightened from tying the laces she was looking at him from the bathroom doorway. She had the flannel blanket firmly secured in towel-fashion above her bosom. She said nothing. Brady put his shirt on and buttoned it. He wanted to get away from her. He found his usual counterfeit impossible. He had no confidence in his own sophistication. His wit had failed him. She had told him she loved him and he — this was what he was feeling — did not believe her. Instinctively he knew the use she habitually put such sentiments to. She was laying traps for him. But he had made his first reputation in laying them for others. "A connoisseur of ambush," Michael Collins had called him once. Brady had the thought that he was afraid of this woman as he once had been of Purcival. A strange thought; he put it away. He stood with his tie stretched around his neck, an end in either hand, but frozen, watching her.

Madeline crossed to the closet and withdrew a red velour robe and, letting the blanket fall, put it on while showing Brady only her back. When she turned around she had knotted the belt at the waist. His eyes went instantly to the sculpted space between her breasts, which he never noticed unless she was clothed. She went to the radio and snapped it on, then got her glass and sat on the edge of the bed with her back to him.

He twirled the necktie around itself and tied his knot.

The static cracked out of the speaker and there was music.

Brady put his suit coat on and stood there, wishing she would look at him. He was feeling suddenly quite devastated because it seemed there was nothing for him to say or do but leave, and if he left then, like that, the end had come upon them unjustly. It was too soon and there was no reason for it to happen like that. No reason. *By God,* Brady thought, *for once that's not enough! When this ends, there will be a reason! A Damn good reason!*

"Will you say goodnight?" he asked softly.

She turned on the bed and was about to speak when the music on the radio was interrupted and a solemnly detached announcer said, *"Ladies and gentlemen, this bulletin from the front in Europe: Belgium has unconditionally surrendered to Germany, and the War Office in London has issued an urgent call to all citizens of Great Britain who own seaworthy craft to assist in the desperate, heroic evacuation of the entire British Expeditionary Force from the beaches of a small French village known as Dunkerque."* The announcer said details would follow, and then the music resumed.

Colman was staring at Madeline. She drained her glass. "Poor bastards," he said. It was his first act of sympathy for British soldiers in years.

"Yes," Madeline said, "aren't we?"

Brady left.

He thought about her for days, how she'd slipped away from him into her dark mood, how she'd retreated into what she was drinking, how she brought him face to face with his own pain. Perhaps he should not call her again, he thought. It would come surely to disaster. But still her image filled his mind when he should have been thinking of other things. She attracted him powerfully.

On the first Saturday in June he was at home at Prescott Street working in his room, going over materials having to do with the series of investments he expected to make with the most recent large sum Anselmo had sent him. He had to plan such transactions carefully to disguise the source of the money and the amount of it. He did the work at his house, where he could be certain of his privacy and freedom from interruption.

But he was interrupted that day nevertheless. Maeve came to his door and knocked timidly. She knew better than to disturb him.

"What is it?" he asked from his chair.

"You've a visitor, Colman. I told her you were busy."

Colman knew immediately that it was she. He got up, went to the door and opened it. "A visitor?"

Maeve stared at him. She let her question show. "Yes. Mrs. Thomson, the lady from fight-night." What was her brother doing receiving visits from a married woman?

"Thanks, dearie," Colman said, slipping by her. It did not occur to him to go to his mirror or to take off his old sweater. It did not occur to him to offer his sister an explanation, though her demeanor made it clear she wanted one. He took the stairs two at a time, boyishly. Madeline's here, he thought. Nothing else registered.

He found her in the living room. She was standing in the bay window and, dressed in white slacks and surrounded by sunlight, she was more beautiful than he had ever seen her. He walked directly to her and, without speaking, took her in his arms and kissed her. All of his reluctance, his worry, his nervousness about her evaporated. He wanted her. He wanted her in every way he could have her.

She responded with a like passion, playing his kiss, prolonging it, holding him at the neck with her arms fast, as if she had let him go for the last time. How strange it was for both of them.

When they parted they looked at each other until Madeline's eyes flicked toward the living room entrance. Colman was immediately uneasy. He did not want Maeve to see him holding Madeline. As far as his sister and their kids were concerned, Colman was a bull spinster, a celibate, a man without women.

"Perhaps I shouldn't have come," Madeline said, but she was teasing him for his embarrassment.

Colman looked toward the door, only to see a flash of blue as Maeve hurried away. He turned back to Madeline and tried to stifle the awkwardness he felt. "I'm glad you came. I've thought of nothing but you since I left."

"Oh, good," she smiled. "Then you have a lot to say."

"Practically nothing. I'm over my head. I admit it."

Madeline was moved by that. She lowered her face, but he, taking her chin in the crook of his forefinger, raised it again. "I look terrible," she said. "Don't look at me so closely."

"You look wonderful."

"I didn't sleep for days. I had a little binge. That's not mascara *under* my eyes."

Colman wondered why she said things like that to him. Did she want him to think of her that way? He wouldn't.

"How would you like some tea?" he asked.

"I'd rather a drink."

"Tea, darling. We'll have a drink later."

Colman led Madeline to the kitchen. Maeve was fiddling with towels at their rack. "Maeve," he said, "you remember Mrs. Thomson, don't you?" Colman gestured. Neither woman spoke. Colman got the drift of Maeve's disapproval immediately. Her face was a mask of it. Madeline Thomson was a married woman. If the laws of God meant so little, why had Maeve slept alone all these years? There was nothing subtle about her resentment. Brady, to his own surprise, understood and did not react to her rudeness angrily. This was not the time or place for tea. "We'll be going out, Maeve," he said.

Maeve nodded but wouldn't look at them.

Colman caught Madeline's eyes, their apology. She felt she shouldn't have come. He took her hand and, stopping at the closet for his jacket, led her out of the house.

They took Madeline's car, a sporty yellow convertible, a new one. Colman drove. "Sorry," he said. "The Irish have no manners." He said it whimsically, but Maeve's response had depressed him.

Madeline laughed. "Don't complain. My people have nothing but."

Colman looked at her. The wind was stirring her hair and she was smiling at him. The hell with Maeve. He felt quite wonderful to be with Madeline again. He slid the car into the traffic on Commonwealth Avenue, heading downtown. "What shall we do?" he asked.

"Do you know the way to Marblehead? I want to take you for a sail."

Ordinarily that would have been the last thing Brady wanted to do, but he understood immediately why Madeline's invitation was extraordinary. Since the death of her son she had not walked by the sea, except with him. Now she was ready to sail upon it. Good for her! Colman was struck by her cockiness, though he knew it for the study it was, and, after the embarrassment of Maeve's showering disapproval, he wanted to indulge it. He followed Madeline's directions to Marblehead and an hour later they were standing at the yacht club slip waiting for the launch to take them out to the Thomson mooring.

"I don't know much about boats," Colman said.

"That's OK." Madeline slid her arm around his waist. "You'll learn about the boat while it learns about you. I'm an expert. Or, at least, I used to be."

"Whatever you say, Captain. Just give the orders."

The gray launch pulled up, driven by a college kid. "She's all rigged, Mrs. Thomson. Just haul away and you're off."

"Thanks, Tommy," Madeline said, hopping aboard. Colman followed her, feeling awkward in his bare feet and rolled trousers. He never had the right damn clothes with this woman. The launch slid slowly through the harbor, threading by hundreds of sailing boats. The breeze was light. Apparently most skippers had decided not to bother. The motor boat drew up to a sleek, narrow-hulled thirty-two-footer. Colman was satisfied to see that it was a larger boat than some of the fragile-looking ones they'd passed. There was a cabin under the mast. But then he wondered if the boat was too big for Madeline to handle alone. He felt an apprehension that embarrassed him and that he stifled. The wind was so gentle. What could happen?

The boy pulled the launch alongside from astern. The words *Desperate Lark* were stenciled in script on the stern. The boat had gleaming brass fittings and white trim around weathered teak. It was a beautiful thing. The mainsail draped elegantly from the boom. The jib was gathered on the forward deck. The lines were coiled. The shine and order of it all were reassuring to Brady. The way the lad handled the launch was, too.

Madeline did not wait for anyone's hand. She hopped aboard the boat even before the kid had stopped his slide along it. Colman followed her, awkwardly.

"We may need a tow, dear," she said to the boy.

"I'll keep an eye out, Mrs. Thomson. But you better watch things, too. They say there's a storm later. I would stay in the inner harbor."

"What, with this wind? We'll be lucky to make the breakwater." She waved and then suddenly, effortlessly, the launch glided away, the boy waving back.

Madeline took her place at the tiller. Colman did what she told him to do. He pulled up the big sail, then the small one. Then he untangled the yarn that dangled from the left guy-wire. He fastened the line that controlled the jib to its hook on the deck. Then he went forward and cast off. Throughout these procedures Madeline was calmly pointing and instructing and using but translating a language in which familiar words were used strangely: *main, sheet, cleat, port, tell-tale, stay.* Other words — *jib, luff, starboard, halyard, gunnel* — were altogether unfamiliar to him. Brady had never been in a sailboat before, but he performed his functions smoothly and efficiently. Madeline, for her part, steered them clear of the yacht club moorings, he thought, superbly. Though the wind remained very light, the boat moved at a handsome clip, which amazed Colman. He decided he was going to like it.

Once out in open water, Madeline fastened the mainsheet to the jam cleat at her feet. "Ordinarily," she said, "we don't do this. We should keep the line free at all times to let the sail out fast in case we have to. But, what the hell?" She smiled at him. "With this wind we can risk it. I want to take my clothes off. Here, take over."

Colman took the tiller from her and began to stare at the compass as she instructed, trying to helm the arrow at a constant 210°. Madeline shoved the cabin hatch back, opened the low doors, then stooped down into the cramped dark space. She stood in the shadow with her back slightly to Colman and began to unbutton her shirt. He watched her undress. But for her tennis shoes, she took everything off. The sight of her nude back loosed his desire and he savored it. He wanted to see her from the front.

"You're too modest," he said. Was she really? No one else could see her. The nearest boats were a quarter of a mile away. He knew it wasn't shyness or prudery. It was her foolish fear of an aging body. "You're too beautiful," he added. She smiled at him over her shoulder and then slipped a red and white striped shift over her head. It was made of terry cloth and covered her to just above her knees. She turned toward him then and said, "Now I'm modest." But he was thinking about her lack of underwear. He imagined her breasts, the patch of hair at her vagina.

"You're luffing," she cried, pointing at the sail, which was flapping away suddenly. He had lost the angle and was steering at 240°. "Pull it in toward you and get it back to two hundred ten degrees," she ordered. He did and the sails filled again. "Do you want to change?" she asked. "There are shorts down there that should fit you, and some shoes." She took the tiller.

"Good idea," he said. He was anxious to get out of his wool pants and linen shirt. "I'll put on the shorts."

"Put on the shoes too, sweetie. If the deck got wet you'd slip all over in bare feet."

Brady didn't see how the deck would get wet. The breeze was light and the boat was riding at an even keel. But that new authority was still in her voice. He put on the shoes as well as the shorts. Both were a bit small on him, and he was glad for the evidence that he was bigger than her husband.

They sailed on for an hour, tacking irregularly. Madeline explained the principle of the air foil that made it possible to sail upwind, and she instructed him in the basic procedures of the sport. Colman thought it all fairly obvious, but he admired her expertise and took a surprising delight at being out of his own element and utterly in hers.

About midafternoon the sea turned flat as the wind died completely. The *Desperate Lark* stopped moving. Its wake disappeared. The sails bounced futilely in the broad even rollers that the waves became.

"What now?" Colman asked.

"Now a drink." Madeline left the tiller — it was impotent anyway — and disappeared into the cabin. When she came out she was carrying a fifth of Cutty Sark and two glasses. She poured them each some. They cheered each other, clinked glasses, and sipped. Madeline stared at him in a way that made him uncomfortable. He turned and stared at the shore.

"How far would you say? About two miles? How will we ever get in?" Colman allowed a faint concern to show itself in his voice. The kid had said not too far, perhaps a storm. Why would Madeline disregard such a warning?

"The wind takes care of its own, sweetheart."

"Will the boat come for us?"

"No. We're too far out. But he'll alert the Coast Guard if we aren't back by dusk." Madeline smiled and drank. Colman tried to take confidence from her but couldn't. He was irritated suddenly by her cavalier manner. She was being irresponsible, he was sure. He did not like being in a boat so far from land with no way to make it move. "The wind will come up," she said. "This is just the midafternoon lull. It often happens this time of year. Especially if there's weather coming."

Madeline stared into the water just off the boat and did not speak again. She seemed calm, if preoccupied. He put aside his worry. It was irrational, he decided, born of his problem, not hers. He watched her. He guessed she was thinking of her son. He secured his drink between cushions and crossed to her carefully, and sat with his hand on her thigh. "You know the sea so well," he said. She nodded. The sea was her old friend and her old enemy. "I'm glad you asked me to do this with you, darling," he said. "Maybe you can master it now, your awful grief."

Madeline stared at him unfathomably. It seemed that her eyes made terrible confessions: my legs are made of straw! My breasts are the pits of discarded fruit! My womb is made of plaster!

"Come here," he whispered, and she turned to him. "Come here," he said again, and she put her drink down between the gunnel and a jib winch and went into his arms. They kissed passionately. Her way of putting her tongue into his mouth excited him immeasurably. He held her away enough to lift the terry smock over her head. She undid his shorts while he knocked cushions from the benches onto the floorboards. She went down under him, urging his body onto her, but in such a way that she could take his penis into her mouth. He felt what seemed the most acute pleasure of his life. It was the combination of the softly rocking sea and the benign sun and the rhythmic flapping of the sails overhead and the exquisite pressure of her mouth — all excruciating and new. He did not want to come in her that way. When he felt the tension peaking he pulled away and down and entered her vagina, which was moist and ready for him.

She exhausted him, repeating his name, demanding that he pour himself into her as if she were the ocean. He realized that she was weeping. She wept throughout their lovemaking, wailing so grotesquely at one point that Brady was unaccountably filled with the urge to tear her clothes off and force himself on her. But of course she was already naked and they were already coupled. It was his strange fantasy at their violent climax.

She did not stop weeping.

When he cupped her face with his hand to make her look at him, her eyes were accusing and bitter. *What are you doing?* they seemed to ask. *Leave me alone! Can't you see I'm dying?* She rolled from under him, crushing herself against the bench. She wept on, crazily.

What was the weight under which Brady found himself flattened then, if not of her self-loathing? He reminded himself that she could not have, as yet, drunk too much. He touched the curve of her shoulder, but she ignored his finger.

He did not mind her weeping, really. He wanted her to turn toward him with it, to let him receive her tears. All his life had been a preparation for that. He was not afraid of her pain. He had his own. He was ready to carry someone else's who would carry his. Her son was dead. Her marriage was meaningless. Her family, her name, her position were as nothing to her. Such misery was not possible to the solitary because, alone, it would kill them. Brady knew about that. If he enabled her to pour it out and be rid of it, he would gladly lie with her even as she rolled away from him. He was not going to flee just because her loneliness faced him with his own. He was not going to submit to the panic that rolled through him when he acknowledged the idea that this woman not only disliked herself and drank too much but seemed at times to be mad.

"Darling, stop it."

"Tell me you love me," she commanded through her tears. She had to make this man like the others. "Tell me you love me."

He said nothing.

She crushed her hands against her face.

He raised himself to look over her shoulder. She was gnawing the knucklebone of her forefinger. It was bleeding. A trickle of blood ran down her hand to the floor of the cockpit. Colman covered the hand with his, pulling it from her mouth. But she struck like a viper, snaring his thumb in her teeth and biting to the bone, an iron clamp.

The pain was excruciating.

"Don't!" He yelled despite himself.

But she would not release him. He could not stand the pain. He felt her teeth wedging into the joint, grinding at the marrow.

"My God!" he screamed. "Aiiiii!"

She *was* mad. She was biting his thumb in two; he could feel it splitting.

He drew his legs up to take his weight off his left arm. He raised his left hand over her head and, not clenching his fist, smashed down on the side of her face.

Her jaw popped open with the blow, and Brady clutched his thumb to his chest. "Jesus Christ, woman!"

Madeline threw her arms around his neck and pulled herself up. "Darling, darling, I'm sorry," she said; "I'm sorry."

He suffered her embrace. What the hell did she expect from him now? The woman had a viciousness he had not suspected.

"I *am* sorry." She released his neck. She had stopped weeping.

Brady nursed his thumb.

Madeline refused to look at it.

"I . . ." She wanted the exact word. "became . . . emotional."

Brady ignored her.

"I didn't intend to do that." She paused, adjusted her weight over her legs. "Are you going to answer me?"

"Sorry," he replied, "I didn't know I was being asked something."

"Will you forgive me?"

"That isn't the main question. Will I lose my thumb?" He smiled at her, a thin, restrained smile.

"Don't be merciless. Your thumb will be all right."

"Have you ever managed to chew one through entirely?"

"No."

"Well, you're not merciless, are you? Cheers." He put his thumb to his lips as if it were a drink.

"Yes. Cheers." She reached past him to the gunnel for her Scotch. She drank, then covered her lap with the striped shift and crossed her arms over her breasts. She was sheepish and silent.

"Madeline, once you mentioned your analyst to me, but you never explained."

"That I'm loony?" She sipped her drink, less compulsively than before, as if the hysteria had left her chastened, exorcised.

"Are you?" Brady asked the question calmly, without accusation, without punishment.

"I have been a patient at a picturesque clinic in Stockbridge. Austen Riggs's. You may have heard of him."

"No."

"He's a swell fellow, a famous sailor. He owns the fastest sloop in New Bedford."

"How charming, the qualifications you cite."

"I was there twice. Once because my son died, and once because I didn't."

"I'm sorry, darling." Brady tried not to show her that he was shocked by her admission.

"Oh, Colman, you mustn't think of me in that way, as pathetic and loony and . . ." — she drained her glass, then studied it before saying, "a drunk."

Brady said nothing.

"Are you going to answer me?"

"What am I being asked?"

"How do you think of me?"

"You do drink too much, you know."

"I know. And I'm an adulteress, and I give my lover rabies, and I cannot convince him that I love him."

He touched her. "You don't have to convince me of anything."

Oh, why wouldn't he say it, she thought? It would be so much easier if he'd say those words, because then she'd know they were not true.

Instead he kissed her. He was trying to quell the uneasiness she stirred in him. This woman, mad, was more alive, he felt, and more sane than he was.

He was surprised to feel his penis asserting itself. It was too soon, wasn't it? She made him feel so young. He moved to kiss her again; he would channel his longing and his fear into this kiss.

But she pulled away from him, urgently away from him. She pivoted on her knees. She had felt an ominous chill sweep over the sea, and was turning to check the horizon. "Good Christ!" she said. There was a black thread across the western sky. A tutored eye could not miss it. A squall was racing out from the land. The water was still calm enough where they were, and the wind, though just picking up, was still off it. But Madeline knew what was heading in on them. She stood, slid the dress over her head and on, and went to the tiller. Brady sensed her mood and copied it. He put on the shorts and tied his shoelaces.

"It's going to blow, darling," Madeline said. "Are you game? We try for the shore on the first wind?"

"What's the alternative?" Brady was staring at the growing black edge. He'd never seen anything like it. The water was kicking up, and he could see the wind dusting the sea and moving toward them fast.

"We could drop sail and ride it. But we don't know how long it'll last. It could carry us out."

Those words frightened Brady. He realized how unfamiliar the sea was to him. He did not want to be out of sight of land. "Let's get in then," he said.

"Right. When the wind hits," Madeline said, "it'll knock us, so hang on. I want you to keep the jib as flat as you can. If it blows too hard, I'll drop the main. Do you remember which halyard? Port, OK? Left, OK? Watch the boom and give us a kiss, love." When Colman leaned to her she pressed his penis through the shorts. He was enormous. "Jesus," she said, and gave him a great smile.

And then it hit, and it did knock them. The boat went a third of the way over and Brady thought they were capsizing. But Madeline let out the line on the main and it slammed open, bringing the boat back to even keel. The wind came from offshore directly behind them and the mainsail was out at a sharp right angle to the boat. The jib swirled chaotically behind it, unable to take wind.

"Get the jib around fast!" she ordered as the boat came about. Brady pulled on the sheet, but there were tangles and he couldn't move the sail. The boat was flying.

"Goddamnit, get it over!" she cried.

But Brady couldn't. The wind kept ripping at the jib and Madeline was having trouble holding course. Brady saw that the lines were snagged on a brass hook on the front of the mast. He crossed to undo the tangle, when a wholly new puff much more powerful than the first, hit the boat. The mainsail was hurled back into the boat with a clap like an explosion, which was Brady's warning. He ducked just as the boom crashed over him, missing his head by inches. It would have killed him. The boat went over again, and this time the end of the boom almost went into the water. Brady hurled himself up to the starboard gunnel and desperately grabbed the ledge of wood.

Madeline was hauling in the mainsheet, ignoring the jib, which was flapping free then. She had wedged herself on the lip of the stern and pressed with her left foot against the port deck. Her right foot was curled around the tiller so that both her hands could work the line. She had to get the main in. She let off a bit, and that brought the boat up. Colman saw what she was trying to do, and he joined her to haul in the main.

"Try that jib again!" she hollered. Rain was pelting them and she wasn't sure her voice had carried, but he moved forward. Since she was beating upwind, the jib line freed itself with the flapping, and he was able to bring the sheet in and around the cleat. He wrapped it around his hands and leaned away as she'd told him to do. It had been so much easier coming out. It had seemed so much safer.

Madeline was eyeing the shore, picking her spot. She could not continue on the starboard tack, though the boat rode well that way, because that would carry them parallel to shore and never in. She had to come about onto a port tack. She picked her spot on the land and made for it, pulling the tiller in and hollering "Hold on!" The boat heeled and the ocean began to wash the deck. This time it went nearly halfway over, and Colman felt the cold water rushing over his feet. He looked up at Madeline, but she was staring at the shore, and the set of her face was so stony that it frightened him further. There was something unfamiliar and eerie in her that manifested itself then. Was it that she was going to die? The thought grabbed him just as a huge wave crashed over the boat, startling him. He was terrified. He fixed his eyes upon her. This was madness. Was she committing suicide? The boat was going down, he was sure. The sail, close-hauled, was making its thunder, the gale snapped along its batten edge. How could she hold it? The measly jib was cutting Brady's hand and he stared at hers, looking for blood.

"Drop it!" he screamed. "Drop it! Let's ride it out!"

But she ignored him. She *was* mad. She was going to succeed this time and she would kill him with her. "Madeline, drop it! Damn it to hell, drop it!"

It was as if he was not there. She was in the boat alone. All of her energy went into three fierce efforts: her eye upon its point on shore; her fists holding taut the main; her right leg keeping the tiller steady. Madeline was not afraid. She was riding the craft on the far edge of its limit. They had to make shore. Ten minutes, with that wind, and they would. Then hell was really going to break. She could feel it. But could she hold for ten minutes?

Brady was furious and terrified. Why wouldn't she look at him? He thought of releasing his line and letting the jib fly, but he didn't know what that would do. It could make things worse. He stared at her, trying to read her. Was it madness? Was there a glee in her flirtation with this disaster? Was she going to take them down? The water was splashing into the cockpit, waves of it. Brady was sure that in seconds he would be up to his neck. He wanted to reach for a cushion, something that would float, but the effort to hold the line and remain wedged against the side of the boat had him paralyzed. He looked away from Madeline and toward the front of the boat in time to take a wave full in the face. When the water cleared, he was shocked to see, dead ahead and very close, land; land! Not two hundred yards away, and not just land, but the point of the harbor behind which they would be safe. He turned to look at Madeline, to see her again. Had he misread her? Was that madness? Or was it only the metal of her will? She had willed them in. She had sailed them along the thin edge, exactly to do what she did then.

She began letting off the main as the boat flashed by the light, and immediately the sea eased. Without being told, Brady whipped across the cockpit and began letting off the jib. When he looked at Madeline, there was nothing of the woman who had wept crazily or who had bitten him insanely or who drank too much or who teased him with her glib intimacy.

Brady thought, strangely, inappropriately, how impossible it was to speak to God. He'd thought he was going to drown, but he had uttered no prayers, no sorrows. He had not sought pardon. Kneeling down or dying, there were no words. Now, before this woman who was grave and rigid as any saint in glass, he felt something he'd never felt before. He felt balked and immobile. He was unable to speak to her. Sitting there, aching at his ropes, was like kneeling for a long time. He saw love in its dark hole and recognized it. His for her.

EVEN IF ONE NURTURED the illusion that things were as they had been in the world, in the nation, in one's own life, one could not sustain it past the moment of crossing the threshold of a massive urban railway station. It was in the railway stations of the United States that the war was most visible to Americans — every third man was in uniform — and most felt: he was saying goodbye to someone.

It was July of 1942, a Friday afternoon. The noises in South Station in Boston filled the vast pseudo-Roman cavern the way confetti fills the air over a parade of heroes. Travelers and welcomers rushed out of their compartments and porticoes at each other, weeping, laughing, squealing like bats released from caves. One woman with a sagging midriff and thick thighs was precariously standing on a girdled suitcase trying to see a train just sliding into its stall. A little boy, his eyes bone-white and dry, was staring up at a man and a woman who seemed intent on eating each other. The boy's eyes did not turn or close. People jumped from trains before they stopped moving; their relatives caught them. Engineers looked down from their perches, not bored, not wondering what the shrieking was about. A fat man wearing a butcher's apron ran in from the street. No one seemed to think him strange. Young boys in brown uniforms wore their dreams of wounds like ribbons, stood holding their inert duffle bags as if they were corpses, and kept repeating the same gesture to their mothers and fathers and girlfriends; raising their wrists to see what time it was. Later they would rest their cheeks against the glass of train windows, wanting nothing but a kind word from the sergeant.

Colman Brady, looking trim and well tailored in a tan cord suit, stood beneath the arch of the entrance foyer that led into the station from Summer Street. He had wheeled his way deftly from the curb where he'd left the taxi, through the crowd that was rushing out the doors. He had been worried that he would miss his train. But now he was stopped, standing still, taking in the scene as if he weren't part of it. It was the sight of all the soldiers that struck him. The soldiers, invariably, were tall and had short brown hair and had great smiles even while saying farewell to the lovelies who clutched at their own hurt more than at their men. The soldiers, invariably, all looked to Colman Brady like Collins.

"Don't you talk to me in that tone of voice!" Brady could still hear himself saying it. It had been months before, winter. Pearl Harbor's aftershock still rumbled beneath everything.

"I'm only explaining, Dad," the kid said with patronizing calm, "that I don't share your prejudices."

"My prejudices are irrelevant. They have nothing to do with your quitting school."

They had the argument on the esplanade of the Charles. The wind whipped up the river from the basin of the Back Bay. The boy wore a flimsy cotton jacket, and his lips turned blue with cold. But Colman had no sympathy for him. Such carelessness was typical. The kid led with his chin habitually.

"It's a leave of absence. It's not quitting. All kinds of fellows are joining up."

"Not seniors, I'd venture. Not now. For God's sake, Micko, you'll graduate in five months."

"But they're offering commissions to seniors now. I'd go in as an officer."

"You will in any case."

"But, Dad, the war's on now. They need us *now*."

"The war's been on for years. It'll wait."

"You're indifferent because it's England."

"As I said, that has nothing to do with it. I'm thinking of you."

"No, you're not." Micko was responding to an instinct he had never felt before, yet trusted absolutely, the way the young do.

Colman Brady, responding to an instinct of his own, slapped his son across the face.

He instantly realized that he was badly overreacting. It was the first blow he'd struck against the boy in years. Where was the infuriating truth in what the kid had said? His son's graduation from Harvard College was far from a matter of indifference to Brady. It mattered more to him then — he would never admit this — than the war did.

Collins took the blow. He showed his father a stoic face which promised never to forget. For once anger outweighed the hunger for approval. Collins Brady had garnered honor and respect from his friends and teachers. He had achieved a habit of such excellence that he took the deference of others for granted. It was inevitable that at some point he should require deference from his father.

"You will never do that to me again," he said evenly.

The son was putting his father on notice; not a grand defiance, a simple announcement. From it, two things, as they say in mathematics, would follow: his own freedom and his father's admiration.

"You will never do that to me again," he had said.

Colman drew back his hand. It still stung from the first blow. He held it poised at his shoulder long enough for Collins to think, *Good God!*

Colman swung his open hand more grandly this time and, in landing the second blow, made Collins gag for breath, turning him from a strapping young man who'd won his prizes into a victim under the kitchen table who only waits for lickings. The boy would not so easily defy him again.

Collins completed the year at Harvard, but, owing to the national emergency, the traditional commencement was canceled, and his father felt a petty disappointment. The pomp, the undulating robes, the dignitaries uncelebrated, the passing of his son into something not his, the sight of him — *magna cum laude* — in their midst: he had wanted it more than he was ready to admit. Ironically, Colman Brady had sent his son to Harvard to be like Harvard and, caring nothing for commencement and intensely for his country, his son was.

Exactly a week after the term ended he went off to basic training and then OCS in Virginia, hoping for an assignment with the Seventh Army, which was commanded by a proper New Englander who, though a West Pointer, had through his family and his years at Groton numerous ties to Harvard. His name was George Patton. Phelps Otis was already one of the junior officers on his staff. Collins, whose instinct for status had not failed him yet, hoped to be another. Indeed, the only sense of failure Collins Brady carried with him when he left at last for the army was that of having cruelly disappointed his father by becoming what he wanted him to be.

Colman, standing under the arch of the entranceway, watched the soldiers bustle in and out of the station. He had forgotten momentarily that there was a train to catch. He was looking at a tall draftee on whom the summer khaki was draped inelegantly. Collins, in contrast, had worn it beautifully, even on his first day. The draftee was saying goodbye to his parents, both of whom were weeping. Brady wondered what the father would say to his son. He took a step toward them to eavesdrop, but their intimacy was mute, a matter of stifled groans and sobs. The boy had a terrified look in his eye, like a snagged beetle in a web. He had a baldysour and pimples and was losing the snot of his weeping off his chin and onto his uniform's ribbonless breast, its first decoration. The sight of the boy transfixed Brady momentarily.

But the announcer called a train, and that brought him back. He was late. Brady pressed his way through the station, banging his small leather bag against other people's knees and apologizing. He made his train, just barely.

He read an abandoned front page, the Hartford *Courant*. The news was all war and bake sales. Hitler could use his U-boats against New York. What would America do without the Pacific Fleet? The Hartford Christian Universalist Church needed a steeple. North of Boston a series of artillery outposts were being constructed; Brady read that item with interest, but it told him nothing he didn't know. One of the companies he had acquired had the contract to provide the cement.

He looked out the window. The train was passing slowly by the rear end of the Back Bay. A quick monotony of scene and sound asserted itself; dreary old row houses, the hard clack of iron on iron. Colman's mind returned to the great hall of South Station from which Collins too had taken his farewell nearly two months before.

Maeve, Maureen, Deirdre, and Jack had all come to South Station and, for nearly an hour, they'd swayed around Collins in uniform like petals around a pistil. Jack was rigid with guilt at his cousin's departure, for as a seminarian he was draft-exempt. He dealt with his embarrassment by, on the one hand, extolling the righteousness of the Allied cause, and, on the other, expressing the hope that the war would last long enough — four years, to be precise — for him to be ordained and appointed a military chaplain. Deirdre, by then a nurse at Carney Hospital, pointed out to Jack the macabre and inappropriate character of this hope. She was more shrill and carping than ever. Maureen said very little, never releasing Collins's hand. Maeve kept giving him orders about food and clothing, to which he seemed to pay close attention. Colman said nothing to his son, standing on the edge of the circle, smoking a lot, keeping an eye on the big clock that hung from the fists of the naked angels over the information booth.

What Colman remembered best about his boy was the lack of fear. His certainty had matched his posture.

What Colman remembered best about himself was how he kept thinking, *The things that boy doesn't know!* But what could he have said? Keep your chin on your chest? Protect yourself? Don't jab with your left unless your right is cocked. Goddamn it, don't confuse sport with fighting for your life. And don't confuse fighting for *your* life with fighting for someone else's. And for God's sake, save your best for *your* fight! Listen to me, son. Your father knows something. Here are the rules: if they come at you with a knife, don't move until they do; if with a gun, wait until you can touch it, then you *must* move first. There are no good shots or bad at ten yards. Remember, you are faster acting than reacting. So is your enemy. Give him nine of what he anticipates. The tenth is yours and will win for you. Never trust the general. Always trust the sergeant, to whom you must never lie. To the general you must never tell the entire truth. Do not feel sorry for the men who die. Do not ride in an open car on roads with ridges nearby and no cover. Do not stop if a dray full of bottles has been turned over in the road. Do not listen to your leader. Do not love him.

Brady was stunned by the string of his thoughts, its final knot, Michael Collins, C-in-C, the big fellow in green with the Sam Browne and the Aussie bush hat, dead. Michael Collins whom he, when younger than his own son, had loved and therefore failed. Brady snapped as a sailor snaps a tangled line that length of memory, and he saw himself standing on the road as Purcival's Lancia screeched to a halt in front of him. He remembered the quick movement with which he had pulled the pistol from his tunic and the force with which he'd pressed it against Purcival's cheek and the authority with which he'd said, "Move and you're dead!" Where the hell, he wondered now, had he gotten such nerve?

He remembered how his son froze when they announced his train. "Capital Limited! All aboard for Washington, Richmond, and points en route! All aboard!"

Colman had looked up at the clock that hung from the angels; seven seconds before three minutes to ten in the morning. It had been a glorious spring day in Boston. Inside the unclothed vault of South Station it was always night. It was always cold.

"I guess, Dad," Collins had said, "this is it."

"Yes, son, it is."

"Well." The boy was still cocky and sure. He seemed to have completely eliminated from his consciousness the winter event of his thwarted rebellion and Colman's blows. Colman, on the other hand, when he was with the boy alone, thought of little else.

"There are some things I wanted to say to you, son, but . . ."

"Aunt Maeve covered it all."

"Right."

"But I wanted to say something to you, Dad."

"You did?"

"Yes. I'm glad that . . ." Collins paused, but more for effect than out of awkwardness. Brady thought his poise remarkable, but — and this was stimulated perhaps by his son's uniform — he wouldn't trust it under fire. ". . . that I finished out the year. It feels right having ended one phase before beginning the next."

"Good, son. I knew you'd see it that way."

"I do, Dad. Thanks for *making* me see it." His son's concession had a depressing effect on Brady. It embodied perfectly what had gone wrong between them. The father wanted the son's acquiescence in everything, but when he had it, he resented his son's surrender. Collins, knowing that, was turning his surrender into a farewell gift, a punishment, an act of vengeance.

"There is something, son."

"What?"

"I'll be thinking about you all the time."

"Me too, Dad."

"And I want you to write to me."

"I will. I must go."

"Goodbye, dear," Maeve said, kissing him. The two girls hugged him. Jack shook his hand manfully, a peer in his own uniform, the black clerical suit and tie.

Collins turned back to his father, whose eyes went back and whose mind went back, back until they were fixed on Nellie saying, "I am. You are. But another time. Not now." How he had loved her! How he loved this boy! How he had hoped to spare him all jeopardy!

They embraced each other, not emotionally, and then his son walked confidently away from him, turning back only when Colman called out *"Amico!"* and waved.

Brady looked out the window. The train was passing through Jamaica Plain, picking up speed, blurring the drab scene of the backsides of flaked gray three-deckers. Here and there families were at their supper on their porches. They waved like laundry, not resenting the intrusion of the locomotive whizzing down the track that kept their houses filthy. Brady had no impulse to wave back at them.

Curley lived in J.P., and Brady thought of him. His house, a white false-modesty on the Pond, was a mile from the spot they were passing. Poor Curley. Demolished by Lodge in '36, defeated narrowly for mayor by his own boy Maurice Tobin in '37, creamed for governor by Leverett Saltonstall in '38, defeated for mayor again in '40 by Tobin, this time hugely. The old codger was talking up a run for Congress in '43, but now he was his own cartoon and everyone knew it but him. All things doomed to die touch the heart. Curley had the capacity to believe himself capable of everything but death.

"Tickets, please!" the conductor bellowed from the rear of the car. Brady bought his ticket from him and then asked the way to the dining car. He went back to it.

In the dining car he found a table by himself, but was soon joined by a pair of spinster teachers whom he resented instantly, not so much for their pursed lips, their bunned-up hair, or their clacking nosiness as for their being not much older than himself.

He decided to order the veal, though he knew he'd get the cardboard box they shipped it in, but before the waiter came one of the women said, "I think I'll have the veal." And the other said, "You can't, Marie. It's Friday."

Neither could he, goddamn it.

"The scrod, please," Brady said when the waiter arrived, a lanky black whose subservience was as artfully creased as his white jacket.

"So will I," Marie said, regret in her voice.

"Are you together?" the waiter asked. He seemed to address the silverware, the dishes, not the threesome.

"Oh, no," Marie said, blushing; "I'm sorry."

The waiter finished taking Brady's order, then, flourishing a new and separate check, began the ladies'.

Brady lit a cigarette. In the silence after the waiter's departure he smiled at the women pleasantly, but took no initiative toward conversation. Neither did they. The three waited for, received, and ate their meal in silence. Brady was the first to pay his bill and leave. He smiled at them again as he excused himself. No sooner had he gone than Marie said to her companion, "For a Catholic, wasn't he rude?"

Brady stopped in the parlor car long enough to have a brandy. By the time he returned to his seat it was dark, the cabin lights had been dimmed, and the window was like an ebony mirror. Brady rested his cheek against it and let the sound of the train wheels cracking the tracks lull him. Gradually his mind gave up its focus and he worked a vacuous hypnosis on himself by staring blankly into his own eyes.

Curley. James Michael Curley. Twenty years before he'd cut such a splendid figure, a man in his prime. Brady told himself again it had been an act of wisdom, not foolishness, to throw in with Curley, despite how it ended. Brady knew what his mistake had been; he'd thought himself exempt from Curley's viciousness merely because he knew about it. The knowledge of evil does not protect from it. Brady felt a rush of his old disappointment. The attempt to conquer fortune can be defeated by time and by death, and by your homeland and by your heroes. All Brady had wanted, really, from the outset was a certain place from which to expend what energy he had been given; a place of his own to share with loved ones and improve a bit and hand on to his son. He had begun by assuming that Four Mile Water was that place, given him by his father, who had lived and died the center of an order which made such grants inevitable and perfect. But that world — how fragile it was! — fell apart when one intruder violated it. Purcival withdrew a linchpin, setting off a sequential collapse which left Brady with nothing, not even the feeling of having caused it. He arrived in Boston with the sense that he had been thrown there and an absolute determination to take for himself what the world had refused to give him. Boston was where, having fallen back on his own resources, he discovered how considerable they were, and how dependable. He understood then that what order and hierarchy his world would have, it would get from him. A dreadful and lonely business, but Brady had taken to it and learned that he was not altogether unsuited for it. By God, he had roared through those first years, throwing off the burdens of other men's prescriptions and expectations until he had only one left: Curley's. If Brady had the feeling he had failed himself — and he did — it was because Curley had discarded him before he had Curley. Curley, like Purcival, like De Valera, like Gavin, had hit him by surprise and changed everything. Brady had had an enormous confidence in his ability to assess the layout of his terrain. Yet he had failed exactly in that and repeatedly. He was the connoisseur of ambush who had been ambushed terribly. Once he went to work for Anselmo he knew that he was again in another man's shadow, a guest in an alien place, a permanent stranger, a man without a spot of his own. If that was what was left to Brady he would take it and, by God, make a masterpiece of it, because now he took his meaning from something new. Colman was living to see that what had happened to him did not happen to his son. If Colman had inherited a fragile niche from his father, Collins would have a place to keep and to be kept by, a trustworthy place, a permanent place. Brady's ironic sense of himself was as a man who had not successfully made it from one side of the ocean to the other. He had made his departure but, finally, no arrival. His son had made the crossing, or was making it, and Colman was behind him all the way. It was not the grand purpose a man sets out with, but it was a purpose, and Colman Brady clung to it for his son's sake and therefore for his own. He watched the boy's growing like a hawk, ready to swoop down and save him from his enemies.

"Stockbridge! Stockbridge!" the conductor cried, disturbing the slumber of the entire car. Brady continued to stare into his own eyes while the train slowed. It seemed to him he could just make out figures running through a wood: a boy, a man, a woman. It was all those years ago, the day he'd met Madeline and they'd chased after Micko, thinking him dead. When he'd begun his affair with Madeline two years before, he'd already come to feel like a traveler without a ticket of his own, and that was exactly what had brought them together. They both had felt that way. Circumstances had dropped Colman between continents and left him there. He met her. She was between continents because her son had died in the ocean, and she had lost the purpose of her life before she knew she'd had it.

Brady was just starting to admit the thought that Madeline had changed things for him in a fundamental way. For two years they had regularly enjoyed each other's company, arranging their meetings to keep them private and taking pains to understand each other and be kind to each other. It had started with that as the simple motive, in fact. They were both so weary of defeat and solitude. Kindness was what they wanted, and the delights of sexual pleasure; such rarities, and they had them in abundance.

Madeline had changed and for the better, and that was evident by her presence in Stockbridge again at last. But Brady now saw how he was changed too perhaps. Nothing required that what he and Madeline were doing had to end in defeat. He had assessed this terrain carefully, more carefully than any before it. He was still cautious, for example, in using language that would make him vulnerable to her. He had not yet told her that he loved her. He could not say that until he was prepared to drag out the old dream of a place of his own and ask her to share it with him. He knew that Madeline was offering a new chance to have a life besides his son's, a life of his own again. The thought of it stirred him — how he wanted it! — and frightened him — how afraid he was of yet another failure! But how he loved her and how he longed to tell her!

"Stockbridge, mister," the conductor scolded. "You paid for Stockbridge."

"Yes," Colman said. "Thank you."

He was the only passenger to disembark at Stockbridge.

A tall white-haired stationmaster greeted him — "Evening!" — with the clipped enunciation of a rural Yankee.

Colman nodded at him, then stood beside him to watch the train pull out.

"She's late," the station man said.

"What time is it?"

"Nine-thirty."

Brady nodded again, and, bag in hand, entered the large room that, with its cubbyhole in the corner, comprised the entire railroad station. But the place was a gem of rough stone, sweeping upward in multiangled lofts. A huge fireplace dominated the space. On its hearth was a polished oak plank with the legend, "Welcome to travelers! Speed the departing guest."

The room was deserted. Brady admired the warmth of it despite its emptiness.

"Stanford White," the master said.

"Sorry?"

"Stanford White. Eighteen eighty-two."

"Oh," Brady nodded.

"He designed Madison Square Garden, you know. Then got hisself murdered, they tell me, by his floozie."

"That so?" Brady touched the stone wall. "Granite?"

"Nope. Rough marble. Looks like granite, though. He used to come up here summers."

"Who?"

"White. Usually get lots of folks up here summers. But this war now, seems like everybody stays home. There's no taxi, not at night." The man tugged at his broad white moustache, openly studying Brady.

"Is the town nearby?"

"Down the road, past the feed barn."

"A hotel?"

"Red Lion. Seventeen seventy-three."

"That right?"

"Yup. Get a drink there, too, if you like."

"Where is it in relation to . . ." Brady paused, then kicked himself for pausing. ". . . the clinic?"

"Clinic?" The man stared at him blankly.

"Austen Riggs's clinic."

"You mean the Center. They don't call it a clinic. Doctor Riggs don't allow no one to call it a clinic."

"Where would that be?"

"Across the street."

Brady turned, as if to look.

"From the Red Lion. Across the street, catty-corner. Main Street."

"Thank you," Brady said. He sensed from the way the man was looking at him that he thought he was an arriving patient.

Brady drew himself up and shook off his uneasiness. He straightened his tie, eliminated his disheveled air and bent posture. He stared at the stationmaster until the latter looked away, as if that small triumph would say to him, *No, mister, not me. I'm not mad, you see, at all.*

Brady turned and walked out into the dark road, leaving the railroad to its memories, and the quaint stationhouse to its connotations.

"I KNOW who you are."

"I can't imagine that you do."

"You're her friend. So am I. I'm Ruth Koch. Nice to meet you, Mr. Brady."

"Are you her doctor?"

"You didn't expect a woman?"

"Well, I . . ."

"Or a Jew, either?"

"I was under the impression this is a very . . . how should I say it?"

"Swish?"

"No. WASPish. A very WASPish place."

"It is."

"I might have known. Italian gardeners. Irish maids. Jewish psychiatrists."

"And Cuban tennis instructors."

"He's quite good, isn't he?"

"So is Madeline. Watch her serve."

"She seems very well."

"She is. She's off to an excellent start. Does she know you're here?"

"No."

"May I tell you something, Mr. Brady? You're very good for her. She's taken hold of herself in part because of you."

"How much longer do you think she'll be here?"

"Oh, a while yet. We mustn't rush it. Our guests are here typically a year or more. Madeline was here twice before, but she didn't stay with it. She wasn't ready."

"I know how much she had been wanting to come here. It took her a long time to feel strong enough, I think. She's not seriously . . . ? I don't know how to ask it."

"Ill?" Doctor Koch smiled. "Who isn't? Madeline's illness takes the form of a chemical addiction that's very hard to break. We do some of the best treatment in the country here, Mr. Brady, and I think you'll sense the difference as time goes along. I think she's on the right road now, and, as I said, that's partly due to you."

"She's a fiery woman, doctor. Hard to keep up with."

"She's had her outbursts with you, hasn't she?"

Brady smiled. God, had she, right from the beginning when she'd nearly taken his thumb off.

"What she needed," the doctor continued, "was someone strong enough to teach her that her expressions of her feelings would not be damaging, even if they were negative ones. She had to have a way to get those feelings out instead of turning them against herself in self-destructive behavior. She's in your debt, Mr. Brady."

"Has her husband been here?"

"No."

"Do you expect him?"

"You should discuss that with Madeline. She would want to know you're here."

"I thought I'd let her finish the lesson. I enjoy watching her play."

"I hope you have a pleasant visit."

"Thanks very much."

"I'm glad you're here. Good-bye."

"Good-bye."

Brady watched the woman walk back across the tailored lawn to the sprawling white mansion — the MOB, the Medical Office Building — that was set like a jewel on the slight crest under stately elms. Adjacent to the MOB was a second white mansion, nearly as gracious; the Inn, where the guests resided. The Austen Riggs Center had more the feel of a country club than a hospital.

Madeline was hitting a series of backhands powerfully and deftly. Her white tennis skirt emphasized the tan of her legs, her long slim legs, which Brady regarded as her best, most seductive feature. From the bench on the low rise where he sat she looked good, very good. Her blond pony-tail swatted the air behind her head. She moved around the right rear corner of the red clay with the grace and lithe ease of a dancer. At the point in her swing where the racquet was extended fully away, her right arm stiff and pointed high, the point of maximum follow-through, Brady could just make out the curves of her breasts. She looked fresh and young and very beautiful. Brady thought, sitting there in the soft morning light, he had never seen anyone so beautiful.

Brady would gladly have spent the day watching her.

But the lesson ended, and she left the court with the dark Latin who'd instructed her politely. They shook hands and separated. Madeline draped a sweater over her shoulders, hooked her racquet under her arm, and began walking across the grass on her way to the Inn. She would have to pass within a few feet of his bench. He did not move.

[308]

She saw him. She stopped dozens of yards away. He read her fear, felt it rolling in on him, waves. "Hello, sweet," he said. She heard him and moved toward him slowly.

He stood as she drew near and opened his arms for her, taking her in silently. They held each other. Each was aware of the other's beating heart.

"Hello, sweet."

"Colman Brady," she said, as if the recitation of his name was an achievement. There had been moments when she feared that even so much as to say his name would be to lose him.

"Colman Brady." There had been other moments when she'd regarded his name as a hoard of ice beneath her tongue for use against the summer.

"Colman Brady."

"Yes. I am."

"Colman, I love you." She spoke the words directly and so self-assuredly that he realized she had decided weeks before to greet him with them.

"I know you do." He had still, after more than two years, not said as much to her. He did not know why. "I'm crazy about you," he said.

She smiled, accepting his profession, and remembered how they were different. Colman was afraid and cautious. She was crazy.

"No," she said, "I'm the one who's crazy."

She did not smile.

"That's true." He lined her chin with his forefinger. "Well, let's say I'm mildly interested in you."

"Well," she cracked, "if that's all, then you *are* crazy."

"Perhaps you should have me committed." He slid his arm around her waist as they began to walk toward the Inn.

"Let me change and we'll do something."

"Are you free?"

"Of course. Even if 'committed.' "

"Funny word."

"Committed? Yes. Hilarious."

"Shall I wait here?"

"No. Come in. They won't bite you."

"Who?"

"The wolves, witches, and warlocks. Neither will the patients."

They entered the Inn by a small back door, went down a dark corridor and into the gleaming entrance foyer. Madeline showed Colman into the living room, a high-ceilinged room with fleur-de-lys wallpaper, a crystal chandelier, a grand piano, an arrangement of Queen Anne wingbacks, and a Chippendale sofa. Fresh flowers in discreet bouquets gave off their scent.

The morning sunlight was streaming in through a large bay window. A breeze graced the gauze curtain.

"In a jif," she said, going off.

Brady stood in the bridge of the window, looking out on the sedate front lawn, Main Street, the gables of a mansion above the trees across the way. He lit a cigarette and wondered how long it had been since a day had passed, an entire day, without a thought of her. He could not recall. He succeeded only in summoning the pain, momentary and intense, that always came with her image in his mind. He had written two letters to her weeks before, shortly after she'd come to Riggs. In one he'd told her that she was everything to him and that he could not think of life without her. In the other he'd said, simply, good-bye. He'd sent neither. Both were still folded in the Bible by his bed, which he never read.

He considered the pain he felt at the thought of her, turning it over in his mind, clinically almost, as if it was someone else's. He wondered what term to give it and considered again that perhaps it was hate. But that was too large a term. Hate was for other things. But hate, he thought, is a pain like this. The pain dissolved when he was with her, and now he would be.

"Ready?"

"That was fast." He looked about for a place to snuff his cigarette.

She was wearing a pleated skirt, a cashmere sweater, pearls. "I don't want to waste a minute."

"How much time do we have?"

"Only all day. It's Saturday. No group."

He found an ashtray on an endtable.

She held her hand out to him. He took it. She started to lead him into the foyer. A pair of women, lean, scrubbed, dressed in white, were going out ahead of them. Madeline dropped his hand, winked at him and whispered, "They think I'm married."

What could he say?

Instead of veering left on Main Street toward the center of the picturesque New England village, as Brady expected they would, Madeline set off in the other direction. They walked by a weathered gray cabin that sat primly on the corner of Main and Sargeant streets. Madeline pointed to it.

"That's the Mission House. Jonathan Edwards or somebody ran a mission to the Indians."

"What Indians?"

"The Stockbridge Indians."

"That's an Indian name, is it?"

She shrugged. "That's what they called them."

"They were probably English Indians. Anglicans, no doubt."

"Not Jonathan Edwards."

"Well, he was probably trying to convert them to animism."

"You're silly."

"I'm interested." He took her hand. The hell with her husband.

"Melville lived here."

"They told us that on Nantucket."

"And Hawthorne."

"They told us that in Salem."

"And Grover Cleveland came here in summers."

"They say that in Washington."

"See that house on the hill? Choate lived there."

"Who's he?"

"As in Choate."

"As in 'Who's he?' "

"The school. Never heard of it? You're kidding. It's like Groton or St. Paul's."

"Anglican animism."

"It's a lovely home. They call it Naumkeag."

"Never trust anyone whose house has a name."

"Stanford White designed it."

"He designed the railway depot."

"He did?"

"Yes. He used to summer here."

"You're making that up."

"No. Really. Just before he founded his school. Stanford. Never heard of it, eh?"

"You!" Madeline twisted his arm behind his back, punching him. He took advantage of her motion to free his hand and embrace her firmly by the shoulders.

He kissed her. They were standing directly in front of a small brown house. She gave him such a weighty look when he pulled his face back from hers that he said, "You don't mind, darling, do you?"

"No, Colman, how could I mind? I'm so happy to have you back."

"You seem grave."

"I felt terrible for weeks about us. I didn't know if I'd see you. I didn't know if I'd hurt you."

"Of course you hurt me. You always do."

"I don't mean to."

A curtain fluttered in a window in the brown house.

"They're looking at us," he said.

"I don't care."

"Even if they think you're married?"

"I didn't mean anything by that. It's just . . . at Riggs there are people who know people that I . . ." She shrugged. "I hate being gossiped about."

"Where's Thornton?"

"He's been in Tangiers. He's coming back."

"When?"

"To Washington, I mean."

Brady could feel her hands working the flesh below the blades in his upper back. She was looking at him intently. He allowed himself to sink into the small concentric circles of her eyes; the black pupil, the blue-green iris with its distinctly dark margin, the field of white. She was drawing him into herself through her eyes, as she always did. At that moment they were gentle and apologetic.

"Do I hurt you really?"

"No," he said quickly. It was a lie. Only lately had he admitted to himself that she did hurt him. The pain of her absence was excruciating. *That* was what he hated. "You make me very happy," he said.

"You say that . . ." — she smiled, still fiercely gazing at him — ". . . so morosely."

"*Delectatio Mortis,*" he said. "The happiness of . . ." He rejected the exact word. The English could be so harsh. ". . . the morose." He shuddered inwardly at having veered so close to the word *death.* All things doomed to die . . .

"You classicist, you."

"No, altar boy."

They resumed their walk, hand in hand.

"Speaking of which," she said, "I want to show you the Catholic church. It's a gem."

"Stanford White?"

"No, the late, great God, I think. An Italian, in any case."

"Is it up this way?"

"No, it's the other side of the village. I've something else to show you first. A graveyard."

They had drawn up to the town cemetery. A white fence bordered it. Dozens of stones, gray, high, narrow, and thin in the old fashion, kept their rigid vigil. Only a few tilted this way and that. The grass was well tended. Altogether, the place achieved an order, warmth, and friendliness that made the prospect of a stroll through it not unpleasant.

Brady said, "And you call me morose."

"But I wanted to show you something," she insisted, leading him in.

She did not speak again for the several minutes it took to walk the length of the cemetery. At the far right corner was a grove of trees, excep-

tionally tall pines, the boughs of which obscured the center of the grove
where there was a small, separate burial place. Dozens, perhaps a hundred
tombstones were arranged in a circle around two large monuments, one an
obelisk, the other a draped marble urn.

"The Sedgwick Pie," she said.

Brady took in the scene silently, unsure what he was expected to make
of it.

The perfect circle of the burials. A perfect pie.

"*Beneath this stone are deposited . . .*" — Brady dropped Madeline's
hand and approached the fifteen-foot obelisk — "*. . . the remains of the
Honorable Theodore Sedgwick who died in Boston, January 24 ad 1813, aged
66.*"

Brady looked back at Madeline, who nodded toward the urn, which
was a mere seven or eight feet high and separated from the obelisk by
barely two full paces.

"*Pamela Sedgwick died in Boston September 20, 1807 aged 54. She was a
Christian humble without meanness, pious without bigotry . . .*" Brady skipped
the saccharine litany to read the last line: "*. . . erected by her devoted
husband.*"

"Erected . . . ," he repeated, looking up at the obelisk, ". . . indeed." He gazed back at Madeline, thinking of her naked. She was reading another stone.

He joined her.

"*Elizabeth Freeman. Known by the name of Mumbet. Died December 28,
1829.*"

The stone showed a pockmarked and weary countenance. Brady
touched it, a soft, dusty surface, perhaps limestone. It was remarkable, he
thought, the inscription could still be read.

"*Her supposed age was 85 years. She was born a slave and remained a slave for
nearly thirty years. She could neither read nor write, yet in her own sphere she had
no superior nor equal. She neither wasted time nor property. She never violated a
trust nor failed to perform a duty. In every situation of domestic trial she was the
most efficient helper and the tenderest friend. Good mother farewell.*"

"Jesus!" Brady said.

"Isn't it touching?"

"Touching?" Colman looked at Madeline, whose eyes were still on the
stone, fondly on the stone.

"No." he said. "It is not touching."

She looked up at him, surprised by his tone.

"Why should the woman be patronized in death?"

"I don't think it's that."

"Oh, come on!"

"They freed her!"

"Freed! She 'never wasted time' or 'failed to perform.' You regard that as freed?"

"Really, Colman, stop."

"Yes, really, Madeline. 'Her own sphere.' We know what that means, don't we?"

"It was eighteen twenty-nine."

"Yes. And this is nineteen forty-two. And what's the difference?"

"Oh, hell, do we have to argue now?"

"Why did you bring me here?"

"Because . . ." She wrung the harshness from her voice. ". . . these are my people." She pointed to a wedge in the Pie, a slice of tombstones that were engraved "Thomson." Some Thomson had married some Sedgwick. "*Nathaniel Butler Thomson. Katherine Sedgwick Thomson, 1904.*"

"Your people?"

"Well, Thornton's."

"You expect to be buried here, with Mumbet and . . ." — Brady kicked his right foot toward a small statue of a dog — ". . . the family pets."

Madeline gave him an expression that revealed not hurt precisely, but the memory of hurt. Would that always be the case now — not pain, but only reminders of it? Brady was aware suddenly that her son would have been buried there had his body not been lost at sea.

"I'm sorry," he said. He meant it.

She turned and walked a few yards to a particular stone and rested both her hands on it. It came to her waist. Colman let his eyes drop to the name. "*William Dwight Sedgwick, April 16, 1873.*"

"He was a leading abolitionist," she said, her voice flat, distant. "They all were."

"That *is* admirable, Madeline. It was harsh of me just then."

"Don't apologize. Please don't apologize. I hate apologies."

"You're right," he said, trying to cauterize what he had been feeling before their visit was ruined. But he was feeling it already was. The cemetery had imposed its mood on them. Brady felt sometimes that there were terrible things awaiting them. He lit a cigarette. "You were going to show me the Catholic church."

"Yes." She faced him.

He did not move. He could not move. He wanted to touch her.

"What do you want to say?" she asked. He was surprised at the simple, direct question, and he knew it was an opportunity, a first one, to let her see what life, what sad life, she sustained in him.

"Nothing," he said.

She crossed to him and put her lips against his cheek. It seemed to him that she was telling him to be brave. He felt her breath on his neck like mist. Unbearable as this is, he thought, it is far better than being alone. His legs threatened to begin shaking. He put his hand at her waist, finding the flesh beneath her sweater at the small of her back. The tombstones were like a crowd of dull people watching them. Disapproval. Be brave.

"Be brave, sweet," he said.

"Yes." When she pulled away from him there was a grove in her eyes, its center obscured by boughs. She had tried to admit him. He had not understood or known how to follow, and he knew it.

He touched her hair, fingered the elastic that held it in a ponytail.

"You look so young with your hair like that."

"It's too long. I didn't cut it this spring."

"Don't ever cut it."

"All right. Never. For you."

It seemed to them both that the bad moment had passed and that they had survived it and that the scent of juniper filled the air. Though they were not sure.

They left the cemetery, retraced their way down Main Street, hand in hand even by Riggs. They sauntered by the shops of the village, browsing the windows.

"That's where Norman Rockwell lives," Madeline said, pointing to a modest white frame house on a corner.

"That's what they say in the *Saturday Evening Post.*"

At Elm Street they turned right and walked past the fire station and crossed the street.

"There," she said, announcing the church as if it were handiwork of hers.

The church was a gothic miniature made of crisp gray stone with a small rose window over the entrance and a strong martial belfry with a notched border around its pinnacle. There were mock buttresses on the sides, separating windows that achieved a modest glory with their pointed arches. Madeline had called it a gem and it was. An embodiment of a sensibility that was medieval and European, it stood on the edge of Stockbridge as a shocking repudiation of the spare native aesthetic. Churches in New England were all white steeples and pillars and clear blown glass and righteous angles. This church was a mistake and a defiance at once.

"St. Joseph's," Madeline said. "Isn't it wonderful?"

Brady loved it. For some reason it made him think of going to Mass in

London the morning after the treaty was signed. He never felt so Catholic as when out of Ireland, out of Southie.

"You like it?" he asked, a little surprised.

"It reminds me of Italy. I love Italy. I love France. I love cathedrals. Have you been to Chartres?"

"No."

"Oh, Chartres is wonderful! You must read Henry Adams on Chartres."

"I have."

"My grandfather went with him once."

"Well, I'm privileged to have such a well-connected guide to the culture of Roman Catholicism." He laughed. "You people!"

"Don't 'you people' me, you!" She hugged him.

"Really," he said, "it takes dull outsiders to reveal genius to itself."

"Great artists," Madeline recited, "require great audiences."

"Precisely. As your fellow Whitman almost put it."

"Damn you, Brady. You never let me up, do you!"

" 'I exist as I am, that is enough./ If no other in the world be aware I sit content./ And if each and all be aware I sit content!' " Brady remembered the scene with the commandant in the safe house. He had pitied him for thinking those lines true.

"Rubbish. Whitman could write rubbish too." She pressed with her arm at his waist. *No stoic solitude for you, mister!*

"What's that stone?" Colman asked. A single tombstone was nestled against the side of the church, neglected and isolated.

"Oh," Madeline said, bringing her hand to her face, "I'd forgotten."

"What is it?" He approached the grave, hauling her after him.

The stone was cracked. The plot it marked was overgrown. The earth was slightly collapsed as if there was a cavity below at just that spot. Brady read the inscription out loud.

"*Jane Sedgwick, Nata in Stockbridge.* Christ, it's Latin! *Februariis XX, MDCCCXX.* What's that, eighteen twenty? *Mortua in Washington, D.C. Februariis XII, MDCCCLXXXIX.* That's eighteen eighty-nine, right? *Fide Fortis et Amore.* Strong in faith and love." He looked at Madeline, waiting for her to explain.

"I'd forgotten."

"So you said."

"She built the church."

"She was a Catholic?"

"Yes. Isaac Hecker converted her. Do you know him?"

"No."

"A prominent Yankee. Brook Farm, Emerson, Thoreau, all that. After

Transcendentalism failed he became a Catholic and a priest. He had a following."

"Even a Sedgwick."

"Yes."

"Which is why she's buried here."

"Yes."

"The only one outside the Pie."

"Yes. In two hundred years."

"Jesus! Mumbet in, Jane out!"

"It's not what you think."

"Oh? What do I think?"

"That she was ostracized."

"Well?"

"It worked the other way, Colman." There was a stern edge to Madeline's voice. "As a Catholic she could not be buried in profane ground. The Sedgwicks were very hurt. They loved her."

Those words affected him. Brady hated himself when he was testy with her. His priggish bigotry was what he pulled over his nervousness. Why was Madeline taking him on a tour of the burial places of her kin? She was making him very uneasy, but he could not tell her that. He could not tell her that he was desperately afraid they'd be impossible to each other. What could he do but disguise his anguish as offended prejudice? "They wanted her for their collection, you mean. She ruined the record."

"That's not fair."

"In any case . . ." — Colman touched the neglected stone with his toe — ". . . this is pretty pathetic, isn't it?"

"Yes, sad. I wept when I first saw it."

"I wonder where the other Catholics are buried. Surely some have died. Surely some have *lived* in Stockbridge."

"Perhaps," she said, "even a converted Sedgwick would desecrate their cemetery."

Colman shrugged. The hopelessness of it. Life teaches, if it teaches at all, that some things just can't be managed. Not even by death.

"*Requiescat in pace,*" he said in a low serious voice.

Madeline put her hand on his arm and pressed it. He covered her hand with his own.

"Amen," she said. "Amen."

They walked to the Red Lion Inn to eat lunch. The inn's dining room, with its red carpeting and embossed windsor chairs, white wainscoting, old chandeliers, hurricane-lamp wall fixtures, and small Victorian mirrors, embodied the constrained dignity of another century. As they were being shown to a table Colman and Madeline noticed the tables in the courtyard just through the French doors, and they asked to be seated outside, where it was warm and brilliant. They wanted, if possible, nothing between them and the day's loveliness.

A waiter made an appearance in the small courtyard, nodded stiffly and asked if they wanted drinks. He was wrong for the place, not an up-country Yankee youth, but a city fellow from New York probably. Efficiency just one side of curtness; like his hair, which was an achievement of wet, black slickness. One could have focused a camera on the thin white line of his part.

"Yes, please," Colman said. "I'd have a beer."

"And you, ma'am?"

Madeline blushed. "No thank you, nothing."

The waiter went away.

Colman studied Madeline, who studied the menu. He had never seen her refuse a drink.

She looked up at him. "I'm an alcoholic."

"I know." He smiled, partly out of affection for her at the innocence of her admission, partly out of amusement at the comfort she took in applying one word to all that chaos. "I've known it for years."

She returned his smile and matched his mood. "Why didn't you tell me?"

"Because I'm not a doctor."

"It *is* a disease, you know. You mustn't moralize with me anymore."

"Moralize? Who?"

"You. The more you moralize the worse I feel, and the worse I feel the more I need a drink. Give me a cigarette, would you?"

He did. "That's the medical theory, is it?" He grinned.

She nodded.

"I thought it was just that you liked the hell out of the stuff."

"I hate it."

The waiter brought Colman's beer. "Will it bother you if I have this?"

She was touched by the concern in his voice. "No, darling, of course not." She watched him drink. "I feel no desire for it at all. Strange." She fingered the checker design of the tablecloth. "Colman, I think I'm really better."

"I think you are, too."

"Do you?"

"Yes." He reached across the table toward her hand. He let his fingers float just above hers like a wing of bees pollinating.

"I've learned some important lessons already," she said.

"Like what?"

"Thirst grows the more you drink. I'm not talking about booze, either.

I'm talking about throwing your head back in the rain, to drink *that*. Or going down into a crystal pond with your mouth open. Colman, the more you live the more you want to live!"

He thought she said that wonderfully, so youthfully, as if she'd just thought it, just discovered it. And of course she had. Wasn't that the point?

"But it's like that with booze, too. The thirst is always . . ." She stopped. "It's just always. That's all."

Brady curled his fingers into hers. "Looking at you is like being able to see the fruit ripen."

"Oh, don't say that!"

"Why?"

"Because I'm overripe and I know it."

He understood what she meant. It was true.

"Do you know what I've been talking about to Dr. Koch?" she asked.

He listened carefully.

"My dollhouse."

"Your dollhouse?" .

"Yes. It's in the attic with the parakeet cage and the mannikins. I've not seen it in years. Yet I've thought of it often and I can describe it in detail, everything perfect and little and inviolate: glazed chickens, a rocking chair the size of your smallest nail, a Lilliputian writing desk with a pewter inkwell and feather-pen like a sliver of dust. It's a good house. The windows open and close. My grandfather's carpenter made it. Every room was papered to scale. What always pleased me most was the canopied bed in the room I'd thought of as mine. I'd always expected to give it to my daughter, that house with the flowers perfect forever and the gleaming fruit that never spoiled. Nothing was ever overripe in that house, do you see? It was . . ." She paused, drawing her fingers out of Brady's and reaching to his face, tracing the edge of his chin, smiling at him, stroking him as if he lived there with her. ". . . incorruptible."

"It still is," he said.

"Yes." She withdrew her hand. "But now as a kind of mockery."

"Do you really think that?"

"Yes. Yes. I tried to make Pride's Crossing into a doll's house in which one would never bid *adieu* to guests or to friends or to . . ."

"Lovers," he said suddenly, surprising himself.

She ignored the word. ". . . or to spring. But rats to that!" She brightened, shrugging off her mood. "Who the hell wants to live in a doll's house? If it was always spring: one, I wouldn't have met you in the winter, and two . . ." She slid her hand into his again. "I wouldn't be here with you in the summer."

Brady was aware of the shifting shadows of fine pointed elm leaves trembling in the shelter of the courtyard.

He received her affection, took it into his own for her, cherishing both affections exactly because they were *so* corruptible. He let his eyes fall to her fingers and stared to see what it was they were touching. The shining curves of her hand stirred the memory of that other curve, the primordial one, of two lying together on a bed of morning light, the curve of flesh.

"What else have you learned?" he asked.

"What the sky feels like before it snows."

He smiled at her fancy.

". . . How stretched and gray and desperate to be released from the tension of what it has been piling up."

"A strange thought for summer."

"Summer is the release."

"I have the impression, Madeline, that you haven't snowed yet."

"Do I seem stretched and gray and desperate?"

"You seem . . . I must be careful, since my last metaphor offended you . . . but it's the quality of, well, ripeness. Call it readiness. Call it release. I think you're approaching it."

"Call it pregnancy."

"What?"

Colman's shock offended her. It said, *"At your age!"*

"A metaphor, darling, a metaphor. I'm giving birth to myself."

The waiter appeared then, his pen poised for their order. They made their selections as much to be rid of him as to have the food prepared. Madeline buttered a piece of bread and ate it, sweeping the crumbs continually. Brady was conscious of their two shadows in the lace of sunlight on the pebbles. He was conscious that shadows did not speak. The bread was crumbling in her hands.

"It's curious, isn't it?" he asked, a vague, deliberate opening.

"Yes."

"How we hate our years, the best ones, until we've left them behind, then, later, scramble for them, trying to remember everything."

"I know so little, Colman, of what you've left behind."

He shrugged. "First Erin. Then Beantown."

"And now?"

"I'm not scrambling yet. For anything, unless perhaps I'm scrambling a little bit, inside, for you."

"It's about time," she said, hiding her pleasure in her embarrassment.

"It is. It's about time I stopped flinging away what I . . ." — he let his reluctance express itself in his hesitation — ". . . will only need later."

"I feel that way too."

The waiter interrupted them again. He served the food. Colman had sole in a lemon sauce, Madeline a minute steak.

"Your son," she said after her first bite, "how is he?"

"Good, I think. Have I told you he's in the army?"

"No, but I assumed that he would be."

"He was anxious to join up. He's in the tank corps."

"Patton?"

"Yes."

"He's from Boston, you know."

"I know."

"Are you worried?"

Colman shrugged. "What can happen with a Beacon Hill general in charge?" He smiled, then cut it abruptly. "Of course I'm worried. This is going to be a vicious war. There's only one way to fight it."

"How?"

"Going in. They have to go in through France. The Germans will destroy them. I hope to God Micko gets a staff job. I've been trying to arrange it, in fact."

"You have? How?"

"Bribery." He stared at her. He was not joking. "An Undersecretary of the Army. I gave him five thousand dollars. I'm waiting to hear."

Madeline did not react. She had no idea how he expected her to react. She felt kicked in the stomach. "Your son would hate that, Colman."

"You're right. I'll tell you something else; he'd hate *me*. But he'll never know."

"Perhaps not." She wasn't eating. She trailed her fork along the vein that angled across her steak.

"And Madeline," he said, sensing her retreat, "I'll tell you something. He'd be wrong. There's no reason in the world why he should die in this war. And I'll stop at nothing to see that he doesn't."

"Well," she said, touching her napkin to her mouth and reaching a long way across her feelings for some lightheartedness. "Undersecretaries, no less. You've certainly come a long way, Mr. Brady."

Colman looked at her. How could he tell her the fact of it, how far indeed he'd come? How far from innocence and simplicity, how far from Ireland, perhaps? He tried to deflect his feelings, which came fast, arrows, shafts of light through the elm canopy. He knew that his admission of bribery had made Madeline uneasy. But the real problem was his fearful effort to manipulate the circumstances of his son's life, which he did because he was so afraid of a life of his own. If Madeline was uneasy it was not with his bribery, but with the default on his own prospects to which it pointed. If he had any hope of changing that, it would be with her, but she would have to understand more, so much more. He decided to try to tell her.

"Madeline, there are things about me you don't know. I wish I could tell you."

She sat forward, listening.

He went on, smiling a bit and showing a gentle irony. "If you and I have a problem it's that you think communion is the result of communication because you're a Protestant. We Catholics think that communion is prior, not the other way. That's why we don't give two hoots for sermons."

"Is that what you wanted to tell me?"

"No. That's just a digression on why this is difficult for me. What the hell do I know about communication?"

"Confession, Colman. You're talking about confession. You Catholics do that all the time."

Madeline's strong and exact statement surprised him. Of course, confession. He decided to start with what was most shocking. "I killed several men when I was young. That changed everything for me. Do you know why? Not because the actual killings were wrong or unnecessary, but because, once started, it made no difference to me whether they were wrong or not. I loved it, the killing itself. I was more alive than I ever was before or have been since, when I was blowing men's brains out." He stopped talking, but the train of thought went on: *but now, Madeline, I've begun to think or hope that I could be more alive even than that with you.* The thought stunned him. Why couldn't he say it? "So what do you think?" he asked.

Madeline thought his statement so self-punishing, yet so devoid of the barest hint of remorse, that she could make no response. He had shocked her not with the revelation of his deed, but with the disgust for himself it left him with. He seemed more regretful of his own loss of innocence than of his victims' loss of life. He was a man who needed a huge dose of both rebuke and forgiveness. Could she, honestly, offer either?

"I don't know, Colman," she said.

Brady let out a faint snort. He could not communicate it, could he? There you were. "Well, it's a long way from honor, duty, and love of country I've come, don't you think?"

"I suppose. It serves me right for asking what raggedy clothing you'd flung off."

"Or not flung off. I think and act in curved lines, Madeline. I'd have expected you to know that."

"We all do, Colman, but there are some times when we shouldn't."

"Like wartimes."

She shrugged.

"You know all about it," he said.

"No."

"Well, I do."

"I doubt it."

"*Don't* doubt it. War, dollhouses, fallen fruit, Austen Riggs. It's all one issue; how to survive."

"All right, Colman. How do I survive? How do you? We have to work that as best we can. For ourselves. But so does your son."

"That's true, but he's not dealing with metaphors. The first five, ten, or fifty thousand blokes out of the ships and onto the ould sod are going to get their heads blown off. It's that simple. And everybody knows it but them. If I can keep my kid off that beach for a week or two, until, say, the generals come ashore, well, I will. And he'll have to take it from there. That's fair enough. I just want my boy to have a chance, that's all."

"I see what you mean. Perhaps it *is* worth the cost."

"Money is nothing."

"Not money. The cost to you, to your — forgive a big word — integrity."

"My integrity? You don't know me well, do you? My integrity weighs less than air."

Madeline decided to lay aside her new reservation about him. She would pretend she had not had that qualm. "I know you well enough. You have never deceived me or tried to bribe me or belittled me to ennoble yourself. I know what integrity is, and what it weighs, and what it costs. I admire you. And trust you. Collins is lucky to have you for his father."

"Thank you." Colman was surprised to find that he was moved by her tribute. She was offering him entry again through her eyes into whatever lay behind them. He took it, thinking for once that he knew; her generous will, which contained him the way the courtyard did the breeze. He could not resist her when she cupped her face with that look. She made him feel that his whole life lay before him like a field of wheat, neck-high, waiting to be taken. He tried to squirm out of her fond gaze and the uneasiness her tribute stirred in him. He said, "I thought we were talking about Collins."

"Bribery," she said, smiling. "We were talking about bribery."

"No, we weren't. I was simply admitting it to you, confiding it in you." He knew what she was thinking; Thornton would never, in a million years, take a bribe or offer one.

"Do you know what I'm thinking?"

"Yes."

"It was bribery before, wasn't it?"

"When?" What *was* she thinking?

"That caused your . . . downfall."

"Not 'downfall,' darling."

"You never told me about it."

"I told you it wasn't what you thought."

"What was it?"

"Why do you ask?"

"I thought we'd admitted it was time we toured each other's closets."

"It had nothing to do with bribery. I arranged a pardon for a man who had me in his debt. Not financially."

"Morally?"

Colman shrugged. "Big word. But yes." The murder of Jerry MacCurtain. Brady had not thought of it in years. The massacre. *Morally?* He laughed, partly to stifle an unexpected grief.

"What's funny?"

"Your curiosity. It has been years after all, our liaison. Doesn't it strike you as funny that we never exchanged these numbers?"

"No." It struck her as sad. They had used their ignorance about each other as a refuge.

"There's much I've never asked you too, Madeline."

"I know. Ask me something."

"No."

"Please."

He wanted to ask her in what way she still loved Thornton. But he did not, he could not. Instead he asked a false and sentimental question of the sort he thought she wanted. "Do you love yourself?"

"When I'm with you, yes."

"And other times?"

"More and more."

He reached across the table to touch her face. "You know, don't you, that what I want is for you to love yourself whether I'm here or not."

"I know. That's what Dr. Koch wants, too."

Brady realized that he had told her the truth, and it seemed suddenly ominous to him. He realized that it was precisely in such a sentiment that love *does* reside. But he could not speak of it further. He let his finger trace the bones of her face. Madeline was very moved, and her eyes filled. She watched him.

When Brady's finger brushed Madeline's mouth she opened it and touched his skin with her tongue. The sensuous, shameless gesture stirred them both.

"I wish we could go somewhere, Colman."

[324]

"We can. My room."

Madeline nodded.

"When we finish?" There was still food on both their plates.

She shook her head and formed a word with her lips: *Now*. Then she bit his finger, almost hurting him. He winked at her.

They laughed and rose. Colman told the waiter to put the bill on his tab. The waiter watched them leave the courtyard and cross the dining room holding hands. A bit old, he thought, to be abandoning food, cutting short meals, rushing off in the afternoon. He put his forefinger, barely the tip of it, to the side of his head, which he scratched affectedly, yet without disturbing a single hair or its sleeve of oil.

Colman's room in the Red Lion was dominated by the great bed, with its tufted white spread, which was all the whiter for the pattern of violet flowers on the walls. Madeline went into the room and drew the blinds while Colman locked the door. She turned to face him from the window and he remained for a moment where he was. He realized for the first time how different she looked. She looked older. She looked sadder. She was not for once wearing the clothing or the expression of her counterfeit youth. She did not look voluptuous, he thought. She looked like the person he knew she was. They walked to each other slowly. While Colman unfastened the clasp of her pearls and the knot at her neck which held her hair, Madeline pushed her fingers between his teeth while rubbing her left knee into his groin until she could feel him stiffening. With a graceful familiarity they undressed each other, fondling the clothing, the snaps and buttons, as though everything were flesh.

When she was naked Colman knelt, his hands everywhere on her. With his tongue he traced her curves, the spaces and vacancies of her body, her breasts, the hollow below them, the line of her hip, her navel, the slight bulge of her abdomen, the hair at her crotch until he moved his tongue to her clitoris, the very tip of it. He began stroking her buttocks with his hands and pressing his tongue ever so lightly against the small knob of tissue which grew as he pressed more firmly, moving his head in a small circle around it.

And cries, low cries came from her, as if she were a creature being dragged across its border. The pitch of response was intense beyond anything Brady had felt from her before. She cupped his head with her hands and pressed him into her belly while he continued to play his tongue on her. She began to come in a sequence of climaxes, which were, he thought, distinct and separate, but which spilled into each other. It was as if she were lying back in water, him supporting her, while unstoppable dizzying waves washed over her again and again and again.

"Come to bed," she said finally, drawing him up, having remembered him, having remembered the ancient secret of women, that the man has so little to do with making that wound whole. Her hand stole down his body and he rose and she took his erection and fondled him. His face was flushed and she could feel the tension in him. She knew that nothing aroused him like her orgasms. "Come to bed, darling."

She lay down and opened her arms and legs and waited for him.

What she was! Without any of her habitual embarrassment, she lay there showing herself to him, and he understood that at last she was not imagining herself a perpetual youth. The lines of her age were all over her body, and finally, Brady understood, they were what made her so ravishing to him. Brady could not love someone whom time had not touched, and it had touched her gloriously. Her skin along the inside of her thighs and up into her pubic hair was like milk with tiny blue veins through it, which trembled as she arched herself up for him. Her legs and arms, her shoulders and her straight neck, were tawny and textured with fine creases. Everything in her ached for him and she let him see that.

"You are beautiful," he said, looking down on her. He held his passion in check for another moment to heighten it. He understood what made them one — the effort to do what seemed impossible. He was ready to risk everything again, not for this woman but with her. "You are beautiful," he repeated, "and so is your miraculous body."

"Take it," she said.

❦ 6 ❧

ON NOVEMBER 8, 1942, eleven months after Pearl Harbor, the American counterattack came. Three hundred thousand invaders, from a convoy of eight hundred ships, rushed in landing craft onto the shores of French Africa, surprising Europe and confusing America. Everyone had expected an assault across the Channel from England, or, at the outside, an attack from the south on the underside of France. But Africa! Few understood that the Allies were far from equipped to meet their enemy head-on in Europe itself.

Colman Brady and tens of thousands of American parents read accounts of the invasion in three, if possible four, newspapers a day. Many like him, who had never particularly formed the habit of listening to the radio, began listening to it constantly. People on buses and on the streets of Boston traded slivers of information as if they were coins.

The operation — code-named Torch — went smoothly. The Germans and the Vichy French were as surprised as anyone, and the Yankee force was unbloodied. On November 23, Eisenhower moved his headquarters from a cavern under Gibraltar to a hill in Algiers, signaling the successful completion of the first great American initiative.

Colman Brady had even less reason to worry than others because his son, 2d Lt. M. Collins Brady, was a communications officer in charge of a pool of radiomen at Headquarters Command. Throughout the invasion he had huddled by headsets, receivers, ticker-machines, and telegraph keys in the tunnel in the bowels of the Rock of Gibraltar. His duty was to organize incoming information into intelligence briefings which other junior officers delivered at half-hourly intervals to senior staff, who further arranged the data into briefings which were presented every two hours to General Eisenhower and his task force commanders, Clark and Patton.

Young Brady had been cruelly disappointed at his assignment.

His first letter from overseas was written during his first break from duty at Gibraltar. *"It is as if this rock,"* he wrote, *"came into existence for the precise purpose of keeping me out of the war. You cannot imagine what it's like to be constantly hearing reports of the progress of the army — to be hearing them from here, the very womb of the earth! I've never been less vulnerable to physical harm in my life than I am now. That's the damn army for you! If you volunteer for the field they bury you in the ground. It's probably the poor bastards who wanted this job who are leading the assault. I gather this is typical."*

It would have suited Colman if the kid stayed inside Gibraltar for the entire war. But he knew that soon enough Collins would be on the line, if not across it, and he expected the boy would feel differently about the rock when it wasn't overhead protecting him.

All three of the letters Colman received from Gibraltar reflected the same frustration, but what began essentially as embarrassment at being safe while so many others were in jeopardy was transformed into resentment at being far removed from the valor and triumph of the unchallenged landing. "A great victory for the Allies," Collins called it. But Brady reserved judgment on that, believing that victories presupposed the engagement and conquering of opponents. That the enemy did not resist the landing meant little to Brady; perhaps the Germans were delighted to have the Allied force harmlessly in North Africa. What the hell was there but an infinity of sand which even the Italians didn't want?

Rommel was there.

The genius of Eisenhower's move revealed itself slowly that winter, for, by landing his force at Casablanca, Oran, and Algiers, he was able immediately to pinch from the west the German who was already under attack by Lt. Gen. Montgomery at El Alamein. The Nazis and Italians withdrew to Tunisia and waited while a massive reinforcement arrived from Sicily. In February Rommel launched his counteroffensive at the Kasserine Pass, and Eisenhower had what he wanted: a head-to-head fight with the elusive and legendary German, the Desert Fox.

Rommel's Stuka dive-bombers and Krupp 88's battered the American tank corps, and, then, in a blitz attack of the sort for which his Afrika Korps was famous, he pushed the Yanks back through the pass, defeating them soundly. He chose not to pursue them because the Allied naval control of the Mediterranean had cut his supplies from thirty thousand tons a month to two thousand. At a meeting with Hitler, he argued for the evacuation of his entire army from Africa, but he was overruled. Hitler wanted to defeat Montgomery and Eisenhower there. He not only rejected the evacuation, but ordered its opposite — a huge reinforcing of Rommel's 15th and 21st Panzer divisions.

Eisenhower meanwhile replaced the II Corps Commander at Kasserine with Maj. Gen. George S. Patton, Jr. Despite his command of the Western Task Force in the initial assault, Patton had spent most of his time in the first stages of the campaign in the cave at Gibraltar, where he nearly despaired with frustration. He hadn't, by God, spent thirty years waiting for the chance to test himself against a Rommel only to find himself too senior — too valuable to Ike — for a field command. He had been delighted when the Germans broke through at Kasserine, even though that put the Allies on the brink of disaster. Eisenhower couldn't refuse him; he *had* to throw his best man into the fray. Patton went into the field at last, and he immediately succeeded in recapturing the pass and establishing a link with Montgomery's army moving in from the east. Slowly the two Allied armies began closing in on Rommel, whose force was bloated with men and tanks but pitifully low on fuel and ammunition.

Patton was determined to get to Rommel before Montgomery did.

Among the officers on Patton's staff was Capt. Phelps Otis, his aide-de-camp. The general had delegated Otis to assemble the junior field staff that would enable Patton to maintain the logistics of a highly mobile command. Otis had recommended Collins Brady for the communications slot. Though Brady was permanently attached to the Headquarters Command, he was assigned on Patton's order to II Corps and promoted immediately to first lieutenant.

I am finally outside an office, have my own Jeep and driver, and a chance to see Africa. Outside of Algiers the land is dotted with Almond trees which from a distance look like fishnet hung on trellises. When you get close to them they look like the apple trees we used to see on our trips north of Boston, only lovelier, if you can imagine. The seeds of the trees are planted on wedding days and the days of funerals so the trees are a kind of memorial. That's why there are so many. Isn't that wonderful, Dad?

Even though he was on the general's staff, Collins Brady had little direct contact with him, dealing mainly with Otis or Colonel Harkins, Patton's exec. Their first encounter came in early May, just when Patton was snapping down on Rommel.

The position Rommel held at the end was an exceedingly strong one. Its left lay on the seacoast; along its front ran the Wadi Zigzaon, a ravine which made a formidable tank obstacle, since it was eighty yards wide and, in places, fifty feet deep; its right rested on the Matmata Hills, an eerie range which was unpassable for wheeled or tracked vehicles. The only way Patton could get at Rommel was through a rugged pass which crossed the hills south of Al-Hamma, but that entailed a sweeping forced march of nearly two hundred miles over broken ground. It would be foolhardy to attempt it. And that was the genius of it. Patton decided to move against the Afrika Korps through the pass as quickly as possible.

When an urgent order came through from Montgomery himself just as the mobilization was under way, Collins Brady knew instinctively that he had to get it to Gen. Patton at once, and, since Otis and Harkins were preoccupied with the move, that was the occasion of their first real meeting.

In the communiqué, Montgomery was ordering Patton to hold his position until he could complete a resupply operation. Patton and Montgomery were supposed to be working in synchrony under Eisenhower, but Montgomery ranked Patton. Patton knew that the Englishman wanted desperately to bring the teeth down on Rommel himself.

When Patton read the deciphered message, he exploded at Brady.

"You asshole! This is wrong! You got this wrong! Even Montgomery wouldn't do this to me now! You asshole! Do it again and get it right!"

"It is right, sir." Brady knew the ciphers backward and forward.

Patton leaned across his desk at Brady. "No, Lieutenant, it is not right." Patton glared at him.

Brady understood what the general was telling him.

"Sir," he said.

Patton was through with him, but Brady did not leave the room.

"Well?" Patton barked, not looking up from his map.

"Sir, I have not acknowledged receipt of this dispatch. I thought you might prefer . . ." How to say it. He went on gingerly. ". . . to miss this transmission, sir."

Patton eyed him carefully. "Because it's accurate, eh, Lieutenant?"

"Yes, sir. It's accurate."

"All right." Patton smiled, more to himself than to Brady, as if to say, *This damn punk lieutenant just got me off the fucking hook.* But all he said was, "Good. I *want* accuracy. Who else saw the . . .?"

"No one, sir. I deciphered it."

"Destroy it."

"Yes, sir."

"Don't acknowledge it."

"Right, sir."

"Receive nothing from Montgomery for . . ." — he looked at his wristwatch — ". . . seven hours."

"Yes, sir." Brady saluted, had his right toe at his left heel, about to turn. But the general stared at him, not returning his salute.

"What's your name, Lieutenant?"

"Brady, sir. Michael Collins Brady."

"Brady. Harvard."

"Yes, sir." Collins reined his delight that Patton knew of him and that he knew *that* of him.

"Otis beat the shit out of you, I understand."

Brady did not reply. It was a knee to the groin. Goddamn Otis.

"Well?"

"Not true, sir."

"He beat you?"

"He did. Barely."

Patton studied him for a moment, making a show of taking his measure. Brady withstood his glare.

"What'd you say your name was?"

"Brady."

"The rest of it."

"Michael Collins, sir."

"Michael Collins? Why that?"

"After an Irish patriot, sir."

Patton nodded slowly. "It's a damn proud name, Brady. Michael Collins was a military genius."

Despite himself, Collins blushed. "I know that, sir. My father . . ."

"You're dismissed. I don't care about your father."

Collins was frankly amazed that anyone would have heard of the obscure anti-British guerrilla. No one outside his own circle of family and friends had ever made note of his name. That General Patton had not only heard of that other Collins, but admired him — Brady wanted to call his father on the telephone!

How superbly the man carries himself! He exercises command not as if the capacity for authority was the highest human achievement — which I believe it is — but as if it were the simplest thing, common to everyone. And it's catching. Even I seem more like an officer, to myself, if not to my men, all nine of whom are older than I am. But lately they seem responsive and I'm trying to make them see that we're not just clerks or message boys. Everything depends on the synchrony of the armored columns, which General Patton conducts as if the army were Symphony. My unit is his baton. By the way, tell Aunt Maeve that General Patton, who's not a Catholic, of course, carries a rosary from the Holy Land, which he intends to give after the war to his old Irish nurse, who lives in Southie now and whose name is Mary Scally. Isn't that terrific!

It took Patton's army eleven hours to break through the pass south of Al-Hamma. Infantry accompanied by engineers advanced steadily through Rommel's main mine fields, clearing two lanes for the armored divisions. Once the mine belt was crossed, Patton's force roared into the heart of the German stronghold, absolutely stunning Rommel's men. If the earth had opened under them they couldn't have been more dazed. Wherever they looked American tanks were roaring past. The German officers of field rank led the flight up the Cape Bon roads, trying for the sea. Patton hurtled past German airfields, workshops, petrol and ammunition dumps, and gun positions in an effort to block their escape. The British force followed the American through the pass, and Patton sent messages to Montgomery telling him to take and hold the positions he was himself knocking over. The German army huddled by the thousands on beaches, abandoned and afraid. Rommel himself was gone. In that climax, Patton drew to a dramatic close an operation in which his force killed a hundred thousand Axis soldiers and captured a quarter of a million more, while sustaining fewer than twenty thousand casualties of his own. History had one of its great military sweeps. The Allies had their first significant victory in a war nearly four years old. And America had its first hero since Pershing.

Even before news of the victory broke in Boston, Maeve was encouraged by the letters her nephew was sending. "He seems not to mind it," she said to her brother one night.

They were sitting in the rear dining room at Prescott Street. The early May wind down from Canada was snapping the night air outside. They were having their tea. Colman was leaning back in his chair, which barely touched the old Carpenter stove, which was warm with the remnant of a wood fire.

"It still doesn't sound dangerous to me," she said.

Colman had recently obtained from his contact in Washington a casualty list broken down by function. Radiomen were a lousy risk; worse than infantry.

"It's not, Maeve. Safest job in the army."

"We're lucky."

"Yes." They'd had this conversation several nights a week for the eight months Micko'd been overseas.

"Peter Boyd was a cook, though."

"The navy's different. If a ship is hit . . ." Colman sipped his tea.

Maeve picked up the letter that had come that day. For the tenth time she began to read it. Brady let his ear drift toward the big radio on the counter in the kitchen. It was on constantly now. A band was playing "Little Brown Jug." The music was irritating and inane. Brady thought of turning it off, but he knew he couldn't.

"He says Phelps Otis was promoted to major."

"Yes. I saw that."

"When will Micko be promoted again?"

"Don't worry about that. If he's on staff, he'll get his promotions." In fact, Brady hoped every day for word that Micko'd made captain, though it was too soon yet. Captains had one-fifth the lieutenants' chance of being killed in combat.

"Isn't it funny they should wind up friends?"

"Who?"

"Phelps Otis."

Brady grunted. His mood prevented him from engaging in their easy and customary chatter about the details of Collins's letter, which was filled with trivia, gossip, and a final paragraph that struck Brady as a bit pious. The kid was a true believer. There was always a nosegay about the nobility of the war. It always made Maeve cry. Maeve knew nothing about the battle with Rommel. News reports were sketchy and vague. Clearly the government wasn't going to make much of it until it was clear the Allies would defeat the Germans. They were hoping to capture the Desert Fox himself. Brady knew from careful reading of everything he could get, including a daily *Guardian* that he had sent over from Manchester by the Cutty Sark people, that the final phase of the fight for North Africa was already under way. It looked good for Patton, not because he was the superior strategist or because his army was better than the Korps, but because, simply, he was far more amply supplied. The essence of desert warfare is supply. Not even Aryans can run tanks on *Geist*. Brady's contact in Washington assured him that the end of the campaign would come soon, with little Allied blood shed. But Brady's worry had fed on itself until he was edgy and irascible.

"We interrupt this program to bring you a special announcement from the War Department in Washington."

Colman and Maeve locked their eyes on each other. She reached across the table toward him. He gave her his hand.

"General Rommel has surrendered. General Marshall issued a statement calling the Allied victory over the Afrika Korps the turning point of the war against Hitler. Jointly commanding the African Expeditionary Force were Lt. Gen. Bernard Montgomery and Maj. Gen. George S. Patton, Jr. Further details about today's victory will follow. But now back to our program."

"Toot toot tootsie," the band blared, "good-bye."

"Is that all?" Maeve asked. "What happens now? I could cry."

"Cry? But why?"

"I don't know. Because he's in a *war*. I forget it's a war. I think most times he's off at school, living in the dormitory, which seems so silly because it's just across the river. And now they're all grown and gone. I never see Jackie." Her face was streaming tears. She was on the verge of hysteria.

"You see him on Sundays at the seminary."

"Oh, Colman, this is silly." She wiped at her tears, trying to control herself. She withdrew her hand from his and began to arrange her hair.

Colman busied himself with a cigarette. How to help his sister through this? She seemed suddenly old to him, nearly overcome with an intangible fatigue, the cumulative effect of her vague worries for Collins and her increasing experience of being left behind by her own children, whose maturity wore the face of betrayal.

"It's not silly, Maeve. If by some miracle I could see the kiddo little again the way he was when we came over, tiny and helpless like your own were then, I would crawl to him on my knees. Everything in me would respond to him. There is nothing I wouldn't give to have it be that time again. It's not silly."

"I worry about him. I worry about them all."

The unsettled experience of parents. Not that Maeve's children were problems to her. Maureen, at twenty-six, was practically a spinster, and her loyalty to her mother was absolute. She lived at home. She was still working for Colman, but now as an office manager for a real estate company he'd acquired. She was bright and happy. Deirdre, twenty-five, was married to a doctor who'd been drafted and who was serving at Fort Dix. She had been living in New Jersey since January. Her letters were full of complaint and misery. But Jackie was doing well in his studies for the priesthood, and Monsignor Keller at Saint Aidan's said he had a very bright future indeed since the new archbishop, Richard Cushing, had singled him out for praise at a recent seminary convocation. It was not at all that the McShane children were disappointments. Only Deirdre had turned out curdled, and she at least had married well. It was not that Maeve had reason to believe that her nephew was in danger; from all reports he was thriving. It was only that . . .

"I'm so tired, Colman."

From where she was sitting by then that night, it seemed to her that thirty years had come and gone almost unnoticed, but for that ache, that weight in her breast. Only a minute before, it seemed, she had been so fearfully in love with McShane. Then, seconds later, she had felt so strong and independent and able. Then there had come Colman and something of which she could never speak, the chill of his shadow. Then the loss of her house, and even of her kitchen and of her Fourth Street circle, to that prosperity which her friends envied and which she, finally, hated. Funny, but it was only since she had had servants to do the cooking and cleaning, only since she'd begun napping in the afternoon — what else was there to do? — that she'd felt continually and totally exhausted.

"I know, Maeve," Colman said, but almost absently, as if he didn't notice the falsehood that had crept into her life. Why the hell should she be tired?

"I think the war's to blame," she said, knowing he would agree with her. It was, after all, the great deception of their generation: to confuse the social spirit of the times, which was savage and evil, with the private one of a domestic life of ennui and resignation.

"Yes," Brady said. One can never get even with history. One can only protect oneself against it and try to quarrel with it as little as possible, and otherwise look for chances to make use of it. By, for example, blaming everything on the war. The damn war. Thank God for it.

Except that . . .

"How much longer can it last now?" she asked. There was a girlish plaintiveness to her voice. What had happened to his Maeve?

"A while yet, darling." Colman rarely even disguised it anymore when he patronized her.

The victory in Africa proved nothing, settled nothing, meant nothing. What counted was Europe. In a way Brady was sorry for Rommel's defeat because now the Allies would have to cross the Mediterranean. A thrust, almost certainly at the Cherbourg peninsula. On the trestle table in his bedroom Brady had a spread of maps — a large one of the Mediterranean and sectional maps of Morocco, northern Algeria, Tunisia, and Libya — on which he had followed the wheeling and cutting of the two armies like a schoolboy. He knew exactly how the Allies would have sprung their trap finally on the Korps and how futile Rommel's evasions had to prove.

And Brady had thought carefully about the next move. It had to be a quick assault on Corsica, where bases could be established, and then a massive landing below Nice, followed immediately by a pincer attack on Marseilles. The only conceivable alternatives were an invasion of Greece to carry the war into the Balkans, but they were too remote from central Europe, where the real test had to be met, or an invasion through Sicily of Italy, which offered the single advantage of keeping the naval operation to a minimum, since the northern tip of Tunisia was only a hundred and some miles from Sicily. But two obvious drawbacks made Brady certain the Allies would not go in through Italy. First, they would have to capture a thousand miles of strategically useless territory before engaging the enemy at a point of significance, the Foggia airfields near Naples, from which could be extended the massive bombing of central Europe. But otherwise Naples paled by comparison with Marseilles as a port of entry to the Continent. Second, in the battle for Italy the real enemy would be geography, for the peninsula was bisected by the Apennines, river mountains which had shaped Italy into a long chain of peaks and valleys, the kind of terrain which infinitely favors defense. Besides, once the Allies succeeded in establishing control over the southern coast of France, it would, by virtue of naval superiority in the Mediterranean, be a relatively simple matter to isolate Italy from the rest of Europe and thereby render Mussolini and the occupying Germans superfluous to the main conflict. But the invasion of France would be savage. Brady assumed that the Nazis expected an assault on the Cherbourg peninsula, and he guessed that they would be ready. Tens of thousands of men would be killed quickly. That was why Brady was hoping Montgomery would be tapped to lead the assault with the British Eighth Army. Let the Brits take the brunt of it. Let the Brits be the heroes.

Colman was certain that if Patton led the attack he would be foolishly and flamboyantly *avant*. And so, therefore, would Collins. Patton was an eccentric, as far as Brady could tell. He would relish his own vulnerability, and his staff, willingly or not, would accompany him — an entourage — into the worst jeopardy. Colman Brady was not going to see his son getting killed in a circus of someone else's glory. If Patton was named to lead the assault on France . . .

Brady made a sudden decision.

"I'm going to Washington tomorrow, Maeve."

"Again?"

"Yes. That tangle with the FTC is still pending."

"Well," Maeve shrugged. Her thoughts had turned to trivial things about the house — a toilet not working, the burn in the linen tablecloth, how to mend it — trivial things that could matter more than the war with Hitler. There were moments, as if of awakening, when she found it incredible that such things could matter at all. But they were the only problems about which she could do anything, about which she had confidence in the value of her opinion. She supposed it was the same for Colman, with his business. If he could go to Washington as if everything were normal, she could have the toilet fixed.

"You're tired," he said. "Why don't we turn in?"

"Yes," she said, so sadly.

And she did.

Colman went to his maps. He wanted to plan carefully what to say to the undersecretary.

The arrangement Brady made the next day with his contact at the War Department had only to do with an invasion of the south of France and only if it should be led by Patton. He was not intent upon sparing his son every risk, but only the most senseless and hopeless ones.

I live now in a *gourbi,* a Tunisian hut sunk into the ground and banked with sand on all sides. Since it's an officers' *gourbi,* ours has a wooden floor and walls and a tin roof. The roof has been covered with sand and alfa grass has been planted on top for camouflage. We have some talented foragers in our group, especially Lt. Woody Woodrum, who just brought in a new tin stove this morning (i.e., jerry can). So we have all the comforts of home (or some, anyway). Sure beats the tent we had before, which was a large circular one with a French stencil on the outside saying it had been rented from a firm in Marseilles and not to fold it wet, but it belonged to the United States Army now. And there were bullet holes in it too, but old ones.

It occurred to Colman that this letter's reference to Marseilles was his son's hint that the invasion would be focused there. The kid was, after all, a cryptographer. But Colman thought better of it. Micko would never try to thwart the censorship of military mail. He would happily write his letters, vacuously, as if he were on holiday.

And so it was that Colman Brady was dismayed when on the morning of July 11 it was announced that an Allied invasion of Sicily was under way. The forces employed were the American Seventh Army of two and a half divisions under Patton and the British-Canadian Eighth of four and a half divisions under Montgomery. Though the free-spirited Sicilians held the fascists of Mussolini — and, for that matter, all mainland Italians —. in contempt, their island was garrisoned by five Italian coastal divisions, five Italian infantry divisions, and two German divisions, totaling 255,000 troops. The Allies had a fierce fight on their hands. Patton moved against Messina by way of Palermo, Montgomery by way of Syracuse and Catania. The Anglo-American command of the air was so unqualified that they had the major advantage of complete tactical surprise, and their advance was steady and quick. The Germans were pushed back from village to village toward Messina. The Italian forces broke and ran before the Allies so consistently that the Germans began placing mines behind them to discourage their retreat.

The people of Sicily are the most destitute and pathetic people I have ever seen. Even worse than the Arabs. They badger us continually for cigarettes. They shout in their funny English, "Down with Mussolini" and "Long Live America!" They throw flowers on the road in front of us and give us lemons and watermelons (huge ones!). But to tell you the truth, I don't trust them. They seem wily and insincere to me. Although I'm told Sicilians have always hated Il Duce, but that's probably because one of the few good things Mussolini tried to do (besides run the trains on time) was stamp out the local mafia (indigenous hoodlums, a swaggering bunch of draft-dodgers). One day when the enemy nearly retook Gela, some of our Artillery killed a few civilians, which was unfortunate. But all the townspeople, including the men, panicked and screamed like hyenas for the better part of an hour.

In late July the Germans and Italians successfully withdrew from Sicily across the Straits of Messina into the toe of the boot. The Allied conquest of Sicily was complete. On July 27, Mussolini resigned his position as head of the government in Rome, and Churchill and Roosevelt called jointly for the unconditional surrender of Italy. But the Germans were pouring thirteen fresh divisions into Italy from all over Europe, and, in a flamboyant declaration of resistance, Hitler named Field Marshal Rommel commander of the German forces in Italy.

In the first weekend in August Colman Brady visited Madeline Thomson at Austen Riggs.

"It's that damn Churchill," he said. They were seated on the grass under one of the large elms on the great lawn in front of the Inn. "Life is cheap to him, always has been. As long as it's someone else's."

"But what's the alternative?" Madeline asked. She hated these conversations.

"We demand an unconditional surrender from them and leave them no alternative but the arms and jaws of the Nazis. All we really need is a provisional truce so we can get into Rome quickly. But not Churchill. He pulled the same song and dance on us."

"Churchill?"

"Yes. Believe it or not, the old bastard was running things in Ireland twenty-five years ago. Same damn thing. If we have to fight the Nazis in Italy it will, you watch, be absurd and tragic."

"But he called it 'the soft underbelly of Europe,' Churchill."

"It's a crocodile's back, and it will be useless."

"You seem so certain, darling. How do you know?"

"Because I think about it, Madeline. I think of little else."

"Have you heard from him?"

"Yes. Shall I read from it?" Colman withdrew a letter from the inside pocket of his white flannel suit.

"Oh, yes, do." Madeline drew nearer to him, pressed his left knee with both her hands.

"Everywhere there are these bizarre pushcarts." Colman managed a movement that was half a shrug and half a shaking of his head. *"They are square boxes measuring about four feet a side, and the corners are set off by wooden pillars which frame painted portraits of the Madonna."* Colman laughed out loud and said, "The damn kid is always trying to edify me." Madeline loved the way his affection for his son showed itself. *"Elaborate scrollwork covers the space between the floor of the cart and the axle, just like the porches of the houses on West Broadway in Southie. Some carts are pulled by mules and horses which wear plumes on their bridles and, sometimes, funny hats."*

Colman stopped reading and folded the letter. "Isn't that the most innocuous stuff you ever heard?"

"Hardly what one would expect from the front lines."

"That's the point. If it's real, the war is the last thing they write home about. Jesus Christ! Carts! The funny thing is, I can remember carts like that in the North End. There's a Sicilian section, did you know that?"

"In Boston?"

"Yes. Along Revere Street."

"I didn't know that, no. I suppose I just thought they're all Italians. And they're all the same."

"They don't think that, believe me. Milanos are claiming now that they're Aryans. Sicilians are Moors, like Othello."

"Well, there's none of them out here in lily-white Stockbridge."

"I suppose not." Brady touched the top of Madeline's nose, a hint of playfulness. "But don't be too sure."

"What do you mean?"

"The Black Hand is everywhere."

"General Patton will protect us."

"Right."

"Do you know what hypnosis is?"

He showed his surprise at her question. "What does that have to do with anything?"

"Psychologists define hypnosis as the filling of the field of attention by one object only."

"So?"

"So maybe you're hypnotized by the war."

"Don't be silly."

"I'm trying to understand. I've been thinking, too. We have plenty of time for that here. The spectator whose participation is restricted to seeing, who is passive, is held in passivity by what he sees. He is spellbound or hypnotized."

"Very Good. A-plus."

"Thank you."

"But I've hardly been passive. I've done what I can to protect the only stake I have in the damn thing."

"Collins."

"Of course."

"But he's in the thick of it, more exposed than ever."

"Not anymore."

"What do you mean?"

"He's not going into Italy. The pursuit is insane and meaningless. It's the exercise of a vain old man at the expense of young ones. They're going after snakes with baseball bats."

"But not Collins?"

"No. He'll remain in Sicily as a garrison commander, part of the force to hold onto what they've taken. He's being promoted to captain."

"Does he know it yet?"

"I don't know. Perhaps."

"Will he be disappointed?"

"Crushed. He loves being with Patton. He hates Sicily, like all good Brahmins."

"That's not fair."

"Which? My slam against your cousins? Or my further act of bribery?"

"Neither. Or either. Both."

"You tell me what is fair, then."

"For him to take his chances as we all do."

"Oh, come along, Madeline. You're not serious."

"Yes, I am. Very."

"What comparison do you find between the pampered life in Stockbridge and, say, a month's worth of slugging along a coastline through a series of towns, each clinging to mountain peaks and each defended by machine gun nests and mortar holes?"

"The pampered life?" Madeline had drawn back from him. She was immeasurably stung by the phrase.

"I wasn't referring to you. I was referring to both of us. We are both in Stockbridge, aren't we? We are both pampered, aren't we?"

"I'm not, no. I have never been less pampered in my life." For the first time ever, Madeline Thomson was faced continually and ruthlessly with the consequences of her freedom. She lived in a constant restlessness the pain of which was exceeded only by the joyous sense that at last she was alive because she chose to be. If there were consequences in that for her, there were for him too. She wanted somehow to warn him.

"Perhaps *pampered* is the wrong word."

"Perhaps it is."

"The point I'm making is about war."

"I get your point, Colman. Mine was that your son is a big boy. When are you going to treat him as such?"

Colman did not answer her.

She touched his knee with her forefinger. "Male mothers," she said, "are like female mothers."

"Do you think so?" The shadow of a self-effacing smile crossed his face.

"Yes." She smiled. "And I sound as if I would be different. If I had a son alive, I'd give everything to see him stay alive."

"Including your honor?"

"If I had any, yes." She threw her arms around his neck. He tumbled backward, saying, "Watch the suit! Watch the suit!" It was too late. The elbows of both sleeves were grass-stained.

Madeline's face was close to his. She beamed down on him. "We're not so different, you and I. What honor do a pair of blatant adulterers have anyway?"

He circled her waist with his arms and held her.

"That's another question," he said lightly, not letting her see that he knew it was a crucial question, whose time was coming sure as victory or defeat was coming in the war. Austen Riggs was a kind of bell jar into which she could receive him from time to time. They could have their passionate afternoon trysts at the Red Lion and their lazy mornings on grass in sunlight. But they could not ignore indefinitely the gestation of their love. What would it bear when she left Riggs?

"How much longer will you be here, by the way?"

"By the way?"

"Yes."

"You know I don't know. When Dr. Koch thinks . . ." — she tacked — ". . . when *I* think it's time to leave."

"Oh."

"I really don't know, darling."

"But?"

"It won't be forever."

"You've been here a year."

"More." Madeline knew that she would be leaving Riggs soon. She was not ready to discuss it with Colman. Over several visits lately his presence had filled her with misgivings, which slowly she was learning to treat as guests that she was obliged to listen to, even if she disliked them.

Brady did not try to express the question that was taking shape inside his uneasiness.

A week later he received a long letter from Collins in which Collins informed him of the promotion and the fact that he'd been given command of a garrison unit that was to remain in Sicily. He was charged with administering the martial rule of the southeastern sector of the island. He had eighty men under him. Collins reported all that crisply, with no hint of how he felt about it. He'd have been thinking of the army censors.

In the piazza back of my house here in Agrigento I can see at this very moment some dogs, a herd of goats, a flock of mangy chickens, an old horse, and half a dozen children, and they are all looking hungrily for scraps on the dusty ground. But you mustn't think all is dreary. My first task here was to secure potable water for my men. But for the two days before we could be supplied with it, we had to drink champagne. A local bootlegger had cached a huge store of it, thinking to make a killing when the Yanks finally came through. Of course we just requisitioned it, and he was fit to be tied. You might know — he's an exportee from New York. And in addition to the champagne, I've met a most gracious and charming man, the mayor of Agrigento, who's an archeologist of sorts, and who took me on a tour of the outskirts of the town, which, it turns out, was one of the earliest Greek cities. There are the ruins of three beautiful temples — to Juno, Concordia, and Hercules. They are connected by a stunning *via sacra* bordered on each side by ancient tombs, all pilfered, of course, and in terrible disrepair. I asked him if the Nazis had disturbed the tombs and caused the destruction. He said, "No. It was done in the other war." I assumed he meant WWI. But when I asked, he explained that he was referring to the war between Carthage and Greece in 255 B.C. Isn't that incredible! Anyway, he invited me to his house for dinner. He has a neat, modest villa, which, by local standards, makes him a very rich man. His wife is huge and good-natured and he has eleven children. The oldest of them is a girl of seventeen who, with pitch-black hair and a perfect oval face, is probably the most beautiful girl I have ever seen. Unfortunately, she speaks almost no English, and she smells bad. They all live on garlic here. It is sold in the streets by old men carrying garlands of it over their shoulders. Her name is Anna.

7

"He's in love with a wop."

"Don't call her that."

Colman hated such words and rarely used them. He was agitated and worried, but it seemed impossible to share that with Madeline, who saw no further, as usual, than his counterfeit bigotry. He and Madeline were walking through Ice Glen on the far side of Laurel Hill south of the village. The deep, drastic ravine ran for a mile between two great mountains. They had continually to mount stones and circle around the thickets of bramble and thorn that cowered in the crevices beneath the stark trees. It was the end of October. The wind had changed, bringing its first frosts.

Their talk was made difficult not only by the fact that Madeline, leading the way, had her back to him, but also by a reticence they felt but had not yet addressed.

"Why do you say 'love'?" She tossed the question over her shoulder.

"He hasn't mentioned her in the last three letters."

"That doesn't make any sense."

"Silence is the surest sign of all. As long as he was singing her praises there was nothing to worry about."

"Why worry?"

"That's easy for you to say."

"Yes. Isn't it?" She pulled ahead of him, closing the subject.

She irked him when she huffed out of conversations like that. *What's the difference to her,* he thought? Now if it was a kid of hers . . . "I just don't want him to get hurt, that's all."

She did not acknowledge his feeble last sentiment.

He was aware of something for which he had no name. It was as if her posture, her back going briskly up the hill, were trying to tell him something. The night before, at Prescott Street, he had watched the waning flames of the fireplace in his room until after midnight. He had gone to bed cold where once the anticipation of seeing Madeline would have warmed him.

"Hey!" he hollered. He stopped walking and put his hands on his hips, laying over his pique a counterfeit pique that he hoped would dispel it. "Is this the way you treat your guest?"

She faced him like a cat facing her opponent down the stairs. The sun preened at her hair, which was loose to her shoulders.

He squinted at her. "You're a harsh, unmannerly woman, Madeline Thomson!"

"Because I don't share your bias against wops?"

"No! Because you defeat me in our race up this blasted mountain."

"Race! Colman Brady! Who's racing?"

"It's a stroll, is it? A nice easy stroll? Why is the sweat pouring out of me like tears from the vale? You come down here right now!"

She did. They kissed and fell to the ground on a grassy place between boulders and kissed again. Then they lay together in each other's arms.

"It's about time," he said. "That's the first warmth from you I've had today. Sometimes, darling, you flow as coldly as spring water over stones."

"Don't rebuke me, Colman, for the way I am."

"But sometimes the way you are rebukes me."

She shrugged in his embrace, but he refused to register her movement. If she was shrugging now, even as he held her, he could not contain the hurt. He refused to feel it as anything but assent.

He felt her weight on his chest and thought of the times she had fallen asleep there. The pain of her body pressing the blood from his arms was one of his great pleasures. She was always the first to fall asleep. He teased her about that, saying she had the man's detachment. He was the one who fluttered afterward, awake and nervous. She said he exhausted her with his manliness, then smirked.

He ran the knuckle side of his forefinger along the soft down of her throat. His mouth was just above her ear. He formed words with his lips, tried them silently, not daring to speak, as if he hoped they would drop by virtue of his thinking them into the well of her consciousness.

"It's All Saints'," he said vaguely, "this week."

"Is it?" she muttered automatically, not knowing or caring.

"Yes."

He toyed with her hair, finding a peace in twirling the blond strands with their gray exceptions.

"We counted ourselves lucky in Ireland if All Saints' Day found our barns full."

"Full of what?"

"Oats. Hay. Food for the winter."

Did she shrug again? Perhaps a shiver. It was cold.

"We had to fold the land under then. It was bitter wet work."

"Did you hate it?" She was snug against him, his mouth still by her ear.

"I hated cleaning out the cow house."

Suddenly his mind was filled with the image of the fire the raiders set that night. He closed his eyes against it and did not move for a long time. He remembered the flames, how they took the thatched roof in one burst. It was as if he were there again, standing by the wall.

"You asked once how my wife died, Madeline." He paused. She did not respond. "It was a fire. A neighbor of mine set it because he wanted me to die, not her; not my brother and sister." Brady had to choke back his grief, which shocked him. "I remember going through the window of our bedroom and crawling toward the sound of our baby. It was Collins. I couldn't save them both." He stopped again, feeling for the first time in years the bottomless remorse; Nellie died because he chose his son. "The roof collapsed and she was gone."

He forced his mind elsewhere, to Prescott Street the night before. He had sat there watching the slow collapse of the ragged embers. It had become so cold. What peasant did not sit by the red of his turf fire and watch till dawn the slow collapse of the world he knew? Brady understood finally that if he had allowed himself to feel his grief for Nell and their world it would have killed him. Perhaps he would have chosen that, but for Micko, whose life alone could redeem Nellie's death. No wonder he had refused to tell Madeline about the fire before. His memory had refused to articulate it because the fire had come to embody the sudden, unexpected catastrophe that ruined Brady repeatedly and to which he had surrendered his hope. But Madeline had changed that. Brady knew that at last he was ready for her.

He felt her body soft and relaxed against him. She was resting with her head on his shoulder. Her eyes were closed. He imagined her trying to picture the fire, trying to put a face on Nell.

He formed the words with his mouth against her ear, only now he whispered them loud enough, he was certain, for her to hear.

"I love you, Madeline. No one has ever loved you as much before. Nor have I ever loved as much before as I love you."

She pulled slightly, ever so slightly, away from him.

He was excruciatingly aware of the fact that he had not spoken such words since Nell. But Nell was dead. She was dead only now that he had said such words again, not to her.

"What?" Madeline said sleepily. "Did you say something?" She shook her hair out. "I think I drifted off."

"No, nothing." Her words blew a hole in his feelings, a huge, terrible hole. "I was just thinking of Micko, and his girl."

[344]

"Oh." She snuggled back into his shoulder.

How ungarnished was her indifference.

But she was smiling, content, peaceful against him. The one language she knew suddenly was this quiet repose inside his shoulder. Perhaps that said everything. "Silence is the surest sign of all," he repeated to himself.

Colman looked up at the thatchwork of branches in the sun. Never voices replied from that sharp sky. Why should lovers reply to each other?

"He's lucky," she muttered.

"Who is?"

"Collins Brady."

"Why?"

"To have someone to love."

She pressed him, covering the unsightly wound her indifference had inflicted on him. He received her pressure and returned it.

"I suppose," Colman said, "but I don't think it's happened before. I don't think he's ever been serious about a girl before. That's a rotten way to fall in love."

"There are no rotten ways to fall in love, Colman."

"They're all rotten."

"God, what a deadly thing to say."

She tried to pull away from him, but he held on to her.

"Hearts and arrows, darling. Hearts and *arrows!* Collins and Anna. Colman and Madeline. Shall we carve it somewhere? *There,* for example!" He flicked her breast with his finger at the place he guessed her nipple was. His callousness was meant to disguise the panic he was feeling at being so vulnerable to her.

"Colman, Christ!"

"Shall we weave sweet tales of love? If you'd spent your proper quota of time on a farm, dearest, you'd know what love is; the itch of cattle at certain times of the year, in certain seasons of life."

"Colman, don't." She tried to pull away from him, but he held her.

"Don't what?"

"You're hurting my arms. Will you let go of me?"

"No."

"Please."

"You see, Madeline, I am trying to spare my son a long life alone in a house filled with wasted effort. It's not the bleeding Nazis I've been trying to protect him from. It's us! I want him to be *different!* Not suspended between disappointments, not terrified to take a step because he'd had the earth open up and swallow him, chew him a bit, and spit him out like cud. I want my son to start his life right. After that, he does it how he does it. But, by God, I will see him started right. That's what I swore the night of that fire. I promised his mother who's dead because he's alive! That's why I brought him over here to the States, and why I refuse to let him bungle everything before I've set him loose. He'll have his start, by God!" Colman was trembling as he spoke. Madeline had never seen him so agitated. He was on his knees and shaking her by the shoulders. His eyes flashed with something else she had never seen — fury. "It's one thing to take a slut — never go to war, boys, without your mistletoe! — but I'll not have him building dream pictures of a life of romance around a scheming dago whore!"

"You're mad! Colman, what are you talking about?"

She pulled out of his grasp and rolled away from him and got to her feet. He remained kneeling and had to look up at her.

He said calmly, "About what every man who's been to war knows, darling. What it does to us. What it does to women. It makes a terrible need for a big dose of the old story and its usual climax, because when so much flesh festers and bone rots you want to believe there's more to it than that. For a soldier out of his trench, the world, the entire world, is like a petticoat. In everything that moves there is a glimmer of flesh. And he wants desperately to believe in it, to make it the opposite of war. When it isn't. It's the same thing as war."

"What are you talking about? I still don't know. Surely not war. Not you, not to me."

"I suppose not. I'm talking about . . ." What was the substance of his feeling? He was furious at her. Why? ". . . Madeline, I just told you that I love you and you were asleep."

"No, I wasn't."

"You weren't?" He sat with his mouth agape, displaying his surprise.

"No. I heard you."

"*That's* what I'm talking about."

"But, Colman, you only said those words as a way to fool me."

"Fool you! What the bloody hell are you talking about?"

"I wanted to hear them very much once. Then, it seemed you were right. They ceased to matter."

"And you stopped saying it."

"Because you wanted me to."

"I didn't."

"The itch of cattle in a certain season, you said. Why should I take anything you say seriously?"

"Because I'm trying to tell you the truth."

"Well, perhaps you should try to *hear* it as well."

"Hear what?"

"I'm leaving the clinic."

That was what he knew! That was what he'd been trying to prepare himself for.

"Well," he said as lightheartedly as he could, "that gives us something to talk about, doesn't it?"

"Yes." She sat by him. She was aware of his hurt and she regretted it, but she didn't know what to say.

But then they were silent, not touching. It was as though their conversation were suddenly mislaid among the noises of the wind and the active woods.

Why had those words of hers not loosed a sense of triumph in them both? She was leaving the clinic! She was taking her life and her future back into her own hands. Whatever the demons that drove her there, she had pushed them back upon themselves.

Brady made a great effort to be sensible. "I'm delighted for you, darling." He touched her bashfully on the sleeve.

She did not answer.

"When do you think you'll . . . be discharged?"

"The week before Thanksgiving."

"That's soon."

"Yes. Time enough, though, to do my 'termination,' as they call it."

"It must be a difficult thing."

"It is, yes, very sad. They've been so good to me. Dr. Koch is . . . I love her very much."

"And you're leaving her."

"Yes. You don't know what it's like," she said, a simple statement of fact.

"Tell me, then."

"I have such a sense of peace and quiet and love there now. It's very different than it was. Last night I dreamed that I was walking on the ocean. It did not frighten me. I had no special need to keep my clothing dry."

"It's been done before, you know."

"I know." She smiled at him with great warmth. "Colman, I've changed."

"Do you think people change that much?"

"I hope to God they do. I was headed for the pit before."

"When you fell in love with me, you mean?"

"That's what saved me." A simple statement of fact.

"And that's what's changed now?" He asked it toughly, leading with his hardness to protect himself from the answer he expected.

"No," she said, "that remains. I love you still. Very much. You are the great love of my life, Colman."

[347]

"Your hyperbole would test the patience of the earth, woman."

He was leading with his pain now. He was at her mercy, but she didn't know it.

She shrugged. What the hell? They couldn't be silent with each other. They couldn't talk to each other. What the hell?

"Let's walk," she said, getting up.

He followed her to his feet, saying, "I hate walking where we must go single file. I want to hold your hand. I think you planned it this way."

"A bit further on it opens up and we can go side by side like children."

"Goody, oh goody!"

"You're silly." She led the way up the ravine.

"No, I'm nervous," he said at her back.

"That's not like you." She wasn't even looking at him.

He aimed his words at a point in the exact center of her shoulder blades. "I know it's not. That's what frightens me."

She did not respond.

The ravine led finally out into a desolate pasture in which hay wafted and bent in regular waves, a neglected somber acre. They stopped on the edge of it.

Madeline sat on a large rock, gathering the folds of her corduroy skirt about her legs, turning up the collar of her blue wool pea coat, adjusting herself in a way that invited Colman to sit by her. He did.

"I've come here at dusk," she said.

"And then made your way back in the dark? How could you?"

"There's a path to the road over there. We needn't go back through the glen."

"Good. I hated it."

"I love it. It's so eerie and gaunt. I guess we're just different."

"Say 'Terrific,' " he ordered.

"Why?"

"Just do it."

"No. Why? Not until you tell me why."

"I've heard you people can say it without moving your jaws."

"You bastard."

"You moved your jaws on that one anyway."

"You double bastard."

"Why don't we just watch the wind move across the grass here? Why do we have to fence with each other?" He took her hand.

"I didn't finish telling you."

"About leaving the clinic?"

"Yes. It's like telling you a secret. I want to finish telling you." She paused. "It's queer that I should feel such regret. I've always counted the days. Now I want to stop them from turning."

"It's hard to say good-bye."

"What's harder is to start again."

"You've a clean slate, Madeline."

"No. That's the trouble. I've wiped my slate and wiped it. It's not clean. There's no such thing. I can read it now for the first time. What's written there."

"What?"

"It's queer. My life. My whole life. My real life is written there, who I am."

"You make it sound predetermined and fixed. It's important, in addition to who you are, who you want to be."

"I'm leaving the clinic now, Colman, finally, because they've become the same thing. I want to be who I am."

"You are Madeline . . ." He let her name drift away.

"Yes. I am also Mrs. Thornton Thomson."

"You're going back to him?"

"I've been thinking of it."

"Madeline . . ." He did not know what he was about to say. ". . . don't think of it. If you think of it, it will become more than it is now, and I haven't had a chance to tell you what I have learned. I told you before that I love you."

"That was your way of avoiding this."

"Perhaps. But it is also true. I want you to come with me. To be with me. To marry me."

"Marry you! Oh, Colman." She began to weep. She wept for some moments.

"Explain to me," he said finally, "what's wrong."

"Oh, it's the *time*, Colman, *time!* If you'd only said that when I was weak and desperate."

"But then you frightened me."

"And now?"

"You still frighten me."

They laughed, both of them, nervously, a bit desperately.

But he went on, refusing the chance to undo the tension. "I am afraid you will rob me of what is most important to me. Perhaps you already have."

"What is it, what is most important to you?"

"A brand new sense I have that the future does not have to be like the past, that I can change my life, that not every surprise is bad, that I've a talent for love after all. Madeline, I'm afraid you will rob me of what you've given me."

They did not speak for a moment.

"Well?" he said.

"Well, what?"

"Jesus Christ!" He slammed his hand down on the stone, jarring himself. Shock and pain ran up his bones to the place in his skull where his brain collected and stored cracked agonies. "I've just asked you to marry me, that's what!"

"Anger is not useful."

"Or did you fall asleep again, goddamnit!"

"No, I did not fall asleep. And I did not surrender my mind to fantasy. And I didn't choose to live in dreams. I am already married."

"Well, get divorced! For Christ's sake, you've been here a year, more! The man has never visited you."

"But he has."

"He has?"

"Yes."

"When?" Colman stood, faced away from her. The burs of burdock weeds caught in the weave of his woolen trousers.

"Last week. I sent for him."

Colman turned to look at her. "Why?"

"Because I had to decide what there was, between us."

"And?"

"There is something."

"You can't be serious. The man has ignored you at a time when you've needed him."

"That's not precisely the case. He communicated with me several times. I refused to answer him. I refused to see him. He came out twice before. He has met with Dr. Koch often. He is in therapy with a colleague of hers."

"This is not what you told me."

"I know."

"I feel besmirched. You've made a fool of me."

"I do not discuss you with Thornton. Why should I discuss him with you?"

"You say that with such exquisite detachment. As if all things are the same to you. As if the two of us taken together, he and I, make one coin for you to flip."

"That isn't fair."

"Your jaws barely move when you say that. Am I heads or tails?"

"Goddamn you."

"But you said you loved me just now. Did it slip? The great love of your life, you said. I did your remark the honor of thinking it hyperbole when it was simply a lie."

"No, it wasn't."

"Well, then, Madeline, marry me. I want you to live with me. I'm sick to death of being without you. Tell me you'll divorce him. I'll have the best lawyers on it . . ."

"You're a Catholic. I'd be divorced, a fallen woman."

"The hell with that. Don't be silly. Why do you say something like that to me? You know it means nothing to me."

"I don't believe that for a minute."

"Don't you tell me what my faith or lack of it means to me. God-damnit, woman, you are infuriating! You keep deflecting me!"

"Into your anger and your rage."

"Yes, goddamnit!"

"Which, frankly, terrify me."

"Will you marry me or not?"

"No."

That word of hers nearly killed him. No? No? He knew at once he had done this to himself. He had used language their liaison would not sustain. He had pressed it past its point. He exerted an enormous control on himself. He had to speak to her or leave her. He could not stand that silence. Silence is the surest sign of all.

"Why won't you? You love me."

"Yes."

"Then why?"

"I can't explain. Except to say I've learned to live within my boundaries."

"That's not recovery, Madeline. It's resignation."

"Colman, I cannot start my life over. Neither can you. I am going to make do with what I have. I am going to accept my limits, my finitude."

"I know, it's because my jaw moves when I say 'Terrific.' "

"No. It's not because of that."

"It's because I've the filthy habit of bribing people."

She hesitated, then said, "No."

"You hesitated."

"You know I've never approved of that. But it has nothing to do with us, except for what it reveals about your idea of love. Your bribery done in the name of love for your son is your way of keeping him in chains to you, even if he doesn't know it."

"I didn't confide that in you to have you throw it in my face."

"I'm sure you didn't. But you're the one who brought it up."

[351]

"I was trying to understand why you won't marry me, since you won't tell me."

"I told you."

"Your boundaries, your limits."

"Yes."

"And mine presumably."

She would not look at him.

"Right?" he persisted.

She nodded miserably, ashamedly.

"I'm still a croppie, papist sod-buster, turf-digger to you, aren't I? I was a fool to mess with your kind."

"My kind?" A sharp anger replaced her misery. "My kind? That's it exactly, Colman. You haven't been fucking me. You've been fucking my kind. Did you confess it? Did you tell your priest every little detail?"

"Yes," Brady said evenly, holding on to himself as tightly as he could. "Every Saturday. I've told him about your orgasms, how your skin turns the color of Christ's blood, which I then drink."

That defeated her. "Colman, don't."

"Well, what a conclusion to our story! Here I've been riding at the end of your string all this time thinking I was a thoroughbred stallion, when what I have become is a whimpering puppy crying for you to only kick me again! Jesus Christ, what a fool I've been! You asked me into your life and showed me your transcendent loneliness. You played me for my Druid sympathies, and you went raving out of your skull, half-killing yourself with booze and convincing me that I was the culprit, that your passion for me had you on the brink of madness. And all this time you've been asking me to unleash my heart and offer it to you so we'd be one in being vulnerable to each other, you were just setting things in a row so that our story would have a right and just conclusion. It wouldn't do to have the yeoman say no to the princess without the *p*, now would it? That's your prerogative, ain't it, Mrs. Madeline Gardner Thornton fucking Thomson! You goddamn devil bitch!"

He slapped her in the face, knocking her half over.

He put his hands together as if they could prevent each other from doing that again. He saw that he had hit her terribly hard. Her eyes were glazed over with the shock of the blow. The side of her face had gone white. Where had all her blood gone? At the thought of her blood, he felt his own veins running dry, as if a wind from Death Valley ran through them.

He had had the feeling before. Once. He had had the feeling after the fire when he'd gone to the Clonmel Barracks at dawn to shoot Gavin. He remembered the dried vomit flaking from Gavin's beard, his misery and self-loathing. He remembered how his eye looked after he'd shot him through it, and he remembered the fever of vengeance, the killing fever that had taken him from one man to another, killing, killing, killing. The last of them he had struck squarely on the head with the butt end of his weapon. He had struck him again, and that blow had been the best one.

"Why don't you do that again?" she said. There was a depth of defiance in her that shocked him and brought him back.

"What?"

"Hit me." Her hand, the back of it, was at her cheek. The composure of her eyes irritated him. They contained no passion, only will.

"Madeline, I didn't mean to hit you. I'm sorry."

"*Au contraire!* You've meant to do that for a long time."

"And you?"

"It is my business now to protect myself. *That,* darling, is what we were talking about. I refuse to expose myself to any of you."

"What do you mean?"

"Concretely, metaphorically, I mean money."

"Money!"

"Yes. Yours, Thornton's, mine. If I divorce him I lose his. If I marry you I lose mine."

"I don't follow that."

"The Gardner money, darling. It could never swim the Tiber or snap Friday mackerels, even if I did."

"Surely money isn't the issue."

"Of course not. There's *your* cryptic fortune. But don't you see at what a price it would come to me?"

"I told you I didn't mean to hit you."

"Not that, not a blow, not a mere moment's viciousness. Oh, Colman . . ." — she leaned forward, practically touching him, suddenly pleading — ". . . don't you see there's so little of me left, and I must protect that little like a child. I am afraid of you. You would eat me. And when or if you spat me out there would be nothing, because I would have died to everything I ever was or wanted so that I could go with you. And I cannot do that. I cannot ever be so utterly at your mercy, or anyone's."

"But if you stay with Thornton, it would be the same."

"He has no power over me. None whatsoever. I do not love him. Which is why I can stay with him. Why I will."

"Madeline, I love you."

The antipendulum of rage, a tenderness he neither expected nor could control, sailed in on him like an ocean-going vessel on the tide. "I love you," he repeated. He did not touch her. He felt overwhelmingly the wrong of his striking her, the sin of it.

"Your love, Colman, cannot rescue me. That is what I have learned. That is what it taught me. It is you who have given me this courage."

"Forgive me if I don't say 'You're welcome.' "

She shrugged, elegantly.

"Perhaps," he said, "I should just say 'Forgive me.' "

"Of course I do." Relief was tangible in her voice. Perhaps things wouldn't end miserably, hatefully. "And you me?"

"No."

"What?"

"I do not forgive you."

She shrugged again. She stood up, and with an infuriating detachment she said, "Well, could you at least kiss me good-bye?"

Brady felt two things at once: how useless it was to struggle against what had already occurred, and a hope that if he could yet say the right word or do the right thing what had already occurred might change. He put his arms inside her pea jacket and around her waist and let his small fingers settle deftly inside the lip of her skirt. But it was not flesh he felt. She was wearing a slip, silken, discreet. Perfume filled his nostrils; he could never dream her scent.

Madeline responded by adjusting her gaze to make clear that only the most chaste kiss would do. It was too late for all the rest.

But Brady worked his fingers against the silk, causing it to slide upward along her back.

"Colman . . ."

He covered her mouth with his, silencing her, stuffing her urgently with his tongue.

One hand was at the buttons of her skirt, undoing them.

She turned her face this way and that, but he kept pressing against her, his face screwed up with the effort. His eyes were closed. He could not see the rough melancholy that filled hers.

His other hand was at her right breast, mashing it against its ribs, forcing the heavy wool jacket half off her shoulder.

"Colman!" she gasped, wrenching her head back and away. He tightened his left arm and held her. "No! No!"

She twisted away from him. He persisted and the loud noise of her blouse ripping was like a horn in battle, which charged their struggle, made it suddenly fiercer and deadlier.

The buttons on her skirt undone, he had it below her thighs, then down. The slip seemed to rise on its own smooth track. He had his hand inside her legs.

She pushed both her hands against him mightily, one at his chest, one at the promontory of his thorax, which must have choked him because suddenly he had her wrist in a bone, his own hand, twisting it back behind her until she thought it would break.

His other hand was in her.

His tongue was in her mouth, and she brought her teeth together on it.

"Oh, Christ!" he screamed, pulling away from her. Blood appeared instantly at the corner of his mouth. He shoved her roughly back against the boulder upon which they had been sitting. She thought for an instant that she was free of him, but he was on her before her spine had diffused the pain it took when her tailbone slammed the rock.

Suddenly Madeline Thomson was supremely indifferent to his touch.

She had found her defense. She went limp, completely, utterly.

Her clothing was more than half off, and she was exposed to him beneath him. He was on the point of entering her when his body registered the inert lifelessness of hers. She was not moving a muscle.

He opened his eyes and looked at her.

How ungarnished was her indifference!

Her eyes were vacant of anger, contempt, and pity.

Slowly he drew himself up, staring at her continually, expecting her to yawn.

He had never been so defeated in his life.

He repaired his clothing.

Still she did not move, but remained sprawled impassively across the flat stone.

Finally she stood, closed her blouse and coat, drew her skirt on, fastened buttons and snaps, brushed herself once, and turned. She walked across the desolate pasture toward the path that led to the road. She did not look back.

Colman Brady watched her until she was gone. He tasted his blood and his self-loathing. That he had done that to her whom he loved, whom he still loved, filled him with such contempt that he thought himself worthy of the final despair which had already closed itself on him like clamps. It was the despair that cauterized his other feelings and that made it impossible for him to weep. Colman Brady understood that he would never be devastated like that again because he would never suffer from such hope again.

Though it would soon be dark, he turned and began to retrace his way through the ravine, Ice Glen, hating it and knowing it was the only way he could go.

⟿ 8 ⟾

GENNARO ANSELMO had a rule; he never met personally with Colman Brady. In the nearly eight years that Brady had been fronting for him, they had met fewer than a dozen times. When he received word that Brady wanted to see him he knew something important was at issue. It never occurred to Anselmo that the matter about which Brady intended to talk to him involved not their business, but Brady's own family.

It was a clear, crackling morning in early March. Colman Brady kicked at a stone in the footpath that ran by the bench on which he was sitting. The stone nearly made it to the edge of the river wall, disappointing him. The Charles River, a dusty cobalt, stretched before him across to Boston. He was on the Cambridge side of the river halfway between the Long-fellow Bridge and the Harvard Bridge just above the MIT boathouse. It was the widest part of the river, nearly half a mile across. Beacon Hill, the golden dome of the State House, the terraced rooftops of the old houses stepping down to the plain of Back Bay, sat across from him primly, self-satisfied, like a Lionel model of itself. He watched the MTA train from Harvard race across the Longfellow Bridge between the salt-cellar pillars and into its tunnel at the base of the hill. He watched a pair of jibless sailboats maintain a perfect synchrony with each other on the same point of sail, on the same gentle wind. A lone oarsman in a shell slithered along the river, marring its surface with a thin scar of a wake.

When the man sat down next to him Brady knew without looking it was Anselmo. Neither spoke.

An athlete wearing a maroon shirt with a gray "H" on its breast ran by them. He was breathing hard and sweating.

"So?" Anselmo said.

Brady hesitated. "So hello. How are you, my friend?" Brady looked at him. The same drooping eyes. Anselmo was always smaller, thinner than he remembered, but now he was older. Anselmo was wearing an expensive wool topcoat over a dark business suit. He was bareheaded. He looked prosperous. His face unaccountably made Brady think of the short riverbank eaten away imperceptibly but steadily by long erosion until the engineers come and build their wall to protect it. "You look well," Brady said.

Anselmo nodded. He was not going to put Brady at ease by engaging in pleasantries.

Brady turned up the collar of his own overcoat, a black cashmere. He looked prosperous, too. He ran his right hand through the loose mass of his hair.

A breeze kicked across the river, quickening it with an embroidery of fine waves. The two boats leaned away from it.

"I need your help, Gennaro."

Anselmo looked at Brady without turning toward him.

"A private matter, having nothing to do with Monument or Christopher." These were the names of the two companies through which Brady funneled Anselmo's money into real estate, shipping, and, most recently, manufacturing. The Christopher Tool Company was making a fortune producing tiny precision ball bearings for use in gyroscopes that were essential for the new generation of navigational gear that airplanes, ships, and even tanks required. The war was turning out to be a boon, a great and rewarding boon.

"So?" Anselmo repeated.

Colman withdrew an envelope from his inside breast pocket, opened it, took out a sheet of paper, which he unfolded painstakingly and gave to Anselmo.

Anselmo read.

Dear Daddo, I want to be short and to the point with this because I know you will not approve. Anna and I are going to be married on the feast of St. Joseph (19 March) here in Agrigento. I know this is not the way you would want it, but perhaps there will be a time when I can explain what I feel and what Anna feels and how compelled we are to wait no longer. I have talked this over with the priest here and he agrees that it is best to marry now. Major Cheever has given his permission. Anna's father approves. I hope you can too. Your loving son, Micko. P.S. Tell Aunt Maeve I'm sorry.

"Agrigento?" Anselmo said.

Brady nodded.

"I didn't know your son was in Sicily."

"Since the summer."

Anselmo looked quizzically at Brady, his eyes showing for once what he was feeling. He could understand neither the sense of Brady's son at war in the homeland of his own parents, nor Brady's impulse to share that irony with him.

[357]

"Why are you showing me this?"

"Because I want the marriage stopped."

"Then forbid it."

"I can't."

"Your son wouldn't obey you?"

"He might. But I can't do it. I can't forbid him."

Anselmo felt something near contempt. It was inconceivable to him that he would involve someone like Brady in a comparable situation in his own family. It was inconceivable to him that he could not control his sons.

"I thought the army might prevent it, but I've checked. Sicily is no longer classified as a combat zone. All that's required is permission of the C.O. Which the kid has."

"Why do you wish to stop it?" Anselmo asked.

The two men looked at each other directly for the first time. They both knew the answer to the question. Boundaries, finitude, limits; Madeline Thomson's words would have put it positively.

"He's too young. He's only twenty-three."

Colman had married Nellie Deasy at twenty-two.

Anselmo shrugged; *It is not for me to contradict you,* he seemed to say.

"We do not know the girl. Perhaps we do not know him. I am afraid, Gennaro, of losing my son."

Anselmo nodded. Every father knows that fear.

Colman was afraid that his voice would let Anselmo hear too much. He did not want Anselmo or anyone to know what a frightful cadence was beating in him. Collins was making the first great choice of his life, and with no reference to what Colman thought or felt or expected or required. That was a pain and a loss for which he had not been prepared. Such faithlessness from his son! It was not just that the girl was a Sicilian peasant; that served only to make the boy's immaturity dramatic. It was that the boy still needed Colman's advice and comfort and support, even if he didn't know it. Everything in Colman was aimed at the single target: getting Collins launched on a different track from his own. Colman wanted Anselmo to know that he was very concerned about this matter. He didn't want him to know he was obsessed with it. He said, as casually as he could, "The great pressures of being away, of being at war — they make the boy impulsive, a bit foolish. Perhaps later, when the war is over, if they still . . . he can return for her. She can visit . . ."

Anselmo raised his hand; *Do not lie to me. Do not pretend that delay would satisfy.*

"Why do you ask my help?"

"I presume on our friendship. I am certain of your influence in your homeland."

"Brady," Anselmo said, smiling suddenly, "you forget. I was born in Worcester. We discussed that once. You are the immigrant. Not me."

Brady could imagine himself saying, "I've lived here twenty years. What do I have to do to be referred to as an American?" And he was an American, even more than Anselmo, who, no matter where he was born, still had the hill dirt of Sicily under his nails, garlic in his eyes if not in his breath.

Brady let his gaze drift across the river to Boston. What the hell, how different were they? His eye followed the silhouette of Beacon Hill up and down its etched contours.

"Right!" Brady said, forcing a laugh. "I'd forgotten. But you know what I mean. I was thinking of your people. I thought you might know someone with contacts in the region."

"Agrigento?"

"Yes. Her father is the mayor of the village."

"Village? It's not a village. Agrigento is the provincial capital. There are fifty thousand people. That's today. Agrigento was the richest and most cultivated city-state of Greece in the fifth century B.C. Then it had several hundred thousand citizens. It is no village."

"Well, in any case," Brady tried to stifle the impatience he felt. "Their name is Taormina. Her name is Anna. I don't know her father's name, his Christian name."

"Taormina, a proud family. I don't know them personally. My people are from the other side of the island."

"But your influence. Surely, you could do something. I want you to offer the man a fortune. I'll pay anything."

"The mayor of an important city, Brady, is not a man to be trifled with. Taormina is not a family to insult."

"I mean no insult, Gennaro. I would not ask you to do that."

"It's an insult nonetheless. If your son's word is given, a grave insult." Anselmo lifted his shoulders and upper torso as if in an effort to ease his breathing.

Neither man spoke for some moments.

"I have nothing further to say, Gennaro."

"Nor do I."

Brady shifted toward the Sicilian and looked in his eyes. He feared that Anselmo was saying no, and suddenly a powerful desperation welled up in him. He took Anselmo's arm and, despite his intentions, he spoke frantically words which, unlike all the others, were unplanned and emotional.

"We are alike, Gennaro! Can't we find each other still, wanderers in this wilderness of lies? Forgive my uncouth ways. Can't you help me to save the one unperishable fruit of my life?"

Anselmo refused to meet Brady's eyes. He was embarrassed for him. He was losing control of himself — Brady! Brady who had mastered the use of mirrors and blue smoke to fool everyone! But he did not fool Anselmo. He never could, which was why Anselmo used him, trusted him, cared for him. Anselmo was considering it. What Brady asked was simply enough accomplished, and he would use his influence in such a personal matter routinely for a neighbor. But Brady was no neighbor, and that was what Anselmo was thinking about. One should not involve outsiders in personal matters, nor should they you. But Brady was important to Anselmo, and this was an opportunity to bind Brady to him again. It would not be unuseful to demonstrate to Brady that Anselmo's power did indeed extend across an ocean. Anselmo could reinforce their friendship and his authority in one stroke.

"I will do it," he said, "yes."

Brady nodded, and though he did not speak, his face showed his relief.

Anselmo stood and left.

Beacon Hill across the water held Brady's gaze until a swift train from Harvard burst out of its tunnel onto the Longfellow Bridge.

For the days after that Colman's attention continually drifted to Collins. How the boy would be hurt when the girl's father rejected him, but how the boy would thank his own father years later for having spared him his own impulse. Colman could not concentrate on anything. He was more anxious, perhaps, than he'd ever been about anything to hear from Anselmo that the wedding plans were canceled. It did not occur to Brady that his anxiety was disproportionate or misplaced. His anxiety was total and unyielding. It seemed to him his son's entire future — not to mention his own — depended on how this regrettable business was resolved.

Nearly two weeks after their first meeting Anselmo and Brady met again at the same place, this time at the Sicilian's request.

It was a similar day, but warmer. Neither man wore his topcoat. The river was gray, more wrinkled. The breeze was strong but benign. A lean spring afternoon. Brady had walked from Prescott Street along the esplanade to the Harvard Bridge, crossed, and come down the path by Memorial Drive. It took him thirty minutes. Anselmo had walked from the North End past the train station and across the dam. It took him twenty. He arrived at the bench first.

When Brady came, he sat down without speaking. Anselmo was reading a book. He did not look up.

"What are you reading?"

Anselmo closed the book. "It is not important."

Brady looked down at it. There were no words on its cover.

"There will be no wedding," Anselmo said. He was staring across the river. There was a sting in his manner. What was it if not sorrow? That perception kept Brady from speaking.

"Do you want to know?" Anselmo asked.

"Yes."

"The girl is dead."

It was wrong to speak such words in mild weather; that was the strange thought Brady had.

"What?"

"The girl is dead."

Which girl? What day was it? What time?

"I don't understand."

"It was unfortunate. Taormina refused. My cousins wanted only to accomplish what they thought was my will. They took the girl. It was a foolish thing to do, but . . ." Anselmo raised his shoulders and lowered them. "Taormina's sons and your son pursued them. They were three days in rough country. My cousins did not know the girl was carrying a child."

"Carrying a . . . ?" The word died in Brady's throat.

Panic like blood coursed through him, leaving behind cold skin which sagged around his bones. Of course she was carrying a child! That explained why his son would defy him, risk his anger and disapproval. The marriage was born of Micko's urgent need to do the right thing. Colman should have known. Of course she'd been pregnant. The damn kid. For honor's sake. The damn kid. How he loved him!

"She died giving birth in the hills. When Taormina's sons came, they killed my cousins, all but one. Now there is war between my family and a stranger's, where before there was peace." Anselmo slowly shook his head, displaying regret and remorse. His cousins had made terrible mistakes, but so had he. He had misjudged Taormina. He had overestimated his own influence. When the mere intimation of one's will is not sufficient to accomplish it, then one's power has already failed.

"My son?" Brady asked.

"I don't know. He won't be permitted to see the child again."

"The child lived?"

"Yes. A son."

Brady's shock began to articulate itself. He glared at Anselmo. "Did you think I wanted you to murder somebody? Who said anything about kidnapping? Did you think I'm like you are, that I don't care how my will is accomplished? That girl's blood is on your hands, Gennaro, not mine!"

But it was on the hands of both, and they both knew it.

Anselmo saw the toil of Brady's face. He could feel the pulse of muscles convulsing under his own skin. What Brady said was true. Anselmo would be at his mercy now, in his debt, instead of the other way around. Anselmo said nothing.

Brady stood up and raved, "It is not merely 'unfortunate' that she is dead! It is the end of everything! Goddamn you, what have you made me do?" Brady stopped, stunned by the thought that Anselmo had made him into Peter Gavin, from whose beard dried vomit flaked. The thought bruised his mind with an eerie calm. He turned and walked up river.

Gennaro Anselmo watched him go and he was thinking what he learned — never again to disregard the strict instinct, never again to let enter his world the most dangerous enemy, a friend.

Brady walked to Prescott Street.

By the time he went into the house he had his clamps on.

"Hello, dearie," he said cheerfully to Maeve. Maeve need never know any of it, thank God.

"Are you in for dinner tonight, Colman? Clara wants to know." Maeve waved her gleaming cigarette holder at him from her chair in the sun porch. She'd been reading a magazine. The damn radio was on.

"Of course. And Ernie's coming over. And I think I'll ask Kathleen."

"Oh, Colman, you should leave her alone. You just get her hopes up."

"Didn't I tell you? I've been seeing her again."

"The poor thing." Maeve was not joking. She drew on her cigarette abruptly.

"Whose side are you on, anyway?"

"I'd have thought that string would break by now, it's so old."

"Like myself, darling. Like myself. Nothing left for me but an Irish spinster."

"You're cruel to women, Colman Brady." He walked over to her, bent and pinched her cheek. He came close to hurting her. "Aren't I, though?" he said and laughed. "I'll be upstairs. I've some letters to write."

He had one to write.

"Dear Micko, I'm sorry this has been so long in coming, but I wanted to think over your news carefully. With luck you'll have this by the nineteenth. I hope so. Because I want to tell you that, though I'm terribly sad not to be with you, your marriage to Anna has my complete approval. I respect you and trust you. If you've chosen her she must be wonderful. If you've decided not to wait, you must love each other very much. I can't wait to meet her. I've not told Maeve. I thought I'd let

you do that yourself in your own way. I love you very much, Micko. And because you do, I love your Anna. I want nothing but your happiness. Always, Daddo."

Brady folded the letter without reading it over. He had no decision to make about sending it, as he'd had none to make about writing it. There were simply no choices to be made in the matter. He was the flawed hero acting out the last scene, the one in which chaos is not loosed upon the world only because he willingly accepts what consequence awaits him. He put the letter in an envelope and marked it. He wrote out a check for two thousand dollars, tore it in half, and wrote out a second for five thousand, which he enclosed.

He then sealed — as it seemed to him — two things at once; the envelope marked "Special," and the eternal damnation of his own immortal soul.

FOUR

1

JANET LINDSAY had been terribly afraid it was a mistake to come to Washington. That was especially so mornings when she'd wake up alone and cold, cast a groggy eye around her chic little room in the cellar of a Georgetown bowfront, find the radium dial and see that, invariably, it was only five o'clock. She could never sleep through until seven. Those two hours were what she hated most. She didn't have to be at her office until half past eight. The *Times-Herald* didn't come until quarter past seven. She couldn't type whatever report she was working on for fear of waking the Davises upstairs. Early mornings were the worst.

Daytime was a swirl of activity around Senator Lodge's office and not so bad. She was one of the senator's seven administrative aides, and the business of answering letters and researching minor legislation was, on the whole, as interesting and as dull as she'd expected it would be. Harold Sisson Evans, her political science professor and advisor — her idol, really — had warned her that the work on Capitol Hill would be an uneven mixture of the exhilarating and the menial. She didn't mind the work. She rather liked it, even though Lodge had turned out to be an aloof and uninspiring mentor who was made so ill at ease by the presence in his office of a young, pretty Smith graduate that he pretended most of the time not to notice her. The senator dealt with Mr. Forbes and expected him to deal with the staff. That was all right with Janet Lindsay. She thought Lodge a bit of a fogy. No wonder he and her father were such friends.

Evenings were worse than daytimes because there were always parties, and Janet Lindsay was afraid to refuse an invitation, partly for fear of being dropped if she offended her contacts, and partly for fear of spending an evening alone. She dreaded being alone. At Smith she had concocted grand fantasies of Washington parties. She imagined them as gatherings of witty and intellectual men — the New Deal Circle — who smoked pipes and took champagne in tulip glasses from trays carried by handsome young waiters. The talk — as she imagined it — was all of boldly saving Greece and boldly stopping HUAC and modestly crowning George Marshall king of Europe. There were never any women at the parties Janet

Lindsay conjured in her mind except herself. And she was always in a corner with Harold Sisson Evans making a point.

In fact, Washington parties were false and stilted affairs. The Young Republican crowd shoved themselves into tiny Georgetown flats with the same flippancy and silliness with which they'd shoved themselves into dormitory rooms at Amherst and Dartmouth. They talked about football and the jobs they hoped to land in the '52 campaign.

Occasionally Janet Lindsay went to a party on Foxhall Road. Embassy people and senior bureaucrats and undersecretaries in tuxedoes abounded. They were nice to her because she was pretty and from Smith and worked for Senator Lodge, whom everyone was courting. At first she'd been buoyed by the feeling of being among the most important people in the country, but gradually she began to notice that Foxhall Road parties tended to be very boring until almost over, by which time the most important people in the country were all embarrassingly drunk. Once, however, at the Harcourts', she met Eleanor Roosevelt, who she thought was as wonderful in person as she was in the papers. But even Mrs. Roosevelt seemed unable to transcend the inhibiting party chatter that seemed to make banalities of the most important questions in life. Janet Lindsay hated party chatter for that reason, and also because she was shy and not good at it.

It was nearly a year after she'd come to Washington before she decided it was not a mistake. In April of 1951 she fell in love. When she woke up before dawn that spring, things were very different. She hopped quickly out of bed, donned her old robe, went to the broad oak plank on two stools that served as her desk, flipped on the gooseneck light, and read for the two hours that seemed to her then a luxury, not a dreaded pit of nothing between night and day. She read the transcript of the hearings of the Special Committee of the Senate Judiciary and Commerce Committees to Investigate Organized Crime in the United States. The transcript was enormous because it recorded the year-long investigation of political corruption and syndicate crime in a dozen cities.

Janet Lindsay, like many staffers on the hill, had been interested initially in the work of the Kefauver Committee, as it was called, because it had generated so much publicity. Its hearings over the year had been carried by national television networks and had been the backdrop against which senators, lawyers, and hoodlums had played out a drama so suspensefully drawn in the bold strokes of good against evil that the nation had been totally captivated by it. And so had she. Though she was put off by the manner of the tall, gangling chairman, whose accent and grammar betrayed his Appalachian background, Janet Lindsay was enthralled by the relentless questioning of the committee counsel, Rudolph Halley, whose detailed probing of dozens of witnesses gave the impression of an incredible grasp of the national crime problem. It was to see him in action that she had arranged to take an early lunch hour one day and sit in on the committee session.

She'd been disappointed. Halley was not conducting the interrogation that day. The witness was a functionary from Roosevelt Raceway in New York, and he was being questioned about the bookkeeping methods of the track by one of Halley's assistants, a young lawyer with a Boston accent. At first Janet had assumed, like most committee members and the press, that the session would be too dull and unimportant to stay with, but the lawyer was very attractive and she was drawn to him. She thought it funny later that after all her time in Washington it was a young man behind the grand dais who moved her. Was it the panoply of Congress, the quiet solemnity of the room, the sacredness of the tradition? No, it had been he, the way he looked away from the witness once right at her, right into her eyes. He had smiled at her. She had blushed. When she left the hearing room, slipping out quietly at the end of her lunch hour, she asked a guard who the lawyer was. He pointed to a name on a page of that day's *Acts; M. Collins Brady, Asst. Coun.* An Irish name, she noted, which didn't faze her nearly as much as it would have her parents if they'd known of her even mild curiosity.

But he'd gone to Harvard, College '42, Law '49. Her friend Sissy Williams checked with a friend she had on the Judiciary Committee staff, who said Halley had recruited Brady for the investigation because of some articles he'd written for the *Harvard Law Review,* but Sissy couldn't find out what the articles were about. There was talk that Brady would join Kefauver's personal staff when the committee disbanded, and that meant he would be on board for the campaign. Everyone knew the senator from Tennessee was going to run for President if Truman didn't.

Janet Lindsay looked up the articles. There were two, one concerned with the civil liberties violations consequent to the televising of government proceedings, and the other a study of the past uses of the contempt citation by congressional committees to elicit testimony from hostile witnesses. Both articles had been written, apparently, in connection with the legal questions rising out of the House Committee on Un-American Activities' 1948 hearings involving Alger Hiss. Though Brady's articles did not express an opinion about the Hiss matter, Janet Lindsay was sure, judging from their preoccupation with the rights of witnesses, that he sympathized with Hiss. She was, of course, pleased. And surprised. She thought all the Irish were insane about Communists.

Janet Lindsay also ascertained that M. Collins Brady was not married. She continued throughout much of April spending what time she could at the committee hearings. Halley was very good, and when Kefauver was conducting the questioning of witnesses, he was impressive for his dignity and drawling innocence. The witnesses at those, the concluding sessions of the investigation, were mainly minor figures whose testimony had not been taken in the on-site hearings. Those highly publicized sessions focused on well-known characters like Frank Costello, boss of the New York underworld, and William O'Dwyer, New York's former mayor, whose reputation had been damaged by testimony before the committee. The April sessions in Washington had the purpose of tying up loose ends before the committee issued its report to Congress with its recommendations for legislation. Even so, Janet Lindsay was fascinated by the process, which seemed to her much more interesting than anything going on in Lodge's office. She considered the hearings and their direct effort to combat a major social problem the most important project in the entire Congress, and she felt that way even when M. Collins Brady was absent.

One day, just as a session adjourned, he approached her. She saw him coming. Walking toward her through the chaos of strewn chairs, television cables, reporters, technicians, an exiting gallery, he was tall and self-possessed. He was running his right hand through his tousled sandy hair. His left hand was in his pocket, and his blue pin-striped suit coat was drawn back around it, exposing a gold watch chain that swung in its perfect curve across his vest.

She thought of running out of the room. If he spoke to her, she would die. If he didn't, she would die.

"Hello," he said, standing above her. She couldn't move in her chair. She couldn't reply.

"I keep seeing you at these sessions," he said. He had a soft voice. When he questioned witnesses it could be hard, edgy, almost cruel, depending on whom and what he was asking. There was something in him that frightened her.

"I'm Janet Lindsay." She was tall enough, when she stood, to feel as though their eyes moved in the same plane. Most of the men who attracted her were too short. He was perfect, even without the dais.

"I know you are."

"You do?" She was looking at him with that cool self-assurance that her parents had spent so much money on at Willow Country Day, and Miss Hall's and L'Ecole de Suisse and Smith. She had an air of competence, achievement, and brain that she never drew over herself except when she was uncomfortable and afraid and nearly speechless. She smiled. He would never know. Men never did.

"Yes, I found out. I'm an investigator, right? You work for Salty."

"No. Lodge."

"A purely legal distinction if it's between Saltonstall and Lodge. In any case, you work for me."

"Sorry?"

"I'm from Massachusetts, too. My name is Collins Brady."

"I know."

"You do?" He was pleased and showed it.

"Yes. It's in the *Record*. You're the assistant counsel."

"Not 'the'; 'an.' "

"A lawyerly distinction."

"What do you think of the hearings?"

She had to be careful. It would not do to gush. "I think they raise some serious problems. At times you seem to be conducting a trial — not you so much, but Halley. One could hardly call it due process."

"We try to be careful of that. One has to balance the rights of the person with the rights of the public."

"Another lawyerly distinction."

He laughed.

"I think the hearings are the best thing happening on the Hill."

"Really?"

"Yes."

"Better than, say . . . ?"

She thought he was going to mention HUAC. He would be testing her, trying to find out her sympathies. Everyone met each other with measuring sticks.

". . . the Neptune?"

"The Neptune?" she replied, surprised. It was a bar on Pennsylvania Avenue, a joint younger staffers went to in the late afternoon.

"Yes. It's a bar."

"I know what it is. I'm just surprised."

"But are you free?"

"Now?"

"Yes."

"I could get free."

She looked at her watch, a sensible watch, an Elgin with a big face and a manly leather strap. The ease with which she lifted her wrist and turned it belied what she was feeling. Here was this man whom she had been watching for a month, whose face she had been holding in her mind just before sleeping, whose name had been on her tongue or just beneath it each morning — here he was asking her to go to the Neptune now.

Something in her rebelled. Why wasn't he asking her about HUAC? Why wasn't he pursuing the point she'd raised? But that had been a ploy. It had been *his* point, after all. He must have known what she was up to,

her old tricks. She had won Harold Sisson Evans over at Smith by flattering him mercilessly with a bombardment of his own ideas, the small puffs
from his books, as if she'd thought of them herself. But that technique
wouldn't work with this man, something told her. Or had it worked already? She didn't want to discuss fine points of law with him. She wanted
to have a drink with him.

"Shall I meet you there, then?" he asked.

"All right."

"When?"

"Half an hour."

"Fine."

Brady couldn't believe his luck. He'd been watching her for weeks. The
sight of her eleven rows back in the grandiose room — she almost always
sat in the same chair — had merely piqued his curiosity at first. Who was
she? She was very tall and slender. She was beautiful, with bright golden
hair down to her shoulders. Whenever he looked up at her she was taking
notes, which made him wonder at first if she was avoiding his eyes. Once
she looked right at him, and he smiled at her and she smiled back. He
had lost his train of thought and forgotten what he had just asked Pete
Incarra about the take at Roosevelt. After that he had looked forward to
seeing her in the hearing room, and he was disappointed when she wasn't
there. And now he was meeting her for a drink. He couldn't believe his
luck.

"Hi," he said. She was sitting in a booth. He had deliberately arrived
late. He slid into the bench opposite her.

"Hi." She raised her beer at him.

"You arranged your schedule, I see."

"I did. I'm en route to L.O.C., if anyone asks."

"Researching?"

"Regulation of seaboard fishing."

Brady nodded.

The waitress brought him a beer and a shot of bourbon. He downed the
shot and sipped at the beer.

His abrupt manner with the drink made Janet uncomfortable, but she
didn't show it.

"I'm glad finally to meet you," he said.

"You said you're from Boston."

"I said Massachusetts. I'm from Brookline. A lawyerly distinction, eh?"

"Quite. I'm from Ipswich."

"And you went to Smith."

"And you went to Harvard, twice. You must have liked it."

"I couldn't get into Yale. Why Smith?"

"My mother went there. Did your father go to Harvard?"

Collins interrupted her with a laugh. "My father's Irish."

Janet raised her brows. She didn't see why that mattered.

"I mean real Irish, from the ould sod."

"Oh?"

They were silent for a moment.

"I met a Negro," Janet said, "who, when I asked him what he did, said he went to Harvard. I was very impressed, and I said, 'Harvard, how nice.' To which he said, 'No, Harvard.' And I said 'Harvard?' And he said emphatically, 'No, Harvard!' Of course he was saying 'Howard.' "

"But with a Harvard accent." Brady laughed. "Actually we had quite a few coloreds there. Four in my class alone."

"How liberal."

"How snide!" Collins liked her very much.

"I was just thinking it probably takes a lot for the average Negro to go to Harvard."

"The average Negro doesn't go to Harvard. Why did you come to Washington?"

"Politics. I'm interested. The job with Senator Lodge looked better than teaching kindergarten."

"Is it?"

"To tell you the truth, it's pretty dull. We have a sleepy office. Mostly it's trying to keep units at Fort Devens and get the new SAC base for the Cape. I write letters. 'Dear Mrs. Gallstone, let me take this opportunity to assure you that I could not agree with you more. I intend to incorporate your contribution to my thinking on the subject in my next speech from the Senate floor. In the meantime I am enclosing the texts of several other addresses, each of which in its own way concerns itself with the broader implications of the question you so usefully raise. Sincerely, Henry Cabot Lodge Junior, period, exclamation point.' "

"What question?"

"Any question. You name it."

"How often do you write that letter?"

"Fifty times a day. *And* I sign it. Blur the initials, but with a flourish."

"Very clever."

"I'm a clever person." She paused. "I don't mean to be so with you. I spend my day counterfeiting and forging. It's hard to stop."

"I spend my day interrogating."

"So we're both still at it? I need another." She held up her glass. When he took it from her he touched her fingers.

"What?"

[373]

"The champagne," she said crustily, "of bottle beer."

Brady slid out of the booth and disappeared.

Janet Lindsay did not know what to do. She had drawn attention to their banter, the light and slightly false set of it. He had noted it with as much solemnity as she. They were both ready for something less quick, flamboyant, self-conscious. She was flattered and excited. He gave her looks of such open interest that she could hardly keep from blushing. When his fingers had touched hers around the glass, she felt innocent and therefore afraid.

Two beers later — an hour's talk about politics and the future and the aftermath of war and the meaning of Korea and the odds in favor of atomic warfare and whether Truman could make stick his relieving of MacArthur of the Far Eastern Command — he leaned grandly back against the leather booth and said, as if announcing the findings of a court, "Janet Lindsay, I believe you are what is commonly called in our era an idealist."

"Do you think so?" She beamed at him. She took his remark as a compliment, even though she was not insensitive to its condescension and the hint of mockery in it.

"I do. And I like idealists."

"You do?"

"Yes. Very much. Especially French ones." She had quoted Sartre.

"Well, I think you're an idealist too, Collins."

He bowed. "In that case," he said, "do me two favors."

"What?"

"One; call me Micko. I'll explain its origin to you sometime. But call me Micko, OK?"

She nodded.

"And, two; have dinner with me."

She nodded again. "But first you must tell me something."

"Yes?"

"What did you think of Alger Hiss's conviction?"

"Why do you ask that?" Their playful, impish mood evaporated.

"It's strange we haven't discussed it. Everyone brings it up first thing. It bothers me not to be able to guess what you think."

"I know what you think."

"You do?"

"Certainly. You think he's a victim of witch-hunters. You think HUAC is dangerous, the *real* un-Americanism. You think McCarthy is a demagogue."

"Don't you?"

"You asked me about Hiss. I don't know the facts well enough to express an opinion."

"You wrote about it."

"I was a student. I knew more about everything then. What I know about now is Frank Costello and Al Capone and Sam Giancana and Crazy Joe Gallo and how to slice parimutuel betting books eight ways so that nobody in the entire world can know how much money a major league track takes in each year."

"I'd like to hear more about it."

"I've said too much already. My work is confidential. Only the Congress can make what I think public. Otherwise everything becomes gossip and rumor-mongering and cheap Hearst sensations. It wouldn't be fair to the defendants."

"They're not defendants, are they?"

"Christ, you're right. That's what I mean. See how easy it is?"

"You set great stock by fairness, don't you?"

"I try to."

"That's why I asked about Hiss."

"The Hiss thing may or may not have been unfair. I don't know. When I wrote about it, the Russians didn't have the atom bomb. They do now. That's not fair. And frankly *that* bothers me more than the fate of Alger Hiss. Joe Stalin frightens me more than Joe McCarthy."

"Said like an Irish red-baiter." Janet tried to smile as if she were joking.

"No. Said like a lawyer. I told you. I don't know the facts. I haven't seen the evidence. Have you?"

She shrugged. What could she say? She had ruined a lovely moment by getting him to expose his dreadful opinions.

"We were about to have dinner," he said.

"Yes." She put her regret aside and smiled at him. He raised his glass to her and drained it, a gesture she accepted with a nod, but did not relish. She wondered if he had a drinking problem.

"But," he said, "it'll have to be a hurried one, I'm afraid. I have to work tonight." Brady was thinking that, after all, she was very young. He was nearly thirty. She was no more than twenty-three. He was thinking she was still enthralled with the opinions of some Smith professor, an old-time leftie, no doubt, who'd spent all his class time defending Hiss and the Rosenbergs. She was practically still an undergraduate. Maybe he wasn't so attracted to her after all.

Their dinner — they stayed at the Neptune and had the menu brought over from the grill — *was* hurried and awkward. By the time they said goodnight to each other and went their separate ways — he to the Senate Office Building, she onto the Pennsylvania Avenue streetcar to George-town — night had fallen and they were both glad to be alone again. But each went to sleep later thinking of the other.

Two days after Collins Brady and Janet Lindsay had their brief dinner together, General MacArthur addressed a joint session of Congress. In the furor surrounding his removal by the President it seemed the Senate had little time for or interest in the concluding hearings of the Kefauver Com-mittee. Brady nevertheless worked tirelessly with Halley and other staff members in preparing the final report. They wanted it out before the summer adjournment. The report was turning out to be several things at once. Senator Kefauver, in the garbled rhetoric for which he was known, described it as "the record of the persons and biography, and then by modus operandi or the technique of how they operate, how they kill, how they hijack and how they work and then by narrative description of the individual cases and the times." One section of the report pulled together various threads of information about syndicated crime and its potential for political corruption. Another presented a set of charges about "the elusive organization known as the Mafia." Collins and two other lawyers argued futilely against inclusion of this section because it contained little sub-stantiating evidence of a national crime cabal other than certain conve-nient factors of ethnicity. Brady was one of the authors of the section of the report that dealt with big-time gambling, which received the bulk of the committee's attention because of the economic importance it had for all other aspects of underworld activity. The incredible sum of over twenty billion dollars was generated annually by illegal gambling, un-checked and unsupervised funds that furnished capital to launch other criminal operations — particularly the burgeoning trade in narcotics — and that made possible the graft necessary to buy official protection of those activities. The final section of the report contained dozens of legisla-tive proposals, the most publicized of which called for the establishment of a federal crime commission, but the most practical of which would have curbed the use of wire services for gambling purposes and would have required more detailed tax records by racketeers. One of the major concerns of the committee was how to prevent the infiltration of legiti-mate business by underworld figures. Brady and others argued that a way had to be found to watch and control the expenditures of the vast sums of money that criminals were known to be accumulating. They focused their proposals to this end on new tax legislation and prepared to shift the bur-den of the anticrime campaign away from the FBI and the Bureau of Nar-cotics toward the Bureau of Internal Revenue.

Collins Brady was deeply committed to his work. After nearly two years he was still consumed by the investigation, and even as the committee's tenure ran out that spring he continued to work, compiling dossiers, reviewing data, scrutinizing testimony, researching the new laws, as if there would always be a Kefauver Committee, as if he would always be a key part of it. He knew that the highly touted TV confrontations between gangsters and senators had revealed little. He knew that the myth about the tight-knit Italian Mafia, which received such publicity, had little to do with the reality of a loosely related collection of individualist entrepreneurs who had nothing to do with medieval pledges signed in blood, and whose activities were benign compared to the images the press had nurtured. He knew that the committee itself had crossed the line repeatedly into areas of unconstitutional procedure, encouraging, indeed requiring, for example, hearsay evidence of witnesses. But he also knew that the committee had focused the glare of publicity on nefarious activities that could survive anything but. He felt an enormous satisfaction to have been part of what Kefauver called a crusade. Brady thought that was not too sentimental a word for it, though he would not have used it himself.

Still, throughout May he was distracted.

He thought continually of Janet Lindsay.

He called her.

"You haven't been at the hearings."

"I know. We've been very busy. We're doing a huge mailing."

"I was afraid it was because of me." As soon as he said that he regretted it as a remarkably self-centered statement. She would think him conceited and arrogant, when the truth was just the opposite.

"No. Not at all."

"Oh."

"I mean, I really have been busy."

"Me too."

"How has it been going?"

"We expect to report before recess after a final flamboyant hearing. The senators want one last blast of TV before going home."

Janet Lindsay couldn't think of anything to say. Surely they weren't going to chat about work and let it go at that. Where were all those clever bits she'd been rehearsing? She had promised herself that if he called she would ask him over for a drink.

"Listen," she said, "I was thinking we might . . ."

"I was, too."

"Don't interrupt me!" She couldn't believe she'd said that, but he was laughing. Did he know he'd interrupted a line she'd practiced? "I want you to come over and have a drink sometime."

"What a good idea! When?"

She took a deep breath. "How about tonight?"

"I'd love to," he said.

She didn't have any bourbon and she worried he'd think her unsophisticated. But she had to straighten the small room, try to bring some order to her desk, then shower quickly and put on her new dress, a beige cotton shift she'd bought at Garfinkle's thinking of him. He'd have to take beer and be satisfied with that, or rum. She had brought a fifth of rum back from Havana when she'd gone there in January. She could offer him rum and Coke.

He took it and said he loved it.

They talked about the Existentialists and each was delighted at how smart the other was.

When he left at ten before midnight he kissed her on the cheek.

The following Friday they went to dinner at the Shoreham on the open-air terrace that overlooked Rock Creek Park. A wonderful orchestra played sentimental music and, after eating, he asked her to dance. Janet was aware of the eyes of the other patrons as they filed through the tables, and she couldn't help thinking they were the best-looking couple there. She was wearing her long black evening dress, which showed her shoulders and drew attention to her breasts. She wore her hair up to display her long neck. He wore a tan serge suit that made him look rakish and cavalier. When she went into his arms they began to glide. The evening was warm, the stars were enormous overhead, the music was lilting and soft. The trumpet player made his instrument sound like a muted, distant bird in mourning. She let her head rest on his shoulder and she felt a tear come to her left eye, it was all so exquisite and lovely. She had dreamed of this before. When they returned to their table the waiter had brought a silver bucket with ice in it and in the ice was a bottle of Dom Pérignon. They toasted each other, and their talk came more slowly than before. When they danced again they were silent. Janet was aware of the pressure of his right hand against the small of her back. When his leg brushed the inside of her thigh repeatedly she shuddered and closed her white gloved arms around his neck.

As they were getting into a cab he pointed up Connecticut Avenue at the Sheraton Park and said that was where he had his apartment. For a terrible moment she thought he was going to ask her home with him, but he didn't. When he took her back to Georgetown he kept the cab waiting. They agreed to spend the next day together, and he kissed her on the mouth.

They went to Great Falls, where the waters of the Potomac fell in a glorious cascade down from the hills of Maryland onto the coastal plain of Virginia.

"Harper's Ferry is up there," he said, pointing upstream. "This falls was the great barrier to the C and O canal. They never defeated it."

"Hence the collapse of trade with the trans-Appalachian interior. And hence the decline of Alexandria as a port city."

"Very good."

"But the advent of railroads made canals irrelevant anyway."

"But too late for Virginia. If the canal had worked, they'd have been tied to the North economically. The Civil War would have been very different."

They were walking along a winding path, woods on one side of them, the falls on the other. They were holding hands. Occasionally they separated to negotiate a narrow place or mount a boulder. But they came easily together again. The sun was bright and warm. Collins was in his shirt sleeves. Janet had her cashmere over her shoulders.

They came to an outcropping that reached far out over the raging water like a sharp tooth snagging the air. They made their way out to its farthest edge, carefully, singly, each with a separate caution. They sat above the roar of the falls, content with their own silence, feeling the power not only of the river, but of the stone that, having been worn to a sliver, still claimed its victory over time.

"You know your history," she said finally. She turned his hand in hers, examining it as if its lines had secrets.

"I'm a child of history, so to speak." He said that without pompousness, and she looked at him.

"What do you mean?"

"I'm named after a character out of the books, Michael Collins."

"Who was he?" She felt ignorant, but not embarrassed.

"An Irish patriot. Do you know the Yeats poem 'In Memory of Major Robert Gregory'?"

"'A thought of that late death took all my heart for speech.'"

Brady looked at her; God, she was wonderful! "He was one of Collins's aides in the early years of the war against England." Then he recited, "Too long a sacrifice/ can make a stone of the heart./ O when may it suffice?/ That is heaven's part. Our part/ to murmur name upon name/ As a mother names her child/ when sleep at last has come/ on limbs that had run wild."

"'Easter 1916.'"

"Yes. Only in my case, it was my father who put name upon name. My mother was killed."

Janet Lindsay felt her eyes filling. Very softly she said, "By the English?" She pressed his hand.

"No. By the Irish. In the *Irish* Civil War. The same faction that killed

Collins. My father was with him. He was also an aide to Collins, after Gregory. I never knew my mother. I was born in the middle of it."

"It must have been . . . terrible." She thought of Yeats's phrase. There was an enormous sadness about Collins. She knew he was feeling the emptiness of never having known his mother.

"Yes." He faced her. "Not for me, of course. But for my dad."

"He must have suffered."

"It 'can make a stone of the heart.' " He smiled at her, a sudden graceful smile. "But it didn't. My father is a wonderful man. Whatever he experienced then made him better, not worse. I admire him more than anyone in the world. I want to be like him."

"What does he do?"

"He used to be in politics. Ever hear of Curley?"

"Are you kidding?"

"My father was his partner in a storefront insurance business in South Boston. During the Depression they devised a system to fund the retirements of city workers. My father was a kind of advocate for the common people, for the Irish, with the mayor and the State House. What they needed in those days was respite from the great insecurity of the times. The Irish lived in dread of the dole and the pauper's house. When the New Deal faltered and it became clear that Social Security was going to be minimal, at least for big Irish families — Catholics, you know — he quit politics to work full-time in the insurance thing to make sure the people would have what they needed when they needed it most. My dad practically invented the mechanism for supplementing the pensions of city workers. Monument Municipal Insurance and Annuity Association. Only municipal workers, blue-collar mainly, are eligible. It caught on, spread from Boston to cities all over the state and then all over the country." Collins laughed. "Of course, he made a killing at the same time. He's not all altruism. He's a very successful businessman now. But he started out just trying to help people who were very desperate. He still does."

"No wonder you're proud of him."

"I look forward to working with him someday. I can't imagine anything better than to be his partner. He doesn't need me right now. The business runs itself."

"You have to get your politics out of your system first."

"I suppose."

"Kefauver's running, isn't he?"

"Probably. Depends on Truman. Frankly, I don't see myself involved in it if he does. I love the law stuff, believe it or not."

"I believe it."

"We've just begun to scratch the surface of interstate crime. I'd like to see it through somehow. I have to wait and see what Congress does with our proposals. As the law stands now, there are a lot of cracks in it. People fall through those cracks and get lost. Innocent people. And others get away with murder, sometimes literally."

"Your father must be proud of you."

"I hope he is."

Janet put her arm around his shoulder and kissed him on the cheek. "I am," she whispered.

"You'd better be careful of that." He hugged her. "You wouldn't want to get involved with the son of an Irish mick, would you?"

"I don't know. What other kind of mick is there?"

He laughed.

"You were going to tell me about your name, 'Micko.' Is that its origin?"

"Michael Collins used to call my father *Amico*. It became their name for each other, shortened to 'Micko.' It's what my dad calls me, and my family. I grew up with my aunt and my cousins, two girls and a boy. He's a priest now in Boston."

"Oh my God!"

"I warned you."

"I couldn't be more Protestant, you know."

"I know. That's why I like you."

"My father would die. He's a member of the vestry at Trinity."

"Just tell him I lived at Phillips Brooks House at Harvard."

"Do you know Lindsay Hall?"

"Yes. Don't tell me. Lindsay Hall in the Yard?"

"I'm afraid so. My grandfather."

"Oh *my* God! Well, we all have to bear the weight of our ancestry, don't we?"

"Don't we ever. You mine, me yours."

"And the C and O canal George Washington's."

They stood and walked back along the path, holding hands and silent.

It was evening by the time they returned to Georgetown. They ate in a small cafe on O Street that was popular with students.

At the door to her flat Janet timidly invited him in. She made coffee. He sipped his once and put it down. He touched her. Janet had prepared herself for that. She was a virgin, and not regretfully. She had never been naked in front of a man, partly because she had accepted the values she'd been schooled in and partly because she'd never met a man she could imagine loving for life. That was the chief value to her, and that was why she was prepared to allow Collins his initiatives. She had been, in fact, looking forward to them enormously. She loved him, and she trusted him and she wanted to give herself to him.

When he kissed her, it was passionate and full for the first time. Janet was as aroused as he was. She kept kissing him and rubbing her hands through his hair and around his neck while he undressed her. They did not speak at all, even when they crossed to the bed, but when they made love Janet repeated the name "Micko" again and again until it too was lost in their pleasure.

They saw each other every day after that, and they made plans to go to Boston together when Congress recessed for the summer.

The Kefauver Committee convened for the final time on June 12 for the purpose of making public its report. All three television networks broadcast the hearing, which was conducted with the solemnity of a climactic scene in a major drama. The committee had held hearings in fourteen major cities: Washington, Tampa, Miami, New York, Cleveland, St. Louis, Kansas City, New Orleans, Chicago, Detroit, Philadelphia, Las Vegas, Los Angeles, and San Francisco. Over eight hundred witnesses had been heard, and the resulting testimony ran to thousands of pages. The committee's success at identifying criminal personalities and activities gave it a prestige probably unequaled by any other congressional investigation.

More people had watched the Kefauver proceedings on television than had watched the World Series, the year before. In the eerie half-light of darkened rooms before small frosty screens, Americans had watched the good men of their government in complete absorption. Never before had the attention of the nation been so riveted on a single matter.

Among those who tuned in the final hearing for the committee's last word was Colman Brady. He sat alone in a corner of his bedroom on Prescott Street. He watched the pale images and heard the static-ridden voices and felt his first real fear in years. Four senators gave their speeches, and Kefauver read a precis of their report. They were unctuous and pious. They didn't frighten Brady because they would turn their attention to their elections and to other business of the Senate. Rudolph Halley outlined the shape of the new legislation. He was a technician and a bureaucrat whose power would fade with the committee's mandate. He did not frighten Brady.

But to the rear and left of Halley, Colman Brady saw the figure of his son, who sat upright and alert, and from whose earnest gaze, even through the damned machine, he could find no shelter.

[382]

2

ARCHBISHOP RICHARD JAMES CUSHING lived in the pretentious mansion on the corner of Granby Street and Bay State Road in the Back Bay. He hated the place. It was a pastiche of molded plaster and false marble and wood pressed to seem crafted, and six-foot oils of Italian bishops hung like trophies on twelve-foot walls. Cardinal O'Connell's seal, with its elaborate pattern of tassels and Maltese crosses, was fixed permanently over thresholds and hearthstones and on china and silver and in leaded windows. It all seemed pompous and arrogant to Cushing, who thought the whole business of being archbishop should be simple, and, well, ascetic. His predecessor, who had required that French or Latin be spoken at his table — he fancied it a table at the court — couldn't have differed more. As far as Cushing was concerned, he wasn't a prince of the Church or a prince of anything. He was a pastor. Who needed a lot of red velvet around to preach the Gospel and feed the poor? He wouldn't stay in that palace for long, he loved to tell visitors. As soon as the new residence was built at the seminary in Brighton, he'd be on his way. A simple life in a place where the people could visit him and not feel awestruck or, worse, scandalized by the showy opulence. Maybe, in another time, the Catholics in Boston needed such an effort at grandeur, such a pathetic attempt to out-Back-Bay Back Bay. But times had changed. The Back Bay wasn't the Brahmin stronghold anymore and Boston Catholics weren't downtrodden anymore. Anyway, the requirements of the Gospel for simplicity, even poverty, in God's priests were perennial. Cushing couldn't wait to move.

He was sitting in his office tugging absently at the gold chain with its pectoral cross that hung at his breast. He was looking out the window across the Charles at the towers and steeples of Cambridge. Sailboats from MIT cut their figures on the blue river, but he didn't see them. The sun sparkled off the water. It was a metallic cold day, but bright and stainless. His gaze rested on the white needles of the churches and distant Harvard houses the way a farmer's gaze takes its ease on hills. Archbishop Cushing knew what steeples were for. That at least was obvious. He was an ordinary man, a bit taller and more gangling than most, a bit brusquer. The ugliness of his face — the dominating nose, the craggy eye-sockets, a brow too thick — achieved a kind of gracefulness by so accurately displaying his mirthful simplicity. He *knew* what steeples were for. One didn't have to think about it. One needed only to let one's gaze rest on them. There was something consoling in the vacancy of his mind as he did so, something peaceful. There was a stark naturalness about Cushing that allowed him periodically such a freedom from the rush of worry. His naturalness was what, on occasion, shocked the refined and, on still others, drew love out of his people the way the earth drains its quota of rain out of the wind. When they looked at Cushing they thought, *Here is a winner of wars. Here is one who will endure as a tree endures.* He knew they loved him. That was why he wanted to move.

His phone rang.

He turned in his chair and reached for it. He loved to answer his own phone. It always stunned them. Imagine the Archbishop of Boston doing that! Where was his secretary? they would wonder. His secretary, Father Kelleher, was in the next room waiting for the third ring. His orders were to let Cushing have the first two for himself.

"This is the Archbishop," he barked.

"Hello, Your Excellency. This is Colman Brady."

"Colman, *hello!* Good to hear you!"

"Thank you, Excellency. How are you?"

"I'm fit as a fiddle for a man our age."

"Now just a minute, Archbishop. You're a man of the cloth. Don't be stretching the truth. I'm not your age."

"You're fifty-three. I'm fifty-six. I call that my age."

"A lot can happen in three years."

"You should know, Brady! What have you been doing with yourself? Why haven't you been down to see me? How's Maeve?"

"She's fine."

"Can you keep a secret?"

"Certainly."

"I'm making her boy pastor of a new parish in Winchester come spring. Just decided."

"That's marvelous, Excellency. That's wonderful. His mother'll be thrilled."

"I expect so. He won't be heartbroken either. He'll be the youngest on the list."

"He's thirty-four."

"No, he's not. He's thirty-three. I checked. That's why I'm putting him out in the suburbs. Won't be any old Altar and Rosary biddies to torture him for his youth. Lots of youngsters. He's terrific with youngsters. He'll have to build the church from scratch, raise his own money, too. It won't be easy. He'll probably come to you for help."

"You know me, Archbishop."

"I do, Colman. You're a very generous man. But I don't want you giving fancy sums to that boy. I still expect you to send your gifts to the Lord through the proper slot."

"You."

"You guessed it."

"I didn't have to. Don't worry, Excellency. It'll be good for Jack to do his own hustling."

"Exactly. And I'm too old to do mine. That's why I keep you around."

"I thought you said I was your age."

"Ouch! *Touché*!"

"I'm calling because I want to see you, as soon as possible."

"Sounds serious."

"If what Father Jack tells me is true, it is."

"What's up?"

"It's my boy, Collins."

"What's wrong with him?"

"Nothing. Quite the contrary, something very splendid. He's going to marry a marvelous young woman."

"What's the problem, then?"

"Well, it's no problem to me, but Father Jack tells me it will be to you."

"What?"

"She's Protestant."

Silence.

"Archbishop Cushing, are you there?"

"Colman, when can you come over?"

"Right away."

"Good."

When Colman Brady returned the phone to its cradle, he sat still for a moment, not turning to face the two young men who were seated behind him, Collins and Father McShane. They were in Colman's study at Prescott Street, a first-floor room jutting off the main body of the house. It had been a sunroom once. Colman loved the way the daylight washed over him there.

Collins was sitting in a colonial rocker with a red tome open on his lap. He held a page down as if marking it, but he was staring at his father waiting for him to explain what the Archbishop had said. He was wearing a dark V-neck sweater over his white shirt and rep tie. Even though it was the middle of the morning in his old home, he was groomed and polished. He had come down from New Hampshire, where Estes Kefauver had just turned the 1952 Democratic political situation upside down by defeating Truman in the primary. Collins had signed on Kefauver's campaign staff to write his speeches pushing the anti-crime legislation. On his way back to Washington he'd stopped at Prescott Street to announce his plans for marriage.

Father McShane was standing behind him. He was carefully decked out, too, but clerically and with such fastidiousness as to seem almost the dandy. He wore his black suit and rabbi, of course, with the spotless high collar which was too tight. His shirt-cuffs, also immaculate, protruded from the black sleeves of his suit, and gold cufflinks in the design of the Chi-rho flashed in the morning sun, as did the highlight of his glistening black hair, which was, as always, perfectly arranged.

"What did he say, Uncle Colman?"

"He didn't say anything yet."

"I mean about me. I heard you talking about me. What's Mom going to be thrilled about?"

"You weren't supposed to be listening to that part." Colman smiled at McShane. The kid had an infallible nose for the scent of his own interest. It would have been an unattractive quality in most men, but Jack's ambition was rooted clearly in a largeheartedness that made him appealing. Sure, he wanted his promotions, but he was working for them and took no shortcuts. He was the best priest in his parish and already had a reputation as a kindly confessor and a whiz with troubled teenagers. McShane could have played on the facts that Colman was one of the leading benefactors in the archdiocese and that he and the archbishop had both begun in Southie, but he was not an operator. If he had a special place in Cushing's fondness it was due to Cushing's knack for singling out exceptional priests. Colman suspected that his nephew already knew about the appointment, or expected it, at least. And that was all right. The trick was to encourage the kid's ambition without helping it to go to his head. Colman believed that success and power are always preferable to their opposites. He decided not to tell Jack what Cushing had said. He turned to Micko. "Well, you're the lawyer. Did you read it?"

"I'm a civil lawyer, not canon. It's in Latin."

"Hell, you went to Harvard. Didn't they teach you Latin?"

"Just enough to read the diploma." He feigned smugness to disguise his defensiveness. He knew what the canon said without reading it.

"Give it to me," Colman said, taking the ancient book. "Even your dumb mick old man reads Latin." He fumbled for his eyeglasses under the papers on his desk. "Which one?"

"Canon ten-seventy," Jack said briskly.

Colman held the book up and read the text aloud with an ease that surprised even him. *"Nullum est matrimonium contractum a persona non-baptizata cum persona baptizata in Ecclesia catholica vel ad eandem ex haeresi aut schismate conversa."*

"Keep reading," Jack said. "Ten seventy-one."

Colman read the next canon and then looked at his son. "It's pretty explicit, Micko."

"Essentially it boils down to 'You can't do it.' Right?"

"Seems that way," Colman said. " 'Disparity of cult,' it's called."

Collins slammed his palms together. "Disparity of cult! What a goddamn phrase! Sounds like a Mafia vendetta ritual!"

"You ought to know," Jack said sharply. He was more anxious about all this than he'd have expected to be.

"Yes, I ought to! I deal with a primitive society all the time. It shouldn't throw me to be dealing with another one."

"That's uncalled for!" Jack retorted.

"Look, I'm just trying to get married to somebody. You treat it as though I'm plea-bargaining for my soul."

"Well, perhaps you are," Jack said.

"That's insane. This has nothing to do with my soul. It's a matter of prejudice, medieval prejudice, pure and simple."

Colman closed the book of canon law, and the noise it made stopped them short. In his glare they both felt miserably caught at their old habit. They had always hoarded resentment toward each other and had often displayed it. But they were too old for that nonsense now. They were not rivals anymore.

"Jack," Colman said, "you and I will be going over to Granby Street. We'll see what His Excellency says." Colman paused. "Will you wait for me at the door?"

Jack nodded and left Colman's study.

Collins stood up, as if he was leaving too.

"Wait a minute, son."

Collins looked at him impassively.

"I want you to understand how I feel about this. We'll have your wedding. I love Janet. You know that. And we can all be proud to welcome Lindsays into our family. So that's no problem. And it's of no matter to me that she's Episcopalian. You know that too. But we must have it done right, with the blessing of the Church."

"But, Dad, if they won't give it, they won't give it."

"They will. Leave it to me. The Church is a little more malleable than most people think."

"Frankly, I'm not sure it's worth the effort."

Colman spoke very softly, with a note in his voice that, while not precisely menacing, was ominous. "Micko, I don't want words like those in this house."

"It's how I feel, Dad."

"We can finesse this, son. It needn't be a rupture. If you have to choose between Janet and the Church, or make the rest of us choose between them, it'll break Maeve's heart. Do you want that?"

"Of course not." Collins hesitated before asking, "How would you feel?"

"We're Catholics, son. That's very simple. It's what we are." Brady remembered Madeline Thomson telling him he was Catholic to the core and himself telling her the Church meant nothing to him. She had not believed him and he knew now she had been right.

"Maybe Catholic is what we were," Collins said.

"No, son. Whatever that means to you or doesn't, it's what we are."

"It doesn't mean I'll crawl to them."

"You don't have to, Micko." Colman didn't complete the statement: *I'm doing it for you.* "Don't worry about it. Let me talk to Archbishop Cushing. He's very liberal. He owes me a favor."

"What, for giving him your only nephew?"

"No." Colman stood and threw an arm around Collins's shoulder. "For *not* giving him my only son."

A few minutes later Colman and Father McShane were walking down Commonwealth Avenue toward Granby Street, which was at the western edge of Back Bay only ten minutes from Prescott Street.

"Listen, Jack . . ." At Cummington Street there was a mess of construction where Boston University was building its new science building. ". . . I want you to help your cousin through this. I don't want you making it worse than it is on him."

"You're right. It was inexcusable."

"I'm not looking for apologies. You have a right to defend what you believe. Just don't pressure him. He's getting enough of that from Janet's people. We're on his side, remember? They want the service at Trinity Church, are insisting on it, in fact. Apparently it hasn't occurred to them that we might have a stipulation or two."

"Or three or four."

"Or a thousand and seventy or a thousand and seventy-one. How many canons are there anyway?"

"Two thousand, three hundred and fourteen."

"Wonderful! How did I live so long without knowing that?"

"As long as you brought it up, I'd like to add something to what you just said, may I?"

"Certainly."

"There are stakes in this business for me, too. The Lindsays are very prominent in this town. The Brady name is not altogether unknown. The wedding is sure to attract attention. If it were to occur in such a manner as to cause the archdiocese embarrassment, it would, I'm afraid, reflect badly on me."

"Jack, I hardly think you've anything to worry about. For one thing, we're going to get the Church's blessing."

"Not at Trinity Church, we're not. It would take a miracle."

"Don't you believe in miracles, Father?" Colman slapped his nephew's shoulder and laughed.

The archbishop's secretary, a portly cleric who had a peculiar way of pursing both his lips and his hands, showed them into Cushing's office. The archbishop met them halfway between his desk and the door.

Father McShane genuflected and kissed his ring.

When Colman began to go down on one knee, Cushing stopped him. "I won't hear of it! You're too heavy to pull up!" He made it impossible for Colman to kiss his ring. Cushing did not hesitate to accept the obeisance of those under his authority, but that did not include Brady, who was one of his "BCL's" — Big Catholic Laymen, a group of trusted associates, even friends, on whom he constantly depended for help and advice. Brady had donated fifty thousand of his own money to the Kennedy Memorial Hospital for children in Brighton, and he had worked with Joe Kennedy to raise the other millions needed. Brady had used his pull with the Teamsters, the Bartenders' Union, and the ABC to get Cushing's cylindrical cardboard coin containers on every bar in Massachusetts, and they were bringing in nearly a hundred thousand a year. Every nickel helped when the Archbishop needed twenty thousand dollars a day to build his new schools and hospitals and to pay the bill for his fabled charities.

When Brady and McShane were seated in the red leather high-backs that faced the large ornate desk, Archbishop Cushing immediately launched into a story which was irrelevant and charming and was intended, like all the stories he began his meetings with, to put his visitors at ease and to display himself as a down-to-earth, slightly buffoonish character. It served his purposes to have his guests think of him as harmless, innocent, and naive. Brady and McShane knew better, of course, but they listened attentively as the archbishop spun his tale in his gravelly, agitated way.

"I was a young priest at the time, see, and I get this sick-call. I was working out of Franklin Street where my Propagation office was. Well, across the street at Jordan's they got this fellow who's had a heart attack, see? And they got him in the first-aid room. And they want a priest, right? So I go over to the store. I never shopped there in my life. I like Filene's. And the guy's on this cot. Well, the nurse tells me he's not dying, but you never know. So I take his hand and I lean down and I say, 'My friend, do you believe in the Father and the Son and the Holy Ghost?' The fellow opens one eye then and turns to the nurse and says, 'I'm dying and he's asking me riddles!' And with that the man gets up and walks out. What could I do? I turned to the nurse and I thump myself on the chest like this and I say, 'Behold the power of the man!' " Cushing stopped to harvest their laughter. Then he set his face in an earnest expression.

"So tell me the story, Colman," he said.

"It's quite simple, your Excellency. The Lindsay family. Know them?"

"J. Bolton Lindsay."

"Yes. The banker."

"Not your average hoi polloi, Colman! You'll be the first Irish Brahmin!"

"Not myself, Archbishop. I'll always be an ignorant harp immigrant."

Cushing turned to McShane and rolled his eyes dramatically toward heaven. McShane, for his part, had already noted again that his uncle's faded Irish brogue had a way of reasserting itself in the presence of the archbishop.

"But it is a problem," Cushing said.

"I know. I've come for your advice. Explain the issues to me."

"Well, you know as well as I do what the issue is. The Church forbids mixed marriages."

"But there've been exceptions. I know there have."

"That's true. Governor Fuller. You know Governor Fuller?"

Brady nodded. Alvan T. Fuller. Sacco and Vanzetti.

"He's as WASPy as they come," Cushing said, "but he married Grace Davenport, good Catholic family. That marriage was approved." Fuller had given Cushing a hundred thousand dollars a year for ten years. "Of course, as is always required in order to get the dispensation, Fuller had to agree to some pretty stringent conditions."

"What would those be, Archbishop?"

"First, there has to be a presentation of reasons, serious reasons, why the dispensation should be given. That's no problem. In your case we could probably say, 'Danger of Catholic party entering into a civil ceremony.' "

"Indeed," Colman said, "or worse, an Episcopal one."

"Good enough. So there's 'urgent and grave cause.' But in order for me to grant the dispensation the non-Catholic party has to sign a sworn statement."

"Swearing to what?"

Cushing ticked off his fingers. "To refrain from the practice of contraception. To do nothing to impede the Catholic party from practicing his or her faith. To raise the children in the Catholic religion."

Colman took in what the Archbishop said, remaining immobile and silent.

"What are the chances she'd convert?" Cushing asked.

"None, I'd say."

"Too bad. It'd be simpler. There's also the problem of the ceremony."

"What problem would that be, Archbishop?"

Jack was aware of the strain in his uncle's voice, and suspected that Cushing was anxious, too, because he was retreating behind an impersonal, officious manner.

"The ceremony would have to be private, in the parlor of a rectory, for example, with only the official witnesses in attendance."

"Why is that?" Brady knew the Lindsays would never agree to such a ceremony. He abhorred the idea himself. If a Lindsay was taking the Brady name, by God it would not be done in secret!

"Scandal, Colman. Even if the Church permits a mixed marriage, it still cannot seem to approve it, or encourage it."

Brady sat forward in his chair. "Archbishop, what would it take to be dispensed from these conditions as well as from the impediment of mixed religion?"

"You mean for these young people to marry as if there was no problem?"

"Yes."

"Won't happen. Not even the Pope can dispense from the requirements about birth control and the children. Those are Natural Law, God's Law."

"What about the ceremony?"

"Colman, I wish I could help you. If it was up to me, I would. You know I just wrote that letter about Adlai Stevenson's divorce, that Catholics could vote for him anyway. I think we should loosen up some of these things, but my hands are tied."

"Could Rome dispense from the secrecy of the ceremony?"

"Yes. That they could. It's a matter of prudence."

'Well, we'd like to apply for that. How long will it take?"

"A long time, six months maybe."

"The wedding's to be early summer, right after the Convention."

"Might not make it."

"What if I went over?"

"What, to Rome?"

"Yes."

Cushing shrugged. "I can't encourage you, Colman. I wouldn't get my hopes up, if I was you." Cushing let his eyes drift to McShane. "Father John?"

"Yes, Excellency?"

"Did you explain to your uncle why this would be a particularly bad time . . . ?"

"You mean about Feeney?"

"I know about Father Feeney," Colman said. Everyone in Boston knew about the fanatical priest. "No salvation outside the Catholic Church, right?"

"Uncle Colman, it's incumbent upon the archbishop to denounce his preaching."

"Hell's bells! I called him in here the other day. I was under orders to silence him. If he persisted, to excommunicate him. I didn't want to do it. But he's been making the Church look awful, especially in this day and age, when things are just starting to thaw out. The Reformation's been a long time healing. Anyway, he walks right through that door. And I say, 'Leonard . . .' But before I can get out another word, he says, 'In the name of the Blessed Virgin Mary, I excommunicate you!' What could I do? He beat me to the draw."

Despite himself Colman was amused and showed it.

The archbishop went on; "We don't want to make things worse than they are, Colman. After all this Feeney nonsense, we're trying to show respect for the other churches. The last thing we need is a brouhaha with Trinity."

"How'd you know it was Trinity?" Colman asked.

Cushing's eyes went briefly and involuntarily to McShane, who lowered his eyes and blushed. What did Colman expect? The kid was just covering his tail. He'd have done the same himself. Maybe. Anyway, priests keep no secrets from their bishops.

"None of us want an uproar, Archbishop," Colman said. "I'd still like to see if we can't smooth the whole thing over."

"Well, I hope you can. But you know my limits now, anyway."

"Right. And I appreciate your position, too."

"I knew you would."

Brady stood, then Cushing, then the young priest.

"By the way," Colman said, "about Feeney. No salvation outside the Church — I thought that's what we believed."

"It was," the Archbishop said evenly. "It isn't anymore."

"It's heresy now?"

"Yes."

"We'd go to hell for holding it?"

The archbishop shrugged. "Let me tell you something, Colman . . ." Cushing stopped and turned to McShane. "Father, would you wait outside?"

Jack McShane, still blushing, turned and left.

Cushing said, "I know what you're thinking: it's all hogwash. I'd like to tell you something as your friend, man to man, the hell with the archbishop stuff. It *is* all hogwash. If I was you, I wouldn't worry about your son's marriage even if it seemed . . ." Cushing shrugged. He had to be discreet. He couldn't seem to give permission explicitly for a violation of canon law.

"Archbishop, that's not how I see it. When my son marries this girl, it will be with a full-blown ceremony and with the complete approval of the Church. When the Bradys welcome the Lindsays into their family, they will do so as people who have not surrendered an inch on who they are. They are Irish, and they are Catholic. I want J. Bolton Lindsay and the Trustees of Harvard and the members at Somerset and everyone else in this town to know that's who they're getting and that's who is getting them."

Cushing was shocked at Brady's vehemence. A sour fierceness showed in Brady that old O'Connell would have understood better than Cushing.

"Colman, I want to tell you something. Even a bishop is a man first and a priest after. I listen for the voice of God, but to tell you the truth, he don't speak my language. What I listen to mainly is pain. Beginning, sad to say, with my own. I spend most nights inside a damn oxygen tent because I got asthma and I can't breathe and sleep at the same time. And next I listen to the pain of my own family. My sister, Colman, she married a Jew. I don't talk about it much. But, well, that was over twenty years ago, and you know what? I listened by accident to the pain of that fellow, that Jew who my sister loved. And you know what else? I was wrong. It didn't matter a damn whether he was baptized or not. That man is good. It's 'cause of him that I knew that Leonard Feeney, that bastard saint, was full of bullrushes."

Colman did not reply. He was very moved by what Cushing had said to him.

"Oh, well, as I always say about Feeney and the rest of them, it's great to live with saints in heaven, but it's hell to live with them on earth! You know what Feeney told them at Notre Dame? Said it was a sign of their damnation that they had Protestants on the football team!"

[393]

The archbishop had Colman by the arm and was leading him to the door. But suddenly he stopped.

"I nearly forgot! I meant to ask you!"

"Yes?"

"Andy Barnes is having a benefit night for me at Rockingham. I was hoping you'd head up a committee."

"At Rockingham?" An alarm, faint and distant but undeniable, went off in Colman. Rockingham Park was the major New England racetrack. Gennaro Anselmo's prints were all over it. "No, Your Excellency, I'm sorry, but I can't."

"You can't?" Colman had never denied him.

"I'm sorry."

Cushing nodded. "Oh. I understand. I'll ask Joe Kennedy. That's all right." He assumed that Brady was denying him because he hadn't been able to grant without conditions the dispensation for the wedding of his son to Janet Lindsay. What could he do?

The next morning Maeve called Janet, who'd come up to tell her parents about the wedding. She and Collins were going to return to Washington that night. Maeve asked Janet to meet her for lunch. She didn't explain, but implied that she wanted to discuss her trousseau and her silver and china patterns and the sort of showers she would want. Janet was rushed, but thought it a nice gesture and agreed to meet her.

But it was Colman who showed up at the English Tea Room on Newbury Street. He'd asked Maeve to arrange the meeting so that Collins would not know about it.

"Janet," he called, crossing between the tables to where she sat. He wore a dark brown suit and cordovan wing-tips. He'd just come from his barber and was shaven, groomed, and manicured. He wanted to charm the apples right out of the young woman's stunning blue eyes.

Janet rose, showing her surprise. "Why, Mr. Brady . . ."

He took her hand. "Aren't I lucky? My poor sister sprained her ankle not an hour ago and asked me to come tell you."

"Oh, I'm sorry . . ."

"Not at all. She'll be all right. She's always twisting the damn thing. She weighs too much. She'll soak it for an afternoon and be good as used."

"Well, I hope . . ."

"But it gives me a chance to take you to lunch myself." He offered her his arm. "May I?"

Janet was confused. They were already in the restaurant, but the English Room was a demure ladies' affair with tiny tables crowded together and no space in the aisles for a man-sized leg, and they served dainty items and no drinks. Janet took his arm.

"How about the Ritz?" he said. "If we're to be relations we must get off on the right foot! And not sprain it, either!"

Janet laughed uneasily and went with him out onto Newbury Street and down the hundred yards to the Ritz-Carlton.

Brady was surprised to find that he was not immune to the pleasure of seeing envy in the eyes of the men they passed on the street. She was a lovely, lovely young woman. Her blond hair trailed back behind her head as they walked. Though she wore a tan cloth coat, it was belted and showed that she had a figure. When they passed the doorman, Brady returned his salute jauntily. Having a girl on your arm makes you younger and happier. No wonder young men are such fools. They can afford to be.

Janet Lindsay felt like a bronze head in a gallery, the way the diners in the second floor salon eyed her as she walked in on Mr. Brady's arm. She knew that they would all have it wrong, thinking she was *his*. It was ridiculous, but she wanted them to think that. They dabbed at their mouths with their napkins. To be so young and yet the lover of such a man! You could look at Colman Brady and see what he had done, what he had been. She was his silver queen, before whose feet he laid his past. Such a past could have made a stone of the heart, but it had not. That was the charm. He had offered his arm as if it were a permanent gift.

"Would you like an apéritif, Janet?"

They were seated, their laps covered with their linen tents.

"Sherry, please, Mr. Brady."

"Two sherries, please, waiter."

The kindliness with which he said that was familiar to her. Collins too was graceful with servants.

She was determined not to be schoolgirlish and shy with him. It would have been so much easier to detail the Shreve's patterns for Mrs. McShane, but she much preferred this chance to be with Collins's father.

"Mr. Brady, Collins, I mean Micko, told me the origin of his name. I found that very moving."

"He did?" Colman lit a Camel and let the smoke disperse. "What did he say?"

"He told me Michael Collins called you that."

"I didn't know Micko knew that. I don't think I told him."

"His aunt did. He told me you are very modest about . . ."

"Modest! Good Lord, darling, there's nothing to be modest about."

She smiled so warmly that he felt invited into her eyes, such flecks of blue.

"I am afraid that I am quite ready to believe the stories of your heroism."

"Ah, there's a difference between the way things happen and how the mind needs to remember them. It's our dreams that breed our heroes."

"You are a hero to your son, Mr. Brady."

"What, for the stuff that befell us before he was born? I'd say that's reason for shame, not pride."

"No, your entire life."

"Oh, my entire life!" Colman laughed. "Did he tell you how I bungled my career in politics?"

"He didn't put it that way. Everyone knows what the machine was like before and what happened if you stood up to it."

Colman said nothing.

"That's what my father said, not Micko. He admires you too."

"If your father thinks well of me, no doubt it's because I had a falling out with Curley."

"We know what kind of a man he was."

"No, you don't, Janet. You mustn't ever think you do." Brady paused. He would never allow one of these people to blast Curley or let them think he agreed with them. "James Michael Curley is a great man, not a buffoon, not a fool, not a criminal. Boston has treated him much more poorly than he ever treated her."

She thought how loyal of him. But he was in no mood for her flattery, that was clear. She fell silent. The sherry came. She sipped it.

"Do you like Washington?" he asked.

"I'd better, hadn't I?"

"Why do you say that?"

"It looks like we'll be there a while."

"I thought things were open-ended, more or less."

"Not quite. There's my job, for one thing. And then Collins's prospects if Senator Kefauver were to win."

"His prospects?"

"The job with Halley. Micko told you about it, didn't he?"

"Oh, that, of course." Colman lit a second cigarette, controlling himself, disguising his ignorance. What was she talking about? And why hadn't the boy told him? Was he hiding something? Was he suspicious already? "I simply assumed it was all very iffy."

"Of course it is. First Kefauver has to get elected. Then he has to actually appoint Halley attorney general. And then they have to actually establish the special unit."

"Micko's unit."

"Yes. The strike force."

"To pursue the investigation."

"Right. It was the only reason he agreed to work on the campaign."

"I know. He feels very deeply about it, doesn't he?"

"He's a very strong and brave man, Mr. Brady. It's nice to know where he gets it."

Colman smiled at her, but he was thinking what a luxury her innocence was. Then it struck him forcefully that his son was pure, ivory pure in just the way that she was. *That* was his son's luxury, and he, Colman Brady, had paid for it, and would pay for it again. He decided to send Adlai Stevenson some money.

"What about you?" he asked.

"I'll stay on with Senator Lodge. We won't be the only bipartisan couple in Washington. Democrat-Republican, that's the real mixed marriage."

"What if Lodge loses?"

"Senator Lodge lose? You don't mean to Congressman Kennedy? Mr. Brady, really!"

Colman made an expression that said, "Anything's possible." Henry Cabot Lodge, Jr., had demolished Curley years before. Brady hoped young Kennedy could pull it off. He had contributed five thousand to his campaign.

"I'll tell you what, Janet. If the impossible does happen, I can fix it for you to keep your job. Of course, you'd have to become a Democrat."

"Would I have to become a Catholic too?"

"Yes." Suddenly Brady was serious.

"I wouldn't do that."

"I didn't think so. Not for a mere job."

"Not for anything, Mr. Brady."

"Not for Collins?"

"He's never asked that of me."

"Janet, I'm asking it of you."

Oh, for the love of God! That was it! That was why he'd brought her here! Poor Mrs. McShane didn't have the stomach for it. Janet Lindsay felt the floor of her brain shifting. Collins had assured her and assured her that she would not be subjected to this. It was bad enough having to face her own father, who vainly tried to disguise his contempt for what Collins was by offering glib tributes about Collins's father, who was sitting here now, poised and cocky, asking her to leap in the Tiber and drown.

"No. Quite simply and emphatically, no. Never."

Brady smiled, and that surprised her.

"I didn't think so," he said. He raised his glass of sherry and toasted her with it. It was such a generous and unexpected gesture that she was moved by it. She had begun to harden herself against him, but here she was melting. She thought she might cry.

"I respect convictions strongly held," he said. It was the sort of thing Collins might have said.

"So do I."

"Good. Then maybe we can help each other."

"Mr. Brady, it's very important to my father that the service be held at Trinity."

"Simply out of the question, Janet. I'm in the process now of trying to get the Catholic Church to bend its rules to the breaking point to bless this marriage. Surely you appreciate that."

"Yes, I do."

"I think I can get the requirement for the service to take place in a Catholic church waived on our side. You must give as much."

"If it were up to me I would."

"Could you imagine having it, say, on your father's estate? It will be summer. There could be a glorious tent. Believe me, my sister wouldn't like it any more than your father. But you and I are caught in the middle. We have to be reasonable."

"But my father . . ."

"Janet, if this wedding takes place in Trinity Church, no one from Collins's side will be there. Collins himself will be formally excommunicated. Both our families will be made to look ridiculous. Is that what your father wants?"

"Of course not. I didn't realize how extreme . . . Collins never explained it to me."

"Collins went to Harvard, darling. He wears a WASP veneer. But you scratch him and he's just like the rest of us."

"Suppose we did have the service at my home. What else?"

"You'd have to allow his cousin, Father John, to marry you."

"Mr. Brady, really! He disapproves of me. He hasn't bothered to disguise the fact, either."

"I'm not asking you to marry *him,* Janet. Just to stand in front of him for a few minutes."

"Would it have to be a Mass?"

"No. A traditional ceremony, much like your own. I've checked."

"In Latin?"

"No. Not the relevant parts, anyway. And I'll make sure he says the rest to himself."

"But my father's oldest friend is the rector. We all thought he would do it."

"Perhaps he could be there, too. Why not? And pronounce the major blessing. Who would know in Rome, right?" He winked at her. "But Jack would have to be the minister of record, signing the forms and so on, the papers."

"I'm not worried about the papers."

"Frankly, Janet, that's all I'm worried about." Fragments of his conscience flickered in front of her briefly. It was not what she expected. "Speaking of which . . ." He pulled a folded paper out of his inside coat pocket.

It was an epiphany of her fear. She looked at the paper even as he held it over to her, as if it were a tool with which one did bad things to flesh.

"What is it?" She wasn't going to touch it until she knew, as if touching it were a promise of some kind.

"It's an application to the Apostolic See for a dispensation from the impediment of disparity of cult."

"What?"

"You're asking the Pope's blessing."

"The Pope?" The very word off her tongue sent reverberations through her body. A medieval woodcut, black figures, the Dance of Death, bubonic plague.

"Yes. Did you think Truman could do it? Of course the Pope, Janet. We're Catholics." Colman was aware of her distaste. Her face even screwed itself up and recoiled, as if he were offering her a worm.

She took the paper. "It's in Latin!" She knew it would be.

"The English is on the right-hand side."

Janet read the document slowly. When she looked up at him her eyes were huge. "You want me to sign this, don't you?"

"Yes."

"But it's no one's business but ours, mine and Collins's."

"I know that, and I apologize for it."

It was the gentleness of Mr. Brady's voice that caused the tears to overflow her lids and stream down her cheeks. She didn't know how to deal with him. If he were brusque and rude like her father, she could fight him and hold him off. But he was so kind. His eyes caressed her and made her want to go into his arms. But no! That was false! He was cruel! Crueler than her father. How else would he give her such a paper, such a blow, even while apologizing for it? He was cheating her of the outrage to which she had every right.

"It means nothing, Janet. No one will ever know. It's simply a document I need to take to Rome."

She looked at it again. "It's already signed."

"Yes. One of the two signatures required. That's Father John's."

"It says he witnessed my oath and my signature."

"I know. Obviously I couldn't have him do it."

"But that's a lie."

Colman did not reply. She had such a vicious purity.

"It says I'm to lay my hand on the Bible."

"Janet, it's only a form. If you sign it . . ."

"Mr. Brady, I could never do that." Her breath was coming in short bursts. She was about to start sobbing quite openly. "Why isn't it Collins who must swear? Why me?"

"Because he's the Catholic. They think they already have him under their control. They must think they have you."

"Well, they never will. I'll never take that oath." She gave the paper back to Brady.

"Then they already do, Janet. The way they 'have you' is if you take them seriously." He folded the paper and put it in his pocket.

She stood, crushing the napkin against her eyes for an instant, just long enough to clamp off the rush of emotion. "Good-bye, Mr. Brady."

"Janet, before you go."

"Yes?"

"One last thing. A great personal favor to me."

"If I can."

"Don't tell Collins."

"Don't tell him what?"

"About our meeting today. About any of this. Let it be our secret."

"Oh, Mr. Brady!" Her mouth twisted miserably. She forced one last sentence out. "I have no secrets from him." And she turned and ran out of the dining room, weeping audibly.

The glasses and monogrammed silver of the other diners were suspended in the air, but only for an instant. They went on eating. They were not crude. They would not stare. In the second-floor dining room of the Ritz-Carlton, nothing like that young woman's outburst ever happened. And so it simply hadn't.

Brady sipped at his sherry and thought.

The waiter came and Brady explained that he wouldn't be eating after all. Before leaving he withdrew a fountain pen from one coat pocket and the folded paper from the other. He spread it carefully on the table and, with a flourish, he signed it in the appropriate space with the name of Janet Bolton Lindsay.

3

"THE BERNINI COLONNADE was constructed between sixteen fifty-six and sixteen sixty-seven, and formed by two hundred and eighty-four impressive columns of Doric style and eighty-eight pilasters." The tour guide was a stout priest who delivered his monologue absentmindedly. He spoke the English as if these were the only words he knew in that language, but he knew them perfectly. His concentration was focused on keeping the broad-brimmed Roman hat, saucer-like on his head, out of the jaws of the April wind. "The columns are arranged in four files, forming three ambulatory covers that measure comprehensively seventeen meters wide. The colonnade is nineteen meters, enclosing an area of one hundred forty-eight meters in breadth and one hundred ninety-eight in length. It is surmounted by a beautiful entablature with a balustrade on which stand out ninety-six statues representing saints and martyrs, that measure three point two aught meters in height. They were sculpted by students of Bernini, and the master furnished the drawings for many of them.

"Remaining at the limits of the square, let us stop to admire the grandiose scenographic effect of all of it together, including the facade of the basilica of St. Peter, the marvelous dome of Michelangelo, the Apostolic Palace, where the Holy Father lives, the obelisk, and the two fountains. The impression that we receive is disconcerting because of the gigantic proportions of every element, especially the Bernini colonnade stretched out toward us, seeming as though it almost wants to receive all of us in a simple affectionate embrace. And, in fact, this was the intent of the genius of Bernini, to make us understand indelibly the maternal greatness of the Catholic Church, ready to embrace all people of every race and color in a single beat of charity and love. The incomparable vision better prepares us to understand the harmonic vastness of the great basilica, to which we proceed now. Follow me. Watch your stepping, please."

Colman Brady let them go.

He watched the bevy of tourists trail after the chunky priest like quail after the lead bird. They moved across the immense stone circle, growing smaller and smaller in the shadow of St. Peter's until finally they assumed the look of one creature, a wandering lonely creature in the most ghostly place in the world.

A ginger tomcat, sly and battered, brushed against Brady's leg. Rome is famous for its stray cats. For centuries they have inhabited holes in the halls and pitted forums where the glory of men mercilessly consumed itself. Brady bent down to stroke the cat, perhaps to comfort it. Even half-wild, the animal seemed to crave an act of human kindness. Its tattered tail was erect, its back arched up. The soft engine of its purring drew Brady down. The cat was rubbing itself against his ankle. But just as he was about to touch the tattered fur, the cat, quick as a flash, flew away, leaving Brady caught in the air of his offer.

There were no pigeons. Brady wondered where the pigeons were. Their absence struck him in a way that the thunderclap of their wings in Boston Common never did. Perhaps there were stories of ravished nests during the food shortage. Had they eaten pigeons during the war? He would have to ask the concierge at his pensione.

Brady began to walk, hunching himself into the wind. He was walking toward the basilica, but his eyes were drawn this way and that, by the obelisk, by the high windows of the Pope's apartment, by the swirl of columns, by the clattering horse-drawn carriages, the men tugging at their black skirts. He scarcely knew what to look at; what sights does one choose when walking into the past? The question carried him across the circle and up the long staircase.

St. Peter's Basilica! In addition to the reputed Chair of Peter, it preserved and displayed the Veil of St. Veronica, the head of St. Andrew, a large piece of the True Cross, and the Lance used to pierce Christ's side.

It was not the size of St. Peter's that stunned Brady as he crossed its threshold, going instantly from morning into night. What stunned Brady was the sure knowledge that the silence and the dark had lashed down on him before in exactly that way. When? Long before. Going into St. Lawrence's on the hill of Four Mile Water. Brady imagined a boy holding his hat, standing just inside the big door waiting for his eyes to find the light and for his nose to adjust to the dank mustiness. That boy believed that God was like a bat who preferred shadows and the chill. Inside St. Peter's, waiting for his pupils to dilate, waiting for the smell to stop shocking him with its familiarity, Brady felt as though he'd slipped into a ring of friends, taking two by their hands to join their circle.

Foreign priests, carrying little suitcases containing their vestments, were looking for altars on which to say their Masses for their mothers. They brushed by Brady, ignoring him.

Brady lowered the collar of his overcoat, smoothing it down. He wished he'd worn a hat so he could remove it. He looked for a fountain into which to dip his hand. He saw it, a huge amber basin, and crossed to it. The sound of his steps on the marble seemed profane. The water was freezing, which seemed right, and filthy. He signed himself and looked for a place to kneel. There were no pews. The church was empty of furniture. He thought of kneeling right there on the marble, but it was too open. They would think him pious.

Every Sunday for thirty years he had gone to Mass. He had hovered away from the pews in the backs of churches with the other men, first Gate of Heaven in Southie, then Saint Brigid's, then Saint Aidan's in Brookline. At the *Sanctus* bell he had always knelt, holding Micko's hand which, at the Consecration, he always squeezed. He always left before communion. Communion was for women. It had never bothered him not to have a pew to kneel in. But now he felt exposed and vulnerable. Inside St. Peter's was like outside everywhere else. He wanted to be still and bask in the silence and the sense of continuity.

That was it; not the size of St. Peter's, but its continuity with everything he believed, had been, and would be.

Trinity Church on Copley Square, the WASP jewel, H. H. Richardson's masterpiece, would be lost in the side chapels of St. Peter's, noteworthy neither for its size nor for its age nor for its beauty nor for the truth of its worship. Let J. Bolton Lindsay come here, by God! A surge of angry pride coursed through Brady, surprising him, a clenched fist of a feeling. He wanted to throw his arms wide and his head back and holler, "Glory be to God, this is ours!"

The grave, devout men, the foreign priests in their fiddleback vestments, crossed the great sweep of marble to their appointed altars. Their demeanor, perfect and solemn, explained that this was the moment they had lived for — to celebrate the Holy Eucharist in St. Peter's. They would never forget it. They were preceded by small Italian altar boys, each carrying a cruet. *Their* demeanor explained that they did this every day. The only excitement for them lay in the luck of drawing an American priest, because Americans were generous.

Brady began to walk.

The long nave of the basilica was like a broad underground highway which, bereft of places to sit, invited movement. The tourists clustered around the whispering guides did not distract. The Shrine of St. Peter's is so large that what would be a bustling chaos elsewhere takes on the air there of choreography. Brady felt himself to be a part of it. He was moving toward the great space of the dome, and his eyes were drawn to it involuntarily. The dome of St. Peter's, designed by Michelangelo at the age of seventy-two, the object of all his effort until his death at the age of ninety. It was the summing up of a life of genius, an enshrined corner of the very heavens. *Glory be to God,* Colman thought again, *this is ours! Michelangelo is ours!* Why wasn't he a saint? he wondered. He should have been a saint! Goddamnit, why didn't they make him a saint?

A few paces away Colman Brady found the *Pietà*. The exhausted Savior, dead, defeated, scourged, crucified, across his mother's knees. Her sorrow was so complete it would not permit the water in her eyes to tear, lest it see what she saw. Brady knelt down on the marble.

He saw in the Madonna's face a vision of the Mary in St. Lawrence's which was a vision — his first in years — of Nellie Deasy. He understood from her dry and perfect gaze why he had never wept in all his years, and why he never would. There is a pain in comparison to which tears are trivial.

Brady knelt not moving, not covering his face, not striking his breast.

Michelangelo Buonarroti, Florentine; words on the Madonna's girdle. He sculpted it when he was twenty-four years old. He spent the rest of his life trying to match the achievement, trying to be worthy of it. It was the only work he ever signed.

It did not occur to Brady to say, "This is ours!" Perhaps because it was that man's only. Perhaps because it was everyone's.

Brady looked up at the dome again. It was the achievement of a sensitivity so fine as to be mammoth. Suddenly his feeling about it was transformed. His clenched chauvinism was replaced by an exaltation that moved him enormously. He had felt it before. When? When first in the presence years before of another masterpiece, Louisburg Square. How was that modest, tidy city park with its brick mansions like St. Peter's? Both were exquisite realizations of what they were intended to be, and in that they shared the same tradition and the same culture. Both were stone monuments to the human quest for excellence. If on one level St. Peter's was Colman Brady's in a way that Louisburg Square was not, he recognized that more basically both were as much his as his own aspirations were. When he had his dreams of being at home they were dreams of having forever the feeling he had then.

After a long time Brady became aware of the slow rhythmic sounds of a bell in the distance. It was ringing outside. At first unconsciously, he counted the gongs. On the stroke of ten he stood. He was late.

He left St. Peter's and set out across the great stone circle to a point where the Bernini portico angled sharply.

A tattered gray cat caught his eye. Still no pigeons.

He felt the seams of the paving stones rough under his feet. He turned his collar up again. The cold of Boston's winter had not chilled him like this Roman spring wind.

He passed two soldiers of the Swiss Guard, living statuary. Brady half-expected them to challenge him, but they remained rigid in their blue, gold, and red costumes as if the sixteenth century had been too much for them. Brady nodded at them. Still they ignored him.

He took hold of a large bronze ring in the center of a massive oak door that displayed its cracks like ribbons and pulled it open. A drowsy cleric sat in a chair, a small table at his elbow, the real guard. Brady showed him the white card that had been given him for the purpose. The man gestured him along, but it took Brady's eyes a moment again to adjust from the spectacular morning sunshine. Brady looked the corridor in the face and saw it emptied of everything but harsh gleams. The floor was polished. Servants worked here; he wondered if they were clergy too. Nuns probably. What kind of faith did it take to be the janitor in God's house?

He walked two-thirds of the length of the corridor.

"Signor Brady."

Another cleric approached him. They had their system.

"Yes."

"Follow me, please."

The priest glided soundlessly ahead of him, as if on wheels. Brady tried to soften his steps. They took four flights of stairs, which were awkward to climb because the vertical space between each pair of steps was a mere four or five inches, as if the Curia were staffed by midgets, like all bureaucracies. The priest did not speak to Brady, whose ear stretched for conversation. He wanted to tell him or anyone that coming to Rome was like coming home. It had surprised him. He never expected to be moved. He never expected to be proud. There was nothing in the Italians he knew in the States to prepare him for such majesty. But even as he entertained that thought, he knew it was wrong. There was Anselmo's silence.

There was the silence of this priest. Perhaps talk was forbidden. Brady tried to walk shoulder to shoulder with him, but the cleric was determined to lead, if only by a step.

The two men mounted the stairs and walked the long gauntlet of a portrait gallery which was hung with dozens of sullen-eyed Popes whose deeds and misdeeds beat the passage. They served the corridor poorly. Their portraits were the opposite, exactly, of windows. Brady's mind went back to that one homely portrait in St. Lawrence's, the Curé d'Ars, whose thin warped hands writhed like a bundle of kindling and whose eyes were heat for the Lord, an ugly thing, but sad as the heart could wish, just right for a boy to kneel before and tremble.

Brady longed to arrive at the end point of the corridors. Each time he thought they had, the dour cleric led him into a new polished tunnel without windows. It was like being inside the very mind of the Church, where the Vatican boasted endlessly of the eyes of its artists and the consecrated hands of its priests and bishops, and where the sternest bragging, the higher and more narrow the corridors, was of the absence of women. Here were these men, breeders all, all with their testicles stabbing the air, all with contractions in their loins, all flogged by the same yearning for a child, here were these men who said, "No!" No wonder they grew cold. What faith did it take to be a janitor? What faith to mangle one's own comeliness?

But how was he different from these? All his women, taken together or singly, had come to nothing, but for Nell, who had come, only, finally, to his son. These at least had the will to make of their barrenness a dare, daring God to make something of it. No wonder they sweetened that will with hate.

The priest opened a large carved door and stepped aside.

Brady entered.

Another priest greeted him with a simple bow and held out his hand for Brady's topcoat. Brady surrendered it without speaking, and brushed the shoulder of his dark blue suit as if it were not perfect. The cleric led him into a great hall of a room, one wall of which was lined with windows. They were covered by thick dark Lenten velvet. At the far end of the room, huge in the light of the one exception, was a desk and, seated behind it, a man. The usher left. Brady made his way across the marble. He was self-conscious about the noise his feet made. It drew attention to the fact that he wore mere trousers and not a cassock. Every Catholic layman feels inferior for that at some time in his life.

The cleric rose behind his desk. He was bespectacled and thin in the fashion of Pacelli. His black robe was made special by its crimson piping and broad crimson sash that extended from his navel to his breast.

Eve alone of all women had no navel; Adam's loss. Brady made an effort to reel in his mind.

"Mr. Brady?"

"Yes." Live boldly, man, and let the dreams be timid. "And you are Monsignor Borella?"

"Yes." The monsignor offered his hand with a grace and warmth that surprised Brady in such a setting. "Ruggero Borella." He was not old. He held himself handsomely in a lithe frame. There was a pleasant modulation in his voice. He could almost have been French.

"Thank you for receiving me, Monsignor."

"I hope I can be of service."

"I appreciate your position and the value of your time."

"I do as well yours also, Mr. Brady. Please sit."

Brady moved a step toward the Catalonian sidechair but did not sit, though the monsignor did. "I have these greetings for you." Brady withdrew two envelopes from the inside pocket of his suitcoat. He handed one to Borella.

"Ah, Archbishop Cushing!" he said, reaching across his desk.

"Yes."

The monsignor sliced it open quite expertly with a blade that had once adorned some prince's tunic, a ceremonial dagger. The envelope contained a letter from Cushing, his personal request for an apostolic rescript, and the petition for a dispensation from the impediment of mixed religion. Also included was the oath of the non-Catholic, signed, witnessed, and impressed with the Archbishop's own seal.

"And this also," Brady added, handing him the second envelope, "from myself. A meager offering."

The monsignor took it and laid it aside. He would open it later.

"And, Monsignor, I bring you good wishes from Gennaro Anselmo." Brady took his seat.

"Ah, Gennaro!"

"His interest in this matter is personal and discreet, but he asked me to convey it nonetheless."

"Ah, Mr. Brady, rest assured. We know nothing here if not the exact measure of discretion."

The two men exchanged the sparest smile, each with his reasons. Borella had an influential new friend in America, where the Church, even among the thorns, had grown to be so faithful and so generous. Brady's journey through the labyrinth had not disappointed. He knew that the preparations for the coupling of the Bradys and the Lindsays would proceed now without further obstacles, and he had a larger sense that other things — as if Borella's smile were God's — would go his way as well. The two conversed easily for some moments then about a range of other matters, since it was clear that their mutual object had already been accomplished. Borella, in response to Brady's polite questions, explained in broad outline how the Papal Offices were administered and the relationship of the Vatican to the Catholic dioceses worldwide. They were two bright and competent executives talking about their operations. When a seemly time had passed Borella stood and ushered Brady to the door and thanked him profusely for his visit, as if Brady had just rescued him and his family from catastrophe and not the other way around.

After Brady's return from Rome the events leading to the wedding unfolded benignly, smoothly, with the apparent acceptance and even blessings of everyone involved.

At the same time, Estes Kefauver, whose campaign against interstate crime and political corruption made him popular throughout America, won every primary he entered save one. Nevertheless, the Democratic party, in convention that summer in Chicago, nominated on the third ballot the reluctant Adlai Stevenson, to Colman Brady's great relief. His son had no connection with Stevenson. His time as a government investigator was over.

Colman feigned sympathy for Collins, who returned from Chicago crushed and defeated. He had become more involved in Kefauver's effort than he ever expected to. Colman remembered his own bitter disillusion with politics.

The afternoon before his wedding Collins asked his father to walk with him for a while. Colman knew what Collins wanted to talk about, and he was ready and glad. They crossed Commonwealth Avenue and Storrow Drive and headed toward Beacon Hill along the Charles. It was a warm but overcast day.

"I hope the weather clears for tomorrow," Collins said. "The wedding will be wrecked if it rains."

"It won't rain, son. Don't worry."

"You've arranged it?" Collins laughed and kicked at a small stone. It scurried down the path scratching like a fingernail down slate.

"No, not me. It won't rain on J. Bolton Lindsay's lawn. It wouldn't dare."

"It'll be the ultimate test, won't it? Of God's position on the matter."

"We know God's position, son."

"You have influence with everybody."

Colman shrugged theatrically.

"I heard a story about your trip to Rome."

"Oh? What?"

"About ten thousand Italians crowded into St. Peter's Square pointing up to the balcony and saying, 'Who's the thin guy in the white robe and funny hat standing up there with Colman Brady?' "

"It's not true, Micko. Don't believe everything you hear about your old man."

"Actually, I wanted to thank you. I never thought you'd pull it off. Jack can't believe it's all on the up-and-up."

"He's got the rescript, Latin and all. He's happy."

"Let's just say he's resigned."

"Don't start in on Jack."

"I'm still irked at him. He insisted on those damn sessions with Janet. 'Instructions,' he called them. I wish I'd been here."

"He's just doing his job, son. He's been a big help in this."

"I thought when Janet refused to sign that paper you'd never get to first base."

"She told you about that?"

"Of course."

"I asked her not to."

"She told me that too."

"I didn't want you to think I was interfering."

"You were."

"I know."

"But it was your right. You *are* the old man, after all. I expect to interfere quite regularly in the lives of my kids."

Collins thought this was the time to tell him, but before he could Colman spoke.

"She told me you have no secrets."

"I guess we don't."

"Everybody has secrets."

"Not us."

"Young love."

"Not that young, Pop."

"I know. I thought you'd wind up an Irish bachelor. What are you, thirty?"

"Not until next month. Don't rush me."

"Once you're thirty, son, you'll never die a young man."

"My first failure."

"And your last."

"Except Kefauver, of course. Poor old Estes."

"It wasn't your failure, for God's sake. It was just that Stevenson's sin — not wanting the presidency — was less grave than Kefauver's — wanting it too damn much."

"I suppose so. You're right about them both having their sins, but you've missed what they are." There was an overt bitterness in Collins that threatened to go miles beyond mere disillusionment.

Colman found that disconcerting, but familiar.

"Stevenson's great sin," Collins continued, "was defending Alger Hiss. But finally *it* was less grave, read 'threatening,' than Estes' sin — attacking the Bosses who've sold their balls to the night crawlers."

Colman remained silent.

"You know what I mean?"

Colman still did not reply.

"They really creamed him, came right out of their ratholes all over Chicago."

"It's just as well you're out of it now, son. I remember how I felt when the steamroller came my way."

They walked along in silence for some moments, letting the subject die.

Collins said, "I wanted to ask your advice about something, Dad."

"I thought you might. I've already spoken to Carson Brown."

"*The* Carson Brown?"

"Brown, Caruthers and West. He'd love you to join the firm."

Collins said nothing.

"Not only that. There's a partnership for you."

Collins stopped walking, forcing Colman to stop. Though they faced each other, Colman looked past his son at the B.U. sailboats, jibless and unsteady on the river. A one-man shell slithered upstream.

"There's only one partnership I'm interested in. The words I was hoping to hear were that you needed me."

"Brown handles a lot of our business, Micko."

"I assumed as much, frankly. That makes your arrangement more convenient than dealing with, say, the Vatican."

"I suppose you want to make your way alone, without any help from your father. It's a little late for that, isn't it?" What was happening? Whence this blade between them?

"That's one advantage of Washington. Don't take this wrong, but I prize the fact that I've made my way down there on my own. Unless, of course, Rudolph Halley owes you something I don't know about."

"Don't be ridiculous. I've never met him. And don't be ridiculous about my offer. I'm not trying to run things for you. You know that."

"You're running the wedding. You've done everything but pick the bride."

"That's the only thing I would like to have done."

They both smiled. They shared an eye for Janet and knew it. They resumed walking.

"Listen, Micko, you said yourself you'd interfere when you had your kids. You'll just have to trust them to let you know where to draw the line. You tell me where and I won't cross."

"You can draw the line at Brown."

"OK. Then we *are* friends." Colman put his arm on Collins's shoulder, but only briefly. "Besides, I only spoke to Carson when I knew your friend Halley wouldn't get the Justice Department. I knew you'd need a job."

"Maybe not."

"How so?"

"The strike force plan is still on, and I'm still up for it. Stevenson offered Justice to Kefauver."

Colman showed nothing.

"Estes asked me to go with him."

"Well, then you're all set."

"Right. I guess so. All that has to happen now is for Adlai to beat Ike."

"And you've decided to stay with it?"

"Yes. I want to see it through. Especially after the job the bastards did on Kefauver in Chicago. Every political machine in this country is controlled by gangsters, and so are most of the police."

"I doubt if that's true here, son."

"Boston is one of the few places we haven't scrutinized. But you watch. All we'll have to do is kick the rock a bit to get the worms moving. They hate the light of day."

"You asked for advice. Still want it?"

"Sure."

"Don't get involved in Kefauver's personal vendetta or effort to even the score. He's not God either, you know. And he's probably no cleaner than most."

"He is clean, Dad. He's a totally honest man. You know why I trust him?"

"Why?"

"Because he's a lot like you."

"Hell, kiddo, you know me! I'd buy and sell your mother."

"I know you would, but she's dead."

It was a bizarre joke, and their laughter seemed cruel and faithless, but they were momentary castaways on a rough sea and couldn't help themselves. They thought they were in the same boat.

"You know, when I married your mother," Colman said with a repentant tenderness, "our wedding was wrecked."

"By rain?"

"Nope. By the Brits. A contingent of Tommies broke it up. They burned one of our houses. Will McCauley's."

"That's quite a memory to know his name still."

"Some things you don't forget. I haven't told you much about those days."

"Maeve has."

"Your mother was a beautiful lass, never more so than on that day."

"Do you have that picture?"

Colman took out his billfold and withdrew an old photograph three inches square, lines like veins all over it, and shades of black and green. Nellie Deasy stared out at them from her place near the bone.

"Some blows don't leave bruises, Micko. Some wounds are never struck. They're the worst."

"You never told me yourself, Dad."

"I couldn't, son. I still can't. Forgive me. She died terribly. She saved you."

"You loved her."

"I still do." He put the photograph back in its cramped womb. They walked.

"But the wedding itself, before Purcival showed, was fine. I forget the priest's name."

"Jack would be shocked. 'Thou art to remember the priest forever!' " Colman laughed.

After fifty yards, Collins said, "Purcival. He's the man you killed."

"One of them."

"I've always wanted to ask you, but I never felt I had the right. I think I do now."

"Then you're a man, son. I guess I've always wanted to tell you. But how to do that without seeming . . ."

"Guilty?"

"Hell no! No guilt at all! I'd do it again! Absolutely."

Collins stifled a shudder and thought, *No man talks of his past in war and tells the truth.* Collins recognized his father's lie — that denial of regret and guilt.

"Anyway, we had a nice wedding up to a point. I wanted you to know."

"I hope my wedding's nice, too. At least we won't be interrupted by the 'Brits.' "

"That's the advantage of marrying one."

The sun shone brilliantly the next day.

An orchestra played the soft bars of its music while the guests arrived at Windemere, the Lindsay estate in Ipswich. A green and white striped tent took up a corner of the lawn, but the chairs, four hundred of them, had been set in rows along the soft incline facing away from it and toward the sea, which was just visible as a thin line of blue above a far ridge. The unmistakable sky of the sea was overhead and the wind brought a peace so deep no chill troubled it.

Maeve was nervous, extremely so. The entire business still seemed wrong to her, but who was she? What did she know? She'd long since learned the chronology of her qualms and the danger of clinging to them past their time. Colman had given her a lot of money for a new gown, a proper yellow one with chiffon sleeves. Her upper arms were not her best feature. She bought a wonderful hat at Bonwit's with flowers in the band that made her look like Lady Davenport. She had composed herself for this wedding the way Beethoven or someone had composed the tune that orchestra was playing. Whoever heard of an orchestra before a wedding? Before church? But of course, she reminded herself, it wasn't church. It was the Lindsays' back yard.

J. Bolton Lindsay was looking out on the expanse of lawn from his study, watching the young attendants usher guests to their chairs. He was composing himself much in the way that Maeve had. A tall, thin man with a modest pencil-moustache and a ring of white hair around his bald pate, Lindsay was aware that his friends and to some extent his family considered him an unfeeling man. It was true that he put his faith absolutely in the human faculty of reason, a matter which caused him no religious conflict because he believed with St. John that God was pure *logos:* that is, Reason itself. *Ipsum Ratio.* But it was also true that there were moments in one's life when it required an act of will to grant reason its proper sway over one's affairs, not to say one's feelings. As now. It was perfectly reasonable for Janet to marry this young man, who was well educated and whose commitments were admirable and whose prospects were adequate. It was reasonable to alter the tradition of the family to have the wedding here instead of at Trinity, especially so since the Brady faction had put aside the more obnoxious requirements of their religion. In point of fact, J. Bolton Lindsay felt a certain limited pride that the marriage of his daughter should be the occasion of an ecumenical ceremony which could well contribute to the relaxing of Rome's stringent attitudes and serve as a model for others. Archbishop Cushing and Mr. Colman Brady were to be commended for their relative open-mindedness. Lindsay, too, was an open-minded person. He was preparing himself now for his role as host. He was Lord of the Manor, after all. The Bradys and their friends would never have a hint of the quite unruly emotion he was only now succeeding in purging entirely as his rational faculty resumed its proper authority. And he was the Father of the Bride, after all. Janet, his most beloved child, would never have a hint that part of him — that most troublesome part — was in deep mourning for her. There was nothing he could do about that, because as a consequence of her choice on this day she was already, secretly but essentially, as one dead to him and his family. He lifted his hand idly and touched the pane of glass and remembered how he had adored her. The focus of his gaze shifted from the lawn and its people to his own reflection, into the eyes of which he looked with the immodesty of a god seeing the will he had composed and the mind he had set. All was ready.

Maureen McShane saw her mother sitting alone in the front row of chairs on the groom's side and immediately felt a stab of anger. Where the hell were Deirdre and her fool of a husband, Horace? Maureen had let them off and gone to park the car. It was a disgrace that Maeve McShane, practically the mother of the groom, should enter the improvised amphitheater unescorted. Maureen clutched her small handbag to her breast and muttered apologetically as she brushed by the other arriving guests. She nodded at the Dugals and Mr. Brace, who was head actuary at Monument and whose wife she had never met. Maureen was the office manager for her uncle's insurance company and as such supervised the running of four entire floors in the Monument Building on Essex Street. She was an exceptionally well organized and competent woman, handling her responsibilities flawlessly. Nothing irked her so much as the sort of unreliability her damn sister displayed in abandoning her mother. A young man stepped in front of Maureen, startling her. He was handsome and smiling. He was offering her his arm. She stifled a wave of panic. She didn't know any young men. She didn't know any men her own age, for that matter. The only men available to a bright woman in her middle thirties were psychopaths or mamas' boys. Maureen did not mind living without a man, nor did she mind living with her mother and uncle. That was preferable, for example, to a life with a fool like Horace. Maureen shook her head at the young man, who stood waiting for her to take his arm; an usher, of course. He offered his arm to anything that moved. She brushed by him and made her way efficiently but without any particular grace to the head of the assembled chairs.

"Hello, Mother. Where's Dee?"

"Oh, Maureen. Here, sit here."

Maureen did not sit. "Where's Dee? Why isn't she here?"

"Horace met someone from medical school . . ."

"This is not the time to socialize. Where are they? Typical. The Lindsays will think we're just a bunch of louts."

"Everyone's talking, dear. Lots of people are socializing."

"If you'll notice, Mother, those are our people. The Lindsays' friends are already seated and attentive."

Sure enough, the chaos in the yard *was* weighted toward the groom's side of the aisle. The bride's side was quiet and almost filled. Brady people were still milling about and filing in. Some were already too loud.

"This is embarrassing," Maureen said, sitting. "Colman will die. No, he won't. He'll kill them."

"Oh, I knew we should of had it in church. They wouldn't be talking if it was church."

"Mother, don't start in on that now."

"There's Deirdre."

"Where the hell is Horace?"

"There he is. He's coming. You shouldn't use language."

Maureen stood and glared at her sister, who ignored her; years of practice, both of them. Deirdre gathered her long skirt, smoothed it, and sat, hoping not to wrinkle it. Horace, a short man and very overweight, took his place beside her. His collar was already soaked with perspiration, which, on his forehead, was slick as Vaseline.

The congregation welcomed the processions by standing. First Father McShane and the Reverend Mr. Bartlett approached the linen-covered table toward which all things pointed. They both wore black cassocks and surplices, but the minister's had a distinctly Protestant cut. McShane thought he looked like an old picture of John Calvin. They walked solemnly and in step from the left rear and took up their places behind the table. They watched as a line of seven ushers in tails entered from the right rear. Then Colman and Michael Collins Brady, both in morning coats and stripes, approached the table. They were a strikingly handsome pair, each with his flourish of hair, Colman's half-gray. Collins had a youthful slimness his father lacked, but never had their physical similarity been more apparent. The Brady side nodded proudly to itself at the figures they cut. Wasn't it lovely that the son's best man was the father? And the Lindsays had to admit they were good-looking men.

The orchestra struck the first notes of Mendelssohn.

The congregation turned toward the center aisle. Young women, seven of them, in yellow gowns with small ribbons in their hair, each with her rose, proceeded into the jealous gaze of the company. They carried themselves with a modesty which, as rehearsed as natural, was irresistible. They were met in turn at the head of the aisle by the ushers, and they stood fanlike at the table.

And then came the bride on the arm of her father.

Where did they learn such dignity?

Janet Lindsay was a snow queen in summer. She had a beauty richer and rarer than the cut of flight a lost heron makes returning from the sea. At the head of the aisle J. Bolton Lindsay kissed his daughter's cheek and stepped with gaunt solemnity out of her reach the way the world's Father stepped aside for Adam. Collins took her, hurting her elbow with his grip to prove how ungarnished was the love he had.

Colman Brady stepped out of their way. J. Bolton Lindsay found his chair. They had not looked at each other.

The marriage rite was swift and neat. It seemed to Brady and to Lindsay like the grass of prim churchyards which covers the wound generation inflicts on generation.

Afterward the orchestra played Gershwin.

Colman found himself standing alone on the edge of things. He had his drink and his smoke. He had a keen eye, wanting to take in all of it. It was a moment he had awaited for years.

He saw Micko approaching him.

"How's my best man?"

"Better."

"How's your drink?"

"Good." Colman smiled. Best, better, good. Everything was upside down.

"I wanted to talk to you, Daddo." Collins took his father's arm and drew him even farther away from the crowd. They sat on a bench.

"What's up, Micko?"

"Two things."

"Yes."

"First, thank you. For everything. For this. It's a great wedding."

"It is, son. I couldn't be prouder."

"It would have been a disaster if not for you."

"Even your cousin seemed to find it tolerable."

"Good old Father Jack."

"Get used to it. Now that he's a pastor, he'll have to find ways to accommodate his conscience all the time. Responsibility has a way of melting scruples. It's as easy as that."

"The heat in the kitchen, eh?"

"Did you notice Carson Brown?"

"I greeted him in the reception line. Good of him to come."

"But you didn't talk?"

"No. Was he going to make me an offer?"

Colman had hoped he'd drawn him aside to tell him he'd changed his mind about the job with Brown. He simply had to find a way to get the kid away from Kefauver. A slot in one of the great Boston firms wouldn't do it, but Colman knew that a job in his own company would. That, however, was unthinkable. It would be impossible to conceal from a sharp eye the discrepancy between incoming funds generated by the insurance and lending aspects of Monument and the much larger outlay invested in everything from real estate to electronic components for airplanes. Monument had turned out to be a modest managing conglomerate with interests in dozens of companies and outright control of seventeen profitable businesses. Seventy cents of every dollar was ultimately Anselmo's. He had to keep Micko a million miles away from that.

"Not that I know of, son. I told you. I don't cross the line you draw."

"It was unfair of me. . . . I'm glad Mr. Brown came. I'll tell him so."

Colman said nothing. His son's surrenders always silenced him.

Collins looked at his watch.

"Your train's at five?" Colman asked.

"Yes. We won't be staying at the hotel tonight. I checked. We *can* stay on board the ship." Janet and Collins were sailing from New York for Europe the next day on the U.S.S. *America.*

"That's good. Be easier that way."

"I think Janet's more nervous about the crossing than anything else."

"I remember when we crossed, you and me. You were three weeks old."

"What was the ship?" Collins asked, disguising his emotion. His father's reminiscence moved him.

"A tub. Practically had sails."

"Dad, I have to tell you something." Collins' voice was abruptly youthful and afraid.

Colman felt the surging of blood through his brain. What was the kid going to say? Did he know something already? Colman faced his son. "What?"

"I have a child." A blatant confession.

"What?"

"I have a son."

Of course he had a son. Colman knew that, but it had never been mentioned.

"What are you talking about?"

"I have a son," he repeated.

"That's impossible, Micko!" Colman feigned incredulity. "Janet could not possibly have had a child."

"Not with Janet."

Colman softened. He touched his boy's knee, could feel his misery. "Tell me."

"With that girl in Sicily."

"The one who got sick and . . ."

"Yes. Anna Taormina. In Agrigento. She was sick because . . . She gave birth before she died. The child is mine."

"Are you sure?"

"That's cruel of you to ask. Of course I'm sure. We were together for a year. I loved her. Or thought . . ."

"But you never told me."

"I know. I have always felt enormous guilt about all of it. About the child because he was what those bastards used — I also didn't tell you that she was kidnapped and practically tortured — to kill her. I didn't ever want to see the child again."

[417]

"Why was she kidnapped?"

Collins shrugged. "Who knows! A family vendetta. She was a pawn. I never understood."

Colman stroked his son's knee.

"I've felt, Dad, very . . . sorry not to have confided in you about the child. At times I thought that it was my refusal to do that that had come between us."

"Did they ever find the kidnappers?"

Collins heard the question as an accusation. He knew that his father would have tracked them down himself had it been his woman, his child. "No. As far as I know, they didn't."

"Are you certain the boy is still alive?"

"Anna's parents have cared for him. I received a letter from Signora Taormina only last month. The mayor died. She worries about the child. She is very old."

"Have you sent her some money?"

"Of course. Right along. But that's not . . ." Collins's voice broke. He bit down fiercely on his lower lip. "Anyway . . . I wanted to tell you."

"I'm glad you did."

"I've decided to get the child."

"What?" Colman had not anticipated that. "It's been too long, son. You should let it go. He wouldn't fit in."

"The hell with that. I've decided to bring him here. Now that I'm married and his grandfather is dead, he needs me. He's my son."

"But what about Janet?"

"She doesn't know yet."

"Yet! You can't tell her!"

"I have to tell her. I should have told her before this."

"Of course you should have. That's why you can't do it now. She'd never forgive you. She had a right to know about this before. Before you married her."

"I couldn't . . ." Collins dropped his head onto the forefinger and thumb of his right hand. Finally he looked up. "Dad, if I couldn't tell you, how could I tell her?"

"You can't do it now, son. It's too late."

"But I must. I'm determined to have my son."

"You could do that still."

"How?"

"Adopt him."

"What?"

"It would be better all around. It would be better for the boy."

"How?"

"Because then Janet wouldn't resent him. He wouldn't be a constant reminder of your first lover, who, being dead, would be her great enemy. If the pair of you adopted the boy, then she could love him as much as you do."

"But I'd have to lie to her."

"How much is your righteousness worth to you, Micko? Enough to deprive the child of a mother's love? Because that's what you'll do if you tell Janet the truth."

Collins touched his forehead again, ran his finger over his brow. Colman recognized the gesture. He hadn't seen it in years. It was the trick his son had always used to ward off tears.

"I was lucky," Collins said, "I had Maeve's love."

"As good a mother, Micko, as anybody could want."

"I think Janet could be like her."

"She's a wonderful young woman, but don't ask her to welcome a wound that would fester in her or in any woman for as long as she lived."

"I have to deceive her?"

"Yes. As little as possible, but yes. The truth can be an act of hatred, son. Forgive me sounding like a father, but when you're my age you'll find that easier to understand."

"You sound like a grandfather."

Collins went into his father's arms then and they clung to each other for a long time.

Collins pulled away from Colman, who would have let him hold on forever.

"I'll tell you something, son. You can't defeat injustice. It's been around forever."

"I'm not trying to defeat it. I would like only to interrupt it now and then."

"Beginning with your own family."

"With my child."

Colman nodded.

"I'll have to do some fast talking with Anna's mother if we're to keep it a secret. And I'll have to finesse the adoption people . . ."

"That's all minor stuff, Collins. It can be arranged."

"What's important, if I do it this way, is that Janet not know. Not ever."

And what's more important, Colman thought, *is that finally Micko the Pure is throwing curves.* Perhaps his son's zeal would ebb now that he was learning how truths and lies are carved together like the hearts and arrows in ancient bark. If truth could be an act of hatred, so its opposite could be an act of love.

[419]

4

THE SUN WAS BOLD in the sky for early morning, its brightness squared by the glimmering surface of the Seine, which coursed timidly through the valley of Les Andelys. Les Andelys was a village fifty miles west of Paris and the home of Solange Pouvelle, who had been Janet's French sister and roommate during her year at L'Ecole de Suisse, and who was now the wife of le Conte de la Rousine, Pierre Pouvelle.

Collins Brady was sitting alone on the terrace of the château where he and Janet were weekending. He was reading *Le Monde,* not without difficulty, periodically looking up to sip his tepid coffee-with-milk and admire the vista. The rear lawn of the Pouvelles' estate ran two hundred yards down a slight incline to the Seine, whose banks at that point were manicured and well favored by a graceful stand of willows.

"*Bonjour,* Michel," the count said cheerfully as he came out onto the terrace. He still wore his pajamas under a floor-length velour dressing gown. A man of about fifty, he had been widowed for some years before marrying Solange, who, at twenty-four, was only a bit older than Janet. Collins liked the Pouvelles. They were handsome, friendly people with that attractive, curious openness at which the rich excel.

"*Bonjour,* Pierre," Collins said, thinking it would never occur to him to call his host 'Peter'; why did he address him by the French for the name he never used anyway? Pouvelle carried a folded copy of *The Times* of London.

"Is that this morning's?"

"No. Yesterday's." He unfolded the paper and dropped it on the table.

"I was about to be very impressed."

Pierre sat. A serving girl appeared with his coffee.

"*Bonjour,* Estelle," he said.

The maid curtsied and left.

"I was just admiring the view, Pierre. It's beautiful."

Pouvelle nodded. "It is a terrible thing to grow accustomed to such a vision. I confess I have."

"The Seine stunned me in Paris, especially the Ile de la Cité, that medieval world rising out of the water, the miracle of Notre Dame. *I* confess I didn't believe such beauty could be made of stone. By men."

The count tilted his head forward, as if accepting the compliment on behalf of the race, as if nuancing Brady's statement with the phrase, by *French*men.

"But the Seine here in all its natural glory . . ." Brady let his eyes bathe in the sight. "It's incomparable."

"Thank you," Pouvelle said, as if the Seine were his property or his achievement. He looked at the newspaper unfolded in front of his guest. "You have *Le Monde.*" He craned to read. "Who is . . . ?"

"Eisenhower. They nominated him by acclamation."

"Ah, wonderful. That is wonderful, no?"

"I was hoping for Taft. I think Stevenson can beat Taft. I'm for Stevenson. I'm a Democrat."

"You will not vote for Ike?"

Collins thought Eisenhower's nickname sounded even sillier on the lips of a Frenchman. "No. I gather you would."

"We love him here, for the most obvious reasons. You would perhaps feel differently if you knew him as we do."

"I served under him."

"You were here?"

"No. Africa. I spent the war in Africa and Sicily. The closest I got to France was Naples."

Pouvelle laughed. *"Tiens!* Not very close, Michel."

Solange arrived at the terrace in a huff. She was dressed formally in a tailored suit, her skirt just to mid-calf. A short woman with pitch-black hair, she achieved her loveliness more by virtue of the brittle fragility of her personality than by her features.

"Pierre! Tu n'es pas prêt? Dépêche-toi! Good morning, Michael."

Collins stood. "Hello, Solange."

But she was at Pierre again. They were due in Paris before noon for the opening of some exhibit, and she badgered him into going off to dress. Just as he went into the house, Janet came out. She was wearing sandals and an airy summer dress that bared her shoulders. She and Solange kissed each other and chattered briefly in French, then Solange departed.

Collins kissed Janet nonchalantly and sat. "What was that all about?"

"That exhibition. They're late. Pierre tends to be a little irresponsible."

"Solange tends to be a little hyper."

"You tend to be a little critical."

"You started it."

"Oh God, our first fight."

"I hope so. I can't wait to get it over with."

"I'm afraid you'll just have to wait. I've changed my mind. I'm not going to fight with you today."

"You guard your temper the way you used to guard your chastity."

"I never guarded it with you, *mon cher*."

"My point exactly." Collins scored it by snapping open the newspaper. "They went for Ike in Chicago."

"Wonderful! Let me see."

"You should cable Lodge that an Eisenhower jacket doesn't have coat-tails."

"What?"

"Nothing. There's *The Times.* Read that."

Janet scrutinized the small headlines of the English paper. Finally she looked at the date. "This is yesterday's."

"Of course, darling. This is France."

"You . . ." — she rolled *The Times* and hit him — ". . . Democrat!"

He grabbed her wrist and pulled her onto his lap and kissed her, a deadly, certain kiss, to which she responded with passion.

"I'm glad they're gone," she said.

"Me too. Let's go back to bed." He had found her breasts beneath the light dress. She was not wearing her brassiere and he felt her nipples rising on their red axles.

"No!" She pulled away. "You mustn't do that! Not here!" She looked around; the servants! "You know I hate to hide . . ."

He shrugged. It is always awful to be refused once the old passions have been aroused.

"Besides, darling," she said, "I want to take you somewhere." She ran her hands in parallel courses down the bones of his face to the hollow of his throat.

She stirred in his lap. It seemed to him she was wearing no panties either. Something new.

"Where?"

"The hills near here, the great lime cliffs upriver. There's an old ruined château called *Coeur de Lion* . . ."

"Heart of the Lion."

"Lion-hearted, Richard, twelfth century. They say he built it en route to the Third Crusade. It's a pun on *cour* as well; Lion's Courtyard. There are caves up there that Solange showed me years ago."

"Sounds enchanting."

She put her lips to his brow. Her tongue brushed it. Her blue eyes harvested all his reticence.

They climbed into the hills that rose up and away from the river. She led the way. They passed three or four strollers early on, but as they went higher they saw no other people, though the terrain leveled at times and opened on hushed meadows that were alive with purple and white flowers.

At last they came to the ruined castle. It sat below the promontory of a hill at the edge of a field. It was unusual for not having been built on the highest point of land. Not even the river could be seen from its parapet.

"Do you believe that about Richard the Lion-hearted?" Collins asked.

"Sure. Why not? He had to spend those years somewhere. It's antinomian to keep thinking that history happens elsewhere, which is the heresy endemic to cynical tourists."

"Who are you calling a tourist?"

"Your idea of Richard the Lion-hearted is Errol Flynn."

"No, he was Robin Hood. I think Cyril Cusack did Richard. But that's not the question."

"What's the question?"

"Whether you know the meaning of *antinomian*."

"I thought you'd never ask."

"Well, do you?"

"*Mais oui!*"

"You can lead a girl to Vassar, but you can't make her think."

"Thank you, Fred Allen. I went to Smith, dear. It happens I do know what an antinomian is."

"What?"

"An angel peeping through cracks in the floor of heaven."

"That's very witty."

"Also true, Micko," she said with infinite cockiness. "Think about it."

"I knew I shouldn't have let you visit the Sorbonne. You think you're Sartre."

"No, you be Sartre. I'm Simone."

"Say something brilliant then, so I can disprove it."

"I just did, and you lost."

"Oh, Christ." He reached for her. "And here I didn't even know it was a contest."

"Not a contest, a race!" She leapt down from the stone ledge of the ruin and ran out across the unmannerly mountain grass. He stayed where he was and watched her go, seeing her wildness for the first time. She ran the way a freed creature runs. He thought of the way she'd walked into Chartres, as if it were hers. He'd never seen awe in her or worship, not before Chartres, not before Notre Dame. Why should he expect either before himself?

She stopped, turned and waved at him. "Well?" she called.

"Well what?"

"You can't catch me!"

"I know!"

She preened at him and took off.

He scooted down from the ledge and crossed the grass swiftly. He could catch her easily and he knew it and she knew it. The weedy earth was hard to negotiate rapidly, especially in street shoes. He wished for his tennis shoes, rising to the bait, feeling suddenly like a boy out to prove something. She had quite a start on him, and he was not closing on her as quickly as he'd expected to.

She dropped over a rise and out of sight, leaving him only the trail of demolished grass to follow. The sod was pitted and rough, and the angle of the land turned sharply skyward until it peaked in the ridge over which she'd disappeared. He still could not see her. Her absence stung him. The land dipped, then rose again. His eyes fell upon a hole in the next hill. It gaped as if the earth there festered, rotting like sheep's flesh in the wind and sun. It was the entrance to her cave, he knew. She had gone in there.

He was hurt that she had left him behind. He ran across the cluttered ravine through a thicket of brambles and low shrubbery. At the cave's mouth he paused, listening. Nothing. The land under him seemed to rise like a boil.

He plunged into the cave, which forced him to bend, then to stoop, then to waddle on his haunches. He lay flat, crawled along the two-foot tunnel on his belly, tasting the bland dust of the limestone. It was too dark in there to see that the dust was white.

"Janet!"

Nothing.

"Janet!"

Nothing.

The cave was tempered to silence. Perhaps she was calling too, but the sounds of their voices just wouldn't carry. It was a bizarre thought and he shook it off. The tunnel mocked him by narrowing just to the point where he began to fear getting stuck and then opening out again, giving him room. He would have given anything for a light.

"Janet! Janet!"

He was filthy. The ragged particles were in his hair and ears and lungs. He had to squint to keep his eyes free of them. He strained constantly to see ahead but to no purpose. His pupils could dilate themselves into saucers; there was no light.

Cave-in! It was a thought he would not admit to his mind, but which would not quite leave its margins. The slow crumbling of the world, not on his head; worse, behind him, leaving him alive, shutting him off, trapping him forever in this stinking colon.

"Janet!"

He saw light, a glimmer at first, then a fist of it. He crawled faster. The ceiling lifted, gave him room to get to his hands and knees. He scurried madly. He saw blue sky. The bright sunshine poured back into the tunnel, but he was oblivious to the pain it caused his eyes. The crawlspace yawned into a man-sized cavern. He was up, on his feet, rushing to the opening wildly. Only at the end, when he was safe, had he succumbed to his hysteria. He was claustrophobic, had always been. Only at the end, when light and space were his again, did he feel the cold blade of his terror. He was hurling himself joyously out of the cave, expecting to fall onto the cushion of meadow grass.

But there was nothing there.

Nothing!

The cave opened out in the sheer wall of a cliff hundreds of feet above the Seine. The vista nailed him, drove him back. Later he would wonder how he had kept from going over.

He fell back on the floor of the cavern, gasping.

When he looked up he saw Janet enthroned in a corner by the shaft of sunlight. She had been waiting for him. She was naked.

"Do you know what I almost did?" He asked her. The calm of his voice surprised him.

"You almost fell."

"You play dangerously."

She raised her arms toward him. The simplicity of the gesture and the classic beauty of her nudity made her seem for an instant a vision, Penelope saying, "This is the way I welcome my man home from the dark journey."

"I love you," she said, with nothing coy, nothing false.

He undressed and went to her. She welcomed him with her legs and, sensing his great vulnerability, she was gentle and reassuring as she guided him into her. She arched herself under him and began to move more sensuously than she ever had. Almost immediately she began to come, and he, joining in her movement, lifted her, kneading the flesh of her buttocks. Perspiration poured off him onto her and they both moaned loudly. He knew that for the rest of his life he would think back on this as the meaning by which to measure every kind of climax. Dangerous? It is the business of love to be dangerous.

Later they walked hand in hand down the slopes to the river valley.

"Aren't we filthy?" Janet laughed, displaying her ruined dress.

"We can say it's not our fault."

"Oh? Whose, then?"

[425]

"Adam blamed Eve. Eve blamed the snake. We can say the earth did it. It will be the truth."

"We should make up a story," Janet said.

"We fell into a rabbit hole."

"King Arthur's hideaway!"

"Richard's! We can say we were attacked by a band of antinomians!"

"Led by Merlin."

They laughed and pressed their bodies together at the hip, an easy graceful contact Collins thought lewd only if done in public.

"Speaking of stories," Collins said.

"Yes?"

"I've been meaning to tell you one."

"About?"

"A little boy."

"Oh?"

"I've been supporting a child."

"What?" The draft in her voice was surprise.

"In Sicily, since the war."

She said nothing.

"Did I tell you about Bernie Packard?"

"No."

"He was a good friend of mine, one of my men, my top sergeant. He was my NCO for almost two years." Collins paused.

Janet's silence was stubborn and articulate.

"He fathered a child in Agrigento, a boy. Shortly after that he was killed by a sniper, one of the last we flushed. I was with him when he died. He asked me to take care of his kid." Collins stopped as if that explained everything.

Still Janet was silent.

"The girl had died in childbirth." He said that as if it were an afterthought, but it had been his first thought and was the most difficult thing for him to say, even though it was, unlike the rest, the truth.

"What did you do?"

"Not much *to* do. The girl's parents had the child. I sent money, still do."

"Have you seen the child?"

"No. Well, once, after it was born. A good-looking kid. I shipped out shortly after."

They came to a string of boulders and had to take them singly. Janet fell in behind Collins, who sprang ahead. He was grateful for the respite, but the worst was coming and he knew it.

When they came together again she did not make it easy for him to take her hand. He said abruptly, "I've been thinking of going down there, to Sicily."

She balked at his announcement.

"What do you think?" he asked.

"Of you going to Sicily?"

"No. Of us going."

"I don't know."

"What's wrong?" he asked, as if she were the one who'd poisoned their mood.

"I don't know, Collins, but something is. I feel very strange about what you're telling me."

She did not believe him. Panic blazed through his stomach. He would never be able to fool her. He could feel the distance opening between them. She knew he was lying.

"There's nothing strange, darling," he said calmly, "just a footnote to the war. I feel some responsibility, I guess. And I just thought since we were over here . . ."

"I had the feeling you were talking about more than popping down for a visit."

"I suppose I am." He stopped and forced her to look at him. They were in the middle of a large meadow. Purple and white flowers showed the wind's kneading. "There is a reason why I haven't told you about him before. It's that I feel guilty, guilty as hell. I can't think of Bernie Packard without thinking that I've cheated on the most solemn promise I ever made until I took my vows to you. I've dealt with that kid the way rich people always deal with the untidy consequences of their selfishness. I sent money, for God's sake. Bernie asked me to take his place with his son, but instead I've been a one-man Marshall Plan."

"But it's not your consequence."

"Janet, I made it my consequence. *That's* what I've been denying. I feel terrible. I'm asking you to understand."

"What are you saying?"

"I want us to think about adopting him."

Janet turned and shot away from him. She was determined to keep from saying the words that were swelling inside her. She knew a lie when it smashed her in the face. Her husband was lying and she knew it.

He grabbed her arm. "Janet, goddamnit! Don't you run away from me!"

She whipped around and slapped him in the face. He was only lucky that she hadn't left her hand a fist or made it a claw.

He knew then that his father had been exactly right. There was no way this woman would ever accept the truth, come to terms with it, forgive him for it. Her rage, the purest emotion he had ever felt from her, taught him that, and its blast destroyed his own ambivalence about the lie and so prepared him finally to convince her it was the truth. After her blow, curiously, he felt strong and free.

"You don't believe me, do you?"

"I don't know."

"You think it's my child."

"Don't make me say that."

"Janet, it *is* my child."

He let the statement sink in before going on. "I *want* you to think of it that way. I want you to deal with it exactly as if it were. Because I'm telling you that as far as my conscience is concerned, it might as well be mine."

"But it isn't?"

He framed her face with his hands and, conscious of the infinite sadness in his own gaze — he had never been so disappointed in his life — he said, "Can you imagine that I would not have told you if it were?"

"No," she said, reaching out suddenly to his earnestness, holding fast to it, and realizing that she would survive. He was not a liar. She had never said he was. "Oh, Collins, I'm sorry!" She crushed herself against him.

Janet stayed with Solange and Pierre while Collins went to Sicily.

Agrigento had thrived on the war. Collins remembered it as a garrison center swarming with GI's and the camp followers who lived off them.

Peace was not so kind. The Americans were gone. The streets were deserted. So, apparently, were the prostitutes and the chewing-gum boys and the old pushcart merchants hawking trinkets. Collins directed his driver to the mayor's house. He had hired the man and his rattletrap taxi at the small airport in Palermo. The driver's name was Guido and he spoke enough English to translate for Collins, but Collins's own Sicilian had come back quickly. He'd had an expert tutor in Anna and all those hours in which to learn.

"This can't be it," Collins said, bending to the window and staring at a shell of a house. A fire had destroyed everything but the stone walls.

Guido shrugged. "You say the piazza at Prima. This is the piazza at Prima."

Collins got out of the car and walked to the threshold stone. An iron bedstead, charred and bent, blocked the way, but only feebly, someone's desperate effort to preserve the precincts of the place, futile effort. Brady pushed it aside and walked into what had been the Taorminas' front parlor. Ashes formed a little hill in a corner where the wind had swept them. One could blow on those ashes forever. They were cold. The fire had occurred some time before. Bits of a splintered mirror flashed up at Brady. The sun was nearly directly overhead.

He walked back into the street. Guido was bored at his wheel. Every town had its ragpickers and its bones.

"I must know what happened," Collins said.

"I only drive," Guido said, but it was not indifference Brady sensed in him. It was caution.

A boy of about ten scurried by on a makeshift scooter. Brady called out to him. He stopped, showing that *his* curiosity at least was unfettered. Collins approached him and managed to ask in the dialect of the place, "What happened to this house?"

"Big fire," the boy said.

"When?"

The boy shrugged.

"A long time ago?"

The boy shrugged again.

"Signora Taormina. Where is Signora Taormina?"

The boy mounted his scooter and slapped his foot at the pavement, off. He was too young even to ask for chewing gum.

Collins walked up the narrow street. A small apothecary he remembered was on the corner. The door was open.

"Hello!" he called.

An old man came from the back, squinted up at Collins, and, though he knew him at once as an American, did not recognize him.

"Signor Tucina."

"*Sì.*"

Brady offered his hand. "Brady. Captain Brady."

"Ah, Captain!" The man took Brady's hand warmly. Brady had authorized his medics to supplement their medicines with purchases through Tucina. Tucina remembered the officer who had regarded him with respect. The Germans had assumed a Sicilian could know nothing of the science Sicilians had invented.

"Taormina," Brady said. "Where is Signora Taormina?"

"Taormina." Tucina shook his head. "He is dead. Consumption. Tuberculosis."

"What happened to his house?"

"There was a fire." It was obvious from Tucina's manner that there was more to the story than that and also that he would tell none of it.

"When?"

"One year. Nearly two."

"So long ago?"

Tucina held himself rigid. He had said too much already.

"And Signora?"

"With the priest."

"Padre Paolo?"

"*Sì*." Tucina pointed vaguely toward the church.

"Signor Tucina . . ." Brady thought of giving the man some money, but did not. He didn't buy anything. ". . . thank you."

The priest knew everything.

In the privacy of his study he told Brady of the terrible blood feud between the Taorminas and the Castillos. Two of Taormina's sons had learned a year after Anna's death that her kidnappers had been Castillos, from the northwest, the far side of Sicily, territory in the control of the Mafia. There had never been mafiosi in Agrigento and no one understood why the Castillos should have come there and taken Anna. The Taorminas were no match for their new enemies. The mayor's two eldest were killed immediately. His third son then killed one of the Castillos. Then he was killed, along with two cousins. That seemed to end it for a long time. But when Taormina's house burned, everyone believed it was the Castillos, but no one was certain. Now that old Taormina was dead, everyone hoped the blood feud was ended. Signora Taormina had meanwhile become sick with what the priest called a sickness of the heart. The priest had taken her in when her husband died, to be his housekeeper supposedly, but she was not much use to him. And yes, Antonio; the priest raised the subject of the boy with a delicacy Brady appreciated.

"He is a strong child, but there is nothing for him here. Only his grandmother. The others here . . ." Padre Paolo looked away. ". . . No one wants the Castillos to come. They leave Taormina alone."

"You said no one knows why they came in the first place."

"No. They were from Cefalù. It is far away. Agrigento was nothing to them."

"But the mayor was a man of some means. They took Anna because they wanted money, no?"

"No." The priest did not elaborate. He sat shaking his head, an unyielding denial of what Brady had hypothesized for eight years. They had not been bandits. It had not been mere extortion.

"Then why?"

The priest considered his words carefully. "Because of you."

"What?"

"You asked why they took Anna. They took Anna because of you."

"I don't understand. What do you mean?"

"They did not want you with her."

"Why?"

"Who knows? The mayor knew perhaps, but he is with God."

"How do you know it was because of me?"

The priest shrugged. He was finished talking.

"I want to see my son."

Padre Paolo nodded.

"I want to take him with me."

"We will care for him here, even if Signora . . ."

"You said they leave Taormina alone here. What does that promise him? Padre, he is my son."

"He has been your son for over seven years, Captain."

Brady lowered his head. There is no shame like the shame before a priest.

"Come." The priest led the way out of his study up two flights of stairs through an eave-ridden hall. There was the dry whisper of wings above them. The priest smiled over his shoulder and said, "Not angels. Bats." He led Brady into a small room in the far rear of the rectory. A boy was sitting on the floor before a pile of wax chips. He had been systematically peeling a candle layer by layer into nothing. The boy looked up at the priest, showing huge brown eyes. His abundant hair was not quite black. He looked directly at Brady. Brady's breath was gone in the memory of what it was he had loved in Anna.

The boy must never know. Brady held himself in check and counted on the priest's silence. It was the most difficult thing he had ever done — not to embrace his son.

"And Signora Taormina?" he asked.

The priest led the way out — the boy resumed his destruction of the candle — and into an adjoining room. It was dark. The priest stepped to the window and drew the curtains back sharply. Brady was shocked by the sight of a woman in the bed. The mayor's wife had been a stately, sophisticated woman. Her letters to him, including the one only months before, had been gracefully composed. Yet, here she was, withered and shrunken. The light was gone from her face, and though her eyes were open they showed no sign that she had registered their presence. Her eyes showed only the dazed contentment of the insane.

"When did she become like this?"

"Weeks ago. She never came back from her husband's grave."

"She wrote to me not long ago."

"She knew what was happening to her. She was hoping you would return."

"For the boy?"

The priest nodded.

"Well, I have."

"You should not feel the weight of obligation."

The hell I shouldn't! he nearly screamed, but didn't.

"We can care for him. He is one of us." The priest seemed determined about it.

"Padre, it is settled. He is my son."

The priest nodded, satisfied.

Collins touched the old woman's hand, but she seemed oblivious still. Even while holding her bright but unfocused eyes in his own, he asked the priest, "Is there any reason why we should wait?"

"No."

"All right." Collins touched her forehead. Still she ignored him. She was in her own world and it was entire and benign.

Brady faced away from her. "There is one thing I must do. What was that village?"

"What village?"

"Where the Castillos come from."

"Cefalù. But that is finished. It is best forgotten. You do us no service if you cause them to return here."

"I must know why. You said it was me. I must know why." Brady walked out of the room. "I will come back for the boy."

"And take him to America?"

"Yes. But say nothing to him."

Padre Paolo pulled the door to as he left the room. He glanced back at Signora Taormina, whose head did not move, but whose eyes rolled toward him like stones.

On the outskirts of Cefalù seven hours later, Brady told Guido to stop. They were lucky to have made it in the beaten old Fiat. Guido had not wanted to make the additional trip. Brady had to double his fee. The driver said he was afraid for his car, but Brady sensed a fear beyond that. Now they were sitting by the side of the narrow road, not speaking. Moonlight illuminated a grove of olive trees on a nearby slope. The trees cast eerie manlike shadows. Brady was thinking. He did not know how to proceed. He had no desire, certainly, to engage the Castillos or anyone else in Cefalù in a physical way. He hadn't come to accomplish the vengeance the Taorminas had failed at. He wasn't a fool. It was as if the knowledge of motive and purpose and his relation to them would have been vengeance enough.

"I must talk to someone," Collins said.

Guido said nothing.

"Where do the men of the town gather?"

Still nothing.

"Take me there," Brady ordered.

"It is late." It was not ten o'clock yet.

"Take me there."

Guido sighed, put the car in gear and drove. The town of Cefalù was on the northwest coast, a marble-quarrying town. Work begins before dawn. Everyone seemed to have gone to bed. The street was deserted, the houses dark. Guido stopped the car in front of a small guildhall. A gasoline pump was on the sidewalk in front of it. A sign over the pump read, "Bolla." Light shone through a crusty window. Brady got out and went in. The place was nearly deserted. Four men sat at one table fingering dominoes. Two sat at another nursing small glasses. Half a dozen other tables were empty. A single light in its tin cone hung from the ceiling, drawing smoke.

Each man looked up at Brady, showed him nothing, waited.

Brady realized he'd made a mistake, a terrible mistake. It was pointless for him to be there, and dangerous, very dangerous. His fear unraveled itself and then spooled quickly around his winch of a throat. He was not certain that, if he opened his mouth, words would come out.

"Castillo," he said. He was in. He had to play.

The men stared at him.

Brady eyed them each carefully. The big man with the dominoes was the one he chose.

He crossed to him and stood directly in front of him. "Castillo. Where is Castillo?"

The man didn't blink.

Brady repeated himself in Sicilian and then walked out of the dingy hall. The street was deserted except for Guido's car. Guido had not been paid yet. The engine was running. Brady got into the back seat, slamming the door after him.

"Turn it off," he said.

Guido shut the engine off and they waited.

Within a few minutes dozens of men walked out of the shadows all at once, surrounding the car. Several carried rifles. One had slung over his shoulder a weapon Brady recognized as a Thompson submachine gun. The circle of men closed on the car until they were within yards of it. Then they stopped moving. Everything was very still. The moon hung over them, throwing its light.

Brady opened his door and slid across the seat away from it. He waited. After a moment a man got into the car beside him and closed the door.

"Castillo?"

"Sì." The man surprised Brady by smiling. He wore a black stocking cap, a tattered leather jacket, soiled trousers and flashing patent shoes. He carried a long-barreled Smith and Wesson forty-five, which he had pointed at Brady's belly.

"My name is Michael Collins Brady," he said in dialect. He waited for a response, but there was none. "What does my name mean to you?"

"Nothing," Castillo said, lying.

"Anna Taormina, you know that name."

"Yes."

"Why did you take her?"

"You are not welcome here. Leave."

"I must know . . ."

Castillo leaned forward and put the barrel of his gun against the flesh of Guido's jowls. "He will die first, then you."

Brady believed him. "All right."

Castillo got out of the car.

Guido, barely able to control his shuddering, got the car going and drove out of Cefalù, praying all the while that his universal joint, clunking away with every shift, would hold.

It was dawn when they arrived at Agrigento. Guido was asleep in the back seat. Brady had driven nearly all the way back. He woke Guido and told him to leave the engine running this time. He banged on the rectory door until the priest came.

When they had bundled the sleepy boy into the car, Brady turned to say good-bye to the priest. Padre Paolo handed over the small bag which held Antonio's clothes and a few toys.

"We have not spoken," the priest said.

"There is nothing more to say."

"What did you learn at Cefalù?"

"Nothing."

The priest nodded. "They are afraid of the American."

"The American?"

"Yes. That is what they call him. Though I am sure you would not think of him as an American. But to us he is."

"Who is he?"

The priest shrugged.

"Silence, Padre, is the vernacular of this place."

The priest shrugged again, eloquently.

5

PROBABLY BECAUSE Kennedy's victory celebration was in the Grill Room of the Parker House, Colman Brady harbored the uncharacteristically Irish sentiment. Indeed, he nursed it like champagne. It was this; better to be lost in the mist than the owner of bleak memories.

Everyone was there, the legion of pols and State House hacks, the ward workers, South Boston boss John Powers, who delivered the city, the Ambassador, Kennedy's brothers and sisters, his mother, for a brief time Archbishop Cushing, Congressman McCormack, Governor Tobin, Mayor Hines, and on the margins the eternal hangers-on.

Colman Brady saw Jack Hurley on the far side of the crowd. Hurley had sworn in the Council that Brady had taken the bribe and everything had followed like greased gears from that. Brady drained his champagne, still eyeing Hurley. He hadn't seen him in years. Colman waited for the hatred to well up in him, but it didn't. Hurley was desperately, pathetically trying to catch the new senator's attention. "What the hell," Brady thought; "better my life than his." Brady's impeachment was ancient history and had been forgotten by everyone but him.

The Kennedys had appreciated Colman's support very much. This celebration of Jack's victory was the first strictly political event Brady had been to in years. He would not have come, though he liked this Kennedy, who was more Harvard than Irish, but Irish enough to move the earth below Boston when he defeated Henry Cabot Lodge, Jr. Brady's attendance was the only certain way to assure his son's, and that was why he'd come.

Collins and Janet had traveled from Washington during the day. Both were exhausted from their opposite and futile campaigns, Collins having worked with Kefauver for Stevenson, Janet for Lodge. For obvious reasons, Janet had no desire to attend the Kennedy bash. But Colman had prevailed upon them both. It would be good for Janet to meet the opposition, and it would be good for Collins to nurture his state connections. Collins, as always, acquiesced. It was not like giving in to an order. Colman never gave orders to his son. He simply drew an outline of the future — "You'll have a grand time!" — and then loved his son for bringing it about. All his life Collins had moved through a complicated web of his father's prophecies, thinking himself free because they were fine and gentle like spider's silk.

Colman wanted his son at the celebration because he wanted him to take a job with Jack Kennedy, who also deplored organized crime, of course. But he did so traditionally, harmlessly. Colman wanted his son out of investigations.

Colman watched from the edge of things while Collins was wooed and courted by a succession of Kennedy's men. People wanted Collins Brady, who knew, well below the line of his tranquil modesty, how to make them want him. Kennedy recognized in the young Brady the same three traits on which he had built his victory: a certain clout in Washington, though Brady's was that of a hotshot lawyer, not of office; a Harvard mind; and an Irish flair just when the times were ready for it. But Brady had long refused to budge from Kefauver's side. That was one thing about him that bothered the Kennedy people. He seemed a bit of an ideologue. It would have been one thing if he'd been motivated by loyalty to Kefauver personally, but Kefauver wasn't the sort to engender that. Kefauver, like all the liberals, was an issue man. Brady was motivated by commitment to his issue. But now Kefauver, runner-up to an also-ran, was finished. With Stevenson's defeat, his dreams of presiding over the eradication of crime as attorney general were dead. He'd be lucky to win his seat in Tennessee again. That left Brady without a mentor, and it was on that that John Powers played, and then Neil Sullivan, and then Billy Reilly. They thought Brady would jump to join Kennedy.

Speaking of bleak memories, Colman said to himself when he saw a willowy woman of middle age approaching him. What was her name? What the *hell* was her name? She carried herself with the slight stoop and dull eye of one who has quite forgotten that once she was beautiful.

"Hello, Colman."

"Hello."

"You don't remember my name, do you?" She smiled at him with a subservience that shocked him. Just as she had learned successfully as a child how to sit up straight, and as a girl to sew, she had learned as a woman to be wounded. She had learned that the beauty of her youth was an accident, something of which, really, she was not worthy.

"I remember laying beside you and thinking you had forgotten my name, Colman. Upstairs in this very hotel."

"You're Mary Ellen Shields; my God!" Why didn't he grab her? He nearly grabbed her.

"Almost."

"You married Eddie Ricketts."

"You didn't come."

"That must be, what? Fifteen years?"

"Eighteen."

"And twenty years since we've seen each other. You look good."

"You never married."

"No. Is Eddie here?"

Colman was already looking past her. She remembered why she had hated him. The ease with which his eyes moved away from her stunned her still.

"Of course he is. You don't think I'd be here on my own, do you?"

"What's Eddie doing?"

"He's the State Rep from Roslindale."

"Roslindale! No fooling!"

"It's not Brookline, but . . ." She shrugged.

Brady was remembering what he liked about her. She was, despite herself, a spirited, feisty woman. What Brady could not know was that she had been that way only with him.

"You've still your blade, Mary Ellen." His old fondness for her was tangible.

"Why didn't you marry, Colman?"

"Because families prefer widowers to stepmothers. You have kids?"

"Four."

"Good for you."

"Yes. And bad."

"Have a drink?" He handed her a champagne off a tray with which a waiter had been twisting his way through the crowd. They raised their glasses to each other. The clink of Colman's against hers brought a smile to both their faces. They liked each other very much suddenly.

"You're lucky," she said.

"Why?"

"Not being married. It's an infinite succession of sacrifices."

"Broken only by nocturnal bliss. I've the other stuff, believe me." He was not going to let her corner the self-indulgence. "We're of an age, Mary Ellen, to understand why the Irish prefer duty to pleasure."

"We are? Why do they?"

Colman burst out laughing, but she didn't.

She was thinking he had not preferred duty to pleasure with her, the bastard.

" 'They!' You don't count yourself among the Irish anymore? You've still got the tongue, Mary Ellen. You're stuck with your Cork lilt."

"Connacht, Colman."

"One forgets."

"I don't. You're from Tipp."

"And the Kennedys are Galway people. Isn't it grand, young Jack beating Lodge?"

"Yes, it is. I never thought he'd win outside the city. How do you account for it?"

"Henry Cabot Lodge began to believe he was Henry Cabot Lodge."

"I heard that," Janet said, approaching from the bar where she'd just had her ginger ale freshened.

"Hello, Janet darling," Colman said, opening his arm. "This is Mary Ellen Ricketts. Mary Ellen, this is Janet Brady, my son's wife, I'm happy to say." He kissed her forehead.

"Nice to meet you," Mary Ellen said. Brady watched her eyes drain, her slate eyes. He remembered their color and their absence of rapture.

"Ricketts?" Janet said, "Is your husband Edward Ricketts, the representative?"

"Yes. How did you know?" No one knew who the pols were, except the other pols.

"I know the district. Roslindale and Forest Hills, right?"

"Exactly."

"I conducted several surveys in the area."

"My daughter-in-law is on the other side. She works for Lodge."

"Aren't you brave to be here then," Mary Ellen said.

"Mary Ellen and I are old friends, Janet. Going back to before you were born."

"Colman!"

"I don't believe it," Janet said gallantly. She wondered if her father-in-law and this rather sad-looking woman had been lovers. Janet had never seen him with a woman.

"It's true," he said. He turned to Mary Ellen. "Janet's going to keep her job in the Senate anyway. I've already fixed it."

"What!" Janet's undisguised anger shocked Mary Ellen.

Colman retreated immediately. He had made a rare mistake. He'd intended to bring it up later. "I'm just kidding, Janet."

Janet was embarrassed. She hated to expose herself, and she had just opened a crack on her secret. Charmed as she was by her father-in-law, she did not trust him. He was a great manipulator. She was very uneasy about the effect he had on Collins. He would not rest, she knew, until she was a properly registered Democrat and, soon after, a properly practicing Catholic. "I'm sorry, Mr. Brady. I didn't know you were joking."

"Of course I was, darling. We couldn't have you both working for Kennedy, anyway." Colman turned to Mary Ellen again. "My son is going to join the senator's staff."

"I don't think he's decided yet what he's going to do."

"Kennedy wants him for his top counsel, Janet. He's just right for it."

Janet made no further comment, but pointedly.

Mary Ellen seemed oblivious to the awkward energy passing between them. She had withdrawn into her own preoccupation and had begun scanning the room to see if her husband was drunk yet.

Janet went to the ladies' room, but only to get away from her husband's father. She should never have come to the damn party. It was probably disloyal of her to be there. But her loyalties were a welter and she was very confused. She would try to find Collins. She would hold onto his elbow and smile at people. Whatever his father's canker, he did not have it. Since the dread moment in France when she'd feared he was lying and discovered he wasn't, her trust of him outweighed her suspicions of his father.

"They're adopting a kid," Colman said.

"Really?" Mary Ellen watched Janet crossing the room.

"Yes. A war orphan."

"Korean?"

"Italian."

Mary Ellen thought it was a little late for that, but did not say so. "That's admirable."

"She'll be a wonderful mother, that Janet. She was reluctant at first, but once she met the kid she melted."

"They have him?"

"Yes. You ought to see her with him. She's learning Sicilian because she can't wait for Tony to learn English."

"How old is he?"

"About seven."

Mary Ellen let her eyes drift back across the room, in search of Janet. She said wistfully, "And she's so young."

"Youth should be illegal."

"I read about the wedding."

"Did you?"

"Frankly, I was surprised. I thought you, well, hated people like that."

"Like what?"

"You know. Like the . . . What was her name?"

"Lindsay."

"Like them."

"I don't hate anybody, Mary Ellen."

"If you did, Colman, you'd probably marry them, or get your son to do it for you. It's the best revenge, marriage."

"You got what you wanted. A warm roof and a cozy fire."

"I wanted you."

"I doubt it." Brady tossed down his champagne. "In any case, darling, what can't be cured must be endured."

"You bastard."

"I doubt that, too, but who knows for certain, women being what they are? I'm off to the lav. Excuse me, dear."

You bitch, he added to himself.

The men's lavatory in the Grill Room of the Parker House was a cavernous hall of dull yellow tile more fitting to a train station than to a hotel. The entire rear wall ran above the notch of a gutter. Against that wall men stood and urinated. Though not the most sociable of situations, two who found themselves wetting adjacent tiles were compelled to carry on as old friends might on meeting accidentally. Silence there and then exposed more than opened pants did.

Colman Brady was a master of talk at the wall, but it was vacant when he entered the lavatory. He was in no mood after Mary Ellen to lean pleasantly across the modest abyss to hear dull words and pretend they were funny or smart. What was with that woman, anyway? How had he hurt her that the wound festered still?

That was the question Colman was mulling when the distinguished shorter man took his place at the wall next to him. It was the ambassador.

"Colman! My God, the sight of you would thaw the piss of an Eskimo!"

"Hello, Joe, how are you?" Brady finished at the wall, closed his trousers and stepped back. That gave him an edge over Kennedy. The camaraderie of the urinal springs from the shared vulnerability. Brady stood back a bit so that Kennedy had to toss his words over his shoulder.

"Couldn't be better!"

"Congratulations on Jack's victory. You're delighted of course."

"Damn right I am. There'd have been hell to pay if we lost. The money I spent, we could have elected my chauffeur!"

Kennedy shook himself and came away from the wall. He moved to Brady's side at the opposite wall, which was lined with gleaming white sinks and a broad ribbon of mirror, through which their eyes met as they washed.

"Colman, I want to say a personal word to you . . ."

"Forget it, Joe."

"You were very generous."

"*Erin go bragh,* and all that. You know me. It's like supporting the Church."

"Well, all you need ever do is ring."

"I know, Joe. I know." Colman wiped his hands on a fresh linen towel.

"There was something else, Colman. Put in a word with that kid of yours, will you?"

"About what?"

"About signing on with Jack. Believe me, Colman, this is just the beginning. This is peanuts."

"U.S. Senate, Joe? The last WASP stronghold. Hardly peanuts."

"Listen . . ." Kennedy pressed the flesh above Brady's elbow. "Put it this way. If the son of a pol from Eastie can become ambassador to the Court of goddamn St. James, what can the ambassador's son become?"

Brady did not respond.

"Well?"

"I know what you're thinking, Joe."

"And I know what you're thinking. Al Smith, right? Well, I say fuck Al Smith, said it then too. This is Kennedy we're talking about."

"For President."

"Vice-President in fifty-six. President in sixty-four, maybe sixty."

"Eisenhower will walk in again in fifty-six, Joe. If your Jack's on the ticket, they'll blame the loss on him, finish him off right there."

"Maybe. That's not our problem right now. We need the best goddamn team in the country, and not for a Senate shit job either. We want your son."

"Why?"

"Three reasons, *deux et trois* for your ears only. One, he's the best, does his homework, works his balls off, gets results. Two, he'll bring in the clout of the committee, all his work on that. He'll scare shit out of machine pols everywhere, just having him around. They'll fall over for us. Three, if he's working for us, he can't work for Kefauver. We see Kefauver as Jack's big competition for the second spot next time. We need your boy on our side."

"That's the trouble, Joe. He's not my boy. He has his own mind."

"Some of the fellows have been at him already, but tell you what. Let's you and me go have a little powwow with him right now."

"I don't know, Joe . . ." But Kennedy was already charging across the tile floor and taking the swinging doors the way Colman Brady had taken Mary Ellen Shields twenty-five years before.

The corridor from the washroom to the Grill Room was a wide, well-lit tunnel with cheerful shops. The white and blue pole jogged Brady's memory, and abruptly he stopped in front of the barbershop. He looked through the glass. The lights were out, and he could barely make out the chairs. Each was draped with its cloth the way some tombstones are hung with mourning crepe. It was eerie and funereal. Barbershops, with ballparks and drugstores, object to being vacant, unlike churches and libraries, which love it. Brady was remembering James Michael Curley sprawled grandly across the center chair, turning his shoe this way and that. He had defeated Curley that day by offering to shine it.

But then Brady realized how his own counterfeit subservience had become real. Habitual falsehood becomes the truth. Brady had pretended, for ambition's sake, to garner less power than Curley, and in the end Curley had creamed him. And then subservience had become the main fact of his life. Brady wondered why he could stomach subservience to Anselmo and not to Curley? Was it that he could never manage the profound bow to one of his own? Or that he could not do it publicly? Brady shuddered and turned from the barbershop, stifling a wave of disgust with himself. How he hated what he had become. But he would not feel it. He almost never did. He tightened his tie and ran his fingers along the line of his hair behind his ear, as if cleaning it.

When he entered the Grill Room Joe Kennedy was already pulling his son Jack toward Collins, who was leaning against a remote pillar, talking to Janet. Colman moved quickly to join them. He was afraid Joe would push too hard and blow it. By the time Colman joined them, Collins was introducing Janet.

". . . the ambassador. And you know the congressman."

"The senator-elect," Janet said with great charm as she took Jack Kennedy's hand. "Congratulations."

"Thank you, Mrs. Brady. I know there's little comfort for you in my election, but I'm honored and pleased that you came tonight. I spoke to Senator Lodge just a little while ago. I told him you might be here with your husband and he said that he'd appointed you permanent spy and ordered you to infiltrate my camp. I told him that I was just delighted and that, as far as I was concerned, that was the first fringe benefit of my new job."

"Are you calling me a fringe benefit, Senator?"

Kennedy could see from her great smile that she liked him. All the women he knew liked him. She took her hand back from his, but not before he had pressed it meaningfully once more. "I guess I'd have to ask your husband about that."

"I'm saying nothing," Collins asserted. Everybody laughed.

"I hope not, son," the ambassador put in, "because we have some questions we want to ask you."

"You do, do you?" Collins held his smile. He had put off Powers, O'Sullivan, and Reilly. Now here was the senator-elect himself, and, more to the point, old Joe. Collins looked at his own father. "What is this, the father-and-son communion breakfast?"

"In that case . . . ," Janet said, starting to leave.

"No, darling. Stay."

Janet loved Collins for that. She leaned into his side.

Collins understood why the Kennedys wanted her to leave. She was not just an outsider, but a Lodge staffer. He knew they would eventually offer her a job, too. For now, they would have to guard what they said in front of her.

"Look, Collins," Jack Kennedy said, "you know what I want to say. I want you to work for me."

"I've heard that, Jack. I wondered if it was true."

"It is."

"What do you have in mind?"

"Chief legislative."

"I thought that's Dave."

"I've something else for Dave. I want you."

Collins was surprised. Kennedy was offering him the plum.

"Forgive my asking, but why me?"

"The work you did for Estes. That bundle of legislation was the best thing out of any committee in years. I know you wrote most of it."

"And the Senate defeated most of it. What are you giving me, Jack? You know how you'd have voted on those bills — with the boys."

The group was stung by Collins's words. John Kennedy flinched. It was not the sort of thing one said to a new senator the night of his celebration after he'd just offered his top post.

"That's an assumption, Collins. I'm not sure what you base it on." Kennedy's stare flogged away at Collins's poise, but apparently without effect.

"We proposed one hundred and fourteen pieces of legislation. Twenty-seven made it to the floor of the House. According to the record, of the twenty-seven votes taken, you were absent for nine, you abstained on eleven, you voted 'No' on the rest. Including the Federal Crime Commission."

"That was a pork barrel for judges and DA's and you know it. Kefauver was trying to pay back all the boys who'd played his tune for him."

"That statement, Congressman, is not only untrue and unfair. It is unworthy of your office, frankly."

"Just a minute, you two," Ambassador Kennedy said. "You're giving me a headache. All this stuff is neither here nor there." He paused to crease the air in front of Collins with his right hand. "It's simple. You need a job. We got an opening. It's that simple."

"Mr. Kennedy," Collins said evenly, "I don't think your son and I are friends of the same people."

"Not a matter of friends, young man. Politics is a matter of allies. Ask your father. He knows what I mean, don't you, Colman?"

Much as Colman detested Collins's arrogance, he would not seem to side with the Kennedys, even though his son had so unnecessarily turned them into adversaries. He said nothing.

"When it came to the Nazis, don't forget," the ambassador went on, "we were allies with the Russians. That's politics."

Which was why, Collins was thinking, young Robert Kennedy signed on as Joe McCarthy's minority counsel. These unashamedly power-seeking men had to cover every base. Collins knew they wanted him for the honesty-in-government base in case that turned out, despite the evidence, to be home plate.

"Look, Collins," Jack Kennedy said, "the goddamn election is over. Your man lost. Our man lost. So we're even on that. But I won, right? I want you on my side. I don't want you against me."

"I'm not against you, Jack. Christ, I married your opponent's best worker to slow him down." He pulled Janet closer.

She said, "Greater love hath no man . . ."

"Well, I certainly owe you one there, don't I? I can't imagine anything worse." Kennedy smiled broadly at Janet, who only then realized what an extraordinary smile he had. "You don't have a sister, do you?" he asked, disarming her and Collins both. It was impossible not to like him. There was something hardheaded and unillusioned about him, but he was utterly lacking in the sinister air that clung to his father the ambassador as the smell of the sea does to a fisherman.

"Jack, the truth is I've had it with the Hill. I don't want to work up there anymore."

"I thought that might be it. My father and I were just talking that over. Let us try something else on you then."

"Work for me," Joe Kennedy said.

"What?"

"I'm pulling together a team to draw up some priorities for Jack and to do some organizing outside the Senate for various constituencies to whom it's important to be of service."

A campaign organization, and Collins knew it. It was stunning to think Kennedy was already pulling one together. No wonder they didn't want to talk in front of Janet.

"You come to work for me, son. You'll have your head." The ambassador shrugged, having said enough.

"A kind of supplementary office outside the Senate, eh?"

"On my payroll, not the taxpayers'."

"To help me be the best goddamn senator down there."

"And we could probably find something for you, too, young lady."

"No thank you, Ambassador. In addition to being a retired Republican, I'm a new mother. We've just adopted a child, who will be my career for a while."

"Congratulations," Jack Kennedy said. "That's terrific!" He had the capacity for leaving aside the unpleasant and plunging on into an expression of warmth that was earnest and touching. "A boy or a girl?"

"A boy," Janet answered. "He's seven."

"That's just great! You guys have real guts. No wonder you're fed up with D.C. I'd feel the same way you do!"

"Jack," Collins said, "I want you to know how honored I am that you would ask me. Ever since I was at the College I've admired you. You were still remembered fondly by a lot of people when I was there, including the old Irish maids at Dunster, who thought you should have been a priest."

"Ha!" Kennedy barked. "You should have asked the young ones!"

"But anyway, I'm going to say 'No' for now. Maybe there will be another time when you think you can use me, and I hope you'll ask again."

"Say something to him, Colman," the ambassador ordered.

"Joe, my son makes up his own mind. I learned that the hard way." Colman's hand rested easily on Collins's shoulder as he said that, one of those perennial parents' sentiments at whose falsehood the minds of their children never seem to balk.

Joe Kennedy left.

Jack Kennedy was not given to graceless gestures. "Collins, I think there will be a time like that, and I will ask you again."

Colman noted the finesse of Kennedy's statement. If he'd indulged his pique and huffed off, then Collins would have had the power that inheres in refusing all offers. By keeping the offer open, Kennedy had kept his power. Colman admired him more than ever. Kennedy was a comer.

"What do you think you'll do?" Kennedy asked.

"I don't know, Jack. I'd like to continue what I've been doing, to tell you the truth."

"But you can't."

"Not with the committee, obviously. Since it's defunct." Collins shrugged. He was not going to say any more. "Anyway, Jack, thank you very much. And again, congratulations." He offered his hand. Kennedy shook it warmly, kissed Janet's cheek, shook with Colman, and then was back in the middle of the crowd dispensing his good humor.

"Let's get out of here," Collins said.

"Where shall we go?" Janet asked.

"We could all go see *High Noon,*" Collins said.

"No thanks, son. I just saw it."

"Yup," Janet said, basso profundo.

The three of them left the Parker House in a cab.

At Prescott Street Janet went immediately upstairs to look in on Tony. Maeve and Maureen were already asleep.

Colman went into the living room and set about building a fire. Collins went to make them drinks. When he came in with them, the fire was ablaze. Colman was hunched on one knee staring into it.

"I've been wanting to ask you something, Dad."

"Oh?" Colman continued to stare into the fire. Collins thought him morose and displeased.

"Do you know any Sicilians?" Collins asked.

A hammer fell on an anvil.

A log fell in the fire.

Colman's mind stopped purring for once. He turned on his knee to face his son. "I beg your pardon?"

"Do you know any Sicilians?" Collins sipped his drink.

Colman thought him very casual with it, shockingly so. "Why?"

"We need a girl to help us with Tony, someone who can talk to him. I do all right with the kid, and Janet's learning. But the help are useless, and English is coming slow for him."

Colman stared at Collins. He laughed abruptly, then cut his laugh short. "No. I know some Italians, of course. I don't think they're Sicilians, though. How can you tell, anyway?"

Collins made a gesture with his head that said, "You'd know."

"I'll ask around, though."

"She'd have to be willing to move to Washington."

Colman did not disguise his surprise at that. He stood, took his drink from the table and sat in the blue wingback opposite Collins's. "I thought you told Kennedy you were sick of Washington."

"Not Washington. The Hill. Capitol Hill. We're staying in D.C. In fact, we're going to buy a house."

Colman whistled. "I guess you *are* staying, buying a house, my God. That doesn't sound like anyone who's up in the air about his job."

"I'm not."

"But you said you were."

"That was to them. I have a job."

"I don't understand you, son. What is all this cryptic meandering about? Why is a clear statement so difficult for you? You hate Washington, you're buying a house. You're looking for a job, you have a job? What gives?"

"I apologize, Dad. I've certainly not intended to be duplicitous with you. It's only that I couldn't know until the campaign was over what our strategy would be. And I absolutely could not discuss it in front of Kennedy; I mean the old man."

"Joe Kennedy is a friend of mine, Micko."

"Then you know about his associations."

"What the hell are you talking about?"

"He's up to his ears in the booze trade. He gets a cut on every bottle of Scotch that comes into the country."

"What's illegal about that? Christ, you sound like a WCTU old biddy. You're not a Calvinist, you know. Sometimes I wonder if you're my son."

"I am your son. That's the point. I can't take things any more lightly than you do. The point about Kennedy is that his business brings him into contact with some pretty unsavory people. He's no stranger to the New York mob."

"Then, indict him, goddamnit, if you've got something on him."

"It's not that sort of thing. I don't mean to imply criminal activity."

What an insane conversation to be having. Collins altered his demeanor and mood. "Strange, isn't it, that Jack Kennedy should epitomize Beantown politics when they've all been in New York for years."

Colman was shocked. He couldn't believe his son was ignorant of the meaning of the peculiarities of Kennedy geography. For all his Harvard years, his son had a lousy education. Indeed, because of his Harvard years.

"Do you know why Kennedy's money and power is New York, not Boston?"

"Has to do with FDR. The old man backed him early and was against Smith."

"It was nothing to do with FDR, son." Colman was being patient. "Joe Kennedy left Boston shortly after I got here after being shut out of his business by the goddamn WASP bankers, who controlled everything and wouldn't let an Irishman within a mile of a boardroom except to empty the goddamn ashtrays. Boston isn't New York. That's right. I'm shocked that you're just discovering that."

"You're talking about that 'No Irish Need Apply' crap. I know all about it."

"No, you don't. That was the tip of it, son. Every city in the country, Collins, is like a ladder. You get off the boat and on the ladder and climb your ass off. But not Boston. It's different here. The only rungs on the ladder are up top, for *them* where they sit with their trust funds and their high interest. Have you tried to climb a ladder without rungs? You've been around. Why is it the Irish have it made in New York and Cleveland and Pittsburgh and Chicago and San Francisco? McDonalds, Coynes,

Cuddihys, O'Mearas, Buckleys, Butlers, Dohenys — you name any Mick money you can think of. None of it is Boston. There's no such thing as a Mick making it in this town."

"There's Brady."

Colman did not reply to that.

"You're a lousy exhibit for your own case, Dad. Kennedy could have stayed here and done what you did. He didn't have to go to New York and be a rumrunner in the shadows thrown by Frank Costello and Al Capone."

"Collins, as long as you're in this house I will not have that kind of talk. Lest you forget, you spring from the same soil as him, even if you are married to an upper-rung. You wouldn't be who you are or where you are if it wasn't for the likes of Joe Kennedy. You even owe the luxury of your sensitive conscience to the likes of him."

"I don't see it that way."

"And you've at least two misconceptions I'd better disabuse you of."

"About?"

"About me. First, 'Brady money.' The Brady money, laddo, is peanuts. By scrambling and building a system out *from* Boston — not in it, mind you — with city workers all over the country, I've made my share. But it's a nickel and dime operation, son. Even taking all the slices of companies Municipal holds, I'd say the annual interest Joe Kennedy collects exceeds by twice our net worth, OK? Two: you are a fool if you think you run a business in this world, especially one like mine, which depends on contacts with unions and the party and city machines, without brushing up against what you call 'unsavory characters.' It's your cousin Jack who spends his time with nuns and priests, not me. Don't forget, Micko, your father was impeached once from public office."

"That's part of why I'm damn suspicious of the whole political arena. I won't let them do to me what they did to you. Frankly, I'm not sure how different Kennedy is from Curley."

"There is a difference, son. Kennedy is better at it than Curley was. And Curley was great."

"He screwed you."

"He was protecting himself. I'd have done the same to him."

"No, you would not have. You're talking to me as if I were a college kid. You seem to have forgotten what I've been doing for a living. It's my business to know about men, to sniff around their heels and guess what they've been stepping on, or who. You like the pose of the cynical, world-weary Irishman who nurses his resentments. But you forget. I've spent a lifetime watching you with people. I remember Curley and I remember even as a kid knowing instinctively the great difference between you. And that same instinct sets you apart from the Kennedy sharpies. And I know how you are with Janet. She's not a top-rung WASP to you, any more than Anna would have been a wop whore to you."

"Collins, I think . . ."

"No, let me finish. The point is, you're my touchstone. When I make my gut judgment about a man — and that's all I do, really — you're what I measure him against."

Colman felt the enormous sadness of a man who had succeeded infinitely well in what he had set out to do. What he could not savor was the truth in what his son had said, nor therefore the irony of it. Colman Brady *was* different from Curley and from Joe Kennedy. "Well, no wonder you find something wrong with everybody. How's your drink?"

"Needs help."

Colman went to the bar to pour the whiskey, then to the kitchen for some ice. It seemed to him he understood his son. For some men — principally those who encountered the universe in books and ideas — only a certain affectedness of soul offered a way to distinguish themselves from the rest. And the need to be so distinguished is absolute. Collins's idealism functioned as its own kind of power-seeking. He who took such solace in being different, even better, was just like all the rest. How to shake him from his lean pride? How to cut him from his purity without killing him? The cruelty of his profound regret at the defects of others! The tyranny of his refusal to admit the real character of his father's life.

But then it occurred to Colman that his son could punish him most effectively for his corruption by refusing to see it. Most of the time Colman Brady felt all right about himself. He was who he was because his own best aspirations had been repeatedly derailed by unexpected and undeserved turns of fate. Had he begun the Irish Civil War? Had he refused Curley the honorary degree at Harvard? Had he murdered his grandson's mother? Most of the time Colman Brady nurtured a careful resignation to the power of evil even as he thought of himself as an essentially good man over whom it had its sway. But in the presence of his son, Colman felt damned. His son's innocence made him feel that he had made not only accommodations with evil but alliances with it. He was living off the blood that gangsters sucked out of defenseless people and without even the nerve to watch them do it. He was without principle, without honor, without respect for himself. He could hide these things from his own eyes except when he was with Collins, because then it took all he had to hide them from his.

"Here you go," Colman said, handing him the drink.

"Thanks."

"Don't thank me." Colman raised his glass. "Thank Joe Kennedy."

"*Touché,* you bastard."

"To a death in Ireland."

"Or wherever."

"Where's the house you're buying?"

"I haven't told you about the job yet."

"You sure you can trust me?"

"If there's a leak, I'll know where it is. I'm going with the Bureau of Internal Revenue."

"What? Say that again."

"Taxes. It all comes down to taxes. Every mobster in the country has a moat around him, lawyers, silence, lackeys. They're very careful. They rarely break the law themselves, the big shots. That's what their punks are for. But everyone of them falsifies his taxes. They have to. That's the trouble with illegal income."

"So, what, you'll be an accountant?"

"No, a new approach. A Bureau assault on crime, using what the committee uncovered. There are thousands of cases just waiting for us. The data's all there. We have to do something with it."

"I had the impression the committee already did quite a lot."

"Sure. Drew up a bunch of new laws that Congress killed. Cited forty-five big-shot hoodlums for contempt. Do you know what happened to those? Twenty-two acquittals, ten dismissals, five convictions reversed on appeal, three upheld, the rest indefinitely continued. Of seventy-nine aliens referred to Immigration for deportation, proceedings against fifty were dismissed, against twenty are pending indefinitely. Five were deported. After two years we got three for contempt, five deported. Terrific, eh?"

"Could be better, you're right."

"The Special Rackets Squad. Silly name, I know, but that's us. We'd have made our move through Justice if Adlai'd won because it all has to end up there anyway, and we could have used the FBI. But it'll work out this way. We're keeping the lid on because we'd just as soon let the targets think the heat's off."

"Rackets Squad. Sounds like the radio, Eliot Ness."

"I know. That's Halley's mania. He wants to get us all guns."

"Guns, Good Christ!"

"Relax, never happen. Ironically enough, we *will* be accountants, just like you said."

"And the Congress is?"

"Once they realize we're talking about three hundred million dollars a year in recovered taxes and probable penalties, they'll love us, even if we also throw some of their dollies in the hoosegow."

"What's your job?"

"Halley's divided the country into regions. The full-court press is on Vegas, Chicago, and Miami. I drew the short stick. I'm heading up the section for the Northeast, but we'll keep a base in D.C."

"Northeast includes what?"

"Northern Jersey, New York, and Philadelphia are the red pins on the map. Most big-time crime action is out west now, but the roots are still in Newark and the East Side."

"What about Boston?"

"Not much in Boston, small fry. Or so we think. The committee never got here. The action in New England is probably all in Providence. Ever hear of Balestrione?"

"No."

"Not many people have. My hunch is that they're either all two-bit operators up here, or they're better at it than any of them. It'll be a tough one to crack."

"Why?"

"Because the whole Mass. system is rotten, from the flatfoot up to the federal bench. We could never trust the locals with anything, none of them."

"That's pretty sweeping, son. Some of those men are friends of mine. A lot of them were at the Parker House tonight."

"You'd be shocked, Dad."

"I doubt it. You just wish more of the State House crowd and the City Hall gang went to Harvard instead of B.C."

"You're damn right I do." If his father had a weakness, Collins thought, it was that the truth sometimes made him flinch.

"Well, you go on over to State Street. That's where your fellow alumni are, and I'm sure their nails are clean."

"You sound like Jack McShane."

"That's funny . . ." — Colman stood to indicate he was finished with this — ". . . because he's the priest, but you're the one who sounds like God."

They said goodnight to each other and went upstairs.

Collins found Janet in Tony's room.

"Why didn't you come down?"

"Shhh." She put her finger to her lips. She was sitting by the boy's bed. The only light was the dim one of a child's night light in the socket and the room was shadowy.

Collins sensed that Janet's mood was splintered. She was basking in the novel fondness of motherhood; she was lonely and sad.

"Is he asleep?" Collins put his arm on Janet's shoulder and pressed.

She shook her head.

Collins looked at Tony, who stared back at him from his pillow with hard, unyielding eyes. The boy had a repertoire of glares.

"We've just been looking at each other," Janet said. There was the sound of a deep hurt in her voice.

Tony looked back at her, as if he heard it too.

Collins pressed her, feeling suddenly very unhappy.

"You know what, darling?" she said softly.

"What?"

"He could almost be yours."

"Why?" Collins was sure the bones in his hand on her shoulder went rigid.

"Because in his eyes I see iron like your father's."

⤙ 6 ⤚

IT WAS NEARLY TWO YEARS before the Federal Bureau of Internal Revenue focused its investigation on organized crime in New England. By August of 1954 the investigating unit, still attempting to downplay the sensational aspects of its work, had changed its name from the Special Rackets Squad to the Special Activities Section of the Intelligence Division. In the northeast sector alone, eighteen thousand investigations had been initiated, mainly in the corridor running from Philadelphia through Newark to New York. Of those, more than five hundred had resulted in indictments and ninety had already resulted in convictions.

Gennaro Anselmo was not worried.

Anselmo still lived on Fleet Street in the North End in a thin brick house from which the posture had been wrung a century before. During decades in which nearly every other section of Boston had undergone enormous change, the North End had changed almost not at all. The streets were still narrow and cobbled. The clustered buildings still prevented the sun from drying any place but the center of the streets, and that only for the briefest time at midday. Slain rabbits still hung from their hooks draining blood onto the sidewalks. Grocers still plied their wares from rickety stands and pushcarts. On Fridays and Saturdays outsiders drifted over from Haymarket to shop in the crowded stalls and bakeries and butcher shops. Fortunately, they stayed away the rest of the week and out of the cafés altogether.

Anselmo could have purchased an estate in any town in Massachusetts. His sons had houses in Newton and Wellesley, but he preferred to stay in the old neighborhood. Not that he ranked it above everywhere else, or that he held its people in such high esteem, but that he was relatively indifferent to his surroundings. He had no need to establish his standing within the community. His standing was a given. Over the years the benign and absolute power of Gennaro Anselmo had become as much a feature of North End life as the ubiquitous espresso. On the other hand, unlike his more notorious counterparts in other cities, he had no desire to attract the attention of outsiders to himself. His sole concern over the years had been to save himself by work and kindness, by, that is, the effective and efficient manipulation of the levers at his hands for the good of his family and his people.

Anselmo's sons were each responsible for a part of the business. Leonard ran the Comose Collection Service, a citywide garbage pickup operation that employed eighty men on forty-two trucks. Rico was vice-president of Othello Wines, the olive oil and wine supplier which was technically based in Naples. Because the company held a foreign charter, its internal workings were subject to supervision only through the State Department Foreign Commerce Section, despite the fact that it operated solely out of the family building on Commercial Street at the waterfront. Marcello, Anselmo's eldest and most trusted son, ran Roma Italian Foods, a small restaurant supply company.

Anselmo's sons had other duties. Through his garbage business, Leonard supervised over nine hundred numbers franchises. In addition to his eighty garbage men, he controlled two hundred independent bookies and nearly a thousand runners. Rico dealt in the import of wine and olive oil and various narcotic drugs, mainly cocaine and heroin. Marcello supervised the regular collection of an informal but exorbitant tax from over two hundred restaurants, hotels, and nightclubs, which were then guaranteed immunity from various calamities endemic to such businesses.

On a Tuesday that August, Anselmo walked out of his office building, a four-story brickfront that had once housed a Boston newspaper. When the weather was nice he customarily took an apple and a wedge of cheese and walked to the end of Commercial Wharf across the street, where he ate sitting alone on a dilapidated bench. But that day the weather was grotesquely hot; the temperature had exceeded one hundred degrees for three days in a row. Anselmo wouldn't have gone out in such heat unless it was necessary to do so. He walked north on Commercial Street. Despite the heat he wore his Borsalino hat, and his black suit coat was buttoned twice.

Across the harbor were the hulking cranes of the East Boston shipyard, the tower of the new airport, and the sleek runways where the old marshflats had been. The tenements, stacked against the water, showed their backsides — swaying laundry, dingy porches — to Boston. They had been Irish tenements; now they were Italian.

Anselmo saw none of it, having seen East Boston from its rear so continually as to be blind to it. At High Street he turned right and right again into a narrow cul-de-sac. He stepped into the alcove of a doorway, faced the street, and waited. No one came. He gave it five minutes.

He began walking up Mulberry Street, which ascended the hill on the peak of which stood the Old North Church. Anselmo did not see it, either. He was blind to the irony of the Yankee church — "One if by land, two if by sea!" — slowly rotting in the middle of an Old World ghetto, neglected and ignored by all but an occasional tourist. Anselmo walked past Copp's Hill Burying Ground, its high weeds sloping toward the harbor and Charlestown, not seeing it. He went down the hill, took two sharp turns, stood in a doorway again for five minutes, then was back on Commercial Street, crossing it, leaving the North End and falling in with the crowd pushing toward the Boston Garden and the Greatest Show on Earth. Ringling Brothers had come to town. Clowns juggled in the street.

But Anselmo bypassed the Garden entrance and made his way through the onrush to the North Station entrance. The ticket windows and outgoing platforms of the train terminal were abandoned. Commuters did not move at midday. There were only mothers with children in tow, circusgoers.

Anselmo crossed the terminal and went through the revolving door that offered access to the lobby of the Hotel Manger. He took his hat off, bypassed the desk, went directly to the elevator and said to the boy, "Eleven."

The Manger was a salesman's hotel. Fifteen stories high, overarching the Garden and North Station, it dominated the skyline on the north of Boston. Its green roof and sand-colored bricks were what caught the eye when one approached Boston from up country. It was not an old hotel. It was managed efficiently if flairlessly. It was a favorite with respectable men who worked the territory. But because of its proximity to the arena and to the dives around Scollay Square and because of the grimy exterior inflicted on it by the elevated train, the Manger was a stepchild among Boston hotels.

Anselmo had a key to room 1134. No one was in the corridor. He inserted the key, turned it and entered the room.

In the lobby, Colman Brady had lowered his newspaper to watch Anselmo cross to the elevator. He put the thin cigar he'd just lit in the sand tray in the corner where he'd been standing. He watched the elevator doors close. Then he folded the paper, tucked it under his arm and crossed the lobby.

"Eleven," he said to the boy.

At room 1134 Brady knocked.

Anselmo opened the door promptly.

The room was about twenty feet square, furnished with a couch, two easy chairs, two end tables with lamps, and a coffee table. There was a door on the left, a closet, and one on the right, the bedroom. The far wall was quartered by two large windows which opened on Boston. The Customs House tower caught Brady's eye. The windows were wide open, but the light lace curtains were still, not a hint of a breeze. The room was stuffy and hot.

"No fan," Brady said, wiping his neck. He thought of loosening his tie, but decided not to.

Anselmo ignored him.

Brady crossed to the windows, lifted the gauzy curtain and looked down. "Ugly damn city from here. Can't even see the State House." He watched a plane making its vector over Southie, angling toward Logan. "Not even an ocean breeze." He took his suit coat off and draped it over a corner of the couch, then sat in one of the chairs.

Anselmo remained by the door.

"How are you?" Colman asked.

"No complaints."

"It's been a while."

Anselmo nodded, but made Brady feel as though he were interrupting something.

"You seem like a street maestro doing his time on the old instrument."

Anselmo's face cracked momentarily into an expression of affection. "I'm sorry. I was remembering. It's good to see an old friend." He crossed to Brady and offered his hand. Brady stood to shake it. A careful fondness showed through the strict distance.

"We have much to talk about," Brady said, pressing the shorter man's shoulder. "So sit."

"No. Not yet."

"Why?"

"My lawyer's coming."

"Who?"

"Costenari."

"We agreed to be alone, Gennaro. I'm offended."

"I don't discuss business alone."

"We've always met alone. What are you talking about?"

"It is different now."

"No, it is not. I refuse to discuss anything with him here."

"Colman . . ." The rare familiarity with which Anselmo spoke was intended to soften the statement. ". . . It is not for you to refuse me anything." He smiled, and assumed the look of one who'd just explained a
complicated truth lucidly. "You know Costanari."

"The lawyer from Worcester."

"The same."

"I don't understand, Gennaro. We never . . ."

"We were never vulnerable, Colman. It's important now to be very
careful."

"I didn't think you'd panic."

"Only a fool confuses panic with caution." Anselmo held up his hand.
They would discuss it no further. They would wait in silence. Anselmo's
face went blank as he assumed a strange martial stance at the door. Brady
channeled his anger into an elaborate about-face. He crossed to the window again.

It seemed to him he could see the heat tying its knots above the city.
When, he wondered, was the last time he'd been in a hotel room like
this? And in the middle of the day. He should have been making his rendezvous with a bosomy girl instead of this dago. He tried unsuccessfully
to conjure up the face of a tart. He watched a bright red ambulance
threading down Cambridge Street until it turned into Mass. General.
Beyond the hospital he could see the medieval walls of the Charles Street
jail.

Anselmo put his hand on the doorknob. He had heard the whirring of
the elevator. He waited. The knock came. He opened it.

A stout man in a black suit entered without speaking. He carried a
briefcase. He was perspiring. His collar had the wrinkled, limp look of
soaked cloth. He stepped between the coffee table and the couch, placed
his bag on the table, opened it, withdrew a pen and a yellow pad, and sat
down.

Colman had been standing with his back to the room. He turned
around.

"Pio!" he said grandly. "My God, it's good to see you!" He took the
space in three strides and shook the lawyer's hand warmly. Costanari was

unaccustomed to such greetings and it threw him off balance for just the instant Brady wanted.

"Mr. Brady."

Anselmo sat in one chair. "Let's begin," he said.

Brady sat in the other.

Anselmo made a minute gesture that indicated to Costanari that he must not take notes. He put his pen down.

"Tell us," Anselmo said to Costanari.

"There have been seven subpoenas, all at the office." The term *office* referred to Balestrione's operation in Providence.

"And?"

"They want Tersa's books and the don's and for the track at Warwick."

"The dog track?" Anselmo was surprised.

"Yes."

"They're fishing. They know nothing. The dog track! Ha!"

"Nothing in Massachusetts?"

"No."

"Seabrook?"

"No."

"Pownal?"

"No. Nothing in Vermont or New Hampshire."

Brady lit a cigar and doused the match by waving it. "It's just starting, Gennaro. Don't get your hopes up."

Anselmo gave him a look that made the day seem cool. "I think it probable," he announced, "that they will center their inquiry there, in Providence. For two reasons. They want Balestrione. They love a villain. Poor Ciro." Anselmo laughed uncharacteristically. "And the court in Rhode Island, the Feds would prefer it."

"I don't agree, Gennaro."

Anselmo closed the tips of his fingers at his mouth.

"It will be Boston," Brady said.

"Colman, it is not like you to be so brittle. You're like the bark of birches. How many years is it now they've been lighting their fires? Capone, Costello, Gigante, Giancana. This is not Chicago. Hoodlums do not exist here. There are no murders in the streets. There are no machine guns. There are no wars. There are no newspaper stories. Why would they come here? They want Ciro."

"Boston it is, Gennaro. I know what I'm saying."

Anselmo's silence was contradiction enough. Costanari looked at his hands which had no opinion.

"Shall I tell you why I'm certain?" Brady exhaled his smoke.

[457]

"Please."

"Because my son just moved back here from Washington."

"Is he still with them?"

"Yes. He's running the whole thing, Gennaro, and he's running it from here. He just bought a house on Beacon Hill. The gangbusters are here, friends. Don't tell me they're not."

Anselmo said nothing.

"They have a whole suite of offices at the courthouse."

"Which courthouse?" Costanari asked.

"Pemberton Square."

Costanari looked smugly over at Anselmo.

"Don't be a fool, Pio. You're the lawyer. They won't move through Suffolk. It's all federal stuff, and the federal bench has three new judges this year alone. Do you own them yet?" Brady paused. "I didn't think so."

"What has your son told you?" Anselmo asked.

"Nothing. Do you think I'm crazy? Should I ask a slew of questions just to draw his gaze my way?"

"There is no reason for you to be upset."

"That's why I'm here, Anselmo. I want to know exactly what there is, what's on your books."

"There's nothing. Don't insult me."

"I intend no insult, but I have a quite specific concern."

"What?"

"We did not start operating through Switzerland until nineteen forty-one. Before that, for five years before that, you made your deposits to that bank in Naples. Then it was transferred to the account at Columbia Savings. And then I drew from that account in the name of Monument. Now that's a connection, a very clear connection. Columbia Savings is no Swiss bank. They can subpoena the teller's grocery list if they want."

"There's nothing. You insult me."

"I apologize, but explain to me why there is nothing."

"The vault with the bank records for that period blew up. All papers were burned."

"When?"

"Nineteen forty-seven, July. During a minor robbery."

"Bullshit. I'd have heard about it. There was nothing in the papers."

"The bank president, Stephen Berman, had been dancing the ballet with his books to the tune of four hundred thousand of his depositors' dollars. It served his purposes to have the records destroyed. After I suggested it."

"But Washington has duplicates."

"It was not a federal bank."

"But Berman could talk."

"He is dead. The bank is dissolved. There is nothing."

Colman thought of asking how the man died, then thought better of it. He worked his cigar, watching its smoke curl toward the ceiling. "So, if they subpoena your books?"

"They can have them. Everything. I am a modestly successful business-man. My sons help me. They are well paid and live accordingly. I draw a salary and live accordingly. They will not find me interesting."

"But the whole North End knows."

"That's nothing. My people will respect my position."

"If there is anything at all to point from you to me, I want to know what it is."

"Brady, I won't listen to your carping."

"Don't cut me off, goddamn it! You're covered nicely, that's obvious. But I am not. I am a sitting duck. How the hell can I disguise the fact that I get nine million dollars a year out of a numbered account in Swit-zerland? Or the fact that I don't have twenty-five thousand goddamn nickel and dime subscribers? That all I have are you and a handful of mick streetsweepers who are counting the days until they can retire on a hundred and fifty dollars a month? The slightest odor of rot from my shop and I'm dead."

"They will have no reason to investigate you. You are thousands of miles away from me."

"Not quite. About eight blocks. Boston's a small town, Gennaro."

"But Switzerland . . ." He shrugged. "We planned for this, Colman. For this very turn of events. Why are you faltering now?"

Brady sat in the balance of his own stare, realizing that he knew nothing about faltering. Faltering? He had no capacity for it. His mind went back and his memory went back, around a lifetime of corners. Fal-tering? Never. Colman Brady's single talent was for doing what had to be done. He always had. He would now.

"Don't misunderstand, Don Gennaro." Brady studied the glowing ember of his cigar. He brushed it into the ashtray. "Only a fool would confuse faltering with caution."

"I beg your pardon, Mr. Brady," Costanari put in, "but you are not vulnerable, or, if so, only minimally."

Brady did not look at Costanari. "Your man should go back to night school — was it Suffolk? — because his ignorance is the rope from which you'll hang."

"One moment," Costanari started.

"Don't 'one moment' me, you guinea shyster! Don't you tell me I'm not vulnerable! I've got four goddamn federal commissions on my shoulder — FTC, ICC, SEC, FIC — each one of which administers a hundred laws. And that does not count the Commonwealth of Massachusetts. I'm out in the cold, friend. Millions of dollars' worth of criminal fraud, tax evasion, and bribery. And all of it is traceable."

"That is what you are paid for," Anselmo said.

"I know the risks. I fall before you do; all right, that's the deal. Just don't let your two-bit Shylock tell me I'm not vulnerable. I'm paid to be vulnerable. I take your loot and go public with it. It's all one finesse, a long dance on thin ice. All right. But this goof isn't going to sit here and tell me I'm not vulnerable. He can tell that to your bookies and your loan sharks and your pimps and your bootleggers and your pushers and your idiot-thugs, not to me. The Internal Revenue is going to hit you hard, Gennaro. If you want my advice, you'd better get yourself a good Jew lawyer. And they'd better not find a hair out of my ass in your stuff, because I'm dead if they do. And if I'm dead, old dear friend, so are you. Get it?"

Brady stood. *Faltering, eh?* he thought. *Blow "faltering" out your ass, you wop creeps!*

The pair of Sicilians sat immobile and expressionless before him.

"Is there anything else?" Brady asked brusquely.

"Yes," Costanari said. "Mr. Anselmo does not wish to meet with you again. You are to meet with me. I will await a complete report on all of Mr. Anselmo's holdings. I want it by one September."

Brady looked at Anselmo. "You've always left that to me."

Anselmo stared through him.

"No more," Costanari said. He seemed to deliberately fan Brady's hatred with the sharp draft of his poise.

Brady started to leave, but Anselmo raised his right forefinger.

"Colman, control your son, eh?"

"Sure, Gennaro. Sure."

Brady left.

Costanari rolled his weight onto his left haunch and pulled a large white handkerchief out of his hip pocket. He wiped perspiration from his face.

"Don Gennaro, we should . . ." — he stared into his bunched handkerchief — ". . . prepare for problems with him."

Anselmo stood. "Pio, he's my friend. I've known him longer than I've known you. Pay no attention. He's Irish."

"He can hurt you."

"No. He can't."

Colman Brady took his suitcoat off when he hit the street. He hooked it over his shoulder, looked for a cab, then changed his mind. He would walk.

His building was on Essex Street below Boylston, a mile from the Manger. On Tremont, the far side of Scollay Square, he went into Er-lich's, the only tobacconist in Boston that carried his cigars, Brazilian crosscut green leafs. Peter Ross, a white-haired Irishman who had been hailing Brady into the shop for twenty years, was at his place by the grand brass cash register. The meerschaum pipe swooped down over his chin, as always. He wore his red cotton smock.

"Hello, Peter."

"Hello, Mr. Brady. Hot enough for you?"

"Hot as the devil's buckle, eh?"

Ross reached into a drawer in the cabinet behind him, drew out a box with the red tinge of cedar bark, and handed it over the counter to Brady.

"Thanks, Peter. I think I'll have a bag today. I'm strolling. Be easier to carry."

"Certainly, sir. And by the way, I thought of you when these came in." He opened a small cigar box. Two dozen miniature cigars were in their row, obsequious and content like all cigars. "It's chocolate from the Netherlands."

"Chocolate?"

"Yes, sir. I thought of your grandson. He seemed to love it here when you brought him in. I remember he kept staring at the display case, and I had the feeling he'd like to imitate your smoking. No harm in choco-late."

"By God, Peter, you're right! He loves to light the match for me. And he's here now, in Boston."

"Is that a fact?"

"His father's been transferred here. They're living on the hill. Actually, they're just moving in this week."

"These could be the lad's welcome-to-Boston present."

"I'll take it. How much?"

"Forget it, sir. A gift from me."

"Come on, Peter."

"I don't take my orders from you, Mr. Brady. Never have. Now, get on with you and give the lad my best."

"You're a thick-headed harp, Ross. You know that, don't you?"

"Indeed I do, sir." He smiled broadly and puffed away on his dull amber pipe.

"I'll bring Tony around so he can thank you himself."

"Do that, sir. Good day."

"Thanks, Peter," Brady said, and left the shop with his two kinds of cigars.

He decided not to go back to his office.

Collins and Janet had found a fine house on Pinckney Street near the crest of the hill half a block above Louisburg Square. From the angle of the bay window in the front parlor, they could see the great lie of the Charles, with its bridges and tailored green margins and the vista of Cambridge beyond with its sparkling steeples. The house had been in one family for nearly a century, the Howes. Before Miss Sheila Howe, the spinster daughter and last heir, died, she had named J. Bolton Lindsay the executor of her estate. She had asked him particularly to assure that the house went to a nice family with a proper background. She would have been pleased to know that it went to his daughter. Collins paid the Howe estate sixty thousand for the house, more, he suspected, than its value, but both he and Janet's father wanted to be certain there was not even the appearance of impropriety in the arrangement.

The subdued elegance of the place made it special. Each room had its hearth with a carved mantel and antique Moorish tiles. Each piece of molding above every door was unique and marked with the sign of the craftsman. The main staircase swept up from the entrance in a swift ebony spiral. The ceilings on floors one and two were twelve feet high and accommodated the crystal chandeliers without flamboyance. Even the maid's quarters on the fourth floor were generous and well appointed. The Howes had long respected the dignity of workers, even to the point of supporting trade unionism.

Janet and Collins loved the place. They worried, however, that there were few children in the neighborhood. The boy was already enough of a loner to make them think they were failing him. He had not mingled well with the other children at the Catholic school in Washington. Janet in particular was determined to help the child find friends.

"Where's Tony, Maria?" Colman asked as he opened the door.

"At the p-p-park, Mr. Brady." Maria was the Neapolitan girl who'd been living with the family for a year. She stuttered and was very bashful. Collins had never found a Sicilian girl to live in. But after his initial hesitancy, Tony had learned English well and quickly, so it didn't matter.

"What park, dear? The Common?"

"Louieburg."

"*Lewis*burg, Maria. Lewisburg Square."

"I think it is French."

"That's a little trap they set for you. They love to correct us."

"Who, sir?"

"Never mind. Is Mrs. Brady home?"

"No, sir. She is shopping. And Mr. Brady is at work."

"Well, I'm taking you from yours, aren't I?" The living room was a mess of cartons and brown paper.

"Th-that is not for m-m-me. The m-men are at dinner."

"Well, thanks. I'll just go find Tony."

There was no sign of the boy at Louisburg Square. The park was as perfectly tended as ever, the great elm canopy over a spotless lawn and dozens of manicured shrubs. Colman walked the complete circuit of the wrought-iron fence. At Mt. Vernon Street he turned back toward the park and saw Tony crouched in the shadow of the badly weathered statue. He was inside the fence. Good for him! The boy grinned impishly up at Brady. He was eleven years old, tall for his age, and the combination of his soft white skin and thin but etched lips and pitch-black eyes and hair gave him a beauty which on boys is always unsettling.

"Well, my old chum Aristides," Colman said to the statue, "how be you? Good! Glad to hear it! Listen, you haven't seen my grandson, have you?" Colman leaned casually on the fence, the gray suit coat dangling from his one hand, the bag of cigars from the other. "You haven't? Too bad. I was hoping to find him. I'm feeling a little lonely this afternoon, and I was hoping he might lighten the burden of my old heart by spending a little time with me." Colman sighed grandly. "Maybe your Italian friend at the other end of the park has seen him. The kid likes Italians, you know." Brady tossed his coat over his shoulder and strolled the length of the park. At the far end he leaned on the fence again.

"Cristofo Columbo! *Ciao! Come 'sta?*"

"*Bene!*" came the boy's voice from behind the statue.

"*Bene! Bene!* Hey, Cristofo, what's a fishmonger like you doing in Louisburg Square?"

"Looking for my grandfather."

Tony popped out from behind a shrub and stood grinning at Colman, displaying his innocent love.

"Tony! My golly! Look at you! How'd you get in there? It's a miracle!"

"I climbed over." There was enough in the statement to indicate it had not been easy.

"Good for you, kiddo." Colman reached his hand through the iron spikes, and Tony took it. "Just like a Brady! We're a family of fence-climbers, kiddo. If they want us in, we get out. If they want us out, we climb in. Right? Right!" He raked the boy's hair.

"Right, Grandfather."

Tony liked his grandfather because he had good strong breath. Even through the fence he could inhale it. And he liked his grandfather because he could see himself in the old man's eyes. The way Colman Brady looked at him was a guarantee of his merit. They had met only a few times and did not know each other well, but Tony knew instinctively that his grandfather was not an impostor like most adults, who spoke to him as if their words were little toy cars they gave him. He had outgrown toys. He hated to have adults treat him like a child. If his grandfather spoke to statues it was not a show put on for him. Tony understood that his grandfather always spoke to the statues whether he was around or not.

"What do you have there, kiddo?"

"My glove." Tony pulled his Eddie Yost third baseman's glove out of his belt and held it up.

"Got a ball?"

He held up a scruffed tennis ball.

"Been playing catch?"

"Nobody to play with."

"That makes it kind of tough, I suppose."

"I was looking for a wall to bounce."

"But not in there, you weren't."

"In here I was looking at the trees. I lay down and look up. The clouds can be animals or ships. The leaves move even when there is no wind."

Was the kid speaking like that because he thought Colman wanted him to? Colman sensed how forlorn and alone the boy felt. Maybe he really did lie on the grass and watch the clouds' meandering.

"Do you like it in there?"

There was no gate, and that made the acre magical to Tony, and private. When he climbed the fence, the little park became his. He nodded. Yes, he liked it.

"That statue, that really is Columbus. You know what he did?"

He nodded. Sure he knew.

"The first one here was from your country. Always remember that."

Tony touched the sandy stone. The statue was only a little taller than he was. "Fourteen ninety-two," he said.

"That's right."

"I read a book about him."

"You like to read?"

He nodded. Janet worried that he read too much.

"You should be very proud of your countryman, Tony."

Were the boy's eyes filling?

"I am a foreigner." The bald statement shocked Brady. It revealed a grotesque shame in the boy.

"Who told you that?"

"Kids."

"At school?"

Tony nodded.

"In Washington?"

He nodded again.

"Well, lucky for you you came to Beantown. In Boston, everybody's a foreigner. Take me, for instance."

The boy listened closely.

"I'm a foreigner. Know where I came from?"

Tony shook his head.

"Ireland. That's why I talk funny. Don't you think I talk funny?"

Tony grinned. He had been accused of that himself.

"In Ireland, they never heard of baseball. Imagine that."

"My mother and father are not foreigners."

"Sure they are. Your mother's folks just got over here a little before you and me, that's all. They came from England. The only people up here who aren't foreigners are the Indians. And the first ones here besides them were from Italy. Good old Christopher there."

"Cristo*fo*. From Genoa."

"Right."

Tony's hand rested familiarly in the crook of the statue's arm.

"And after him came a fellow name of John Cabot, fourteen-ninety-seven. And his folks, Cabots, live right up the street here. I can show you their house. I'll tell you a secret. They think they're English, but they aren't, because his real name was Giovanni Caboto and he was Genoese too. The English King who hired him, Henry the Eighth — a bugger if there ever was one — made him change his name. So even the first English in this town were Italians. Get it?"

The boy nodded and grinned.

"Now then. Aren't you glad you came to Boston?"

Tony thought about it, then nodded again, vigorously.

"Tell me something else, kiddo. How the blazes are you and me going to play catch with you inside that fence?"

"I'll come out."

"Good." Colman put a cigar in his mouth. "Because I got something for you."

While the boy hoisted himself over the fence, Brady opened the bag and took out the small cigar box. Tony was grateful that his grandfather was distracted by his packages because climbing the iron pickets really was hard.

"Here," Colman said.

The boy opened the cigar box.

A gooey mass of chocolate; the cigars had melted in the heat of the day.

"Ugh!" Colman said, "You might know."

Tony laughed.

"Anyway," Colman said, "mine didn't melt." He handed Tony his matches. "Give us a light, kiddo."

Tony lit his grandfather's cigar solemnly.

"OK. Now for a little catch, eh? We'll go to the Common. It's better than this place. More room, no damn fences. Best darn park in the world, Tony. Know why they call it the 'Common'?"

The kid shook his head, clutching his box of goo and sliding under Brady's arm.

"Common property, kiddo. It belongs to everybody. Including you and me."

7

COLLINS BRADY could not have articulated it, but the work of his life was nothing but the effort to redeem the injustices that had been inflicted on his father. The world was a place in which to be on your guard; that was what he had learned. If his father, who was a better man than almost anyone, could harvest defeat and disappointment, then a drastic watch had to be kept. Collins's ambition was to make his father proud of him, and he knew how to do that, by bringing the Brady name honor. Collins understood his advantage, his freedom from economic struggle and moral conflict, and he was determined to use it. As the son of an immigrant he had the extreme energy and motivation he needed to make the New World his world. Having had an elite liberal education, he had an attachment to an abstract ethic that set him apart from his father and from his father's kind. But if he was preoccupied with justice and with principle, it was because he embodied in himself the conflict between the two worlds — his father's and his wife's — in which justice and principle were given such different meanings. The mission of Collins Brady's life was to reconcile those two worlds for himself and for his family and for the two worlds themselves. Integrity was an ultimate value for him because that conflict was violent and huge, and only a strict personal ethic could spare him its chaos. It could break a man. It nearly had his father. It nearly had, once, Collins himself. His great detour from strength and integrity had been in

Sicily during the war. It had killed Anna and left him with a shameful secret. He knew with certainty such a detour would not happen again.

At seven-fifteen on the morning of the first Tuesday in September that year Collins Brady walked across Bowdoin Street into Pemberton Square at the foot of the east side of Beacon Hill. Pemberton Square was dominated by the new courthouse, a seventeen-story granite building with narrow windows that seemed like the slit eyes of a magistrate. Only the courthouse separated Beacon Hill from the dregs of the city at Scollay Square. At that hour in the morning drunks were stirring from the doorways in which they'd huddled fitfully all night. They wanted to be gone before the merchants came. They wanted to get onto the street to forage for breakfast. None of them approached Brady because of the way he walked.

The elevator operator was not in yet, so Brady climbed the five flights to the office of the Special Activities Unit of the Intelligence Division of the Bureau of Internal Revenue. There was nothing on the opaque glass of the door he approached except the number 674. There were no signs of life in the broad corridor, but when he opened the door a burst of light and the noise of machines spilled briefly out into the hall. His people were at work already.

Though they had been operational in Boston less than a month, their routine had been established for the nearly two years they had worked as a roving unit in Newark, Trenton, Philadelphia and at their base in Washington. The office was one room half again the size of a basketball court. There were desks — uniformly the clumsy maple ones that had been distributed throughout the bureaucracy after the war — for sixteen special agents and twenty-four clerks and typists. The agents occupied the north end of the room. Five of these were lawyers; the rest were CPA's. Of the lawyers, two had been on Brady's staff on the committee, one was on loan from the FBI, and two were from the BIR legal office. The accountants were all veterans of the BIR, and most of them had been involved in the haphazard, slapdash investigations of crime figures that predated Halley's mandate.

Collins Brady's office was a glass-enclosed cubicle in the far corner. As he walked past the desks of his agents, several raised their heads from their folders, several did not. Brady noted that all but three — Hughes, Sanford, and Martin — were in.

When Brady passed Deke Thomas's desk he stopped. Thomas was the assistant supervisor and Brady's number one. They had worked together for Halley and were close friends. Thomas's desk was just outside Brady's office.

"Deke, I want you, Dawson, LeBlanc, and Martin inside."

"Martin's not in yet."

If anyone was going to get to work after Brady, Martin was. A fifty-year-old accountant, he'd been nailing underworld figures for tax evasion since the thirties. He was lackadaisical and headstrong and not much on the new-breed methods. But he was brilliant, and his instincts were acute.

Brady went into his office. Thomas moved discreetly among the desks, tapping the other two. Dawson and LeBlanc were both lawyers. Thomas ignored the resentment he could feel aimed at him by the accountants. They knew that Brady's inner circle were the law jocks, the hotshot outsiders. There should have been at least one of the CPA's at the meeting. Was that why Brady'd asked for Martin, Thomas wondered briefly, so that the token math-wizard would be late? No. Thomas knew damn well what was on Brady's mind. Anselmo. And that was Martin's case.

In his office Brady unlocked his drawer and put his hand into the sleeve of a nearly empty carton of Camels. He withdrew the last pack and dropped the carton into the basket under his desk. He started to close the drawer, but stopped when he saw the gun. It could still shock him. In the two years he'd been an agent he'd never fired it outside the range in Virginia, where he was obliged to qualify three times a year. He'd drawn it on men twice, though, both times in the middle of raids in Newark. He'd nearly shot Jerry Cappella, whose specialty was torching restaurants, and surely would have had the mobster not dropped his gun instantly. Brady let his fingers rest lightly on the blue steel of the .38. His forefinger found its way naturally inside the half-oval trigger guard.

"Martin's not in yet, Chief," Thomas repeated as he entered the office.

Brady took his hand out of the drawer and closed it.

Len Dawson and Richard LeBlanc followed Thomas into Brady's office. Dawson carried himself with a bit more swagger than the other two. He was the FBI agent and did not like being outside the familiar terrain of his own bureau. He would not have accepted the assignment to BIR had the request come from anyone but Mr. Hoover. At first he'd thought it ludicrous to sic tax cops on the heavyweights, but that was before Newark, where Brady's unit alone got seventy-two indictments through. Who cared if thugs like Zwillman and Adonis were convicted for punk tax evasion, as long as they went up? Dawson had long since stifled his resentments. Besides, Brady was the best of the dozen supervisors under Halley. For a man not FBI, he was all right.

"What do you have, Len?" Brady asked, waving out a match. Brady was seated. Dawson, Thomas, and LeBlanc were standing opposite his desk.

"We were right. It's numbers. The base is numbers. My guess is they clear a cool fifty big ones on the city alone."

"That's news?"

"I mean as *opposed* to loansharking. It's two separate operations, and only the numbers racket is controlled from here."

"What are you talking about?" LeBlanc demanded. "The two go hand in glove. We've never seen them cut apart."

Dawson shrugged. "You can read the shit yourself. It's all there." He gestured out toward his desk.

"Give it to me again, Len," Brady said. "How do you see it?"

"Balestrione leaves the numbers completely alone in the Commonwealth. He takes his cut from the loansharking. The local Shylocks turn over sixty percent to the office in Providence."

"Sixty!" LeBlanc said, "Impossible!"

"That's the trade-off."

"What's the take?" Brady asked.

"A guess, sixty or seventy-five big ones."

"Sixty million dollars!" LeBlanc was apparently determined to undercut Dawson's briefing. "I don't believe it."

"That squares with the ratio, LeBlanc," Brady said. "Sharking to numbers, five to four. What I want to know is how it works. Either Balestrione controls the turf here or he doesn't. If he does, why no numbers take? If he doesn't, why do they give him the gravy?"

"Balestrione's the thug. Nobody in Boston swings a mace like him. He has the soldiers. That's why loansharking fits. His people can collect. They have the muscle. It doesn't take muscle to run numbers."

"Why wouldn't he run it all, though?" Brady paused. He needed more on Balestrione's nemesis, the North End honcho. "Where the fuck is Martin?"

The three men looked through the glass partition toward the frosted-glass door on the far side of the office. As if on cue, the door opened and Bill Martin walked in. He made for his desk, but one of the agents touched his sleeve and pointed toward Brady's office. He crossed to it without rushing. He was white-haired and paunchy, and looked not at all like a crack BIR agent. He had compiled the dossier that formed the basis for the successful tax prosecution of Al Capone.

"Get your folder, Martin," Thomas said.

Martin's eyes went involuntarily to Brady, whose nod was perceptible only to him. He returned to the outer office, to his desk, which he unlocked. He withdrew a key from the top drawer, then crossed the room to the northeast corner, in which sat, stolid and massive, the vault. He turned the combination until the door opened, then he inserted the key into a drawer lock. Out of the drawer he took a brick-colored folder tied with a brown lace. He returned to Brady's office.

"What do you have?" Brady asked.

"I was under the impression my report was not due . . ."

"Cut the crap, Martin," Thomas said. "This isn't school." One of Thomas's services to Brady was to be the mean bastard.

"Bill," Brady said, "we've been trying to get an angle on how far Balestrione comes into Dearo. What can you tell us?"

" 'Dearo'?"

"The North End. It's what the Irish call it."

"Oh." Martin shrugged. "It's all Anselmo. It's that simple. I don't see Balestrione's prints anywhere in Boston."

"What about loansharking?"

"No way of knowing. The books I have don't break it down."

"Give us the highlights," Brady said.

Martin opened the folder and, as he talked, had continual reference to it. "There are twenty-two companies whose records we have, all North End and, presumably, Anselmo's. His three sons, Leonard, Rico, and Marcello, run seven of them. Marcello is college-educated, went to B.U., where he lost an eye playing hockey. Their businesses run the gamut, the usual stuff: wines, Italian foods, pasta, real estate, two restaurants, a garage, warehouses, garbage trucks, so forth. Waterfront stuff. Anselmo's been the big don in the North End for twenty years."

"What's the total take, from what you've seen?"

"All twenty-two concerns?"

Brady nodded.

"Neighborhood of two and a half, three million dollars, I'd think."

"Total?"

"That's the *tax* figures, remember."

"And the companies are legit?"

"Seems so. No chunks of unexplained capital. And they all do *something*. I checked out the physical stuff first. I don't think he's using any of these companies for his laundry. These books are clean."

"Any connections with Providence?"

"None that I see."

"That's not much help. We were trying to figure the connection between him and Ciro Balestrione."

"What's the question?" Something in Martin's voice said, *All right, you punk lawyers, ask me. I'm an old pro at this. What do you want to know?*

Brady gave his eye to Dawson.

Dawson said, "They've split numbers and sharking. Anselmo gets one,

Balestrione the other. Balestrione has the guns. Why couldn't he take it all? It doesn't figure. Boston's his cherry, like Cicero belongs to Giancana or Jersey City to Lucchese. Does Anselmo mind the store for him? That's my guess."

"Len, I'll tell you," Martin said, touching him, not concealing his condescension. "Anselmo doesn't mind anybody's store. He killed Zorelli himself. I mean *Zorelli!* When Anselmo blinks, lights go out for a millisecond all over the North End."

"Not in Providence," Dawson said.

Martin turned a page in his folder. "If he's a storekeeper, why does he have a Swiss bank account?"

Brady leaned forward. "How do we know that?"

"His name was on a list of seven numbered accounts Kefauver turned up in Miami. Nobody'd heard of him then. It took two years to figure out what the numbers were. They were his accounts at a bank in Basel. Turned out one of his bagmen had taken a little detour on his way to Switzerland to try to sell dope on Anselmo's system to Johnny Dio in Florida. Dio refused the deal and told Anselmo about it. But apparently Dio kept a copy of the numbers just in case, which, apparently, Anselmo never knew."

"Let me see it."

Martin handed Brady a page with fourteen sets of numbers on it. One set was circled.

"Christ!" Brady said, "If we could only get inside *that* vault."

None of the men spoke. They were all more than familiar with the inviolability of the Swiss banking world.

"Do we know what bank it is?"

"Yes. The Kurfürst Royale. The first two numbers indicate that."

Brady stared at the numbers as if they would tell him everything.

Again silence settled over the office.

Finally Dawson said, "It's clear Anselmo has more clout than shows through at first. Maybe the son of a bitch owns G.M."

"If he owned G.M. he wouldn't need guns," LeBlanc said.

"I think," Martin said modestly, "you've the wrong impression of Anselmo because of the contrast you've drawn between him and Balestrione."

"What do you mean?" Brady was getting impatient with Martin's posturing.

"Anselmo has his soldiers, his guns. You know that bagman?"

"The courier who went to Dio?"

"Yes. Gaetano Castillo. His body turned up in a boat floating in Miami harbor, cut from ear to ear."

Brady stood with an abruptness that startled the others. "What'd you say?"

"Ear to ear. They cut his throat. Anselmo's capable of all that shit."

"No. What'd you say his name was?"

"Castillo. Gaetano Castillo. He was a cousin of Anselmo's even, from the same town as his mother. Her name was Castillo."

"What town?"

"Wait a minute . . ." Martin started flipping through the folder.

"Cefalù," Brady said.

Martin looked up at him. The others were staring at Brady, whose expression had gone strangely waxen.

"That's right," Martin said.

For Brady to recall such a detail, the others knew there had to be a significance in it of which they were ignorant. One thing they had in common was the detective's irritation at his own ignorance.

"Where was Anselmo born?" Brady asked.

Martin looked in the folder. "Worcester."

"So he'd be what you'd call . . ." — Brady paused strangely — ". . . an American."

He was gripping the edge of his desk, trying to contain his shock, not to show it. Gennaro Anselmo had caused Anna's death. The realization had come at him totally unexpectedly. He felt as though a boulder had fallen at his feet, just missing him, nearly killing him. What had Gennaro Anselmo to do with him? How were their lives entwined? A sharp blade of intuition stabbed him suddenly, but before it could assert itself another took its place, and tried to push the first one away.

"Well," Martin said, "he'd be a citizen. We couldn't deport him. We'd have to indict him."

"That's not why I asked."

They did not know why he asked. Their ignorance again.

"How do we get him?" Brady looked at Dawson.

"I think it'd be a mistake to focus on him, Chief. The guy with the muscle is the guy with the enemies. Balestrione's goons are the ones who lean on you when you fall short. A shit-load of dagos out there would love to see the office fold. They'll help us make it happen. That's why Anselmo stays clear of loansharking. Too many enemies. The street will protect Anselmo. We'll never nail him."

"I did not ask 'if,' Len. I asked 'how.' "

"It's obvious," Martin said.

Brady shifted his glare to the white-haired man.

"The Swiss account," Martin said. "You can bet that loot doesn't just sit there. Where do you suppose it goes? What does Anselmo have going that keeps Balestrione at bay? What's the take per annum?" Martin looked at Dawson.

"Fifty million in numbers alone."

"OK, add another twenty for miscellaneous. Seventy million dollars a year for what? Say six years. Forty million for ten before that. And a lousy fifteen million for, say, four before that. That's eight hundred and eighty million dollars. With minimum compound interest over twenty years, it's up near a billion. Now, let's suppose for a minute Anselmo hasn't settled for interest all these years. Suppose he has it working for him. Suppose instead of three percent, he's been revaluing at ten or twelve. Shit, the guy *could* own G.M. The Swiss account. That's how we find out. That's how we bring him down. His clout runs only as deep as his secret does."

It was LeBlanc who asked the obvious question. "How are you going to crack the Swiss bank, Bill?"

"Let's put it this way. If it was your account and Anselmo wanted the dope on you, he'd get it."

"How?" LeBlanc asked.

Martin shrugged.

There was something Sicilian about that shrug, and Brady noted it. Martin had become like his prey.

"A bag job," Dawson said quietly.

They all stared at their hands. Just like the FBI.

"You ever been to Basel, Len?" Martin asked. Dawson shook his head. "Only folks could break in those banks, you G-men finished. Bonnie and Clyde."

"I was thinking of Capone," Dawson said feebly.

"It would have to be the government," LeBlanc said, so innocently. "Maybe we could get Dulles to do it."

"Allen?" Martin asked, enjoying himself, "Or John Foster?"

"CIA."

"Shit," Dawson said.

"I agree with Len," Deke Thomas said. "You guys are all full of shit. The secrecy of their banks is guaranteed by their constitution. The government has to stand by it. If they didn't the whole thing would fall. Even the Nazis didn't crack Swiss banks. Nobody can."

The men were silent again, and gradually their bickering evaporated beneath the mute look of Collins Brady, who was leaning back in his chair, smoking his cigarette. "All right, men. You're excused. We'll pick this up later."

The four agents started to leave.

"Not you, Bill. I want a word with you about something else."

Martin and Brady stared at each other until the others were gone. Deke

Thomas stood in the door waiting to be told to remain also. But Brady ignored him. Thomas closed the door after leaving through it.

"Go on," Brady said.

Martin shrugged.

"Don't try my patience, Bill. Tell me what you're thinking."

"What I'm thinking is illegal. If I say it and you hear it and neither of us reports it, we're both guilty of a crime."

"Bullshit. I'm the lawyer. You're the accountant. You're confused. Tell me."

"I know a man who can get us the records of that account, amounts, signatures, deposits, withdrawals, everything. It'll cost us."

"Bribery."

"I told you."

"Who is he?"

"A guy I know. I heard he was used on something for our side during the war. It is not true, by the way, that the Nazis didn't crack the Swiss banks. This guy was a faucet, a neutral faucet. He told whoever turned his head anything they wanted to know. He is accustomed to being paid well. He will accept only gold, no currency. It is my impression that he was paid at times by the Germans with the fillings from teeth."

"Who is he?" Brady did not like to have to repeat a question.

"Ernst Müller. He is a senior official in the Commerce Ministry. His responsibilities include supervising the security of banking information. It is a simple matter for him to see any record he chooses. He is reliable and efficient."

"How do you know?"

"Are you asking me if I have previously bribed him?"

"Exactly."

"I will not tell you, Mr. Brady. There are limits to my confidence."

"We could not make use of such records in court."

"Of course not. Nor in any other public forum." Martin's brows came down on his eyes as he leaned over Brady's desk and put his weight on his stiff arms. "A source in Switzerland is worth hundreds of millions of dollars to the American government in prevented evasions, but zero in recovered funds. If we choose to make use of Müller, we must do so judiciously. He can give us all the leads we want. It'll be up to us to get them into court."

"How much?"

"For the records of one account? Fifty thousand dollars."

"Jesus, Martin!"

"In gold."

"Forget it."

Martin shrugged. Brady was a lightweight after all. No, that wasn't fair. Anselmo was the lightweight. Capone had been worth it. Who the hell ever heard of Gennaro Anselmo?

Even while Brady seemed to reject out of hand what Martin had proposed, he was wondering where he could get the money. He had a limited budget and, on the face of the evidence gathered, no justification for a special request of Washington of such enormousness. And Halley would never cooperate in the bribery of an official of a foreign government, no matter what the possible payoff. The ends don't justify the means.

Bullshit, Brady thought, *if the ends don't justify the means, nothing does.* It was a new thought for him, uncharacteristic and therefore powerful. He turned it over in his mind as if it were a coin, or a corpse. He savored it — if the ends don't, nothing does — as if he were the first to think of it, as if he were the first to discover that every absolute and unyielding principle carries inside itself its own opposite.

"Forget it, Bill," he said again. "That's out of the question. Besides, you were right. It would be illegal."

Martin shrugged and left Brady's office.

Brady sat in his chair for a long time. The sharp instinct which he had turned aside before asserted itself again. His mind had seized upon the problem of how to ferret out Anselmo while exactly avoiding what it was stalking now. There was one possible connection between himself and Anselmo.

He put the thought out of his mind. The issue was Anselmo. Collins knew he was having an emotional reaction to the discovery that Anselmo was the one behind Anna's death. Further speculation at that point was uncalled-for and unhelpful. He had to adhere to professional method, now more than ever. Personal feelings should have as little weight as possible. He considered his next move.

It was better to proceed without Martin. Ernst Müller; Brady would search him out himself. If he was going to buy an official, better to do it alone. Who knew, finally, the margins of Bill Martin's loyalties?

Brady turned in his chair to face away from the cavernous office as if he didn't want his people to see his face while he laid out his plan.

Through the slats of the window blinds the golden dome of the State House was harvesting the gleaming early sun. Under the roofs of Beacon Hill houses with their potted chimneys and bundled angles, the indolent city dawdled over coffee. Thin fingers of smoke tested the day; calm and fair.

Where could he get fifty thousand dollars in cash?

Brady pulled his drawer open to hook his leg over it. He saw the gun, thought of closing the drawer, but didn't.

He had just put down thirty thousand on the house on Pinckney Street. He had less than twenty in his own account. He could cash in some bonds or go to the trust, but he'd need Janet's signature for those. He had to keep her out of it.

His mind drifted as though he were sitting by his fire and watching the slow crumbling of the wood. His eye was balanced on the sharp gleam of the State House dome. The sun dragged itself out of its own embers every morning and snuggled the Bullfinch breast, the gold tit.

Gold, where would he get it? Another set of laws to break. He'd have to smuggle it out of the States. Getting it into Switzerland would not be a problem since, surely, Swiss customs inspection would be perfunctory. The Swiss economy depended on a tolerant discretion. They would not question his purpose once he displayed his credentials. He'd have to be careful to keep the consul out of it.

But the money, and the gold. He could buy the gold in Panama, where the thriving black market in pressed bars drew the artificially inflated dollars of Latin despots. But if he bought there, the rate — fifteen percent at least — would push the price to sixty. But sixty thousand was peanuts. Anselmo's take a year was sixty million. Those were the stakes; it was important to remember that. If the Swiss account did crack Anselmo's secret and lead to substantial penalties and recovered taxes, there was some likelihood that Halley would see to Brady's post factum compensation. He would have to keep records to later prove his outlay.

Brady realized he didn't give a shit about post factum compensation or recovered taxes or what Halley thought. What he wanted more than he had ever wanted anything in his life was Anselmo and his secrets. He needed sixty thousand dollars. Suddenly he knew two things at once: how to get the money, and how to exorcise that terrible suspicion; he would go to his father. He would tell him about Anselmo and he would ask him for the money. Was he laying a trap? Perhaps. But for his father's sake and his own. If the end doesn't justify the means, what does?

He looked at the gun.

He looked at his watch. Eight-fifteen. If he took the long way to Essex Street, his father would be there by the time he arrived. He decided to do it.

A few minutes later he was crossing Beacon Hill. At Mt. Vernon Street where it meets Joy Street a cluster of children were waiting for their bus, and Brady paused to watch them. The boys shoved each other jovially. A couple were Tony's age, about eleven, but most were younger. The older boys seemed a bit like bullies.

Collins had finally yielded to Janet on the matter of Tony's school. In Washington the boy had gone to a parochial school outside the neighborhood. He had hated it, had no friends, and was reclusive enough to worry Janet intensely. She wanted, since he had to change schools with the move to Boston anyway, to enroll him at Milton Academy, the posh Protestant boys' school outside Boston. Both Janet's brothers had gone there, as had her father. Janet wanted Tony to go there even though his boarding would deprive her of his presence, which — to her own great surprise and Collins's — she had come to cherish. Collins at times was frankly jealous. But on that street corner that morning watching the children, he felt an exceptional fondness for his own son.

Brady walked down Joy Street to the Common thinking of things to do with the kid that night.

Essex Street is in the quarter of the city that snuggles up to the southwest corner of the Common, so Brady's route took him diagonally across it. From the summit of the hill in the center of the Common, Brady looked absently down on the old sheep meadow that sloped toward the Public Gardens.

He was surprised to see a labyrinth of wooden fences. Workmen were off-loading a heavy steam shovel from a flatbed truck, and another machine, a bulldozer, was already tearing up the lawn. Brady remembered reading about the new five-hundred-car garage they were going to build under the Common. He flinched at the thought. The place would be a mess for years. Where would Tony play? And they'd probably never put the grass back. After three hundred years, a disembowled, asphalted Common.

"Christ," he muttered. He turned and plunged down the back side of the Common, passed the Parkman Bandstand, and made for the corner of Boylston and Tremont.

Boylston Street was lined with gawdy stores that sold musical instruments and displayed them, gleaming, in their windows. There were also two theaters, half a dozen restaurants with formica tables, a joke shop and an army-navy surplus store. Brady pushed along the sidewalk with dozens of others who'd come up from the subway and were on the way, barely conscious, to work.

At Washington Street, Boylston Street ended and Brady angled across to Essex. Looming office buildings and wholesale houses engulfed the street, covered it with shadows, and made it seem narrow and morose. The commuters went into these buildings which were as sad and dull as they were.

At the corner of Lincoln and Essex the pace of the wind quickened in the open of the broad boulevard. The intersection was dominated by the Monument Building, and Collins, waiting for the light to change, stood on the corner and looked up at it. He had admired the building ever since his father'd bought it in the early forties. It was six stories high, a block long, and half a block deep, and it was a masterpiece of neoclassical understatement. Dating to 1896, it had been designed by Sears, whose most famous work in Boston was the Isabella Stewart Gardner Museum on the Fenway. The Monument Building, on a more massive scale, made use of the same brick arches and pillared ledges and achieved a simplicity of line that made the building a perfect example of utilitarian beauty.

The light changed.

Brady crossed Lincoln Street. A policeman stood on the opposite corner looking benign and bright. He touched the beak of his cap as Brady passed. Brady nodded, but his eyes went to the policeman's gun.

Five of the six floors of the Monument Building were given over to the uses of the Monument Companies. In addition to the Insurance Association, there were business offices for the rayon plant in Haverhill; the headquarters for the real estate company, Suburban Developers, which had holdings on the fringes of two dozen large cities; Gyro-Instruments occupied the entire third and fourth floors manufacturing precision navigational equipment for airplanes. It had recently been decided to move Gyro-I, as it was called, to a new plant in Waltham.

Colman Brady's office was on the third floor. Collins entered the elevator with his usual tremor. The open-grill cage of the elevator with the exposed cables and shaft had always both exhilarated and frightened him slightly. The elevator was Colman's pride. The tile floor and the fancy iron scrollwork and the ivory organ stops that served as floor buttons and the long draping cables that undulated as the cage rose, rattling away, were what had made him want to buy the building in the first place. Then he set about making the rest worthy of the elevator, worthy, he would almost have admitted, of mercantile London in its late nineteenth-century heyday.

Each of the office floors was arranged as a hollow square. The center was the work space for clerks and secretaries, and on the periphery were offices of company managers and executives. The partitions were built of polished walnut and trimmed in a dull-finished bronze. Only leaded glass was used in the dividers, and all of the light fixtures were of leaded glass as well. Doorknobs were glass on silver. Walls everywhere were lined with the leather-bound books of the company. The officers all had rolltop desks with pigeonholes. The clerks sat at partners' desks. An economy of space precluded crowding, though each floor had dozens of workers. The standing desk in one office, for example, provided the innards of a filing cabinet in the next. The offices of the Monument Companies were unusual for their restrained, tasteful, and quiet elegance. They embodied Colman Brady's idea of a nice place for his people to work.

"Hello, Dad," Collins said, briskly entering his father's office. He had asked Colman's secretary not to buzz him.

Colman was surprised and delighted. He looked up from the *Herald* and took off his glasses. "By God, look who's here!"

They'd seen each other only days before, but it had been years since Collins had come to Essex Street, where he'd always loved seeing his father in the full sway of his realm. Colman, for his part, had displayed it to him as though from the pinnacle of the Temple. They shook hands warmly.

"Sit down! Sit down! How about some coffee?" He pressed the intercom. "Marie? Some coffee. Regular." He looked up brightly at Collins. "Regular, right?"

"No, Dad. That's the way you take it. I take it black."

"Black, Marie. One regular. One black."

Colman's desk, a great, sensuous rolltop out of Dickens, faced the wall. There was nothing between him and Collins but the six-foot expanse of an exquisite Oriental for which Colman had paid too much money.

"It's the poor beast's portion," Colman said, "to live for his whelps. You know that now, I suppose." His son had always had the power to shrivel the concerns of business by merely walking into the office.

"I was thinking about him on the way over just now. He starts school next week."

"At Cathedral?"

Collins hesitated. It surprised him to realize that he hadn't told his father yet. "No. Milton."

"Milton! What the hell is that?"

It also surprised Collins that his father had not heard of one of the best schools in New England. "Milton Academy. It's in Milton."

"How's the kid going to get there?"

"He'll live there. But I didn't stop by to talk about that."

"It's Protestant, isn't it?"

"Yes."

"Jesus Christ, wait'll Jack hears."

"The hell with Jack!"

"Now, son!"

"No! The hell with that sanctimonious creep. He's not the kid's father. Tell him to stay the hell out of it."

"I'm sure you'll get the chance to tell him that yourself. I'm not a referee in a match between you two. I'd be the one to get slugged."

"He drives Janet nuts."

"He means no harm."

"Let's drop it, can we?" Collins was shocked by his outburst. His emotions were seething below the surface of his composure. He was miserable and afraid and already feeling traitorous for what he had been thinking. He made an effort to control himself.

Colman shrugged. He didn't care about the school, but he thought Collins a little touchy on the subject. All things being equal, Tony'd be a step ahead if he got one of those superb horse-country WASP educations. It was all right with Colman. But of course all things were not equal, never were.

Marie brought the coffee in. They waited for her to leave.

"Well?" Colman said.

Collins looked up from his cup. "I need a favor."

"You name it."

"Sixty thousand dollars."

"A loan or a gift?"

Collins laughed inappropriately and falsely. "I recall a priest asking me, 'Alone or with others.' I'd told him I 'took impure pleasure in sex.' I think that's the last time I went to confession."

"How the hell did it turn out that I raised a heathen?"

"You who are known far and wide for piety."

"It's true." Colman grinned. "Are we avoiding something, or what? Why did you jump from the subject of money to the subject of impure sex?"

"Did I do that?"

"Just now."

"God, the weedy trails of my psyche, eh?"

"You didn't answer my question, son."

"A loan, of course."

"Are you in trouble?"

"No." He stood and went to the window, where he looked down on Lincoln Street. He held his cup at his breast. His back was to his father. He was trying to control what he was feeling. "I found out this morning who had Anna killed." It was like pushing words through iron to say this. "It will take sixty thousand dollars for me to get him."

Colman sipped his coffee. "Tell me about it, son."

"It wasn't local Black Hand extortion at all. They were sent. They were Castillos from a village in the northeast called Cefalù. They were sent by a man they called 'the American,' and he sent them because of me. I still don't know why. I found him today. He lives right out there, maybe ten blocks from here. His people are Castillos from Cefalù, but he's an American, born in Worcester. They're still frightened to death of him."

"What his name?" Colman asked sadly.

Collins faced his father and stared at him. "Gennaro Anselmo."

"I know him."

"You do?" Collins felt a surge of complex emotions. He had not expected this admission. Was his suspicion accurate? But his father's candor disarmed him. Wouldn't he try to hide the fact that he knew him?

Colman noted the quaver in his son's voice and he knew he had to move his pieces very carefully. But they were all identical, and he did not know which to protect. "Yes. A long time ago. He was up for a pardon when Curley was governor. I met him."

"Why was he pardoned? He's a thug."

"Boston had its problems in those days about fair trials for Italians. Ever hear of the 'two fried wops'?"

"Sacco and Vanzetti."

"Yes. Anselmo tried to get the truth out about that holdup in Braintree. A hood named Zorelli did it."

"Anselmo killed him."

"So they say. I don't know about that."

Collins was surprised by the turn the conversation had taken. He didn't know what to make of his father's mood.

"I do know," Colman said, "that Zorelli killed some friends of mine. Ever hear Maeve and me talk about Jerry MacCurtain?"

Collins nodded.

"Zorelli gunned him down, him and a dozen other Southie lads. We didn't keen much when Zorelli got it. I didn't care who killed him, still don't. He was a festering sore."

"You sound pretty knowledgeable about it."

"Son, I've been alive all these years, you know. It's a big city."

"Yeah."

"What else do you know about Anselmo's pardon?"

"Nothing. Just that it was Curley. I assume he was bribed."

"It wasn't him, and there was no bribe. It was me. I'd have thought you'd know that by now. My name is on the pardon. It's public record."

"I didn't know that!" Collins felt a burst of anger at Martin and the others who had prepared the brief on Anselmo. They should have known that! Christ, they should have told him that. Collins held a line on his feelings. "I'm glad to hear that from you. I'd have been surprised to come across it myself, to say the least."

Colman nodded. He decided to tell the kid everything that he would find out anyway.

"You remember my — what shall I call it? — setback?"

"Yes. Nineteen thirty-seven."

"Thirty-six. That was the issue. I was accused of taking a bribe. I didn't. They impeached me anyway, *in camera* so Curley wouldn't be em-

[481]

barrassed. That was the deal. I did recommend the pardon. It seemed wrong to me that Anselmo should be in jail for the murder of Zorelli. There was no question of a bribe. It was a question of right and wrong."

"Anselmo was innocent?"

Colman shrugged.

"Don't shrug, goddamnit! Everybody goddamn shrugs!"

"Relax, Micko."

"Relax! The son of a bitch who killed the first woman I ever loved, the mother of my son, you tell me he's an old . . . what? . . . of yours! Relax! Goddamnit! The fuck I will! What are you telling me?" Collins was trembling. His knees were unsteady and he was perspiring freely.

"I'm telling you I met the man, had something to do with him, was on the fringe of the same battle once twenty years ago. It's a long time, son. I'm telling you that before you make your final judgment about a man you ought to make allowance for the terrain he's crossed."

"I know all I need to know about Anselmo. He's an emperor of carnage and misery. I know his kind inside and out. He's a night crawler. He's a fucking murderer."

"And you're going to get him."

"You're goddamn right I am."

"Because of Anna?"

"I'm going to find out what the hell this son of a bitch had to do with me and her."

"I don't tell you your business, son."

Collins caught himself, slowed it down, dropped his voice and said, "But I need your help."

"The money?"

"Yes."

"What's it for?"

"Anselmo has a Swiss account. It's the trapdoor. I have to find out where his money goes."

The one language Colman Brady never wanted to learn was the shrill scream, its nuances, the violent cracks of a breaking voice. He sat there looking at his son. The silence between them was vast and hard.

Colman knew that the game was up. It was inconceivable that his son would not find out now. Colman was deciding whether to tell him the entire truth immediately. He could at least try to make him understand that he had never intended Anna's death, that he regretted that more than anything else in his regrettable life. But he knew that he could not tell him. He understood that his son was embarked on the mythic journey. He had a right to it. The last act was begun and it had to be played out.

Greek fates had written this, he decided, and consoled himself that at least when this blow landed he would have been prepared for it.

So he had to finesse his son yet more; Micko the Innocent. That thought set loose in him a wave of laughter that surprised Colman and stunned Collins, and the laughter itself, though genuine, was all the finesse he needed.

Colman put his cup down and laughed until his eyes watered. Then he stopped. "You want the money for a bribe."

"Yes." Collins was shaken. His father had seemed insane to him while he was laughing.

"Dear Christ, Dear Christ . . ." Colman sat shaking his head. There was an irony so huge as to be its own rebuke. "Dear Christ, Micko . . ."

"I didn't think you'd react this way."

Colman slammed his fist down on the desk, and anger poured out of him. "You didn't! How in God's name did you expect me to react? You come in here as if I was *your* goddamn Swiss account. You who prides himself on his independence! On his Harvard degree! On his Pinckney Street house! On his Smith wife! On his blowsy righteousness! You come in here to get your lucre to accomplish your purpose no matter how, no matter what laws, what principles, what norms are violated. There are some things I don't do with my money, Collins."

"I thought you'd understand when I told you . . ."

"I do understand. The world you live in, son, has very narrow margins. It's difficult for you to see beyond your own wants, your own questions, your own pains. Not that they are not real and important, but that, well, we each have our own set of wants, questions, and pains just like yours. I do. Even old son of a bitch Anselmo does."

"You won't give me the money."

"That's right. You drew a line with me once. I'm drawing one with you."

"I'm sorry."

"That's life. I haven't said 'No' to you enough."

"I mean, I'm sorry I asked you. I didn't know you'd take it as an insult."

"I did. Now it's over. Forget it."

"All right."

"One other thing. I'm curious. Who were you going to bribe?" Colman Brady had the small sudden hope that he could get to the fellow first with a fortune.

Collins slowly and deliberately lied to his father for the first time. "I don't know his name. I would have gone through an intermediary."

"So you're not going to do it?"

"No." His second lie. "I feel differently now that I've seen your reaction. I was wrong." Collins put his cup and saucer down on the table, but as he did his hand shook convulsively and the china rattled loudly for an instant. "I'll see you later," he said, and left.

Colman Brady sat in silence for a long time.

Collins went to his bank.

By noon he had renegotiated the mortgage to the new house, closed out his own account and his joint account with Janet. He left the bank with a cashier's check for seventy thousand dollars. If the man's price was fifty in gold, certainly he would take seventy in cash.

He went home and lied to Janet. He told her he was going to Washington. It was more crucial than ever that no one know of his trip to Switzerland.

A day and a half later he knew.

Two signatories were authorized to deposit and withdraw from the account; Gennaro Anselmo and Colman Brady. By the time Collins saw the photostat of his father's bold scrawl he was not surprised. He was numb. A seal had been pressed on his feelings, like sod onto turned earth. His father was not only part of what killed Anna, but was also the permanent accomplice of brutal hoodlums. Why, by then, wasn't he surprised?

When he returned to Boston it was late afternoon. He went from the airport to his office briefly, and then to Prescott Street. His father was in the solarium that he used as a den during the good weather. Come October he would use the proper den upstairs.

"You're back," Colman said, looking up from his papers.

Collins dropped a manila envelope on the desk in front of his father.

Colman did not look at it. "You lied to me, son."

"That's right, Dad. I did."

"Well, how about that. You learn slow, but you learn good."

"You are a master. You've been Anselmo's front for years."

"Is that what they're saying in Switzerland?"

"You had Anna killed."

"I think it was more complex than that, Micko."

"I have to arrest you. I'm sorry." He said those strange words precisely as he'd imagined himself doing all the way back from Switzerland. It was simple. All he had to do was follow the plan. All he had to do was enact a sequence of silhouettes.

"No, son, you don't. You don't have to do anything."

"But you are a . . ." Collins's voice broke. His lip trembled. ". . . criminal." His eyes overflowed and his face collapsed. He began to weep.

Colman stood and crossed to him. He put his arms around him.

Collins fell against Colman and sobbed uncontrollably. "Perhaps I am, son. But right now I'm your father and I love you. I love you, Micko."

Colman hugged his son with all his strength, wanting to give him some of it, but relieved beyond words for once that his son had none of his own.

❦ 8 ❦

JANET DREADED the Sunday dinner, but she just could not put it off any longer. The one enormous disadvantage of the return to Boston was living in proximity to her husband's family. She had to have them over. She had never entertained the McShanes and the Bradys at her own table. By the second week in September she was as ready as she'd ever be.

Collins was no help at all. He'd returned from Washington an abrupt shadow of himself. She read his troubles the way a farmer reads the wind, but she could not bring herself to ask what had happened to plunge him into such a bleak mood.

Maeve, Maureen, and Mr. Brady arrived first. Tony was a gem for the way he greeted them and took their coats. Janet watched him delightedly. He was turning out to be such a perfect young gentleman. By the time Collins had taken them on a tour of the house, Deirdre and her stuffy husband Horace arrived, and, on their heels, Father Jack. Collins ushered everyone into the front parlor, which, Janet thought, had turned out just elegantly. The Queen Anne settee was the perfect piece for the bay of the window. On opposite sides of the fireplace were a pair of crafted cabinets with blown-glass doors, in which Janet set out her china collection. She thought it the most exquisite display imaginable. It surprised her how important it had become to impress her husband's family. Basically they were very simple people.

Everything went smoothly until they gathered at the dinner table. After each had been served — Maria was quite a competent table servant after two years in Washington — Janet invited them to begin. But they did not. An awkward beat fell as she raised her fork. She thought perhaps they were waiting for a toast, and she looked toward Collins.

Maeve said, "A word of Grace perhaps?" Janet knew Mrs. McShane did not mean it as a rebuke, but she was stung. Grace! Of course! Christ!

[485]

All looked at Father Jack, who blessed himself, and all did likewise except Janet. Even Tony blessed himself.

"Bless us, O Lord, and these Thy gifts which we are about to receive through Thy bounty through Christ our Lord, Amen."

They began to eat happily then, but the meal was ruined for Janet. It was stupid of her not to think of Grace. It had been the custom, on Sundays, in her own family. But no one said Grace in Washington. One's habits changed.

The second blow came when Mr. Brady said grandly, "Well, Janet, what do you think of your husband's new job?"

She tried to smile. She forced herself not to look immediately at Collins. These people would not see her surprise or her hurt any more than they would see the cleft rocks over which the tranquil sea sleeps. "Whatever Collins enjoys, I enjoy," she said. Only then did she look at him. He was staring at his plate.

"I don't know about any new job," Deirdre said. "What's the story?"

"He's coming to work for me. About time, too."

"I think it's wonderful," Maeve said. "Brady and Son."

Colman dropped his large hand on Tony's head. "And then this one! Brady and Son and Grandson!"

Tony smiled up at Colman, but only briefly. He was an exact barometer of his parents' mood, and he knew that, while his mother was mystified, his father was clutching inwardly at something awful.

Collins was staring at his plate as he said, "I've always wanted to be Dad's partner."

He looked across the length of the table at Janet. "And now that we're back in Boston, it seemed like a natural time. My crusading days are over."

A look of such bereft pleading crossed his face for an instant that Janet would have taken his hand in her own if the table weren't between them, and she'd have said, "You can do what you want, darling. I'm with you whatever you choose." It surprised and saddened Janet that Collins had found it difficult to confide his decision in her, much less to consult her about it. She could not imagine why he should not have told her. It was a right and natural thing for him to go to his father's firm. She had always assumed he would at some point. She smiled at him. She wanted to assure him it was all right with her.

But he dropped his eyes again.

"I have some news to announce, too," Father Jack said. "Pass the salt, Dee, would you please?"

"What, dear?" Maeve asked. "You sound happy about it, whatever it is."

"I am, very. I spoke to Father Alban at Portsmouth Priory, and he's agreed to take Tony."

Janet's fork hit her plate. "What?"

"That's right. They're willing to waive the exam. Tony'll go right into the second form."

Everyone was very quiet. Janet understood immediately that she alone did not know what he was talking about.

"Bob Kennedy went to Portsmouth. Tony'll love it. It's the best school in the country." The priest had pointedly not said "best Catholic school." He went on. "The English Benedictines are . . ."

"Tony's going to Milton Academy, Father," Janet said calmly. "We're driving out this week."

Tony wanted to vanish. A terrible panic unraveled itself in his chest.

Father McShane touched his napkin to his lips. "I had heard that."

Collins said, "Perhaps this isn't the time . . ."

"Tony," Janet ordered, "see if Maria needs help in the kitchen, would you?"

The boy left his place. No one spoke until he was gone.

"You can't send him to Milton," the priest said gently.

"We are not discussing it, Father. Not with you." Janet had never been more sure of herself. "This is a matter between me and my husband."

"I hate the thought of interfering in a family matter, Janet, honestly I do." The priest spoke with a tangible sincerity. He was clearly proceeding reluctantly, without relish or rancor. "But in a way this is my family, and this is a matter of faith and morals. I feel obliged by that. Besides, I looked into it at your husband's request."

Now Janet's head did whip toward Collins. "Is that true?"

"I said he could look into it, but I never thought he'd do that."

"Really, Janet," Father Jack said, "Portsmouth is a wonderful school. The monk who's the headmaster is a convert from Anglicanism, and before, he was headmaster of St. George's in Newport. Surely you know about St. George's?"

"I don't care who he is or was. Tony is going to Milton."

"Milton Academy is a Protestant school," the priest said.

"You needn't say the word as if it were filthy. I'm a Protestant, Father."

"I intend no disrespect of your beliefs, Janet, but Tony is a Catholic."

"We're not changing his religion. Just his school." Janet was trying to keep the fury out of her voice. She was trying not to look at Collins. Why was he permitting this humiliation?

"But Janet, my dear," Father McShane said firmly but not unkindly, "you must respect your husband's solemn obligation."

He paused, letting his words gather mass the way dust does. He would have preferred it if it hadn't come to this, but it had. "And you must respect the oath you took."

"Oath!"

Janet stood, knocking the table. Her water glass fell and shattered. It was a cut crystal heirloom, but she ignored it. "I never took an oath!"

It was between her and the priest, simply, totally.

"You did. I saw it. I saw your signature."

Janet's glare went to Colman.

Colman sat unmoved behind a benign mask. He was not even blushing.

Janet said to him, "You signed my name!" The authority of her statement surprised even her. She was incredulous. She could not believe this was happening.

"I'm sorry, darling," Colman said. "What?"

"You signed my name."

"Janet," he said, "you're upset."

"You're damn right I'm upset. You forged my signature."

"I did nothing of the kind. You may regret it, but you signed that oath yourself. I saw you."

Janet sat down. Colman's statement, the baldness of it, the certainty and, yes, the gentleness, was like a blow to the groin. She covered her mouth with her hands as if in an effort to prevent the air from escaping her body. Janet Lindsay had never been lied to before.

"So," the priest said softly, "we are simply enabling you to keep your word."

"Never," Janet said, but in a tone barely above a whisper.

"What do you say, Micko?" Father Jack asked.

Collins shrugged. He had nothing to say. "This isn't the best time to deal with this."

Janet yelled at him. "Don't let them think they'll have their way on this. Tell them."

"We want the boy in Milton," Collins said.

"I forbid it," the priest said. He was damned if his nephew's immortal soul was going to be put in jeopardy by this woman.

Collins looked at Colman, but Colman's eyes showed him nothing. He wasn't getting into this one.

"You're the father, Collins," the priest said. "You tell her."

Collins dropped his eyes.

The priest looked at Janet as if he had scored.

[488]

Janet leaned toward him, and pointed a finger at him. "I've as much right to make choices for the boy as he does." She looked at Collins. He raised his eyes to meet hers. "Isn't that true?" she asked.

He did not reply.

"Isn't that true?" she repeated. On the word *true* her voice cracked. She could keep the panic away no longer. She had just asked him the question she had sworn never to ask again.

Collins sat there mute and immobile. It was all the answer she needed. At least his father had the spine to give words to his lie, and even credence. Collins could not look at her and she knew it, and she knew that Tony was his. She hated him for that. Did he know it? Was that why he leaned forward, gave the priest a deadly, brooding look — a falcon's look — and said, "The matter is closed. Tony's going to Milton Academy."

But it was too late. Something unforgettable had just happened to Janet, something unredeemable. The sense of it, amorphous and vague, spread upward and outward from a place in her breast like a stain. It changed the hue of everything the way a gaunt brown lens brings out the ugliness in scenes. She would have scrubbed her very skin with coarse sand if that would have smoothed her permanent gooseflesh. She would have chipped at her own bones with an iron wedge if that would have softened the cracked edges in her. She would bicker with herself about it for a long time, trying to believe that this was the sort of graininess that gave each family its particularity, its cunning for survival. She wanted nothing so much as to find herself wrong, too WASPish, too righteous. But she had too much brain and too much self to settle into such a lie. She was not what they were. That was the point. The killing fact was plain and simple. There was something evil about her husband and his people. Something quite evil.

There were only two things into which, after that Sunday, Janet Lindsay could settle: a fierce determination to save Tony from them because by then her love for him was irretrievable, and a mannered, private despair at the terrible mistake she had made with her life.

❧ FIVE ❧

1

"MEMBERS OF THE COURT, Honored Guests, Ladies and Gentlemen, the President-elect of the United States of America."

They rose together and turned expectantly. They were the senators and representatives of the Commonwealth of Massachusetts, each at his dark desk in the House chamber. They were the clerks and out-of-office pols lining the walls and filling the spaces on the margins as usual. They were reporters in one balcony, family and friends of the Court in the other, and guests of the President-elect in the third. The applause of the assembly cracked into a loud sustained *hurrah!* which did not fade but hung in the domed ceiling, the curve of which was timid compared to its exterior, the cocky Bulfinch gold on top of Beacon Hill.

Handsome, deeply tanned, forty-three years old, Kennedy took the chamber by his party's aisle. The sight of him whipped the crowd to even louder cheers. They were almost raucous, yet singly each person fondled him with the gentlest eyes. Those nearest reached out to him, but he held his hands hooked together easily at his waist — a characteristic posture — and did not touch them. He was a hoarder of dignity, no campaigner now. When he touched them it would be as from a slight rise. He would no longer merely give his attention or affection. He would bestow them. He mounted the platform on which the squat rostrum waited, taking four steps in two strides. He faced them, not raising his arms above his head, not waving, not playing on their applause. He simply received it and waited. Only his smile let them know how much he cared for them, how proud he was to be their son. He was a son of Massachusetts. On January 9, 1961, at five-thirty in the evening, he had come before his own to be celebrated and sent forth.

Finally, after nearly five minutes, the assembled members and guests stopped clapping and cheering and took their seats.

In the balcony reserved for guests of the President-elect sat his wife, Jacqueline, his mother, Rose, two of his sisters, their husbands, and several dozen family friends and political associates. Among these were Colman Brady, M. Collins Brady, his wife, Janet, and their son.

In the interval between the end of the applause and the final quiet after the audience was settled, Collins leaned across to his father. "Where's Joe?"

Colman looked toward Rose. "I think he's sicker than they're letting on. I should call him tomorrow. Remind me, will you?"

Collins withdrew a notebook with gold corner-guards from his coat pocket, wrote a word and closed it. "We should put Joe and Cush on the same porch. They could compare charts." Cardinal Cushing had been in an oxygen tent almost continually since Christmas. He was absent too.

"Not humorous," Colman said.

Colman Brady was sixty-two years old. He was heavy now. Though he still carried himself proudly and cut a striking, strong figure when he entered a room, his stomach was a thing on which to settle his arms when he sat. On time's diet one grows fat. If even one's son has gray hair . . .?

M. Collins Brady was as handsome as John Kennedy, but, though younger by a couple of years, his looks were not penny-bright. His sideburns *were* gray. He had the solid, graceful aspect not of a groomed politician, but of a diplomat or a breeder of fine horses. He wore his looks the way other men his age wore new young women.

Janet Brady sat next to him. She would not think of not being at her husband's side on such an occasion, and she was elegantly turned out as usual. She had nurtured her beauty and it had flowered. Her blond hair flashed against the mahogany panels of the hall. She was thirty-two. Others in the chamber, noticing her, thought she was escorted by the dark young man with the dramatic eyes at her other side, her son Tony, who was a senior at Milton Academy.

"I have welcomed this opportunity to address this historic body," Kennedy began, "and through you the people of Massachusetts, to whom I am so deeply indebted for a lifetime of friendship and trust."

Inside Tony Brady's head the tune had started, the tune of his worship; he worshipped Kennedy. Once, the year before, Kennedy had come to the Academy and after dinner had asked the headmaster to call Tony over. Kennedy told Tony what a proud name Brady was.

"For thirty-three years — whether I was in London, Washington, the South Pacific, or elsewhere — this has been my home; and, God willing, wherever I serve it will always remain my home. It was here my grandparents were born — it is here I hope my grandchildren will be born."

Did Janet stiffen at that? Collins's body was touching hers at the knee and along the curve of the thigh. The row was crowded, otherwise they'd have pulled slightly apart from each other. Collins turned his head slightly, enough to see her. Her flesh in the hollow of her long thin neck was like warm milk. He could taste it. He wondered what she thought when Kennedy adverted to his grandchildren. They had decided to have no children of their own. There was and would be only Tony.

"I speak neither from false provincial pride nor from artful political flattery. For no man about to enter high office in this country can ever be unmindful of the contributions this state has made to our national greatness."

Collins was still looking at her. She held herself stiff as a bell. Her eyes were fixed on Kennedy, but Collins could tell that she had merely assumed that upright posture of perfect attention. It was one of her showpieces. Janet was a maestra of appearances. When they were alone they were friendly enough, and they had good moments together now and then, but it was clear to both of them that theirs was a partnership maintained for public purposes. Janet never intruded upon Collins's business, except for the occasional social function that required a display of their intimacy. Collins never inquired about Janet's activities, but he had the sense that the reduction of their relationship over the years pained him far more than it did her. Collins's love for her would not fade and it showed him no mercy.

He turned his head away from her. She had not acknowledged his gaze with so much as an altered rhythm to her blinking. He looked toward the rostrum but saw Jacqueline a few rows ahead, and he stared at her, at the perfect curve of her neck.

"And so it is that I carry with me from this state to that high and lonely office to which I now succeed more than fond memories or past friendships. The enduring qualities of Massachusetts — the common threads woven by the Pilgrim and the Puritan, the fisherman and the farmer, the Yankee and the immigrant — will not be and could not be forgotten in this nation's executive mansion."

Kennedy's faith in himself as he delivered his speech seemed absolute. His listeners had never seen a man step onto the podium from which command is exercised with such confidence.

Colman Brady had the eerie sense that he'd listened to young Kennedy's speech before. He recalled being in a gallery looking down on the pompous well of a legislative hall, though in fact he hadn't been there. He had followed the great Treaty Debate by newspaper, but he had imagined it all so vividly that now he remembered it as if he'd been present. He remembered the tall, burly figure of Commandant Michael Collins in the center of the Dail pleading with De Valera. He remembered De Valera collapsing and the great leaders of Ireland weeping. How they loved their defeats! How they lived for their deaths! Colman Brady remembered what it was that had driven him then from Dublin back to his farm and from his farm to Boston. He had been fleeing the Irish worship of sad tales, even while telling a new one, the tale of his life.

But Kennedy! A stalwart brilliant man in control of himself and his audience. Thirty-five million people believed in him, but none as he did in himself. Colman was certain he had heard those words before — Pilgrim and Puritan, fisherman and farmer, Yankee and immigrant — yet Kennedy spoke them as a roll call of people he represented. He was unquestionably their superior. He had been summoned forth by America because he was its best. In the excellence of his temper and the power of his achievement, the old distinctions and factions were blurred and obliterated. Yankees and immigrants, eh? John Fitzgerald Kennedy had entered the sanctuary on Beacon Hill to absolve Boston. He was the new high priest.

"I have been guided by the standard John Winthrop set before his shipmates on the flagship *Arbella* three hundred and thirty-one years ago as they too faced the task of building a new government on a perilous frontier. 'We must always consider,' he said, 'that we shall be as a city upon a hill — the eyes of all people are upon us.' "

Brady could not help but think of Kennedy as a newer Michael Collins, as a newer Jim Curley. They were men who had harbored such sentiments about themselves, even if they had never had the gall to so proclaim them. The eyes of all people are upon us; it was an all too familiar assertion to Brady, and the arrogance of it was still stunning. Had Kennedy not heeded those ghosts? Didn't he know how futile were grandiloquent expectations like theirs and his? Kennedy's reputation was for more savvy than that. He knew his history, didn't he, and its humbling lesson? But then Colman Brady recognized Kennedy as the exact opposite of the old Irish patriots; while they idolized defeat, he idolized victory. But they were not so different. They were alike in their idolatry.

"For those to whom much is given much is required. And when at some future date the high court of history sits in judgment on each one of us — recording whether in our brief span of service we fulfilled our responsibilities to the state — our success or failure in whatever office we may hold will be measured by the answer to four questions."

Brady listened to the litany of his own questions. Does the future have to be like the past? Can we endure the accusations of our loved ones at how we've failed them? Who could stop us Irish if we learned loyalty to the living instead of to the dead? Was Kennedy trying to teach us that? Colman held himself still and attentive, hanging on his words. He reminded himself that this was Joe Kennedy's kid. They had bought the damn election in Cook County. A fortune had put him on that podium where he was twinkling like silver and spinning out silk webs; how adept he was at manipulating his hearers and their dreams of glory. It made Brady weary, more of the usual God-talk. These guys all thought they were preachers. The high court of history — shit!

But Brady could not do it; he could not dismiss or demean or deny what he was witnessing. His usual cynicism crumbled between his fingers, which would have touched Kennedy gladly then for his power. He discerned in him for the first time more than a hint of greatness. Maybe the future did not need to be like the past. Maybe the rough world could be shaped to the measure of a young man's hope. Nothing John Kennedy had said or been before could contravene what he was to Colman Brady at that moment — the herald of a victory he had dreamed of for years. Colman turned his head, hoping for his son's eye.

"First, were we truly men of courage — with the courage to stand up to one's enemies and the courage to stand up, when necessary, to one's associates, the courage to resist public pressure as well as private greed?"

Collins looked at his father and he guessed how moved he was. Collins would have given anything to have been Kennedy at that moment, not for the glory or the power or the achievement, but for the pleasure of having so moved his father. Collins understood implicitly that Kennedy represented the repudiation of his father's habitual cynicism. How he would have rejoiced to have been as much.

"Secondly, were we truly men of judgment — with perceptive judgment of the future as well as of the past, of our own mistakes as well as of the mistakes of others, with enough wisdom to know that we did not know and the candor to admit it?"

Collins knew that he had as much right to that sort of language as Kennedy did. If his own career had taken a surprising turn, Kennedy's had all the hardness and cruelty of fox-hunting in it. Collins Brady was studying his hands. They were hands that had done what was required of them. He had been biting the nails of both forefingers again. Soon he would be at work on his thumbs. It was his only overt weakness, nail-biting. And he always had it ninety percent under control.

"Third, were we truly men of integrity — men who never ran out on either the principles in which they believed or the men who believed in them — men who believed in us — men whom neither financial gain nor political ambition could ever divert from the fulfillment of our sacred trust?"

The roof of the place was listening to him. Collins lowered his eyes to his hands again, then raised them and let them drift over the heads of the legislators below. They were men who had heard such words before, but never so simply, so starkly. It was the simplicity of Kennedy's rhetoric that held them. It was the purity of his nerve they ached for; good looks and brain and no problem that could not be defeated by the right ideal. They were weathered pols who knew better, yet the great image of the man's innocence struck root in their hearts, and Collins Brady saw that in them.

"Finally, were we truly men of dedication, with our honor mortgaged to no single individual or group and compromised by no private obligation, but devoted to serving the public good and national interest?"

Colman Brady was watching Leverett Saltonstall for a sign that he was bored or resentful or contemptuous of Kennedy. But Saltonstall was as rapt as any harp. Was it the ancient patrician disguise? No, it was that Saltonstall could look at the new President and see, like Brady, an image of himself. That was Kennedy's secret and his joke. Out of that irony came his humor.

"Courage, judgment, integrity, dedication — these are the historic qualities of the Bay Colony and of the Bay State — the qualities which this state has consistently sent to Beacon Hill here in Boston and to Capitol Hill back in Washington. And these are the qualities which, with God's help, this son of Massachusetts hopes will characterize our government's conduct in the four stormy years that lie ahead. Humbly I ask His help in this undertaking, but aware that on earth His will is worked by men. I ask your help and your prayers as I embark on this new and solemn journey."

He was finished.

No one moved.

He stood before them like a shadow on a wall of plaster, with that much silence, that much mystery. John Kennedy sensed the awe in them; the knowledge that it was awe for him pressed on his shoulders and went into his back, making it stiffer yet. He could no more break that silence than they could. He could not walk out of it.

The legislators were coming solemnly to their feet and applauding the President-elect with a dignified restraint that was far greater tribute than the boyish exuberance with which they had greeted him before.

Colman rose, as did everyone in the balcony when Mrs. Kennedy did. While he applauded he turned toward Collins, who gave him a look of respect and affection. Colman looked past Collins and Janet and saw that there were tears up to the brim of Tony's eyes, and that surprised him. Tony was an aloof young man not given to an easy display of feeling. He was a loner. He had resources that he didn't get from his parents or share with them. He had steadfastly refused to choose between Janet and Collins, one at the expense of the other, and maintained a firm politeness in relation to both of them. It was as if he'd decided years before that if he could not belong to both he would not belong to either. Colman guessed that was the secret of his strength. Colman had kept an eye on the kid and knew there was something inexhaustible about him, something unfathomable. The kid was an object of fascination for Colman. And more. Colman suspected that Tony, for all his dark looks and Italian moods, was more like him than Collins was. That was why Colman was surprised to see the boy's eyes brimming in response to Kennedy, and why he was glad. The young should love Kennedy, he thought. But he couldn't reduce Tony's response to Kennedy to ingenuousness, any more than he could his own. Tony looked toward his grandfather, who winked.

The applause died abruptly when Kennedy stepped back and John McShane, Auxiliary Bishop of the Archdiocese of Boston, approached the podium. The bishop intended to take what they were all feeling and hand it back to them as a prayer, and that was what they wanted. Kennedy had as much as said it; he had all the applause he could use. What he needed now were prayers.

One of Cardinal Cushing's first acts after receiving the Red Hat from Pope John in 1958 had been to name John McShane an assistant bishop. There were three others, but they were all older men whose power was negligible and whose duties consisted of confirming children and consoling old folks. When Cushing could not make the State House ceremony, there was no doubt that McShane would take his place. He was forty-two years old, nearly bald, and just portly enough in his crimson robes to look like an ecclesiastic with a future.

He adjusted his red skullcap and coughed briskly. "Almighty God," he intoned, "we commend to Thee Thy servant John, on whom Thou hast so graciously bestowed gifts of wisdom, fortitude, and comeliness. Be with him as he embarks on his sacred journey and takes onto his shoulders the solemn weight of governance. Guide his mind. Enlighten his soul. Strengthen his heart as he leads us into the new frontier where we hope, through Your bounty, to find peace and harmony for all mankind. Graciously bestow upon the United States of America and all elected officials Your infinite blessings. And in particular upon this man, our son and brother and friend, our President. Be with him now and always, through Christ our Lord, who lives and reigns with Thee in the unity of the Holy Ghost now and forever, world without end. Amen."

Bishop McShane, having been moved nearly to tears by his prayer, turned toward Kennedy and opened his arms. It is the prerogative of bishops to hug people. Kennedy suffered McShane's embrace the way he would a Frenchman's pair of kisses.

Then the sergeant-at-arms, a dour figure in tails, struck his mace once on the floor, turned on his heel, and led the way up the right aisle. The governor, the bishop, the senate president, the speaker, and Kennedy filed off the podium. The legislators burst once more into applause, only now with their earlier exuberance.

The reception was held in the Doric Hall just inside the grand portico that overlooked the Boston Common.

"Hell of a speech, Colman, eh?" Jerry McBride, a man of about seventy who'd been a faithful crony of Curley's, had joined Colman Brady on the edge of the crowd. "Too bad the mayor wasn't around for this."

"The mayor hated Kennedy, Jer. You know that."

"Hell, that was Joe. Everybody hates Joe. This Jack is different, always has been. There weren't a dry eye in the place. Even the goddamn Republicans love the guy. Where's the booze, Colman?"

"I don't see any, Jer. Not likely to have it here."

"The hell! I never heard of such a thing!" McBride went off looking for a table with white linen on it and bottles. He would look in vain. The Kennedys wanted the reception to be brief. The President-elect had to fly to New York for a dinner at eight. The *Caroline* was already revving its engines at Logan.

"What do you think, Dad?" Collins asked.

"About the line?"

"Yes."

"I suppose we should."

"Tony'd like to meet him."

Kennedy was standing between his mother and his wife receiving the legislators. William Keegan, an aide, was standing a step back from him and whispering the names of those approaching.

When the Bradys drew near, Rose Kennedy stepped toward them. "Colman," she said warmly. He was a friend in a crowd of strangers.

"Hello, Rose. How's Joe?"

"Could be better," she said. Then she smiled. "Could be worse. He went ahead to Florida. I'm going down tomorrow."

"Give him my best, darling, would you?" Colman kissed her.

"He'll want to see you in Washington. We're staying at the Sheraton Park starting a week from today. Here, Jack, say hello to Colman."

"Hello, Colman. Good to see you here."

"Mr. President." Colman bowed slightly, then grinned. The title would be a bit funny for only a little while longer.

"And the whole clan," Kennedy said. He reached out to Janet and Collins.

"It was a stunning speech, Jack," Collins said.

"Thanks, Collins. By the way, did Keegan here talk to you?"

"No."

"I was hoping you could stop by Arthur Schlesinger's house tonight. I won't be there, but Bobby is. There's something we want to talk to you about."

"Well, really, we were going out . . ."

"Come on, Brady! This is your country calling!"

"Funny, I thought it was you." Collins paused to let Kennedy laugh, then said, "Say hello to my son, Mr. President. You've met Tony."

"Sure!" Kennedy took Tony's hand in both of his. "We talked at Milton, right?"

"Yes, sir."

"This is your last year, right?"

"Yes, sir."

"What next?"

"I've applied to Harvard, Mr. President. I hope to go there."

"Good as done. If they give you any trouble you call me up. I'm an Overseer now, you know." Kennedy turned to Colman. "The only way one of us could get on the board was to get elected President. That's the real reason I ran."

"Now you should invite the Jesuits in to run the place."

"Good idea, Colman. I was over there today going over the students' grades with President Pusey." Kennedy drew Janet away from Rose and kissed her on the lips. "Jackie, look who's here."

Jacqueline greeted Janet warmly. They were friends.

"When are you coming down?" Jacqueline asked.

"The night before the ball, the eighteenth."

"Come to Georgetown. We'll be up late. We'd love to see you when it's not so rushed."

The President-elect said to Tony, "And you, son, I want you in Washington next summer working for me."

"Yes, sir. I'd be honored."

After a flurry of kisses, the Bradys moved off and the Kennedys greeted the next well-wishers.

"What was that all about?" Janet asked Collins.

"I don't know."

Her look said, "I don't believe you."

"Honestly, I don't."

"He's got a job for you, clearly," Colman said. "Bobby's recruiting at Schlesinger's."

"Are you going?" Janet asked.

Collins looked at Colman. Colman showed him nothing.

"I don't know," Collins said.

"Well," Janet said softly, "when you've decided, do let me know, darling, won't you? I'm the one who'll have to arrange things, aren't I?" Janet looked toward her son. "Tony, will you walk me home, please?"

"Certainly, Mother," Tony said, but he wasn't able to disguise his disappointment. He wasn't ready to leave. He was feeling surprised and excited that his family should have been received so warmly by Kennedy. That his father could be offered a job in Washington filled him with anticipation and pride, neither of which he could express because his habitual response to his father was one of polite detachment. He did not understand his mother's frostiness just then. He wanted to say, "Good for you, Dad," but nothing in their manner with each other made such an expression possible.

Before Tony and Janet left, Bishop McShane joined them.

Janet Brady would not think of rendering herself vulnerable to him, of all people, by an act of discourtesy. She would wait the seemly few minutes before departing.

"Well," the bishop said, "the gang's all here." There was nothing in his greeting to show his resentment. The gang was not all there. The place his mother should have occupied had been taken by Tony. Maeve had insisted that the boy go, but McShane knew that Collins and Janet had again succeeded in making her feel unwelcome.

"Hello, Jack. That was a wonderful prayer."

"Thank you, Colman. Hello, Micko."

Janet offered him her cheek; he pecked it.

"And Tony!" the bishop proclaimed. "Aren't you the grown-up today!"

The boy looked spiffing in his blue suit, and he knew it. "Hello, bishop." Tony offered his hand, but ignored the bishop's ring. He was well aware of the underlying current between his father's cousin and his mother, and he responded to it with an exquisite aloofness. He habitually showed the bishop a courtesy that was every bit as icy as his mother's. The bishop habitually treated him like a child, but in fact he was mystified by the boy, who was unlike any other he'd known.

"How's the cardinal?" Collins asked.

"Not so good. The doctor says if he takes it easy all week he might be up to the trip to Washington. He doesn't want to miss the inauguration, you can bet on that. So, for once, he's following orders."

"Will you do it if he can't?" Collins asked.

"Heavens no. They'd get Spellman, or O'Boyle. Has to be a big shot."

"Your turn'll come later, Jack," Colman said. "How about joining us for dinner?"

"You fellows go ahead," Janet said. "I'm going home." She slid her arm into Tony's. The men knew better than to invite a change of mind or to ask a reason for her leaving.

"Where'll we go?" Colman asked.

"How about the Parker House?" Collins said.

"Christ, the same old place! How about something different? The Union Club, now that Jack Kennedy has cracked the barrier!"

The President-elect had lunched at the Union Club on Park Street the day before. It had been a highly publicized event since, as far as was known, he was the first Irish Catholic to eat in the fifth-floor dining room since it had served as the maids' quarters in the nineteenth-century town houses of the Lawrences and the Lowells.

The bishop flinched when Colman said, "Christ!"

"How about the Ritz?" Bishop McShane said.

Colman and Janet did not snag each other with their eyes at the mention of the Ritz.

"Sure," Colman said. "The Ritz, why not?"

Janet ushered Tony away from them. He looked back and gave them one of his strange looks.

The three men watched them go.

There was a commotion from the center of the hall as the Kennedys made for the rear exit. Their cream-colored Lincoln was waiting for them under the arch at the top of Mt. Vernon Street.

William Keegan walked quickly up to Collins Brady. "The President asked me to repeat his request, Mr. Brady. Robert Kennedy will be expecting you at nine sharp."

"Thank you, Mr. Keegan."

But Keegan waited for him to say he would report as requested.

Brady waited him out.

Keegan had the derived arrogance for which Kennedy's aides were already famous. They basked in their own power, but seemed able to experience its pleasures only by blasting people with curtness.

"What shall I tell the President, Mr. Brady?"

"You tell him good luck and God bless."

The hell with this guy, Keegan thought. He turned and walked away, confident that Brady would not make the team. Suddenly he began to run when it occurred to him that the cream limousine might not wait.

"Who is he, anyway?" Colman asked.

"Harvard whiz kid. Irish Mafia. About like I was fifteen years ago. Only all I had backing me was Daniel Boone. He has God."

"I wouldn't say that, Micko," McShane said.

"That's your job, Jack — *not* to say what the rest of us think. Are we going to the Ritz, or what?"

Colman and his nephew looked at each other a bit helplessly. When the mood was on Collins there was nothing to be done. The mood was always on him in Janet's bitter wake.

"If we go to the Ritz," Colman said, "you'll never make your meeting."

"Do you think I ought to go?"

"I never saw the point in offending friends without a damn good reason."

"But I have to offend them at some point. You know what they want."

"Bobby wants you with him at Justice, I presume."

"I presume so, too."

"Well, why don't you take it?" the bishop said. "It'd be an honor to all of us."

"Because I just replaced Harvey Brace as chief counsel for the corporation and I'm chairman of the board for two of the companies. Any other questions?"

"Colman got along without you before."

"This isn't the time or place, fellows," Colman said. "What the hell, let's go to the Parker House."

"I have to change from these robes. Give me a minute."

"There's a phone booth in the basement, Superman," Collins said.

The bishop laughed despite himself and said with mock indignation, "Very funny! No respect in this family at all!" Then he went off, shaking his head.

"Micko, don't get into it with him. You don't owe him any justifications. And don't get into it with the Kennedy people, either."

"What'll I say?"

"Just say 'No.' Can't you say a firm, polite 'No'? You should have mastered that one years ago."

"That's what I get for never saying 'No' to you."

"That's right, blame it on me. You want me to go with you and hold your hand?"

"I get the point."

"I hope you do. You've got the most powerful men in the world doing somersaults in front of you. Enjoy it! Goddamn it, use it! Let them think the hook is still in your mouth. Let them think they can still get you. Give them reasons to keep wooing you. It's always nice to be wooed, and it can be damn useful also."

"That depends on what they're wooing you for."

"Any ideas?"

"You kidding? Not Civil Rights."

[504]

"Well, you'll find out soon enough."

Arthur Schlesinger's house was a rambling three-story Victorian on the tract of semiwooded land abutting Harvard property near the Divinity School. When Collins Brady drove his black Chrysler into the driveway at five past nine, two men swept out of the shadows at him.

"Good evening, sir."

"Hello."

"Mr. Brady?"

"Yes."

"This way, please."

Robert Kennedy was sitting alone in Schlesinger's study. He was wearing a white shirt with its collar open and no tie and the sort of shapeless brown cardigan that Perry Como had pioneered and George Gobel made ludicrous and Arnold Palmer glamorized. When Brady was shown in, Kennedy was up and waiting for him, though he'd obviously been sitting in the stuffed leather chair where the floor was covered with loose papers and stacked reports.

"Collins, good to see you."

"Sorry I'm late, Bob."

"What are you talking about? You're right on time. I've been dealing with professors all day, damn guys operate on sundials. Not in D.C. they won't, though. Sit down."

"Thanks. You've been seeing people?"

"Interviewing the shit out of Cambridge. I think I've talked to everybody but Pusey's houseboy. He's probably next." Kennedy grinned and leaned back in the chair, pushing his hair up from his forehead. "It's good to see a friend."

Collins nodded, but thought it a strange comment. He barely knew Bob Kennedy. They had been in Washington and on the Hill at the same time, both counsels for Senate committees, but Kennedy had been with Joe McCarthy while Brady was with Kefauver. In those days Bob Kennedy had been a loud and abrasive devotee of the theory that the Reds were the number one internal threat to America. He'd seen the anticrime effort in Congress as competition to be beaten back. But that had changed. Just before McCarthy's disgrace, Kennedy had landed a job with the new McClellan Labor Rackets Committee, where he'd made a name for himself as the handsome scourge of corrupt union officials. That job had given him a new respect for the threat mobsters posed and, Collins supposed, a belated appreciation for what they'd been trying to do with Kefauver years before.

"Do you know what Orville Freeman said yesterday?" Kennedy asked.

"Ed Newman or somebody asked him why he was picked for the Cabinet. He said, 'Probably because Harvard doesn't have a school of agriculture.' "

Laughing, both men could smell their youth in the harmless chauvinism of fellow alumni.

"So it's true, eh?"

"What, that we're looting Harvard? Shit, yes. MIT too. Jerry Wiesner's on board. Signed him up today. The best fifty men in the world, Collins, live within three miles of this chair. And they're coming to Washington."

"You make it sound like Athens."

"Maybe. But . . ." — Kennedy leaned forward — ". . . it's Sparta I want to talk to you about."

"You lost me."

"We need your help. Are you open?"

"To tell you the truth, Bob, not very. I couldn't budge Janet out of Boston, and I like what I'm doing, a lot."

"What *are* you doing?"

"Monument. My father."

"I know, but what?"

"Legal department, I run it. I do the troubleshooting. I'm director of a couple of our leaky vessels."

Kennedy stared at him over the mound his hands made at his chin.

"You look like you have another question or two, Bob."

"I do."

"What?"

"I'm not sure, frankly, that I should pursue it."

"Feel free."

"All right." Kennedy stood abruptly and picked up the telephone, cradle and all, and carried it to the bookcase, tugging at the cord several times. He put the phone down in front of the speaker of a large Philco radio, which he snapped on. The radio crackled. Kennedy twirled the dial until he found a station that was playing a mad rendition of "Lullaby of Birdland."

"Erroll Garner," Kennedy said, resuming his seat. "This is Norman O'Connor's show."

"Dial 'M' for Music."

"Right."

"But why?"

"Did you see that movie, *Dial 'M' for Murder?*"

Collins did not answer him.

"You know why."

Collins nodded, barely. The telephone could be bugged. What in hell was happening?

"Why did you quit, Collins?"

"The BIR?"

"The IRS, as we know it now."

"That's a long time ago, Bob. Why do you ask?"

"Because . . ." — Kennedy picked up a folder — ". . . it's the last thing we have on you in our file. We have files on everybody whose help we want."

"I assumed you would."

"Well, it seems a little strange, how you resigned. It was very abrupt, wasn't it? And at the outset of a major new investigation."

"Frankly, I don't recall."

"You don't recall?" Kennedy's retort had the exact inflection of a Senate committee interrogator.

Collins realized he'd invited it with his measly dodge. "The point is that my father needed me very much just then. He'd been pressing me to join him and I did. It was that simple."

"But why 'just then'?"

"I'd have to get into the dynamics of the business to make you understand."

"Go ahead."

"Do you know what 'critical mass' is?"

"Sure. Fission. Neutron splits atom, which sends out neutron, which splits atom, etcetera, until critical mass and the release of power, near-infinite power."

"Very good."

"Harvard."

"The business equivalent to that has been happening in Monument. There's a critical mass to money. At a certain point it has its own power, its own energy. You have to ride it. Six or seven years ago Monument stopped being a big insurance company with holdings in several dozen companies and outright ownership of a few, and it became something else, something new."

"Conglomerate."

"That's a word they're using, yes. And, as you know, the basis in law for the conglomerate phenomenon is Kefauver-Cellar, 1952, and the antitrust package that followed. Damn complicated stuff, Bob. It happens I was in on some of the drafting when I worked for Estes. I wound up an inadvertent expert in the area, and my old man badly needed what I knew just then in fifty-four. The business took off and it could have come apart. None of his people knew what was legal expansion and what was monopolistic. Frankly, they didn't know exactly where the loopholes were, and, since I had helped put them in, I did. It would have been an act of disloyalty on my part not to go to work for the old man."

"You had just moved the Strike Force here from Newark."

"Jersey City, actually."

"You had just opened the book on Gennaro Anselmo."

Erroll Garner was sliding through a satiny version of "Teach Me Tonight."

"Do you recall that?" There was the barest sarcasm in Kennedy's voice. He turned pages in the folder, but absently.

"Of course."

"The investigation died when you quit."

"It was all going down the drain, anyway. Halley quit too."

"That was later. There were tax indictments brought against mob leaders in every section of the country except New England."

"There was less going on here."

Kennedy looked up from his folder. "Anselmo nets a hundred million a year. Balestrione twice that. And you knew it. It's all in the files of your own squad."

"Not net; gross. But it doesn't matter. We couldn't get to them."

"Well, the President thinks it's time we did. The first priority of my office is going to be the mob. That's why I wanted to talk to you tonight. I thought you might like a chance to finish what you started."

"I'm not interested in going to Washington, Bob. That's absolute."

"You won't have to."

"You're not offering me U.S. Attorney for Boston?"

"No."

"What else is there?"

"I'm not offering you a government job. Not a public one, anyway. We offered you a job eight years ago." Kennedy let the silence say, *You refused us and we don't forget.*

"You've lost me."

"I want you to be my eyes and ears inside Anselmo's operation." Kennedy grinned.

"What the hell are you talking about?"

"Why did you go to Switzerland?"

"What?"

"Who's fronting for Anselmo?"

"What are you asking me, Bob?"

"I'm not asking you anything. I'm telling you. We know, Brady. We know the whole story, what Monument is, what your father is, what you are."

Collins sat still. Any movement, he thought, would bring down the remains of his composure.

"We want a bust and soon. We want a couple of big game trophies for the White House wall. I want Anselmo and Balestrione."

"You don't want much, do you?"

"Not considering what we already have. You."

"How'd you put it together?"

"Are you kidding? Your father pardoned Anselmo, for Christ's sake. Dozens of people noticed that at the time, and some of them don't forget. He's just lucky the fucking Yankee DA's they've had in this state can't see the shit for stepping in it. My father's had your father's number for years."

"They're not so different, Bob."

"My father never stowed his balls in a wop's pocket. They're *very* different. You're just lucky we're the ones who know."

"Your loyalty to the clan is very touching."

Kennedy's right arm shot out and his forefinger stabbed toward Brady. "You're goddamned right it is! I could have you in Danbury right now, *and* your father. Don't forget that!"

"But what's a pair of jailbird micks, right? You want your wops, the big ones."

"That's right."

"What about Sam Giancana? Why don't you go after him? You've got the inside on his mob, too."

"Fuck you, Brady."

"Fuck yourself. Don't you come on with me like I've a corner on this shit. You're up to your ears in it too, with Joe and Jack both. I could have puked at his speech."

"You puke your heart out, friend. That won't change things. There's a very important difference between you and me."

"Oh really? What?"

"I'm the Attorney General. I can throw your ass in jail."

"Go ahead."

Kennedy took a page out of the folder and handed it to Brady. "Read it."

Collins read it. "This is an indictment."

"That's right. Of one Colman Brady. The blank spaces are for the exact sums, which we wouldn't know until the audit was complete. We'd fill them in before we presented it to the grand jury. That's about a hundred and twenty years' worth of criminal fraud and tax evasion. And those are just the federal charges. I'm prepared to press every one to the full, and then tip off the locals to see what they dig up."

"Unless I become your sneak."

"You figured it out."

"And what happens to this?"

"We have no need to slam your father or Monument or you. And we won't. Frankly, I could care less about it, but my parents would hate it if something tragic like that happened to Colman. I think we should try to make our parents' last days as blissful as possible. Don't you?"

"Yes."

"I thought so. We have an agreement?"

"But what do you want me to do?"

"For now, insinuate yourself into Anselmo's operation. I assume you have little direct contact with it."

"Almost none."

"Create some."

"How? They're not the K. of C., you know."

"Through your father, obviously. He and Anselmo are old friends, or colleagues at least. Take advantage of that. And you know the rules of evidence as well as I do. Start collecting. I'll have some spook shit for you eventually, microfilm and bugs, when the time is right."

"Bugs!" Collins looked at the telephone. Erroll Garner was smothering it with "Misty." "You can't take this to court!"

"Of course not. It's between us. No one will know but you and me and the man I'm putting on it. I swear."

"But without a court order it's not legal."

"Fuck legal."

"That's right. I forgot." Brady stood up. "Who are you putting on it?"

"Remember Deke Thomas?"

"Yes. We were friends. You have to tell him everything?"

"He already knows."

"Christ." Brady started to leave.

Kennedy dropped the folder on his pile, but remained seated. "Do you know what greatness is, Collins?"

"No, Bob. What?"

"The capacity to get small men to do big things. We have that greatness."

"You are smug bastards. Do you know that?"

"Just do your big thing for us."

"Not for you."

"For whomever. Just do it."

"It's bigger than you think. You don't know these guys."

"But I know you. You went to Harvard."

❧ 2 ❧

POPE JOHN XXIII sat in the dark red velvet throne on a gold dais beneath the high baldachin at the head of the Hall of Benedictions. The Sistine Choir was making its way through *Veni, Creator Spiritus*. It was the feast of St. Paul, January 25, 1961, and the event was John's fourth consistory, the ecclesiastical senate to which he announced the names of new cardinals. As the Pope peered out over the stately gathering of his crimson-robed princes, only the brilliance of television lights and a camera crane at the far end of the hall suggested that the scene was not a Renaissance painting.

One prelate who was absent was Richard Cardinal Cushing of Boston. He had been excused because of the inauguration of the new American President. He hadn't felt much like going, anyway. His asthma was killing him.

"Turn that damn thing down, Jack. I hate that song."

Bishop McShane crossed from his chair to the television and adjusted the volumn down.

"His Holiness will be speaking soon," McShane said.

"We can turn it up again, can't we?" Cushing's mood was less morose than his gruffness indicated, and McShane knew it. "Though what the hell's the point? It's all in Latin, anyway."

His complaint was part of his simple Irish prelate pose, and McShane took it for granted and played into it.

"The commentator will translate."

"Fulton Sheen, that pretty boy! He should of been a violin player, that fellow. Fix us a drink, Jack, would you?"

McShane looked sharply at the cardinal. It was only eight-thirty in the morning. The consistory, broadcast live on the new Telstar satellite, had preempted the Today Show.

"What would you like, Your Eminence?"

"Bourbon."

McShane went into the small pantry off the cardinal's sitting room. He poured the drink, bourbon and water, a lot of ice. He made it very light.

"Thanks, Jack."

"This won't be over by nine."

"So what's the diff?"

"You have the major superiors coming in."

"Oh God, I should have went to Rome. I should be there, then they'd leave me alone. I'm staying right here until I hear Larry's name. How do you say 'Larry' in Latin?"

"*Laurentius.*"

Lawrence Sheehan, Archbishop of Baltimore, was one of those whom the Pope was about to name to the College of Cardinals.

Cushing spilled a few drops of his drink on his crumpled white shirt. A collarless shirt, it was the sort that all men had worn once; now only clergy wore them, openly only in private. The cardinal's legs were up on a leather hassock. His black trousers were baggy and shiny.

"I wonder how many he'll add this time?" Cushing said. "Last time it was what, thirty?"

"Thirty-five."

"Used to be the most exclusive club in the world, now everybody's a cardinal."

"You sound like one of the old-guard Italians."

"I'm not complaining. Hell, Pius — that dingaling — would never of given me my hat. Thank God for Pope John."

"He loves you, Cardinal."

"I know it. I should of went. On the other hand, like Groucho says, who'd want to belong to a club that would admit people like me?"

"Speculation is that there'll be two non-Italians for every Italian this time."

"I hope so, Jack. Give the Church back to the world. Too many damn Italians — that's the trouble with Rome. Of course, you — you'll live to see the miracle."

"What miracle?"

"A non-Italian Pope. That's the point of revamping the college, isn't it? Tilt the majority the other way. Get Bea in there. Or Tisserant. A German fellow, or a Frenchman."

"Tisserant's too old."

"Hell, you might even see an American get it."

Cushing turned in his chair toward McShane, raised his drink to him and proclaimed, "Hell, Bishop, you might even *be* it!"

"What?"

"Pope! Pope Jack the First!"

Was Cushing drunk? Had he been at the juice before Mass?

Cushing sensed that he'd embarrassed McShane and had the thought that the guy took himself too seriously. His one real flaw. By God, the fellow probably *could* see himself as Pope.

"Not likely, Your Eminence."

"You never know these days. Look at those blacks from Africa in the Hall there. Think they ever thought they'd be cardinals? It's a new ballgame. How old are you?"

"Forty-two."

"Roncalli was seventy-seven when they elected him. That gives you thirty-five years, Jack."

McShane blushed. He had missed entirely the mischievous aspect to Cushing's words.

"A lot can happen in thirty-five years, Jack."

"Maybe they'll elect you."

"Yeah. Head bottle-washer. What are they saying?"

McShane turned the volume up.

Pope John had put on his old-fashioned gold spectacles and was reading an address. He gestured with his free right hand, emphasizing points in rhythm, but the precise Latin phrases were lost below the droning whisper of the translator.

"Venerable Fathers, the latest and humble successor to the Prince of the Apostles, in order to assist once again the magisterium of the Church in order that this magisterium, taking into account the errors, the requirements, and the opportunities of our time, might be presented in exceptional form to all men throughout the world . . ."

"That's some sentence, eh, Your Eminence?"

"Quiet, Jack. What's he saying?" Cushing had dropped his feet to the floor and was hunched over his bony knees. His glass was empty.

The television camera had drawn in close on the Pope. His face, an arrangement of pink curves, soft angles and jowls, was radiant. He read his statement as if he knew it for the surprise it would be.

"The Church must always take note of the new conditions and new ways of life introduced into the modern world which have opened new avenues and offered new challenges to the Catholic apostolate."

"You know what he's leading up to, Jack?!"

Cushing's excitement was palpable. He held his hand up to cut off the conversation he had begun himself.

The effect of the two voices intermingled — the soft, uninflected voice of the announcer and the high-pitched, electric voice of the Pope — was to force attention.

It was impossible not to lean toward the television and listen closely. One could imagine the cardinals, their miters atilt, leaning toward the Pope in the hall of the consistory.

"Unfortunately, the entire Christian family has not yet fully attained unity in truth. The Catholic Church, therefore, considers it her duty to work actively toward the fulfillment of the great mystery of that unity which Jesus invoked with fervent prayer to His heavenly Father on the eve of His sacrifice. The Church exults greatly at seeing that invocation extended even among those who are outside her fold."

"You don't think he's . . ."

"Quiet!" Cushing barked.

"Venerable brothers, our voice is directed to you and through you to the world, that we might summon the Church's best energies to prepare and consolidate the path toward that unity of mankind which is required as a necessary foundation in order that the earthly city may be brought to resemble that heavenly city where truth reigns, charity is law, and whose extent is eternity. Sanctity and moral confusion exist side by side in villages, cities, and nations throughout the world. In order to proclaim the truth and reanimate the faith of Christians, we have, after prayerful deliberations and with full knowledge of our solemn responsibility, decided to call a council of the Universal Church."

"*Sì! Sì!*" Cushing said, jumping to his feet. "*Un concilio!*"

McShane thought Cushing was going to embrace the television. He loved to portray himself as old, bumbling, and ignorant, yet he spoke Italian fluently, and the words had burst from him.

"I never thought he'd do it! Oh, I should of went! I should of went!"

"Listen, Your Eminence! Listen!"

". . . to meet in solemn assembly beginning the Feast of Saint Teresa in the year of our Lord nineteen sixty-two."

"St. Teresa," Cushing said. "When the hell is that?"

"October thirteen."

"My God! He really did it! They said he'd never do it. Alfieri must be pissing!"

Cardinal Alfieri, secretary of the Congregation of the Holy Office, had tried to dampen Pope John's enthusiasm for a worldwide council — the Church had not had one in a hundred years — by urging him to call a synod of the Italian Church. The Pope had done so, but the synod had not discouraged him. For obvious reasons, the established Italian bureaucrats of the Church looked with alarm on the prospect of all the bishops of the Church assembling to debate political and theological questions. The bishops in assembly could do anything and probably would. The Vatican inner circle who had enormous power to lose if the council altered Church structures included Alfieri, Archbishop Enrico Belli, the papal master of ceremonies, Cardinal Pietro Croce, of the Congregation for Seminaries, Cardinal Emilio Carducci, the secretary of the Consistorial Congregation, and Cardinal Ruggero Borella, Assessor of the Holy Office.

"Good for good Pope John! I guess we go to Rome after all, Jack!"

In response to a question put by Frank McGee, Fulton Sheen was saying, "There have only been twenty ecumenical councils in the entire history of the Church. This is truly momentous, Frank, truly momentous. A council is a great event."

"But what's it for, Bishop?"

"The Pope's favorite word, Frank, is *aggiornamento,* which means bringing things up to date."

"But does the council intend to change the Church or to change the world?"

"Both, Frank, both."

"Turn that guy off, Jack," Cushing said. "Gets on my nerves. We got to watch for when he names the new cardinals."

"It's nine o'clock, Your Eminence."

"Oh damn, my nuns."

"I'm afraid so."

"How about you take it for me, Jack? Tell them I'm sick. Why'd what's-his-name schedule it for now anyway?"

"I'll be glad to take it for you, Cardinal." McShane stood. Cushing looked up at him and it seemed to McShane a forlorn expression moved quickly across his face. The man *was* sick. He hadn't been able to sleep since returning from Washington. He looked exhausted and haggard, and he'd been drinking too much, far too much.

"Can I do anything else for you before I go?" McShane asked. He felt his great affection for Cushing flowing in.

"Yeah, Jack, would you get me another drink? There's a sport. And turn up the set a bit. Maybe Uncle Fultie is off."

McShane fixed the drink, feeling guilty as he did so.

"Anything else, Cardinal?"

Cushing's eyes were full. He had just seen Larry Sheehan on the screen and remembered the day of his own elevation. "Aw, Jack, damn me, I should of went! I could of been there to hear him call the council!"

"But now you'll go to the council itself."

"You too, the both of us. It'll be great!"

"Sure will, Cardinal. I'll see you later."

McShane met with the nineteen major superiors of women's orders of the archdiocese for an hour in the chancery library. The nuns were worried about overcrowding in the classrooms. The parochial school system was nearly bursting, and the nuns wanted more schools. Cushing had already built two hundred and twelve in ten years. It seemed to McShane that pastors spawned churches and nuns spawned schools the way the Catholic people spawned the kids. He assured the sisters that the cardinal was about to launch a new building drive. And then he poured tea for them himself.

Then he went into his office, closed the door, and made a phone call.

"Colman? It's Jack."

"Why, Your Excellency! Top of the morning to you!"

"And to you. Did you hear the news?"

"News?"

"There's to be a council."

"Of which tribe?"

"Don't josh. Pope John just called an ecumenical council this morning. It was on television. There's going to be a council."

"Is that good or bad?"

"Depends on who you are. No doubt a matter of indifference to most. For Roman *curiales, aggiornamento* is a disaster. For Americans, a great opportunity to be vindicated. The American Catholic Church will come of age finally, out of the shadows. John Courtney Murray has been hoping for a council for years, and Gus Weigel."

"And you?"

"That's what I want to talk to you about. Can I see you?"

"Sure, when?"

"As soon as possible."

"Sounds like you've something in mind."

"Your friend in Rome."

"Who, Borella?"

"Yes. Ruggero Cardinal Borella. I do have something in mind."

"Come on over. We'll have an early lunch. You like Chinese?"

The bishop did not like Chinese, so they walked to Jake Wirth's on Stuart Street. It was a raw blustery day and, though it was not snowing, the sidewalks were caked with frozen slush. By the time they arrived at the restaurant they were both chilled. Colman wore no hat, as he hadn't for years, even before John Kennedy.

"*Cuius Quique*," the carved legend over the old bar read. Wirth's was a nineteenth-century saloon — now a picturesque lunchroom featuring plain German food — that had survived everything.

"To each his own," Colman said, raising a mug of the special dark beer. Bishop McShane, who did not drink in public, sipped his coffee.

"How's Mother?" McShane asked.

"Not so fine," Colman said. "When are you coming over?"

"I was over Sunday."

"She feels neglected, you know. You're busy, but . . ."

"I'll be over Sunday. I haven't missed a Sunday in years. You know that. Is that neglect?"

"That's just how she feels. It's the medicine that drags her down."

"I'll be over. Tell her I'll be over."

They watched their drinks.

The waiter came, a short old man with slick gray hair. He wore a long white apron beneath his waistcoat. He took their orders and left.

"Now," Colman said, "what's this about Monsignor Borella?"

"He's a cardinal now, Colman, and a very powerful one."

"I still think of him as 'Monsignor.' "

"Have you had any contact with him lately?"

"I got a Christmas card. I sent him a greeting myself." Colman took a deep draft of his beer. He was trying to analyze the quality of his nephew's nervousness. "Why?"

"The council. Borella is the Assessor of the Holy Office."

"So?"

"The budget for all of the council preparations has to go through him, and he'll be in the middle of the administration of all the commissions."

Colman considered what the young bishop was saying.

"Let me explain something to you, dear uncle." McShane smiled a bit condescendingly. "Every bishop in the world will be at the council. Any idea how many that is?"

"None."

"Twenty-seven hundred, give or take a few dozen auxiliaries. In that crowd of cardinals, archbishops, and ordinaries, auxiliary bishops like myself will count for nothing. Each bishop will be assigned to a particular area of responsibility. The likes of me will be put in charge of drafting a detailed, cubit-by-cubit description of Noah's ark. I don't want to waste my time on ecclesiastical inconsequence, Colman."

"I don't blame you. What do you want?"

"A position of importance and influence, as much of both as I can get."

"Surely, Cushing pulls some weight . . ."

"Very little. You'd be amazed. He has the same simple touch of Pope John, the same sort of peasant style. But they can ignore Cush; he's not Pope. John loves him like a brother. The rest write him off, and he knows it. He won't dent the council. I need another *patrono.*"

"Borella."

"Yes. If you can interest him in me."

"What can he do for you?"

"Get me appointed secretary to the Commission on Bishops and the Government of Diocese."

"That sounds pretty dull."

"It will be dull. The glamour will be with the reform of the liturgy and the Christian unity stuff, but Government is where the real battles will be fought. That's where the power center will be, and where critical decisions will be made, and I want to be there."

"You've given this some thought, and not just since this morning."

"I have. Ever since speculation started that John might do it I've been asking myself two questions. How can I be most useful to the council?"

Colman raised a finger. "And how can the council be most useful to you?"

"Right."

"Ask not what your conciliar commission can do for you . . ."

"There's no shame in asserting oneself. I intend to help fate along if I can. I want to be at the right place at the right time."

"So you can do the right thing." Now it was Colman's turn to condescend a bit.

"Exactly." McShane was telling the truth.

The waiter delivered their plates like a blackjack dealer his hits and left. Colman broke a piece of bread and buttered it.

"You should understand something about my relationship with Cardinal Borella, Jack."

"I'm interested."

"He's a political man."

"Of course. Nothing wrong with that."

"He arranged that dispensation for Micko's wedding for two reasons. One, it was commonsensical to do so. There were no good reasons not to."

McShane worked at his food. He did not want to hear what his uncle was going to tell him.

"And two," Colman said, "money."

The bishop felt a rush of guilt. It was wrong, what he was thinking. He had come to his uncle to ask him to use his influence to get him a position of significance at the council. The council was what mattered to him. He firmly believed that the Holy Spirit had inspired John to call the council to prepare the Church to face the great crises of modern life. A certain lethargy, a turpitude, had crept into the lives of Catholics. McShane believed that the Church had moved too slowly in facing up to the challenges posed by the loss of moral values and old certainties, and people were increasingly confused and indifferent to the faith. The business of the council was going to be nothing less than a new Pentecost to inspire confidence and zeal in the laity and in theologians and bishops and cardinals and the Pope himself. McShane wanted to be part of it, a significant part of it. But speaking of the loss of moral values, here he was listening to his uncle talking about bribing a member of the Holy Office.

McShane was not naïve. He knew that the normal transactions of the Church — whether a baptism or a Mass or a dispensation — involved offerings and stipends. But there was all the difference in the world between the payment of such modest sums and the outright bribery of officials. McShane had tried to ignore his assessment of his uncle's relationship with Borella, but now he was feeling his great qualm because he knew and could not ignore it. He was prepared, even, to benefit from it.

"A lot of money," Colman said.

"I guessed as much," the bishop said. "It was a rare dispensation, hard to get."

"Borella's a very influential fellow." Brady paused. "And he's still mindful of our family."

"He is? Why?"

Colman shrugged. "Because I had a feeling you and I would be having this conversation someday. I've been saving Borella up for you, Jack." Colman leaned forward and gave his nephew a weighty look. "You're not just thinking about the council, Jack."

"I am, Colman. The council is what is on my mind. It's going to make a great difference for the Church, a difference for the good. Most bishops don't appreciate how necessary it is, but I do. That's why I don't want to be shunted off to a side altar somewhere."

Colman nodded. "I agree with you. Do you know why? Because *you* could make a great difference for the good, Jack. That's what I think. And not just at the council." Colman put his spoon down and touched his napkin to his lips. "May I speak boldly?" He paused. "You're forty-two. You have the inside track on Cushing's chair. He's a sick man. In three years, maybe five, he'll be replaced. I'd like to see him replaced by you. You'd have the Red Hat by the time you're fifty. Boston is one of the largest archdioceses in the world, right?"

"The second largest."

"Right. And I know that Cushing sends more money to the Peter's Pence than anyone anywhere. Cush doesn't want the power, Jack. If he did he could be running Rome."

"If he wanted the power he wouldn't be Cushing."

"No," Colman said, "I suppose not."

McShane had to overcome a shortness of breath to say to his uncle, "You don't seem to be through telling me the future. So I'm the cardinal archbishop of Boston at fifty. Then what?"

"Depends." Colman was being as low-key as he could be. He was having outlandish thoughts, but not for the first time. Once he had had them about his own career.

"Depends on what?" McShane was troubled. His uncle was speaking with a certainty that seemed wrong somehow, but it was what made McShane desperate to hear him out.

"On two things. The kinds of alliances you can make at this council. And, two, it depends on getting a solid non-Italian majority in the College of Cardinals. I'm talking about you becoming Pope."

Bishop McShane did not speak for a moment.

Colman sat there looking grave, as if that proved he was serious.

"I know you are," the bishop said finally. He was stunned by the scope of his uncle's ambition — ambition for him. He was trying to ignore a feeling that this entire conversation was wrong.

"Obviously," Colman went on. "I'm not talking about succeeding John. He's how old?"

"Eighty."

"He'll go before Cushing. And then one of those Italians will get in, right?"

"No doubt. The club members. They're all old men, though." McShane was catching on. Time. Time was on the side of youth. "You're on to something, Colman. The next pope will reign for ten years, fifteen at the outside."

"You'll be sixty something."

McShane calculated. "Sixty-five. Just old enough to be venerable."

"Like I am." They smiled at each other.

McShane assessed his uncle openly. There was a patience about him which seemed appropriate to what they were talking about. McShane had never been able to visualize a future for himself beyond what he was — Cushing's favored assistant. That had been ambition enough until the council was called. Suddenly the range of his hopes had broadened considerably, and his uncle had pressed them so much further still as to make them nearly unthinkable. But his uncle spoke about the future like a Greek who knew where his planets were. That was what compelled McShane.

That was what made Brady faintly uneasy about what he was doing. He knew damn well that the certitude that simplifies everything to smooth surfaces can be misleading and dangerous. One can slip on such surfaces. Brady had. Was he setting up his nephew for some dreadful fall? Where was this sudden urgent energy about Jack's future coming from? And wasn't it finally ridiculous? Pope? But what surprised Colman was how reasonable he'd made such an ambition seem.

[520]

McShane shook his head. "I believe in lending fate a hand, Colman, but it's still fate. A lot can happen or not over a couple of decades."

"It's true. I've been painting by the numbers. But it's because I know what a contribution you could make to the Church, beginning with this council. I was getting the impression you were thinking of the council as your last step up. It might be your first. I don't think the Lord wants you to sell yourself short, Jack."

McShane laughed because that was just what he was thinking. "Anything's possible, Colman. As Saint Thomas says, potency precedes the real."

"Absolutely. Saint Thomas and JFK. If a mick can be President, what else can happen?" That was what Colman was feeling; if Joe Kennedy could do it, he could do it better. A mick can be pope, that's what else.

"I'd be satisfied to get on that commission, Colman. For now." The bishop sugared the request with his smile.

Colman nodded. He would get in touch with Borella. They both understood that.

Then, as if changing the subject, McShane said, "You know, I wish that Collins had taken that job."

"What job?"

"Whatever Bob Kennedy offered him. As long as I'm allowed to be self-interested, my stock would have gone a lot higher in Rome if I could have pointed to a brother in the subcabinet."

"Oh, when he's in the cabinet, your cousin's your brother, is he?"

"It's the same word in Italian, Colman. And anyway we are brothers. We have the envy that's peculiar to siblings."

"Envy, Excellency?" Colman smiled, bitterly. "I'll tell you something, Jack. If Collins had your gall he'd be President, not Kennedy. I want some coffee. Where's that damn waiter?"

Colman turned away from what he'd just said. Disappointment in his son? If so, he rarely allowed himself to feel it. Disloyalty to express it before McShane? What if Collins knew he'd said that? Collins would have pointed out quickly that since he was born in Ireland he was not eligible for the office. That was how he'd have avoided the hurt his father's words would have inflicted.

But Jack was a priest, not given to scoring points with idle chatter. One could say anything to a priest.

"Coffee, please, waiter," Colman said, overgraciously.

They waited in silence for the waiter to return and serve the coffee. Bishop McShane declined a refill.

"What's the job again?" Colman asked.

"Secretary to the Commission on Bishops and the Government of Dioceses. It's an appointment that wouldn't in the normal course of things be announced for months. I hope it would not be inappropriate for you to ask."

"Leave that to me, son."

Son?

Had he said *son?*

Colman could feel the blood rushing to his face. He hoped Jack hadn't noticed the word. He hoped he wasn't blushing.

"Colman," McShane said awkwardly, "you must be discreet in how you broach the subject."

"I'll take care of it. You just be open to the Will of God, Bishop, and let the laity arrange it for you."

After they left Jake Wirth's they walked to Lincoln Street, where they parted. Brady returned to his office. McShane went west on Lincoln as far as Washington. He thought of hailing a cab to go back to the chancery. He wondered if Cushing had collected himself. He wondered if Cushing was stewed. Then he thought he should go to Prescott Street. His mother, Maeve, would be in bed but awake, watching the soap operas. But he had to be very careful about visiting her. She expected him on Sunday and only on Sunday. If he went other times as well, she'd begin to expect him daily. It was not that he was parsimonious with his time. For her own sake he had to keep a clamp on her demands, which were like jaws. She would eat him. She would eat herself. She would eat like a gull, from pure reflex, even if she were not hungry.

The sky had cleared. It was cold but pleasant. He decided to walk down Washington Street to the South End. He would stop at the cathedral and sit in its permanent twilight and pray for a while.

It took McShane twenty minutes to walk to the Cathedral of the Holy Cross. While he waited for the light, he looked up at the grotesque iron structure of the el. The Forest Hills line ran on the track above Washington Street. For fifty years the black filthy thing had hurled its soot against the great marble church, throwing its shadow onto the grand stairs that led up to what should have been an entrance fit for royalty. The elevated train had ruined the cathedral by making its exterior cold, dark, ugly. The pink stone had been black for years. It had ruined the cathedral on the inside by demolishing its silence every four to seven minutes with the noise of the roaring monster uptown and down.

McShane recalled standing as a lad on that very corner with his uncle. He could hear Colman Brady yelling up at the el, "And *they* did it, the Brahmin bastards!" Colman had arrived in Boston about the time it was being completed. "They took one look at that masterpiece with real Carrara marble," he would say, "and, by God, they just couldn't stand it, the jealous Yankee roundheads with their little wooden steeples and sterile altars! So the old circus dogs pulled one of their last tricks before James Michael Curley drove them from the ring." Colman always claimed they moved the street trestle six blocks over from the Roxbury tracks, where it would have thrown its shadow, dirt, and noise harmlessly down onto the railroad pit, to Washington Street, where it cut through the heart of an Irish neighborhood and desecrated God's holy temple, O'Connell's Holy Cross.

McShane squinted up at the church. It was a shrine to the resentment his uncle still wore like an undersheen to his polish, the resentment McShane could surprise like a sneak thief in himself now and then. He shook himself free of it, crossed the street, climbed the cold stairs, and went into the church. The huge bronze door opened easily, still a perfect balance. However sooty and besmirched the door was now, it had begun as a masterwork of craftsmanship.

McShane slipped into one of the rear pews, his eyes blinded for the moment.

His sight found its focus again on the blue flickering of the votive lights that burned at the feet of the Blessed Virgin Mary at the far front of the church. McShane could barely make out the features of the pale ivory statue, but, as always, he was transfixed briefly by the mournful beauty of God's mother.

His own mother was sixty-eight years old and only mournful. She was diabetic, and her refusal to maintain her diet only made her weaker and more morose. It was one of the mysteries of Jack McShane's life that his mother should have turned out to be, finally, unhappy. He hated visiting her. He assured himself again that that did not mean he did not love her.

"Hello, dear," he would say on entering her room. Then he would kiss the air by her cheek. She would offer him her litany of complaints — nothing long-suffering about Maeve McShane — to which he would add his pointless nuances as if in sympathy. Then they would sit in silence for a while, and then Marie would bring their dinners on trays. She would ignore her food while insisting that he eat each morsel of his. He would promise that the cardinal would be over soon. He would stand over her and bless her. He would take the dishes out with him. She was always weeping when he left.

He looked at the Blessed Virgin and prayed for his mother. He prayed on her behalf for the grace of a happy death. If she was still living when the council convened, she would never forgive him for going off to Rome.

"Unless you abandon mother and father and wife and brother and sister for my name's sake, you cannot be my disciple."

McShane idled over his prayer, wondering what God's mother made of his wish for his own mother's death.

He knew that he was only pressing his thoughts with the word *prayer* as if it were a stamp, as if he could mail them then to heaven. What else does a man on his knees in a dark place do?

He prayed for Cardinal Cushing. The man was an alcoholic, but McShane did not judge him. That was for God to do. McShane loved Cushing.

He prayed for Pope John and for the success of the Second Vatican Council. And, humbly, he offered his life to God in its service, invited Him to make of it what He would. McShane pressed his hands against his eyes trying to press out of his mind the enormous new conflict that seethed there just below the surface of his familiar concerns. The papacy for himself? It was ridiculous. Cushing's chair? How even to imagine that without feeling disloyal? McShane pressed and pressed. He wanted to feel a dose of his customary zeal for the Church, how it needed the council, how it needed his own dedication, fresh and unselfish. McShane felt that he had a special mission. He was young enough to appreciate how the Church needed its *aggiornamento,* yet as a bishop he was prepared to defend her tradition. Sensibilities like his were exactly what was needed. He assured himself of that. He assured himself that there was nothing wrong in wanting to put himself at the further service of the Church. He prayed that the Will of God in his life and times be successfully accomplished. He was sure, one way or the other, it would be.

Especially with his uncle's help. Jack McShane was kneeling to his own hopefulness. He would always remember the day of Pope John's momentous announcement. After this day the Church, unchanged utterly for four hundred years, would never be the same. He knew he would look back on it later in life as the day the earth tilted slightly on its axis, tilted toward him. Was that pride? No, it was the truth. There is nothing shameful in the truth.

In addition to everything else, this was the day on which Colman Brady had called him son.

"WHEN WE PULL the string," Collins Brady was saying to his father, "we would clear ten and a half to eleven million dollars."

Colman Brady sat with his back to his rolltop desk. Collins sat in a straight-backed oak chair by the refectory table on which papers were stacked and on which a gray leather attaché case stood open at a rakish angle. It was a warm summer afternoon, Thursday, June 10, 1961, but the windows were not opened. Brady had installed central air conditioning in his building the year before. Both men wore suit coats and ties.

"We buy three hundred thousand shares of Percy-Dentler at thirty dollars a share." Collins referred to the notepad on his knee. "We hold it for two months. By fall the stock will increase in value at least four hundred percent."

"How?" Colman's dark look was on his son. He was beginning to think the kid was better at it than he was.

"The key is San Francisco. It's an American-listed stock. We go through McDonald. We pull Transnational off the board. A month later we get SWG to be noncommittal while word floats that they are about to liquidate, seeming to leave Percy-Dentler on top. The demand then would be instant and strong. We hold. We help the rise along with McDonald and, say, Van Heuval, who start bidding. We still hold. We hold until it's two hundred a share."

"When."

"October, the latest."

"Have you talked to McDonald?"

"Of course not, but he'll have to come in."

"I meant to ask you what he was like these days. He wasn't always out west, you know. He was a friend of mine."

"He's old."

Colman did not like the bald curtness of his son's statement. Of course, Jim McDonald was old, near seventy. But Christ, he was only a step or two ahead of Colman.

"He's my age."

"No, he's not, Dad." The certainty in Collins's voice was like a perch on which his statement sat.

"He's the best damn broker in the business. I'm lucky to have him."

"He's lucky to have you." Collins was thinking that the best in the business would not have been suspended from working as a registered representative by the New York Exchange. But that disgrace twenty years before had been a stroke of fortune for Brady, since it led to McDonald's move to the American in San Francisco, where they needed him now.

"What's the liability?" Colman asked.

"The obvious one. SEC stock manipulation and fraud. You're the director."

Colman was frankly surprised to have such a proposition laid out by his son. They both knew the importance of avoiding outright criminal activity. Their entire enterprise was criminal, but subtly so, designed to attract as little attention as possible from the regulators. Stock manipulation and market fraud; Colman thought about it. The kid seemed to have great hopes pinned on the thing.

"Why not do it through Instrumentation?"

"You'd have to bring in Harper, and since you're a company officer, you'd still be liable. Frankly, if we go through Monument, we can keep the risk at an acceptable level. We own Sullivan. Even if there were bubbles and he had to move on us, he could hold it down. The deal would be voided. The worst you'd have would be civil."

Colman brushed his right hand through his abundant white hair. "Sullivan? I didn't know we had him. Since when?" Colman let his voice display surprise and respect. Peter G. Sullivan was with the Securities and Exchange Commission.

"Since May seventh. I took him to lunch at Bassin's, an eighty-thousand-dollar lunch. I have a photograph of him accepting the envelope from me."

"*L'audace,*" Colman said, "*toujours l'audace!*" Collins had already committed an enormous act of bribery. Where had he been hiding his balls all these years? Colman folded his hands at his lips and considered what his son had proposed. "There's another problem."

"The Monument shortfall."

"That's right. Dividends just went out. I doubt if we have five million."

"We don't." Collins looked at his notepad. "Four and a third."

"And we'd need?"

"Ten five. It has to be cash. Percy's giving us a depressed price to get cash."

"Ten million cash! Don't be ludicrous!"

"Not in green, not in bills. But immediate credit in his bank. For Christ sake, Dad, that's what 'cash' means now."

[526]

"I thought 'cash' meant cash."

The two men looked at each other. Collins's smooth face was waxen, immobile, waiting for his father to speak. Colman could sense how much Collins wanted this deal. It was something he'd worked up on his own, and it looked very good. It wasn't the enormous sums they would make that interested Colman. The innovation of it did. His son was cutting his own path across the field and Colman liked that very much. But still it was out of the question.

"I'm sorry, son. There's simply no way we can swing it."

"What about a short-term on Monument assets?"

"We'd have to disclose to stockholders. Out of the question."

"There's another way."

"What?"

"Anselmo."

Colman did not respond. He remained still, fingers a steeple at his lips.

Collins wanted to weather his father's silence, but could not. "What do you think?"

"Gennaro Anselmo. Why do you think of him?"

"It's obvious, isn't it. He's our alchemist."

"Lead into gold," Colman said absently. He studied his son's face. *Genius,* he thought, *reveals itself in the eyes.* He studied his son's eyes. "I had the impression you were content to leave him to me."

"I am. And he is to leave me to you."

"Yes. He's a great respecter of sons, but he doesn't trust former cops."

"It's curious what part of my life I have to be ashamed of."

"Shame is an indulgence, son. The point is this isn't Anselmo's kind of deal."

"How much is in the Swiss account?"

Colman shrugged. "Come on, Dad, this is me! How much?"

"More than enough."

"Why won't you tell me?"

Colman stared at the hard image his son threw back at him, a mirror. "I don't know, Micko, how much is in the account."

"I don't believe you."

"It is true, nonetheless. I haven't seen the figures since April."

"How much was there then?"

"Seven million, and you want six."

"Yes."

"He'd never agree. He believes in cash. That account is his mattress. There has to be five in it at all times."

"Let me ask him."

"He won't see you."

"He will if you bring me. Look, Dad, once he sees what a sure thing this is he can't say no. He can double his stash in three months, and there's no risk."

"There's always a risk in the market."

"No. They want you to think there is."

Colman registered the awful confidence of his son's generation. They had begun their lives with the great victory over Hitler. They had bare memories of the Depression, of the Crash, but they had no scars. They believed in the absence of limits. Their money, their plutonium carried the same secret; limitless rapid growth means limitless power.

"Anselmo doesn't see things the way you do, son. Having five now is more important to him than maybe having twenty in the fall."

"We're either in business or we aren't. This kind of deal is what it's all about. What the hell does he have us out front for if not for this? Good Christ, Dad! You can't just buy up nickel and dime shoe stores and then tally the cash register every night. Like it or not, we *have* to pull this scheme, or one like it, and very soon. If we don't expand we shrivel. That is what Anselmo is paying us to know. Otherwise we might as well just move into the fucking bank vault with him and whack each other off."

"He doesn't live in a bank vault. He lives in a slum." They could also be very crude, Colman thought, his son's generation.

"Still?"

"Yes. The money is nothing to him. It never has been. *That* is why he brought me in."

"Don't kid yourself; he loves the secret hold he has on things through you. He loves the fact that unlike all of his flamboyant bullshit brothers of the Unione, his fingers touch something besides dope peddlers, hookers, bookies, and Vegas sharpies. And when I tell him that he can make the stock market dance a minuet to Aaron Copland and pull off one of the coups of the century, he'll wet his pants to get in."

"When you tell him?"

"Yes. I want to see him."

Colman lowered his hand. Maybe what the kid needed was a dose of the wop. "He won't know who Aaron Copland is."

"Do you?"

"*Rites of Spring.*"

"That's Stravinsky, Daddo."

"I wasn't talking about the music, son. I was talking about you."

Collins grimaced. He should have known.

Colman decided to go with it. As for the fraud, what the hell, it was all fraud. There was something showing in Collins that he had not seen before, and he liked it. If he was disappointed at all, it was that his son

had not displayed such nerve a long time before. Colman turned to his
desk, picked up the phone and dialed. He waited. Then he spoke.

"I must see you."

He waited.

"Very soon, as soon as possible. Yes. That would be good."

He waited.

"It is not about that. We can discuss that, but I have nothing to . . .
All right."

He waited.

"One more thing. I am bringing my son. Yes, Gennaro, my son."

He waited.

"I insist. You must trust me. All right."

He returned the phone to its cradle and turned to Collins. "He thought
I had something else in mind."

"What?"

"The killing at Revere Beach two days ago. You didn't read about it?
A Gallagher kid killed a Maguire, over a girl, for Christ's sake."

"What's that to Anselmo?"

Colman wondered momentarily if his son really did not know. "Gallagher runs Anselmo's operation in Southie. Maguire runs it in Charlestown and Somerville. Bennie Maguire declared war on Gallagher this
morning."

Collins did not react.

"Do you know what that means?"

"Certainly. If Anselmo can't keep his boys in line Balestrione will come
up and do it for him. Nobody wants a gang war now."

"Not with the noise Bobby's making at Justice. It's head-in-the-
trenches time."

"But the Irish don't know it."

"Stupid harps."

"Anselmo should relax, Dad. Bobby's after the Midwest boys, Chicago,
Detroit."

"Suppose you tell that to him."

"Politely, eh?"

"Very."

"When's the meeting?"

"Now. Let's go."

Outside Colman hailed a Checker cab and told the driver to take them
to Castle Island.

Castle Island was the park on the far tip of the South Boston peninsula.
It had not been a true island since Curley's landfill project on which Brady
and Anselmo had first met.

"Forty years ago, nearly," Colman said.

"It seems to me I can remember when this was an island."

"Impossible. You were two."

Collins paid the driver.

On top of a hill was the colonial battery that gave the island its name, a massive stone fort that achieved a medieval aspect with its angled notches and cannon slits, the blinded eyes of war. Boys carrying fishing poles passed Colman and Micko as they stood in the parking lot looking up at the castle. There was a fishing pier at the north base of it. To the south was an expanse of lawn that drew picnickers on weekends. On that Thursday afternoon, typically, there were only the young fishermen, a few solitary strollers and a pair of hand-holders. Colman led the way along the walk that encircled the fort, past the obelisk honoring David McKay, the builder of clipper ships. On the harbor side of the castle they leaned over the iron railing and watched the surf breaking on the rocks twenty feet below. The harbor islands were like a fleet of ships waiting for their pilots.

"They used to burn the horses there," Colman said, pointing to a ruined smokestack on the nearest island. "Rendering plant. Render unto horses."

"And unto glue what glues."

Colman looked sharply at his son with surprise, not rebuke, in his eyes. It was an impiety once not typical of Collins, like the crude language.

Colman looked at his watch. Four forty.

"Castle Island," he said. "Because it has a castle on it. Don't you wish everything was so simple as the name of this place."

"But it's not an island. Is that 'simple'?"

They stared out over the harbor from their similar postures, hunched over the railing, hands clasped.

"There's a rock out there," Colman said, "to which they used to tie pirates for the vultures to eat."

"And for other pirates to see. I remember you telling me about it. Those were the good old days."

"When they tied pirates to rocks?"

"No, when you told me stories. I loved coming over here with you. I used to come out here by myself a lot. Once or twice from Harvard I came over here."

"With a girl?"

"Nope." Why was it hard for his father to imagine him coming out here alone? Because by the time of college he spent as little time as possible alone. That was before Janet, of course. Now he was alone continually, but for such rare moments as this with his father. It was like being a boy again.

Colman looked at his watch. Four forty-seven.

"The next parish over, your Aunt Maeve used to say, is Dingle."

"It's Portugal. Ireland is due east of Newfoundland."

Colman stared at the swells of water as if he saw faces in them. "You've a new habit, I see."

"I do?"

"Contradicting your old man. You used to have respect."

"That was before you hired me."

"I pay you to contradict me, do I?"

"Don't you?"

"You've no poet in you, Micko. It disgusts me to think that when you look out at that horizon you see Iberia, not Kerry."

"I see the horizon."

"You're hopeless."

"No. Just not Irish."

"Exactly what I mean. How the hell did you end up a son of mine?"

Collins shifted his weight on the railing to look at his father. Though the question had been asked lightly, it sliced through Collins. He wanted to show his wound no more than his father had shown his blade, but he could not help but lift a corner on what he was feeling. "I've often wondered that myself, Daddo. If I'm a disappointment, it's as much to myself as to you."

Colman was stung by his son's simple statement. *A parent,* he thought, *who wants to be everything to his child hates the child when he is.* He felt that he had failed his son miserably. "You're not a disappointment to me, son."

"If there's a difference between us, it's not your brogue or my flat *a*. It's that you live in the world you were born to, however much it keeps changing on you. I don't. I don't even live in the world I was trained to."

"You do all right." Colman was thinking of the stock deal he had put together.

Collins was thinking that his entire life had become layered with deceit. He was deceiving his father now, even while trying to tell him the truth. There was no point in pressing it. He didn't say anything.

Colman mistook his son's silence for mere moroseness. He couldn't figure the kid. One minute, driven and enthused, the next, done in by self-pity. Colman thought nothing was so smug as self-pity.

He looked at his watch. Four fifty-eight. He pushed himself away from the railing, casting one last look at the harbor. A tanker was sliding in from Boston Light. An Eastern Constellation with a fuselage the shape of a cigar angled down toward the runway at Logan. Colman headed up the grassy slope toward Fort Independence.

Collins followed him.

In 1634 Governor Thomas Dudley persuaded twenty of his fellow Puritans to subscribe five pounds each for the fortification of the island in the middle of Boston Harbor. "We find our defense here," he said; "now let our history begin." But it was not until 1776 that the granite fort engaged an enemy. On March 5 of that year Lord Percy, under orders from General Howe, directed a withering fire from the fort against the very people its guns were meant to protect. When the British fled Boston they left the castle ablaze and, on their way out of the harbor, blew up Boston Light as a final gesture of contempt. The fort had five bastions and two dozen casements from which heavy cannon covered Boston.

Colman, and after him Collins, walked through the narrow passageway that cut the east wall in half opposite the huge gate entrance in the west wall. An elm grew in the center of the courtyard and cast its shadow sharply down. Its leafy branches reached to the level of the ramparts fifty feet high. Other smaller trees grew from the soil that covered the bastions on the site of gun emplacements.

Collins saw a discarded condom in the corner of the passageway where it opened on the inner fort. He heard a rat scurrying away and felt a predictable revulsion. He expected to see condoms and hear rats in such places.

Colman took his place under the elm. Collins joined him. They stood stiffly. No one else was in the courtyard. Colman looked at his watch. Five.

He looked toward the low arch of the entrance gate and saw the figures of three men, silhouettes, in the tunnel. They walked with a similar swaying, right to left. One was quite short. All three wore dark business suits.

Colman knew Anselmo and Costanari, but the third man he recognized only because of the eyepatch. Anselmo's son Marcello had lost his eye, ironically, in a youthful hockey accident.

"Hello, my friend," Colman said. He stepped into Anselmo's arms and they embraced not quite perfunctorily.

"This is your son?"

"Yes. Michael Collins Brady." Colman pushed Anselmo lightly by the elbow toward his son.

Collins had been looking at Marcello, who was as tall as he was and about the same age. He had pronounced lips that were out of proportion with his other features, incongruously so. Such lips were a sign of softness and inexperience which clashed with the gleaming leather eyepatch and with Marcello's reputation as a rough player.

Collins turned to Gennaro and his impressions came quickly: a short man, losing his hair, sixty, not fat, nothing soft about him. Collins tried to recall the facts about Anselmo's operation, tried to conjure up the data sheet with its figures and names: Comose Collections — garbage and numbers; Othello wines — bootlegging, smuggling; Roma Foods — the lead arm, Marcello's. What were the sums involved? What laws habitually violated? What were the points of conflict with Balestrione? What would the Irish gang war mean? Collins was, while staring at Anselmo, trying to think of anything but Anna.

He nurtured a juxtaposition of opposing convictions about Anna's death. On the one hand, it was an accident which resulted from his father's overzealous and misguided effort to protect him. His father had been gullible and naïve about what was involved in preventing the marriage, and he regretted Anna's death as much as Collins himself did. On the other hand, Anna's death was the result of brutal behavior by gangsters who were murderously indifferent to the value of human life. Anselmo had had her kidnapped and, as Collins saw it, was only vaguely disturbed that she had died. Collins had transferred all the hate and rage he might otherwise have felt for his father to this callous man who was standing in front of him. But he would not feel it. Collins would show Anselmo nothing.

"Good to meet you after all these years," he said.

"Yes," Anselmo said. "You've been with your father a long time now."

"Nearly seven years."

Colman put his hand on his son's shoulder. "He gets the works when I retire."

"As it should be," Anselmo said.

"But he'll never retire," Collins said. "That's the catch."

"Also as it should be." Anselmo touched Colman. "We must beware the ambition of our sons, eh?"

"Indeed," Colman said, but Anselmo's statement put him in mind of his nephew's ambition, not his son's.

Costanari's impatience was palpable. "There are two points to this meeting, the don's and yours. First, the don's."

By virtue of Costanari's rudeness Anselmo could be polite. "You know Gallagher," he said to Colman.

"I knew his father, P. J. He was with Jerry MacCurtain. You remember Jerry MacCurtain?"

"You know Gallagher," Anselmo repeated.

"No. Maybe I met him when he was a kid. I don't think so."

"I know him," Collins said. "They lived on Seventh, right?"

Colman nodded.

"We were altar boys together. P. J., Junior. I know him."

Anselmo had entirely ignored Collins and continued to do so. "You know Maguire, the oldest one."

"Yes," Colman said, "I know Bennie. I don't know his brother."

"No matter."

"Why?"

"He is dead. Gallagher walked up behind him on the street at City Square and put his gun to his ear and blew his head off."

"Christ," Colman said, "Bennie'll murder him."

"He will not," Anselmo said.

"You don't know Bennie. If they killed his brother, they'll make Chicago look sweet. You've got a problem."

It seemed to Marcello his father did not need an Irishman telling him he had a problem with Irishmen.

"I want to see them," Anselmo said.

Colman said nothing.

"I want you to arrange it."

"They're your boys, Gennaro. I'm out of touch with that stuff. I haven't seen Bennie in years."

"My friend, I am asking you to help me keep the peace of Boston. Your Irish brothers understand only one word from me. I would prefer not to speak it."

"I have no influence with them."

"They are your people."

How to explain to Anselmo that micks are not wops.

Collins shocked Colman by saying, "You have more influence than you imagine. I think Mr. Anselmo's right."

Colman looked sharply at Collins. The kid and his contradictions. *Colman,* Anselmo had said, *control your son.*

Colman led Collins away from the tree to the point where the passageway intersected with the courtyard. Colman stood with his back toward the others so that his son had to circle around him.

"What in hell do you think you're doing?"

"Anselmo's right, Dad."

"It's his problem, not ours. I stay out of the street. I have always stayed out of the street."

"But if these punks start bumping each other off you know what follows — press, TV, editorials, outraged citizenry, pressure to investigate, starting with Anselmo, ending with us. We have to help him cool it."

[534]

"He thinks I'm some kind of harp chieftain. Gallagher and Maguire would laugh me off the block."

"I'll do it."

"What?"

"Let me do it."

"You're kidding. You don't know your ass from your elbow out there."

"I know Gallagher."

"Altar boys, Jesus Christ!"

"And you can get me to Bennie."

"Collins, listen to me. We have no public link to Anselmo. We do not want any now; can't you understand that?"

"Our secret is not worth a damn if a major gang war opens up. The one reason the arrangement has worked is because Boston has been peaceful. If Gallagher and Maguire start knocking heads, then Anselmo moves in on both of them. If he doesn't, Balestrione moves in on him. If *he* doesn't, the national syndicate moves against him. One's house in order — the first rule."

"For want of a nail, the shoe."

"Alarum sounds. Exit Richard to be slain." Collins paused. "It's not such a big thing to ask Gallagher and Maguire to sit down." He paused again. "All right?"

"All right."

They returned to the tree.

"I've decided," Colman said, "to have my son arrange it."

"I want you," Anselmo said.

"No."

Anselmo studied Colman's face. That jaw was set.

Anselmo nodded, barely.

"The meeting," Costanari announced, "will be Saturday at three o'clock at the Cantina Reale."

The Cantina Reale. Could Colman Brady be doing this again?

"I will arrange it," Collins said. "That brings us to point two."

Costanari gave Collins a sharp look. He was the one to announce the points.

Brady ignored him. "We have an extraordinary opportunity to establish the economic power of Monument on an international level. The details are too complicated to go into."

"Go into them," Costanari said, but Collins was addressing himself to Anselmo.

"There are only two dozen companies in the country that could make the deal I'm proposing, and they don't know about it. It boils down to buying out the largest copper company in Latin America, waiting long enough to make it seem that its holdings are going to be multiplied by the purchase of other companies, letting the stock soar, and selling at four hundred percent."

"A public corporation?" Costanari asked.

"Yes."

Costanari shook his head at Anselmo.

"The SEC will approve everything we do. We'll be operating in a legal gray area. The regulations governing multinational transactions are a thicket of contradictions and vagueness. In any case, we have the SEC tied up."

"What do you want from me?" Anselmo asked. "I don't concern myself with these things."

"Six million in cash to add to the four we have."

Neither Costanari nor Marcello spoke. This was Anselmo's.

"Why should I trust you with that much money?"

"For the same reason you've trusted us with any," Collins said. "Because you don't want to underuse your capital. You hired my father to pull in chits for you, and he does. He hired me because I know things he doesn't know. The law, for example, and how to work it in your favor. And I know that at a certain point in business, money has its own momentum, and one had better either be prepared to run with it or get out of business altogether. Frankly, Mr. Anselmo, your alternative to this deal is a savings account at First National."

Anselmo said slowly, "You want me to risk the money to make money."

"No. That is not it at all, and you know it. I want you to take the opportunity you have to score one of the major coups in the history of the stock market."

"Which would attract attention."

"Not to you. Not to us if we don't want it to. It's paper talking to paper. We control the transaction and its aftermath absolutely. Obviously Monument could be a big-league operation after this. I assumed that was what you wanted."

Anselmo looked at Colman. Colman understood that he was being asked for his endorsement. "I'd go with it, Gennaro. The kid has done his homework. And I think he's right. We either go with the boom or we start shutting down."

"Eventually, you're talking about an international company," Anselmo said, showing his interest.

"A collection of companies," Collins said. "A conglomerate, controlled by no one government and subject to the regulation of no one commission. There is a huge crack in the wall and we can be one of the first through it. We need the six million."

Anselmo turned slightly toward Costanari, who nodded.

Collins understood immediately that Costanari kept the books. He would be the Swiss shuttle. His were the hands that touched things.

"When?" Anselmo asked.

"Tomorrow."

Costanari shook his head. "Six million dollars. It is not in my desk. It means a journey."

"My father can go," Collins said.

"No," Costanari said blankly.

Anselmo and Colman stared at each other. There was a second account in Switzerland. Colman was not privy to everything.

Collins, aware of the magnet lock between the two, understood the revelation he'd forced and was embarrassed for his father. All these years — a second account. But Colman was not embarrassed. He understood Anselmo. He'd have had a second account himself. Anselmo probably had a third, of which Costanari was ignorant.

"I must be here for the meeting with the Irish," Costanari said.

"If we're going to make the deal," Collins said, "we have to do it at the latest Monday morning."

Anselmo was still staring at Colman. "Is it good?"

"Yes," Colman said.

"You will go," Anselmo said to Costanari.

"But I will . . ."

"I have decided."

Costanari sagged with disappointment.

Collins was thinking the man's office would be vacant all weekend.

⪻ 4 ⪼

P. J. GALLAGHER ran a flower shop on Broadway. Ordinarily a Friday in June was the worst possible time for him. In addition to the regular Sunday displays that had to be readied for the high altar at Gate of Heaven, there were always at least a dozen weddings. If a Southie boy caused the sweat to flow on the palm of a girl's hand, he married her, just in case. Gallagher was convinced that half the brides who just knew they were pregnant had also just never been penetrated. South Boston was the only place in the world — outside Tipperary — where the miracle of conception occurred in the woman's mouth.

If Fridays were usually bad, that one was worse.

The flower shop was closed. The hell with the customers for once. P. J. and seven of his boys were huddled in the main room upstairs. P. J.'s wife, Judy, and their four kids were off at her sister's place in Dorchester. Gallagher did not expect Bennie Maguire to hit him there, but you never knew. Not after what he himself had done. The day after you blow some fucker's head off from a foot away, you just fucking turn into jelly wondering what the hell you've done. But P. J. wasn't going to let anybody see how he felt. Let the fuckers come. He'd blow them all away. When the shit settled he'd be running everything from Highland Ave. and Bunker Hill to City Point. He watched the traffic on Broadway from the corner of the window. He gave every appearance of confidence and brain, as if this war was what he'd always wanted. In fact, he'd felt continually that day like throwing up.

It wasn't noon yet when he saw the guy in the suit up the block by Doran's. Gallagher studied him. What was there about him? He was coming toward the shop. P. J. wore his mind out trying to remember. He watched the guy coming.

"Somebody's coming," he said.

The others jumped. They pulled their guns. They were all sick with fear.

"A fellow, dressed up."

There was a loud knocking on the door downstairs.

No one moved.

The knocking was repeated.

"Hell," P. J. said, getting up, "probably wants a fucking bouquet." Nobody he knew dressed like that, cufflinks and all.

He went downstairs. He put his gun in the pocket of his windbreaker, but he did not take his finger off the trigger.

"Yeah?" he yelled through the door.

"I want to see Gallagher, Peter Gallagher, Peter Joseph Gallagher."

"Who does?"

"Mick Brady."

"Who the fuck is Mick Brady?"

"Is that you, P. J.?"

The voice plucked at Gallagher's memory, the wire of it. He had the gun aimed at the door. He opened it.

[538]

"I told you."

"Mick Brady?"

"That's right."

"Christ, I remember you." Recognition crossed P. J.'s face. "Fourth Street, right?"

"Right. St. Eulalia's."

"They call it St. Brigid's now. Monsignor Connor changed the name after his mother."

"I didn't know that."

"You been gone quite a while."

"Yes."

"Quite a fucking while."

"Can I come in?"

"What for?"

"Because I'd just as soon not be in the street in front of your place right now. If you don't mind."

Gallagher let Brady enter. He did not lower his arm or release the feather hold he had on the trigger.

"And don't shoot me, P. J., if you don't mind."

P. J. let the barrel of the gun fall inside his coat. "What do you want?"

"I came to invite you to a meeting you won't want to miss."

Gallagher circled Brady slowly, a loitering crow.

Collins was thinking he and Gallagher should have grown up friends, though he found everything about him distasteful, including the film of oil on his forehead and the blackheads awash in it.

"I'm listening," Gallagher announced.

"Tomorrow at three at the Cantina Reale on Hanover Street."

"Fuck! Anselmo?"

"You guessed it."

"This is none of his shit."

"That is not how he sees it."

"You tell him to stay out."

"You can tell him yourself."

"Bullshit. Maguire be there?"

"That's the point."

"I'll be goddamned if I will."

"Possible. What is certain is you'll be dead if you won't. What chance would you have against both Maguire and Anselmo?"

Gallagher considered this.

"Why are you setting this up?"

"I'm a lawyer. I set up a lot of things."

"You work for Anselmo?"

"Let's just say I work for the peace of the city, P. J. Some concerned citizens would like to help you and Bennie avoid the Hatfield-McCoy bit. Anselmo couldn't very well send over one of his wop thugs, now, could he?"

"You going to be at this meeting?"

"Yes."

"I don't trust that fucker."

"Anselmo or Maguire?"

"Either one of them."

"Nobody's asking you to trust them. Just come."

"That's not trust, you dumb shit?"

"And, P. J., no hardware."

"Fuck you, no hardware."

"And come alone."

"That's not trust? Jesus fucking Christ!"

"Bennie will be there, Gallagher. He'll be delighted if you don't show. He'll have the don's ear all to himself, and your absence will say all Anselmo needs to hear."

"Fuck."

"OK?"

"Fuck you, Brady."

"I'll see you tomorrow, P. J. Three o'clock. *Ciao, bambino,* as we say in Dearo."

Maguire's house was next to the school on the square around the Bunker Hill obelisk. It was the sort of house Bostonians were accustomed to find on Beacon Hill, a grand Federal bowfront with wrought-iron grillwork on the windows and crafted spiral balusters supporting the brass handrails that framed the seven stairs of the entrance. The brass was brown and caked, however. No one in Charlestown knew what a shine the metal would take. The doorbell did not work. Collins banged on the wood of the door. The beveled glass shook, and a piece of ancient dried putty fell. No one answered. He knocked again and still no sounds came from the house.

Monument Square was a broad expanse of lawn, unfenced. Collins surveyed it, then let his eye drift up the granite shaft, the Washington miniature. As every obelisk once imitated Egypt, now it did Washington. The Bunker Hill Monument was two hundred and twenty feet high. A single window, a monster eye, topped it, Bunker Hill cyclops. Collins Brady saw a flash of white in the window, the sleeve of a shirt pulling back quickly. He waited for it to reappear, but it did not. Someone was up there watching him. It was a good place for that.

Brady crossed the lawn.

" 'A dear bought victory,' " the plaque read. " 'Another such would have ruined us.' — British General Henry Clinton after the Battle of Bunker Hill."

"Something eh?" the guard said from his little house.

"Yes," Collins said, "something. How much?"

"Ten cents."

Brady paid, went into the monument and started to climb the stairs, two hundred and ninety-four of them.

He had not climbed more than a few dozen when he heard the footsteps from above, rapid and increasingly loud. Someone was running down the stairs. The passageway was very narrow, with barely room for three men to stand abreast, winding upward at such an angle that only the next seven or eight stairs could be seen. Brady retreated four stairs to get away from the meshed bulb from which light poured conically on a small space.

The runner spiraled down on Brady without seeing him. Brady clamped a bearhug on the man and pinned him to the cold rock wall.

It was a boy.

"Let me go!"

Seventeen, no more than eighteen, Tony's age. He was thin but strong. Brady had to strain to maintain his hold.

"Let me go, goddamn it!"

"Shut up!" Brady pressed the kid hard until he felt him give. "I want to see Bennie Maguire. I'm a friend of his. Where is he?"

"You're a cop."

"No, I'm not. Were the cops here?"

"Last night, yesterday, all day."

"Where's Bennie?"

"I don't know." The kid began to struggle again. "I don't know. Let go of me."

Brady released the boy and stepped back. The boy bolted, but Brady grabbed his arm. "Listen. You tell Bennie I'll wait upstairs, you hear? You tell him Colman Brady's son Micko is upstairs. OK?"

"Let me go."

"What are you going to tell him?"

"Brady."

"That's right. Colman Brady."

The view from the monument was unlike any Collins Brady had ever seen of Boston. It was Boston from behind, and because it was unfamiliar — the Manger and North Station and the Garden and the court at Pemberton Square were in the foreground for once, and Beacon Hill seemed stunted and minor in the background — the rents and tears in the tapestry were visible. The shoddy roofs of Scollay Square, the scarred

[541]

railroad yard, the beaten hotels, the tenements of the West End, and the wharves and warehouses along Commercial Street below Copp's Hill in the North End — the worn side of the city was showing. Yet, because he had never seen it that way before there was a freshness to it, as if his gaze were enough to repair time's damage.

Collins never heard him.

"So you're Colman's boy." It was the brogue that told him it was Maguire.

Collins turned slowly to face him, expecting the gun. Maguire had it pointed at Brady's head.

"Yes, I am. He sent me to you."

"Why didn't he come himself?"

"Because I'm a lawyer. If I cross with the police I'll have reasons. They can't touch me. Privilege of the court, attorney-client secrecy, all that."

"And who would your client be, counselor?"

Maguire was tall and very thin. His features were rugged, sharp as a woodcut. His hair was white. Collins guessed he was near sixty. Perhaps he should not have had him climb those stairs, but he seemed strong, unwinded. His accent made him sound just over from Ireland, but Collins knew he'd been in Boston nearly as long as his father. His father's brogue was softer, more mannered than Maguire's. His father's ear had had other tones to learn from.

"Don't fire," Collins said, smiling, "till you see the whites of their eyes."

Maguire did not show whether he got the allusion or not.

"No 'dear bought victories' today, all right? Put the gun away, Mr. Maguire. You don't need it with me." One of life's first rules — never address your parents' peers by the Christian name or by the surname without its title.

Maguire looked at the .38. "I hate the thing anyway." He slid it into the back pocket of his baggy wool trousers. "So?"

"I've come to deliver a message."

"From Colman?"

"No. From Anselmo."

Maguire's smile was as swift and nonchalant as an usher's tearing a ticket into two pieces. He knew.

"Oh?" he said.

"There's a meeting tomorrow at three at the Cantina Reale."

"With Gallagher?"

"Yes."

"I have to kill him. Anselmo will understand that."

[542]

"I can't speak for Anselmo. He wants you there."

"Will Colman be there?"

"No."

"I want Colman there."

"That's impossible. I'll be there."

Maguire did not speak.

"All right?"

Maguire remained silent.

"Mr. Maguire, you don't want this war."

"Of course not. I want that animal Gallagher. It's just between him and me. You tell Anselmo that."

"You can tell him yourself."

Nothing.

"All right?"

Maguire nodded, then turned and disappeared into the narrow winding staircase.

Collins turned to the window and stared out at the city of Boston, still from the wrong angle. A tired old lady whose memories made her almost beautiful.

The next day Collins Brady entered the North End feeling like a member of the public entering a private garden. The streets were crowded with pushcarts and children. Men, retired sentries, stood in their tame clusters on corners. Crones watched from windows, their beefy elbows on stained cushions. Three blocks in on Hanover Street was the Cantina Reale. When Brady went into the restaurant, it was dark and chairs were upended on tables. A man behind a small bar was washing glasses.

He gestured with his head toward a door in the rear.

Brady followed the winding aisle between the tables. The door opened on a staircase, which he ascended.

At the top of the stairs a large man in shirtsleeves sat on a straight-backed chair. The leather straps of his shoulder holster pressed furrows in his flesh. He stood. Brady took his place in front of him and raised his arms. The man ran his hands down the length of Brady's body, was satisfied, stepped back, and opened the door. Brady entered the room.

Anselmo was behind a desk.

Two men were seated on a tattered vinyl couch to Anselmo's left, both nattily dressed. A third, Marcello, was standing at Anselmo's right elbow.

Anselmo nodded at Brady.

"My sons," he said, gesturing to the seated men, "Leonard and Rico."

The two stood and shook Brady's hand with a stiff courtesy. Both were on the wrong edge of youth.

"And Marcello you know." Marcello, older and more subdued than his brothers in dress, was like his father.

"It's time," Marcello said.

"They'll be here," Brady said. He looked at his watch. It was two minutes before three.

Standing in the stare of Anselmo and his sons, Brady thought that was what it was to stand in court. They were waiting for the liturgy. There was that peculiar silence floating in the air like the sun's dust. Brady slowly turned, studying the room. There were no files, no drawers, no shelves. It was not a room from which business was administered. Anselmo's desk, a table really, was clear.

Behind Anselmo was a door. What was its secret?

"Before our friends come," Brady said, "is there a bathroom I can use?"

No one moved or spoke.

Finally Leonard stood up and said, "Sure." He pointed to the door behind Anselmo and took a step toward it. But Anselmo pointed to the door through which Brady'd entered the room and said, "Out there. He'll show you."

That was what Brady wanted to know; Anselmo did not want him through the other door.

The man with the shoulder holster took Brady down the corridor to a tiny closet barely large enough to accommodate a man over the toilet. The place was clean.

When Brady returned to the meeting Maguire was there. Relief transformed the Irishman's face when Collins entered. He guessed that Maguire knew what had happened in that room nearly thirty years before.

"Where is Gallagher?" Marcello asked. It was not clear to whom he was speaking.

"He'll be here," Collins said.

Leonard and Rico continued to sit. Anselmo was motionless at his desk. Marcello and Brady stood straight and still while Maguire shifted his weight uneasily from leg to leg. He was too old for this nonsense. A punk like Gallagher he could handle, but Anselmo scared the hell out of him.

There were loud footfalls on the stairs outside. Too loud to be one man.

A voice, presumably the holstered guard, barked a command, but the door muffled it so the men could not make out what he'd said. Another voice, Gallagher's, responded cockily and too loudly. He was drunk.

Anselmo's eyes brushed Rico and Leonard, both of whom were up instantly, guns drawn, and at the door. Rico flung the door open and Leonard went through. P. J. Gallagher was standing over the guard brandishing a pistol. The guard's hands were up. Behind Gallagher were two other men, apparently not armed.

"Well, fuck me," Gallagher said, staring at the barrel of the gun Leonard pointed at him. "Looks like a fucking standoff."

Gallagher staggered slightly. He was quite drunk.

Marcello touched Leonard's shoulder from behind. Leonard stepped aside. Marcello leveled the snout of a Thompson submachine gun at Gallagher's belly.

"Oops," Gallagher said. He laughed insanely and insanely cut his laughter short. *"Was* a fucking standoff."

Rico crossed to Gallagher and took his gun away from him. Gallagher grinned at Rico, then at his companions. He shrugged grandly. *Oh, well.*

Marcello looked back at his father, who flicked the tip of his thumb with the tip of his forefinger.

Marcello turned back to Gallagher. "You can leave now."

"No fuck," Gallagher said. He grinned back at his friends, weaving. "Fucking-A I can leave now. You tell that truck-fuck Maguire P. J. Gallagher says blow it out his ear!" Gallagher craned past Marcello. "You hear, you fucking asshole?"

Marcello stabbed Gallagher in the belly with the snout of the machine gun.

"All right, shit, all right." Gallagher backed off. "And you tell the Top Wop P. J. Gallagher's fight ain't with him, OK?" Gallagher backed over the uppermost step and fell drunkenly down the flight. His companions scurried after him.

Marcello listened until they were gone. He gave the guard a look of infinite scorn, returned to the meeting room after Leonard and Rico, and closed the door behind him.

Collins Brady watched Anselmo. He gave no signal. He said nothing, but Gallagher, all understood, was dead.

"There will be no peace," Anselmo said.

"I want him," Maguire said.

Anselmo shook his head once.

"But hit him quick," Maguire pleaded. "If his boys blast any of mine, I can't stop what happens."

That was the issue and Anselmo knew it. What did authority mean to these fools? How to keep one's grip on slime? How to keep one's grip on Boston? If he didn't, Balestrione would.

"You control your people, Bennie. If you don't I will." That was the rule. Anselmo's rule. Balestrione's rule.

"Shit, I . . ."

"Control them!"

Maguire stood mute and stooped, looking ashamed. He could control the old guys, but those kids . . . "OK," he said finally, "I will."

"Good," Anselmo said. He smiled.

Collins Brady thought it was one of the nicest smiles he had ever seen. Its warmth and the Italian's evident affection for the old Irishman struck a more discordant note in Brady than the gunplay had, than the sentence passed on Gallagher had. It occurred to Brady suddenly that he was indifferent to the fate of P. J. Gallagher with whom he should have grown up friends. His indifference did not shock him. He was indifferent to everything but saving his father, which alone was why he'd come to the meeting. He had to see Anselmo's office and find the place to plant the microphone. He stared at the door behind Anselmo as if he could see through it.

Then he bade the Italians farewell and walked with poor Maguire out of the dear old North End.

That night, in the last hours before dawn, he returned.

Nothing was moving in the North End, not even the early merchants, since it was in fact Sunday morning. The small transistorized microphone-transmitter that Brady carried in his windbreaker pocket was the twin of one developed by the FBI laboratory in Washington for use in the main conference room of the Soviet embassy on Sixteenth Street. It was a radically new device for eavesdropping, one which the Soviets might anticipate, since they had their equivalents, but which gangsters would never suspect. It was the perfect way to penetrate their secrecy since it had no telltale wires and was not part of a predictable telephone tap.

Collins Brady entertained the thought that his would be the first government-sponsored burglary, but of course he knew it was not. The FBI had been breaking into the embassies and consular offices of foreign countries regularly since the war.

What he did not know was that his importance to Robert Kennedy had as much to do with Kennedy's conflict with J. Edgar Hoover as with his touted assault on organized crime. Hoover refused to respond to pressures from above. He refused to create a special unit in the bureau to concentrate on organized crime — the General Investigative Division dealt with security checks on pimply-faced applicant clerks as well as with investigations of known hoodlums. Hoover also successfully resisted the establishment of a national anticrime unit outside the FBI. But Kennedy was not going to be thwarted. He intended, despite Hoover, to enlarge the Racketeering Section of the Criminal Division at Justice to coordinate investigations and handle intensified prosecutions. And he intended, under the national security principle, to authorize the extensive use of bugs and wiretaps as intelligence sources if not as the means to collect admissible evidence. But to justify that authorization and to withstand the blast he knew would come from Hoover when he learned of it, he needed a pilot case, a fait accompli, a bug which had turned up irrefutably invaluable information about the Syndicate. Hence Collins Brady's importance to Robert Kennedy.

Robert Kennedy had an equal importance to Collins Brady. Terrified and reluctant as Collins was, the mission made him an infallible protector of his father. He would plant the microphone and he would monitor its tape. Perfect. He would be the source of everything the government learned about the Anselmo family and the censor of what it would not about the Brady.

Entering the North End at that time of night was like entering a church, silent, familiar, foreign. Brady crossed into Hanover Street on soft feet. He was wearing tennis shoes, twill trousers, a navy windbreaker, a black knit cap, and driving gloves. He felt falsely calm and assured about what he was doing, although he compulsively held his breath for long stretches as he strode by the stores, the locked stands, the coffee bars, butcher stalls, and pizzerias. He passed no one. Not a curtain in a window stirred at his passing. He was less to that street than a breeze. The only sound in his ear was of his manic heart.

At the Cantina Reale he stopped.

He had the keys and a tool in his left pocket. He studied the lock on the door to the restaurant, a simple bolt, as he'd noted. He slid the thin metal edge of the tool inside the crevice between the jamb and the door. He pressed: click! Open. He went in. He stood in the vestibule and leaned his face against the wall and made a cup around it with his gloved hands. In that dark shell the pupils of his eyes dilated rapidly.

On the inner door was a snap lock. He opened it easily.

The restaurant seemed in the dark like a chamber in a mausoleum. The chairs up ended on their tables achieved a rigid eerie grief as for some pharaoh or Druid king. Brady stifled a shudder. He moved swiftly through the tables to the door in the rear.

Meanwhile Pio Costanari was waiting for a cab at Logan airport with as much patience as he could muster. He had left Geneva at noon Saturday for Paris, just making his connection to Idlewild. He arrived in New York before midnight, but it had taken an hour to clear Customs. A pilot in the line had told him there was an alert out for a Rumanian defector, but still Costanari worried that they would discover the false wall in his suitcase and find the banknote. They had not, but he missed a flight to Boston, and had to wait an hour and forty minutes and now he was waiting for a cab. He was exhausted and angry, but mainly he was worried. The cashier's check made out to Monument was for six million dollars. Costanari would not relax until the check was secure in the safe in the office. That was why he would go there before going home.

Brady was at the door behind Anselmo's desk. It had three complex locks. He had expected that. If it led to what he thought it did, it would have such locks. With as much patience as he could muster he was making his way around the circle of thirty-two manufacturers' master keys which Deke Thomas had provided with the microphone.

But it took time. Key by key, and each attempt drilled the room with its noise. It seemed like noise to Brady. Finally the lock he had been working opened. It had taken seventeen keys. He had gone to work on the next one. Eleven keys and it had opened. But the third lock was proving impossible. As he approached the thirty-second key he could barely hold on to the ring because his hands were so slick with perspiration. They trembled so that in addition to the noise of the keys into slots, there was the new noise of the keys rattling against each other.

The last key. Brady inserted it with extra care. He turned it gently at first, then firmly. Nothing. He applied more pressure. Nothing. He pressed the key until his fingers hurt so badly he had to stop. Nothing. He could not believe it. He was convinced, irrationally, that the thirty-second key was the right one, and so he tried turning it again. He slid it in and out of its slot and tried again. Nothing.

It had to be one of the other keys. He had missed it. He forced calm down on his hands and on his mind. He slowed his breathing and told himself there was no hurry.

Costanari's cab pulled up in front of the Cantina Reale. Costanari told the driver to wait.

The eighth key opened the lock and Brady nearly yelled with relief.

He opened the door on an office just spacious enough for two wooden chairs, two desks and a man-sized floor safe. There were three telephones on each desk. Behind one desk was a door ajar on a cubicle showing its toilet shamelessly. The safe was snug in a corner and abutting a radiator. A radiator. That was what he wanted. Brady took a step toward the radiator. Then he heard the sound.

A key in the lock. It was a sound — a subtle combination of sounds — branded on his mind by then, but this one was coming from the door in the rear of the restaurant downstairs. Brady held his breath. The door opened. There were shoes on the stairs, coming up.

Had he locked the door to the meeting room behind him? Yes.

He would stay in the office.

He swung the door closed and bolted the three locks quickly, hoping the excruciating noise of their actions would be lost on the corner in the sound of his own feet.

He looked around the office.

He crossed to the toilet cubicle and closed himself in it and stopped breathing.

That was when it began to happen.

The space, the utter lack of it, pressed down on him or, more precisely, on his pumping heart. If your heart makes noise when you are hiding you must clamp it in a vise and turn.

He covered his ears and pushed into the corner over the toilet and then vowed never again to move a muscle.

Claustrophobia is mental. It is not real. There is nothing to fear. Those were the slogans he was repeating.

But still he was not breathing, which was foolish, he knew, because finally when he gasped for air he would explode with noise and they would catch him and slice him from his bones before killing him, and his father would never understand why.

He made an effort to breathe and that made things worse because the dust on the nodules of his nostrils took him elsewhere. It took him to France where he was running down from the château and across the grass as swiftly as he could after Janet. He remembered cutting through a thicket of brambles and coming upon a cave into which he dreaded going. But he loved her. She was leading him there. She would make it safe for him. But, going in, he could not find her. Collins remembered the taste of limestone — was that the dust? — and remembered crawling on his belly and the awful feeling that the cave was going to collapse. He was having that exact feeling again. He pressed his hands against his ears harder, trying to squeeze the panic out of his head, trying to make the memory go away. But it would not. He remembered the light, how when the cave opened he hurled himself toward it, but there had been nothing and he had nearly fallen from the sheer cliff. He recalled turning to find Janet naked and alluring, waiting for him. He had gone to her and made love with her, but that image eluded him. What he saw, even as he kept his eyes shut against it, was an image of himself flailing her, kicking her, pulling the flesh from her bones. He was tearing at her eyes and clawing her and pounding her. He saw blood splashing from his hands. He was killing her and he could hear himself screaming, "Ma! Ma! You're smothering me! You're smothering me! Get off, Ma! Get off me, Ma!" And pushing her and clawing at her and not breathing because there was no air, only smoke, and not breathing because his mother was lying on top of him and his face was lost in her belly, and not breathing because he was choking with his weeping and his father was squeezing him in his terrible embrace and saying, "It doesn't matter, Micko, because I love you." All Collins Brady knew was that he was locked in too small a place with no air and it took everything in him not to cry out because he was dying of it.

He opened his eyes.

He was hunched over the toilet bowl.

He covered his face with his hands, which were wet, and he feared in the dark that it *was* blood, his mother's, his father's, his wife's. But it was tears and perspiration, his.

Ma? Had he cried Ma? What Ma? Was he crazy? Had he killed Janet? Was his father smothering him? What had happened?

There was the noise of a key turning in the lock. And then a second. A third.

He listened.

There were no other sounds.

Still he listened.

There was nothing.

After a long time he opened the cubicle door. The office was empty.

He crossed to the door and began to open its locks.

But he had not hung the microphone. The hell with it! He wanted out. He had to get out.

But he forced himself back. He took the device from his pocket, turned the switch as he'd been instructed, then lowered it on its wire a foot and a half below the level of the radiator. Only when it was securely in place, hidden, did he turn, cross back to the door and leave.

On the street, going west toward Boston, he knew that he had just lost his mind. He had just killed Janet, calling her "Ma." He had lost his mind and would never find it again. Why shouldn't he, when the sun finally came up, have been walking along the esplanade of the Charles weeping?

An MDC police cruiser on its regular patrol along the river drew up behind him. The lone officer might have passed the man by — there was nothing illegal about walking the esplanade at dawn — but there were several peculiarities about him. Peculiarities are what police look for. First, he did not move off the center of the path so the cruiser could pass. He seemed oblivious that an auto was trailing at his heels. Second, there was a purposelessness to his walking, a vagueness that reminded the officer of the way inmates walked around the yard at the State Hospital in Westboro. Not walking; ambulating. Third, the man was sobbing.

The policeman stopped the cruiser, put it in neutral and got out.

"What's the matter, fellow?"

Brady kept walking.

The policeman touched his elbow. There was something so sad about the guy that the policeman was moved. He wanted to be kind.

"Can I take you home, fellow?"

Brady stopped and faced him. "Take me, please, to the bishop's house."

Jesus Christ, the officer thought, *it's a priest!*

"You mean the cardinal?"

"Bishop McShane. Jack McShane."

Yes. He had to be a priest. Who else would call the bishop by his first name?

"Sure thing, fellow." He would not embarrass him by calling him "Father." "That's up at St. John's, eh? At the chancery?"

Brady nodded.

"Sure thing." He was glad, really glad to help, after all the good things priests had done for him. Priests were human too, right?

When Bishop McShane saw the police cruiser from his window he answered the door himself. He wanted to give the officer ten dollars, but he wouldn't hear of it.

He gave his cousin an ounce of brandy in a tumbler.

"What happened, Micko?"

Collins looked up at Jack from the large easy chair, a dazed, frightened expression on his face. There were dried tracks of tears on his cheeks. His cousin was standing over him with a strong hand on his shoulder.

Collins loved the feel of that hand. "Oh, Jack. Oh, Jack." Then he began to cry again.

The bishop sat on the arm of the chair and put his arms around his cousin. His cousin, hell! His brother. "It's all right, Micko. It's all right," he repeated.

Through his sobbing, Collins was saying, "I'm so evil, so evil, so evil."

McShane rubbed the flesh below Collins's shoulder blades. "I'm with you, Micko, no matter what."

Then Brady stopped saying anything, and soon he stopped crying.

For a long time he sat hunched in the hollow of McShane's strong embrace.

McShane had never seen his cousin vulnerable before, and here he was shattered. He'd come, thank God, to the right place.

When after nearly an hour Collins seemed to have a hold on himself, the bishop said, "Do you want to talk about it, Micko?"

"I guess, Jack, I'd like some coffee."

"Sure." He crossed to his hot plate. "Instant OK?" He put a kettle on the burner and took a seat opposite Brady.

"I don't know how to tell you, Jack."

Brady could feel his mind closing its shutters on its secrets. He owed a serious and truthful explanation to his cousin, but he would say nothing that pointed to his father or that demeaned himself.

"I'm involved, Jack . . ."

The bishop thought he was about to say, "With another woman."

". . . with the Mafia."

"The Mafia!"

"Yes. Have you ever heard of Gennaro Anselmo?"

"No."

"He's the don of the North End. Tonight . . . It was awful . . . I had to sit silently while he ordered a man killed in my presence. I felt a part of it, there was nothing I could do."

"I don't understand, Micko."

"Jack, I'm a special undercover agent for Bobby Kennedy."

The whistle on the kettle exploded.

McShane got up and prepared two cups of instant.

Collins was in complete control of himself now. "I had something of a trauma this morning because I'd broken into Anselmo's office to plant a bug and was nearly caught. I had to hide in a closet and, well, I guess my old . . ."

"Claustrophobia."

"Yes."

"You couldn't even hide under the bed when we were kids."

"I know. I was in there for a long time." Years.

"That must have been terrible for you."

"It was, as you saw. And, frankly, my mission, in which I believe and which Kennedy is counting on as a major breakthrough against crime, still makes me feel dirty, filthy, sneaky. And then this thing with the order to in effect murder a man, well, I feel awful about it."

"There's nothing you can do about that, is there?"

"No."

"Then you're not morally responsible, Micko. Your conscience should be clear."

"You think so?"

"Yes. I assure you."

"I think, Jack, I feel . . ." — Brady paused, knowing this was the truth — ". . . evil."

"Would you like absolution?"

Brady studied his cousin. That was not what he was talking about at all.

But, well, maybe it was.

"Yes, I think I would."

The bishop laid his coffee aside, crossed to his bureau, from which he took a thin purple stole. He donned it and stood over Brady with his hands on his head. *"Absolvo te,"* he intoned, and deliberately made his way through the Latin phrases, thinking meanwhile that he really did, after all these years, love this man intensely.

When the bishop finished, Collins took his hand and kissed the green stone of its ring. He looked up and said, "What I've told you, Jack, it's very secret."

"Of course, Micko," the bishop said. "The seal of confession. And who would I tell anyway?"

⟿ 5 ⟾

TONY BRADY did not look like a Harvard freshman. His complexion was a shade too dark. His eyes were black and very deep-set, which made him seem older than he was. He carried himself with an exceptional erectness that made a breezy casualness impossible. When he walked from his dormitory across the Yard to Widener it was utterly without any show of gregariousness. He was a self-possessed slightly aloof young man who, in his starched white shirt with open neck and closed sleeves, seemed a bit out of place among the Ivy button-downs.

He sat on the steps of the library to wait for his grandfather. He had not finished unpacking his trunk and his room at Hollis was still in chaos. He would like to have spent the morning putting his things in order. He wanted his room to be ready when classes began the next day. But his roommate's parents were still hovering awkwardly in the corners, making it impossible for him to stay there anyway. They had been uneasy with Tony and he had sensed it. When they'd asked him where he came from, as people do, he had startled them by saying Sicily, which they'd treated as a joke. But then they'd looked at each other and asked him nothing else. When his grandfather called and expressed an interest in seeing the campus with him, he welcomed the idea.

"There you are."

Tony stood and turned. Colman Brady, dressed as usual in a dark three-piece suit, was coming down the broad stairs. He'd been inside the library.

"Were you here already?" Tony asked. He did not like to be late.

"I got here early, laddo, and I've been touring the library inside. Been in yet?"

"Not yet. They say it's a great library."

"Indeed. The best."

Tony nodded. He understood that about Harvard. He was ready for the place. He had an exceptional intelligence, had done very well at Milton and was going to do very well at Harvard. He took it for granted that it was the best, but without a freshman's cockiness.

"Do you know the story of it, Tony? The library?"

Colman sat on the lowest of the terraced granite blocks that bordered the yawning staircase. He hiked his trousers, pinching their creases. He ran his right hand through his sandy gray hair.

"No, I don't think so." Tony sat on the step again, below his grandfather.

"It's named for a fellow — Harry Elkins Widener — who went here. His folks, of course, were loaded, and when he graduated they gave him a trip to Europe as a present." Colman paused to make sure he had the kid's attention. He did. What Colman liked about the kid was how he listened. It seemed he missed nothing. He listened the way Colman did. "He had a great time, presumably. But he came home on board the *Titanic*."

Tony said nothing. He stared at his grandfather. He understood exactly why he'd told him that. His grandfather had once been very moved by that story. That, more than the story itself, moved Tony.

"His mother gave the library in his memory," Colman said.

"When was that?"

Colman squinted up at the great pillared portico. The late morning sun blinded him for a moment. "Well, the *Titanic* went down in nineteen twelve. I was practically your age." Colman laughed at the truth of the statement. He'd been fourteen. "That's why grandfathers are grand, kiddo." He tousled the boy's hair.

"How did you know about Widener?"

"You can read about it inside. There's a collection of his books." Colman paused. How did he know? "A former ladyfriend of mine told me."

Tony rubbed the fingers of one hand in slow circles around the fingers of the other. He knew a confidence when it was offered him. "Ladyfriend, Grandfather?" Tony smiled.

"Yes. A long time ago."

"How did she know?" he asked, instead of *What was she like?*

Colman looked at him seriously. What the hell, why not the truth? "Her husband was on the Board of Overseers. She had a son whom she lost at sea. I think the memory of the Widener lad was precious to her."

Colman stopped. He was surprised by a rush of feeling. The boy did not avert his eyes. They sat looking at each other. Colman wondered where the urge to tell the kid more was coming from. "You know when I met her?" he asked grandly.

Tony was charmed by his grandfather's sudden expansiveness. "When?" he asked.

"On the day Prohibition ended. Your father and I were stealing a Christmas tree from her land and she caught us." Colman saw Madeline standing by the bar in that dark parlor. She had poured him a glass of Bushmills. He remembered how her hand shook slightly as she poured. "Do you know what she said to me, Tony, when she gave me a drink? She said, 'Doesn't taste nearly so well, does it, when it's legal?' "

"Did it?"

Colman shook his head slowly. "What she and I had, it was never legal. Your father never knew about it. It tasted marvelously." He smiled, but less grandly. Why was he saying these things? Colman found it very easy to show his sadness to his grandson.

"You have a girlfriend, son?"

"No," Tony said.

"You will. It's a wonderful thing, men and women."

"Your wife was killed in Ireland."

Had they never talked about that? "That's right. Your grandmother." Colman realized as soon as he'd said it that he'd never thought of Nell as Tony's grandmother. But of course she was. Then Tony gave him a look that reminded him that Tony didn't know it. Tony thought his grandparents, his real ones, were all Sicilian. Tony did not know, Colman thought, that it was Irish blood keeping him so sad.

"I never saw her picture."

The kid's past had so few faces. Colman reached inside his coat and withdrew his billfold. He rarely looked at Nellie's photo. He didn't remember when he last had. He unfolded the paper that held it and gave it to Tony.

"She's very beautiful," the boy said. "She is so young." After a moment he looked at Colman. "I remember my grandmother in Sicily. She was old. I remember her smell. She was very good to me, I think."

"Yes, I think she was." Colman took the photo and wrapped it carefully and replaced it. He did not study it as once he would have because he was still thinking of Madeline.

"Shall we walk?" Tony said, standing up. It was not a question.

Colman thought he'd grown into a wise young man. He knew when the edge of a mood had been reached and how to draw back from it.

"Lead on, kiddo," Colman said. But both he and Tony knew that he would be the leader of this tour. It was a pattern they both relished. Since Tony was young Colman had taken him places and told him stories. What those stories almost always showed was that Tony's grandfather was no more a part of his parents' world than he was. Tony had no stories to tell Colman, except what he remembered vaguely and what he read about Sicily. His grandfather was not curious about Sicily, though.

"Tell me about Harvard, Grandfather."

"What do I know about Harvard? You should ask your father." Colman paused unfortunately, long enough for them both to have the same thought. Tony kept his distance from his parents' pain by keeping his distance from his parents. No, he would not ask his father about Harvard. No, his father would not tell him.

"I do know some things, though," Colman admitted. "I was here for the Tercentenary, nineteen thirty-six."

"You were?" Tony was impressed and curious and showed it.

"Indeed. I was holding the governor's horse."

"Who was governor?"

"Himself. Curley."

"I thought he was just mayor."

Christ, Colman thought, why was such ignorance allowed? "No, laddo. Curley was one of everything except President. That wasn't his fault. It was his father's for not being Joe Kennedy."

"I remember when Curley died. We had a special civics class on him."

"November twelve, nineteen fifty-nine." Brady summoned the date effortlessly. "Curley would have been thrilled to know they noticed his passing at Milton Academy."

"It must have been difficult, working for him."

"Why do you say that?"

"He was . . ." — Tony wanted the proper word — ". . . unscrupulous."

Colman did not comment. It was true, of course. But the truth was not worthy of Curley. It didn't begin, the mere truth, to describe him.

They were halfway across the Yard, walking toward the entrance to the Memorial Church.

Tony felt the weight of his grandfather's silence. "My father told me you had it out with Curley because you were too honest."

Colman looked at Tony and smiled. The boy's father would say that. "I'll tell you, Tony, Curley and I had our differences, no doubt about it. But those folks at Milton and these at Harvard have a special cause to make you think poorly of him. He was a good friend to people like us when we were just getting started."

"Like us?"

"The Irish."

Tony wanted to remind his grandfather that he was not Irish, as if that were his secret, and that he was not a WASP preppie, as if that were. Tony's secret was that he was Sicilian. He wanted to ask what Curley had done for *his* people, but he said nothing.

"I want to show you something, kiddo. Can I?"

Tony followed his grandfather up the stairs and into the Memorial Church.

It was a lot like the chapel at Milton, very white, a soft deep red rug, gleaming mahogany railings and trim. But it was much larger than the school chapel. No one was there. It was very still.

Colman crossed to the aisle that cut the nave and stopped practically in the dead center of the church.

"Look." His voice was hushed. He gestured to the north wall which was covered with names. *Men of Harvard Who Gave Their Lives in Defense of Their Country.* The columns of names were divided about equally beneath the two headings, *The Great War* and *World War Two.* A third smaller and new section was headed *Korea.*

Colman was reading the names.

Tony imitated him.

It was a litany of Anglo-Saxon surnames, all those families. Here and there, an Irish name — more in the second war than in the first.

"See it?"

"What?"

Colman pointed. "Third column, halfway down."

He saw it, the name of Joseph P. Kennedy, Jr.

Colman said softly, "Tony, I want you to know what a victory it is to have any Irish names up there at all. The great victory it is to have Kennedy. You know that, don't you?"

Tony nodded. He felt a kinship with the President all out of proportion to his usual responses. He was a lad with shrewd insight into the falsehoods of adult lives. He saw with devastating clarity through the manners and values and ideals that had been urged upon him by his mother and his father and his schooling. His keen-sightedness was what kept him slightly apart and emotionally distant. But his response to President Kennedy was one of strong attraction. What Tony sensed in Kennedy was a strength that came from a solitude about which Tony knew nothing except that Kennedy had it. Because he was slightly alien to his time and place he could, as President, embody them perfectly. It was an alienation of which Tony was acutely aware. Kennedy had mastered it, had made it his great asset, and that was why Tony believed in him intensely. Because he did — and not because of the urgings of his teachers and his parents — he had come to Harvard.

"There are no Italian names up there," Tony said.

Colman faced the kid. "There probably aren't," he said, though he was sure there were some. The kid seemed always to erect a barrier like that. It seemed to Brady at first that Tony was just indulging his hurt at not being — as he thought — biologically a member of his own family. But then, looking at him and seeing his strong dark eyes, which showed not a hint of self-pity, it struck Brady that the kid was not erecting a barrier but trying to collapse one. He was Italian, after all. Why should that not be as important to him as being Irish was to Brady? Tony never adverted to his roots around his parents, sensing perhaps that his origins were part of what kept his parents separate. By his simple statement now he was entrusting his grandfather with something that was precious to him. Colman was shocked by what he saw suddenly in Tony. The moody, insistent autonomy, the self-serving stubbornness, the refusal to forget how things began or to expect that they would end differently — Colman recognized those qualities. He knew them inside and out. They were why he himself had survived his own youth. They were why he himself was alone. They were — and this is what shocked him — his grandson's! It was as if he had seen a peculiar dimple in the boy's chin and recognized it as his own. The boy *was* his grandson. Tony's heart beat with *his* blood, even if he didn't know it. And if that strange, rough inner terrain had passed from Colman through Collins, whose surfaces were so smooth to this boy, why should he not be glad? Colman understood then that the very thing that kept Tony apart from him was what he admired most in the kid. Colman put his hand on his shoulder to press it and to let some of what he was feeling flow into him. But Tony turned away — there it was — and led the way out of the church.

They circled the Yard together, paused dutifully at the statue of John Harvard, crossed to Massachusetts Hall, the oldest building, and toured it quickly.

They were waiting for a break in traffic to cross Mass. Ave. to see Radcliffe when Colman pointed to the MTA kiosk on an island in the middle of Harvard Square. A subway from there would get a man to Park Street in ten minutes. "Do you know the story of that kiosk, laddo?"

"I didn't know it had one."

"There's a story for everything."

"Tell me."

The light changed, but they stayed on the curb looking at the faded green graceless little building that had an air of substance only by comparison to the newspaper stand next to it.

"The subway building wasn't always there, you know."

"No kidding. It looks like it's been there since Genesis."

"It was very controversial when they put it up. Cambridge wanted it, of course. Harvard, of course, didn't. Anyway that's the background for what will probably go down in history as the most memorable headline from the old Boston *Examiner*."

"What was it?"

"Well, that's half the background. The other half has to do with Abbott Lawrence Lowell. Ever heard of him?"

"No."

"He was this thin, bespectacled, prissy fellow who never went anywhere without his wooden staff like he was Moses or a bishop and his little prissy cocker spaniel named Phantom. I mean all you need to know really is that he was a very proper and tight and, well, Puritan patrician. You know what I mean?"

"I get the picture. We had a dozen of them as teachers at Milton."

"Good. Well, one day in the middle of that controversy over this damn thing, the *Examiner* runs a page-one story with the headline in big bold letters, 'President Lowell fights erection in Harvard Square.' "

Tony was shocked.

Colman started smugly across the street. He knew he startled the boy, and he loved it. Tony, like all eighteen-year-olds, thought he was among the first in history to feel the stiffness in his pants. It was the source of their ultimate embarrassment and therefore of their most extreme laughter. But Tony's appreciation was wry and subdued.

On the other side of Mass. Ave., Tony said, "If I told that to my father he'd blast me for two things; talking dirty and not showing respect."

"It's not talking dirty to mention Abbott Lawrence Lowell," Colman said, "unless you do it in church. I won't listen to your complaints about your father."

Tony was offended by the quick rebuke, and Colman knew it immediately for the overreaction it was. The lad's manner stirred up more feelings in Brady than he expected. For one thing, he felt guilty and disloyal toward Collins for being disappointed in him. Tony was tougher than his father, that's what Colman thought.

They walked down Church Street to Brattle and up Brattle a block. "Come along here," Colman said. He left the sidewalk and cut between two hedges, following a path that the girls used as a short cut. It led into a yard bounded on one side by the gracious colonial curve of the dormitory and on the other by a serpentine brick wall. Colman made for a point in the center of the wall where a fountain spilled a trickle into a raised pool. "Look at this."

Tony saw an arrangement of dots on a plaque.

"It's braille, kiddo."

Tony let his fingers run over it.

"Ever hear of Helen Keller, son?"

"Sure. *The Miracle Worker.* Who hasn't?"

"She went to Radcliffe. This fountain is here because *water* was the first word she said."

Tony put his hand in the water, as if he were dipping to bless himself.

"Do you know who her teacher was?"

"No."

"A girl from Boston. Annie Sullivan. An Irish girl. In fact, kiddo, she was from *South* Boston. She lived about six blocks from our old house."

"No kidding."

"That's right. And she stayed with Helen Keller right through, even through Radcliffe."

"You have a sort of a thing about the Irish." Tony smiled ironically.

"Around here, Tony, the only men who talk the way I do are janitors. And the only girls who do are maids."

"That's not true anymore, though."

"Not for you, son. I hope you appreciate why. I don't want you to start thinking of your people the way they do here."

"I don't."

"I'm sure you don't. I want you to be proud of where you come from, and I don't mean Milton Academy."

"I know." The boy fell silent, and Colman guessed what he was thinking: if the point was to be made, he comes from Italy, or, worse, from Sicily. "I'm glad," Tony said, "of where I come from." Tony looked away. It was not Colman's place to tell him more.

"Ever been to Southie?"

"Sure. The beach a couple of summers ago."

"When you couldn't get to Ipswich, eh? Want to go over there? I'll show you where we lived when your dad was a wee infant."

"Could we? I'd love to."

"Sure, we can. You can't know where you're going unless you know where you come from."

"That sounds like something they'd teach you at Harvard."

"Only they'd be talking about Athens and Sparta, not Fourth Street."

"What about that war?" Tony asked suddenly.

"What about it? Think they'll know we came over from Cambridge and bump us off?"

Colman made Tony's hesitation seem silly, but for months the gang-land-style killing in South Boston and Charlestown had dominated the news. Over twenty men had been murdered.

"That's what I mean, kiddo." Colman misunderstood the boy's hesitation. "The Irish aren't a bunch of vicious animals. Lots of folks live in Southie besides hired guns. There's nothing to be afraid of."

Tony stared at his grandfather. What there was to be afraid of was the fact that the war was between the Irish and the Italians. Tony had secretly been obsessed by it. He had, during the just-ended summer, taken to strolling through the North End as if he lived there, trying to understand how such violence could involve such lively, generous-spirited people. He had even taken to teaching himself how to read and write Sicilian, and to polishing his ability to speak it, not lost since childhood. He loved to ease along Revere Street chatting with the old ladies, who would not have understood if they'd known his name was Brady. The newspaper accounts of each fresh killing bothered him more and more because he could not imagine the people he saw on the streets of the North End doing what reporters and police said they did. But he couldn't imagine the Irish doing it either. Given his own reactions, it seemed to him his grandfather was bothered very little by the worsening spiral of that violence.

"What do you say, kiddo?" Colman said. "We can take the subway from Lowell's erection. When all the Cambridge cookies get off at Park Street on their ways to Shreve's, we can stay on three more stops and get off in the world of Cardinal Cushing, Speaker McCormack, Annie Sullivan, and — God forbid! — James Michael Curley. Southie's a wonderful place, the Irish Riviera. You'll love it!"

Tony said nothing, but thought, *A wonderful place? Why had the Bradys moved?*

So little ever happened there, that was why. Walking up Broadway that day could have been walking up Broadway thirty years before. The rough and merciless tenement flats with lamplight and cellar toilets were gone. In their place was the new D Street public housing project. But still the west end of Southie was a concentration of howling families with banshee mothers, drunken fathers, and foul-mouthed children. Colman and Tony walked by some of each. On the corner in front of Doran's Bar they had to step between an unconscious inebriate and a mangy dog who lay in the sun shrugging spastically at its fleas.

Colman snorted, "It's not all like this."

"Oh, this isn't . . . ." What could he say? The place was exactly what he thought it would be. ". . . that bad." But it was that bad. The North End was paradise compared to this. That was what Tony thought. His grandfather's obvious revulsion relieved him.

"But it's not all like this, I'm telling you. You wait."

At Dorchester Heights Broadway makes a sharp jag left, and everything changes. It had been so in the twenties and it was still so. There were the grand bowfront brick mansions the old families had built before the Irish came, and there were the neat three-deckers of City Point beyond Flood Square.

"See that hardware store?"

"O'Houlihan's?" Tony asked, reading the sign.

"That was a speak in my day. A speakeasy. You know about speakeasies?"

"Prohibition."

"Right." As they went by the place, Colman remembered the massacre from that other war which had lasted only minutes. He thought of Jerry MacCurtain. A fond memory, it was, of Jer trying to get him to quit politics. Colman thought briefly how differently his life might have looked. MacCurtain might still have been alive. But the Bradys might still have been in Southie.

Colman remembered what he used to say to his friend, and he said it out loud to Tony. "You know what O'Casey said, don't you? 'A man should always be drunk when he talks politics. It's the only way in which to make them important.' "

Tony took in what his grandfather said, thought it strange, and did not reply.

"This is City Point," Colman said as they crossed L Street. The neighborhood took on a scrubbed look, not the groomed aspect of Beacon Hill perhaps, but a look as healthy, fresh, and clean-smelling as a nun. The houses on both sides of the street stood their watches like matrons eyeing children. At L Street and Fourth the Tuckerman School disgorged a legion of them just as Colman and Tony were passing.

"I see the kids still go home for lunch," Colman said. "That school is new."

"It doesn't look new."

"Well, forgive me. I mean new since the war."

"Who was Tuckerman?"

"No idea."

"Well, make something up."

Colman looked sharply at him. Tony was smiling, that irony again. "Don't vex me, you!"

Halfway down the block they stopped. "Well, there it is."

An ordinary three-decker with a nearly fresh coat of gray paint.

"We lived up there at first." Colman pointed to the third-floor flat. "Maeve owned the place, shocked hell out of me when I got here. She seemed rich to me."

"It's a nice house."

"See the first floor? I had my insurance business in there. That's where it all started."

They continued to walk on Fourth Street toward Marine Park and Castle Island.

"What do you think you'll do, son? Now that you're in the majors."

"I don't know, Grandfather," he replied. "Maybe a lawyer."

Colman hated it when the kid called him that. Janet. It was so formal, stilted, goddamn British. Like *pater*.

"Like your old man."

"Like Kennedy." Not like his father. "But I've also been thinking about the Peace Corps. You know, I mean after college, before law school, for a couple of years."

"Africa or someplace."

"I'd love to go to Africa. I want to go everywhere."

Colman remembered that feeling. The young have a right to it.

Marine Park is an expanse of lawn at the tip of City Point which runs gently down to the beaches that lie like cuticle on Paradise Bay, the lagoon formed by the causeway and breakwaters at Castle Island. At the point in the middle of the park where Morrissey Boulevard, the beach road, and Broadway intersect, there is a large statue of Admiral Farragut, whose bronze gaze is fixed on the sea. The statue, imposing and handsome, is a point of pride for the people of Southie and a common meetingplace. On warm, lovely days like that one, the benches in its shadow are always crowded in the mornings with the teenaged mothers who sit gossiping with one hand on the chrome handle of the baby's pram, and in the afternoon with old men who amiably share their brown-bagged bottles.

Colman and Tony were half a block from the statue, approaching it, when they heard the screams of women.

They ran toward them.

A group of seven or eight young mothers and old men — the benches' shift was on since it was midday — were clustered at Farragut's feet. At their feet lay the body of a man.

Colman and Tony were paralyzed momentarily with the shock of the sight. The corpse was grotesquely twisted.

"Wait here!" Colman commanded.

Colman crossed to the stunned group and pushed through them. Two women were holding each other. An infant was screaming in its pram; its mother was hysterical. The old men just stared stupidly down at the corpse.

A trickle of blood seeped out of a large hole in the head, and there were the dark caked stains of old blood in a dozen different splotches on the body. Whoever it was, he'd been gunned to death some time before.

"What happened?" he asked the man at his elbow. The man looked blankly at Colman. He was very old, toothless, unshaven. He clutched a wrapped pint to his breast.

"Sure, they just drove past and he fell out."

Colman recognized the lilting accent of his own county, and a bitter distaste welled in his stomach; the goddamn Irish bum!

"When?"

"Just a minute ago."

"It's Mugsy Malloy," one of the other men said in a sudden fit of recognition. He'd been craning down to see the less damaged side of the man's face. "Mugsy Malloy! Oh, Mugsy!"

"What'd he ever do to them?" another asked.

And one of the women let go a fresh shriek at the mention of Malloy's name. If that mass of goo and red pulp was Mugsy, woe was her! Mugsy Malloy was her husband's cousin.

Colman turned away.

He bumped into Tony.

"Goddamn you! I told you not to come over here!"

Colman's hand was open and ready to slap the kid. It was the horror in Tony's eye that stopped him, for that was the mirror of his own — horror at this corpse, at these people, at this rage spilling from his own throat like vomit. Tony's horror, so articulate in his beautiful dark face, stopped Colman cold.

He might have hit the kid.

He might have killed him.

He did not want him to see this. He did not want him to know.

"When I tell you to do something . . ." He was not speaking angrily now. He was speaking with an aloof, chastising sternness to protect both of them from that other thing.

But Colman could not continue because Tony was devastating him with the expression on his face. Tony was reading his anger as an assault, an act of vengeance, as if Brady cared that Italians — not Polish — had done this. Suddenly Colman saw what Tony saw — a war between his real people and those who had somehow stolen him from them and whom it was Tony's misfortune to have come to need and depend upon. Colman had ushered his grandson onto that harsh spot where he could see nothing but murder between his family whom he did not know — the Sicilians — and an enemy — the Irish — whom he loved.

"It's all the same, Grandfather, don't you think?"

Tony had seen it before, such blood. Colman understood for the first time, really, that the kid had been born in Sicily and had lived through terrors there. His first family, Colman remembered, had all been murdered in the war between Castillo and Taormina. Colman could think of nothing to say. He wanted to embrace the kid, to hold him against his breast, to take him inside the great old ache. But before he could, Tony turned and walked away from him.

That loosed a huge rage in Brady. "You come back here," he hollered.

Tony walked, not hurriedly, up Broadway.

"Goddamn you," Colman yelled. "Don't you walk away from me!"

Colman Brady was screaming at the top of his voice, like the women. He was one of them.

His son had never done that to him, defied him so. His son had never looked with such horror on who he was.

"Goddamn you," he said one last time, still staring after his grandson, but he said it softly, to himself.

He looked at the corpse.

This was insane.

This had to stop.

Such horror as Tony's was exactly right. For the first time, Colman Brady felt it.

By the time he got to the cab stand at Broadway and P Street, police sirens resounded from three directions.

"What's that?" the cabbie asked.

"Who knows?"

"Where to?"

"Hanover Street in the North End."

Gennaro Anselmo was sitting in his accustomed place at a table in the far corner of the Cantina Reale. The restaurant was crowded with lunch business. Anselmo could watch everybody from his place.

He was the first to see Brady. He watched him wave the maitre d' aside and walk deliberately into the restaurant, his head turning slowly, looking at the people, looking, Anselmo knew, for him.

Anselmo remained motionless in his seat.

Brady saw him and crossed.

"I want to talk to you."

Anselmo made a simple gesture toward an empty chair. Pio Costanari was slurping minestrone, ignoring Brady. Marcello was staring at him.

"Not here," Brady said.

The sharp omen flashed in Brady, confirming what Anselmo thought. He had expected Brady before this. He was, after all, Irish. Anselmo was repeating Zorelli's slaughter, only systematically and efficiently, more ruthlessly. He had killed all the leaders of the South Boston, Somerville, and Charlestown gangs, all but Maguire and a few other old ones. They were alive because there was still something sentimental in Anselmo.

"As you wish." Anselmo stood.

Costanari and Marcello both rose.

"Not them," Brady said.

"Ah, but my friend . . . ," Anselmo began.

"Not them."

Anselmo faced Marcello. "Stay."

He dropped his napkin and started to come out from the corner. Costanari prepared to follow.

Brady stepped into Costanari and grabbed his arm and hissed, "Not you!" Brady caused him such pain, squeezing the flesh above his elbow, that his jowly face drained of color.

Marcello was ready to hurl himself on Brady.

"Come, friend," Anselmo said.

Brady released Costanari, who grabbed his arm and rubbed it.

"Finish your meal, Pio," Anselmo said. "Keep my son company. It is not good to eat alone." Then he led Brady up to his office.

Anselmo sat in his chair and leaned back in it as he usually did. The vertical slats of the chair rested against the radiator.

"Call it off, Gennaro."

"Please, sit."

"No."

"It is off. It's all finished."

"Shit! Your creeps just dumped a corpse at my feet in Southie."

"Malloy."

"Yes."

"He is the last."

"I don't believe you."

"Have I ever lied to you? Nothing more will happen, unless they do it."

"You know they will, somebody will, some damn punk."

"If that happens" — Anselmo shrugged morosely — "what can I do? I must protect my people."

"Shit! What about my people? It's their cadavers that have paved over the cobblestones in this town."

"Don't speak to me like this."

"You're Al Capone, Gennaro! What the hell happened?"

Anselmo only stared at him.

"Are you that afraid of Balestrione?"

Anselmo still said nothing.

"If you are, then kill his boys. Leave the dumb mick shitheads alone. They can't hurt you. Call it off."

"I won't defend what I do, or explain it."

"You goddamn have to!" Brady slammed his hand down on the table that separated them.

A small grin transformed Anselmo's face. "You forget. You wear my livery, Colman, not theirs. If they were really your people you'd have been here before now. I killed Gallagher a year ago."

"Gallagher asked for it. But these other guys are nobody. Malloy, for Christ's sake! Who the hell was he?"

"He was on the list."

"Jesus Christ! You're mad!"

"No. Quite the contrary. I am maintaining control of what I am responsible for. In this instance, that requires the elimination of the undisciplined. They are eliminated now."

"And Balestrione's off your back."

"Ciro Balestrione is my friend."

"Don't shit me, Genarro. When did you ever lie to me, eh?"

"Colman, you are either dangerously ignorant or losing your grip on yourself."

Anselmo's tone contained warning enough. "Ignorant about what?"

"Ciro and I cannot afford pointless rivalry now. We are both targets of the same investigation."

"The IRS shit?"

"No. Much more serious, I'm afraid. Kennedy."

"Kennedy! You mean he's doing something?"

"I'm disappointed not to have learned about it from you. I was under the impression that your son had maintained some contacts for the purpose of our protection."

"What's the investigation? Tell me."

"A secret grand jury is to be convened here in Boston for the express purpose of bringing indictments against Balestrione's family and mine."

"Christ!"

"You didn't know?"

"I thought Bobby'd shot his wad with Hoffa."

"He's just been warming up. Have you ever heard of the Defense Intelligence Agency language school in Monterey?"

"No."

"They teach their spies Russian and Chinese and Cuban."

[567]

"So?"

"They have just added a new language to their program." Anselmo waited several beats. "Sicilian."

Brady refused to show any reaction to this.

"Why, my friend, do you think they do that? To come among us as one of us? No. It is a mystery, isn't it?"

What the hell was he driving at?

Anselmo shrugged. "Who knows? Of course, if they had ears . . ."

"I want out, Gennaro." Colman shocked himself. He had not planned to say that.

Anselmo let the grin creep back across his face. "Out, Colman? Where is 'out' for you?"

"We had an understanding, Gennaro, from the beginning. This was not Chicago. We were not murderers. I want no further part in things."

"Things? There are no 'things.' There is only history. History, Colman. You cannot get out of that. That is what we have together."

"What we had together died at my feet this morning."

"We are two sides of one coin. How do we separate two sides of one coin? Tell me that. You have a company, many companies. You are a powerful man. But you own nothing. You rent. Rent, Colman, from me. Tell me how you can get 'out' of 'things,' Colman."

Colman said nothing. He looked at Anselmo the way the dead look at their progeny from portraits.

Anselmo, oblivious to that hatred, maintained a voice and manner which were fond and benign. "We wear the same shackles; that is our history, Colman." Anselmo let his chair come forward away from the radiator. "If Kennedy moves on me, he moves on you. If my people are troubled, your people die. If my sons have reason to fear, your son will not sleep for as long as that is so. 'Out'? No, friend. Not you, not ever. We wear the same shackles, Colman. They are terrible in every way but one. They are what made us friends."

6

AT EIGHT O'CLOCK on the morning of Thursday, October 11, 1962, a line of men half a mile long proceeded down Bernini's *scala regia,* across

St. Peter's Square, and, wheeling right, up the great stairs into the largest church in the world. They were the bishops of the Catholic Church, immaculate in white damask copes, tall in pointed white miters. And they were the Sacred College of Cardinals, scarlet. And in their wake, innocuous, Angelo Roncalli, peasant, riding in oriental splendor on the *sedia gestatoria*, the Pope blessing everyone, collecting their tears.

To that man a few moments later, after he had taken his place in the Chair of Peter, each bishop came forward, bowed, knelt, kissed his ring and made obeisance to the See of the Fisherman.

Then Pope John rose and in strong voice he proclaimed his sermon on the occasion of the opening of the Second Vatican Council.

"The council now beginning rises in the Church like daybreak, a forerunner of most splendid light. It is now only dawn. And already at this first announcement of the rising day, how much sweetness fills our heart. Everything here breathes sanctity and arouses great joy. Let us contemplate the stars, which with their brightness augment the majesty of this temple. These stars, according to the testimony of the Apostle John, are you, and with you we see shining around the tomb of the Prince of the Apostles, the golden candelabra — that is, the churches confided to you.

"In the daily exercise of our pastoral office we sometimes have to listen, much to our regret, to voices of persons who, though burning with zeal, are not endowed with too much sense of discretion or measure. In these modern times they can see nothing but prevarication and ruin. They say that our era, in comparison with past eras, is getting worse and they behave as though they had learned nothing from history, which is, nonetheless, the teacher of life. They behave as though at the time of former councils everything was a full triumph for the Christian idea and life and for proper religious liberty."

Pope John paused and looked out at the massed prelates sitting in their tiers along the length of the nave. The hush was such that whispers uttered in the corners years before seemed to hover in the dark, vast reaches above them.

"We feel we must disagree with these prophets of doom who are always forecasting disaster, as though the end of the world were at hand.

"In the present order of things, Divine Providence is leading us to a new order of human relations which by men's own efforts and even beyond their very expectations are directed toward the fulfillment of God's superior and inscrutable designs. And everything, even human differences, leads to the greater good of the Church."

". . . *ad majus bonum ecclesiae.*"

The Pope was speaking in Latin.

Latin was the language of the Church. The speech of the ancient

Romans was alive, and never more so than at this gathering. French-speaking blacks from Africa met their German brothers and spoke in Latin. Asian prelates, courtly and reserved, listened and nodded while their Italian colleagues spoke in Latin. A peasant bishop from the Amazon explained himself to a venerable cardinal from Vienna in Latin. *L'Osservatore Romano* had run an advertisement which read, *"Hertz Automobiles Novissimae Locantus. Securitatem Hertz. Amplius Confert."*

But while John was delivering his stirring mandate-sermon, Richard Cardinal Cushing nodded sleepily, as if Latin were his sedative. He stabbed his breast repeatedly with his chin, a dangerous weapon.

At a preparatory meeting of the commission to which he'd been assigned he had risen and begun to speak in English. Monsignor Felici, the secretary general, admonished him.

"Eminentissime, violes regulas ordinis. Aut response lingua Latina aut tace."

Cushing had looked at Felici, stunned. Even if he hadn't heard the words he'd have caught the drift of the Italian's rebuke. He was expert in reading the tilt of noses.

He'd looked at the man next to him and wished it were John McShane. He could have made a show of asking McShane what the wop had said, but McShane was on *Bishops and Government* — God knew how he landed that!

The bishop next to Cushing had been from Rhodesia.

"What's he say?" Cushing had asked, leaning down.

The Rhodesian shrugged. He wasn't going to get involved in that.

Cushing turned and glared at Felici, whose dark contempt came back at him as from a glass. Cushing turned back to the Rhodesian and, in his booming voice, said, "Your Lordship, you speak Latin?"

"Of course," the archbishop mumbled.

"Then will you kindly tell that ding-a-ling that I am here representing the Church-outside-the-walls!"

With that Cushing had left the room.

Now, during John's address, he was bored stiff. He'd personally told the Pope that he would gladly contribute the sum needed to install a United Nations–type translation system, but no. Everybody knew these Italian fellows weren't really speaking Latin, anyway. They were just speaking their regular wop, a little slower was all, and without the hand-spaghetti. Except for His Holiness, of course, who wasn't like the rest of them. Not at all.

After the Pope's sermon and during the break before the first session, Cushing went over to the Bar Jonah, the coffee shop for Council Fathers that had been set up in a spacious corridor leading to one of the side entrances of St. Peter's. The Pope himself had suggested the accommodation, even though some thought it violated the sacred character of the Basilica. "If we don't provide a place for them to smoke," he'd said to the cardinal in charge, "the bishops will be puffing under their miters."

Cushing thought a little coffee might be just what he needed.

The narrow shop with its buffets and stools was crowded with fathers and observers, with waiters in red busbies carrying trays, sliding between the chatting pairs of prelates. Cushing stood on the edge of the bustle for a moment looking for somebody to speak English to. He saw McShane.

Jack McShane was talking familiarly with Ruggero Borella. *A sacristy snake if there ever was one,* Cushing thought, approaching them. What the hell was McShane doing with that guy?

They were conversing in Latin.

Hotshots, Cushing thought.

"All right, Bishop," he said loudly, "enough of that gobbledygook!"

"Hello, Your Eminence. You know Cardinal Borella?"

"Indeed. *Eminentissime,*" Cushing said impishly, *"Dominus vobiscum!"*

"Good morning, Eminence," Borella said, extending his hand with warmth and even — was it possible? — a hint of deference.

"Wasn't that a wonderful sermon, Cardinal?" McShane asked Cushing.

"I wouldn't know. I didn't catch a word of it."

"Come now . . ." McShane blushed. Why did Cushing have to continually play the buffoon? McShane eyed Borella briefly to see if he were displaying his disdain.

Borella showed nothing. His face, thin and ascetic below rimless spectacles, was composed like a diplomat's. He was nearly as tall as Cushing. McShane, between the two of them, had to look up; he had long considered his short stature one of his failings.

"I met your Mrs. Kennedy, Cardinal Cushing, when she was here for her audience with the Holy Father." Borella had withdrawn a silver cigarette case from a pocket inside the tunic of his cassock. He was tapping a filterless cigarette on the case.

Cushing was staring at the engraved embellishment on Borella's silver case; it was a *Chi-rho,* the ancient Greek symbol for Christ. *That's a little much,* he thought.

Borella, noting the stare, offered his case.

"No, no. Not with my asthma. Then I *would* be finished. So you met Jackie. A great girl, Jackie."

"A woman of poise and charm. Americans are right to be proud of her."

Cushing nodded, accepting the compliment. Jackie Kennedy was his daughter.

"May I get you some coffee?" McShane asked. "Either of you?"

"None of that cappuccino stuff, Jack," Cushing said. "See if they have Postum, will you?"

"Postum? They probably don't."

"Well, lace it with a lot of milk, will you? Make it like American."

"Certainly." McShane turned to Borella. "Eminence?"

"No, Bishop, thank you."

McShane went off thinking, *Make it like American, indeed!* What an embarrassment the Cush could be!

Borella was thinking how like Roncalli Cushing was. "Cardinal Cushing, I can arrange, if you like, to provide you the text of His Holiness' remarks. In English, of course."

"Never mind."

"It must be done in any case, for the Protestants."

Cushing knew a slam when he heard one. "No, thanks. I got the gist of it."

"Your promotion of the vernacular is well known."

"Why call it the 'vernacular'? I was just promoting understanding. I don't see why things should be carried on in Italian."

"In Latin, Eminence. Because it is the Holy Father's wish."

"The Holy Father is getting bad advice."

"Latin must be preserved as a sign of unity. It is the language of the Church, a sacred tongue."

"Sacred? It was the tongue of the fellows who nailed the Lord to a pole, as I recall. I don't think Jesus knew Latin, do you?"

"That is irrelevant."

"I suppose so."

"You have a firm position, I see." Borella's smile was intended to be ingratiating. Its condescension only piqued Cushing further.

"You're kidding yourself if you think half these bishops know what's being said."

"That may not be the most important thing." The ash on his cigarette was nearly an inch long. He let it fall to the marble floor.

Cushing made a point to watch the ash fall.

"Oh? What is the most important thing, Eminence?"

"Preserving the deposit of Faith."

"How does a little translation system put the deposit of Faith in jeopardy?"

"If you admit the vernacular into the proceedings of this most sacred forum, then soon there will be agitation for its use in the very prayer of the Church, the Holy Office and the Eucharist."

"Nobody's talking about changing the Mass."

"Yes, Cardinal, that is exactly what the issue is. And if the tongue of the Mass can change, what cannot, eh?"

"Why is it dangerous if people understand what's happening? The way it is, there will be just a few of you fellows talking to each other about the 'deposit of Faith.' You make it sound like a bank account."

"What should be discussed if not that?"

"How to be of service to the world."

" 'The world,' Eminence, is what threatens the Faith."

"Ah, I see. And the way we protect it is by keeping its head in the sand of mumbo jumbo. I think you're in for a surprise or two, Cardinal, at this council. Or do you think the Holy Spirit only understands Italo-Latin too?"

Borella would perhaps have not replied to that anyway, but he did not have to since McShane arrived, holding two cups of coffee. Under his chin he had pressed one of the cheap aluminum ashtrays.

"Here we are." He sensed their mood. "Sorry to interrupt."

"That's all right, Jack." Cushing took his coffee. "We were just talking about the prevarication and ruin of modern times. Cardinal Borella was just telling me how our era, in comparison with past eras, is getting worse."

Cushing's eyes twinkled as he toasted Borella with his coffee cup. He had heard the sermon and understood every word, and he knew, as well as Borella knew, that Pope John had already labeled such sentiments as Borella's as the prophecy of gloom.

Cushing cast one more glance at the ashes on the floor, turned and walked away.

Borella snuffed his cigarette on the ashtray McShane held for him.

"Your cardinal is a very shrewd man."

McShane wondered what prompted that. He watched Borella, whose eyes were following Cushing.

"Is it true he is an intimate, authentically an intimate, to Kennedy?"

"Yes. The President calls him once or twice a week."

"Remarkable." Borella's expression suggested that Cushing's relationship with the most powerful man in the world — and that relationship alone — was reason to take him seriously.

"When President Kennedy needed the million-dollar ransom for the Bay of Pigs prisoners, it was Cardinal Cushing he turned to."

"But it is only a formal contact, no?" Borella was trying to assess Cushing's power, his real power.

"No. Quite personal. The family seeks his counsel on a range of matters."

John McShane considered himself an astute judge of the motives of others, and he assumed that, like most Romans, Borella was enthralled with Kennedy. Hence his interest in Cushing. He assumed that Borella was alert for ways to exploit the President's Catholicism, the potential of which as an opening on power had so far been missed by the Church. McShane guessed that in Borella's estimation Cushing was not shrewd enough to take full advantage of his relationship with the most powerful man in the world. Cushing was all too lacking in the sophistication required to move comfortably at such altitudes. Borella had it. McShane assured himself that he had it.

But McShane's assessment of Borella's interest in Cushing's connections was off the mark. Borella was not enthralled by Kennedy, and he knew that the man's religion, like that of most Americans, went no deeper than the tan he nurtured for his television appearances. The Church had no particular need of Kennedy. Borella's interest was in Cushing himself, only because it is important to know the exact measure of a man's potential before dismissing him utterly.

"Perhaps a bit of air, Your Eminence, before the session?" It was bold of McShane to suggest that he, a relative underling, and Borella, a senior official of the Holy Office, should go outside together. The garden stroll was an act of intimacy at the Vatican, a sign of peership. Cardinals in the Curia did not lightly bestow it on mere auxiliary bishops.

"Certainly, my friend. Certainly."

Borella had his purposes for everything.

The pair left the coffee bar and walked the length of the nave of the Basilica. They crossed through the cavernous sacristy behind Bernini's columns and went out into the manicured garden that nestled between St. Peter's and the Vatican apartments.

It was a glorious fall day, crisp yet not cool enough to require a cloak. The sky was the color of robins' eggs.

No one was in the garden.

The chips of marble with which the paths between the boxed shrubs were paved crackled beneath their swaying red cassocks. They walked slowly, each with his hands clasped behind his back. Borella carried himself more erectly than McShane. They made one complete circuit of the garden before Borella spoke. Both knew it was his place to begin the conversation.

"So, John, the work on the commission goes well?"

"Yes, Eminence. The first draft of the report is nearly complete."

"Fine. Fine. I am told my trust in you was not misplaced."

"I am glad."

"But enough about the business of the council. That is for the chamber."

"Yes."

"How is your good uncle?"

"Splendid, splendid. Although my mother is ill, not faring well at all."

"I am sorry. I will think of her. I will put her on the Paten."

"Thank you, Eminence. She would be most consoled and honored."

"I will mention it to His Holiness."

"Cardinal, that would be wonderful."

Borella touched McShane's shoulder, as if to say, *It's quite all right, my friend.*

McShane was surprised at how moved he was.

"And your cousin?"

"He is fine. He works for my uncle now."

"Ah, he is not with the government?"

McShane remembered the morning Micko'd come to him, what he'd said. "No." He regretted his inability to score a point about his own influence with Kennedy.

"And the marriage? He married well, as I recall."

"To a Protestant, I'm afraid."

"I recall."

"But they've a fine son, an Italian lad, in fact, whom they've adopted and raised as their own. A fine Catholic boy who goes to Harvard."

"Harvard, ah!"

"Yes."

"Give them all my blessing."

"I certainly will, Eminence."

Borella tugged once at his cincture, then gestured toward a bench with his bejeweled hand, a long, thin hand with manicured nails, a hand by El Greco. "Let us sit, John. We must speak *cor ad cor.*"

They sat. McShane felt the pitch of his nervousness go up. Borella's show of intimacy startled McShane. He felt flattered to be treated like more than an underling, but he was also wary.

"I am very concerned, John."

"Concerned, Cardinal? About what?"

"About His Eminence, your Ordinary. Cushing."

McShane dropped his eyes. It was no secret that Cushing had his enemies in Rome. Borella was probably one of them. McShane had the strange thought that he was crossing a minefield. He resolved to be loyal to Cushing no matter what. "You are concerned about the cardinal?"

McShane said, a bit too innocently. "But why? Because he objects to Latin?"

Borella smiled. "Ah, I wish it were that. But no." He shook his head sadly. "He is not a well man."

"He's well enough. He has the asthma under control."

Borella glared at him. "Not asthma. His asthma is well known." He softened. "He is in great pain most of the time from his condition."

"Yes, he is. The Cardinal carries on, in my opinion, heroically."

Borella nodded. "I'm certain of it. But the pain, how does he get relief from it?"

McShane did not want to answer him.

"What does he take?" Borella insisted. "We inquire only out of the most profound charity."

McShane noted the use of "we" and that disturbed him. Was this an official inquiry of some kind? Obviously they knew the answer already anyway. "On occasion he depends on alcohol for the relief of his pain."

Borella nodded sympathetically then asked, "Daily?"

"Yes."

"He is inebriated?"

"Sometimes, yes."

"Daily?"

"Yes," McShane said and felt an immediate qualm. Had he just betrayed Cushing? No. No. McShane reminded himself that the drinking was killing the Cardinal even more than the ailments that drove him to it.

"He appears in public . . ." — Borella paused — ". . . inebriated?"

"Almost never, Your Eminence," McShane said quickly.

"But on occasion?"

"Yes." McShane dropped his eyes to his hands, expecting blood.

"We have great sympathy for the weaknesses of the Lord's shepherds. But the people must not be given cause for scandal."

"Cardinal Cushing is a holy man. He is the most loved man in Boston." McShane felt miserable.

Borella ignored his testimony. "Your brother priests in America, John. They seem susceptible to this dreaded weakness. The drunkenness of God's anointed is one of the thorns in the heart of His Holiness."

"It is a grave problem," McShane said, thanking God that he didn't like the taste of whiskey.

"But the Shepherd! Such scandal not only to the people, but to the priests who must be shown good example! Something must be done." Borella slowly turned to face McShane. He wore such a look of mournful worry that the American thought at first he was going to cry. "We must pray, first of all, for our poor brother."

"Of course."

"And perhaps, now I am speaking confidentially, something could be found for His Eminence that would both lighten his burden and lessen the possibility of public scandal."

"Something?"

"A new mission, perhaps here in the Vatican."

McShane suddenly felt the weight lift slightly from his conscience. Borella was proposing an appointment to Rome, not a disgrace. Perhaps this was not betrayal after all. At the same time, McShane guessed that for Borella to discuss this with him was a sign that his own prospects to succeed Cushing were good. He felt a surge of excitement, but checked it and determined to play the hand out cautiously. He said, "Cardinal Cushing would perhaps be happy to be here and close to Pope John, whom he loves so much."

"Ah, but there is the problem. As you know, His Holiness holds your Ordinary in highest esteem. He has an exceptional affection for Cushing."

"I know. They are much alike." McShane paused, then added hastily, "In their virtues."

"But, you see, His Holiness would never remove Cushing against his will. His Holiness has a weakness of his own. His large heart."

The echo McShane heard in Borella's statement said, "His small mind."

Neither man spoke for a moment. McShane was at a total loss for what to say. If Cushing couldn't be transferred, why were they talking like this?

Borella touched McShane's sleeve. "Excellency, I will tell you something in sacred confidence. His Holiness is failing. There are a number of problems that will not be tended to until his successor takes his place on the throne of Peter. His Holiness will not see the full turning of this garden again."

"I had no idea."

"You must guard the secret."

"Am I not a priest?"

Borella smiled and pressed the flesh above McShane's right knee. "And you must help us to choose a worthy successor to Cardinal Cushing when the time comes."

McShane nearly gasped. There it was. How could it be already? How he would have preferred that this turn could be taken without his feeling that he was involved in Cushing's downfall! If he had hoped to have

Cushing's Chair, it had been a hope for later when Cushing was prepared to step aside or when his health failed dramatically or, God forbid, when he died. But this seemed like conspiracy. McShane forced himself not to flinch from it because they were talking about his being Archbishop of Boston, and John McShane knew that, if anything was true, he would be a good archbishop. He had convictions and commitments about the new era dawning for the Church that would make his service invaluable. He believed in Pope John's *aggiornamento* and knew it would take younger bishops like himself to implement it. He felt called to serve God in exactly that way. He was convinced that he was responding not to self-interest or ambition — although he too was susceptible to those — but to an authentically discerned vocation. Even so, it was not without difficulty that he said, "I am at your service, Eminence, in this and all things."

"I think the new Ordinary should be of the archdiocese, don't you?"

The vein in McShane's fleshy neck jumped. "Yes. I do."

"Boston has been so good to the Church with the gift of so many of her sons."

"There are many fine men."

"None, John, finer than you, in my estimation."

"Why, Your Eminence, you embarrass me."

"It is not my purpose to do so, but I must know, before I make certain arrangements, whether you would accept the call to office as Ordinary of the archdiocese?"

McShane's chin fell, a studied show of surprise. "I don't know what to say."

Borella smiled. "Say 'Yes.' Say '*Adsum.*' "

"You honor me, but of course I'd have to pray . . ."

"Of course, of course. But are you inclined for yourself, supposing that later it is perceived as God's Will?"

"I would never refuse a call to serve the Church."

"Good. As you can imagine, there will be problems."

"Yes. I am young. Younger than most Ordinaries."

"And Spellman would want one of his. And there would be others to contend with. But leave that to me."

McShane's mind took an unexpected turn then. It occurred to him that Borella was expecting him to offer some money in return for his sponsorship. The idea panicked McShane, not that he thought it wrong by then — he knew that large sums of money flowed into the Curia and that most senior Vatican officials lived very well — but that he had no idea how to broach the subject. It had to be done delicately, he knew. "Perhaps there will be expenses," he said.

Borella silenced him by raising his hand.

But when McShane said, "I will have my uncle make an offering through you," Borella nodded.

Then McShane, feeling a new burst of guilt — was this treason? was this bribery? — said, "The important thing is the physical and spiritual wellbeing of Cardinal Cushing."

"Yes," Borella said, "but also of Boston."

"MR. ANSELMO, would you please answer the question?"

"I would like to consult my attorney."

"You may be excused to do so."

Anselmo pushed his chair back from the small table. The panel of twenty-four men and women watched him collect several small pieces of notepaper. He arranged them neatly, deliberately lining up their edges. He did not look up.

They were the members of the special federal grand jury which had been convened by the United States Attorney for the purposes of conducting an investigation into the activities of organized crime in New England and, if appropriate, bringing indictments against its members. They had been in session since the first day in May, nearly two weeks. They had listened to Deke Thomas, Assistant U.S. Attorney, interrogate a succession of witnesses. They were familiar by now with the routine. The attorney asked his question. The witness asked to be excused to consult his lawyer, who was forbidden to be present in the hearing room since the proceedings were conducted with elaborate secrecy. Permission for the witness to leave was granted. The witness left the room. The panelists then had to wait in silence. There was nothing to do but read the paper or count the slats on the Venetian blinds which filtered the light on the room's four six-foot windows. If the blinds were up they could stare at the Customs House Tower, which was directly across Post Office Square from the Federal Building. They could watch the clouds float by. It was, they all felt, a waste of time to be pinned up in a drab room in the lovely month of May listening to these guys say nothing. The witness invariably came back from consulting his lawyer to plead the Fifth Amendment.

Anselmo hated going out into the corridor because he had to wade through the mob of loitering reporters.

"Mr. Anselmo!" one shouted, falling into step with him. "Do you agree with Mr. Balestrione, who said that this grand jury is designed to grab headlines for the Democrats before the elections?"

"No comment." Anselmo walked slowly, calmly toward the small room beyond the lavatory, where Pio Costanari was waiting for him.

"Do you agree that Robert Kennedy hates Italo-Americans?"

"No comment."

"You have been called the head of the mob in the North End . . ."

Anselmo opened the door and closed it behind him.

He leaned against the door.

Costanari was seated at a table in the tiny windowless room.

" 'Mob,' " Anselmo said, "What kind of word is 'mob'? Do they think this is television?"

Costanari shrugged. "It is television. They want a new Valachi."

Anselmo closed his eyes. Never had he suffered such insults. A lifetime of quiet, private life was being ruined.

"What is the question, Gennaro? Come, we must talk."

"For what? I'm saying nothing to them."

"What is the question?"

"Another from inside."

Anselmo put one of the pieces of notepaper down in front of Costanari, who read it without touching it. The question read, "Do you have personal knowledge of the present whereabouts of Joseph Bonanno?"

Bonanno was a well-known New York crime figure who was in hiding in Montreal. Anselmo's son Rico had driven him across the Canadian border in Maine several months before.

"How can they connect us with Bonanno? There is nothing!" Anselmo was angry and showing it.

Costanari held his hand up and let his eyes fly around the ceiling. "Do not speak," he said every way but verbally. "Not here!"

Costanari wrote on the top page of his yellow pad, "That's it! They have someone inside N.E." Inside the North End.

This was the fourth consecutive question about matters for which there were no records. They were not asking about any of the North End business fronts Anselmo's family ran. They were asking about his associations with nationally known crime figures. Anselmo had guarded against such associations and the few he had were models of a discretion which bordered on secrecy. But each of the questions put by Thomas indicated that the government had penetrated that secrecy somehow.

Costanari scratched out what he'd written, then wrote, "C. B.'s juror?"

They knew that one of the jurors had already been bought by Ciro Balestrione. The juror would feed the Providence don information about who had been asked what and what, if anything, he had said. Balestrione had not yet been called to testify, but the government seemed not to be in a hurry. They were fishing. The grand jury would be seated for months.

Anselmo shrugged. He had no idea which of the jurors was Balestrione's.

"Find him!" Costanari wrote.

Anselmo nodded. He knew that Balestrione's spy had the purpose of protection as much against himself as against the government. If Anselmo gave testimony that could in any way damage Balestrione, the Providence don would know it immediately and would kill him. Costanari was right. If they could discover the spy, they could use him too. They had to make the traffic run both ways on that street if they could.

Anselmo took a chrome Zippo lighter from his pocket and struck it. He held the flame out ceremoniously. He did not smoke. He had brought the lighter for this purpose. Costanari ripped the bottom half of the yellow page from the pad and put it into the flame. He pushed his chair back from the table and held the burning paper by its edge until the writing was consumed. Then he dropped the fire into the metal wastebasket. He did the same to Anselmo's notepaper. They conducted this burning solemnly, rubrically, as if it were the first ritual of *omertà*.

Anselmo returned to the grand jury room.

The Assistant U.S. Attorney repeated the question. "Do you have personal knowledge of the present whereabouts of Joseph Bonanno?"

Anselmo stared at the jurors. They were seated at small wooden schoolroom desks, which were arranged in four neat rows as if for a class in high-school civics. Thomas paced back and forth across the front of the room, the teacher. The jurors were looking up from their newspapers and copies of *Time*. One woman was knitting and the click-click of her needles was the only sound.

Anselmo stared at her.

"Mrs. Walsh," Thomas said politely, "if you please."

She stopped knitting.

"Answer the question, Mr. Anselmo."

Anselmo watched another juror, a gray-haired man in a tweed sport coat, lighting his pipe.

Another, a small effeminate-looking man, was rubbing his forefinger up and down the hollow between the bridge of his nose and his cheek.

"Mr. Anselmo?"

A Negro woman dropped her eyes when Anselmo looked at her.

A fat man with long, greasy red hair, wearing a sheeny purple jacket with an embroidered yellow dragon on its left breast, glared at Anselmo impassively. He was Irish. Anselmo recognized the hate.

"Mr. Anselmo, please."

Anselmo looked at Thomas. "On the advice of my attorney and based on rights accorded to me by the First Amendment, Fifth Amendment, and Seventh Amendment of the United States Constitution, I respectfully decline to answer the question on the ground that to do so may tend to incriminate me."

Thomas rolled his eyes toward the ceiling.

Mrs. Walsh resumed her knitting. Anselmo had the impression that she clicked her needles more loudly than was necessary.

"You people all have the same script-writer, don't you?" The Assistant U.S. Attorney bent over his small table and made a note.

One of the jurors stretched his legs forward, sliding his desk backward. It scratched unpleasantly on the floor.

The man in the tweed coat held a new match to his pipe.

"Well," Thomas said, not looking up from his pad, "I don't suppose there is much point in going on with this, is there?"

Anselmo ignored him. He was still studying the faces of the jurors. He was waiting for his instinct to tell him which of them was the one.

Mrs. Walsh? It was the only name he knew, a slight indiscretion on Thomas's part to use it. Their names were secret.

"In that case, Mr. Anselmo, you are dismissed." Thomas looked up. "For now."

Anselmo stood and, without looking at them again, left the room. He did not know.

Whom did Balestrione own? Who, of Anselmo's associates, was providing the government its clues?

As he left the Federal Building with Costanari at his heels, Anselmo turned over in his mind again his most familiar thought. Deke Thomas had been Collins Brady's assistant on the strike force eight years before. Thomas and Brady had been together with Kefauver. Was that the link? Was that the key? But the younger Brady was privy to nothing that was not at least as incriminating to his father as it was to Anselmo. Neither Brady had knowledge of his relationship to Bonanno. The government knew things that only members of the North End inner circle knew. Since he was scrupulous in using only pay telephones for business calls, it couldn't be a tap. It had to be one of his own people; that was the weight that bent Anselmo. That was what stirred this unfamiliar rage. He had to know who the Judas was. He had to kill him.

Meanwhile at Prescott Street, Bishop McShane was trying to make his mother understand why he had to leave.

"Ma," he said, touching her emaciated upper arm through the sheet, "I have to go to Rome."

"Why? Why do you?" She was going to cry again.

"Because Pope John is dying, Ma."

"What about your ma? I'm dying."

"No you're not. You're fine. I just spoke to Dr. Schaeffer, and he knows how you are."

"No, he doesn't. I'm the only one that knows that."

"Look at me, Ma."

"No."

"I want you to look at me."

"You want me to die."

"No, Mother. That hurts me to hear you."

"You want me to tell you to go ahead so you won't feel guilty."

"That's true."

"When I die."

"You're not dying."

"You hope."

"You just said I hoped you were. I have to go, Ma."

"I abandoned my own mother in the old country. This is God's punishment. I should never have come. She asked me not to."

"You had to come. So did Uncle Colman."

"He didn't leave until she was dead. You shouldn't leave, son, until I'm dead."

"I'm not leaving you, Mother. I'll just be gone a few days."

"Until he's dead."

"Who?"

"The Pope. The Pope gave me his blessing."

"I know. He's praying for you."

"But you said he's dying."

"He is."

"Well, what good are *his* prayers?"

"He's the Pope, Mother."

"But he's dying. So there. What's he dying of?"

"Old age."

"I'm older than he is."

"No, you're not. He's eighty-four."

"But I have it too, old age."

"You're only sixty-nine."

"What's the difference?"

"Fifteen years."

"Don't be smart with me, young man."

"I'm sorry."

"You should be."

"I have to go, Ma. My plane's in forty minutes."

Silence.

"Ma?"

"Give us a kiss, Ma."

Rigid silence.

"I'll give you my blessing. May the blessing of Almighty God, the Father, the Son, and the Holy Ghost, descend upon you and remain with you forever. There."

Colman was waiting for him downstairs.

"She didn't take it very well," McShane said.

His uncle nodded. "I didn't think she would."

"How could she? Her son is leaving her deathbed for a stranger's."

Colman touched his nephew's sleeve. "Jack, it's been her deathbed for a while. Dr. Schaeffer said she could linger indefinitely."

"Coombs said she could go any day."

"He said that a month ago."

"And yesterday."

"Jack, you're torturing yourself. Your mother would keep you by her bedside for years if you let her."

McShane nodded. "It is the Pope, after all. Bishops from all over the world are going for the vigil. I'll be back next week. It won't be a problem."

Colman didn't say anything.

"That is if His Holiness and Ma time their deaths to suit my schedule." McShane allowed his contempt for himself to get the better of him. Nothing could devastate him like the feeling he had failed his mother. She knew that about him and she played it like an instrument.

Colman said, "You'll see Borella?"

"Yes," McShane said. He did not know or want to know what Colman had sent him, and he refused to think of Pope John's dying as the beginning of the process that would get him Boston. He did not want to talk about Borella. He said, "I wish you could buy more time for Ma."

Colman did not reply.

"I have to go. I'll miss my plane."

Ruggero Cardinal Borella would not see McShane for three days.

McShane was a nervous wreck. He spent the time pacing his room in the *pensione* at the Dominican convent on Via Veneto or kneeling with the other prelates in the Sistine Chapel, praying the rosary and reciting the psalms in Latin. He prayed as earnestly as he could for both his mother and the Pope. He tried continually to abandon himself to God's Will. He asked the Blessed Virgin Mary to intercede for him with her Son.

Periodic bulletins were issued on the pontiff's condition by the attending physician, Doctor Piero Mazzoni. The Pope's stomach wall had ruptured and the internal hemorrhaging was proving impossible to stem. They were fearful that peritonitis would set in any moment. Once that happened . . .

Finally Borella sent for him.

McShane was ushered into the cardinal's office, a stern, ascetic room, which, by its spaciousness, by its view of St. Peter's, and by the aged simplicity of its oak furnishings, nevertheless achieved a kind of medieval grandeur.

"Your Eminence," McShane said, kneeling to kiss Borella's ring.

"My friend." The cardinal lifted him, but there was an edge in Borella's voice. "How good of you to come."

"It is the most unhappy time for the Church and for the world. All America mourns."

"Ah, His Holiness is not dead, yet, my son. We must not mourn the living."

"But he is near death."

"Yes." Borella took his place behind his desk. He was nodding sadly. "The Lord is very close. Please sit."

McShane sat in the carved abbot's chair opposite. He wished they were walking in the garden behind the Papal Apartments.

"He is a saint, this one," Borella said solemnly. He might have said that saints are better prayed to than respected.

"Yes, he is."

"This morning he gathered his family at his bedside. He said in the Bergamasque dialect, 'Remember Mama? Remember Papa? I am going to see them. Let us pray for them.' "

"How very moving."

"He is a man of his people. He loves his family dearly."

McShane refused again to feel his guilt. Such choices as he had made were the work of Providence.

"And how is your family?" Borella asked, falsely smiling. He lit a cigarette.

"My mother is unwell, Cardinal. Quite seriously unwell."

"I am sorry to hear that. You should be with her."

"I came to pray for His Holiness."

"It is His Holiness who should pray for us."

"Of course. I have also looked forward to seeing you."

Borella nodded, but said nothing.

McShane took a deep breath. He had decided to press Borella. If Cushing, whom he loved more than ever, was going to be replaced anyway, then he was going to do what he could to see it was with himself. Besides, wasn't Cushing committing a slow form of suicide with his drinking? It was not love or loyalty to pretend otherwise. "In fact, Eminence, I wanted to convey to you the impression that my fellow clergy share in Boston that the situation with Cardinal Cushing is growing worse." McShane paused. "It should be . . ." — he waited for Borella to look up from his cigarette — ". . . resolved quickly."

"Situation? I am not certain I know what you refer to."

McShane was stunned. Did Borella require a more explicit explanation? Obviously not.

"You said when we talked . . ."

"At the council?"

"Yes. That when Pope John died . . ."

"But Pope John, dear Bishop, is not dead." There was a viciousness to Borella's smile that caused a shudder to climb up McShane's spine.

"I know that, Eminence, but . . . the next Pope must . . ."

"Bishop, it is not appropriate to discuss the duties and burdens awaiting the next Pope. John is Pope."

"But you said . . ."

"I said nothing."

McShane stared, disbelieving, at Borella, who had accepted, he was certain, thousands of dollars from Colman Brady. Did he think that money was meant to purchase rice for pagan babies?

Borella was growing impatient. There was nothing subtle about this McShane. He dripped with ambition. He was utterly lacking in discretion. He had no patience. What an offense against the Church it was for him to bare his hunger in this way. Roncalli was not yet dead!

"It is unseemly for you to be here," Borella began.

McShane interrupted, his voice cracked by panic. He saw that he had made a dreadful mistake. "I'm sorry, Cardinal, Your Eminence. I meant no harm."

Borella silenced him by abruptly raising his hand; *do not interrupt me!*

It was clear to Borella now that McShane would not do. It was too bad. More of his uncle's money would have been useful, but, after this recent hundred thousand dollars, he had gleaned enough. McShane was all too American. He had no sense of the decorum of things. The Pope was dying, after all. This was not the time. "You should be with your mother."

"Yes," McShane said, defeat and shame in his voice. He sensed how vast and awful was the disaster that had just occurred. He was totally destroyed. He *had* betrayed Cushing. He *had* abandoned his mother. He *had* profaned Pope John's dying. He was a hugely sinful man to himself. He stood. He wanted to get away from Borella. He wanted to go home to his mother. But he had to find some way to redeem, if only partially, his dashed hopes. He needed one last rope to grab. Where was it? His mind whirred. What to say to recoup his dignity, to make Borella think well of him again? McShane knew instinctively that now only under the guise of small talk could he make a new point. While going the infinite distance from Borella's desk to the office door he had to think of what could reverse this disaster. Something under the outward ease of family gossip; it was the terrain on which polite moves came so easily to both of them. Something to do with Kennedy would be best of all. The Italians loved Kennedy.

As McShane stepped back from his chair he said, "By the way, I discovered since our talk at the Council that my cousin Michael Brady went with the Kennedy government, after all." What harm was there in saying that?

"Oh?" Borella had come out from behind his desk and was taking McShane by the elbow to the door. "Your uncle must miss him at the company." Borella was barely interested. He wanted McShane out of his presence.

But McShane couldn't leave him with the impression that Micko'd left Monument, since that wasn't the precise case. "Well, he's still with my uncle. He does that also." What a feeble statement. "He does some confidential work with Kennedy. I mean for Kennedy."

Borella stopped. They were at the door.

Suddenly Borella seemed less impatient. He took out his silver case and withdrew a cigarette. "Confidential?" he said. He seemed impressed.

McShane relaxed a bit. "Yes. He works directly with Robert Kennedy."

"The Attorney General. How very important his work must be."

"Yes, although I know almost nothing about it. It's very secret."

"Having to do with crime."

"Yes. Against the underworld. Against mobsters. He and Kennedy meet all the time."

"A secret agent?" Borella smiled. "Like your hero, James. . . ?"

"Bond." McShane laughed. "Yes, like that. James Bond. Only Collins works against the Sicilians instead of the Russians."

"Sicilians," Borella said, smiling broadly. "I am Sicilian."

"Oh." McShane blushed. "I didn't mean Sicilians. I meant . . ." McShane thought he would die. He wanted to end this and get out.

"The Mafia."

"Yes."

"A terrible thing, the Mafia." Borella dragged on his cigarette, shaking his head. "They have been bad for our people for years. It is good that men like your cousin work against them. You should be very proud."

McShane relaxed some. "Yes."

"So your cousin works against them in Washington."

"No, in Boston."

"Oh? Is there Mafia in Boston?" Borella dragged on his cigarette. "I did not know that."

McShane panicked. Had he revealed something he shouldn't have? Had he broken the seal of that confession Collins had made? He tried to back off what he'd said. "But you're right. I think mainly he works in Washington. I don't know of any underworld in Boston either."

But Borella seemed suddenly uninterested. He opened the door. "You have a fine family, John. That is another reason why the Church is privileged to have your service."

"It is my privilege, Eminence."

"We are all privileged, aren't we?"

McShane felt that perhaps his mistakes had not been so drastic, after all. Borella seemed to regard him affectionately still. But the question nagged; had he violated Micko's confidence? Of course he had. The seal of confession is absolute. "Eminence." McShane lowered his voice so that the secretary in the outer office would not hear. "What I've told you, of course, about my cousin is *sub secreto.*"

"Am I not a priest, John?"

"Thank you, Eminence. May I have your blessing?"

McShane knelt.

Ruggero Cardinal Borella blessed him, then said, "Pray, dear Bishop, for His Holiness."

"Yes, Cardinal, of course. Always."

Borella closed the door on McShane, then crossed to the large window that cut the north wall of his office in half. He looked out at the dome of St. Peter's and lit a second cigarette from the stub of the first. *Gennaro,* he thought. *Gennaro.*

McShane stopped in the Basilica to pray.

He felt better. Perhaps his cause was not lost after all.

He knelt before Michelangelo's Pietà and let his eyes bathe in the suffering of God's Mother.

He asked her to forgive him.

He had violated the seal of silence for the first time in his priestly life, but not gravely. He had shared the secret, but only minimally and only with another priest, and not casually, not without reason. God's Mother would understand.

He asked her to grant Pope John the grace of a happy death.

He asked her to sustain his own mother in her time of trial. What evil could befall her under the benign glance of Mary?

McShane hurried back to his room to pack and catch the next plane home. It seemed to him that things were not nearly as bad as, for a moment, he had feared.

But that was before he arrived at the *pensione* and found the telegram from Maureen. "Mother died," it said. That was all.

❧ 8 ❦

"SAD, EH?"

Collins said it half to his father, half to his son. The three of them were coming down the stairs of Holy Cross Cathedral onto Washington Street. It was early evening, Monday, June 3. They had just attended a Holy Hour in memory of Pope John XXIII, who had died that day.

"Yes," Colman said. He was between them. He took their elbows. "I'm glad you both could come." When Colman heard the news of Pope John's death, even though it was expected, he was unaccountably moved. Cardinal Cushing had called him then and, in the middle of their conversation, the old prelate had begun to weep. The cardinal asked Brady to come to the impromptu service at the cathedral. Brady thought he would have attended even without his old friend's request. He asked Collins to go with him, even though, aside from Maeve's funeral, it had been ages since he'd been in church. Then Colman had thought of asking Tony. He hadn't seen much of him in the past year and knew they had never really recovered from that day in Southie the autumn before. Colman had correctly guessed that John XXIII meant something special to Tony.

"The family that prays together stays together," Collins said goodnaturedly. But there was an edge to his statement, and Tony got it. Since the term had ended a few weeks before and Tony had moved back to

Pinckney Street from Harvard, there was more tension than ever between them. Collins had finally concluded that Tony was not going to outgrow his sourness, after all. He thought his son habitually moody and self-absorbed and indifferent both to himself and to Janet.

Colman knew how Collins saw it and his awareness of the distance between Collins and Tony made him think that fathers are never satisfied with their sons. He knew that he understood Tony better than Collins did. Grandfathers have so much less at stake than fathers. "I think we ought to walk back," he said. "Where'd you park, Tony?"

"A block or two from your office, Grandfather."

"Good. I'll leave you two there. I've got some work to do. Let's walk."

"Good idea," Collins said.

They cut through Union Park. The once elegant green with its oval of bowfront mansions was now a slum. Garbage was strewn on the sidewalk. They had to step over two decapitated pigeons.

"Christ," Collins said, "I hope it was dogs did that."

"This place has been ruined," Colman said. "Those coloreds sure can speed up the work of time."

Collins winced. He hated the ease with which his father blamed Negroes for the state of the city. "It's been downhill for this neighborhood since the Irish moved in forty years ago. Right, Tony?" He touched his son, expecting his alliance on this at least.

But Tony did not reply.

"Why Mick Collins Brady!" Colman said, "You souper!"

"What's a souper?" Tony asked, trying to join in. There was an awkwardness about their mood, but they were all resisting it.

"What your father is," Colman said jokingly, "a traitor to his people." Colman slapped Micko's shoulder, then began, "During the great hunger . . ."

Tony interrupted. "You mean the Irish famine?"

"It wasn't a famine. We called it 'the hunger.' A famine is an act of God. The 'hunger' was the act of the British. In a famine every crop fails, but in Ireland only the potatoes failed, and potatoes were what they let us eat. We weren't allowed to eat the grain we were growing for the landlords who lived in Sussex and Lancashire."

"I didn't know that," Collins said. His tone showed genuine surprise.

"You see what I mean, Tony. How I failed!"

It seemed to Tony that his grandfather meant that, and he felt a sudden pang for his father, which he deflected by saying, "So anyway, soupers?"

"The British set up a relief system to feed the starving. You know how humane they are. They'd kill us if we ate the corn we'd slaved to harvest, and then they expected us to be grateful when they offered us a brown water they had the nerve to call soup."

"You speak about it as if you were there." Tony was surprised by his grandfather's seriousness. This was not banter anymore.

"I was."

"You weren't even born," Tony said.

"I was there, nonetheless. We all were. Six million people died to Ireland one way or the other in the Hunger. Same as the Jews. Only the indifferent world didn't ask us to forgive it the way it has them."

"You can't compare the British to the Nazis, Daddo," Collins interrupted. He tried, but how could such a thing be said lightly? "The Irish deaths took place over forty years, not four."

"You think that matters? Ask the dead."

"So the British were serving soup," Tony put in. "What then?"

"They served it from their churches. In order to have a smidgen of the stuff you had to convert."

"What, become a Protestant?"

"Yes. Almost no one did it. People habitually chose to starve. Those who took the soup . . ."

"Were called 'soupers,' " Tony said.

"Yes. Like MacNamara."

"Bob MacNamara?" Collins was incredulous.

But Colman was insistent. "He's a Protestant, right? With a name like that? Somebody in his family took the soup, sure as hell. Kennedy never should have put him in his Cabinet."

"Come now."

"You Harvard fellows stick together, don't you?"

"He was at the B-School. Hardly counts, does it, Tony?"

But Tony refused his father's lead again.

"They used to say that if anyone in a village took the soup, no one from that village and no descendant of it would ever receive the gift of a vocation to the priesthood."

"So no one from your village took it," Tony said, "since Uncle Jack's a priest. I mean a bishop."

"A lot of us starved, Tony," Colman said. "Your great-great-grandmother, for example."

Tony looked away from Colman and at his father and, with more than a hint of rebuke said, "You never told me that."

Collins didn't say anything, and Colman understood why. How could he have told Tony such stories? The very point of Tony's aloofness was his refusal to take on the weight of the pasts of his father and his grandfather.

[591]

Tony considered himself exempt from the awful bloodline. Colman savored the irony of a heritage so wily it made Tony think himself free of it, when that deception proved he wasn't. But because the kid thought he was orphaned he had bidden his ghosts adieu and as far as Colman could tell, lived without them. Which was why the kid had such power, perhaps, over his parents, over Colman.

Their mood had gone completely sour. It was dangerous stuff for a stroll. They turned toward town on Tremont Street and walked a block in silence. Then Colman said, "You know, Tony, stories like that are sacred things. My grandmother is who we were talking about; the British murdered her. That's how close it is to me. But if your dad never told you that, it's because it's almost that close to him. It's a difficult subject. Just because we crossed the ocean doesn't mean we left it behind, either of us." Colman was feeling a very powerful sense that things could not have turned out other than they had for his son. Collins had not made a successful crossing, that was all. Tony was ruthless, it seemed to Colman, in his accusing detachment.

Collins looked sideways at his father, who was saying two powerful things to him. One, you did not turn out to be what I hoped you would. And two, it's all right if you didn't, because neither did I. Collins knew he had no capacity — not yet — to say the same thing to Tony.

"This was a lovely street once," Colman said. "When I came to Boston it was still very posh."

"You wouldn't know it now."

"The coloreds are ruining Boston," Colman said.

"I'd have thought the Irish would have been able to sympathize with them," Collins said.

"The Irish never threw their garbage out the front window, son." Colman paused, looked across at Collins, wanting to rescue their amicability. "Just out the back one."

Collins laughed, relieved.

"You should both come to Ireland with me on a trip. I'll show you Four Mile Water, Ballymacarberry, Clonmel, Tipperary. Maeve always wanted to go back. I should have taken her."

"First Maeve," Collins said soberly, "then Pope John. A lot of death lately. We used to say in the war it comes in threes."

"Makes a fellow think, that's for sure," Colman said.

Collins felt a surge of concern for his father. There was an unusual sadness about him when he said that. "What's a fellow been thinking about?"

"I'm sixty-five, Micko." He did not continue, as if that announcement explained everything.

They waited at Berkeley Street for the light to change. Collins could not think of anything to say. His father's morose mood filled him with uneasiness.

"You know what sixty-five is, son, don't you?"

"What?" Of course he knew.

"Retirement age."

"Christ, Daddo, you're years from that."

"Who says?"

"I do."

"I do too," Tony said.

Collins and Colman were surprised at Tony's intervention. He shared that much with his father, a great need to have Colman steady and strong. This first faint hint of aging disturbed them both.

"That shows what you fellows know," Colman said. "I make all my clerks cash it in when they hit my age." He said this with a deliberate resignation. Colman knew exactly what he was doing. His calculated display of an elder's ennui had the purpose of distracting Tony and Collins from their mutual antagonism. Colman hoped that their common affection for him might be a bond between them yet. Colman was not going to dwell on the other thing he was feeling; the weariness, of which he was showing them the smallest part, was real.

But it dawned on Collins then that his father was in fact betraying his anxiety about the grand jury investigation. There was every reason for him to fear it because he would expect Anselmo's tracks to lead immediately to him. Collins wanted somehow to reassure him and to tell him that he would be spared the jury's scrutiny. But how? He could not tell him that the government was building its own wall around Colman to protect him from its own investigation, because he'd have to tell him what he was doing to earn that. In any case they couldn't discuss it in front of Tony. But then it occurred to Collins that retirement was just the thing to get Colman off the target range before the shooting started.

"Maybe retiring's not a bad idea, Daddo."

The equanimity of Collins's statement and the reversal it represented surprised Colman, but he decided to play it out. "You could take over Monument, son."

"Sure."

"You practically run it, as it is."

"Would you think about selling Prescott Street now that Maeve is gone?"

"What, the whole street? Let's cut over and see the swanboat."

They walked a block along Arlington to the Public Garden. The swanboat was gliding under the rococo bridge that halved the pond.

"Did I tell you about the time Curley drowned 'Old Man Prohibition' in the pond here?"

"Yes. Many times," Collins said.

"Really stuck in their craw, that one."

"Whose craw?" Tony asked.

"Your neighbors, kiddo, the Pinckney Street crowd. No, I wouldn't think of selling the house." Despite himself Colman felt a surge of panic at the thought of going back there alone that night. He tried to press the old confidence back into his voice. "Where the hell would I go? Back to Southie?"

"You could take your trip to Ireland," Tony said.

"I was joking. Didn't you hear? Ireland hit an iceberg and sank."

"You could move in with us," Collins said, and then he surprised himself by putting his hand on Tony's shoulder. "Couldn't he, son?"

"Sure. Sure, Grandfather. You should do that."

Colman thought better to ram the iceberg than live in it. "No thanks," he said. This business had gone about far enough. Colman could hear the pity in their voices. He hadn't bargained for pity. Colman Brady hadn't come all this damn way to be patronized by his offspring, not by a distance! "I don't know about you two, but I got to get back to work." Authority was crisp in the statement.

"Why don't you come have dinner with us?" Collins said.

"No. To tell you the truth, I'm not in the mood. You'll be cutting across the Common?"

"I have to go down to Essex to get my car," Tony said.

Collins touched his son again. "I'll go with you," he said.

The three of them left the Public Garden together and headed down Boylston. They walked several blocks without speaking, all carrying the same weight and each feeling he carried it alone. The sidewalks were clear of shoppers and workers. Everyone had gone home. They crossed to Essex and entered the strange, dark tranquility of Chinatown, an edge of it which was all warehouses and lofts. There was almost no traffic. At the corner of Essex and Columbia, they stopped because Tony's car was down that block. None of them noticed the dark green Buick that started its engine half a block up Columbia.

Collins was reluctant to let his father go off alone. "You know, Daddo, I was thinking."

"You were, eh?"

"That perhaps I'm fairly Irish, after all. Even if I don't hand on the tradition like a troubadour." He looked at Tony. They smiled at each other for the first time.

"What makes you think so, Micko?"

"That ballad you used to sing me."

"Which one?"

" 'Their songs of war are merry, Their songs of love so sad.' "

Colman pressed his son's shoulder. Damn, it could hurt to love this man. But Colman put a brake on his emotion, and withdrew his arm. He looked at Tony. Such a pain filled him for them both that he couldn't stay there. He shook their hands, warmly if a bit formally, and said goodnight and headed down Essex.

Tony and Collins watched him for a moment. Then they walked into the shadow that the tall buildings threw on the deserted narrow street. Neither of them paid attention to the green Buick moving toward them until it accelerated rapidly. Collins was only a yard or two to the left of Tony but, since he was walking on the curb, that was enough. The driver picked him off cleanly, lifting him on the horn of the left headlight and taking him away.

Like that he was gone, and the car was around the corner and gone.

Tony ran to the crumpled bloodied form that lay in the street where Essex crossed Columbia. He stood over his father, trying to make a sound come out of his throat, but he could not. For what seemed a long time to him, he had his mouth open and was forcing a huge pressure up at it from his chest, but nothing happened. Then a loud word, a single word came out: "Grandfather!" And it came out again: "Grandfather!"

Colman had crossed Lincoln and had his key out to open the building when he heard it.

"Grandfather!"

He turned and began to run. He cut back across Lincoln Street, a broad four-lane with light traffic, timing two cuts to miss cars that passed very close. And he knew even as he ran that he had done it before, the very same dash, the very same terror. After he'd seen the army lorry with Gavin roar out of the darkness he'd whipped his horse mercilessly to get to his burning house. He had that same feeling again, that driving, desperate flight *toward,* not from, the most awful thing imaginable.

"Micko!" he cried. He strained to see Tony bent over the form of his son, but the image filling his mind was of Nellie's body, inert and leaden, on top of the baby, covering him, all but his small head, which protruded from between her legs as if — he remembered the thought quite clearly — he was being born a second time. It seemed to Colman that his entire life had been a running toward that child. The day he'd met Madeline he had run like this after the horse came back riderless. He had been so certain that the kid had fallen onto a blade of a stump and was impaled. But the boy had been safe and Colman had hit him — for being safe? And Madeline had screamed, "You're mad!" and had run from him and he had been alone again with only his son.

"Micko! Micko!" Colman fell on him, lifted him as gently as he could onto his lap. Blood gushed from him everywhere. "I'm sorry, Dad," Collins said. "I'm so sorry."

Colman cradled his son's head, touched it with his cheek. "For what, Micko? For what?" He was not asking, but was telling him he had nothing in his entire life to be sorry for. "For what?"

"Ask Deke," Collins said. Then he died.

Colman crushed Collins to himself and held him, then frantically he tried wiping the blood from Collins's face with his hand, then his sleeve, then the corner of his coat. It was a futile, insane frenzy. The blood had stopped gushing because the heart was not pushing it out anymore. Colman thought if he could just rid the body of blood Collins would be revived, but the red juice would not clean. Collins was smeared and stained everywhere with it. Colman pressed him to his breast again, and then he lifted his own face and let go an animal wail, a roar, but it was a word, one long agony of a word; "Anselmo!" He repeated it, a fury loose, "Anselmo!" He slammed his right fist onto the street, and the pain of the blow shot up his arm. He remembered slamming his fists against the Dolmen stone and it had not moved. He roared and slammed his fist down again. It was the hardest blow he ever struck, and still the earth did not move. "Anselmo!" he cried again.

"Grandfather!" Tony took a firm hold of Colman's shoulders. He was afraid his grandfather had gone insane. Such mad roaring, such violence in a sound. And why was his grandfather crying out "Anselmo"? Tony knew the name; the North End chieftain notorious in the war against the Irish. Tony tried not to think of it. What did Anselmo have to do with his father's death? Was his father murdered? The boy would not think of it. "Grandfather," he repeated, and he held his shoulders firmly to keep him from hitting the concrete. Colman continued throughout to cradle Collins with his left arm, and for an instant he rested against Tony and finally stopped roaring that awful name.

Tony craned around to look at Brady's face. He wanted to ask his grandfather what to do, but again his voice failed.

Colman was staring at Collins. He was filled with an overwhelming urge to wash his son, not now to revive him, but to prepare him, to stroke him, to take care of him one last time. He had to clean the blood off him. He had to strip his body and anoint it. He had to lay him out on the old table. But no, this was America, not Ireland. Here other men did those things. Colman put his cheek against his son's.

He had to get the police. He had to get an ambulance. That was how to get his son off the cold street. And then he would get Gennaro. Gennaro had done this, he was certain. But he had to know why.

"Here," Colman said to Tony. "You take him." Colman wanted the boy to take his place, a cradle for Collins's body. Tony stepped back despite himself. He was filled with horror at the thought of having that corpse in his lap. It was like that corpse in South Boston. It was murder. His father and his grandfather and Anselmo and all those killings all mixed together, all a piece. The shock of it paralyzed him. He would touch none of it, take none of it in his arms. Colman lifted his son slightly and then looked up at Tony again. He guessed what Tony was feeling, but he would not tolerate it. Once he would have yelled at the boy, tyrannized him, beaten him with his own heartless cowardice. But now he said very softly, "We can't have your pa laying on the ground, Tony. I have to go and call."

Tony replaced Colman, taking his father's body across his lap and into his arms, but his senses revolted and he felt as stiff and lifeless as the corpse did. Tony watched Colman run down Essex, across Lincoln, and into his building. The boy did not want to be alone with this man. But he forced himself to look again closely and to touch the face. How cold it was. And in Tony's mind, a refrain, were those words his father had spoken, nearly his last. "I'm sorry. I'm so sorry."

Colman forced himself to wait for the elevator, though his impulse, despite being more winded than he'd been in years, was to take the stairs two at a time. But his mind was clicking; he would need all of his strength for what was ahead. In his office he called the police, identified himself, and requested the ambulance. Then he looked up Deke Thomas in the phone book, wrote out the address, and then dialed the number. A man answered the phone: Thomas. That was what Brady wanted to know. He hung up. He took his raincoat out of the closet and belted it closed over his bloody suit. He crossed to Collins's office, opened his safe and withdrew his son's .38 caliber police special. Brady took it out of its holster and put it in the raincoat pocket. Then he went back down to the street.

The police were there. Tony was still holding Collins. When Colman arrived, Tony said strangely, "I wouldn't let them take him, Grandfather."

Colman said, "It's all right, Tony. They'll take care of him now." Colman answered their questions. Tony described the car. The police offered to drive them home, but Colman declined. He and Tony went to the boy's small Austin-Healy. "You drive," Colman said. "Take me to Back Bay."

Deke Thomas lived at 133 Marlborough Street. Tony channeled his tension into the driving, gripping the wheel and the gearshift as if the muscles in his fists were what made the car go. It took them six minutes to get there.

Colman got out of the car. "You go home," he said. "Tell your mother."

But Tony stared up at his grandfather. "No," he said. "I'm staying with you."

Colman couldn't believe it. The kid would not defy him now. Rage surged through Brady. This arrogant snot had deprived Collins of the pleasure and joy and satisfaction that should have been his as a steadfast, loyal father. The kid had forever defied Collins. He would not do it to Colman Brady! Not now! Not ever! "You get your ass home, I said. You belong with your mother. You didn't give a shit about your father. Just now you could barely bring yourself to touch him. Get out of here! Get out of my sight!"

Tony gave Colman a look of such fierce resistance that he thought he was going to disobey him, and the boy's eyes said something else to Colman, something terrible. Colman had killed his real mother. Did he know it? Was that the hate he saw in him? The lust for vengeance? Vengeance for that other murder? "Get out of here!" Colman repeated.

Tony popped the clutch and the sports car squealed away.

Colman went up to the Thomases' house. His rage at Tony had broken the dike in him, and huge unmanageable feelings, waves of them, rolled through him. He pounded on the front door repeatedly until Deke Thomas answered. Without speaking Brady grabbed Thomas by the shirt and pushed him back against the staircase. Thomas fell. There was a scream from the living room, Thomas's wife.

"My son is dead, you son of a bitch, and I want to know why!"

Thomas was sprawled on the stairs, a look of pure horror on his face. He thought Brady was going to kill him with his hands.

"Get up!" Brady said. Then he turned toward the living room where Thomas's wife was standing with her hands covering her mouth. "Mrs. Thomas," Brady said evenly, "you go on upstairs and be quiet. No one's going to be hurt."

Thomas stood and straightened his shirt. "Do as he says. I'll be all right."

She crossed in front of Brady, not daring to look at him, and went by her husband up the stairs.

Thomas led the way into the living room. "What happened?" he asked. His voice shook.

"They killed him just now, hit and run. I want to know why your name was the last word my son uttered."

"Really, Mr. Brady, I don't think this is the time."

"You tell me, Thomas, or I'll kill you."

There was no question that Brady meant it. Thomas crossed the living room and went into a small den. "In here," he said. Brady followed him. Thomas closed the door behind them. He went to the bookcase and removed a row of large books behind which was a wall safe. He turned the combination dial, shielding it from Brady. The safe opened. He withdrew a reel of magnetic tape and crossed to a desk on which sat a portable tape recorder. He reeled the tape, pressed the button and turned to watch Brady's face.

"What about this woman Walsh?" It was the voice of Pio Costanari.

"No. She looked at me. She was not afraid." It was Gennaro Anselmo.

"The nigger then."

"Perhaps. She would not look at me."

"I'll find out who she is."

"There are so many. It could be any of them."

"Not the red-haired man."

"No."

"Not the woman Walsh."

"No."

"Not the pipe."

"No."

"So, you see. We know something. It is too bad they had no more questions. You would have known."

"Perhaps this man Thomas."

"He has never received gifts."

"Still. Perhaps. We could bring it up with . . ."

The tape began to buzz. It buzzed for half a minute. Thomas let it run.

The voices resumed.

"Call Rico," Gennaro said, "I want Rico in here."

Thomas snapped the machine off.

"They are trying," he said, "to discover which juror Balestrione owns. Obviously, it is very useful to me to know that one of my grand jurors has already been bribed."

"How did you . . . ?"

"Isn't that obvious to you?"

"Collins."

"Of course. He planted a bug on Anselmo two years ago, a very sophisticated one which transmits without wires. He has been delivering tapes to me all along."

Colman showed Thomas nothing.

"You noticed the static interference? The inaudible?"

"Yes."

"That was when your name was mentioned. The tapes always somehow seem defective when they mention you, or when, for example, you call."

"How long have you known?"

"Years. I suspected it when Micko quit the strike force. But Kennedy knew before that."

To his horror Colman could feel his legs beginning to tremble, a quivering in the hollows behind his knees. He felt his bowels turn. He rammed iron down his spine. *You will not feel this!* But Kennedy knew!

"Your son has kept you out of stripes, Brady. You should know that. We'd have thrown everything at you."

Here was this bloody WASP Harvard Brahmin bastard telling him that he and Kennedy would have doubled on him, Colman Brady. But that was nothing. Here was this stranger telling him that he did not know his son, did not know how much more he was than he had ever suspected. At the end doesn't the child always carry his father across the ford? And isn't the child always, finally, the one who saves? His son had saved him! His son had fooled him! Colman had thought him so weak and lacking in nerve or real principle. Yet his son had found a way to do both the things he was raised to — to work for justice and to protect his father from the world. How Colman had misjudged him! How the boy had loved him and what pain it must have been to be so unknown. Colman closed his eyes against a rush of misery and grief. He had made all the wrong choices with his life, and Collins had known it. He had chosen Anselmo, and that choice was what killed Collins.

Colman looked at Thomas. "So presumably Anselmo discovered."

"Presumably. Any idea how?"

"Someone in your shop."

"No. I'm the only one who knew, aside from the attorney general. That's why this stuff is here. If it's any consolation to you, this tape I just played will get a kind of revenge for Collins."

"What do you mean?"

"We've decided to use Balestrione's informant. I'm going to announce to the jury tomorrow that Anselmo's son Marcello has agreed to testify."

"He'd never do that," Brady said.

"I know it. But when Balestrione hears it from his plant, well, he'll have to do something, won't he? We can't get them in court. We've decided to get them in the street. If Anselmo and Balestrione are at each other's throats they'll do society a lot less damage."

"Jesus Christ, you guys will do anything."

"To get those bastards? Yes, we will."

But Brady only wanted to get one of them. "I'll tell you something, Thomas," he said. "We're all those bastards."

Brady left Thomas's house and walked quickly down Marlborough to Arlington Street, where he caught a cab. He did not notice the small Austin-Healy following.

In the cab Brady had to press the hand-grip and hold on to it all the way to the North End. He could feel the pounding of blood through his veins; the pulse at his right temple seemed to resound in his ear. Was this vast surge of mere grief and remorse? He had failed his son so. Was it fear? He was an old man trying to kill a ruthless, well-guarded gangster. He would not survive this one and he knew it. But he was not feeling fear, nor mere grief nor mere anger. He was in the grip of that old killing fever which had begun everything. The spasm of killing on the road from Clonmel that day had generated an emotion in him which he recognized now as the truest, most vital thing about him. How he had relished killing Peter Gavin with a bullet through the eye. How he had been lifted and exhilarated by that orgy of violence against Nellie's murderers. Violence at the heart, the love of it. Colman Brady shivered in the back seat of the cab. He was watching the twilight city pass, but not seeing it. He was cold in the blast of his own self-knowledge. Here he was doing it again and feeling not old, not vulnerable, not confused, not lonely, not disappointed; feeling the strength and clarity and freedom and perfect power that come after the decision to kill a man. Why had he never found a way to transfer that vitality, that purity of emotion to the rest of his life? Then he could have loved Madeline. Then he could have known his son and been known by him. Then he could have protected himself from Curley and even Curley from Curley. Then he could have said no to Anselmo decades before. But all of that was idle and useless remorse. The point was that the future is like the past, exactly. Why had it taken him so long to admit it? In the great struggle, it is darkness hands down. He remembered how he put the barrel of Purcival's own gun against Purcival's cheek and fired. He pressed his hand around the barrel of the gun in his pocket. He was willing and ready and he hoped to God his legs wouldn't fail him or his eye or his steady hand. *But no, not tonight,* he thought. *I have it. I have it in spades. It is what ruined me. It is what turned my people into murderers, destroyed my home, burned my wife, wrecked my dream of America, and killed my son. And I have it and I love it.*

Brady directed the cabbie down Hanover Street as far as Fleet Street, then right to Revere, then left. He began to count the houses. As they passed by Anselmo's in the middle of the block, Brady looked discreetly out. Three things: the lights were on, two men stood by the door, and the building was, as Brady remembered, a row house joined like all the others to its neighbors. The guards and the lights told him that Anselmo was there. He instructed the cabbie to go left up to Hanover again. Brady got out and paid him. He went three doors down Fleet Street and entered a building.

That was when Tony lost him. He parked his car and ran the length of Hanover Street looking for his grandfather. Then he went into a cafe and struck up a conversation with two boys less than his age. He spoke to them familiarly and confidently and partly in Sicilian.

Colman climbed the dark stairs of the building, remembering the rancid odor of the North End Prohibition stills. But that odor was gone. The stairs smelled of garlic. People were preparing and serving their dinners. As quietly as he could Colman went through the door onto the roof. He let his eye drift along the outline of the chimneys and uneven ledges of the buildings. He saw that there were several walls to hurdle, but it seemed possible. The buildings were all connected. He moved silently, slowly from one to the other, scaling the walls and crawling through gardens and under clotheslines. He guessed that he would not confront a guard until he came to Anselmo's roof. He was hoping for a guard, in fact, because that would tell him for certain which was the building he wanted.

Tony Brady bought espresso for his two companions. He told them he was staying with his father's uncle and that he had arrived only that afternoon from New York. When the boys told him where their parents and grandparents were from in Sicily, Tony rhapsodized about Agrigento. The boys had never been to Sicily and they loved hearing about it from someone their own age. They invited him for a game of billiards in the back room. Tony accepted, but said he had first to let his aunt know he would not be eating. As he started to leave he said he was not sure of the house number and asked if they knew his father's uncle, Gennaro Anselmo. The boys were impressed and they reminded him gladly, not only of the number but of the street.

Brady saw the guard, a man sitting in the shadow of a tall thin chimney with a shotgun in the crook of his arms. Brady crept as close to him as he dared. Then he threw a stone against a small water tank on the next building. The guard stirred, looked, then began to hoist himself up. While he was in the act of standing, Brady came swiftly up behind him and struck a fierce blow on his head with the butt end of Collins's weapon. *Not bad,* he thought, *for an old man.* The guard went down and was out cold, but Brady hit him again. He had to be certain the man was unconscious, for if he had any chance of escape at all it would be back across the rooftops. He stood over the slumped form for some moments waiting for his breathing to normalize. The exertion even of the simple blows had taken his wind again.

He went into the building and down the stairs. The dining room, he thought, he had to find the dining room. The first landing he came to was on a bedroom floor, and there were no sounds. Brady knew that Anselmo's sons lived with their own families. With luck, there would be only Anselmo and his wife. With more, the two guards on the street would not be alerted until it was too late. He went down the stairs to the next floor. Still no sounds. Doors were open on a parlor, a lady's sewing room. Brady started down the next flight. The stairs creaked and he froze, but there was only the muffled sound of talk from the floor below. There were sounds of silver on china. That was what he wanted to hear. A pair of sliding double doors faced the bottom of the staircase. Brady stood in front of them. He wiped the perspiration from his gun hand. He gripped the door firmly and slid it open. He stepped into the room and closed the door behind him.

There were only Anselmo and his wife. They froze with their forks at their food. Anselmo and Brady stared at each other for a long time across a distance of only four yards. Colman thought that Gennaro, with his collarless shirt and suspenders and napkin at his throat and sauce in the corner of his mouth, looked old and vulnerable. How wonderful to have caught him in the act of eating! A man never feels more exposed than when he is eyed with his mouth full. There is nothing more foolish or graceless or more undignified than closely watched chewing. Anselmo had either to chew his meat or spit it out. He chewed and swallowed, then brought his napkin across his lips and down. His wife knew enough to stare at Brady's gun and not move.

"You're a dead man, Gennaro," Brady said.

"So are you, Colman, if you do this."

"The difference is I don't give a shit." Colman had not realized how bottomless was his despair until he'd said that.

"Colman," Anselmo said softly, shaking his head. "Colman," he repeated with genuine regret. "You understand how it is. I had no choice." It was a statement, not a plea.

It was true and Brady knew it. Collins had known what the stakes were and he'd dealt himself in. Once Anselmo learned who the informant was, he had to kill him. There was nothing personal in that. He had not meant it as an act of betrayal against his old friend, and, in a way, Colman did not take it as such.

"I do understand, Gennaro. Exactly. You and I are enacting what someone else wrote for us. You had no choice." Colman opened his raincoat to display his bloodied suit. "Neither do I."

Anselmo's eyes went up and down Brady's body; blood covered him from his knees to his chest. "I misjudged you," Anselmo said; "I didn't think you loved your son that much."

Brady had to deflect his emotion. He wanted to cry out again, to slam his fist on stone. It was not only his son he loved at that moment, but his power, finally, over Anselmo. He'd been wanting to stand over him like this for thirty years, and here he was doing it. The son of a bitch, he repeated to himself, killed Micko. "We are old men, Gennaro. What else is there but sons?"

Anselmo nodded. He understood that. He regretted very much what he had been forced to do. He would not willingly have taken a son from any man. Certainly not from Brady.

There was a faint sound outside the door. Brady saw Anselmo's eyes dart to it and back. Without hesitating Brady took two steps to Anselmo's wife. He pressed the muzzle of the gun against her cheek and he fixed his stare on Anselmo.

A faint knock on the door.

Brady shook his head, barely.

Anselmo turned toward the door and grunted. A man frantically called through the door, "Don Anselmo, we have a boy here who tried to come into the house. He refuses to talk."

Anselmo's eyes went to Colman Brady. Brady was stunned by an instinct that seemed absolute to him. He knew who it was and he knew that just when the world had spread itself out before him once again, he was once again being taken from behind by what he never expected.

He nodded to Anselmo, who barked an order. The door opened and Tony was shoved into the room by the two guards, each of whom had him by an arm and each of whom had a pistol. "Drop the guns," Brady ordered, as he pressed his own harder yet against Anselmo's wife. The guards looked at Anselmo in a way that said they would not drop them; they wanted the standoff. But Anselmo wasn't having it. He would not give Brady reason to kill his wife. Anselmo nodded and the guards dropped their weapons, but continued to hold the boy's arms.

"You bloody punk!" Brady said to Tony. "What are you doing here?"

Tony looked at Colman, but only briefly. He faced Anselmo, who returned his stare unflinchingly. Anselmo knew that this was the Taormina boy. How he regretted the death of the boy's mother and the deaths of the war that followed it. He wondered if the boy knew. Was that why he stared at him so? Or was it only this recent death, his father? Anselmo would like to have explained to the boy what dreadful turning the earth does.

Colman was shocked at the animal stare that locked Tony and Anselmo together, and then he realized that of course they were of the same blood. They were like each other in the power of their detachment. That was why he could never defeat either of them, and that was why he envied them.

"Take a good look at him, kiddo. He just killed your father," Colman said. Should he tell him the other part, that Anselmo had also killed his mother? He would have, but Collins would not have forgiven him. "Take a good look, kiddo," Colman repeated. Brady was having trouble reading Tony, whose stare showed almost nothing. "What do you say, Tony? What should I do with him?"

Then Tony turned slowly toward Colman and his face began to change, to twist, to contort itself into the most awful expression of rage and hate that Brady had ever seen. "Kill the bastard!" the boy screamed. "Kill the bastard!" And then there was a stream of invective — Sicilian, Brady guessed — and then the words, more shrill and piercing: "Kill him! Kill him! Kill him!" The guards held Tony as he lunged toward Anselmo, but the fit continued. "Kill him! Kill him! Kill him!"

And Colman Brady saw, that simply, that clearly, what the killing fever looks like. He saw himself in the boy and he saw what his life had come to. Is the future like the past? Exquisitely. But from Tony! Such rage, such hatred, such vengeance! From the aloof, detached, mysterious kid whom Colman could not manipulate and could not control and could not destroy. But his power had depended on his detachment, and that had evaporated totally, instantly, as Colman's own had once. Such a feeling for Michael Collins Brady! Only love could inspire such hate. Colman recognized the blood in his grandson. It was his own. The boy faced Colman with an image of himself, and suddenly he realized how much he loved him. The overwhelming love of a family for itself, of an old man for his youth, of one Brady for another — it was with those loves and a simpler one that Colman loved Tony, and that made everything different. The question was not then whether to spare Anselmo, but whether to spare Tony. Killing upon killing upon killing; lifetime upon lifetime upon lifetime. Everything in Colman revolted against those words — *Kill him!* — from his son's only son. He loved him. That changed everything.

Brady dropped his gun and crossed to Tony, who was held rigid by the two guards. Tears were streaming down his face and his lips were still moving, though silently, around the words, "Kill him! Kill him! Kill him!" Colman stood before the boy and shook his head slowly. His own eyes overflowed and he could not speak.

Anselmo made a motion with his head to the guards and they released the boy, who threw himself on his grandfather, holding on to him so tightly that Colman Brady, for a change, could not breathe in someone else's embrace.

The guards had their pistols ready, but Anselmo said, "Get out," and they left the room.

For a long time Colman stood inside his grandson's arms. Finally, he turned the boy toward the door, opened it and gently led him out. Before closing the door he said to Anselmo, "Gennaro, your son Marcello; protect him from Balestrione."

Anselmo eyed him carefully. He asked the question by opening his hands.

"Don't misunderstand, Gennaro. You are not forgiven, and we are not friends. And you will have my hate forever. It is not your family I want spared of this. It is mine. It's myself." Then Brady left.

On the sidewalk, Colman said with a great effort at lightheartedness, "We're walking, kiddo. I love to walk in this city. I'll tell you a story or two on the way. You see that house down there? Honey Fitz was born there. What do you think of that?"

Tony was walking inside his grandfather's arm. Tears still flowed freely down his face and he could barely take in what his grandfather was pointing to. But the old man's words affected him and he made his own effort. He nodded and said, "In eighteen sixty-three he was born there." And then he smiled at Colman, who hugged him harder. Neither of them spoke again until they were out of the North End and well past Haymarket.

"Grandfather," Tony said simply, "I loved him. I loved him as if he was my real father."

"I know it, son," Colman said. He wanted to press the kid closer and tell him that Collins *was* his real father and that he himself was his real grandfather. Brady wanted to tell Tony that he was his and he always would be. He wanted to take the kid in like air, like food. But he knew instantly that that was how he always ruined what was precious. Brady wanted once to love someone without eating him.

And there was Janet. This young man was all she had. It was for her to tell him what his bloodline was or not to tell him. It made no difference that Tony did not know. What mattered was that Colman knew, and that knowledge was air enough and food enough. And so he said, "You should always think of him as if he were your real father, Tony. He loved you that way too, and so does your mother. Let's go tell her what happened. Let's tell her everything."

Tony draped his arm around his grandfather's shoulder, and they crossed into Boston Common.

But when they got to Olympia, the doctor encountered a revolting development.

God help us all!

So much of what happened during the invention of Seattle baffled the pious part of the pioneer community, it ended up crediting the creation of our town to a little bit of Divine Intervention here, and a smidgin over there. The whole thing gets dropped into the lap of The Lord on the grounds that He moves in mysterious ways to do His thing.

If He was responsible, the Lord sure did it the hard way, because what happened was that while Doc Maynard was in California, a young fella went south with $60,000 belonging to Mike Simmons and kept on going. On November 18, 1851, Mike ran an ad in the *Oregon Spectator* reading:

"Notice—My late partner, Charles Hart Smith, having absconded with several thousand dollars belonging to me, and having besides defrauded every other person in this vicinity whom he could, under false pretenses, persuade to credit—this is to notify the public that the partnership lately existing under the name of Simmons & Smith is hereby dissolved, and all persons are warned not to trust the said Smith, under any circumstances, whatever. M. T. Simmons, Olympia, Lewis County, O.T., November 18, '51."

You'll notice the ad didn't say anything about the sixty thou. And the chances are that at that stage of the game Mike didn't know that he had one foot on a banana peel and the other on financial oblivion. At any rate, he sure didn't show it in regard to the romance between the doctor and Catherine Broshears. And, of course, he had all of the help he needed from the eligible bachelors around the Pacific Northwest who descended on Catherine like a bunch of bees attracted by the honey.

Prosch says, "Notwithstanding the newness of things and their primitive character, life at the upper end of Puget Sound was not uninteresting to the widow." (After all, she was thirty-two, going on ninety-six, a well-preserved hunk of woman.) "Men were many enough compared to women, there probably being three or four to one. Women were correspondingly in favor. Nothing was too good for them. They could have what they wished for the asking.

"Mrs. Broshears soon found herself to be in high favor with the bachelors and widowers, and she was evidently regarded by them as a 'catch' of the best character. Her people speedily saw the direction of things, and they tried to direct it into quarters to suit themselves and their own ideas of propriety and desirability. They found out that the beginning of a romance had developed on the plains, east of the Rocky Mountains, and that it had attained with the passage of weeks and months such life and strength as to be quite serious.

"Knowing that Dr. Maynard was a married man, from his own admissions, they disapproved the bent and inclination shown by him and their widowed sister. They made suggestions of other men, introduced them, and did what they could to break up the alliance between Maynard and Mrs. Broshears. They restrained her somewhat of her liberty, and prevented her from going with him when they could.

"More than once they were on the verge of stopping by force the marriage."

Do you think Doc Maynard took this lying down?

Hell, no!

Instead of going on to Seattle, he set up shop in Olympia.

And that really did screw up the works in Mike's clock. The doctor introduced a totally new concept to the Mike Simmons monopoly.

It was known as "competition."

Doc Maynard had bought and equipped a general store for ten-cents on the dollar. What he did was start selling stuff for the same prices merchants were getting for it in San Francisco, Portland, Oregon City and Salem. Catherine would say later that his action created "quite a disturbance in the trade," and she was right. Mike previously had been getting ten times the going rate for his products.

But with Smith gone . . . And the $60,000 gone . . . Charging ten prices for things was not a luxury, it was a necessity. The Simmons Empire teetered on the brink of collapse. With Doc Maynard's store in town, Mike's financial demise was guaranteed. If he went under at the hands of the doctor, the family pressure against Catherine's marriage to Maynard would become unanimous and irresistible. And suddenly Catherine was on a very hot seat indeed. Her "go away, stay" attitude toward the doctor suddenly was crystallized out of the solution and into direct action.

"If you leave," she said, "I'll marry you."

To the family, she said, "It's going to be David Maynard or nobody."

A few months later, one G. A. Barnes set up what he advertised as a "Cheap Store," and broke Mike Simmons.

But by that time, Doc Maynard was long gone.

The return of the Native

While all this was going on, Chief Seattle was hopping around on one foot and the other like he had to go to the bathroom. He had the greatest grapevine on the Sound and knew that the doctor's primary interest in life was a hunk of land at the mouth of the Duwamish River.

The Chief had been in the doghouse with the members of his tribe ever since he had opened his big mouth about protecting the Nisquallies from Patkanim four years earlier. They were in pretty good shape as long as they stayed at Suquamish, which is on the west side of Puget Sound, but the fishing there was lousy. And, with Patkanim threatening to wipe them out if they came near their favorite camping ground at the mouth of the Duwamish, their traditional fishing ground had become a precarious place indeed.

They had to sort of "sneak" the fish out . . . ready to beat a strategic retreat when Patkanim came thundering down on them from his headquarters at the mouth of the Snohomish River.

For all of his bellering and bluster, Chief Seattle was *that* close to a recall election. His hopes were raised in the winter of 1850 when Doc Maynard survived one of Patkanim's cheap excursion trips around Puget Sound. And his native intelligence told him there was something in Doc Maynard's little black bag which commanded Patkanim's complete respect.

Respect?

Patkanim was scared to death of that bag.

Maynard, who was not unaware of the Indian Political Climate, had a whole bunch of merchandise on his hands . . . and Felker was off some place like San Francisco. What he needed was some cheap transportation to Elliott Bay with the ingredients for his store.

And it was a lot of stuff.

There were, for instance, several barrels of whiskey . . . brandy . . . rum . . . nearly two tons of molasses . . . half a ton of hardtack . . . three tons of flour . . . a box of pots and pans, axes, tobacco, raisins, shoes, boots and medical supplies . . . a quarter-of-a-ton of sugar . . . several dozen hickory shirts . . . a dozen window sashes . . . a box of eight-by-ten-inch window panes . . . a case each of mustard . . . salt . . . pepper and pepper sauce . . . a dozen grindstones and a half-dozen each of files and crosscut saws . . . several roles of calico and a bale or two of domestic—and more brooms than the chief had ever seen.

That was mid-March, 1852.

For the first time in four years, Chief Seattle and his tribe were returning to their Duwamish fishing ground in time for the spring run of Chinook salmon.

Opening day at the Seattle Yacht Club when thousands of boats of one kind and another pass through the Montlake Cut and into Lake Washington past a reviewing stand is a pretty and impressive function in our town annually . . .

But it never could equal the triumphant procession which marked the return of Chief Seattle and the 200 members of his tribe to the mouth of the Duwamish River and the home of his ancestors.

The sun could have been shining.

The sun had to be shining!

The sun was shining in Chief Seattle's heart—regardless of the kind of climate that The Lord visited upon that part of the earth around Alki Point on the particular day in question.

The chief lined up a flotilla of floating craft, the like of which never had been seen before in the town of Olympia . . . canoes . . . scows . . . sailing vessels—the works.

They departed Olympia on the morning of March 23.

With all that crowd it took 'em nine days to reach Elliott Bay.

What a triumph for Chief Seattle, Chief of the Suquamish and Allied Tribes, Chief of the Duwamish and Allied Tribes, High Muckamuck of the Most Exalted . . . returning in triumph from exile. There he was in full regalia at the head of the procession, lolling in the stern of the lead canoe . . .

Beside him was the impeccably clad Dr. Maynard with his broad-brimmed fedora . . . immaculate white shirt, black tie, flowered vest and flowing cape . . .

And his little black bag.

Unlike opening day at the yacht club when everybody is having a great time, there were mixed feelings among the folks on shore. There was, of course, the irrepressible Charlie Terry, looking like the Cheshire cat that just has swallowed the canary . . . he only recently had stolen the location from under the noses of the people from Cherry Grove and had named it New York after his native state.

Also there, however, were the people who had lost the battle for ownership of the new town on Elliott Bay. They weren't on speaking terms with the ones who had won the townsite. Some of them weren't even on speaking terms with one another. There was, for instance, the forthright young Louisa Boren, who had been trying for forty-five days to get the menfolk in her group off their duffs and moved over to a town-location which they had staked out at the head of the bay five miles away. Some of these people were sick of one another and the others were just plain sick . . .

But the sickest of the shore bunch was Patkanim.

That was *his* canoe Chief Seattle and the doctor were riding in!

Doc Maynard, not unmindful of the political situation between the two Indian Chiefs, and appreciative of the efforts to which Seattle, his new whipping boy, had extended himself, decided to make the Chief's day complete.

"What I'm going to do, Chief," he said, "is name the most important town in the world after you."

"Besides," he reflected, "it sure will tick off Patkanim."

And so Seattle was named.

Bye bye mudhole

You don't have to dig deep or read far to find out that a bunch of teetotallers from a presently non-existent town called Cherry Grove, Illinois, landed at Alki Point on November 15, 1851. The folks had had a terrible time coming across the continent . . . what with Indians and all like that.

By the time they got to Portland, half of the party wasn't talking to the other half, and they split up—one half remaining in Portland and the other half heading for Puget Sound. Leader of half the party was John Denny.

The other half was headed by his son, Arthur Armstrong Denny, who was sick with malaria at the time and sent his younger brother, David, to explore the Puget Sound country. When Arthur was well enough to come, he brought his half of the party with him . . .

Only to find himself euchred out of Alki Point by the brothers Charlie and Lee Terry. And here the party split again into two non-communicating groups.

What they knew for sure was that they were broke. And what they found out was they could get eight cents a running foot for piling. So, what they set about doing was finding the best place to get piling.

In the process, they went up and down the Duwamish River a few times—never noticing a particularly obnoxious mudhole at the mouth of the river. On February 15, 1852, four of the folks who were speaking with one another, Arthur and David Denny, William N. Bell and Carson Boren, paddled around Elliott Bay and found a place where it was easy to cut trees and roll them down a steep bank to deep water where they could be loaded aboard ship.

Here, they staked adjacent claims that ran from approximately the Kingdome to the Space Needle. David was too young to stake a claim. Arthur took the center cut, which was thick with beautiful, straight piling material, and they handed the bottom of the barrel to Carson Boren, Denny's brother-in-law, who was only there because his wife told him he had to be. What Boren didn't like was his wife. What he did like was hunting and fishing . . .

So *what* if he got the mudhole?

When Doc Maynard appeared on the scene, Arthur Denny was laid low again with malaria and the doctor was summoned to ease his pain a little . . .

During the course of which time Maynard maneuvered a little in a most un-medical manner. Today, the Hippocratic Oath hanging in his office would be ripped up and he would be stripped of his medical buttons by the Committee on Medical Ethics of the King County Medical Society.

The sick man bemoaned the fact that Charlie Terry had done him in. He felt awful. When they landed at Alki, it had been raining. The women and children had been in tears and now everything was going to hell in a handbasket.

The doctor administered some soothing syrup which consisted largely of alcohol into which opium had been dissolved. And as the elixir took hold of the patient, the doctor ventured the opinion that he was looking around for a hole in which to go fishing. He mentioned diffidently that he had a full-scale general store.

The place that interested him a little . . .

For a fishing camp only, you understand . . .

Was the punker part of Boren's claim.

That was the part that was under water when the tide came in. However, the Indians had been using this fishing camp on the point.

Boren's claim! Denny perked up.

Here was a chance for a country boy to take in the city slicker.

It could be arranged for the doctor to have that hunk of property. Denny felt that he could induce his brother-in-law to give a little. The doctor demurred. He wasn't at all sure this was what he was looking for.

Denny pointed out how welcome the doctor and his store would be.

The doctor relented a little . . .

Well, maybe.

Denny swiftly closed the deal.

He did not learn until later . . . much later . . . that, teetotaller or not, he'd been on an opium jag and given away downtown Seattle . . . on April 1.

Doc Maynard got busy.

The town is born

Two days later, Dr. Maynard and his crew of Indian volunteers hauled the ingredients for his store and the goods of the Boren and Bell families to the new location. Bagley writes: "On April 3, Bell, Boren's family and Doctor Maynard moved from Alki to their claims, leaving behind A.A. Denny who was too ill with the ague to come over until a house could be built. At first Bell camped on the north side and Boren on the south side of the claims continuing thus until they could build cabins . . . "

The doctor, who had other eggs to lay and other fish to fry, lacked their degree of leisure. Bagley covers this phase of our founding with: "Maynard's official entry named April 3, 1852 as his date of settlement. With his accustomed energy he at once set to work to provide himself with a store building, availing himself of white and Indian labor, and in a few days was selling goods in it. It was eighteen feet wide and twenty-six long, with an attic in the front half of it. The walls were of logs and the roof of shakes, the usual name for split boards about four feet long. It stood at the northwest corner of First Avenue South and Main Street. The unbroken forest was a few feet away on the east and the steep bank above tidewater on the west. The stores of that period included under one roof the necessaries of pioneer life as far as attainable, clothing, hardware, groceries, tools, ship chandlery, and Maynard's was the first of its kind in Seattle although Low and Terry had conducted a similar business at Alki."

The doctor called his store the "Seattle Exchange."

It was the first structure of any kind, size, or shape in our town and, as such, we ought to know what it looked like.

The top side of each log was hewn into a triangular shape and the bottom was notched to accept it. About eight feet from the ground, the logs were continued up another four to six feet, but in shorter lengths that created a peaked roof. Rafters about four feet apart extended from one end to the other and were covered with cedar shakes, which were fastened with wooden pins. The logs then were chinked with clay, which was plentiful in Seattle's birthplace. And this in turn was covered with slats inside and out.

Doc had plenty of cedar to work with. This was split and formed into a puncheon floor with an adz that in the hands of a good workman could be as smooth as a modern kitchen floor and just as waterproof. The cedar also was fashioned into tables, benches, stools, and a door which was made with an upper and lower section, with hinges and bars that defied all ordinary attempts at breaking it open. A bar served as the lock. Pivoted at one end, it dropped into a slot. At this end, a leather thong from the bar led through a hole above the door. In peaceful times, the thong was not drawn at night, giving rise to the phrase, "the latch string is always out."

The double door had a double purpose. When the upper section was open, it provided both light and ventilation, while the lower section kept out dogs, chickens, pigs—and, hopefully—unwanted Indians. There usually was an opening six feet square left in one wall, which led to a fireplace built outside of the cabin.

Lighting at night was provided by tallow candles or fish oil placed in a shallow bowl with a cotton wick in it . . . and by the open hearth. Wooden pins driven into the walls supported shelves made of split cedar. Uprights driven into the floor supported a platform that was covered with fir bows to serve as a mattress on which blankets were spread for a bed.

In this 18x26-foot-square structure, Doc Maynard housed the town's first combination hardware, drug, grocery and clothing store. It also served as the first hospital, polling place and meeting hall. And a few months after it was built, it became the first restaurant in town.

Doc Maynard was a one-man band.

I'm drawing on Bagley for a good deal of this information in spite of the fact that his history of Seattle was paid for by the people whose biographies appeared in it. In the biographical sections, the families controlled exactly what was said. But Bagley was too much of a reporter to saccharinize the historical truth in the non-biographical section.

He wrote: "Among his other activities (the doctor) immediately set to work to put up salmon for shipment. That season he sent to San Francisco nearly one thousand barrels of salmon. The barrels were made on the ground where they were packed, though where he got the coopers is not recorded. Procuring the fish was a simple matter, as the Indians supplied him with all he could use. On its arrival in San Francisco most of the shipment was found to be spoiled, and his venture proved almost a total loss.

"During this time he had men skilled with broadax squaring timbers, and others cutting piles and shaving shingles. A cargo of these was shipped to San Francisco on the brig *Franklin Adams*; 12,000 lineal feet of squared timbers, 8,000 lineal feet of piles, 10,000 shingles and 30 cords of wood. All of this found a ready market at good prices and from it he more than recouped the loss on the salmon."

As it was, he lost about $700 on the salmon deal . . .

And made about $20,000 on the "wood goods" in the same shipment.

Of course, all of the above is just something the doctor got under way in his first month in the new town. The chances are that if he had given the salmon packing deal a little more of his personal attention, it wouldn't have gone bad on him.

But, he had bigger fish to fry.

There were monumental enterprises afoot like getting a new territory started north of the Columbia River and, of course, obtaining a divorce from the Territorial Legislature. A man or woman with the right connections in the legislature could have a bill passed granting him or her a divorce—without ever bothering the other party to the marriage.

And to get the ball rolling, he had to help elect his friend, Isaac N. Ebey to the Oregon Territorial Legislature.

IV

The Great
Magoozle

Except for the people who live in the fourth and ninth grades where the teaching of Washington history is required by law, and those getting a master's degree in history, there aren't many people around who give a good goddam how Washington got started as a separate entity. Well, the people who write history books have got to know something about it, too . . . and for the most part, their attempts at figuring it out have resulted in a great deal of confusion for the people who are sentenced to nine months of Washington History in the fourth and ninth grades.

But in Doc Maynard's time, the creation of Washington Territory was BIG.

To be or not to be a new territory was the burning question of the day. It wiped all other news like who shot whom and where off the front pages of the paper . . . and it was the main tavern topic from the Canadian to the California borders. They even knew clear back in Washington, D.C. that there was some kind of a rumble going on in the northwest corner of the country.

The reason for all this was that the folks living south of the Columbia River got more money from the federal government than the folks living north of the Columbia River. And the question was, could everybody get more money from the federal government if there were *two* territories out here in the northwest corner instead of one. Or

would Congress just continue with the same appropriations for both
. . . which would result in the folks south of the Columbia getting less
money.

And that's how Doc Maynard got into the Great Magoozle.

(A magoozle, for the benefit of those who have retired or not as yet
awakened, is a method by which we get things done in America. It's
neither legal nor illegal, but it gets the job done.)

Everything always happens at once, and, naturally, the Great
Magoozle was coming to a head right at the time the doctor was
starting Seattle, which was why he couldn't fool around with a lot of
vacillating opinions about what the town should be named or where to
locate the downtown business district. He moved some of the
dissidents to the new location on April third, and he had to get going
on the magoozle by May third.

The doctor had participated in many a magoozle in the past, and
would engage in his fair share of magoozles in the future . . .

But this one was the GREAT Magoozle.

In it, he created Washington Territory . . . and won King County as
kind of a booby prize . . .

And they were only incidental to his real objective.

The light that failed

It takes a little doing to follow this, which is why the people in the
fourth and ninth grades flounder a lot on the question of what happened when and where, but I'll try and ABC it. While the doctor was
cutting his woodpile and the Denny Party was watching another
Indian bite the dust on the Oregon Trail and Mike Simmons was the
big frog in the small pond, some fellows tried to get the new territory
going.

At the Annual Fourth of July picnic in Olympia in 1851, one J.B.
Chapman made a big pitch about the creation of a new territory north
of the Columbia. This was nine months before Doc Maynard moved
the folks from Alki Point to his new town. Mr. Chapman really didn't

care much whether there was a new territory or not. It was just that his brother was big in the development of Portland, and J.B. wanted the folks back home to know that he was just as big of a shot as his brother.

To that point, Mr. Chapman had a singular record of failure.

He had tried to get a town going on Grays Harbor. It was one of the other twenty-five towns that advertised as being the terminus of the transcontinental railroad. That one never got beyond the planning stage. So, he tried to get another one going farther up the Chehalis River and that one went belly-up, too.

So then he got thinking that Lafayette Balch, who had started Steilacoom and advertised it as the terminus of a railroad that would come through Naches Pass, had the right idea. Balch called his place "Port" Steilacoom. Chapman started a town across the street and called his place Steilacoom "City."

This move annoyed Lafayette Balch all to pieces. He had tried to get going in Olympia, but Mike Simmons, with his monopoly going full blast, had thwarted the attempt. So Balch loaded his general store back on his boat and moved it a few miles north. Now, the shoe was on the other foot. He was getting a competitive store right across the street.

But Chapman was a pretty good con man, and he suckered both Balch and Simmons to back his plan for the new territory on the grounds that if they could get it, there would be enough in the deal for all of them.

So, they joined forces with him and kicked off the campaign for the new territory at the Fourth of July picnic in Olympia.

And Doc Maynard, who took to politics like a big dog takes to steak, interrupted his wood-splitting to get into the act. At the picnic, Chapman called for a thing that has come to be known as the "Cowlitz Convention." This was held at Cowlitz Landing on the Cowlitz River, which probably is why it was known as the Cowlitz Convention. At any rate, Chapman, Balch and Simmons ran the Cowlitz convention.

Right into the ground.

For a while there, Doc Maynard thought it was legit.

Then he realized the trio in charge couldn't have cared less whether or not a territory was created. Chapman's real problem was that he needed a job. If he could make a big enough name for himself, then the Oregon Territorial Legislature would name him as prosecuting attorney for the Puget Sound District. What Balch wanted was for Chapman to get the job as prosecuting attorney so he'd get the hell out of Steilacoom City and leave Port Steilacoom alone. And what Mike Simmons wanted out of it was an entity called "Simmons County."

Maynard first tumbled to the truth in the fall of 1851 before he took his load of wood to California. The way he found out about it was that Isaac Ebey told him. And the reason Ebey told him about it was that Ebey also wanted to be the prosecuting attorney for the Puget Sound District.

And when those two got together, the other guys didn't have a chance.

Doc scooted back from San Francisco in time to attend the session of the Oregon Legislature in Salem in the winter of 1852—before he moved to Seattle. When Chapman showed up with fifty-five signatures calling for the creation of Simmons County, the doctor and Ebey lobbied around the legislative halls and got things changed around some. The county was created all right. But the name was changed from "Simmons" to "Thurston," which is the way it is today.

Then came the matter of prosecutor for Puget Sound District. Chapman got two votes for the job. Ebey got fourteen. But there still was a small detail that had to be corrected. The new prosecutor had not as yet been admitted to the bar in Oregon Territory. So what they did was hurry on up to what we know of today as the Jackson Courthouse (which still is extant south of Chehalis) and get Judge William Strong to admit Ebey to the practice of law.

Balch was the only one of the original three who got anything out of it.

Chapman's Steilacoom City folded.

But, before all of this happened, the doctor had made the concluding speech of the Cowlitz Convention and in it he had caused an interesting paragraph to be inserted in the petition to Congress. The insertion notified Congress that if something wasn't done about creating the new territory by May 3, 1852, we'd hold another convention . . . and at this convention we would form our own state. And, if we formed our own state, the next time they heard from us, we'd be seeking admission as a state, not a mere territory.

That's where things stood when the doctor initiated the construction of Seattle.

And, that's why he only had thirty days to do it.

Strong Medicine at Saunders' Bottom

One of the first people that Doc Maynard met when he came to Oregon with Catherine was J. R. Jackson, proprietor of the establishment which has come to be known as the Jackson Courthouse. Jackson, a one-eyed man who disputed Mike Simmons' claim of being the first man to settle north of the Columbia, was married to the best cook north of the Columbia River. He also was sheriff of Lewis County when it extended all the way from the Rocky Mountains to the Pacific Ocean and all the way north to Alaska. His establishment became a place where, for a fee, you could get citizenship papers. You also could get other kinds of justice.

The Jackson Courthouse was located about ten miles south of Saunders' Bottom, (named for the muddy condition at this spot of the trail between Cowlitz Landing and Olympia). Ten miles north was S.S. Ford's farm, where the circuit court also held sessions.

Judge Strong was strong in the judging business at the time, although he was even stronger in the gambling business. Judging didn't pay well in those days, so he had a line of gambling paraphernalia which he sold from the "bench" when court was not in session. And here, the profits were enormous. The big item, of course, was the playing cards. He bought them at a penny-a-deck in New York, had them shipped here at government expense by the gross . . . and sold them for $1.50 per deck.

He was not a medical man and the title to this segment does not refer to anything connected with the human body. However, it had a great deal to do with Saunders' "Bottom" and the creation of the new territory in which Doc Maynard became deeply involved.

A month or so after the adjournment of the Cowlitz Convention, the judge was called upon to do his thing in Lewis County. At that time, there was no county seat and, acting under procedures adopted by the legislature, the county commissioners were authorized to set the location for the sessions of the circuit court. Intensely aware of the road conditions at Saunders' Bottom, the county commissioners cannily set the site for the court at Sidney Ford's. But Judge Strong, whose appreciation of the road conditions in Saunders' Bottom equalled that of the county commissioners, had other ideas. He peremptorily ordered the jurors to appear for court at J. R. Jackson's. Bancroft notes that the jurors refused to do so "on the ground they had been ordered in the manner of slave-driving, to which they objected as unbecoming to a judge and insulting to themselves. A public meeting was held, at which it was decided that the conduct of the judge merited the investigation of the impeaching power . . ."

There were other irritations involved, but this was the one that launched the second attempt at dividing the territory north of the Columbia from the rest of Oregon.

For reasons of his own, Doc was in the thick of it.

And this time, the First Team got into the act.

George N. McConaha, the "rail sitter"

Fate has methods of moving people around for reasons not available to the normal man . . . but all as a part of the Grand Plan. And such was the case with George N. McConaha, who got moved around more than most.

McConaha, who became Doc Maynard's lawyer, was born on January 4, 1820—making him twelve years younger than Doc. He studied for the bar in Cleveland at the time that Doc was doing his thing in that town. And they may have met then, but they most certainly met when Doc was in California.

In 1850 McConaha defended a man in a murder case and got an unexpected windfall of $750, which he used to join Weller in California.

McConaha always comes off as a big hero in Seattle history, but that's not the impression you get from some of the California papers at the time he departed from that scene. He was billed as a degenerate alcoholic who consorted with prostitutes and other people of low character . . . and presumably was run out of Sacramento wearing a coat of tar and feathers and riding on a rail.

He arrived at Doc Maynard's doorstep six months after they had met in California. Doc greeted him with open arms. By that time Doc had given up the notion of by-passing the intermediate "territorial" step and now he proposed to petition Congress to become a territory. However, that territory would need a delegate to Congress. And he saw no reason why McConaha wasn't the man for the job.

Doc also had an immediate and urgent need for a personal attorney. The city of Seattle was under way by then, and how would McConaha like a nice corner lot at First Avenue South and Washington Street (where the Maynard Building is located today)?

McConaha shook hands on the deal . . .

And the creation of Washington Territory took another step forward.

Fun and games at a Fourth of July picnic

If you think you're confused by all of this, think of the hapless historians who have spent the last century-and-a-quarter trying to figure the whole thing out themselves . . . and then explain it to the millions of fourth and ninth grade students.

No wonder the kids hate history.

But now everything will be made clear.

On July 4, 1851, J. B. Chapman, for his own special reasons, initiated a movement to create a separate territory north of the Columbia River. This was followed a couple of months later by the Cowlitz Convention at which Doc Maynard got carried away by his enthusiasm for the project and obtained passage of a resolution that if Congress didn't get off its ass and give us a territory by the following May, we would meet again, form our own state and request admission to the Union. I doubt if Doc really thought that would happen, but he figured it was good pressure politics.

A month after the Cowlitz Convention, Doc trundled off to California, sold his pile of wood and met McConaha. He returned in January to help Ebey into the prosecutor's job and thwarted the effort to name it Simmons County. (Mike's dislike of Maynard became more pronounced.) That was in January, 1852.

In March of the same year, he arrived in Seattle, looking for a new place to live with Catherine.

In May, they were supposed to have another convention and form a state, but by then everybody'd had time to think things over and they decided it was better politics to take another run at creating a new territory instead.

Meanwhile, McConaha appeared on the scene and took on the responsibility—among other things—of doing the doctor's legal work.

That's when the Great Magoozle got under way.

The movement which resulted in the creation of Washington Territory was initiated at another Fourth of July picnic in Olympia a year after Chapman had taken his run at the project and had fallen flat on his face.

One D. R. Bigelow, who had been making Fourth of July speeches all over America for years, had arrived in the Pacific Northwest eight months earlier, and the backers of the movement recognized that he was an expert in the field. Subsequent historians have remarked at the fact that, unlike Chapman, Bigelow did not call for a convention to draw up a memorial to Congress requesting a separate territory. To date, historians have pointed with pride that Bigelow's speech sparked the grass roots movement which became a prairie fire . . . sort of a spontaneous combustion.

But "grass roots" movements don't grow on trees.

Somebody has to plant 'em.

Bigelow's job was to raise the flag and see who saluted. He was to leave the rest of the operation to the guys in the smoke-filled room backstage. The most-often quoted part of his speech goes like this:

"We are now assembled on the verge of United States soil—no monumental shafts erected on the revolutionary battlefields meet our eyes to stimulate our patriotism and awaken our sympathies. We are far removed from all such scenes, farther than the most enthusiastic actors in those scenes ever expected the results of their labors to extend. But the scene exhibited here today shows that the great national heart sends its pulsations, actively, healthfully, patriotically even to this distant extremity. We see the flag of the Union waving over us, and we feel that beneath its ample folds we are at home . . . "

There were half-a-dozen principals in the backstage operation, of whom only Doc Maynard and his friend, J.R. Jackson were holdovers from the participants of the previous year's convention. They had at least the tacit backing of the two legislators from north of the Columbia, F.A. Chenoweth and Isaac N. Ebey. In addition, they brought in R.J. White, Quincy A. Brooks, Charles S. Hathaway and F.A. Clarke . . .

And, of course, Doc's attorney, George N. McConaha.

What the fellas did after the speech was take a reading of the reaction to the speech. They knew going in that they had the people around Puget Sound in the palm of their hand. What they had to find out was whether men living along the Columbia River like Seth Catlin and F. A. Clarke figured they were close enough to Salem to get what they wanted without all the bother of creating a new territory. These two men represented the preponderance of the population and if they didn't choose to go along, the whole project would be dead.

It was no different in those days than today. The people along the Washington side of the Columbia River owe a greater allegiance to Portland and Salem than they do to Seattle and Olympia.

The men in leadership positions along the Columbia didn't respond with what could be called overt enthusiasm. But, at least, they wouldn't oppose the movement. And Chenoweth even agreed to active participation in creating the new territory.

Anyway, it was enough to spend a few bucks on.

The first thing they needed was a newspaper with which to beat the drums for the project, and McConaha, who saw himself becoming the first delegate to Congress from the new governmental unit, talked his law partner into starting the first weekly publication north of the Columbia. I'm sure that the doctor, who always put his money where his mouth was, participated in financing the venture.

At any rate the first issue of the *Olympia Columbian* appeared on the newsstands on September 11, 1852. It was dedicated to the principles of the Democratic Party and to the creation of what they hoped would become the new territory of "Columbia."

The first issue of the paper carried the full text of D.R. Bigelow's speech.

The object of their affection

The magoozlers knew they could convince the folks living north of the Columbia of anything they thought might bring in more federal money. The folks south of the river could tumble one way or another . . . also depending on who got how much money and when. The seat of power was in Salem, and there were no public opinion polls.

Well, that wasn't entirely true.

There was Joseph Lane, Oregon's delegate to Congress. If they could find out which way he blew, they would know the direction of the political winds. Lane had been governor in 1849-50. Under him, the territorial legislature had sent a memorial to Congress asking for a railroad and telegraph to the Pacific Northwest although, as Bancroft put it, "there were not enough people in all Oregon to make a good sized country town."

"There was an ingenuous vanity about his public and private acts, a happy self-confidence, mingled with a flattering deference to some and an air of dignity to others, which made him a hero of certain circles in Washington as well as the pride of his constituency."

It was this quality that enabled him, as a Roman Catholic, to be elected as delegate to Congress from a territory primarily nested by Methodists. The fatal error committed by Chapman, Simmons and Balch had been that they didn't clear with Lane before firing their memorial off to Congress. This was accompanied by the fact that they made their try during his first session as delegate. And he followed the precept that in case you're not sure what to do, the safe route is to do nothing.

So the first step was to find out which way Lane blew.

Lane allowed as how he could go for the deal if they could drum up support among the constituency north of the Columbia. He had produced money for Oregon before and assured the folks south of the Columbia that the creation of a new territory north of the Columbia would mean double the federal funds in the Pacific Northwest. They wouldn't lose money on the deal because they could spend the entire amount they got south of the Columbia without those folks north of the river yapping about it.

Lane told the magoozlers that if they could draw up a resolution and get backing for it, he would drop a memorial from a "citizens' group" in the hopper on the opening day of the session and do his level best to buck it through. He cautioned them not to make the mistake that the Chapman axis had made the previous year. Chapman had made a big point of the fact that there were 3,000 people living north of the Columbia.

"Without at least 10,000 people, Congress won't even think about you," he cautioned. "Let me see some signs of activity before I leave in mid-October."

Hail Columbian!

The heavy artillery was initiated by the *Columbian* on September 25 with specifics like calling for the name of "Columbia" for the new territory. The paper pointed out that the area north of the Columbia River was five times the size of Missouri . . . six times the size of Illinois . . . seven times larger than the state of New York and five times the size of all of the New England states put together.

Here's a sample of part of an editorial:

"That a country of such vast extent, so geographically situated, and of such great prospective importance, should remain under one territorial government, constituted as it is at present, is, we believe, destructive to our own interest as citizens, and injurious to those of our general government. Nature has pointedly divided the territory by the Columbia River; that portion to the south has hitherto (received) all the fostering care of, all the benefits arising from the act of Congress approved August 14, 1848, establishing the Territorial Government of Oregon . . . while that portion north of this river . . . has been utterly neglected . . . "

The editorial pointed out that we had a sufficient number of legal voters to be entitled to four out of twenty-five legislators, but until recently had only one . . . petitions for improvements invariably have been disregarded . . . funds from Congress for public buildings have been expended only in southern Oregon . . . sales of public lands have been for improvements south of the river . . . the surveyor general and superintendent of Indian affairs never came north of the river . . .

In the same issue of the paper, there was a letter signed by "Elis" suggesting that there be a meeting on October 25 at the home of J. R. Jackson where preparations could be made for the election of delegates to a convention at Monticello a month later where duly-elected citizens would draft a memorial to seeking a division of the Oregon Territory.

Those were busy days for Doc Maynard and his young attorney, George McConaha. They had a lot of legal and political material to put together before the meeting at J. R. Jackson's. By mid-October, the arguments for division were completed and carried in the *Columbian* so that the folks who gathered at J. R. Jackson's on the 25th would know what they were supposed to do . . .

And Lane would have them all done up in a nice package with a blue ribbon around it.

Because of its historical significance, the resolution is repeated here:

"1. The present Territory of Oregon, containing an area of three hundred and forty-one thousand square miles, is entirely too large an extent of territory to be embraced within the limits of one state.

"2. The said territory possesses a seacoast of six-hundred and fifty miles in extent; the country east of the Cascade Mountains is bound to that on the coast by the strongest ties of interest; and, inasmuch as we believe that the territory must inevitably be divided at no very distant day it would be unjust that one state should possess so large a seaboard to the exclusion of the interior.

"3. The territory embraced within the boundaries of the proposed "Territory of Columbia," containing an area of about thirty-two thousand square miles, is about a fair and just medium of territorial extent for one state.

"4. The proposed "Territory of Columbia" presents natural resources capable of supporting a population at least as large as that of any state in the Union, possessing an equal extent of territory.

"5. Those portions of Oregon Territory lying respectively north and south of the Columbia River, must, from their geographical position, always rival each other in commercial advantage, and their respective citizens must, as they now are and always have been, actuated by a spirit of opposition.

"6. The southern part of Oregon Territory, having a majority of voters, have controlled the Territorial Legislature, and Northern Oregon has never received any benefit from the appropriations made by Congress for said territory, which were subject to the disposition of said Legislature.

"7. The seat of the Territorial Legislature is now situated, by the nearest practicable route, at a distance of five hundred miles from a large portion of the citizens of Northern Oregon.

"8. A great portion of the legislation suitable to the south is, for local reasons, opposed to the interests of the north, and inasmuch as the south has a majority of the voters, and representatives are always bound to reflect the will of their constituents, we can entertain no reasonable hopes that our legislative wants will ever be properly regarded under the present organization.

"9. Experience has shown that in states having a moderate sized territory the wants of the people are more easily made known to their representatives and there is less danger of conflict between sectional interests, and more prompt and adequate legislation can always be obtained."

The arguments for division also made note of the fact the land north of the Columbia was rich in natural resources and presented unparalleled inducements to emigrants who would swell the *present large population* (italics mine) and that the population was rapidly increasing and required the attention of a separate and independent legislature.

"Present large population . . ."

That was the great masterpiece of overstatement.

Oregon made it into the ranks of the territories with a mere 10,000 white residents for the good and simple reason the United States didn't want the land to fall into the hands of the British. But the proposed new territory—even taking in all the land from the Pacific Ocean to the summit of the Rocky Mountains—had fewer than 4,000 and the vast majority of these were living along the north bank of the Columbia River. The total population of the Puget Sound basin ran around 200—and they were the ones who really wanted the new territory, not the people living along the river. Future territories wouldn't make it with less than 50,000 to 60,000.

When Joe Lane trundled off to Washington City with the petition from the settlers, it carried eight signatures. For four of the eight the signatures on that document it was their only appearance in Washington history. They were at the right time and the right place to put their names on a piece of paper . . . then they disappeared into the rain and mists.

Let's see how it added up: George N. McConaha (they spelled it McConaher in the *Congressional Globe*) had only been around for three months. R.J. White was listed as secretary. That was his only appearance in our history books. And apparently he was only here for a day or so because future correspondence was carried on by Quincy A. Brooks. The other one timers were Charles S. Hathaway, C.H. Winslow and F.A. Clarke.

The only two signators whose names also had appeared on the Chapman petition of the previous year were J. R. Jackson and D. S. Maynard.

America in action . . . "grass roots" department

Joe Lane left for Washington, D.C. sometime between the middle and tail end of October, with the memorial seeking the division of Oregon Territory as it subsequently appeared in the *Congressional Globe*, predecessor to the *Congressional Record*, safely tucked in his pocket.

Now all the magoozlers had to do was get the citizens to go along with what already had been written.

And so it was with this in mind that the *Columbian* began to "hype" up the Monticello Convention.

On October 23, the *Columbian* pointed out that the only solution to all of the wrongs that had been visited on the people north of the Columbia River was a "LEGAL DIVORCE FROM THE SOUTH—the formation of a new territory north of the Columbia, with full power to legislate for ourselves, and be entitled to all the rights and privileges which such separation may guarantee, as allowed to territories in general."

The editorials touched all of the emotional bases in the book. "Are we, as American citizens to be thrust aside as unworthy to be the recipients of national bounty, and with none so poor to do us reverence?

No, fellow citizens, such is not, cannot be the spirit and intention of our government, but we are in the hands of the Phillistines, and it depends upon ourselves to put a stop to their boastful language, 'we shall rule and you shall in thralldom serve . . .' "

The *Columbian* promised that with the territorial status would come steam sawmills . . . roads . . . mail routes . . . postoffices . . . courthouses . . . a university.

On November 6 the paper took a gratuitous shot at the Chapman-Balch-Simmons axis with, "Let us take warning, at this stage of our proceedings, and profit from the former abortive movement for bringing about the results which we now have in view . . ."

One of the great gimmicks utilized by the magoozlers was the business of making the delegates to Monticello "official." Here's a sample of what the newspaper pitched: "LET ALL THE DELEGATES BEAR IN MIND TO PROCURE CERTIFICATES OF THEIR APPOINTMENT FROM THE OFFICERS OF THE GENERAL MEETINGS . . . REMEMBER THE DELEGATES ARE TO MEET AT MONTICELLO, (mouth of the Cowlitz River) THE LAST THURSDAY IN NOVEMBER . . ."

I loved the parentheses above.

Monticello has come down to us in our history books as the spot where the spirit of the people attained some kind of spontaneous combustion that blossomed into a new U.S. territory.

But the guys operating the magoozle believed in killing flies with sledgehammers. They knew that half the delegates would get lost if the location of the big event wasn't carefully spelled out. And, of course, they were right. Monticello was an extremely wet farm location owned by one H. D. Huntington. (It periodically flooded out until 1923 when capitalist R. A. Long built a big dike around the place and built a town called Longview.)

So, every news story carried detailed instructions on how to get to Monticello.

The Monticello Convention—a master magoozle

I've heard it said that if the news media had reached the present state of its art a couple of hundred years ago, the fellas never would have been able to put the United States together. A television reporter poking around among the delegates to the Monticello Convention would have blown the whole operation before it ever got started.

The way the magoozlers had it set up was that if Lane would drop the resolution in the hopper at the opening session of Congress, they would produce a grass roots movement with enough bodies to impress Congress before the matter came up on the floor for debate.

Key to this phase of the operation lay in the opening words of the resolution: "The memorial of the undersigned, *delegates of the citizens of Northern Oregon, in convention assembled . . .*"

I've italicized portions of the above to draw your attention to the fact that the organizers of the convention wished to leave the impression that each of the delegates to the convention had stood for election in his own community and represented a whole slew of other people residing back there in the underbrush someplace and whooping it up for territorial status. The newspaper did nothing to disillusion either Congress or the other delegates on the subject. Nearly every issue of the *Columbian* for a matter of two months emphasized the importance of holding elections at the precinct level and arming the delegates wth official credentials signed by the chairman of the grass roots meeting.

But it didn't always work precisely that way.

And the matter of Edward J. Allen is a case in point.

On May 19, 1852—six months before the Monticello Convention, Edward J. Allen, who was twenty-two years old and had not as yet cast a vote of any kind in any election—departed from Pittsburgh, Pennsylvania, for Oregon. Allen was a sickly young man; his doctors had informed him that if he remained in Pittsburgh he wouldn't live to vote for anybody.

If the truth be known, he was considerably more interested in the state of his health than in the state of the Union. Right off, he sprained his ankle on the Oregon Trail. He had to walk on that ankle several hours a day and the resulting pain left him with insufficient sleep. The trail, itself, left him with insufficient food and water.

Allen reached Portland in October and got himself a job in a sawmill where he worked twelve hours a day, six days a week, trying to recover his health and put together a grubstake to continue his journey to his destination on Puget Sound. He had reached Cowlitz Landing on the Cowlitz River on November 24, the day before the Monticello Convention. At the time, he had about as much knowledge of the Pacific Northwest as a native of New Guinea.

Allen tells us in his memoirs that he was preparing to initiate the long walk to Olympia when he met a group of men heading down river in the other direction. Because he previously had met Quincy Brooks, one of the group, back in Pittsburgh, he fell into conversation with the men in the group and they informed him that they were headed for Monticello.

"What," he asked, "is Monticello?"

Monticello, they told him, was the location of the convention.

"What convention?"

"To form a new territory."

"What territory?"

One of the men said he thought it was going to be called "Columbia." Whatever the name, the people north of the river wanted to be separated from the people south of the Columbia.

The idea intrigued Allen but, as he noted in his memoirs, he'd only been in this part of the territory for a couple of days . . . represented no constituency . . . had no credentials.

"What the hell," somebody rejoined. "Your credentials are as good as some of ours."

Going to Monticello seemed like a good idea at the time, and Allen had nothing else to do, so he headed back down the river with his new-found friends. Some fifteen of them were put up in the loft of a barn where they drank and sang and played mumbletypeg all night.

The next morning, a sleepy, hung-over and bewildered Allen was approached by somebody whose name he couldn't remember and informed that he was a member of the committee to draft a resolution to Congress requesting the creation of a new territory north of the Columbia River.

Happily for posterity the complete text of the proceedings at Monticello were printed in the December 11, 1852, issue of the *Columbian*. And this was one "railroad" that ran on schedule. The entire operation previously had been scripted. It proceeded with the precision of a well-oiled grandfather clock.

The story noted that "Pursuant to a resolution adopted at a meeting of the citizens of Northern Oregon, held on the 25th and 27th days of October last in the courtroom for Lewis County (J. R. Jackson's log cabin) a convention of delegates from the different precincts and settlements of Northern Oregon assembled in the town of Monticello (Huntington's farm) on the 25th day of November, 1852."

One W. W. Plumb called the convention to order.

This was Mr. Plumb's first mention in Washington history.

It also was his last.

The newspaper reports that thereupon "Mr. G. N. McConaha was chosen president by application," and "on the motion of Quincy A. Brooks, Dr. R. J. (or R. V., nobody ever got that straight) White was unanimously chosen Secretary." (This mention at the Monticello Convention was Dr. White's only appearance on the stage of Washington history.)

The convention operated without a hitch.

McConaha took the chair, giving his grateful thanks for the distinguished honor they had conferred upon him and adding, "I can assure you gentlemen, that this distinction has been as unexpected by me as it was unsolicited. I am proud to have been chosen of so large and intelligent a body of men." He suggested that they had over-rated his abilities. However, he was "cheered by the hope that whatever errors I commit, they will receive immediate correction by your generous cooperation." He said he would not presume to dictate what should be done at the convention. He noted that it was the job of "all of us." It was their job to carry out and perfect the instructions which the delegates had received from their constituents.

He added:

"You come fresh from the people with positive instructions, knowing their grievances, and cannot, therefore, fail truly to reflect the popular will . . ."

After a certain amount of additional butter in the same vein, Quincy A. Brooks arose to name a committee of thirteen to draft a memorial to Congress. He then proceeded to nominate himself, Doc Maynard, J. R. Jackson, William Plumb, Alfred Cook, E. L. Finch, A. F. Scott, F. A. Clark, C. S. Hathaway, E. H. Winslow, Seth Catlin, N. Stone, and E. A. Allen.

For eight of the thirteen, it would be their only appearance in Washington history. Where they had been before nobody knows. And they disappeared without a trace after the convention. Like E. A. Allen—who is not counted among the eight—they just happened to be at the right place at the right time.

Well, that was the end of the morning session.

Two hours later, at two o'clock, they reconvened and, *voila,* there was the memorial from the Monticello Convention all printed up and ready to go.

Two hours to create a new territory.

No fooling around like they do nowadays.

The pioneers did things fast.

Actually, the whole thing was like being against sin and in favor of motherhood. The fellows voted for everything that was presented to them. The newspaper report reads, "On motion of Dr. Maynard, the report of the committee was taken up and considered *seriatim.*

"The various portions of the memorial were discussed and adopted without a dissenting vote.

"Before taking the final vote on adoption of the memorial the convention was addressed by Messrs. PLUMB, CATLINE (misspelled) MAYNARD, JACKSON, MILES and others." Quincy A. Brooks then gave a speech that the secretary said was too long to record. Brooks then sought and got a resolution that they would meet again the third Wednesday of May, 1853, at Olympia so they could take further action if Congress had not acted in the meantime. He also introduced resolutions urging that the memorial be sent to Delegate Lane and to all newspapers locally and nationally.

Having endorsed and signed the memorial to Congress, and arranged for its dispatch to various and sundry places, the delegates got down to the real point of the convention.

They voted to send D. S. Maynard to Salem with a copy of a petition asking the Oregon Legislature to endorse the proposed new territory.

They didn't know this was the point of the convention.

Only the magoozlers knew that.

The doctor thanked them for putting their trust in him on this important mission. He then introduced resolutions that were unanimously endorsed thanking the president and secretary for their services and F. A. Clarke for his kindness and attention and the use of his "hotel."

Mr. Clarke responded to the doctor's kind words and moved for adjournment.

The Monticello Convention was history.

(Historians, and the poor kids who have to try to understand what they wrote, have had a terrible time with the Monticello Convention. The convention adjourned on November 28, 1852. There was no possible way a memorial passed at that convention could reach Washington, D.C., on December 6, eight days later. Bancroft took the easy way out. He said the convention was held on October 25. When Meany wrote his *History of Washington* in 1909, he went along with Bancroft. But after thinking about it for thirteen years, he did a piece in the *Washington Quarterly* in 1922 in which he opined that Lane "must have acted on his volition or *upon initiative from some other source.*" *(Italics mine.)* Snowden took the position that Lane must have used the memorial that had been sent the previous year by the Cowlitz Convention. But that was not the case.

Arthur Denny, who must have been aiming at being named the father of Seattle for a long time, saved every mention of his name that had ever been printed. The copy issued to those in attendance at Monticello was one of them. In 1889, when statehood came to Washington, he was giving reporters the low-down on the important role he played, but somebody noticed his name wasn't on the list of petitioners in the *Congressional Globe* . . . only Doc Maynard's—on the memorial Lane had taken back with him before Monticello.

The doctor—long dead—had done it to Denny again!

Dissolution of marriage—1852 style

From the pure standpoint of physical exertion, the creation of a new territory in the United States did not require the same amount of muscular strength as cutting a pile of wood containing 400 cords. And, I might add, the doctor enjoyed the magoozle with a greater degree of enthusiasm than was his in the cutting of the woodpile.

But he did it for Catherine just the same.

She was having all the trouble she could take care of with her family the way things were . . . without finding herself named as correspondent in a court divorce case . . . or without having the doctor's name spread all over the pages of the newspapers with the juicy material he had to produce in order to get a legislative divorce.

But the doctor was a big man in the territory at the time and just imagine what the newspapers could do with this kind of "privileged" news in today's media marketplace . . . His petition read:

"To The_____

"The Legislature of the Territory of Oregon. The undersigned Your Petitioner Humbly represents to Your Honorable Body, that he was Lawfully married to Lydia A. Rickey in the State of Vermont on the twenty eighth day of August A.D. 1828, that the undersigned and his wife Lydia continued to reside in the State of Vermont until the Autumn of 1834 when they removed to the State of Ohio in which State Lydia still resides.

"And Your Petitioner further represents to Your Honorable Body that he and his aforsaid companion continued to live together as man and wife until the Spring of 1841, that in the month of April of the year last aforsaid on returning home from visiting a patient at about the hour of ten o'clock in the night found his wife lying with a certain John Hemrick in an obscene manner. That the undersigned had previously doubted her chastity but had never before seen anything positively confirming his suspicions, at which time the usual relations between man and wife ceased.

"And Your Petitioner also represents to Your Honorable Body that his wife has had two children, The Eldest a Son Born in The Year 1830 named Henry C. Maynard and The Youngest a Daughter Born in the Year 1834 named Frances J. Maynard, which Said Children still reside in the State of Ohio, That Your Petitioner verrily believes said children to be his own, and that he desires to bring them to Oregon where the undersigned has permanently settled.

"And Your Petitioner further represents to Your Honorable Body, That until of late Your Petitioner had not determined ever to making application for a Divorce on account of the tender regard which he had for his Children. But that time and the advice of friends has in that respect worked a change in the mind of Your Petitioner. And further that Your Petitioner has written to obtain testimony from Ohio but owing to emigration from that country and other causes set forth by Correspondents from Ohio, he has not been able to obtain testimony of Material Witnesses. And Your Petitioner represents that his Correspondent in Ohio informed him by letter that it will be impossible to obtain positive testimony until persons in California can be found which said letter will be laid before Your Honorable Body.

"Finally, Your Petitioner would Humbly represent to Your Honorable Body, that as it is impossible that he and his wife can ever again live together, and as it is at present and perhaps ever will be out of the power of Your Petitioner to procure the testimony which might be required in a court of Chancery to entitle the undersigned to a Divorce from his said wife, And believing that his sufferings of mind have been born long and patiently and believing before God and Man, that he is justly entitled to the relief which he seeks, has as a last resort appealed to the wisdom and magnanimity of Your Honorable Body.

"It is with Great reluctance that the undersigned presents his petition to the Peoples Representatives. He deeply regrets to consume one moment of their valuable time. And the undersigned will here state to Your Honorable Body that he has always provided for, and kept his wife in a comfortable living until he left Ohio for Oregon Territory. And that at the time of leaving for this Country, he left her provided with a comfortable Home and a means of living independently at which home the undersigned will further State That he never Quarreled with or abused his wife, Either before or after the discovery of her unfaithfulness.

"Wherefore Your Petitioner believing that he is without other remedy Humbly prays Your Honorable Body to pass a law Divorcing him from the Bonds of matrimony now existing between him and his wife. And as and for such he will ever pray,

D. S. Maynard"

"personally appeared before me Samuel Parker a justice of the peace fore the county of marion David S. Maynard and after being duly sworn says that the facts set forth in this petition is true to the best of his beliefs. Sworn to before me S Parker J.P this the 10 day of december A.D 1852

Samuel Parker J.P"

Doc Maynard came close to tossing in the sponge on this next one, but his attorney, McConaha, who had been through the mill on this kind of thing many times before, reminded him that, "If you don't make your case, they'll throw your petition out."

So the following letter dated August 4, 1852, also was put into the record . . .

"Dr. Sir   I recd yours of the 25th of May and was much grattified to learn that you were in good health I also seen and read your letters to Payne and Grimshaw and they both requested me to say to you that they regarded it as impossible to git the evidence which you desire unless you were here in person Your many acquaintances here are unanimous in the desire to aid you in procuring the evidence which you desire but Candor compels me to say to you that I do not believe that if you were here yourself that you could succeed in procuring the evidence of a positive character as to the incontinency of your wife.

"I have seen and talked with Sprague Brown and others on the subject and whilst we all agree in opinion that your wife has been in time past and still is addicted to the habits of adultery yet this is only our opinion it is true that it is the belief of the community generally that she is unchaste.

"Yet how can her want of chastity be proven Who will sware that he had carnal connections with her Ormsby says to me in confidence that he could sware to her want of chastity but that he would flee his country or die in jail before he would tell what he knows & say that he well knows that you deserve a divorce in every sense of the word but that he cannot and will not divulge anything that he knows on the subject & so say the others.

"I saw her a short time since and asked her if she had got any letters from you She said no but that you wrote regularly to Henry She said she had written one letter to you since you had gone to Oregon just to let you know that she was as independent as ever & declared that she was much happier in your absence than she had ever been in your society said you had been jealous of her for many years and she hoped you would remain in Oregon for the remainder of your life

"I asked her if you had ever mistreated her She said no, not in any other way than by your jealousy & indifference Said she knew people had talked about her but disregarded it

"I spoke with Wilson as you directed me but he thinks that your only chance of succeeding will be before the Legislature. He says that that public Rumor without Specific proof offered of some want of chastity on her part will not be sufficient on your part before a court.

"The truth is Doctor that people here are unwilling to give evidence in the matter She is shrewd and sly & keeps good lookout & another thing her friends & relatives here are respected very much and on their account people hate to say what they know or believe about her.

"William Craig is in California. also Harper & Miles If you could only find where abouts they are you might readily procure the desired proof Craig you know is a man that will neither lie or flinch & if you could find him he would testify that he caught her and Ormsby *kissing* and that too in the bushes—but persons here who are known to her misconduct are loth to communicate what they do know for the reasons which I have before stated

"Doc, I trust that you know that I desire to serve you if in my power and indeed I believe that there is not one of your acquaintances in this community but deeply sympathises with you in your unhappy Situation It is true as you say in your letter you have suffered long and patiently and God knows you ought to be relieved— My family are all well & Sarah sends her best regards to you Your son Henry has a situation on the railroad and says he is resolved to come to you next spring

"Frances is at school She is a lovely girl but I will come to a close hoping that you will write again ere long Yours in truth
C_____.

W. G. Oliver

"To Dr D. S. Maynard

"P.S. McNair and Sarah Stevens are married at last after their Seven years Courtship."

The above, along with signed affidavits of a bunch of other prominent men in the Territory stating that the doctor was a moral man who richly deserved the divorce, could have been just the meat of such newspapers as the *Oregon Spectator* which carried the story that McConaha had been ridden out of one town on a rail . . . had consorted with pimps and prostitutes and spent his time in low company in the saloons of Sacramento while his wife and children languished at home.

As it was, the doctor's plan worked.

Through his friend, Isaac Ebey, a petition asking for support from the Legislature for the division of the Territory was dropped in the hopper in Salem on December 6, 1852.

This was the same day the companion piece was dropped in the hopper in Washington, D.C., by Lane. (A service to the community which moved Doc to provide his town with the name of Lane Street six months later when the plat of Seattle was filed.)

Doc Maynard slid his divorce petition right in behind the petition for getting the Legislature's aid in securing the new territory. And sure enough, the newspapers were baying down the trail of the new territory.

There wasn't word one about the doctor's divorce . . .

It has remained in the Archives of the Oregon Historical Society for the past 126 years.

The perfidy of Isaac N. Ebey

The doctor didn't come out of it without a scare, though, and it was well he had followed McConaha's advice to let it all "hang out."

The scare came from his friend Ebey.

Going in, Ebey had introduced the doctor's divorce petition and accompanied it with an affidavit stating that he had met the doctor two years earlier and believed him to be a moral man, well thought of in his community and someone who had a divorce coming. That was on December 10.

On December 15, Ebey came up with this: "Mr. Ebey's Report From the Minority of the Committee On D. S. Maynard's Bill for Divorce." It started out: "The minority of the select committee, to whom was referred the petition of D. S. Maynard, praying the Legislature to dissolve the bonds of matrimony existing between him and his wife, beg leave to submit the following as some of the reasons that have led him to dissent from the decision come to by the majority of the committee:

"Without entering upon the consideration of the facts connected with this case, it will be sufficient in the opinion of the minority of said committee, to state the general principles of law on which he predicates his opinion that the prayer of the petitioner should not be granted.

"The position assumed by the report of the committee in favor of the prayer of the petitioner, is, in the opinion of the minority, not tenable, either upon the principles of sound morality or law . . ."

In the shocker that followed, Ebey wrote a complete brief on the concept that marriage was a civil contract that only could be changed through the courts. The Legislature couldn't just write a new law and knock out the contract . . .

Especially without consulting with the other party to the original contract.

Doc Maynard, who had helped Ebey get the prosecutor's job and then had functioned as Ebey's campaign manager when he was elected to the Oregon Territorial Legislature six months earlier, was not appreciative of Ebey's concern with the theory of law in this instance.

But Ebey had his own guilt complex to deal with.

He'd been married for six years, himself . . . and four of those six years he'd been peregrinating around the west while his wife languished at home in Missouri wondering if, as, or when she'd get a notice like the one Lydia was about to receive—telling her that her husband had found another woman. She had but recently arrived in the Pacific Northwest with her two kids, only to find she saw almost as little of her husband as she had when the two of them were separated by most of the continent. To top all of this off, she was terminally ill with tuberculosis (although nobody knew what tuberculosis was at the time).

When she heard her husband was sponsoring the doctor's divorce, she blew her cork.

"Look, Doc," Ebey said, "I've got to keep the home fires burning. You're going to get your divorce, but this minority report gets me off the hook with my wife."

The doctor's failure to appreciate this caused Ebey to sweeten the pot. "I'll tell you what I'm going to do. You've got a nice little town going up there. How would you like to have a county to accompany it?"

Well, the doctor's divorce was granted on December 21.

The next day Ebey introduced a bill creating King County and naming Doc Maynard's store as the County Seat.

Doc Maynard high-tailed it for Olympia . . .

And Catherine.

"The bells are ringing for me and my gal!"

Thanks to the kindly ministrations of her family, Catherine's opinion of herself was at a low ebb . . . and one of the poultices that seemed paramount to her ego was a church wedding. It was an emotional condition of which the doctor was completely aware. And while a Justice of the Peace could have made her marriage with the doctor as legally binding as any performed in a church, she wanted that show of respectability.

The Reverend Mr. Benjamin Close recently had been named to represent the spiritual needs of the people in northern Oregon by the Oregon and California Conference of the Methodists.

On January 15, 1853, Dr. and Mrs. Maynard were married by Mr. Close at the home of friends in Bush Prairie. Those in attendance were Catherine's brother, A. J. Simmons; a brother-in-law, Joseph Broshears, and his wife, and Mr. and Mrs. Gabriel Jones.

Conspicuous by their absence were Susanna and Samuel Rider, and Mike and Elizabeth Simmons.

Catherine and the doctor spent the five days of their second honeymoon traveling from Olympia to Seattle . . . where together they would share the further invention of our town . . . with the joint ownership of 640 acres of land.

Nor did Mr. Close go away empty handed.

When he attended a meeting with his bishop, E. R. Ames, he would have his own brand of contribution to the continued mission of the church.

The second paper recorded in King County was a conditional quit claim deed from David S. and Catherine Maynard to the Methodist

Episcopal Church dated July 15, 1853. What it did was provide the church with a beautiful piece of property overlooking Elliott Bay from the top of what we know as Yesler Way.

Thirty beautiful acres in what the doctor faithfully promised Mr. Close would be the biggest town in the Pacific Northwest.

The condition of the conditional quit claim deed was that the church must do something—anything, toward the development of a school of higher education with it no later than the end of March, 1856.

V

Madam Damnable &
The Stout-hearted Men

An integral proportion of Seattle's creation evolves from and reverts to Madam Damnable's whorehouse, and those idiots in charge of writing our history left her out of it completely.

I can't believe it!

Oh, yes, I can. And the Divine Comedy herein lies in the fact that she functioned in the finest structure in the entire town plat. Nowadays only the rich own view property. But back then Madam Damnable's was the only house in town with a view . . .

There's a picture of her house in every history book.

They left out her occupation.

When I try to pass along to you the essence of our beginnings, I can do no better than quote a man who talked about the beginnings of Charleston, South Carolina: "From the beginning, the people of Charleston were different. They drank. They dueled, gambled, raced horses, wenched, baited bulls, pitted cocks, pulled geese, sailed yachts. They were a grand lot and quite different from the blue-nosed Puritans who settled the up country."

In our case, the Blue-Nosed Puritans were only four or five blocks up the street, but they successfully isolated themselves from the essence of the town . . . and then would have us believe they *were* the

MME. DAMNABLE
HER MANSION . . . HER CLIENTELE

essence, when all they really did was run around the outskirts of the action wringing their hands and wondering how they could curb it.

One wonderful irony which illustrates the point lies in the fact that the much-touted "White Church" in our town went belly up during its first year of operation . . . and stayed empty for the next four years while the white house of Sin rose to dizzying heights of glory, famed throughout the world during this same period of time.

David Swinson Maynard was not about to have a whorehouse in his town that was just like your average, run-of-the-mill whorehouse in the usual seaport town. He had to have the best, and only the best. There never was one like it before and none since.

The doctor, directing the destiny of our town with Machiavellian skill—and a will of steel—was essentially a moral man. He knew, on the other hand, that if Seattle were to fulfill the destiny which he had in mind for her, the oldest of all professions must be integrated into the scheme of things. While he ran the show, Madam Damnable's—like the animals permitted on the Ark—was the only example of the species permitted in the place. He required that it be operated with finesse and discretion. Madam Mary Ann Boyer, the diminutive lady who operated the place, crossed him only once . . . to her everlasting regret.

Doc Maynard recognized the need for this kind of facility but he was not about to have a Barbary Coast like the one in San Francisco take root in his town. Court records show that in later years more prostitutes per square inch were arrested in Seattle than any other town in the Territory . . .

But not while Doc Maynard was running the show.

Discretion was the order of the day.

Dignitaries rested their tired bodies in Madam Damnable's luxurious public rooms, probably without even knowing about the function of the place—unless, of course, they responded positively to the question, "And what is your pleasure?" Madam Damnable's functioned with such discretion that the United States of America felt perfectly proper in holding federal court sessions in the structure. And, as a matter of fact, the only encounter with scandal came when Judge

Strong essayed the sale of his gambling equipment from "bench" when his circuit court was not in session.

Doc Maynard thought about that one for a while and concluded that the game was worth the cards.

Doc Maynard gathered around himself a group of men who could understand the importance of Madam Damnable's presence . . . and it was on this basis that he fulfilled the words of the famous song about "Give me some men who are stout-hearted men and I'll soon give you ten thousand more . . ."

The "mew" with the view

A century or so ago, the Voelker family of Bavaria moved to Pennsylvania to participate in the development of a section of this country populated by what have come down to us as the Pennsylvania Dutch. Most of them became Quakers or continued as dedicated members of the Lutheran Church . . .

While they were in Pennsylvania they opted to change the family name to Felker.

And it was inevitable that in the prodigious reproduction process that was popular in those days the family would spawn a few black sheep who at the age of twelve ran away to become cabin boys on sailing ships. At any rate, one of them did and ended up important in the founding of Seattle.

Thanks to the sanctimonious souls who got into our history business early on, Captain Felker has been virtually deleted from our history books . . .

Except for that one picture of Madam Damnable's piece de resistance.

Pioneer National Title Company records show that Doctor Maynard sold all of block four to Leonard M. Felker for $350 on August 24, 1853. This was three months and one day after the doctor had filed the plat of what would become the central business district of the city of Seattle for the next fifty years.

It was the biggest real estate transaction in our town to that date . . . thirty-five times what the average lot was selling for in the average town in the Pacific Northwest and 280 times what you could buy land for from the federal government at the time.

It was the choicest piece of property in town.

And at that, more than half of it was under water at high tide.

Until the landfills were made that created our present industrial district and Harbor Island beginning in 1895, this piece of property was known as "Maynard's Point," midway between Jackson and King Streets on the west side of First Avenue South.

In those days Seattle was shaped like a teardrop, beginning at sea-level at First Avenue South and Washington Street and running south to a bluff twenty-five feet high above the Duwamish River which was a healthy stream forty yards wide at First Avenue South and South King Street.

One of the great tributes to Doc Maynard's sagacity—and a little trick he had picked up during his years in Cleveland—was the existence in all his deeds of sale of the proviso that "a substantial building be constructed on the premises within three months." The doctor has come under some scrutiny as an "unscrupulous" real estate man—our city's first, by the way—for selling the same lot several times to different people.

But this was his reason:

It discouraged land speculators and brought in the kinds of people he wanted for the construction of a major city. He appointed himself as the sole judge of what constituted a "substantial" building . . . and he sold lots for as little as ten dollars to somebody with the skills needed to make ours the major town on Puget Sound.

Felker was such a man.

What he did was provide Seattle with a Southern Mansion.

The front entrance of the two-story structure was flanked by the square columns of the period and supported the traditional second-floor veranda. There were the four customary "nine-on-nine" windows (nine panes of glass above and below) on each floor, with the door centered in the structure. Entering the grand, eight-foot front door with ornamental lamps on either side, one faced the broad bannistered staircase which parted into two smaller ascending sets of stairs on either side about halfway above the first floor.

On either side of the front entrance hall were magnificent paneled rooms with fireplaces, an architectural design to be found throughout the South in those days that was duplicated on the second floor. In the fashion of the time, there were wide floorboards cut from southern pine and imported from Baltimore as were tongue-and-groove boards of the white exterior. An addition in the rear that was perpendicular to the main structure housed the kitchen and what would have been the small cubicles designed for servants in the South.

There were no slaves in Seattle, however . . .

And the services provided in the small rooms were of far greater economic impact on the embryo town than those provided by the negro servants as cited in *Gone With the Wind*.

The exercises conducted in the upstairs rooms were enjoyed by men who were gone with the wind, but it was the kind of wind that propelled the ships which came to our town in huge numbers and spread the fame of Seattle throughout the world . . .

Especially the fame of one Mary Ann Boyer—nee Conklin. Mary Ann was known by sailors in the far corners of the earth as "Madam Damnable" (a name that was altered by our historians to "Mother" Damnable) because "she swore like a trooper."

That's the one that really bugs me.

A musical comedy with the title, "Call me Madam!" makes sense . . .

But, "Call me *Mother?*"

Naval engagement at Madam Damnable's

Thomas S. Phelps, who became an admiral in the United States Navy, was a mere lieutenant on board the sloop-of-war *Decatur* on

January 26, 1856, when a ragtag bunch of desperate Indians made an abortive assault on the town of Seattle.

Lieutenant Phelps was pretty partial to the United States Navy, which he credits with saving Seattle in its hour of desperate need—but he also had a sense of humor that was overlooked by our first historians. Phelps was the kind of a man who kept copious notes of the interesting things that happened in his career. And the so-called "Battle of Seattle" was one of them. Some seventeen years after the fact he revisited the town and the local folk persuaded him to assemble his notes in some kind of permanent form. And in 1881 the notes appeared in an article—along with a map of Seattle as it was at the time of the Indian Rebellion—in a Navy publication called *United Service.*

The servicemen were steeled for an encounter with savage Indians.

But they weren't prepared to meet Madam Damnable.

Six days after the Battle of Seattle the Navy strategists sat down and determined upon a program for the future defense of the city. Essentially, it consisted of burning anything that stood in the line of fire between the Navy's cannon and the potential approach of hostile Indians.

Indians loved to creep through the bushes.

So the Navy burned down the underbrush in town . . .

Except for the bushes around Madam Damnable's whorehouse. Madam Damnable figured that they were *her* bushes on *her* property. The success of her entire operation hinged on privacy. And if the United States Navy burned *down* the bushes, they burned *up* the customers. If they burned up the customers they wouldn't attend her services and she couldn't pay the rent to Captain Felker.

Phelps' description of the scorched earth policy resembles the operation of a present-day real estate developer. He wrote: "Both officers and men entered upon the work with a spirit worthy of the occasion, and the stumps too large to be extracted with levers were burned, the fires being kept alive night and day till reduced below the surface, when ax and shovel completed the rest, and in a few days, South Seattle assumed the appearance of a well laid-out town."

Except for Madam Damnable's.

That still was surrounded by bushes.

Phelps again writes: "On an elevation near the southwest point of the peninsula was situated a large boarding house, kept by a stout, coarse Irishwoman, who, for some reason, was called Madam Damnable, perhaps in consequence of her masculine build and the vile language constantly flowing from her lips, or it may have been from her resemblance to her prototype of that appellation, a famous French woman, formerly residing in Callao (the principal seaport of Peru)."

Phelps was under orders from his commanding officer, Guert Gansevoort, to burn down Mary Ann's bushes.

Mary Ann, who understood exactly what was going on, hated Gansevoort with a passion which transferred itself to everybody in the commander's crew. Phelps noted that she was a terrible woman, and a terror to the members of the crew who found her tongue more to be dreaded than the entire Indian army that the sailors and marines had faced a week before.

The problem lay in the fact that the commander insisted that roads be built in what today is the Pioneer Square Historic District so that if the

Indians attacked again there would be easy lines of communication within the perimeter of the town. This meant clearing the brush off First Avenue South as far south as Madam Damnable's mansion and then clearing them east along Jackson Street, which was thirty yards north of the mansion. What the commander really wanted to do was denude her property so it would stand out like a sore thumb on the landscape, exposing all of the sinners who approached the place to the eyes of the clucking Puritans up the street.

Work parties were sent out from the *Decatur* every day but each party "sedulously" avoided the part of the project near the "female dragon's house" until the rest of the landscape was the ideal of a developer's dream and as bare as a baby's posterior . . .

Phelps wrote: "Every imaginable device was adopted to complete this road, but the moment our men appeared upon the scene, with three dogs at her heels, and an apron filled with rocks, this termagant would come tearing from the house, and the way stones, oaths and curses flew was something fearful to contemplate, and, charging like a fury, with the dogs wild to flesh their teeth in the detested invaders, the division invariably gave way before the storm, fleeing, officers and all, as if old Satan himself was after them."

These were the same guys who had stood up to the horde of a thousand attacking Indians only a week earlier.

Phelps reported that Captain Gansevoort had on a number of occasions been the victim of her most intense vituperation . . . and being averse to facing her, himself, "satisfied his conscience" by ordering his subordinates to "do their duty." Phelps comments at this point that these orders were all well and good, but the big question was *"how* to do it." The first and second divisions mounted assaults on the premises and were driven off. And it became Phelps' turn to face the inevitable.

"Plucking up all the courage we could muster," he wrote, "and with trembling knees, we essayed the task set before us. For once, the house seemed deserted, not a sound issued from behind its silent walls; not even a dog could be seen or heard; and thus encouraged, we sprang to our work with all the energy of desperate men. The road rapidly progressed, the house reached and nearly passed, while our spirits rose with the joyful thought that the old dragon was either absent or overcome with constant vigils, had at last succumbed to exhausted nature, and when on the eve of relieving our suppressed feelings with congratulatory shouts, the door flew open, and this demon in petticoats, who had bided her time, shot out upon us like a bolt from a catapult, and, to our astonished senses, the very air seemed filled with sticks, stones, curses and dogs, and the division, a moment before so firm and hopeful, now, blanched with fear, first wavered, and then broke, and incontinently fled in every direction to escape this whirlwind of passion.

"It is, perhaps, needless to remark that I did not volunteer to again undertake the completion of that road . . ."

For the next twelve days, the military strategists developed and rejected plans for storming Madam Damnable's. They tried doing it under the cover of night, but the dogs were alert and roused Mary Ann. They tried the diversionary tactic of sending half the crew in small boats to approach from the water side of the structure while the other half of the crew attacked the garden. This, as Phelps reports, "fell to the ground."

Finally, Captain Guert Gansevoort summoned the entire ship's company for a frontal attack . . . and put Phelps in charge.

A hundred and fifty men armed to the teeth with hand guns, bayonets and howitzers . . .

Against one woman.

It was a greater concentration of fire power than had been applied in one location against the combined armies of the eastern and western Washington Indians.

Gansevoort, of course, was safely back on the poop of the sloop, three blocks away.

There is no telling what mayhem Madam Damnable might have visited upon the honor and prestige of the United States Navy and the Marine Corps combined if it hadn't been for Quartermaster Sam Silk. Phelps reports that Sam, "a veritable old-time salt," ventured the opinion that he might be personally acquainted with this lady. He couldn't tell from a distance of thirty yards because his eyesight was failing. But close up, he could tell for sure . . .

And so it was that Sam Silk and Midshipman Francis G. Dallas advanced under a flag of truce.

Mary Ann, with a billet of wood in hand and ready for action, eyed the two approaching men suspiciously. As they got closer, Silk began chuckling. "It's Annie," he told the nervous midshipman by his side. "I used to know her when she operated a whorehouse at Fell's Point in Baltimore."

Sam Silk approached Mary Ann with extended arms, "Why what do you mean, you damned old harridan," he said affectionately, "raising hell this way? Don't you remember the good old days at Fell's Point?"

He told her the United States Navy was not trying to put her out of business, just clear a temporary road for military purposes.

"For old times' sake, Annie?" he pleaded.

With Mary Ann, the customer was always right.

"Very well," she responded, "for old times' sake."

She dropped her sticks and stones, called off her dogs and went back into the mansion.

Sam Silk was the hero of the day.

With liberty and justice for all

What with Madam Damnable's mansion being the fanciest structure on Puget Sound, it was no more than natural that it serve as the first courthouse as well as whorehouse. Doc Maynard had himself named as the first court clerk and it was a simple matter for the clerk to make the necessary arrangements for the administration of justice in a spot where his friend, Felker, could pick up a few extra bucks.

And fancy prices, indeed, were charged for the use of one of the first-floor parlors during the daytime—Monday through Friday—leaving the premises upstairs available for other enterprises on the weekends when the loggers and other men came to town looking for fun. In the first ten-day session in October of 1854 when Washington became a territory, the territory was charged $25 for use of the parlor, plus an additional $4 for the use of the furniture . . . an outrageous $10 for use of some of the rooms in the "slave quarters" for the use of the jury and an additional $66—at a shocking fifty cents apiece for the meals of everybody concerned with the operation. (A full course chicken dinner only cost two-bits.)

The young prosecuting attorney protested the exorbitant prices levied against the territory by the landlady, but she laid her sticks and stones bit on him and he backed down.

In those days the Duwamish River debouched upon 1,500 acres of tideflats that subsequently have become Seattle's industrial district. The course of the main channel was shunted north by three low-lying islands with the imaginative names of "Island Number One," "Island Number Two" and "Island Number Three." The river flowed north along the base of Beacon Hill on what subsequently became (1) the River Road, (2) Duwamish Way and now (3) Airport Way, flowing west between what today is the Kingdome Stadium and the Pioneer Square Historic District . . .

And past Maynard's Point, where it dropped into deep water.

All traffic to and from the Duwamish Valley passed through Doc Maynard's claim . . .

And Luther Collins generated most of that traffic.

In his own way, Luther was as great a promoter as the doctor. He set about single-handedly to populate the Duwamish Valley with farmers—having jumped somebody else's claim to get his own. And as a result the valley became the breadbasket of the Puget Sound basin. He and the others boasted cabbages that weighed forty-seven pounds and turnips weighing twenty-nine pounds . . . four-pound potatoes . . . twenty-nine-pound beets . . . two-pound onions, and apples and peaches sixteen inches in circumference. By 1855 he had 200,000 apple, peach, pear and cherry trees for sale in his nursery. Truck gardening vegetables of all varieties were raised here and shipped around the Sound, along with chickens and eggs, pigs and dairy and beef cattle.

The farmers came to Seattle to sell their products and to buy their supplies.

All of this contributing to the economic growth of Seattle.

When the doctor obtained his divorce from Lydia, Luther signed an affidavit that Maynard had sufficient cause for complaint and it was evident to him "that the Evil disposition of his wife had caused him to seek peace (in Seattle) where we have Every Evidence he intends to spend his days."

In return for the favor, the doctor had Luther appointed as the first commissioner of King County.

From time to time, however, the doctor had his hands full taking care of Luther, who was his own kind of a wild man. He was in continual court ruckuses with his neighbors over one thing and another.

Luther was what you would call an "active" man . . . and the court dockets are loaded with many of his activities . . . as attested to by the following which are taken verbatim from the archives:

"October 13, 1861. This day came Diana Woodbridge, and made oath, that on the day and date above written Luther M. Collins did come to her house and strike her on her shoulder and her arm three times and threaten to shoot her and further that the said Luther M. Collins was armed had his pistol in his belt and his rifle gun in his hand cocked and that he commit [sic] this violence and made these threats on the complainants premises in King County."

The same day one John Martin came before the court with the charge that Luther did "willfully and maliciously and with premeditation commit an assault with intent to kill him the said John Martin with a revolver pistol first and then afterwards with a rifle gun . . ."

When the judge got it all sorted out he found that one Joseph Farris had stolen two of Luther's hogs of the "aforesaid L. M. Collins, which hogs were worth twenty dollars."

Luther, taking the law in his own hands and hunting for the thief, shot up the neighborhood, scared the hell out of all the neighbors and got himself thrown in the clink.

Luther was a wild man, all right.

But Doc Maynard was his principal protector . . .

And on one occasion that protection turned out to be *real* important to Luther.

Luther was hauled into court on a charge of defacing his own property. What he had done was tack several Indian scalps on his fence. The prosecutor admitted that one or two scalps was within the bounds, but a dozen or more was tacky.

Luther countered by stating that he had taken the scalps only from "unfriendly" Indians. He said he kept them tacked up on the fence posts as "good luck charms . . ." pointing out that he lived some distance from town and he never knew whether the Indians who appeared at his place were friendly or not.

Luther also pointed out, for example, that he was very friendly with his Indian mistress, a young lady of handsome proportions who drew official attention to her boy friend on two subsequent occasions. Once was during the Indian Rebellion, when all friendly Indians were supposed to have moved to the west side of Puget Sound. Indians who remained behind were presumed unfriendly. Commander Gansevoort lodged a complaint charging Luther's girl friend with being a hostile Indian and Luther won the case by pointing out she was the friendliest Indian he had ever met . . .

Which brought up the second court case on the subject.

Luther's wife, Diane, divorced him, on the grounds he was too friendly with this friendly Indian.

Luther's most interesting date with a judge came on Friday, October 27, 1854. The handwritten court record reads: "Comes now into open court Luther M. Collins in the custody of Sheriff Thomas Russell . . . Frank Clarke prosecuting the cause of the Territory . . ."

"The charge?"

"Murder."

So there was Luther behind bars.

And there was the doctor on the outside of the bars saying, "Luther, what am I going to do with you?"

"I have faith, Doc," Luther pleaded. "Get me off the hook!"

The record doesn't show how the doctor did it, but when the court reconvened ten days later, the prosecuting attorney appeared before the judge and "begged leave to no longer prosecute said cause . . . " Luther was set free to carry on a rigorous life that ended abruptly a few years later when he drowned near Orofino, Idaho, where he had gone during a gold rush.

If you have ever wondered whether or not the present county commissioners are setting precedent by getting away with murder, you can rest your mind.

They've been getting away with it from the beginning.

Crazy like a fox

The thing to keep in mind about that complicated human being we know of as David Swinson Maynard is that he liked living high on the hog, and used the real estate which he owned as his primary source of income. He and Catherine had twice as much land as any of the rest of the married couples.

His idealistic objective was the construction of the greatest town in the territory. And he played chess with that real estate until the day he died. There are those who have made the point that Seattle's development has been the result of a series of gigantic real estate promotions . . . which isn't far from the truth.

As usual, Doc was the one who established the formula.

In this connection—what with one reason or another—some 80,000,000 cubic yards of earth were moved in this town . . .

Before the freeway was cut through.

The doctor had got his training in the importance of landfills in Cleveland. Cleveland, in turn had gotten its from Boston, Boston from London, London from Paris, Paris from Venice, Venice from

Rome—or in some such progression of real estate promotions. The other settlers thought he was out of his mind, for instance, because he was willing to stake his claim on land, half of which was under water when the tide came in. He didn't intend for that land to stay under water for any appreciable length of time. One can safely say that the idea of the industrial landfills south of the Pioneer Square Historic District were the product of his original plan. This would include the construction of Harbor Island . . . and in its own way the construction of the Lake Washington Ship Canal. In the original instance, the plan was to construct that canal along Spokane Street. Even today on the side of Beacon Hill, you can see the hole where the digging of that canal was initiated.

In those early days, the doctor was too busy putting together a city to run for public office. But he did have need of a few jobs that were interconnected with his real estate transactions and he had himself appointed as a Justice of the Peace, Probate Judge and, of course, Notary Public. But the neatest of all his magoozles on this front was the appointment he secured for himself as the Clerk of the United States District Court.

We were a little low on federal judges in those days, and the circuit court judge only came to town when his judgment was needed. He left the details of arranging things up to his clerk, who was happy to take the responsibilities off of the judge's shoulders. (Knowing how justice was rendered in those days, I have to admit to the possibility that the Doctor cut the judge in for a few bucks just for the privilege of handling the details of justice. After all, one of the travelling judges sold gambling equipment when court was not in session . . . and when the court was in session, it was in the leading whorehouse in the Pacific Northwest.)

To understand the depth of the doctor's magoozle on this front, we have to keep in mind that there once were a couple of mountains in the heart of our town. One was called the Jackson Street hill. When we first were trying to figure out what to do with the Jackson Street hill, the plan was to put a tunnel through it like the tunnel through Twin Peaks in San Francisco. To obtain a mental picture of that hill, just imagine that an eight-story building constructed on the freeway at Jackson Street today would just have reached the top of that hill.

In later years, that mountain was dumped into Elliott Bay to give us the land on which the International District and the Kingdome Stadium rest today.

Then there was the Denny Hill.

Part of it was used to fill in the waterfront from the Pike Place Market down to Pioneer Square.

The major part of it, however, was moved to create the Denny Regrade . . .

By taking it out and dumping it into Elliott Bay . . .

Millions of tons of it . . .

Dumped in Elliott Bay.

Keeping all of this in mind, we go to the very first sale of the very first piece of real estate in what has become the city of Seattle. On May 16, 1853—seven days before the doctor and Arthur Denny filed the first plats which created our town—Maynard sold two lots for a grand total of ten bucks.

They were, unobtrusively enough, lots three and six in block two of the doctor's donation claim.

At any rate, the very first land sale of any kind by anybody to anybody else was made by the doctor to Felker a week before the original plats of the town were filed. The two lots were immediately north of the doctor's store on the northwest corner of First Avenue South and South Main Street . . .

And one of them was under water at high tide.

And that's the one that was worth the money . . .

A hundred times the money.

The early court records show that on a number of occasions, ship captains were hailed into court on a charge of dumping ballast in the harbor. Most of the cargo obtained in Puget Sound by the early sailing ships consisted of piling, hewn timbers, shingles and oysters and salmon destined for the San Francisco market. Therefore, the captains came north weighted down with ballast. They dumped this wherever they could.

Doc Maynard took advantage of the fact that there are a lot of harbors in the United States which can't take dumping of ballast. So the doctor had a nice federal law against indiscriminate dumping of ballast going for him.

He also had a lot of holes in his donation claim that needed filling.

So, there he sat in court. A captain would be hailed before the District Court judge on a charge of dumping ballast. Actually, all the judge did was issue warnings that this was illegal. The alert court clerk cornered the captains outside the court room and informed them that he had a nice spot, handy to everything, where they could dump their ballast.

For a mere five bucks a ton.

Felker was one of the captains.

His appreciation of the doctor's ingenuity was heightened when he learned where ballast could be dumped . . .

On lots three and four in block two. What with being the owner of lot three, Felker was the happy recipient of half the take . . . well, maybe not half. The judge must have got his cut.

Anyway, this was the first landfill in the city of Seattle. In the next forty years, enough ballast was dumped at this spot to form what was known in the 1890's as "Ballast Island." Somewhere between 30,000 and 40,000 tons of rock from Telegraph Hill in San Francisco were dumped and the island subsequently was filled in completely and today is engulfed by added fill. And the Alaskan Way viaduct runs over the whole thing.

While the doctor didn't live long enough to see it, his entire donation claim has been filled today, creating the land for the Kingdome Stadium and the industrial district of the city south of King Street.

On the other hand, the doctor and Felker—and maybe the judge— got their fair share of that first 30,000 to 40,000 tons that were dumped . . .

At five bucks a ton.

Doc Maynard—matchmaker

Although he was largely omitted from Seattle's original history books, it is impossible to underestimate the importance of Charles Plummer in shaping the destiny of this city. Bagley lists him as second only to Doctor Maynard . . . saying of him, "Next to Doctor Maynard in the activity of his business enterprise came Charles Plummer. He came to Seattle early in 1853 and continued in the mercantile business until his death (August 29, 1866.) Plummer was full of energy and enterprise and from time to time widened his activities wherever he saw an opportunity."

Bagley concludes with: "The writer regrets that more information regarding him is not available."

In one respect, Plummer comes in third . . . being ranked after Felker. Felker was the first man with a considerable amount of capital that Doc Maynard was able to interest in his town. Felker invested heavily in the doctor's enterprises with the construction of Madam Damnable's house and as a partner in the doctor's fishing enterprises. Felker also provided the doctor with a shipping advantage to San Francisco. But Felker never lived here . . . and disappeared from the Seattle scene sometime within the first decade of the town's existence.

Plummer, on the other hand, not only saw eye to eye with the doctor on how the town should grow, but established himself here—and above all had a lot of money to throw into the pot. The doctor always overextended his capital in the development of the town. And he might not have made it without this man. Plummer developed the town's first brick yard. He bought a lumber mill and coal mine on the Black River which fed into the Duwamish and provided the original industry of what now has become the industrialized Duwamish Valley. He provided the first water system in town, the first public pier, the first dance hall, bowling alley, billiard parlor and saloon.

His was the second store in town—directly across the street from the doctor's Seattle Exchange.

And he was the second postmaster.

He and Charlie Terry were the strong men of the first board of Town Trustees . . . and together, they invoked the doctor's policies with a degree of ruthlessness that routed the Prohibitionists completely and at least for the first half-century of the town's existence.

We don't know where Plummer came from, but early histories refer to his "Yankee" ingenuity. And we don't know how old he was although a logical educated guess is that he was about Charlie Terry's age, which puts him at about twenty-three years of age when he arrived on the scene. The chances are that he left New England in 1849 to participate in the California gold rush and that he hit it fairly big there, because he had that most priceless asset in the Pacific Northwest at the time . . .

Cash.

The doctor was stuck with Arthur Denny, who was upright and up-tight, but he chose as his friends men like Plummer in shaping the personality of the city. And the logical conclusion is that Plummer, like the doctor and the others who constituted Seattle's first "establishment" found California a little too wild and raw. Unlike Arthur Denny, who stumbled upon the place, Plummer came here on purpose and put his shoulder to the wheel because he liked the way the doctor was mounting his metropolis. They were men to whom the molding of the city was a matter of choice rather than accident . . .

And they prevailed.

The statement of today that the United States is on a tilt and all the nuts roll down to California was as true in those days as it is now. You had to climb uphill to get to Seattle.

Plummer appeared on Puget Sound some time in 1853.

He had cash and every town proprietor on the Sound wanted it and him. It is known that he visited Olympia, Steilacoom, Port Madison, Port Gamble, Port Townsend, New York-Alki and Bellingham. He almost staked a claim in the latter place, where coal already was discovered and being mined.

But Doc Maynard got him with one of the slickest tricks of his career.

The doctor introduced him to Ellender Smith.

Maynard previously had enticed Dr. H. A. Smith, a fellow practitioner from Ohio, to Elliott Bay. The two men agreed that Elliott Bay would be the terminus of the transcontinental railroad. And they worked together to bring it here. They disagreed only on where the actual terminus facilities would be located. Maynard figured they would be on his claim at the south end of the town. Smith thought they would be at the north end. So, he staked his claim at what we now know as Smith Cove.

As it was, both of them were right.

Today we have railroad yards in both places.

Smith, who was twenty-two years younger than Doc Maynard, came close to being a carbon copy of this town's founder. Young Smith completed his medical education in Cincinnati, Ohio. He set forth for the California goldrush with his mother and his sister, treated cholera en route and for some reason was diverted to the Willamette Valley . . . the only difference between the two men being that Doc Maynard was diverted by a dame . . .

And Smith was just diverted.

Smith, who couldn't make up his mind whether he wanted to be a doctor, a writer or an orchardist, left his mother and sister in Portland when he fell into the hands of Luther Collins, who was pitching the orchard business with every ounce of energy he had. Smith arrived on Elliott Bay with Luther in the spring of 1853, but neither Luther nor Doc Maynard was able to sell him on locating along the Duwamish.

However, as it turned out, the timing was perfect for the future of this city.

Smith completed his log cabin at Smith's Cove in the spring of 1853 and sent for his mother and sister that summer . . . the two of them arriving about midsummer . . . to be greeted by Doc Maynard, who was not so antiquated that he failed to note that Ellender Smith was a comely young maiden indeed.

Plummer showed up in late July.

Sly old Doc Maynard introduced him to Ellender, and while Plummer still was in a bemused state, the doctor took step number two . . .

On August 6, 1853, he *gave* the young man lot four in block eleven, the second best piece of view property in town. It was on a bluff overlooking the Duwamish River and the Cascade Mountains at what today is the northeast corner of Occidental Avenue South and South Jackson Street.

The doctor wanted Plummer so badly that he might have given him the property at the Point . . . but he already was negotiating with Felker for that one for hard cash. If he was going to give away some property, it wasn't going to be the best piece he owned. Or, the chances are even more likely that he knew, with Ellender in there to sweeten the pot, he didn't need to. Whatever it was, he knew what he was doing . . .

Because it worked.

The doctor inserted his usual "condition" about constructing a substantial building . . . and Plummer, eager to impress Ellender, went into competition with Felker to provide the finest structure in town. By the fall of 1854—when other towns around the Sound were lucky to get log cabins—Doc Maynard had under construction in his town two mansions that would be in the mansion class even by today's standards.

As Justice of the Peace, the doctor performed the ceremony by which Charles Plummer and Ellender Smith were married in January of 1855.

The doctor, who was an eminently practical man when he chose to be, provided the happy young couple with some brooding hens along with a rooster or two as a wedding present . . .

And Plummer, being the kind of operator he was, constructed a chicken house as big as the average settler's cabin.

Doc Maynard, the Plummers' friend

On January 16, 1854, Doc Maynard sold Plummer lots two and seven in block three—directly across Main Street from his own store. And it was here that the young man established the second store in the town. Two years later, he sold him the two lots immediately south—giving Plummer the four lots at the north end of block fronting on what today is First Avenue South and South Main Street. And here Plummer subsequently would build what has come down to us as both Plummer's Hall and Snoqualmie Hall, the main tourist at-traction—outside of Madam Damnable's—in town. All in all in the first two years, the doctor sold Plummer forty lots in the heart of the business district . . .

And Plummer used every inch of land to help develop the town.

Plummer developed the Duwamish Mill Company, which brought both lumber and coal down the river and past the main entrance of the town. He built the town's first brickyard along the banks of the river and the record shows that at one time he shipped a single cargo containing half a million bricks. Plummer at times had two different partners in the mercantile business, H. A. Stone and S. B. Hinds. And, in combination with the doctor's store, the waterfront at First Avenue South and South Main Street became the original heart of the original business district.

Thanks to the machinations of the doctor, the county seat was located in his store. All business conducted by anyone with the county had to stop at Plummer's pier and the latter ran an overhead water system from a stream on the side hill a dozen or more blocks away. He also laid in a supply of cordwood for the propulsion of the new steamers that were beginning to appear on the Sound.

Within a short time, every ship of any kind which visited Puget Sound found it necessary to stop at Plummer's pier . . .

Up to and including the mailboat.

But here, they ran into a little problem.

Arthur Denny had somehow wangled the postmaster's job without the doctor's knowledge. And, naturally, he had located the post office in his little log cabin way to hell and gone north of Plummer's pier in the wilderness at First Avenue and Madison Street—nearly a mile away and with no docking facilities. All of the mail landed at Plum-mer's pier and had to be hauled to Denny's cabin and then hauled back again to the center of town where the business was being conducted.

"It doesn't make sense to me," Plummer said.

"No sweat," the doctor replied.

The Democrats were in charge of Washington Territory and of Washington D. C.

Denny was a Whig.

And the doctor informed his friends in key positions that Denny not only was a Whig but an offensively partisan Whig. It was a statement as easily confirmed as the nose on your face.

Three months after Denny got the postmastership, the rug was jerked out from under him. In due course, the job was awarded to Plummer.

East side, wet side, all around the town

While Leonard Felker and Doc Maynard constituted the team that put Seattle together in the original instance, Felker never did take up residence in our town . . . and as time went by his presence here became less frequent until he finally disappeared from the records about 1860. But the doctor moved Charles Plummer into a key position so smoothly that Felker's absence never was missed. And, beginning in 1854, the two men became Seattle's second Establishment.

And their first problem was Prohibition.

Neither the doctor nor Plummer wanted a wide open town. Madam Damnable—alone and away out there on the Point, which was a block away from the nearest store or restaurant—ran an unobtrusive operation. Actually, she was six blocks or so from the nearest resident Bluenose . . . and they just pretended she wasn't there. On the other hand, the doctor and the Plummer had no intention of letting the Prohibitionists turn Seattle into a closed town.

Things came to a head early in 1854 when the county government was created and Plummer got the first liquor license in King County. Plummer immediately put the license to work in his store at First Avenue South and South Main Street.

He installed the city's first saloon, a place with a honky-tonk piano, relatively ornate bar and a couple of pool tables. He didn't do much business with the Christers who lived north of Yesler Way, but the sailors and miners, and fishermen and loggers came to Seattle in droves on the weekends. And Plummer did a roaring business— below the line (the line for the next half-century or so being Yesler Way.)

During April of the first session of the Legislature in 1854, a bill patterned after the Maine Liquor Law was introduced. Maynard and Plummer, with their Masonic and Democratic connections in the legislature, saw to it that the bill got short shrift. But the next year, the women's groups pressured the legislature into passing a liquor law.

The Wets countered that move by arranging for the first referendum vote of the people in the history of the territory. The vote was 564 in favor of Prohibition and 650 against . . . a difference of eighty-six votes. The Drys hollered "fraud" on the grounds that ballots which were not marked one way or the other were counted as being against Prohibition. But they never were able to make anything come of it.

And that was the closest the territory—as such—ever came to enacting a ban on the manufacture and sale of alcohol during the lifetimes of Seattle's founders. From then on the Drys made a lot of noise, and occasionally they would elect someone to office—but it never mattered much until the debacle of 1909 when the Blue Laws were passed.

The Blue Laws making anything that was any fun illegal.

From 1854 on, licensed premises proliferated in Seattle and within a decade we had "squaw" saloons, regular saloons, cheap saloons and classy saloons with such wonderful names as the Dolly Varden . . . the Gem . . . the Snug . . . the Alhambra . . . Oro Fino . . . Bank Exchange . . . Billy the Mug's and such colorful spots as the Sample Room and the Collar & Elbow Room.

In 1859, the stout-hearted Plummer built the forerunner of Seattle Center when he established the finest entertainment spot on Puget Sound and called it "Snoqualmie Hall." He put a bowling alley in the basement, moved his pool tables and bar to the first floor and added a dance hall and meeting room on the second floor.

It was here that all of the major indoor entertainment of the town was brought for about a decade . . . exhibitions . . . magicians . . . elocutionists . . . instrumental and vocal concerts . . . lecturers . . . dancers . . . comedians and meetings . . .

Yes, meetings.

This was Seattle's first convention center.

And one of the more amusing events evolved when the hall upstairs was rented for a convention of the Order of Good Templars. The Order of Good Templars was· an international temperance organization. Snoqualmie Hall was the biggest place in town and that's where they heard the temperance story and sang the temperance songs like "Come Sign The Pledge," "Some Poor old Mother at Home," and "A Picture from Life's Other Side" . . .

While on the floor below, a bunch of drunks trying to keep time with a tinny piano were hollering at the top of their lungs such popular pieces as "Turkey in the Straw," the "Arkansas Traveler," "Oh! Susanna," and "Wait for the Wagon!"

Plummer played both ends against the middle.

Seattle's first "Lady?"

Nobody knows and the record doesn't show when Madam Damnable died, although it was some time prior to 1863. But she was just as colorful here in the "hereafter" as she had been in the "here."

Doc Maynard, who provided cradle-to-grave service for the people who came to his town, had designated land for a cemetery along the banks of the Duwamish somewhere in the vicinity of Fifth Avenue South and South Jackson Street. When Mary Ann died, she was buried in the doctor's cemetery.

Then, they needed room for the first gasworks in town and it became necessary to remove the bodies. David Denny offered some of his land up where Denny Park is today at Dexter Avenue and Denny Way. By that time, there were 223 bodies and the gas company contracted with a gentleman to move the bodies to the new location.

When they got to Madam Damnable, they found to their astonishment that the coffin weighed about five hundred pounds . . . and when they opened it, they discovered that due to a judicious mixture of seawater and limestone, she had turned to stone in her grave.

There's no record of whatever happened to her body, but the rest of the bodies were moved to a new location on what was a view spot on an area known as Denny Hill.

All seemed well for a while, but then the folks decided to remove Denny Hill and the process had to be repeated . . . with the final destination of the first 223 people who died in town being what we know of today as Lakeview Cemetery.

The digger with the contract for moving the bodies did a sloppy job and when the steamshovels started biting into the hill, they came up with a miscellaneous collection of shinbones, skulls and ribs. This, in turn, resulted in a great hue and cry about the desecration of the graveyard. In response to the screams of the proletariat, the ingenious contractor disposed of that hill between midnight and eight o'clock in the morning . . .

Giving rise to the first use of an expression in current use today: "The graveyard shift."

Seattle's first fish factory

Fish-packing always has been up there in the top ten basic industries of our town. And Doc Maynard, who fell in love with the flavor of salmon on the Oregon Trail, was the first person in town to try and preserve it.

Among the twice-told tales of Seattle history is the one about the doctor's original experiment with the preservation of salmon. The way it reads in our traditional history books is that the doctor was a dumb cluck who tried to salt salmon down for the San Francisco trade. The salmon spoiled and he lost money on the deal . . .

The way it's put is "Doctor Maynard had this wonderful scheme about preserving salmon," as though he were out of his tree.

The facts are that the Hudson's Bay Company had been engaged in this kind of salmon packing for twenty years before the doctor showed up. It cost a dollar a barrel to salt the salmon down. They sold for twenty-dollars a barrel in San Francisco. The doctor, who was elsewhere at the time, contracted with someone else to salt down a thousand barrels, a shipment on which he and his partner, Leonard Felker, stood to net $19,000 from an investment of $1,000.

The salmon spoiled.

Each of them lost $700.

But in the same shipment were piling, shingles, squared timbers and cordwood on which they made $20,000.

They learned from the "fish fiasco" and after that they, and everybody else in the business on Puget Sound made money on salted salmon . . . until the mid 1860's when somebody figured out how to can salmon . . . and then it became one of the major factors of this city's economic growth.

But that wasn't the entire story.

And Bagley provides us with additional details . . .

After pointing out that Dr. Maynard was the first person in Seattle to get into the salmon trade, Bagley says: "During the next twenty-five years, the fishing industry on the Sound depended on its revenue upon salted fish and fish oil . . . San Francisco offered a good market for this salted fish, also for the oil which was expressed from the lower grade fish and offal."

But even that wasn't the whole story and Bagley covers that one, too, with: "Maynard's salmon enterprise carried with it another important industry, that of barrel-making. In pioneer days, the cooper made all his barrels by hand and of wood. The hoops were of split hazel or small vine maple, shaved on the inside, notched at each end on the lower side in a way that the notches would engage. These hoops were strong and endurable. They continued in use into the '70's when iron hoops superseded them. Salmon, beef, pork and later lime were all put in barrels and kept large numbers of men busy in making them."

"Hoop making was an art in itself. Men went into the woods and cut straight hazel or vine maple bushes from six to ten feet long and an inch in diameter at the top. These were carried to a shed or central station and there split and shaved, tied into bundles and carried . . . to the riverside and taken to town. Contracts for 100,000 or more to be sent to San Francisco were not unusual . . . "

Fortunes were made in this business.

And the meat of the coconut lies in: "When ready for market they (the hoops) were put in big canoes or bateaux and brought (to town) by way of Lake Sammamish and river, Lake Washington, Black and Duwamish rivers . . . "

All of them past Maynard's Point.

All of them contributing to the growth of Maynard's town . . .

"Everybody makes mistakes. That's why they have erasers on pencils."

In *Sons of the Profits,* I wrote about Henry Yesler under a chapter entitled "The Bastard," and there's nothing during the intervening ten years that either I or other researchers have come up with which changes the context of that designation.

The sawmill which he brought to Seattle always has been billed as the most important industry in town at the time . . . the basis of our whole industrial complex.

Well, God help us if all of our industries were run the way Henry's was!

On the other hand, no one can deny that in the field of bastardry, he was the most stout-hearted man we had.

The doctor brought Henry Yesler into the act in the original instance because he needed the publicity for his embryo town. He didn't care whether the sawmill ever amounted to a tinker's dam—as long as it was in his town. Every town north of tne Columbia River—and there were a dozen or more trying to survive—needed a steam sawmill worse than it did anything else on earth. Prior to that time there only had been hydraulic mills which couldn't cut boards straight enough to compete in the San Francisco trade. The town that could get the mill as its basic industry could, like any other basic industry, attract satellite industries like shipbuilding, metal-working, housing, and shipping.

It was the general consensus that the town which got the first steam sawmill would have an unassailable advantage over the other towns.

The doctor handed Henry ten half-lots in the platted portion of his donation claim (two of which were under water at high tide) and persuaded Boren to give Yesler three times as many in his claim in order to get the first mill in Seattle. Charlie Terry, who was beginning to have doubts about his location at Alki at the time, offered Yesler the whole town. Yesler also was offered whatever he wanted in Olympia, Steilacoom, Port Townsend and Bellingham Bay on Puget Sound and in the incipient town of Charleston in Grays Harbor as well as as many free lots as he wanted in Portland.

But the doctor got him.

And, the doctor exercised a not inconsiderable influence in the *Olympia Columbian,* which was the only paper north of the Columbia River. And on October 23, 1853, the following item appeared:

". . . there is a new steam sawmill in process of erection by Mr. H. L. Yesler at Seattle, north of the Duwamish River, and which, we are told, will be ready to go into operation early in November, next and no mistake. Huzza for Seattle! It would be folly to suppose that the mill will not prove as good as a goldmine to Mr. Yesler, besides tending greatly to improve the fine town site of Seattle and the fertile country around it by attracting thither the farmer, the laborer and the capitalist."

To approximate that announcement today, you'd have to be watching John Chancellor on the national news announcing that the Boeing Company had landed a billion dollar contract with Pan American World Airways. In this respect, Yesler's mill was a major shot in the arm for the incipient city.

Within a month the doctor was mighty glad he'd only given up five-and-a-half lots to this intellectual imbecile.

Henry had served his purpose.

From then on, he was only a headache for Doc Maynard.

Henry Yesler's wife, who was really a very nice person, had made the arrangements with a friend in Massillon, Ohio, for the $15,000 that Henry needed to build a sawmill. And had arranged to have the machinery shipped to San Francisco. Henry had worked as a carpenter back in Massillon and had come west with one John Stroble who had been in the sawmill business in Ohio. Henry didn't know beans about building or operating a mill. And he really needed Stroble to get it all together.

The newspaper article noted that the mill would be in operation in November, yet, when the doctor showed up with Catherine in January, he got a rude awakening. Catherine later told a newspaper reporter that Stroble prepared her first breakfast in Seattle, and was a man with whom she formed an immediate friendship. (She told the same reporter she always felt that Yesler was a "worthless fellow.")

Anyway, it was during that breakfast that Stroble dropped the news on the Maynards that he and Henry had quarrelled and that he was headed back to Ohio. As it turned out, there was nothing the doctor could do to patch up the quarrel and Stroble departed, leaving Henry in charge of the operation.

For purposes of understanding the subsequent events, it is necessary to know that all of those little sawmills in the early days were relatively simple to put together. When Cyrus Walker, the Puget Sound manager of the Pope & Talbot Company put that company's first sawmill together in Port Gamble later in 1853, it was exactly one week from the time the machinery arrived to the time the first lumber was cut.

It took Henry *five months!*

And that was only the beginning of his troubles.

Henry never did make money on that mill.

Yesler was pointed out as a perfect example of total inefficiency.

Commenting on the *Columbian's* prediction of Yesler's "goldmine," Thomas R. Cox says, "Yet a goldmine it was not." He goes on to say that some mills suffered from poor management, others from faulty equipment . . . Henry's suffered from both. He notes that: "Henry Yesler's mill in Seattle, the first steam sawmill in what was to become the State of Washington, is an excellent case in point. One of the partners . . . commented 'Yesler has disappointed us in nearly everything . . . ' "

Doc Maynard couldn't have said it better.

Pausing a piece for Snoqualmie Pass

Snoqualmie Pass was then, is now and probably forever will be the lowest and best pass through the Cascade Mountains, which separate the wet from the dry side of the state of Washington. The mountains have an hour-glass shape, being 100 miles wide at the Canadian and Oregon borders and fifty miles in the middle.

The pass runs through the middle and is about a thousand feet lower in elevation than the next nearest pass.

The Puget Sound basin is eighty miles long and eight miles wide and so deep you wouldn't believe it unless you saw a model of it at the Pacific Science Center—which is where you can see a model of it. But to relieve you of suspense on the subject, it runs to depths of 900 feet . . . with some of them right up to the shoreline. Seattle is in the middle of the east shore of this inland sea and, as a crow or an airplane flies, Elliott Bay is the nearest and best harbor to the lowest and best pass.

The Indians have known this for something like 5,000 years. The Hudson's Bay people had known it for a quarter of a century before Doc Maynard appeared on the scene. And with all that knowledge floating around, I can tell you one thing for guaranteed sure, the doctor found out about it fast . . .

And did some worrying about it.

In his day, there were no highways through the forests, except those provided by the rivers. And the river out of Snoqualmie Pass is rather reasonably known of as the Snoqualmie River . . . which, in turn, has three forks in the mountains—known with deadly logic as the "North," "Middle" and "South" forks of the Snoqualmie River. These converge above Snoqualmie Falls and at that point, the river flows abruptly north where it combines with the Skykomish River eight miles east of Everett to form the Snohomish River, which in turn empties into Port Gardner, where the city of Everett is located.

When the doctor explored Puget Sound in the fall of 1850, he had intime' chats with various and sundry Indians, trappers, prospectors and inquisitive men who just like to explore things. They gave him the lowdown on the eleven rivers which flow into Puget Sound and where they originate . . . and the various and sundry bays into which these rivers empty.

His problem was whether to opt for the mouth of the Snohomish where the harbor wasn't one, two, three with Elliott Bay, and be sure the trans-mountain traffic was coming his way . . . or to go for the best harbor and hope to abort traffic to his town above the falls. Accordingly, and although Catherine doesn't evidence the slightest notion of why they were doing this, she and the doctor spent weeks prowling around the rivers that came down out of the mountains and into the Duwamish. The thing she does remember is how nice the trees were around one of the rivers and its source, and how, to please her, the doctor named them Cedar River and Cedar Lake.

But Doc Maynard wasn't merely on a sightseeing trip.

He was trying to find a way of hooking up Snoqualmie Pass to the Duwamish River and consequently to his town on Elliott Bay. What he did was find just that. And he did a great deal more. He became the first person to traipse across the pass, meet wagon trains at the Grand Ronde, and lead them back to his town through Snoqualmie Pass. He later headed up the committee which raised the funds to build the first wagon road through the pass.

And, don't think he was without competition.

Lafayette Balch was doing the same thing with Naches Pass, giving away free lots in Steilacoom to people who came over that pass and settled in his town. He was fighting a losing battle. Some of the more traumatic experiences of the early days are related by the poor pioneers who took his advice. Today, as anybody around these parts knows, Naches Pass is closed in the winter. Even with all of our heavy snow removal equipment, we can't keep her open.

When Governor Isaac I. Stevens won the appointment to survey the northern route for a railroad from the head of the Missouri to the Strait of Juan de Fuca, he took on the 2,000 miles across the Rockies and assigned his good army buddy, George B. McClellan, to find the lowest and best pass through the Cascade Mountains. Stevens, who read omnivorously of the western explorations, had a pretty good hunch Snoqualmie was the lowest and best pass.

McClellan, on the other hand, knew which side his bread was buttered on . . . and that was on the side of Jefferson Davis who was at the time the Secretary of War. The war between the states was shaping up. He had strong southern leanings and he sure as hell didn't want a railroad built across the northern tier of states.

That would just tap a whole lot more land that would become anti-slavery and lend more support to the cause of the North. He rightly figured that the government probably only would give full financial support to one transcontinental railroad. If it did, he wanted that road to run through the southern states.

So Stevens would order McClellan to find Snoqualmie Pass.

But the big boss simultaneously would quietly countermand Stevens' order and require that McClellan *not* find Snoqualmie Pass.

They couldn't beat the physical evidence of the existing geography and soon the whole United States would know that Snoqualmie was the lowest and best pass to the most commodious harbor on Puget Sound.

What follows is the story of how that happened.

Doc Maynard meets the tiny bandy-legged tyrant

Isaac Ingalls Stevens was the kind of a guy of whom it could be said, "to know him was to hate him." His secretary, Elwood Evans, later a prominent historian in our state, was in an eminent position to make a judgment when he succinctly described his former boss as a "tiny bandy-legged tyrant." I presume that Evans was close enough to him over a long enough period of time to write with authority about his bandy legs, because there are no pictures of Stevens which show his body below the waist. That's because he would smash the camera of any photographer with the temerity to shoot the lower part of his anatomy.

There was, however, an additional reason for Stevens' ban on full-length photos . . .

Washington's first governor was only five feet, three inches tall.

He might have topped Madam Damnable by an inch.

These days, he couldn't have made it into the sacred walls of the United States Military Academy, because even on tip-toes he couldn't reach the physical entrance requirement. In those days, he not only made it, but became the valedictorian of the class of 1839. And, despite his physical stature, he looked down on anybody who (1) wasn't a graduate of West Point and (2) wasn't the valedictorian of the class of 1839.

In his heyday, he successfully provoked quarrels with the President and the Congress of the United States . . . the Secretaries of War and Interior . . . Great Britain . . . the Governor General of British Columbia . . . the Chief Justice of the Supreme Court of Washington Territory . . . the Washington Territorial Legislature . . . the Commanding General of the United States Army on the Pacific Coast . . . all the members of his immediate retinue . . . and a whole passel of Indian Chiefs in a hunk of ground that reached from the California and Canadian borders and the Pacific Ocean to the summit of the Rocky Mountains.

The only guy he never could get in a fight with was Doc Maynard.

Yet every time he entered into a confrontation with the doctor, he ended up on his tokas—without ever understanding how he got there.

Stevens' first encounter with Doc Maynard came on January 10, 1854. We're indebted to David and Catherine Blaine, Seattle's first full-time Methodist minister and wife, for the date. The Blaines were prolific letter-writers and somebody at the other end saved the letters for posterity.

Under the date of January 11, 1854, David Blaine wrote: "I have just seen Governor Stevens. He came to Seattle last night; is expecting to go up our river tomorrow to visit our coal mines and make arrangements for the exploration of our country back to the pass in the Cascade range, with a view to ascertaining the most feasible situation for the terminus of the Pacific railroad. Many in this territory are sanguine in the opinion that this terminus will be at some point on Puget Sound. This place (Seattle), in view of the natural easy route hither and our excellent and commodious harbor, said to be the best on the Sound, will probably be the place."

That was the week that was for Seattle.

On January 1, the Governor had set sail in a small sailing craft, the *Sarah Stone,* with his ethnological advisor, George Gibbs for a visit with James Douglas, the head of the Hudson's Bay Company in Victoria, and a quick look at Pacific Northwest Indians . . . but mostly in search of the terminus for the transcontinental railroad. He had left the upper waters of the Missouri River some six months before with instructions to survey the route of a "Pacific Northwest Railroad." With a crew of 175 technicians, mule drivers, etc. he had surveyed a swath of land 200 miles wide and 2,000 miles across untracked wilderness.

Now he had to determine on the terminus.

His orders were to locate it on the closest feasible spot to the Strait of Juan de Fuca. That he had anticipated it would be considerably closer to the Strait than Elliott Bay is indicated by the fact that he later bought land in Anacortes. But, on January 10, he fell into the hands of Doc Maynard.

The doctor met him at Plummer's pier along with Plummer, McConaha, W. J. Wright, who had replaced Arthur Denny as postmaster, Luther Collins and one William Heebner. These gentlemen escorted him to the most luxurious accommodations he yet had encountered on Puget Sound, a second-floor suite at Madam Damnable's, who was, among her other attributes, one of the finest cooks in the Pacific Northwest.

The next day, the Committee, with Chief Seattle's men providing the paddle power, escorted the governor on a tour of the backcountry . . . a trip that involved heading up the Duwamish and Black Rivers to a place which we know of today as Renton where the governor was shown a functioning coal mine with easy access to tidewater. It was some of the finest coal on the Pacific Coast and later would make King County the most important coal-producing county on the coast.

He was introduced to Seattle's prolific hinterland en route, showing the Duwamish and Kent valleys as the bread basket of Puget Sound . . . and then taken up the Cedar River (which entered Lake Washington a hundred yards east of the Black River . . . and then taken between Rattlesnake Mountain and Mount Washington to the confluence of the north, middle and south forks of the Snoqualmie River).

As an experienced engineer, he was fully cognizant of the fact that he had been taken through what could become an easy, low-level railroad route to Elliott Bay, and what obviously was the best harbor he had seen since his arrival in the Puget Sound country.

Six days later, on January 17, Catherine Blaine penned the following: "Our governor is now arrived and we are to have a Territorial Legislature. The members are to be elected next month. The governor's home is at Olympia at present. He was down last Friday with Governor (she meant "Judge") Lancaster, the nominee for congressman. They both addressed the people here . . . They gave very good satisfaction. I did not see the governor, but the judge called on us twice. He appears well, has the reputation of being a fine man, a Christian.

"The governor is as rough in his appearance as any of our back-woodsmen. They say he wears a red flannel shirt, no white one, coarse clothes and unshaven beard . . . He unhesitatingly declares the advantages of the northern route and thinks, as we all here know, that if such a route is ever built, its western terminus will be somewhere on the Sound . . . He pronounces himself pleased with the country, considers its resources abundant, and says he is astonished at the degree of intelligence he finds wherever he goes ."

Chief Seattle and the other Indians, as well as the members of the committee, who had explored the pass themselves, assured him that the valley where the town of North Bend is located today, was connected by gradual grades with the lowest pass in the Cascades. It was a conclusion the governor had reached during previous interviews with Hudson's Bay people, trappers and Indians on both sides of the mountains.

The governor was impressed.

Under normal circumstances, the governor would have followed the Snoqualmie River to its mouth. That would be the natural flow of traffic. On the other hand, he hadn't even seen the Snoqualmie River until after he had been shown an alternate route aborting the natural flow of traffic to Elliott Bay. The doctor casually reminded him that the mouth of the Snoqualmie was thirty railroad construction miles north.

At $60,000-a-mile.

To a man fighting the overall construction costs and under an injunction to reach tidewater and the best harbor by the "*shortest* and most feasible route*." the doctor's argument was persuasive. The problem was that the governor's trusted Lieutenant, George B. McClellan, had informed him that Snoqualmie Pass was impassable in the winter.

"My man Tinkham will be trying to come through that pass any day now," the governor informed his hosts. "If he confirms what you say, you have a railroad terminus."

"We'll have some Indians meet him when he comes through," the doctor replied.

Under the doctor's instructions, Chief Seattle appointed some of his most knowledgeable braves to see to it that the governor's man was met as he came through. Under normal circumstances the man would follow the course of the river to its mouth. The doctor impressed on Seattle the importance of intercepting the explorer and showing him the easy route to Elliott Bay.

Unbeknownst to any of them, George B. McClellan, who had explored and *not* found Snoqualmie Pass from eastern Washington, was exploring and *not* finding the pass from the west side . . . at the very moment the doctor was showing the governor the same river.

How they missed one another at Snoqualmie Falls is one of the great mysteries of mischance in history.

But, at that same moment, one A. W. Tinkham, who had ranged far and wide seeking the best railroad route in the governor's survey party across the continent, was approaching Snoqualmie Pass from eastern Washington. And the diary he kept of that exploration is the most critically important document that has been neglected in Seattle history to date:

"On the 7th of January, with two Wallah-Wallah Indians, I proceeded up the Columbia till it receives the waters of the Yakima River, and then taking the latter stream, turned westwardly to trace its waters to their source, in the close vicinity of which also spring the headwaters of the Snoqualme [sic] and White Rivers, emptying into Puget Sound."

He then goes into a considerable description of the Yakima valley, the terrain, Indians and Roman Catholic missions. On January 17, Tinkham reached what he spelled as Kle-al-um Lake and found the snow to be two feet deep. He described the approaches to the pass as being favorable to a railroad line, noting that the valley rose gradually on either side of the river, adding that "Here, too, commences the wooded region extending to the shores of the Pacific, and where exhaustless stores of firs and cedars will not only furnish the building material for a railroad, but will, from its resources, with suitable means of transportation, supply the wants of the country east of it, lacking in timber and fuel."

On January 20, he camped on the edge of what he spelled as Lake Kitch-e-lus. He continues with: "Wishing to know the real difficulty to be apprehended from the passage of these mountains in the winter season by railroad trains, I gave particular attention to the measurement and examination of the snows on the route. From Kitch-e-lus Lake to the summit, some five miles, and where occurs the deepest snow, the average measurement was about six feet, but frequently running as high as seven feet . . . The whole snow was light and dry . . .

"These snows present little obstruction to removal in comparison with the compact, drift snows of the Atlantic States, and would cause very little detention to the passage of trains. Passing on to the western slope of the Cascades, the snow rapidly disappears; fourteen miles from the summit there was but eight inches of snow, and gradually it fades away as the approach is made to the shores of the sound."

Tinkham points out that "It should be borne in mind that this examination was made in mid-winter, from the 20th to the 25th of January, and in a winter known to be one of unusual cold, and that the accumulated snows of the winter were but six feet in their greatest depth, and this only covers some half dozen miles of route . . . "

Tinkham arrived in the general area of North Bend on the twenty-sixth or twenty-seventh and was met by Chief Seattle's Indians. He notes that: "Without giving the details of the remainder of my journey to the sea-board, which in a more extended report may be noticed, I reached the vicinity of Seattle, under the guidance of Indians, on the night of January 27, tracing a very excellent railroad connexion [sic] from the valley of the Snoqualme [sic] to that commodious and beautiful harbor."

Where he spent that night in a commodious and beautiful bed at Madam Damnable's.

That was twelve days after Governor Stevens had spent a comfortable night in the same comfortable bed.

Of course, during the intervening period, the bed had been kept busy . . . and they *did* change the sheets for Tinkham.

Convention city

Seattle became the convention city of the Pacific Northwest in that same happy January . . . and if ever the Lord intervened on the doctor's behalf, that was the month he did it. Come to think of it, the Devil demanded equal time of the doctor's soul and there was all hell to pay for a while there.

It started with George B. McClellan, the guy that Secretary of War Jefferson Davis ordered *not* to find Snoqualmie Pass. With Fate intervening in successive waves, McClellan spent New Year's Day with one of our old acquaintances. And, if I hadn't seen it in McClellan's own report, I wouldn't have believed it. As it was it bade fair to knock me off my perch.

He spent New Year's Day with Chief Patkanim at the mouth of the Snohomish River. McClellan wasn't very good with the Chinook jargon, but he sure learned quickly how to speak Patkanim. What he did was use "sign" language.

Dollar sign.

He explained to Patkanim that the Great White Father in Washington, D.C., wanted him to go up the Snoqualmie River and look for Snoqualmie Pass. But that the Great White Father also had ordered him *not* to find Snoqualmie Pass. By this time, what with his experience with Doc Maynard a few years earlier, Patkanim concluded that the white man was nuttier than any Indian fruitcake he'd ever met. But if the guy wanted to spend his money not finding some place, it was quite all right with Patkanim if the price was right.

So, what they did for the next nine days was take a leisurely trip to Snoqualmie Falls, arriving there on January 9 . . . a day on which the Lord smiled on McClellan's cause by dropping a load of snow on the pass that extended well down into Rattlesnake Prairie. If I know Patkanim, he took credit for the snowfall and charged extra for it. And if I know McClellan, it didn't come out of his pocket.

The federal government coughed up the extra charges for *not* finding Snoqualmie Pass.

And, man, did they beat a hasty retreat.

It took them nine days to go from what we now know as Everett to what we now know as North Bend.

It took 'em two days, the tenth and the eleventh, to get back down to the mouth of the Snohomish River again.

McClellan then proceeded with his usual speed, exploring bays and harbors of the coast in the general direction of Seattle. He found Elliott Bay on January 15 and probably spent the night at Alki Point, proceeding to take soundings in the bay that day and the next, arriving in Seattle on the night of the sixteenth.

To appreciate the picture, it is necessary for us to understand the activities of the Lord at this juncture. Stevens beat his way out of Seattle through snow, wind, rain and sleet, bound northward to find out if his hosts had indeed been telling him the truth about Port Gardner . . . and to look in on a few other places, like Fort Victoria on Vancouver Island. Snow, wind, rain and sleet were no deterrents to the complusive little tyrant.

But they sure slowed down McClellan.

And, as luck would have it, McClellan was wending his weary way from Alki Point to Seattle on the same day that the governor courageously sailed into the teeth of the weather headed past Smith Cove on his way to his appointment in the north. They passed one another without contact.

Imagine McClellan's delight at being met by a committee of genial men with a deep understanding of creature comfort, a bottle or two of Kentucky bourbon and the luxury of a hot bath at the finest hotel he had encountered since he'd left San Francisco more than six months before.

There was one discordant note in this symphonic paradise.

These guys guaranteed him a quick run up the Duwamish, Black and Cedar rivers and an easy trip to Snoqualmie Pass the next day. How in God's name would he avoid taking the trip with them?

This time with witnesses!

But the Lord let His countenance smile on McClellan.

George woke up the next morning to a spectacular view of Mount Rainier and to an even more awe-inspiring view of the Duwamish River which lay immediately below his second-floor room in Madam Damnable's establishment.

That was January 17, 1853 . . .

The coldest day in the memory of any human being on Puget Sound to that date.

The Duwamish River was frozen solid.

They couldn't make the trip.

Thank you, God!

The Saints and the Sinners

When you read the average history about the pioneers of our town—they never were just pioneers, they were "hardy" pioneers—and they needed to be hardy for reasons which shortly will be explained. But, before getting into that, let me give you one of my favorite passages from one of our history books.

After explaining that the efforts of our pioneers "required a fortitude and staying power seldom equalled in the history of human effort," this book continues with: "But above all and beyond this, they carried the profound convictions of Christian men and women, of patriots and martyrs. They battled with the forces of Nature and implacable enemies; they found, too, that their moral battles must be openly fought year after year in the face of riotous disregard of the laws of God and man."

Talk about the forces of Nature.

She, he or it, sure was doing her thing on that January 17, and Catherine Blaine took occasion to write home about her hardships. To appreciate the situation, you must understand that the Blaines had brought formalized Methodist Episcopalian religion to Seattle a month earlier. The Blaines came here under pressure exerted by Arthur Denny. They didn't have a home of their own at the time, but as they wrote to their relatives back east, "Brother Denny" found a place for them in his little log cabin located where the Federal Building at First between Marion and Madison is today. The Denny family huddled into one room of the two-room structure, turning the other room over to the newly wedded Blaines. The windows consisted of thin white cloth.

Here's a verbatim excerpt from Catherine Blaine's letter:

"The present week is the coldest known within the memory of the oldest white inhabitant. This morning it was ten degrees above zero. Our room is so open that we can look through cracks in every direction. It freezes within five feet from the stove where we have as much fire as we can get into the little thing. I washed before school this morning, standing over the tub with the shawl on and my teeth chattering with the cold . . ."

And there was McClellan taking a bath in a big tub of hot water in Madam Damnable's whorehouse six blocks away with windows on the lines of a southern mansion . . . nine panes above and nine below the sash. Rainier, the mountain that the Indians called God, thrust its pristine glory into the azure sky. A crackling fire in the huge fireplace shone on the highly polished floor and reflected in the lath and plaster walls and ceiling. A bottle of bourbon sat on the night stand along with a pitcher of ice, if that should be his pleasure. From the kitchen below wafted the comforting aroma of bacon frying and hot coffee.

The river was frozen.

All was well with the world.

McClellan rang for room service.

The wages of sin . . .

On January 30 and 31 and on February 1, Stevens, McClellan and Tinkham wrote varying reports on the conditions in Snoqualmie Pass.

But they had one thing in common . . .

Total praise for the town of Seattle.

Stevens wrote: "Mr. Tinkham reached Olympia from Snoqualmie Pass, bringing information of the most important character; the snow deposited in layers of one or two feet, but six or seven feet deep for some six miles, and one and a half foot or more for only about forty-five additional miles, and undisturbed by wind, and offering not the slightest obstruction to the passage of trains. The grades good to Seattle, with a tunnel of considerable length. I herewith enclose a copy of Mr. Tinkham's report, and cannot too much commend the energy and judgement which he has shown in crossing, in mid-winter, the Cascade Range, and actually bringing to the Sound the route of the Snoqualme [sic] Pass, and thus accomplishing what had not be [sic] done by any previous labors of the expedition." (The last a reference to McClellan's failure to find the pass.)

McClellan ducked the pass issue completely, noting in his report:

"The result of my examination as to harbors is, that of all the harbors between the north end of Whidby's Island and Olympia, that of Seattle is by far the best, being well protected against the wind, having thirty fathoms of water, a most excellent holding ground, being easily approached from the Straits of Fuca, and having a good back country. It is, therefore, in my opinion, the proper terminus for any railroad extending to the waters commonly known as Puget Sound."

Madam Damnable's establishment had served the town well. And today we have McClellan Street just south of Doc Maynard's original claim.

Tinkham's copious report noted there were no substantial difficulties in crossing the mountains, stating, "It should be borne in mind that this examination was made in a winter known to be one of unusual cold . . ." and concluding with the words that were music to Doc Maynard's ears: "tracing a very excellent railroad connexion [sic] from the valley of the Snoqualme [sic] to that commodious and beautiful harbor."

That material went into the official reports which then were fed to the news media. And for the next twenty years, every newspaper in the country automatically referred to the Northern Pacific Railroad from some place on the Great Lakes "to the town of Seattle on Puget Sound."

Then, three months after Maynard's death, when Arthur Denny was in charge of the negotiations for making Seattle the terminus of the Northern Pacific Railroad, he got the now-famous telegram from the two representatives of the railroad:

"Kalama, July 14, 1873
"A. A. Denny, Seattle.
"We have located the terminus on Commencement Bay.
"R.D. Rice, J. C. Ainsworth, Commissioners."

Tacoma?

Nobody had ever heard of Tacoma before.

The man who traditionally has been referred to as the "father" of our town had blown the most important assignment of his entire public career. And it would be fifty years from the time that Doc Maynard sold the world on the importance of Snoqualmie Pass that it reached the full utilization that it enjoys today.

The Madam and the Master

Madam Damnable was the only one among those who knew what was happening who failed to appreciate the significance of the doctor's accomplishment. As far as she was concerned, all of this "pro bono publico" time she had been required to give to visiting dignitaries during the month of January was for the birds.

It cut into the profits something awful.

And when the Madam considered that something was awful, she let the world in general know about it . . . and the person who inflicted that something awful heard about it specifically and graphically . . . this time it was Doc Maynard.

He responded with the only incident on record in which he resorted to physical violence. What he did was turn Mary Ann over his knee and give her a good paddling on the "seat of learning."

Mary Ann promptly went to Justice Sam Holderness with a charge against the doctor of "Trespass against a person." Sam, who was well aware of the entire situation, found for the doctor and Mary Ann appealed the case to the Circuit Court, which showed up in the shape of Judge Strong in one of the Madam's parlors on the first floor.

This time she had enlisted the aid of Prosecutor Frank Clarke, who had changed the charge against the doctor to "Assault and Battery." The case came to trial on April 24, 1854. Judge Strong upheld the decision of Sam Holderness and added his own fillip to the proceedings. He levied court costs and lawyers' fees against the plaintiff.

Where Doc Maynard was concerned, Mary Ann was a good girl from then on.

VI

The Doctor and the
Tiny Bandy-legged Tyrant

One of the little details that is largely overlooked in our history books is that under international law the United States had to figure out some kind of a legal gimmick to separate the land of the free and the home of the brave from its original occupants. It was a matter that caused a certain amount of friction then and is providing the legal profession with a field day right now . . . with the U.S. Supreme Court periodically being dragged into the fracas on account of trivia like who owns the state of Massachusetts.

Locally the conflict crops up from time to time in the headlines like when the state of Washington built a nice million-dollar bridge across a river in the Quinault Reservation and the Indians wouldn't let us hook up Highway 101 to either end . . . or when the Indians cast their fishing nets upon the waters of the Puyallup River in the town of Tacoma . . . and we had to call on the Tacoma Fire and Police Departments to try to quell the "rebellion."

Well, all of this stuff started back when Doc Maynard was inventing Seattle. You don't find much in the way of Indian trouble in Seattle for the simple reason that the doctor decided that the best way to avoid Indian trouble was to keep the Indians and the troubles with the Indians away to hell and gone out of his town.

He had a relatively fine needle to thread on this one because about ninety-eight per cent of the population felt the most efficient and economical method of solving the problem lay in the extermination of the aborigines.

The Methodist missionaries, who were big in the Pacific Northwest at the time, had an attitude on the subject which was reflected in a history of the missionary movement written by The Reverend Mr. Gustavus Hines and published in 1850 with a paragraph that reads: "The doom of extinction is over this wretched race, and the hand of Providence is removing them to give place to a people more worthy of so beautiful and fertile a country."

So, in addition to more guns, we had God.

Participating in the extinction of the wretched race was doing God's work.

On a more practical front, there was one Isaac Ingalls Stevens, first governor of Washington Territory . . . the principal exterminator . . .

Subsequently referred to by his disenchanted secretary as "that tiny bandy-legged tyrant."

Doc Maynard didn't believe that human beings should deliberately set about killing each other, regardless of whose side the Lord was on . . . so he found himself in a nose-to-nose confrontation with his peers in general . . . and the tiny bandy-legged tyrant in particular.

But he also had his own goal . . .

Creation of the world's greatest city.

How he coped is one of the great unsung songs of our history.

Give the little man a big hand

At this point, it is essential to regroup the sequence of events for the sake of understanding how they progressed. Stevens left the nation's capital for his transcontinental trip in about June, 1853. He arrived in Olympia late in November and initiated a number of enterprises . . . the assembling of the survey information on the railroad that would fill three volumes . . . issue the necessary proclamations for the creation of the new territory . . . find Snoqualmie Pass if he could . . . and, finally, try to find out what the Indian problem was all about.

On December 1, five days after Stevens arrived in Olympia, Secretary of War Jefferson Davis had dictated a letter to the governor telling him to forget the whole blamed railroad survey. The letter would take ten weeks getting here . . . and it was during that time the governor prowled Puget Sound seeking Indians and Snoqualmie Pass.

The record shows that he visited Seattle twice, once between January 10 and 15, 1854 . . . and then returned two weeks later to address some 2,300 Indians that Doc Maynard, with the aid of Chief Seattle, had summoned to Elliott Bay around and adjacent to Doc Maynard's store. This was the first meeting between Stevens and any substantial number of Indians.

And it was at this place and time that we get into what has come to be known as "Chief Seattle's Speech." (Written twenty-five years after the fact by Dr. Smith, poet laureate of the pioneers.) The gist of it was, "Take it easy on us, you guys. You're liable to be in the same boat we are some day, and the Lord will look upon you with a greater degree of compasssion if you behave like Christians." It was a speech of such mellifluence that Shakespeare might have been moved to comment, "Man, I wish I'd said that!"

The only problem is that Chief Seattle didn't . . . couldn't have said it. He not only didn't speak a word of English, he couldn't even converse in the trade language, Chinook, which was bastardized from several languages. He could speak only in his native Duwamish dialect which consisted at the most of about 800 words.

Dr. Smith, who was there, says that the meeting took place in front of Dr. Maynard's office at the foot of Main Street. The doctor got up and introduced Stevens as the Commissioner of Indian Affairs, and the man who held the destiny of the Indians in the palm of his hand. Doctor Smith describes the scene with: "The bay swarmed with canoes and the shore was lined with living, swaying, writhing, dusky humanity."

Stevens, who was a very short man, like five feet three inches, and conscious of his lack of physical stature, made up for it by being both overbearing and condescending. He talked to what he considered a bunch of ignorant aborigines in the kind of language he had picked up from a first primer of the *McGuffey Reader* . . . sentences like, "I see a cat," and "Oh, see Jane run."

And the Indians behaved like a group of frolicking first graders, chasing each other, talking among themselves and generally behaving in a manner calculated to give rise to the governor's gorge.

Then Chief Seattle stood up.

I have to give you some of Smith's prose because it's an image of the chief for whom our town is named filtered through his rose-colored glasses of a quarter of a century. He described Chief Seattle as broad-shouldered, deep chested and finely proportioned, where in most of the pictures and statues of the chief he really looks like kind of a dumb cluck. Here's Smith on the subject again: "His eyes were large, intelligent, expressive, and friendly in repose and faithfully mirrored the varying moods of the great soul. He was usually solemn, silent, and dignified, but on great occasions moved among the assembled multitudes like a Titan among Lilliputians; his lightest word was law."

If you want to get a picture of what the chief *really* looked like, imagine one of Seattle's mayors . . . any Seattle mayor. If he matches the above description, that's how close Chief Seattle matched it.

Here's Smith on Chief Seattle again: "When rising to speak in council or tender advice, all eyes were turned upon him, and deep-toned, sonorous and eloquent sentences rolled from his lips like the ceaseless thunders of cataracts flowing from exhaustless fountains, and his magnificent bearing was as noble as that of the most cultivated military chieftain in command of the forces of the continent . . ."

Not exactly the mental image projected by the chief when he spoke to the assembled Indians about Patkanim on Whidbey Island a few years earlier.

Anyway, in the 1881 edition of the affair, Dr. Smith has Chief Seattle, who was over six feet tall, arising "with all the dignity of a senator who carries the responsibility of a nation on his shoulders."

Stevens, who had arrived here thinking he was the star of the show, was ruffled by the fact that these rambunctious redskins had talked through his short dissertation. If Smith remembered correctly, the governor would have been even less impressed by what happened next. "Chief Seattle's trumpet-toned voice rolled over the immense multitude, like the startling reveille of a brass [sic] drum, when silence became as instantaneous and perfect as that which follows a clap of thunder from a clear sky."

What happened then wasn't in the script the governor had visualized when he first set up this session.

The chief thundered on for half an hour.

To the governor, who couldn't understand a word of what the chief was saying, it sounded like a demonstration by the winner of an Iowa hog-calling contest.

But that was only minor.

Chief Seattle raised his right hand to the sky . . . and that still was only part of it. He placed his left hand on the head of the little governor . . . and it stayed there for the duration of Chief Seattle's dissertation.

Five-foot-three Stevens, who never allowed a full-length picture of himself unless he was astride a horse, already had a low opinion of Indians.

Chief Seattle, with that graceful placement of his left hand, became the low man on the governor's totem pole.

Bad medicine at Medicine Creek

Governor Stevens' first meeting with any substantial number of Indians in Western Washington occurred in front of Doc Maynard's store in the latter part of January, 1854, when the doctor—through Chief Seattle—produced an estimated 2,300 members of that aboriginal race.

The second took place eleven months later on Christmas Day and the day following.

We all would have been better off if the governor had spent the holidays with his family.

But he didn't and we aren't.

Location of that second meeting with the Indians was at Medicine Creek where the first and worst treaty with the western Washington Indians was signed on December 26, 1854. Medicine Creek parallels the Nisqually River which, in turn, enters Puget Sound via the Nisqually Flats, a piece of geography located about halfway between Tacoma and Olympia, There were about 600 Indians present.

Governor Stevens' son, Hazard, whose version of the affair has dominated most of our history books, goes like this:

"The messages and exhortations of the governor, promising them protection, pointing out the way of bettering their condition, and even imitating the envied superior race, broke upon them like a lighthouse in a dark night upon the storm-tossed mariner, relieved their fears and anxieties, and gave them hope. They hastened to assemble at the appointed council grounds, eager to listen to the new white chief, and learn what he offered them from the Great Father for their benefit."

Judge James Wickersham, of the Alaska fame, provided a somewhat different version of the affair forty years later when he opined: "The treaties constituted a contract obtained through over-persuasion . . .

deceit . . . promises not on the record . . . contracts obtained by the strong, from the ward, by the guardian, the child from the parent.

"They were unfair, unjust, ungenerous and illegal."

Outside of that they were pretty good.

A sidelight was provided later by the chief interpreter, George Gibbs, who was taken by the fact that the governor was drunk . . . and at the same time lectured the Indians on the evils of alcohol. (Consumption of alcohol by Indians was prohibited in the treaties.)

To further set the scene, the brightest Indian of the bunch on hand for that treaty-signing was Chief Leschi, the richest and most influential of the associated Nisqually tribes.

The thing that must be kept in mind here is that the smart Indians in the Pacific Northwest had been doing business with the Hudson's Bay Company for thirty years—a whole generation. The Bay Company men were tough, but when they made a deal, it was a deal. If they bought a piece of ground from an Indian, they paid for it in cash or the equivalent in goods at a fair price. The same was true of furs. Bay Company rules against the sale of liquor or other crimes applied equally to whites and Indians. Bay Company people intermarried with Indians. And Dr. William Tolmie, the Bay Company factor at Fort Nisqually, had told Governor Stevens that Chief Leschi was an extremely intelligent Indian and a leader of the other Indians. "Get Leschi on your side and you've got a good head start," he said.

And so it was that the governor gave Leschi a slip of paper appointing him as a chief. (As there weren't enough recognized chiefs to go around, the government had to appoint chiefs so it could negotiate the treaties to make everything legal under international law.)

Here's how the governor approached what was probably the most sophisticated Indian in the Pacific Northwest:

"My children! You are not my children because you are the fruit of my loins, but because you are children for whom I have the same feeling as if you were the fruit of my loins. You are my children for whom I will strenuously labor all the days of my life until I shall be taken hence.

"What will man do for his own children? He will see that they are well cared for, that they have clothes to protect them against the cold and rain, that they have food to guard them against hunger, and as for thirst you have your own glorious streams in which to quench it. I want you as my children to be fed and clothed and made comfortable and happy . . . We want to place you in homes where you can cultivate the soil, raising potatoes and other articles of food and where you may be able to pass in canoes over the waters of the Sound and back in the mountains to get roots and berries . . ."

He then went into the subject of *The Great Father*.

Some of his quotes went like this: "The *Great Father* desires this . . . I want to know your grievances and report to the *Great Father* about you . . . I have been to the *Great Father* and told him your condition . . . I made a journey of fifty days to the *Great Father* on your behalf . . . I went to the great shores of the east to report to the *Great Father* . . . I told the *Great Father* I had traveled six moons in reaching this country and had never found an Indian who would not give me food, raiment and animals to forward me and mine to the great country of the west . . . I went to the *Great Father* and you all know I have come back."

The *Great Father* was Franklin Pierce . . .

The pro-slavery Democrat named on the forty-ninth ballot at the Democratic Convention.

"Take that . . . and that . . . and THAT!"

The governor then offered the Indians 4,000 acres of land that had been agreed upon in conference with his Indian agents in Olympia before he approached the treaty grounds. I'm sure that he was not there to deliberately insult the Indians, so it has to be presumed he knew absolutely nothing about the lands he offered the Indians at that treaty. This is further confirmed by the fact that nine months later he met with them and gave them exactly what they asked for in the first place.

But it was too late then.

A lot too late.

Congress, for once, had ratified the Medicine Creek treaty three months after it was made. The rest of the treaties wouldn't be ratified for four years.

Of all the treaties, this had to be the one they ratified fast. It was on this one the Indians based their subsequent actions.

The governor was totally unprepared for Chief Leschi's response. He apparently didn't know that the chief had farm and grazing land of his own that was greater than what the United States government offered to all of the Indians represented at the Medicine Creek treaty grounds. Leschi already was engaged in farming and knew the value of farm real estate. He also ran a string of some 150 horses . . . and the reports were that he had discovered gold in the Cascades. At the least, he was an extremely wealthy Indian. The other appointed chiefs signed, but Leschi's response was one of outrage.

The gist of his reply was: "You tell us you want us to be farmers. But what happens is that the white settlers grab off all the good farm land and you try to palm off this useless junk on us."

This was the last response Stevens had anticipated from an aborigine.

He blew his cork: "You'll take this ground and like it!"

Chief Leschi tore up his appointment as Indian "chief" and threw it at the furious governor's feet.

The chief then stalked away from the treaty grounds.

His last words were: "I'll fight rather than take it!"

For years an uneasy peace had been maintained between the whites and the Indians in the Oregon Territory—primarily through the efforts of the Indian superintendent, Joel Palmer—but now the news that spread like wildfire throughout the Indian nations was that the white man finally had shown his true colors. He was trying to steal the Indians blind.

The Pacific Northwest was a tinder box . . .

And what was this piece of land so despised that Chief Leschi would rather fight than take?

I hate to mention it because the people living there already have been put down often enough . . .

It was Tacoma.

Pop goes the weasel

If I had to nominate any one thing as the slickest magoozle Doc Maynard ever perpetrated on behalf of his incipient city, it would have to be the one he slid past everybody involved in the treaty at Point Elliott on January 22, 1855.

This one was Doc Maynard at his Machiavellian best.

To get the picture, please remember that one year earlier he had collected some 2,300 Indians to meet the new governor of Washington Territory in front of his store, the Seattle Exchange. Four weeks earlier the tiny bandy-legged tyrant had instigated the disastrous Indian Rebellion in the first Indian treaty at Medicine Creek. The signing of a treaty at Point Elliott was to be the second one attempted. And Point Elliott, for the benefit of those who never heard of it, is known today as Mukilteo, the spot just south of Everett where the ferry leaves for Columbia Beach on Whidbey Island.

Stevens had provoked an Indian rebellion liberating relatively few acres from the Indians during the negotiations at Medicine Creek. But now he was into the first major Indian treaty . . .

Extinguishing the Indian title to 5,177,600 acres of land . . .

King, Snohomish, Skagit and Whatcom counties.

All the land on the east side of Puget Sound from Seattle to the Canadian border . . . today the most valuable land in the state of Washington. And would you believe it, history records there were exactly the same number of Indians this time as had been in front of the doctor's store the previous year . . . four times as many Indians as had been at the signing of the Medicine Creek Treaty. This apparently was Doc Maynard's basic supply of Indians.

Governor Stevens, of course, was delighted at the turnout. But then, he was drunk again and really didn't know what was up from what was down. Ezra Meeker notes that the governor knew as much about the Territory as a passenger on a railroad train does about the foreign country the train is traveling through.

But Doc knew what the stakes were . . .

Another treaty like Medicine Creek and a massacre of the white population on Puget Sound would begin.

On the one hand, he had the governor to contend with . . . a man with characteristics described by Meeker with, "He would take no counsel nor brook opposition to his will . . . it may be said of his appointment of others to fill numerous offices were made to fill up a personal following rather than for fitness."

In those days men seeking to get into the Indian agent business would part with payola of from $500 to $5,000—just to get a job as Indian agent. Bancroft estimates that once they got it, eighty per cent of the money appropriated by Congress for the Indians slid into the pockets of some of the Indian agents. There were some honest Indian agents. General Joel Palmer was one. Mike Simmons was another. But for the most part they were a bunch of unmitigated crooks. It was a sorry chapter in our history. But the point is that there was nobody around the governor willing to brook his wrath or tell him something he didn't want to know . . .

Except, of course, Doc Maynard . . .

Who was a lot smarter than that.

The doctor had his own objectives here . . . and they were largely selfish objectives . . . but then again, he didn't want any killing and he was not about to light the fuse leading to a firecracker like Stevens.

A magoozle was in order.

The doctor's primary objective was simple . . .

As the only real estate man in Seattle, he already had sold a large section of the downtown business district to people he felt would help him construct the greatest city on earth. But there was a little problem here. The land wasn't as yet his to sell. It didn't even belong to the United States government . . . and wouldn't belong to the United

States government until this treaty was signed and the Indian title to it had been extinguished.

Now we get into the complications.

Over 5,000,000 acres were at stake . . . but the doctor's interest lay in a mere 54,790 acres. That was the amount of land he considered as the ultimate acreage of the city he had in mind. It extended from Point Pully on the south (known today as Three Tree Point), and a place called Four Mile Rock on the north, a location directly west of Lake Washington. The land then ran generally south along the west side of Lake Washington . . . and then generally west again to Point Pully . . .

In other words, Seattle's city limits today . . .

Well, not quite.

Our city today goes a mile or so north of what the doctor envisioned and encompasses 58,603.84 acres, not the 54,790 acres he had in mind.

The doctor's objective was to extract that 54,790 acres from the 5,177,600 at stake in the total picture at Point Elliott. He needed a separate treaty to get it . . . and this is where Chief Seattle earned the right to be the doctor's whipping boy. He stood up and was counted. This was the territory that belonged to the Duwamish and allied tribes, of which he was the supreme chief . . . and by God . . .

God?

Well, yes.

He had been converted to Roman Catholicism by that time.

Anyway, by God, he wanted a separate treaty, covering his allied tribes.

Doc Maynard was condemned by his peers as an "Indian Lover," than which there could be nothing lower . . . but there wasn't much love in this deal.

Not when it came to the construction of his city.

So enter his second objective.

DUWAMISH LAND
POINT ELLIOTT
TREATY LAND

McDONALD LAKE

M'LAISLAND

MAY CREEK

CEDAR RIVER

MERCER ISLAND

LAKE WASHINGTON

BLACK R.

GREEN R.

DUWAMISH RIVER

SEATTLE

ELLIOTT BAY

FOURMILE ROCK

ALKI

POINT PULLY

There was a need for Indian reservations . . . reservations with a lot more land than had been awarded the Indians at Medicine Creek . . .

But he didn't want them in Seattle.

As a matter of fact, it was far better that they be some place else. Everybody else may have been a little bit fuzzy about things, but Doc Maynard saw the picture with utter clarity. The Indians were safer some place else. So were the whites. And the development of the city was far more propitious if there were no Indian claims to cloud the title to the land. He magoozled a square mile for the Indians on some of the best property on Puget Sound, and some land elsewhere . . . the most significant of it being at Port Madison on the west side of the Sound where Chief Seattle had been born.

And, out of the Point Elliott Treaty the Indians got some 40,000 acres instead of the 4,000 that had been awarded them at Medicine Creek.

Oh, happy day!

Governor Stevens was surprised and delighted at the response he got from the Indians at Point Elliott, although he never did figure out why the Indian chiefs put in such a plug for Doc Maynard . . .

Up to and including Patkanim.

The process went like this:

Chief Seattle initiated the round of thanks by saying: "My heart is good toward Dr. Maynard. I want always to get my medicine from him." This sentiment was echoed by Chief Choitshoot who said, "My mind is the same as Seattle's. I love him (Maynard) and send my friends to him if they are sick." Chief Goliah brought Maynard up with "I shall be glad to have a doctor for the Indians."

Even Patkanim got on the bandwagon with: "We want everything as you have said, the doctor and all."

After each mention of Doc Maynard there was thunderous applause from the 2,300 Indians present.

And this goes to show you how little Governor Stevens knew about what he was doing. The Indians were thanking the doctor for providing them with a place where they could survive. Stevens thought they wanted a doctor to make house calls in their tepees.

His response was: "My friend Seattle has put me in mind of something I had forgotten. You shall have a doctor to cure your bodies and I trust your souls also."

From then on he provided for the inclusion of a white doctor in all of the Indian treaties . . .

A singularly bad move with the Walla Walla treaty.

The Indians over there had killed Dr. Whitman because they thought he was poisoning them.

But what a fine real estate deal it was for the doctor. The federal government paid the Indians three cents an acre for the Seattle townsite—and turned around and gave it to Doc Maynard for free. And he had no reservations on his land . . .

With the exception of mental reservations.

He already was selling that land at an average of $290.95 an acre.

You can fool some of the people

We have spent so many years busting our elbows patting our backs about the "Great Northwest" that we've come to the uneasy point of almost believing it. And most of the people writing most of the history books have contributed to our delinquency. But the truth is that we had a bunch of people here who weren't very nice at all.

Nationally, the Great Northwest had a bad reputation.

To begin with, you can't confine Seattle's history to the things that went on within the city limits. In 1852 and 1853 the folks back east didn't even know there was a city here—let alone a city limits. In more modern times, we've had incidents like the Watts riots in Los Angeles erupting between the white and black races . . . except that between 1852 and 1856 the race riots in the Pacific Northwest were between the whites and the reds. For comparison, you have to extrapolate the

Watts riots from a neighborhood in the Smog City to an area extending from California to the Canadian border.

Bancroft gives us a tip on what it was like in 1852, the year the folks were driving their stakes in the land that became our town: "With such a rough element in their country (The Rogue River in southern Oregon) as these miners and settlers, many of them bloody-minded and unprincipled men, and most of them holding the opinion that it was right and altogether proper that the natives should be killed, it was impossible to have peace. The white man, many of them, did not want peace. The quicker the country was rid of the redskin vermin the better, they said. And in carrying out their determination, they often outdid the savage in savagery."

On June 1, 1853, the *Yreka Herald* hit the nail on the head with, "Let our motto be extermination and death to all opposers."

In March of 1854 Major General John E. Wool, commanding army officer on the Pacific Coast, wrote a much-publicized letter to his superiors in the War Department charging that the settlers initiated a war against the Indians in order to bring in more federal troops . . . and in turn sell supplies at exhorbitant prices to the military. Federal soldiers, escorting an Indian to jail, fired upon and killed attacking miners who had killed their prisoner. Villages of Indians were massacred by the whites. And Wool wrote that he was forced to deploy his troops in the protection of Indians rather than the whites.

Bancroft writes of Indian women in the Rogue River fights risking their lives to provide water for wounded soldiers, adding, "I find no mention made of any such humane or Christian conduct on the part of the superior race." In another instance he tells of a treaty in southern Oregon acquired at gun point, "placing the conquered wholly in the power of the conquerors, and in return, for which they were to receive quasi-benefits which they did not want, could not understand, and were better off without."

The Rogue River War of 1853 cost the lives of a hundred white people and several hundred Indians at a cost to the federal government of $7,000 a day.

Bancroft referred to it as a "bloody carnival."

And don't think the hostilities were isolated to southern Oregon. Washington became a territory that year . . . and got a new governor . . . and all of the residents of the Territory looked to see whether or not he would pour oil on troubled waters or use it to further the conflagration. Stevens didn't get here until December, 1853. He was back in Washington nine of the twelve months of 1854. His only conclusive action of that year was the totally unacceptable treaty signed with Chief Leschi and the chiefs of the upper Sound.

And Doc Maynard didn't need any diagrams to tell him what was happening to our town.

In 1853, concomitant with the joyous news that Washington had become a territory, the doctor sold eighty-seven lots in his new town.

In 1854 sales dropped to fifteen lots.

In the first four months of 1855—in spite of the favorable treaty signed at Point Elliott in January of that year—real estate sales dropped to zero. Charlie Plummer was the only investor who saw any future in Seattle . . . he bought a whole block on May 22 for $175.

The governor could fool some of the whites about his intentions . . .

But not the ones who put out money for real estate.

The easy route out

In those early history books about Seattle and/or Washington Territory, you get ten pages of who conquered what molehill and how. For a while there, the Indians were beating the pants off of the United States Army and the Volunteer Militia combined. And it was all very exciting when, after about four years, the "good guys" won. But in order to be the good guys, they had to win and win big against overwhelming odds. The script called for a pitiful handful of gallant settlers against the savage horde.

We needed the money.

And Congress was mighty suspicious.

But it wasn't until the 1890's that historians like Bancroft and Judge

Wickersham and Ezra Meeker began to blow the whistle on the operation. But by that time we had all the money we were going to get in war reparations. So it didn't hurt to let the folks know that once more history had been written by the big battalions. We didn't have any more brains, but we had a lot more firepower than the Indians.

It was not a heroic period for the superior race.

Among the things that came out later from his closest aides was the fact that Stevens upended a lot of bottles of booze during his negotiations with the Indians . . . and that he was, to say the very least, a difficult man when he had a load of corn on board. While the drys were in Olympia making King County alcoholically arid, the doctor was at Point Elliott watching Stevens. Here was a man whose sense of values was based on whether or not a fellow officer had graduated from the United States Military Academy at West Point. The aborigines were located on the scale of living things in about the same category as any other kind of rodent.

How he must have *loved* Chief Seattle's hand on his head!

The doctor was a witness to the two sides of Governor Stevens. A year earlier he had been on hand when Stevens, the engineering genius, had conquered the vast wilderness of America and carved out the route that would be followed when the first transcontinental railroad was constructed to the Pacific Northwest. At Point Elliott, he saw the face of hate based on fear . . . which is the most virulent there is.

It was disguised by the mask of the *Great Father* who had been nominated on the forty-ninth ballot at the Democratic convention. But I wonder how many people it fooled, up to and including the Indian Chiefs who got up and put the arm on the doctor by thanking him for the role he'd played in the negotiations.

Doc Maynard was the only "outsider" on hand.

The rest of the negotiating team was subject to the whim of the governor.

The doctor had obtained what he came after—the land for his city. But he also was the same person who had stuck with a shrewish woman for nine years when it would have been the easy route out for him to be a hero and join the army in the war against Mexico. He was the same man who had witnessed the killings in California and, as Prosch said, "it was too much like a continued battle to please the peaceable physician." Now, he was faced with the same prospect in his own home ground. And it wasn't just Stevens. Stevens rapidly was moving into the position of the chief executioner, but the growl of public opinion was with him.

Which brings us to the key issue.

As a matter of convenience in Washington D. C., the local Indian superintendents were asked to gather as many Indians as possible into big reservations. The prospect of keeping books on a whole bunch of different tribes loomed as horrendous in the nation's capital. So Stevens' instructions read like this: "In concluding articles of agreement and convention with the Indian tribes in Washington Territory, you will endeavor to unite the numerous bands and fragments of tribes into tribes and provide for concentration of one or more of such tribes upon the reservations which may be set apart for their future homes."

These were standard instructions to the Indian superintendents, and the key word above is "endeavor" to locate the tribes on one big reservation. Stevens, who was a thoroughly literal man, took these instructions literally.

Superintendent Palmer, who had the same instructions and tried to carry them out when possible, also knew what the circumstances were locally and knew how to yield.

Bancroft explains: "But the opposition made by all natives to being forced upon the territory of other tribes, or to having other tribes brought into contact with them, on their own lands, caused Palmer to select, an alternative to the first proposal of putting incompatible groups of natives on one reservation." Governor Stevens, who had negotiated with Indians for fewer months than Palmer had years, possessed no such insights.

Bagley sums up the fatal flaw of the Point Elliott Treaty. He points out that the Tulalip Reservation, occupying a whole township north of Everett, accorded the Indians in the Point Elliott Treaty, gave considerably more satisfaction than the Medicine Creek Treaty, but adds: "But Governor Stevens made the serious mistake of, also, ordering the Duwamish Indians and allied bands to be moved thereon within a year. This included the Indians inhabiting the upper White River and other streams forming the Duwamish.

"The Snoqualmie and Snohomish were allied tribes under the leadership of Pat Kanim, [sic] a wily, turbulent and dominating personality, who terrorized over the smaller and weaker tribes living in the vicinity. The latter had good reason for refusing to be placed on a reservation with semi-hostile tribes under such leadership, and leave their place of abode, hunting grounds and fisheries where their forefathers had dwelt for centuries."

The governor reached his decision to consolidate the tribes at the end of the Point Elliott Treaty-signing . . .

And nothing could induce him to change his mind at that time.

The die is cast

Doc Maynard may have susained some hope that Governor Stevens would not plunge the new Territory into war—until about mid-May, 1855. After all, the governor's instructions from the Bureau of Indian Affairs were specific on one front. Except around existing settlements, he was to take it easy on the Indian treaty business.

The actual wording of his instructions were supposed to have left him with no leeway: "You *will* at present conclude treaties with such tribes *only* as are located immediately adjacent to the settlements of the whites, and between whom and our citizens animosities prevail, or disturbances of the peace are apprehended." And to further put the emphasis on the above, the department added that it was "*desirable* that the stipulations to be fulfilled annually on the part of the United States be few in number." (Italics mine.)

The "will" and "desirable" above provide totally different emphasis. They go along with instructions that the governor should "*endeavor*" to unite tribes on one reservation. Treating with the Indians near the settlements only was an order. Uniting them on one reservation was a suggestion.

Stevens, of course, read it the way he wanted to read it.

The whole Indian question was a chance for Stevens to make a big name for himself. He was legit when he went from the Point Elliott Treaty to another at Point No Point a few days later. There were lumber mills functioning at Port Madison, Appletree Cove and Port Gamble. And he was acting within reason when he treated with the Clallams and Makahs on January 31. Port Townsend already was a functioning town.

But he went away out in left field when he tried to treat with the Quilleutes along the coast.

He had struck out with Chief Leschi. Doc Maynard had saved his bacon at Point Elliott. Then he completely and unnecessarily blew it with five tribes at the Chehalis Treaty grounds in February.

James Swan, who was there, corroborates this with: "The governor certainly erred in judgment in attempting to place these five different tribes on the same reservation; but his motive was, that as they were so few, being mere remnants of once powerful bands, it would be better to have them concentrated at one point. They, however, did not think so; their ancient prejudices were as strong as ever, and they well knew that they never could agree to live together."

The tenuousness of his position would have given pause to a more reasonable man . . . together with his specific instructions to consolidate his gains around land that already was settled. And further evidence was available to the governor. Two Roman Catholic priests familiar with conditions in eastern Washington warned the governor and other U. S. authorities that their part of the country was a tinder box. The weight of Superintendent Palmer was added to that of the priests. No treaty had even been attempted with the warlike Indians in either eastern Oregon or Washington.

But all of this came to naught when General Wool suggested that eastern Washington be declared off limits to white people until the tribes could be brought under military control.

If Wool was against it, Stevens was for it (this is where you get into one of those incredible situations which change the course of history. General Wool and a bunch of his army buddies were swapping lies that had been irrigated by corn whiskey in a bar in San Francisco and Wool, who really did have a lot to do with it, opined that he had won the battle of Buena Vista in the Mexican War. The general was in his seventies and headed for retirement at the time, and whether they agreed with him or not, the other fellows went along with the gag . . .

But not the tiny, bandy-legged tyrant.

He *had* to tell Wool that Zachary Taylor was the commanding general at Buena Vista, and *he* was the one who won the battle.

And, in his own inebriated state, Stevens had to rub it in by pointing out to the assembled group of army officers that Wool wasn't even a West Point graduate.)

Stevens dispatched Indian agents to Walla Walla to initiate the treaty-making process . . . and on May 12, 1855, left Olympia—with his teen-aged son accompanying him—for Walla Walla.

No bunch of redskins was going to intimidate him!

George Gibbs tried to warn the governor not to get into the Walla Walla Treaty. Recalling it later he wrote: "All that summer, rumors came in of the intention of the Indians to break out. Indian women living with white settlers warned their husbands to take care of themselves; but these reports were disregarded, because we had so long slept on the volcano that we did not believe it could burn . . ."

"That the governor's treaties had a great deal to do with fomenting this war there is no doubt. Those on the Sound were much too hurried, and the reservations allowed them were insufficient; but his great blunder was in bringing together the Nez Perces, Walla Wallas, Yakimas and others into one council, and cramming a treaty down their throats in a hurry."

The governor did not take readily to advice, which is why he totally disregarded an important piece of information supplied him by Bishop A. M. A. Blanchet, who had been dealing with eastern Washington Indians for nearly a decade.

Blanchet condemned A. J. Bolon, the governor's appointee as Indian agent for eastern Washington.

He said that in visits to the Yakima Indians, Bolon had shown a complete incapacity for his job as Indian agent. He "has, 1. Associated with and given all his trust to that which is the most vile in this nation; 2. He has made himself, by his acts, the initiator of games of chance prejudicial to the Indians; 3. He has carelessly rewarded thieves, and by doing this has incurred theft among the Indians; 4. He has shown with regard to the missionaries of this nation a vile conduct which the missionaries would never have expected from a government agent; 5. He has by his general conduct, lost the trust of all that is good among the Indians to the point that in my opinion Mr. Bolon can no longer perform in this nation the good that the government expects of its agents in the midst of them. [The Indians.]

"For these reasons I think it my duty to solicit his changement (Removal.)"

It was advice that fell on deaf ears.

The governor initiated the treaty-signing on May 21, 1855. The big chiefs of the eastern Washington tribes didn't even show up at the treaty-grounds for a week. Where treaties were completed in a matter of a day or two in western Washington, it took nearly a month to get the signatures at Walla Walla.

There were about 100 whites present . . .

And 5,000 warlike Indians.

During that summer, gold was discovered near Fort Colville and a lot of miners headed into the war zone. The Indians said that somebody among them "outraged" one of the women of the Yakima tribe.

Make no small plans

The future of Seattle was bleak indeed in the summer of 1855 . . . no matter which way the inventor of the place looked at it. A majority of the people of the Pacific Northwest looked at extermination of the Indians as a great idea. They would have preferred to just wish the problem away, but it wasn't going to disappear that easily.

But all that was needed was a leader and a spark and the superior race would dispose of the inferior.

Looking at it from both sides, the doctor could see that Chief Seattle in particular and the other Indians on the west side of the mountains were between a rock and a hard place. There was no safety for them. The whites were itching to shoot them. The warlike Indians in eastern Washington promised them that if they sided with the whites, they would be considered as the enemy. The men would be killed . . . the women and children taken as slaves.

There were between 6,000 and 7,000 Indians in eastern Washington . . . Between 8,000 and 9,000 in western Washington.

The doctor had one thing going for him.

Stevens was in eastern Washington . . . and would continue to be away from his post as governor in Olympia for the next six months, because after he finished treating with the tribes in eastern Washington, it was his intention to head east of the Rockies and treat with the Blackfoot tribes at Fort Benton. And while the governor was away, Charles Mason, Secretary of State, acted as governor.

Mason was in his early twenties, and a contemporary described him as well-equipped by "education, by temperament and by mental calibre for the duties devolving upon him. He was possessed to a great degree of that rare faculty of listening patiently to counsel . . . then to weigh it and act upon his own judgment, while throwing all prejudice aside. He was a courteous gentleman, not headstrong, but firm; not opinionated, yet self-reliant; easily approached, nevertheless dignified in his bearing, while not in the least self-conscious as to his own importance in the difficult position in which he was so suddenly and unexpectedly thrust."

Following the governor's departure in May, Doc Maynard approached the acting governor with a proposition that was too reasonable to be ignored. The instructions from the Bureau of Indians Affairs clearly stated that the principal thrust was the separation of the Indians and the whites around the various settlements. Stevens was spending all of the money allotted for Indian Affairs in the purchase of presents and financing the payroll for the eastern Washington treaties.

What the doctor would do was take over the role that was supposed to have been played by the United States government. He would, in effect, get the children off the streets in the event of war.

But he didn't have the immediate cash.

What he proposed to do was sell the land in Seattle which he and Governor Stevens had agreed would become the terminus of the railroad.

You can see that land today.

It's where the passenger terminals of the transcontinental railroads are located on South Jackson Street at Fourth and Fifth Avenues South.

Mason responded well to the suggestion.

He didn't have the cash, himself, but there were a couple of other guys in the administration who did. They were Major H. A. Goldsborough, the territorial tax collector . . . and James P. Tilton, surveyor of public lands.

On August 4, 1855, Dr. Maynard consummated the largest and most important real estate transaction in Washington Territory to that date—with a consortium composed of Mason, Goldsborough and Tilton.

He sold the terminus of the transcontinental railroad . . .

For $2,400.

He used the money to buy one sloop and charter another belonging to Luther Collins . . . and bought the supplies necessary to sustain about twenty-five percent of all of the western Washington Indians for a period of four or five months.

Mason did his part by negotiating with another man whose role in Washington history has been sadly neglected, one John Swan. Swan, an Olympia resident, saw eye-to-eye with the doctor and Acting Governor Mason on the necessity of isolating Indians near the settlements in the event of war. He would try and locate another contingent of Indians on Fox Island, near Steilacoom.

The doctor sold ten lots in the heart of the town and 121 lots covering all possible railroad approaches to the town—as they would come in on stilts across the tideflats.

At that point his total real estate sales—from the time he disposed of his first lots to Henry Yesler in January, 1853—consisted of some thirty-acres of the 640 he had obtained for nothing in his original donation claim.

All hell breaks loose

It would be erroneous to presume that Doc Maynard thought of himself as some kind of a hero in the events of the next few months. Unlike a number of the others involved, who collected and preserved every scrap of paper they could lay their hands on, Doc Maynard didn't save anything . . . didn't record anything that was not absolutely essential. His wife, who was not the brightest lady who ever came down the pike, didn't even know what he was up to half the time. A lot of other people resented what he was doing and wrote letters to the editor about it, but the doctor was too busy keeping his town from going belly-up to notice.

Except on two noteworthy occasions—once against the Indians and once against the Methodists—he didn't even lose his sense of humor.

And his strength during this stressful period did more to set the character of the city of Seattle than anything else which he had done to that point in our history.

At about the time that Doc Maynard completed his transaction with the consortium in Olympia, word reached civilization, after an Indian maiden was "outraged" by gold seekers, that the Indians in eastern Washington would deal "peremptorily" with prospectors. It was one of the many pieces of clear evidence that the vaccination of the Walla Walla Treaty had not "taken." Indian agent A. J. Bolon proceeded to the country with the objective of trying to reason with the toughest chief of the bunch, Kamiakim, head of the Yakimas. He last was seen alive on September 18, 1855 at a Catholic mission near the present site of the town of Yakima.

That was one-and-a-half months after the doctor's real estate sale. A few days later, Bolon's body was found.

Somebody had shot him in the back, then cut his throat, then burned him and his saddle bags and his saddle and his horse.

Somebody was sure sore at Bolon.

There were any number of reasons such as the five that Father Blanchet had outlined in his letter to Governor Stevens. The Indians had an eye-for-an-eye and tooth-for-a-tooth philosophy. In western Washington the classic example was the beheading of Isaac Ebey. Ebey was not even remotely involved in the incident which resulted in his death. Bolon's murder could have been the result of the incident in which the Indian maiden had been ravished by the gold miners.

It could have been even more direct.

Maybe Bolon was caught cheating at cards.

Whatever it was, the time had come for blood-letting.

And the whites chose to make Bolon the *cause celebre*, the Archduke Ferdinand of the Indian War.

When war is declared, truth is the first casualty

Granville O. Haller was dispatched from Fort Vancouver to chastise the Indians . . . and he got his pants licked off. Lieutenant William Slaughter was dispatched from Fort Steilacoom and got to the summit of Naches Pass where he realized the place was swarming with hostile Indians infiltrating western Washington. Wisely he fell back.

The whites used Indian hostility to get help from the federal government, saying they were under siege by a savage horde. The Indians also used it to try and get western Washington Indians into the affray.

It should be pointed out here that a state of war existed between the whites and the Indians from the time that Haller and Slaughter marched. Well aware that the 7,000 to 8,000 Indians in western Washington were a potential source of allies, fifth columnists sneaked across the mountains with an interesting and—to the local Indians— believable set of arguments.

Kamiakim announced he had enough war material to fight for five years . . . that "all tribes were invited to join him, and that all who refused would be held as foes who would be treated in the same manner as Americans—the adults killed and the children enslaved."

He pointed out with a certain amount of logic that, regardless of what they said, the whites were primarily interested in getting rid of the Indians. Either they would be exterminated or returned to the land of darkness from whence their ancestors had come.

The picture painted by the fifth columnists was one which caught the imagination of our local redskins. They would be crammed into steamships and hauled away. Except that they didn't call them steamships. They called them fire ships . . .

And not without reason.

Those early steamships on Puget Sound had a tendency to blow up, scattering the arms and legs and heads and torsos of the occupants all over the place. The local Indians were as afraid of the fire ships as they were of the white man's cannons.

Once packed like sardines in the fire ships, they would be hauled off to a place called "Polakly Ilahe," where no ray from the sun ever penetrated; where there was torture and death for all the races of Indians; where the sting of an insect killed like the stroke of a spear and where the streams and water were foul and muddy and unfit to drink."

In other words, Siberia.

The whites had been speculating for some years about the origins of the Indians and the general consensus was there once had been a land bridge across the Bering Straits. Western Washington Indians had landed in eastern Washington and had been driven to the coast by the tough Indians living in that part of the country. And enough of this had rubbed off on the Indians to make it believable.

The exterminators, of course, had no intention of doing that.

They were going to shoot 'em on the spot.

The Indians got plenty of demonstrations from the white men that whatever it was, their fate was not very good. Picnicking families of Indians were mowed down. Their ears, noses and hands were cut off, dried and shipped to friends elsewhere as trophies of the war . . . a little practice that had been initiated by the whites in Oregon a dozen years earlier.

The red brethren in eastern Washington had one clinching argument.

If the weak-kneed Siwashes in western Washington didn't join up . . .

And if the whites didn't ship 'em off or kill them on the spot . . . then the war parties from eastern Washington would treat them the way they were going to treat the whites . . .

With torture and death.

Doc Maynard makes his move

Doc Maynard, the only man in western Washington who had prepared for the problem, moved swiftly to thwart the ambitions of the hostile Indians in eastern Washington and any of what he later referred to as "troublesome whites in Seattle" who might take it upon themselves to shoot some of the local Indians.

Having handed Mason what the latter knew would become a fortune in land, the doctor exercised plenty of clout in the councils of war in Olympia. And one of the first orders to emanate from the territorial capital was the evacuation of Indians on the east side of Puget Sound to Port Madison on the west side of Puget Sound. Mason ordered Mike Simmons to appoint the doctor as a sub-Indian agent in charge of the Indians at the internment camp which was named Fort Kitsap.

Putting Chief Seattle on the same reservation with Patkanim added up to signing Chief Seattle's death warrant. Chief Seattle would have to fight or die. He would have to fight the whites or he would have to fight Patkanim if both chiefs were on the same reservation.

But Doc Maynard had got his land out of the treaty . . . his city was named, owned and operating. And he no longer needed Chief Seattle. All of a sudden, he was a liability. In some of the biggest corporations of the civilized world of today, what a man in Chief Seattle's spot would get would be what we call "dumped."

The doctor moved with characteristic vigor.

Within a month of the outbreak he had the bulk of his 2,000 Indians at the internment camp. Armed with the necessary carpentry tools and lumber from the nearby sawmill operated by George Meigs, they were constructing buildings for what the doctor believed would be a long stay . . .

At least for the Indians.

He wasn't about to see Chief Seattle located at the Tulalip reservation with Patkanim . . .

Ever.

Nobody knew how many eastern Washington Indians had penetrated western Washington. But as far as rumor had it, the woods east of Lake Washington were loaded with belligerents ready to shoot the head off of any white man they could get in the sights of their guns.

Demonstrating considerably more courage than anybody else in town, the doctor insisted on covering the territory east of his town to collect any stray Indian families that might be caught between opposing forces in the war zone.

Governor Mason furnished him with an armed guard.

Bagley writes: "On November 9, he (Dr. Maynard) went up the Duwamish and Black rivers, thence along the east shore of Lake Washington and notified all Indians to come to Seattle to be conveyed across Puget Sound."

The doctor combed those fearsome forests for a whole week . . .

Realizing that at any moment he could be shot in the back.

He returned with some seventy-five Indian men, women and children. By November 20, 1855, they were joined by another 175 who had come to Seattle in their canoes from elsewhere on the Sound and were accordingly shipped off to Fort Kitsap.

Before anybody knew what had happened, the doctor had swept the east side of Puget Sound clear of non-belligerent Indians.

And the squawks weren't long in coming.

Henry Yesler blows his whistle . . .
his cork and his stack

At five o'clock in the morning of November 21, Henry Yesler blew the whistle of his steam sawmill to summon his cheap Indian help to work.

And nobody showed up.

By November 24, he had rounded up some of the other members of the local business community who also were suffering from a lack of cheap labor—and feared that this lack might continue for some time.

And they fired off a letter to Acting Governor Mason.

It's a letter that never before has made any of our local history books and it's too good to leave out any longer:

"Seattle, Nov. 24, 1855

"Hon. C. H. Mason

"Sir we would beg leave to state that a short time since Col. M. T. Simmons came here and requested a meeting of the citizens for the purpose of determining the most suitable place to locate the friendly Indians during the present hostilities; stating at the same time that he only wished to know the will of the majority and he would be governed by the same. Accordingly it was determined by said meeting (called at his request) that the Indians should be located in this place on a plot of ground designated by a committee appointed by said meeting, in all of which the Indians have acquiesed [sic] with as little complaint as could reasonably have been anticipated.

"But just at the time when they had got their houses built and fixed to live in, they were required to break up and move on to their reservation; which is causing great dissatisfaction, and we fear will tend to provoke hostility with well disposed, and friendly Indians. A clear and decided majority of the inhabitants of this place have decided (as Col. Simmons well knew before he left here) that it was not safe to remove the Indians of this vicinity to their reserve, in fact it was to all appearances tantamount to a declaration of war against them.

"We would also respectfully state our firm conviction that the department can never give satisfaction to either whites or Indians in this part of the territory through the agency of D. S. Maynard inasmuch as it is *utterly impossible* for the department to obtain reliable information from him, owing to the fact that he scarcely consults any other Indian than Seattle, when the large majority of the Indians here are not his people and do not acknowledge him as their chief. Hence discord and difficulty must ever exist here until a different course is pursued.

"We must say in conclusion that we do not wish you to understand us, as preferring a charge against the government. But simply as wishing to give such information as will prevent trouble in the future. Confidently believing that the department has not heretofore been well appraised of the circumstances surrounding us here. Our request (as democrats) in the present case is, that the Dwamish [sic] Indians be permitted to remain here. They having voluntarily given up their arms to Captain Hewitt, and declared their willingness to obay [sic] his orders, and submit to his authority in all things, if they can be permitted to remain here. Will you please answer immediately in order that we may know how to act in this emergency and if possible prevent unnecessary bloodshed.

"With high considerations of respect
we are sir
your obedient servants

"H. L. Yesler
David Phillips
C. C. Lewis
S. Lamson Grow
Thomas Mercer

"P. S. If this does not belong to your department please send it to the proper person.

"H. L. Yesler."

I got a particular charge out of Henry's reference to the fact that all of the signators of the letter were Democrats. Mason just happened to be a Democrat, too.

It was politics as usual.

On November 27th, Mason replied to Yesler's complaint with:

"I have the honor to acknowledge the receipt of your favor of the 24 inst. and in reply to state that this office still places great confidence in ability and discretion of Mike Simmons, Esq. in Indian matters. Whether he agreed or not to be governed by a decision of a majority of the people as to the disposition of the Indians in your neighborhood, I know not; but have simply to state that the expression of the opinion of a majority can have no controlling influence upon the actions of the Indian agent—In addition to this, complaint already has been made by Col. Simmons that an unwarranted influence has been exercised by some of the citizens of Seattle with his efforts to provide for the Indians.

"As to the charge of 'unfitness' made against D. S. Maynard, Esq., 'it being impossible to obtain reliable information from him because he scarcely consults any other Indian than Seattle,' I have to state that 'Seattle' is recognized by the Indians as the head Chief of the Duwamish Indians, and it is part of the policy worked out to make the chiefs as influential as possible in order that they may have more responsibility. In conclusion I must say that I decline to interfere with any steps taken by Col. Simmons."

A war in the town of Seattle had begun.

Not between the whites and the Indians . . .

But between the whites and the whites.

Meanwhile back at the ranch

Until the incident of Indian Agent Bolon, the killing of Indians around Puget Sound was kind of a sometimes thing. For instance, Luther Collins might decorate his fence with Indian scalps, but he didn't go out *hunting* them. And when Masachie Jim got obnoxious, the entire population of Seattle had a hand on the rope that strung him up. The folks were horrified when they learned that Territorial Supreme Court Justice Edward E. Lander, newly-arrived in town, was serious when he said the parties who had participated in the hanging would, themselves, be hung if found guilty. So, the jury found everybody not guilty.

For their part, the Indians would cheerfully shoot somebody in the back, but a nose-to-nose confrontation wasn't anybody's idea of how to handle the situation.

Bolon's murder changed all that.

Well, not so much Bolon's murder . . .

People could understand that.

But killing his horse, too?

That *did* change everything!

Those eastern Washington Indians were really serious about this. We got the next horrible example of their seriousness on October 28, 1855, when nine people in the White River valley were massacred by Indians. Leschi became the goat and got hung for this, but post mortem testimony revealed he couldn't have been there at the time . . . and he said he wasn't there, even when they were putting the rope around his neck. And there's little doubt in my mind that it was those tough eastern Washington Indians who sneaked over the mountains and perpetrated the deed. But the massacre made one thing quite clear. This was no casual incident. It was deadly serious . . . so serious that a week later, Doctor Maynard had himself sworn in as a sub-Indian agent and started moving nonbelligerents to Port Madison, which he named Fort Kitsap.

And where was Stevens, the guy who had stirred all this up?

Clear off on the east side of the Rocky Mountains, treating with the Blackfoot Indians . . . a couple thousand miles away.

Under the initial enthusiasm of the murder of Bolon's horse, Acting Governor Mason was able to get together a troop of men who volunteered to make their way through the war zone east of the Cascades and bring home our chief executive . . . obviously the right man to direct the extermination of the redskins.

There was one problem.

The troops had no guns.

So, in a forced march, they descended upon Fort Vancouver, but by that time, General Wool had reached the conclusion that Stevens' objective was the extermination of the Indians. So when the volunteers arrived at Fort Vancouver and asked for guns, they were told by the regular army people something like, "that's a pretty dangerous mission. Somebody could get hurt. One of you guys might shoot himself in the foot . . . and besides, General Wool has declared eastern Washington off limits to white people."

So they didn't get any guns . . .

And gratefully abandoned the mission.

Somebody had to make the trip, though, and it devolved on W. H. (Bill) Pearson, who had been the governor's expressman on the railroad survey and still was in the employ of the federal government.

On October 29, the day after the White River massacre, he leapt from his exhausted horse and stumbled into the light of the campfire where Governor Stevens was relaxing, a day's journey west of Fort Benton.

Pearson dropped his bombshell.

One historian was able to give us the direct quote: "A thousand blood-crazy warriors are massed in the Walla Walla valley. They lurk behind every hill, in every swale, to kill the Governor and wipe out his train. Kam-i-ah-kan, Pu-pu-mox-mox, Young Chief, Five Crows, are in command. They are spurred to savagery by the waving of fresh and gory scalps torn from unarmed settlers and careless prospectors. The Yakima passes are closed by thousands of warriors; the Walla Walla country fairly crawls with them; the Columbia River trails, both lower and middle, are blocked. The only open trail leads down the Missouri River. Which way do we head from here?"

Presumably, after that, Pearson took a breath.

One of the dispatches in Pearson's pouch was from General Wool.

It explained in no uncertain terms that he (Wool) had declared all land east of the Cascades off limits to white people. Six or seven thousand Indians—nobody knew how many at that point—were ranging the country on fast horses looking for an expeditious method of bloodying their tomahawks . . .

Preferably with Stevens' scalp.

Wool was not about to give a bunch of hot-headed but naive villagers the opportunity of exposing themselves to death and burning. So there wasn't going to be any rescue party. And he had a suggestion or two. Inasmuch as Stevens was the firebrand who had lit the torch with his precipitous treaty-making, the best interests of all concerned would best be served if Stevens absented himself from the scenery for the next six months or so while the regular army brought things under control again.

Wool would have preferred having Stevens return by way of New York and Cape Horn, with possibly a long visit to Washington D. C. enroute. What he suggested was that Stevens try going down the Missouri and Mississippi Rivers, to New Orleans, the Isthmus of Panama, San Francisco . . . and then take a leisurely cruise back to Olympia.

Stevens was not amused.

The man and the muscle

Doc Maynard was not as much pro-Indian as he was anti-annihilation. In the development of his city he had from time to time ridden rough-shod over a number of people, but he usually did it in a way that you couldn't pin it on him. What usually happened was something like Denny's deprivation of the postmastership. One day he was post-master, and the next, this little plum had been snatched from his grasp just as he was about to take a nice bite. But, when Doc placed himself on the side of the Indians, he became a clear-cut pariah to his peers.

The most powerful of these peers, of course, was Governor Stevens. Stevens was a friend of the President of the United States. His was the power of the office of Governor . . . the superintendency of Indian Affairs.

And more than either of these, the power of public opinion which was ninety-nine and forty-four one hundredths percent with him.

Yet, above and beyond all of this was the personality of the individual involved. And, in order to gain further understanding of the doctor, it is essential to appreciate that of his principal opponent during the Indian Rebellion.

To begin with, Stevens was a born over-achiever, with a father who compounded this particular form of delinquency. Stevens' biographer makes note of the fact that Stevens tried harder than anybody else in school and was driven to even greater lengths by his father . . . to the point that the man who would become our first governor begged for relief from his schooling for a time.

Isaac's notion of relaxation was a job in a woolen mill, working ten or twelve hours a day, six days a week.

He was ten years old.

The biography continues with: "So Isaac went to work in the factory . . . rising long before daylight that he might eat a hurried breakfast, walk a mile to the factory, and begin the day's work at five o'clock in the morning, and toiling ten to twelve hours a day. The best weavers were women, it seems, and able to run two spindles apiece. Isaac determined to excel the most capable; and before he left the factory, succeeded in reaching the goal of his ambition, and managed four spindles unassisted."

Enroute home after a year at the factory, Stevens saw some hot gingerbread that cost a penny. But he didn't buy it. His puritannical upbringing required that he give his father all the money he had earned during the year. And what did his father say when Isaac asked for one penny out of that year's earnings?

"No!"

Father did one more small favor for Stevens. This one was physical rather than psychical. He drove the boy so hard in the haying fields that the lad got the rupture that plagued him for the rest of his life.

Stevens was constitutionally incapable of slowing down to a walk. There are regular references in his biography like, "in his zeal, he overworked himself, and was prostrate with severe illness in consequence." Another goes: "Mr. Stevens was never a sportsman or fisherman; indeed, he kept himself in work as never to have time for field sports." A schoolmate noted that Stevens was a small, insignificant boy . . . "But the impression of insignificance vanished as soon as one regarded his large head, earnest face, and firm, searching and fearless dark hazel eye."

He was a whiz at mathematics . . . A hell of an engineer . . . And the victim of continuing pain from an inguinal hernia.

The principal exterminator

When Governor Stevens returned to Olympia on January 19, 1856, there was an urgent message on his desk from Captain E. D. Keyes, commanding officer of the army headquarters for the Puget Sound District.

Keyes wrote: "I have heard directly and indirectly from Leschi, and the temporizing course I am pursuing, I feel certain, is the reason why he and the hostiles have ceased their depredations . . . *I deem it necessary to record my opinion that a forward movement at this time would not hasten the termination of the war, but might and probably would, induce the hostiles to recommence their depredations* . . . " (Italics mine.)

A day or so after Stevens arrived, the *Olympia Pioneer and Democrat* reported, "All was joy and gladness. The cannon was charged to the muzzle and our citizens seemed to look upon him as their deliverer— their hope."

I'll say the cannon was charged to the muzzle.

They gave him a thirty-eight gun salute.

Seventeen over what the President gets!

On January 19, the governor spoke to a joint session of the legislature in which the fellas were hanging from the rafters.

He said: "The war will be prosecuted until the last hostile Indian is exterminated . . . I am opposed to treaties; I shall oppose any treaty with these hostile bands. I will protest against any and all treaties made with them.

"Nothing but death is mete punishment for their perfidy!

"Their lives shall pay the forfeit!"

I don't know whether they fired off another thirty-eight gun salute, but

Stevens was able to gather from the thunderous applause that he had hit the nail of public opinion on the head.

Doc Maynard would quote Chief Seattle in writing to the governor later as saying that the whites were unable to determine through the sights of their guns in the woods which Indians were hostile and which ones were friendly. At that point, the number of friendly Indians killed had equalled the number of hostiles who had met their demise.

Governor Stevens carried his great message of extermination to the residents of Seattle on January 25, adding, "The town of Seattle is in as much danger of an Indian attack as are the cities of San Francisco or New York."

The next day, Seattle was under attack.

The Battle of Seattle—Part I

The "Battle of Seattle," which occurred on January 26, 1856, always has been billed in our history books as the turning point in the so called Indian War in western Washington. And the most-often quoted authority on the battle has been an account written by then Rear Admiral Thomas S. Phelps in 1881.

According to Phelps, 2,000 Indians attacked the town.

Opposing the hostile horde were ninety-six U. S. sailors plus eighteen marines and five officers . . . 119 men from the sloop-of-war *Decatur*. They subsequently were joined by seven civilians, four of them from G. A. Meigs' mill at Port Madison . . .

North of the blockhouse was a deep and difficult ravine at about Columbia Street. The main access to town was a well-beaten trail that ran up Yesler Way and continued on out to Lake Washington, which was where most of the hostile Indians from eastern Washington were supposed to be coming from.

After the attack, a breastworks consisting of timbers five feet high and eighteen inches apart—filled in between with dirt, and a blockhouse at Occidental Avenue and South Main Street would be built. But neither the breastworks nor the south blockhouse—presently occupied by the

Pioneer Square Branch of the Seattle First National Bank—was there at the time of the attack.

Oh, yes, I forgot.

According to Phelps, there were fifty "volunteers" from among the residents of Seattle and a few other places . . .

Unfortunately there were two doors in the blockhouse . . .

A front door . . . and a back door.

And only one sergeant-at-arms.

With his loaded carbine, he could drive the volunteers out one door to join the battle, but they just circled the fort and came in the other . . . and he finally gave up. At least, that's the way Phelps tells it. Our history books say: that was a "damned lie!"

After the smoke of battle cleared at the end of the day, there were two casualties. One was a young boy who poked his head out of the door of the blockhouse when he should have kept it in and the other was a soldier who got up to get a drink of water at the south end of town.

No, there were three casualties.

Before the attack of the Indians a sailor from the *Decatur* got drunk and tried to rape a young lady. Her thirteen-year-old brother shot the intruder in the head with a small fowling piece and killed him.

Maybe, you would have to say four casualties.

Years later Dexter Horton, Seattle's first banker, was warming his behind at a stump being burned for clearing land when one of the old shells from the *Decatur* went off . . . with the result that for some time thereafter Mr. Horton worked the front counter of the bank standing up and ate his meals on the mantle-piece at home.

This absence of casualties with 2,000 savage Indians attacking 126 stout hearted men was clear evidence that The Lord was watching over us. He was especially helpful at noon on the day of the attack. Phelps could see that about a thousand Indians were about to descend on him and "strike for the annihilation of my division."

His "division" consisted of himself and fourteen men.

Phelps continues with: "Quickly arranging my command to meet the tremendous odds to be launched against it, I had only time to impress in their minds with the certainty of our scalps ornamenting an Indian wigwam in the event of any weakness on our part in the assaults to be made . . ."

And it was here in the heart of the battle that Phelps recorded the great quote of the war.

The fourteen men said in unison: "Never fear for us, sir; we will stand by you or die in our tracks."

In the midst of battle . . .

Fourteen men, as one, came up with the greatest quote in Seattle military history.

At least, Phelps put quotation marks around it.

Now picture this. A thousand armed and angry Indians came within ten feet of Phelps and his fourteen men . . . The Indians were firing as rapidly as they could load their guns.

Phelps writes: "At this moment the fate of Seattle hung by a thread. With two bounds, three at the most, the third division of fourteen men would have gone down like grass before a mower's scythe, and in a few moments the battle would have been won, the people given up to indiscriminate slaughter, and the village in flames; but failing to make those bounds, the town remained in our possession, and the Indian cause was forever lost."

Man, talk about God being on our side . . .

None of the men was even scratched!

Well, that did it for the Indians. When they saw that God had stuck out his invisible shield like that and was on our side they slunk off into the underbrush and never came back.

Battle of Seattle—Part II

A good many of the more naive residents of Seattle slept in the blockhouse for most of 1856, but Seattle merchant, J. R. Williamson was not among them. Williamson was the guy with the spy in the Indian camp who had alerted the military officials on the night before the attack that this time the thing was for real—Governor Stevens to the contrary and notwithstanding.

Williamson also was privy to the fact that this was the first and would be the last attack on the town by the Indians. He had his own peculiar intelligence system and one which he had found to be entirely reliable. And while it hasn't as yet made any of our history books, it is to be found in a letter which Dr. Maynard wrote to Governor Stevens, contributing to Stevens' education on the subject.

Maynard may have been at Port Madison, but he was completely apprized of anything and everything that happened in his town. And what he wrote to the governor was that Captain Lander had been tipped off that the few remaining hostile Indians were leaving town to join with the hostile Indians on the east side of the mountains. Inasmuch as it was Williamson who had tipped off the folks about the original attack, it probably was Williamson who tipped them off that the last detachment of hostiles was headed east.

The doctor writes: "The Duwamish Indians being suspected of visiting the enemy rather often, and not altogether to our advantage, a company of the volunteers under Capt. Lander went up to an advantageous point enroute and watched their movements. Sometime towards morning three canoes with upwards of thirty Indians in them arrived, many with guns. On their drawing near, the volunteers fired upon them, killing two and supposed to have killed more . . . They took one canoe from them which had on board a quantity of provisions . . . which it is supposed they were carrying to the enemy, all of which, together with the canoe, was destroyed . . ."

It was not without irony the doctor wrote: "The history of this case will convey somewhat of the feelings and disposition of these Duwamish Indians. I believe they will bear close watching and careful management for a while, especially their leaders, Tecumseh, William and Curley."

Some of Governor Stevens' best friends were Indians . . .

Chiefs like Tecumseh, William and Curley.

The fun part of all of this is the role played by Williamson.

The day before, he had sold to the Indians the arms and supplies which Lander confiscated the next day. In other words, he cheerfully had been trading with the enemy.

No wonder Seattle became the major city.

No wonder Williamson ended up owning Ballard.

Battle of Seattle—Part III

The question of how many Indians participated in the attack on Seattle has steadily been revised downward with the passage of the years. In 1881, Phelps' estimate of 2,000 sounded pretty good to the people of Seattle because—nearly thirty years after the fact—we had been unable to collect all of our war reparations from Congress. A dozen or more years later, when the money either was collected or given up as hopeless by the second generation of the creditors, Phelps, himself, dropped the figure to 1,000.

In the 1920's, it had dropped to 300.

The most recent estimate I've seen was thirty.

Now, if there's one thing you can be sure of, it's that the merchants of Seattle—not the Christers who were marching around and pointing their guns at things—had a pretty good yardstick of what was going on. The local Indians were not what you could call a very belligerent bunch. Charging them with participating in the attack was like suggesting that the family dog had joined a union and was marching against its family. Everybody, with the possible exception of Stevens, knew which Indians he could trust or not trust.

On the other side was Commander Gansevoort of the sloop-of-war *Decatur*.

After the attack, Gansevoort insisted that guards be posted all night. On the first night, volunteers were assigned the duty. Phelps writes: "At 9 P.M. these volunteers were sent to their stations, and at ten o'clock, when the officer went on his rounds, every soul of them had gone home to bed, leaving their guns behind to represent them."

Gansevoort played the military game by the book.

Years before when he was the executive officer of a Navy training ship, he had played the game by the book with a bunch of midshipmen who had been charged with mutiny. What he did was string two of them from the yardarm.

One of the two was the son of the Secretary of War. Gansevoort was able to beat the court martial. But he wasn't able to beat the "system."

His future advancement had passed . . . and he was handed the rock-bottom assignment of the whole Navy—a little mudhole called Seattle.

But he still played the game by the book.

He couldn't control the volunteers, but he could control the men in his command. So, in addition to working all day at hard labor, like clearing away stumps in front of Madam Damnable's, they had to stand guard duty at night.

Phelps, who also belongs in the eager beaver class, suspected that the men from the Decatur were not attending to that night duty as seriously as they should be. The real casualties of the Battle of Seattle were beginning to come in.

Not from enemy bullets . . .

But from head colds.

Head colds which they caught when they decided during the night to take a nap in the frost-bitten ditches on either side of the road. Phelps' spies suggested that these were not called "naps" in Navy parlance, but "passing out."

Phelps, got out of his warm hammock to check on what was happening on January 28, 1856—two days after the attack on Seattle.

He provides another significant word picture.

"The occasional barking of a dog alone disturbed the stillness of the night, which was passing quietly away, when, at two o'clock in the morning, the most unearthly yells that ever greeted mortal ears, accompanied by oaths in the highest order of blasphemy, arise from the hen-coop (Plummer's), which instantly brought me to the scene, feeling sure the savages had succeeded in eluding the sentries, and were at their deadly work of slaughtering my men, when, pushing open the door, spectacle presented beggars all attempts at description.

A whirligig of arms, legs, heads and bodies met my view. Ten out of the twelve occupants were 'roaring drunk,' and mingled in a promiscuous mass of revolving humanity, fighting, biting, kicking, shrieking, and cursing, rendering futile all unaided efforts on my part to untangle this human ball of raving maniacs . . ."

The military authorities squawked to the merchants for selling liquor to the sailors.

The merchants protested indignantly that what with the war and all these men were the only customers they had.

Two weeks later, though, more men reported to sick bay with severe head colds.

It was the bloody end for Captain Guert Gansevoort.

He declared the town his men were supposed to be guarding "off limits to military personnel."

The scarlet letter

Along about the time that Doc Maynard was moving a whole bunch of Indians to his personally-financed reservation at Fort Kitsap, Lieutenant William A. Slaughter reported from the field that Chief Patkanim and a bunch of his tough warriors "are dogging my footsteps." Slaughter, who had been around for a while and knew Patkanim well, feared that this bunch of Indians was up to no good and asked Mason to haul in some of the Chief's relatives as hostages. The idea was to help Patkanim "keep the faith" and not get off on a killing spree.

Arthur Denny offered to lay his life on the line by going after Patkanim and bringing him in, but the authorities wouldn't hold still for it. Denny's argument was that Patkanim was the best Indian friend the whites had and why should we antagonize him. People who knew Patkanim from another picture were, at the very least, suspicious. History generally has concluded that Denny was right, that Slaughter had made an unaccountable mistake. On the other hand, Patkanim and his men were loose in an area that had been declared as a "war zone." Any Indians in that zone were supposed to be presumed hostiles.

And unknown Indians killed Slaughter.

At the same time, Doc Maynard, who was moving nonbelligerents to Fort Kitsap, wanted Patkanim and his wild bunch on the reservation about as much as he wanted a couple cases of cholera. But what are you going to do when all nonbelligerents were supposed to be on the west side of Puget Sound and out of harm's way?

The doctor was equal to the occasion.

Patkanim was a son of the profits . . .

And the thing to do was put him on the payroll.

So out of it all came one of the more remarkable documents in the military history of the Indian Rebellion . . . a letter to Acting Governor Mason attested to by Mike Simmons, Lieutenant A. D. Drake and the doctor. Dated November 4, this interesting missive has heretofore eluded historians:

"I learn slanderous reports are in circulation regarding my actions and tumtums. I therefore improve this opportunity to state facts as actually exist.

"First I will furnish 100 Good men Subject to Your order at the Inst. of Your Call, to fight, anywhere this side of the Cascade range, But I cannot at this time consent to go onto the other Side of the Mountain.

"Second, I will arrest any and all Such as I can find within my Jurisdiction who May appear as Enemies to the Bostons, and forthwith Bring the Same before you.

"In consideration of the above I require that You furnish adequate means to carry the Same into Effect—& Compensate us as the other Bostons are paid.

"I will *see* you in answer to your order without delay.

"To the Above I subscribe myself
"Respectfully yours to serve

"Patrick "X" (his mark) Canam"

That first proviso was pure Patkanim for you. He didn't want to get stuck waging war against those tough eastern Washington Indians.

(This may be where Arthur Denny got the notion of giving Patkanim two names. Actually, the copy of the letter in the state archives is not in Doc Maynard's handwriting. It's in that of a young navy lieutenant named A. D. Drake. Patkanim couldn't read anything in the letter but his own "X," and wouldn't have cared, anyway. Subsequent scholars have concluded that it was all one word. Otherwise we'd be referring to some of the other chiefs like "Leschi" as Les Chi, and "Kitsap" as Kit Sap . . .

"Sap" County, Washington.

I'm sure the people living in Kitsap County wouldn't sail for it.)

In those days, friendly Indians frequently were used as hunters, scouts and expressmen in the communications network. Patkanim would go for whichever side could pay him and his men more money.

So, he was wandering around loose in the war zone when Slaughter was killed. The Denny family figured he was maligned and helped erect a monument to him in the 1920's. The local newspaper obituary at the time he died sixty years earlier opined that it was just as well that he had gone to his great reward because "we never trusted him anyway."

But Doc Maynard was reasonably assured of knowing where he *wasn't* . . .

At Fort Kitsap.

Charge!

Governor Stevens launched his plan of annihilation with his accustomed zeal, vigor and energy by addressing the legislature and announcing that "I am ready to take the responsibility of raising them (an armed force independent of them (the U.S. Army) . . . Let not our hearts be discouraged, I have an abiding confidence in the future destiny of our Territory. Gloom must give way to sunlight. Let us never lose sight of the resources, capacities, and natural advantages of the Territory of Washington. Gather hearts. Do not now talk of leaving us in our hour of adversity, but stay till the shade of gloom is lifted, and await that destiny to be fulfilled. Let us all put hands together and rescue the Territory from its present difficulties, so we may all feel that we have done our whole duty in the present exigency."

The governor's son reported that "to this manly and clear-sighted appeal the legislature made haste to respond with alacrity and heartfelt sense of relief, and renewal of hope and courage, with which men in the extremity of danger ever turn to a natural leader, and, so far as lay in its power, gave him unlimited authority to take measures necessary to save the settlements from extinction."

Then came the Battle of Seattle.

Man, alive!

Those damn Indians shot back.

Two of our guys got *killed*.

We had cannons . . . and we had rifles . . . and we had pistols . . . and we peppered the hillside behind the town with enough cannon balls and bullets to "salt" a lead mine. There wasn't a leaf left in a tree and enough stuff was expended to keep explosions going during the land-clearing operations for a decade and nearly blow the behind off of the town's leading banker . . .

And we didn't hit a single Indian.

Our Leader had assured us the night before the attack that Seattle was as safe from an Indian attack as were the cities of New York and San Francisco. That night, the governor assured the assembled townfolk that with "ten good men, I can kill off every hostile Indian between here and Snoqualmie pass."

Stevens was in the approximate position of a coach giving a pep talk to a team that trailed its opponents by ninety-one points at the half. If The Lord was trying to promote the extinction of the Red Race, he sure was exhibiting some mighty mysterious methods. Those guys were shooting *back*.

Then, General Wool sent in a bunch more federal troops under Lieutenant Colonel Silas Casey who, on January 31, informed the governor that he now had a sufficient number of troops to replace the volunteers and "occupy all those points now held by your men, (the volunteers) and which I consider in any way necessary for the protection of the country within the region of recent hostilities." Casey, who had mustered two volunteer companies into the service of the United States army, announced that he did not need any more of the governor's volunteers.

The fact is that after the Battle of Seattle, the Indians on the west side of the mountains were in a retreat that amounted almost to a rout. They were able to stage one final battle on March 10 at a place called Connell's Prairie, near Puyallup. But that was the end of it for the Indians in western Washington.

But, it wasn't the end for Stevens.

Acting under the authority granted him by the legislature, he issued a call to arms for eighteen companies, twenty captains, twenty First Lieutenants, eighteen Second Lieutenants, and 1,002 non-commissioned officers and privates for the territorial militia . . . a total force of 1,060 men. The response around Puget Sound was lukewarm to say the least. Ultimately, he was forced to recruit down as far south as northern California to fill his quotas. He finally was able to submit a bill to the federal government for a payroll of 133,259 man days . . . with a price tag of $1,019,090.20.

But that was a year or so later.

Before he negotiated his first Indian treaty, the governor wrote a letter to the Bureau of Indian Affairs in Washington, D. C., saying: "The great end to be looked to is the gradual civilization of the Indians, and their ultimate incorporation with the people of the territory. It is obviously necessary that a few reservations of good lands should be large enough to give each Indian a homestead and land sufficient to pasture their animals, of which land they should have exclusive occupation.

The location and extent of the reservations should be the peculiar wants and habits of the different tribes . . ."

"In conclusion, I would express the hope that the administration of Indian affairs in this new and interesting field may illustrate not so much the power as the beneficence and paternal care of the Government."

But now the governor had forgotten about the "great and good end" was the civilization of the Indians . . .

What he wanted was blood . . .

Redskins' blood.

And that's the frame of mind he was in when Chief Patkanim's letter floated to the top of the pile on his desk in Olympia. Here was a fighting man after his own heart!   And, as his son was wont to say, he "threw himself into his work with even more than his accustomed zeal."

If the whites wouldn't kill the Indians, then he would have the Indians kill Indians.

There were 4,000 to 5,000 Indians lolling around on reservations like the one at Fort Kitsap. They weren't even being shot at. The least they could do was provide him with a bunch of Indian battalions. So he broached the subject to Chief Patkanim . . .

And Chief Patkanim said, "I'll tell you what. I'll make you a deal . . ."

The comical side of the Indian war

I suppose every war has its comical side and the way our history books have handled it, it was Chief Patkanim who did it for the one with which we presently are concerned. Lieutenant Phelps started it, but it's been generally quoted since. Phelps tells about Patkanim's appearance on one occasion upon his return to Seattle from Olympia "after being paid off." "He was arrayed in citizen's garb, including congress gaiters, white kid gloves and a white shirt with standing collar reaching halfway up his ears, and the whole was finished off with a flaming red necktie."

Paid off?

For what?

Patkanim was hired by the governor to kill hostile Indians. The deal was that the chief and his men would get eighty dollars a head for every chief he killed and twenty dollars a head for the average run-of-the-mill Indian. James Swan makes note of the fact that he accompanied Patkanim on the first expedition. "The chief brought the heads of his slain as trophies to Colonel Simmons, who did not participate personally in the fight, except by being *constructively* present, that is, in a tent nearby."

(Mike served as sort of a federal government meat inspector. It wasn't as good as being the Territorial Delegate to Congress which Mike had tried for and missed, but it was a living.)

The heads were taken to Seattle in a big bag and placed on board the sloop-of-war *Decatur* which then, with its crew of 156, sailed off into the sunset, depositing the heads on the governor's lawn where they were counted and payment made.

Patkanim soon objected to Mike Simmons' presence on the grounds that the chief was an artist and couldn't do his best work with a government inspector looking over his shoulder. Furthermore, there was no need to use a whole U. S. battleship to haul the heads. For a few extra bucks, he would take them to Olympia for the count, himself.

And that's the way it worked.

There are those of today who are somewhat skeptical that this kind of thing was done, but, preserved in our state's archives, is a sample receipt issued by the Washington Territorial Government to this Indian chief. And inasmuch as it is an integral part of our history and the character of Doctor Maynard, it needs to be bound between the pages of a book instead of moldering away in the archival vaults.

This is what Patkanim got for his work:

30 Printed Handkerchiefs
60 Yards Muslin
30 Yards Muslin Delaise
6 Covered Pans
6 Covered Pans
50 Yards Green Baize
50½ Yards Scarlet Baize
30 2½ Point Blankets
44¾ Yards Bed Ticking
2 Pounds Thread
36 Thimbles
4 Pairs Fine Cloth Pants
2 Pairs Fine Cloth Pants
12 Pairs Fine Cloth Pants
1 Pair Fine Cloth Pants
20 Pounds Crop Wire
89 Cotton Shirts
24 2½ Point Blankets
2 Pairs Large Hose

The aftermath of this is that on June 29, 1924, a beautiful monument to Patkanim was unveiled at the Tulalip Indian Reservation. One of our Eagle Scouts blew "Assembly, out of respect to the military character of the Chief," according to Edmond S. Meany in *Washington Historical Quarterly*. "Skookum George, Chairman of the day, then called on Father O'Donnell, of Marysville, who opened the program with a prayer. The American flag was then raised." This was followed by addresses by a number of Indians and by Arthur Denny's granddaughter, "Mrs. Florence Heliker, (who) gave a brief address referring to the fine old friendship between her grandfather and the great Chief in whose honor the meeting was assembled."

Without Mike Simmons on hand, Chief Patkanim reverted to his normal system of profiteering. What he did was cut off the heads of some of his slaves—worth only twenty bucks—and sent the heads in as those of chiefs—worth eighty bucks.

Which in time came under the scrutiny of the Territorial Auditor, who apparently brought the entire operation to a standstill with the charge that the territory was paying for too many chiefs . . . not enough Indians.

Target numero uno

Bancroft notes in his chapter, "Extermination of the Indians," that, "It was the unpopular side to defend the Indians during this war. There were (however) many among the officers and servants of the United States brave and manly enough to do this."

(They were the ones who made the difference in the Pacific Northwest as opposed to the exterminators of Nazi Germany eighty years later.)

In the Washington Territory, there were two of record, Doctor Maynard and John Swan, of Olympia. And neither man was under any illusions about the precariousness of his position. Except for some relatively casual comments about the fact that attempts were being made to murder him, the doctor passed the whole thing off in his letters to his commander-in-chief as a normal, run-of-the-mill business.

Doc Maynard had about 2,300 Indians in his charge. To give you an approximation of what he was up against, it is noted that the number of Indians he was caring for constituted a population twenty times that of any white settlement on the Sound. Indians were encamped all around him in a dense forest. His camp consistently was infiltrated by the enemy fifth columnists. And there was no way he could tell how many hostiles from eastern Washington surrounded the camp. At the time of the attack on Seattle, he and his wife were the only white people in this crowd . . .

Two in two thousand.

If the hostiles could have persuaded even a hundred to join with them on the attack on our town, it would have fallen.

He was target numero uno.

Here's how he handled it in his correspondence after the attack: "We have some hostiles in our camps—how many, I do not know. On

Tuesday the Fifth at about half past seven in the evening one of them was discovered crawling about my camp and trying to look in at the apertures . . . last night they were discovered again and an attack was expected."

His final commentary is illustrative: "These symptoms of trouble and danger I must acknowledge rather absorb all other matters. But with the apparent determination of the Indians to fight when they do come, I am in for one frolick at all events unless I learn their numbers are too small."

The doctor and the head-hunter

Immediately following the attack on Seattle, Governor Stevens launched a program of enlarging in the scope of Patkanim's activities by enlisting head-hunters from the tribes on Squaxon Island, Fox Island, and the Chehalis and Cowlitz Rivers. His theory was one of deadly simplicity. If he could get Indians killing other Indians—and getting killed themselves in the process—the total number of aborigines would be reduced.

The doctor's objective was the prevention of just that.

How he did it is as reflective of his character as anything in this book.

The correspondence on this one is a little bit one-sided because only the doctor's letters are on file. What the governor was up to has to be pieced together from other sources. But you must keep in mind that Stevens was lethal in direct confrontations. When he was in the army, he went up against his own Chief of Staff during the presidential campaign in which Franklin Pierce was elected. He came within an ace of getting James Douglas fired as Governor of British Columbia, and only a miracle avoided his precipitation of the United States and Great Britain in a shooting war over the controversy about which country owned San Juan Island. He took on the Secretary of War without getting himself fired on the question of the Northern Pacific Railroad. And, before he was through, General Wool was recalled. He gave Company "A" in Seattle a dishonorable discharge . . . and threw the Chief Justice of the Territorial Supreme Court in jail and got away with it.

Doc Maynard, on the other hand, was a different matter.

He never let Stevens get a clear shot at him.

It started when Stevens ordered the doctor to produce a troop of Chief Seattle's braves to join with Patkanim and Captain Lander in an attack on the hostiles at the confluence of the Snohomish and Snoqualmie Rivers.

Here's how the doctor handled that one. He wrote that he had recruited 103 braves who were ready, willing and able to march immediately, adding, however, "I believe the enemy are aware of the movement in sending out the Snoqualmies (Patkanim's men) but have no evidence of it to lay before you. I have the names of 103 men under my charge which list I will send you in by next express. Please advise."

"Please advise," that's the way the doctor whipped him. By the time of the next express, of course, Captain Lander had marched on the enemy at the confluence of the two rivers and had learned, as the doctor had predicted, that the enemy was not there.

The governor then apparently told the doctor he needed some volunteers to beat the underbrush east of Seattle to search out hostiles. And Maynard replied with an inquiry. "Chief Seattle and his band," he wrote, "have heard that volunteers in the militia are being paid to stand guard in the settlement of Seattle and they wonder if they, too, shouldn't be paid for standing guard at Fort Kitsap. Please advise."

The governor then apparently pointed out that Patkanim and his men were making a small fortune killing hostile Indians at eighty dollars a head for chiefs and twenty dollars a head for other hostiles. Doc Maynard immediately upped the ante. He wrote the governor, "I have posted a bounty of $100 for the scalps of the Indians around the camp who have been trying to murder me," adding, "Am I justifiable in offering a bounty for the scalps of the enemy under these circumstances. Please advise."

Meanwhile, the list of the 103 willing warriors never appeared to be produced. The governor sent Captain Lander to Fort Kitsap demanding it. This time, a list was forthcoming. In it were the names of the Indians, but the bottom line of the resolution read: "We will fight whenever we have the consent of our Indian agent, the aforesaid D. S. Maynard."

Stevens blew his cork.

He demanded that the doctor produce the warriors. Doc blandly replied, "Some of my Indians have expressed impatience and are anxious to engage themselves in scouring the woods east of Seattle, but I do not feel safe in guaranteeing their fidelity. I do not wish to be understood as trusting these volunteers, yet I would be glad of further evidence of a fixed determination to render themselves profitable on such an undertaking. As soon as I am able to determine the number of volunteers at this point—I will report same to Captain Lander."

At this point, Stevens ordered the doctor to come to Olympia and laid down the law. The doctor carefully responded in writing after his return to Fort Kitsap.

"On my return from Olympia, I found them unwilling to risk themselves in the field exposed to the threat of the whites about Seattle. I conferred with Captain Lander about the subject and he expressed doubt about their safety at present. Please advise."

The problem was that all Indians looked the same in the sights of the settlers' guns . . . and everybody concerned—including Stevens— knew that the settlers would welcome the opportunity of shooting an Indian, any Indian, in the back. The doctor was not about to expose Chief Seattle and his men to such a risk.

And that's when the governor played his ace.

I wonder why it never has appeared in a Seattle history book.

What he did was call upon the talents of his wife's sewing circle in Olympia. The story appears in Stevens' biography: "The ladies of Olympia, under the head of Mrs. Stevens, made blue caps with red facings, with which these red allies were equipped to distinguish them from their hostile kindred."

Doc Maynard trumped the governor's ace.

He wrote that Chief Seattle and his men were hot to trot under the captainship of Lander, but added: "I submit to the governor their expressions and await instructions what course to pursue. I find, however, they are destitute of guns. They say they have been unfortunate in gambling (with the enemy infiltrators in camp) for some time back and have lost all their weapons . . .

"Please instruct me by return express."

Mrs. Stevens' sewing circle made baseball caps for eighty-two of Chief Patkanim's men . . . fifteen for Squaxon Island Indians . . . seventeen for Chehalis Indians . . . nine for Cowlitz Indians . . .

And none for Doc Maynard's Indians.

At that point, the governor threw in the sponge.

VII

"Having accomplished my purpose . . ."

Somewhere in the neighborhood of ninety-nine per cent of the Indian Rebellion in western Washington took place in King County. What with the county running from the summit of the Cascades to the Pacific Ocean, however, it wasn't hard for the folks to get in the fighting without stepping out of the boundary. At any rate, the last battle was fought on Connell's Prairie on the White River on March 10, and the doctor submitted his resignation as "Special Indian Agent" on March 28.

By that time, he had successfully thwarted Governor Stevens' enthusiastic efforts to exterminate the Indians. He had arranged for Secretary of State James Mason to go back to Washington, D. C. and obtain $300,000 to take care of those same Indians.

Our history books say that the doctor remained at Fort Kitsap for a year, when it actually was only four months. I guess the history books rely on the memory of Catherine Maynard to whom it *seemed* like a year. But it only was four months, and the doctor was a busy man indeed during those additional eight months . . .

Preparing for the peace.

At any rate, and for whatever reasons, the doctor's letter of resignation has lain moldering in the State Archives for 118 years now. And since it provides us with such a splendid example of how he behaved in that period of his life, it must be incorporated in our history if we are to know who we are.

The letter, written in Olympia, probably because the governor had refused to even talk to him, reads:

"Dear Sir: Not having had an opportunity and failing to make report (as I designed), to Lieut. Col. Crosby at Seattle, I therefore report to your honor at this place. There has been no material change among the Indians under my charge since my last report. Col. Crosby is evidently deeply engaged in so regulating the troops at Seattle as to render them useful that he has found little time to assaying matters of our Indians, or rather the troublesome whites. I understand he has called at my camp since I left. Of which he will undoubtedly report. I am requested by Chiefs Seattle and Now-Ohisy to report to you the conduct and disposition of, Stuttering George, Enoc-O-Lin and One-Eyed Tom, which I do in their own words, to wit:

"They are bad men and evil disposed toward the whites, have threatened to kill me (Ed. note, Maynard) and twice drawn their knives to do it but were stopped by Chill-Whale-Ton, are spending a part of their time with the Duwamish Indians who are urging them on to evil acts, are dangerous *Tamahnous workers* and are about to cause all them to sicken and die.

"They earnestly pray that these three be taken from among them and either closely confined or put to death. I believe this matter should be noticed and suggest that it may be attended to as soon as may be after the report of Col. Crosby upon the subject.

"To further acquaint yourself with the matters, I refer you to Col. Simmons and L. M. Collins.

"My Asst. at Fort Kitsap having ingraciated [sic] himself meritoriously among those under my charge together with the assurance of having effected the object of my appointment *(at all events the object I had in accepting it)* [Italics mine] together with the impairment of the health of my wife appear in justification while I ask at this time to be discharged from further duties and responsibilities under my appointment as Spl. Ind. Agt. [sic] and ask that Mr. Haley, my Asst. be appointed in my place.

"I await your decision upon this matter and most cheerfully I continue to submit myself.

Respectfully yours to serve
D. S. Maynard, Spl. Ind. Agt.
Seattle Division, W. T."

In matter of Chief Curley

The doctor's reference to the hostile Duwamish Indians needs some background information to be understood. There was almost as much antagonism between the members of the Duwamish tribe and Chief Seattle as between Chief Seattle and Chief Patkanim . . . even though Chief Seattle gets listed as the principal chief of the Duwamishes. It dates back to pre-Maynard days when Chief Seattle was chief of the Suquamish Indians. the fishing wasn't much over at Port Madison. And the Suquamish Indians liked to come to Elliott Bay and fish the mouth of the Duwamish. It was for this purpose the Suquamish Indians had a fishing camp at Maynard's Point.

The Duwamish Indians, under their chief, Curley, had their main camp at about where Renton is located today. Under the cover of darkness, it was their wont to swoop down on the Suquamishes, kill the men and take the women and children as slaves.

One night Chief Seattle, who owed most of his success to the grapevine he maintained, heard there was going to be a raid and had his men fell a tree across a bend in the Black River, which fed into the Duwamish. The first canoes of the raiding party hit the log and dumped their occupants into the water. Chief Seattle and his men, who were lying in ambush, jumped into the river and killed the raiders. The following canoeists beat a strategic retreat and were forced to submit to the rule of Seattle as their new chief.

Chief Curley wasn't even invited to be a speaker at the Point Elliott Treaty. His resentment, already smoldering, grew as he watched Doc Maynard unobtrusively appropriate what once had been his domain for the city of Seattle. The resentment flared into active resistance when the doctor tried to force him to live with Chief Seattle at Port Madison. The doctor, who was sensitive to the situation, provided the

Duwamish Indians with an eight-acre tract on Bainbridge Island, across the port from the main band of reservation Indians.

Most of the Duwamishes went peaceably to the new location.

But not Chief Curley.

In those days, Indian chiefs attached themselves to the white man they figured could do them the most good. Chief Seattle lucked out in making himself Doc Maynard's "dog robber." Patkanim attached himself to Arthur Denny. And Chief Curley performed the same service for Henry Yesler.

In other words, politics worked the same in those days as it does today.

Being under the aegis of Yesler, Curley was not required to place himself at Fort Kitsap. So he was loose in Seattle at the time the hostiles arrived from eastern Washington. He counselled them on the attack of the town, specifying that Henry Yesler's life was to be spared when the other townsfolk were killed. Curley made himself useful to the hostiles by supplying them with guns and ammunition and information about what strategy the whites had in mind.

When he placed the Indians at Fort Kitsap, the doctor had in mind protecting them from extermination. But when it came to Curley, the doctor sought to protect the whites. He wanted no part of Curley anywhere in the neighborhood.

The doctor, who didn't want Indians to get a foothold anywhere near his town, intervened and forced Curley and the remaining members of his tribe to move to Bainbridge Island.

In the summer of 1856, the whole thing came out in the open when Commander Samuel Swarthout of the *U. S. S. Massachusetts* and newly assigned to duty on Puget Sound, listened to Henry's side of the story and dispatched a letter to Governor Stevens. It's a letter which provides us with an insight into the rebellion on the part of some of the whites to the doctor's arbitrary rule.

It dates back, of course, to the fact that Henry always was in financial trouble . . . and was in even worse trouble after the doctor had removed the cheap help from the mill at the end of 1855.

Swarthout's letter, written on August 31, 1856, reads like this:

"A short time ago "Curley" and his tribe of Indians, were removed (agreeably to their wishes and with your approbation) from the "Seattle" reservation to a Reservation contiguous to "Alki Point" and nearly opposite this town, where they are living happy and contented, molesting no one and interfering with nobody; perfect harmony prevails among themselves and between them and the white inhabitants of this vicinity, and yet, I am informed, there are some evil disposed persons exerting all their influence to disturb the tranquil state of affairs by having these "Indians" removed again; the most prominent actor among these mischief makers is an individual named "Maynard" for whose character the most respectable people of this town entertain no respect. I am constrained to place reliance upon the report alluded to because I know that Captain Hewitt, who was appointed a Sub-Agent over "Curley's" tribe, by Col. Page, with your acquience [sic], has been lately removed by Col. Simmons, through the interference of this man "Maynard." I will submit to you, Sir, that if an effort is made to remove these "Indians" against their wishes, they will resist and it can be accomplished only by coersion [sic], in which case I will decline rendering any assistance toward so unjust a proceeding. I have, however, an abiding confidence in your sense of equity which, I flatter myself, will prevail over the influence of these designing men."

The Swarthout letter, instigated by Henry Yesler, was an attempt at rebellion on the part of the folks who chaffed some at Doc Maynard's arbitrary rule of the town.

At this stage of the game, the governor was a little leery about the unexpected things that happened to him when he crossed the mild-mannered doctor . . . and he let the order stand.

Doc Maynard retained control of his town.

The "education" of Arthur Denny

The most venerable building on the University of Washington campus is called "Denny Hall" in tribute to the fact that Arthur Denny donated the piece of prime land so Seattle could get the first university in the territory—and the thirty thousand bucks it cost to build it.

This generally is accepted as the most important single contribution that Arthur made to the town. In understanding it, you also must understand that he was the world's most notorious tightwad. That's what shocked the folks out of their socks. Further consideration must be given to the fact that his principal asset was keeping his ass set on downtown property.

What Denny gave was eight-and-a third acres of land where the Metropolitan Tract containing the Olympic Hotel, IBM Building, Stimson, Cobb and Rainier Tower are located today. How he happened to give it generally has been attributed in the Denny-dominated history books to his deep spirit of altruism.

But how it came about is quite another story.

Providing the town with an institution of higher learning was part of the doctor's grand plan for the city . . . and it was with this in mind that he set aside a thirty-acre tract of land at the top of a hill overlooking Elliott Bay for that purpose. This was a big deal for the Reverend Mr. Benjamin A. Close who, as you will recall, performed the ceremony uniting the doctor and Catherine in marriage. Close was new to the Methodist-Episcopal Conference, and it was a great feather in his cap to report at his first conference—as a new minister— that this generous gift had been made.

The Methodists were hot for this kind of thing at the time. They had a university at Salem . . . sold lots around it . . .

And made lots of money.

Normally, the doctor required that some kind of a building be constructed within three months on any land he sold or gave away. But because of his friendship with Mr. Close, he gave the church three years to do something—anything—with the property that would indicate it would be used for purposes of higher education.

Denny, being the leading layman of the church in Seattle, was made chairman of the board of trustees and instructed to see that the conditions of the conditional sale were fulfilled. Others on the board were Edmund Carr, Nelson Barnes, Philip Northeraft, R. H. Lansdale, George Hughbanks and William Morse.

Of course Denny was so busy trying to bring about Prohibition that he neglected to do anything about legally acquiring the property.

Now, under ordinary circumstances, the doctor would have let things go along until the church got around to taking advantage of his offer. But he was in big disrepute among his peers for thwarting their ambition to dispose of the Indian "problem" with bullets. But every time they went after the doctor, things boomeranged and somehow they found themselves kicking their own posterior extremities.

Catherine was different.

She didn't stay home and raise a brood of kids. She helped the doctor in his medical practice—which included treating paupers, Indians and even Negroes if they happened to be sick. She sank to a low ebb by accompanying the doctor to Fort Kitsap and helping him take care of the members of what officially had been determined as that "wretched race." (To understand the spirit of the times you have to keep in mind that the first session of the legislature had passed a law providing a fine of up to $500 against any minister who made so bold as to perform a marriage between any one hundred per cent white person and anybody who was more than twenty-five per cent any other color.)

But most significant of all was the matter of Catherine's premarital relationship with the doctor on the Oregon Trail. During the Indian rebellion, the Christers concocted the bright idea of entering into our history books that Catherine had planted the first dandelion in the Pacific Northwest. The other women planted sweetbriar, or roses, or pansies, or sweet William, or clover . . . but Catherine planted the dandelion.

The barbs they sank in her emotional hide were invisible, but they hurt just as much as any you could put in a blow gun.

And so it was that when the Maynards returned from Fort Kitsap Catherine was located by public opinion on the "other side of the railroad tracks" . . . twenty years before we even got a railroad.

Doc Maynard blew his cork.

And when he got mad, somebody got hurt.

His very first act upon his return was to notify the church that the terms of the conditional sale of the thirty acres had not been met and that he was cancelling the deal. No amount of pleading on the part of anybody would change his mind.

The deal was cancelled on April Fool's Day, 1856.

And the elders of the church would never let Denny live it down.

So it was that the Reverend Mr. Daniel H. Bagley came to Seattle five years later at the behest of Mr. Denny. Mr. Bagley had this great ambition to create a new university in the territory, but he had to have a bunch of land on which to put it. Knowing the background of the situation, Bagley leaned on "brother" Denny for the land. And it was with that in mind that the two men prowled Denny's donation claim for a suitable hunk of real estate. Denny tried to pawn off the side hill below the present site of the Pike Place Market.

But Bagley knew he had his parishioner on the spot and would sail for nothing but the best piece of view property on Arthur's donation claim. On April 16, 1861, Denny signed a quit claim deed to eight and one-third acres . . . land that was rounded out to 10 acres by Charlie Terry and Edward Lander—both of whom have halls named in their honor on the campus today.

Doc had his sweet revenge.

Today the University derives between four and five million dollars a year in leases on the property.

The post war real estate boom

While the eager beavers of the governor's extermination corps were out giving the Pacific Northwest a bad name by killing off berry-picking Indians and sending dried Indian scalps, ears, noses, and hands to friends who weren't able to be here and enjoy the fun, Doc Maynard set about the business of reconstruction.

On April 15, 1856, he sold Plummer and Chase seventeen town lots for an average of $130 apiece . . . a total of over $2,200. This was the highest price he had obtained for a single lot and nearly as much land as he had disposed of during the entire previous year. And later the same day, he nearly doubled that amount by selling Franklin Matthias, the housing contractor, two lots for $500.

The fifteenth was a big day for the doctor. By that time, it was becoming evident that it was unnecessary to dedicate the finest piece of property in town to a whorehouse. The men bent on whoring would happily take their business where this occupation was practiced—without regard to the view. And it was then that the doctor sold to Seymour Wetmore a piece of property next to the garbage dump that would in time become the basis of the town's red light district . . . which would arrive here along about the time we got the University.

On the seventeenth he sold W. D. Van Asselt and Jacob Maple a pair of lots real cheap, like for $100 and later an adjoining lot for another $100. These men already owned land in the Duwamish Valley, but they subsequently would bring to town the first furniture factory. On the eighteenth, he liberated $1,000 from J. R. Williamson. Williamson previously had made a small down payment on a couple of lots in the block where the Grand Central Arcade is today. Williamson had made a lot of money supplying both sides in the Indian Rebellion and paid the doctor $1,000 to get a warranty deed. David Maurer, who wasn't all that bright anyway but owed the doctor for keeping his head out of a noose after hanging an Indian, punked up $500 for the restaurant in the same block as Williamson . . . where Maurer already was operating the best restaurant in town.

On the twenty-ninth, the doctor collected $100 from Lewis Wyckoff, around whom has been based one of the favorite legends in our history.

The legend, of course, has been used to beat Doc Maynard's reputation to death on a post-mortem basis. The idea is to show how stupid the doctor was. He was trying to get a blacksmith shop going— just for no reason at all. There wasn't a horse within fifty miles of town. Along came Wyckoff, who was a blacksmith . . .

And the doctor gave him the land and the shop . . .

The whole works for twenty bucks.

What doesn't come into the legend was that the doctor had been advertising for a blacksmith for a year before he made the deal with Wyckoff . . . that he had to have a blacksmith shop if he wanted the town to grow. Henry Yesler's mill, for instance, was shut down as often as it was operating. He had to have parts made in Portland or San Francisco and remain closed down until the order could go south, the part made and returned . . . or send to Port Madison where G. A. Meigs had a blacksmith shop. In which instance Henry had to pay triple the going rate for the part.

In those days Seattle had four major rival towns—Olympia, Steilacoom, Port Madison and Alki. Port Madison had the blacksmith shop and because of it was outdistancing its rivals.

Wyckoff's foundry was to be the other metal industry that would start to make up Seattle's industrial district on Doc Maynard's claim. This, in turn, would make Seattle competitive with Port Madison as the Sound's other ship-building town.

So, he *needed* a Wyckoff.

At a time when the going rate for lots in any town on Puget Sound was between twenty-five and a hundred bucks, Wyckoff's first twenty bucks was the down payment. He made the next payment of $100 for the property on April 29.

That was the same day that Dan K. Howard, a Seabeck lumberman, was eased into a lot in the doctor's claim for a measly thirty dollars.

"Typical of the doctor giving away land!" the history books have said.

The truth is that Doc Maynard never disposed of his land just for the fun of making a sale. If he sold it cheap, he had a reason for selling it. And he had a good reason for selling a lot for thirty bucks to Daniel K. Howard of Seabeck. It isn't apparent on the warranty dead. And, unless it's linked up to the reason for the sale, it doesn't make sense.

Doc's reason for selling to Daniel K. Howard will shortly be made apparent.

In the meantime, in the month following his retirement as Special Indian Agent, the doctor sold $4,500 worth of real estate. If you discount the more or less forced sale to the Olympia consortium the previous year to finance Fort Kitsap, the sales in the month of April, 1856, constitute about half of all the income he had derived from real estate sales during the previous three years.

Postwar inflation had set into Seattle real estate six months before any of the other towns on Puget Sound had come to the realization that the war was over.

And, on May 1, he made one of the most significant sales in Seattle's financial history.

Dollars from Dexter Horton

Doc Maynard always was on the lookout for bright, hard-working young men in his embryo town.

One of the bright young men who impressed the doctor was Dexter Horton, who had an engaging personality and a capacity for work that had employers in Port Townsend and Port Gamble bidding for his services. In the spring of 1853, the twenty-eight-year-old Horton did a little work for William Bell at $2.50 a day. He was lured to Port Townsend with wages of ten dollars a day for a short-term job.

Then in September he fell into a bonanza.

Cyrus Walker, the big boss of Puget Mill, which was the local operation of the Pope & Talbot people, made Horton and his wife an offer that no sane couple could refuse. In those days Walker could hire a man to work an eleven-and-a-half-hour day for thirty dollars a month. He worked from six o'clock in the morning until six at night, with a half-hour off for lunch, six days a week. He could be sure of a roof over his head and good food.

The cook, on the other hand, arose at four o'clock in the morning to prepare breakfast for the mill hands and worked until eight o'clock at night.

What Walker did was hire Horton and the latter's wife, Hannah, as a team for the 60 men in the mill . . . with room and board thrown in.

Not for thirty bucks a month . . . or sixty bucks a month . . . or even a hundred and twenty bucks a month.

They got $130 a month!

When Dexter Horton went to work for Cyrus Walker, he was fifty dollars in debt to Thomas Mercer for financing his trip here. His clothing consisted of a pair of overalls, a hat and a pair of somebody else's cast-off boots. In the nine months they worked at Port Gamble, the pair paid off their debt, acquired suitable wardrobes and saved $1,100.

He was just the kind of a man we needed in Seattle. Henry Yesler offered the couple more money cooking for his crew of fourteen men along with shorter hours. The job required their services from one o'clock in the afternoon until midnight. So they went to work for Henry in June, 1855, and worked there until the Indian Rebellion shut down the mill five months later.

Then Horton went to work hunting Indians for Governor Stevens.

Five months later Doc Maynard talked Dexter Horton into going to work for himself. The doctor persuaded him there was need for another general store in town and sold him two lots on the northwest corner of First Avenue South and Washington Street. Horton acquired as a partner one David Phillips.

And on May 1, 1856, the doctor issued the two men a deed to the two lots for $100.

There was a small detail that had to be taken care of here. Three years earlier, on September 1, 1853, the doctor had sold the same land to one Miles Fowler. But Fowler hadn't constructed a building on the premises and the doctor repossessed the land.

The rest of the story is one you can find in any history book on Seattle. Horton & Phillips became an important general store. The two men warranted the trust of the people in town . . . started holding gold dust, etc., in the bottom of a coffee barrel in individual sacks.

Fourteen years later Horton opened the first private bank in Washington Territory at this location. In time his establishment acquired the name that it has today . . .

The Seattle First National Bank . . .

And the site?

It presently is occupied by a branch of the Seattle Trust & Savings Bank, which has become one of the most imaginative loan institutions in betting its bucks on the rebirth of Seattle's birthplace in Pioneer Square.

(In fairness to Seattle First, I am compelled to note that it has a colorful Pioneer Square branch at the site of the old South Blockhouse at Occidental Avenue South and South Main Street.)

The passing of the bar

Doc Maynard quit his job as sub-Indian agent on March 31, 1856 . . . just three weeks after the last battle with the Indians on the west side of the Cascades. On May 1, he made that significant sale of real estate to Horton & Phillips.

Then he disappeared from public view for the next six months.

Meanwhile, the volunteer army marched around killing stray Indians wherever they could find them. These included a Hudson's Bay Company employee plowing a field for the company . . . and a party of thirty-one Indian women, children and old men picking berries on the banks of the White River.

During this period Governor Stevens threw a Territorial Supreme Court justice in jail twice and handed dishonorable discharges to the members of Company "A" in Seattle for insubordination.

Then, on October 30, Adjutant General James Tilton disbanded the Volunteers of Washington Territory, noting in the process that "the most cordial thanks of the commander-in-chief are given for the signal gallantry, resolute endurance and excellent discipline they have maintained during the six months' arduous, faithful and efficient service. The people of Washington Territory will know how to honor for all time the devoted and fearless men who have maintained the foothold of civilization upon the remote frontier."

They knew what to do all right.

They elected Stevens to Congress.

Why?

That six months had cost the federal government nearly a million dollars in scrip to pay for the wages, supplies and ammunition of the volunteer army. A century later, historians Charles M. Gates and Dorothy O. Johansen would comment that the army expenditures and circulation of scrip with which the volunteers were paid was "advantageous to farmers and merchants alike . . . This was not an insignificant sum in a frontier economy."

The doctor was among those who derived the greatest benefit. Downtown Seattle had been cleared of stumps, at a cost of $175 an acre. At federal expense the blocks had been surveyed, the streets laid out, and ditched . . . a leveling process that had enhanced his real estate sales in April and May. Of the fifty buildings in town, forty-five were located on his town plat.

But the doctor was off on another tangent at the time.

The doctor could look with pride on his accomplishments to that date. In the first place, Alki had gone out of business at the time and young Charlie Terry was evidencing great interest in becoming a part of Seattle, an interest which the doctor looked upon with great favor. Charlie was the liveliest young man on Elliott Bay. He already had bought a sizeable chunk of land from Carson Boren and saw eye to eye with the doctor on what was needed for the construction of a city.

Doc Maynard was nearing retirement age and, as the biggest land-owner on Elliott Bay, looked to the future for a comfortable living in real estate sales. However, there was a missing ingredient in town. His own lawyer, George McConaha, had drowned in a canoeing accident off Vashon Island two years earlier and the town was without a member of the legal profession.

So, while the rest of the male population was marching around the territory and quarreling among themselves, the doctor applied himself to the studies necessary for admission to the bar in Washington Territory. And, at the October session of the District Circuit Court in Madam Damnable's establishment, his efforts bore fruit. The court record reads:

"Elwood Evans, Henry R. Crosbie, and William H. Wallace testified that having examined the qualifications of David S. Maynard for his qualifications for admission to the bar as an attorney and counsellor, and having reported favorably, Maynard was, by order of the court (Judge Chenoweth) admitted to practice as an attorney-at-law and solicitor in chancery in all courts of the Territory."

Elwood Evans, who originally had served as secretary to the governor, got a choice lot in the heart of the central business district in Seattle for a mere fifty bucks out of the deal.

Doc believed in making his land work for him.

Half a loaf is better than one

I have mentioned on more than one occasion that Arthur Denny's principal objective in life—aside from making money—was the creation of a "dry" town. He introduced Prohibitory laws in the legislature in 1854 and 1855. On the second occasion, the rest of the territory voted "Wet," but King County voted "Dry," primarily because the big mill towns on the west side of the Sound were operated by New England prohibitionists like Walker and G. A. Meigs. (You will recall that at that time, King County extended from the summit of the Cascades to the Pacific Ocean.)

Doc Maynard had no intention of permitting his county to be dry, but the Indian Rebellion intervened in 1856 and he was too busy to do anything about it. And so it was that after he had passed the bar examination, he could turn his attention to the little matter of thwarting Denny again.

While the latter was killing Indians, Doc got busy.

He had to get rid of that dumb ban on the sale of alcoholic beverages which had been imposed in the county by the big Denny Prohibition Project.

The Doctor selected as his vehicle one Timothy D. Hinckley.

Mr. Hinckley arrived in the area in 1853 and took up a donation claim on Lake Washington. He was one of Doc Maynard's fellow

Democrats and the two men became friends at the regular meetings of St. John's Lodge of the Masons, which the doctor created. Hinckley found that farming wasn't that hot and after the Indian War got a job as engineer for George A. Meigs at Port Madison. The record doesn't show whether Hinckley was for or against booze . . . just that he wanted a good hefty license of $500 a year on the people who sold the stuff. He also bought a lot of property and subsequently would develop the Hinckley Block at Third and Columbia, where the Seattle Chamber of Commerce is today.

Having persuaded Hinckley that his investment in town lots would pay bigger dividends if Seattle was a wet rather than a dry town, and when the legislature convened in December, 1856, they went to work.

With the following results:

On January 9, 1857, Hinckley presented a petition as resident of King County, praying that the west half of King County be set off in a new county to be named "Madison." The county boundary was to commence in the main channel of Colvo's passage and go along the old boundary of King County to Case's inlet, thence westerly to the head of Hood's canal and then following the main channel of the canal to Admiralty Inlet; thence following the main ship channel of said inlet to its junction with Colvo's passage; thence following the main channel of said passage to the point of beginning.

The bill became law on January 16, 1857.

King County was cut in half.

It had taken exactly one week.

King County was "wet" again.

A face that only a father could love

You read the average description of the town of Seattle at the end of the Indian Rebellion and you get a pretty unprepossessing picture. For one thing, there were no streets north of Yesler Way, which was the northern boundary of Doc Maynard's claim. There were, however, seven ravines, one of them as deep as a seven-story building, lying

between the doctor's claim and what we know of today as Belltown, about a mile north . . . all along what we know of today as the downtown business district. Today, First through Fourth Avenues provide us with a gradual upward slope of some twelve blocks. But, if you looked under the streets, you'd find either fill or trestles. You also would find a labyrinth of drainage pipes.

If they ever got clogged up, downtown Seattle would slide into Elliott Bay.

It was twenty years before the city council took the bit in its teeth and ran streets through rather than around stumps.

In Doc Maynard's time, there were two ways of getting from Maynardtown to Belltown. You took a boat from the level land of Maynardtown across a crescent-shaped bay to Belltown, or you drove along what was called the "Beach Road." The Beach Road failed to function at high tide. Maynardtown was at sea level. Belltown was about 175 feet above the beach. So, you had to be prepared to climb.

What there was of Seattle was Maynardtown.

An eight-acre pimple at the northeast end of 1,500 acres of tideflats, but the doctor saw beyond the mud.

His vision encompassed trade with China . . . with Seattle as the major U. S. port for that trade . . . and in this connection it is of interest to note some comments by William Bunge who was employed by the State of Washington to do an economic study of the Puget Sound Region a century later. Bunge noted that shipping costs over oceans are one-tenth those of land, adding: "In terms of economic distance, Seattle is closer to Tokyo than it is to Chicago . . . within a few years these Oriental economies can mean to the West Coast what the European economies mean to the East Coast . . . China's annual economic growth is an astronomical twenty -three percent."

But Bunge has an even more interesting commentary to make on the population movement within the Puget Sound Region.

He points out that for about a century, the trend of migration has been from the rural to the metropolis. The general store which once served the hamlet now has moved to the middle sized communities. "The driving force is the change of transportation which shrinks the cost and time to cover the longer distances . . . The rural hamlet depended for life on the inconvenience of travel. Now the farmer's wife can reach downtown Seattle department stores easier than she could formerly hitch up the team and is obviously going to frequent the Seattle stores with their wider variety and special services. In a study of Marysville Washington (1960 before the advent of Interstate 5) it was found that the improvement of U. S. Highway 99 caused a loss of 83 percent of the higher functions . . . doctors, dentists, entertainment, etc . . ."

Bunge's study clarifies the cutting edge of the town that Doc Maynard invented when it is placed in juxtaposition with a similar analysis resulting from observations made by Bagley a century earlier.

Bagley points out that at the end of the conflict with the Indians there were thirty-nine ships of one kind or another functioning on Puget Sound. Seattle was located at the geographic center of the Sound. It had the best harbor, the best port facilities. It became the principal port of call for every vessel.

Writing in 1916, Bagley sums it up like this: "Port Blakely, Port Orchard and Port Madison all built large vessels in the early days. These points across the Sound were like suburbs of Seattle, for all of them did their shopping and marketing here. Like the street cars of today, which bundle the suburbanites off to the city markets every Saturday evening and return them to their homes in the outlying districts, loaded down with provisions for the week, the water craft of the pioneer days were the public service vehicles, which brought the shoppers to the Seattle market."

Bagley went on to say that in "1857 King was the banner county of Puget Sound."

He continued with: "Large mills were in operation at Seabeck, Port Gamble, Appletree Cove, Port Madison, Port Orchard, Alki and Seattle. In 1857, when Kitsap County was taken away from King, all but the latter two were taken away but their trade and friendly intercourse remained as before. This was particularly true of Port Madison and Port Orchard and later of Port Blakeley.

"The company store in each milling town supplied the standard foodstuffs and the clothing for the men but the women came to the little town in King County for the finer articles of women's and children's apparel.

"Gradually men and families came to Seattle for better school facilities, social opportunities and business investments.

"From Seabeck came Capt. J. R. Williamson who put up a large mill across the bay at West Seattle, and Marshall and Blinn who made a large fortune at Seabeck invested largely in Seattle town lots and King County timber lands. Also, from there came Daniel K. Howard to make considerable investments.

"From Port Gamble came John Collins, John S. Condon, Stephen Hovey, Hiram Burnett, M. S. Drew and Cyrus Walker. All these made large investments in Seattle and King County, but small in comparison with those of Pope and Talbot, who were the Port Gamble Milling Company. Their holdings were large and today (1929) are almost beyond estimate in value, including many buildings scattered about Seattle. (In 1857 when all of this began, Cyrus Walker, for all practical purposes, *was* the Pope and Talbot company on Puget Sound.)

"From Port Madison came John Webster, Capt. J. W. Edwards, Capt. John Cosgrove, Andrew B. Young, P. J. Primorose, William A. Jennings and others although A. J. Meigs, the founder of Port Madison contributed little toward the early growth of Seattle and King County, nearly all the wages of its employees were spent here. Meigs brought with him down-east views regarding temperance and morality and made of Port Madison a 'closed town.' He established a large community hall and reading rooms, but the rough element of the logging camps and mills and deserting sailors preferred to come to Seattle to spend Saturday evenings and Sundays and holidays, of course."

Where they spent their time, of course, was at Madam Damnable's, Charlie Plummer's pool hall and what Bagley dismisses as the "usual assortment of saloons."

During the day, however, they found the widest variety of goods at Horton & Phillips, Plummer & Hinds, J. R. Williamson or Bettman Brothers, nee Charlie Terry's. There usually was one general store in the little hamlets on the Sound.

There were four sets of aggressive merchants in Seattle. The circuit court still functioned at Madam Damnable's . . . And real estate . . . Doc Maynard was the *only* real estate man in town. He also was the only doctor . . . the only lawyer.

The nucleus for the major city in the Pacific Northwest had been established. All it had to do was divide and grow.

The heir apparent

Doc Maynard lifted his nose from his lawbooks during the summer of 1856 to make the arrangements for Seattle's first spectacular wedding. What he did was set it up for Charlie Terry to be married by Chief Justice Lander in Patkanim's canoe . . . with Chief Seattle along in the canoe as Charlie's "best man." The event occurred in Fort Kitsap's front yard in the middle of Port Madison, with a couple thousand delighted Indians watching the show from shore.

It was the Doctor's way of telling the world at large and the Indians in particular that he had selected Charlie as his heir apparent in the construction of his town.

The event took place on July 13, 1856.

Charlie was married to Mary Jane Russell, daughter of King County's first sheriff, and those of you who have read *Sons of the Profits* will know that he was the only man in town besides Doc Maynard who had a sense of humor. It was at his house at Alki Point that David E. Blaine, Seattle's first minister-in-residence, gave his first sermon— even before taking up his residency here. Charlie took up a collection afterwards with the famous quote, "I don't know much about Methodism, but I sure know about this." Later, when Mary Jane heckled him for some chamber pots, he sent a wagon around to every store in town and had a whole wagon load dumped on the family front porch.

Charlie, who gets even more of a kiss-off than the doctor in Seattle's early history books, disenchanted the Dennys by stealing Alki Point from under their noses before the doctor arrived on the scene. He committed the further heresy of selling liquor in his store.

Charlie was an admirer and emulator of Doc Maynard—the sincerest form of flattery. Twenty-two years the doctor's junior, he didn't have the slightest idea of how to put a town together. When he first established his town, he named it New York after his native state. But when he saw the doctor's success in naming his town, Seattle, Charlie changed the name of his town to Alki.

When the doctor platted a town, Charlie platted a town. When the doctor got Henry Yesler to establish a sawmill in town, Charlie got William Renton to build a sawmill at Alki. When the doctor advertised his town in the *Olympia Columbian,* Charlie advertised in the *Olympia Columbian.*

The only basic difference between the two men was that while Doc Maynard couldn't care less about making a buck, Charlie had a deep interest in the pursuit of the dollar. The doctor, of course, had no way of knowing that he would outlive his pupil, who died at the age of thirty-seven in 1867 . . . but not before he had acquired a huge amount of land in town and served as the chairman of the first board of town trustees.

Doc Maynard had been on hand to watch Cleveland and Ohio City behave like the Gingham Dog and the Calico Cat, eating one another up . . . with the exception that in Ohio, real human blood was shed. Maynard did not believe there was room for two towns on Elliott Bay, but Charlie was stubborn, which the doctor had to admire. But it wasn't Maynard who persuaded Charlie to come to Seattle. It was the lack of protection from the north wind, which caused Renton to move his mill to Port Orchard a few months after he got it started. And it was a lack of a sufficient supply of running water.

But the doctor wooed Charlie from the beginning.

On June 6, 1855, for instance, he sold Charlie four lots in Block Eleven for $150. This was Charlie's first tentative investment in Seattle. The site later was occupied by Lou Graham's fancy whorehouse. Today, one of the lots is occupied by the unique park which United Parcel Service, which got its start at the spot, has given to the city of Seattle.

The following year, Charlie bought out Bettman, and then on July 11, 1857, the doctor and Charlie effected the big exchange which has made all of the history books . . . in a way that has been designed to make Doc Maynard look like the village idiot. What the doctor did was swap Charlie 260 acres in the vicinity of downtown Seattle for Charlie's donation claim of 320 acres at Alki Point.

Some cogent details have, naturally, been left out.

The property which the doctor swapped with Charlie was outside the platted part of town. It ran from Dearborn Street south to Holgate Street, and from the waterfront to Thirteenth Avenue South. If you take the time to look at a map, you quickly will learn that half of this property was under water at high tide . . . and the other half of it was on the side of Beacon Hill.

What Charlie bought the property for was a nice piece of fertile land along the Duwamish where he could establish an onion farm. And he had good reason. Onions were selling for $4.58 a pound at the time . . . three times what Charlie and Judge Lander paid per acre for their purchase of their acreage from Carson Boren.

So that was the swap between the two men.

One other detail has been left out.

The doctor sold Charlie 55 lots in the platted part of his claim for $3,300 . . .

Which surpassed the sale to the Olympia consortium by $800 . . . and became the biggest real estate transaction in any town on Puget Sound to that date.

Doc Maynard acquired a $5,000 mansion at Alki Point in the bargain. To that date, including the sale of the huge acreage in the unplatted part of town to Charlie, the doctor had disposed of 320 acres of land. Because he and Catherine had arrived earlier than anyone else, they had started with 640 acres. So they still owned 320 acres . . .

Which was what all of the other couples had started with in the first place.

There always has been a big hoorah about the real estate exchanged between the doctor and Charlie Terry. The way it goes is that the doctor exchanged downtown property that was "worth millions" for worthless property at Alki Point. The doctor got $3,300 for his property—seven months after the Indian Rebellion was history and real estate values on the Sound were as close to zero as they ever got.

So what about the millions that Charlie realized on the deal?

Millions?

Not quite.

Charlie's estate was probated on July 29, 1875—when Seattle already had become the major town on the Sound.

Charlie's executors had sold the land for $18,736.

Shell-a-bration

There must have been other occasions, but Chief Seattle's ineptitude only appears on the record three times. The first, of course, was on Whidbey Island in the presence of every Indian on Puget Sound when he opened his big mouth and got himself in a pickle with Chief Patkanim. The second big one came when he made the "Great Speech" with his left hand on Stevens' head. Finally, there was the matter of the big social gathering on Puget Sound.

It was the fore-runner of the Seattle Seafair Celebration . . .

Only this one was to be the world's biggest clambake.

Chief Seattle and the members of his tribe undertook the responsibility of providing the clams.

Charlie, who was deep in the mosquito fleet business himself as captain of the steamer *Fairy*, which was engaged, among other things, in hauling coal barges down the Black and Duwamish Rivers and in delivering his crops of onions to market, worked out a trans-portation deal with Captain John Scranton.

This was a big splash.

Scranton was captain of the *Julia*, originally named *Julia Barclay* by one of her California owners. But she was the first steamer built on Puget Sound, and the pride of every person on the Sound. She was a sleek, fast, 145 foot sternwheeler and everybody on the Sound wanted a chance to ride her. Obtaining her services for the first big celebration on Puget Sound was the first of many similar coups that has made Seattle the major city.

Charlie Terry's brand new mansion on the onion farm near the present site of Georgetown, was the headquarters for the visiting dignitaries. There was to be a big ball in the Snoqualmie Hall that night and it was here that the ladies were to change their clothes . . .

And see Charlie's fancy new home.

What Charlie needed if he was to be sure that the ladies could be hauled up the Duwamish without getting stuck on a sandbar someplace was a high tide . . . and he was just the kind of a guy to think of that kind of thing. Chief Seattle, on the other hand, was the kind of a guy who would say to Doc Maynard, "yessir, boss. Anything you say, boss!" whether he intended to or could do what he promised or not. And in this instance the hopes of the chief were incompatible with the needs of Charlie Terry.

"In order to give zest to the entertainment," the advertisements read, "Dr. Maynard, hyas tyee of the Seattle tribe of Indians, will superintend the grand clambake. The clams and other shellfish will be cooked on heated stones in the ancient style of the aborigines of our territory."

The town put its best foot forward. Madam Damnable's normal operation may even have been suspended for the occasion. It, along with Charles Plummer's and Charlie Terry's mansions would be the first opportunity for most of the folks on the Sound to see real lath-and-plaster buildings . . . together with the new-fangled green blinds that you pulled right down in case the sun was shining, or if you didn't want any Indians peeking in the windows at night. Other novelties for a number of the folks were the glass-paned windows, polished floors . . . and a magnificent fireplace in every room.

Seattle had cornered the mansions on Puget Sound.

Two hundred people—everybody on Puget Sound who could borrow, beg or steal three bucks for the tickets and could get himself loaded on board the *Julia* came.

And Seattle set out to show them that this was the biggest, finest and most important town on the Sound.

To begin with, we had the biggest population. There were 123 grown men . . . twenty-five women . . . thirty-four children.

One-hundred-and-eighty-two white people.

Wow!

And every one of them with his best foot forward. There was Yesler & Denny's sawmill, kind of dinky alongside of some of the big mills on the Sound, but shined up fit to kill.

Outside of the huge mansions, center attractions were Horton & Phillips, Williamson & Greenfield, Plummer & Hinds and Charlie Terry's stores. The stores contained a myriad of household supplies, outfits for logging camps, carpenters' tools, agricultural instruments, ships' stores, flour and feed, coal, coal oil and tobacco . . .

And booze.

You couldn't buy booze at Steilacoom or Port Madison, or Port Orchard or Port Gamble or Port Ludlow—the other big towns on the Sound. But in Seattle you could get every potable beverage in the books.

L. C. Harmon had the hotel you could write home to mother about. David Maurer, Manuel Lopez and S. B. Simon had the restaurants. A whole bunch of people had saloons, but those didn't get mentioned in lists of enterprises in Seattle at the time. The only one which slid through the automatic censorship was Plummer's and that only made it because he was the first man in King County to punk up the $500 necessary for a liquor license.

Doc Maynard had gone out of the grocery business, but the shingle on his door informed the folks that they could get either legal or medical services. And he was immediately adjacent to the mail dock operated by postmaster Plummer.

At that point Doc Maynard had a corner on both the medical and legal services in town. Dr. Smith, lived way out at Salmon Bay. There was another man, Josiah Settle who advertised himself as a doctor, but the local historians commented that he was "more of a nurse than a doctor." In listing the other lawyer in town, Jasper W. Johnson, the commentary was, "he had little professional employment excepting conveyances and notarial work."

Thomas Mercer, L. V. Wyckoff and Hillory Butler were the teamsters who handled the merchandize from the docks, "the cordwood down the hill and the lumber about the village. Mercer and Wyckoff also had good farms that occupied their spare time." Wyckoff, of course, also had the blacksmith shop.

Mercer also had another sideline. He had invented a patent medicine that was liberally-laced with opium and advertised as curing everything from falling of the womb to cancer.

Charles H. Gorton and Harvey L. Pike were the housepainters . . . and Pike was an adept sign-painter. Henry Atkins, William H. Surber and William Cheney dominated the pile-driving business on the Sound and had their headquarters in Seattle. Besides Charlie Terry, there were Samuel D. Libby, H. H. Hyde, John S. Hill and his brother, David, in the steamboating business.

Having served his purpose in creating the new county, T. D. Hinckley had moved back to town. George Frye was Yesler's other partner and head sawyer in the mill. And then there was Nils Jacob Ohm, mentioned so prominently in *Sons of the Profits* as the chief sawdust dumper of the Yesler-Denny mill.

John Pike, Franklin Matthias, Thomas S. Russell, Harry Hitchcock and Solon B. Abbott were the carpenters and housebuilders . . . with Matthias in his cabinet shop next door to Plummer's store by far the biggest. M. D. Woodin and his son did all of the tannery business on the Sound. Jacob Wibbens ran Charlie Terry's bakery and cracker factory.

Others in the act were: L. B. Andrews, gunsmith; Hugh McAleer, plumber and tinsmith; William W. White, blacksmith; John Welch, tailor.

Plummer had a brick factory and commercial carriage house in addition to his other activities . . . and most of the 664 barrels of salmon that were shipped out of Puget Sound were processed in barrels that had been made in Seattle. Coal from Renton, while not big, produced several hundred tons a year. It was a good quality and came down the Duwamish in scows along with the prolific supply of gorgeous fruits and vegetables which were on display in the stores to impress the visiting folk.

All of the businesses were in the Central Business District, which was on Doc Maynard's claim in an area that had come to be known as "Maynardtown." Only half of Yesler's mill was on Doc Maynard's original claim. The other half was on Carson Boren's.

The Doctor was so busy with his other preparations he didn't pay attention to Chief Seattle's promise to produce the necessary shellfish. A computer analysis providently provided to me by Ron Westley of the State Department of Fisheries and Eugene Collias of the University of Washington's School of Oceanography reveals what the chief's problem was. Chief Seattle, who had been digging clams around Puget Sound for the previous fifty years should have known what the computer of today revealed. He was faced with what today are termed "climbing tides" beginning on July 18. On July 17, there was a .1-foot tide. The next day there was a 1.1-foot tide. And that was really his last chance to dig enough clams for 200 people.

Doc Maynard got madder at Chief Seattle over those damned clams than he had for any of the dumb things his whipping boy had done in the previous seven years . . .

They had this big clambake . . . And there were no clams.

Mine the miners

Two months and ten days after the doctor informally turned the reins of his town over to Charlie Terry, Dr. William F. Tolmie of the Hudson's Bay Company inserted the first of a series of small classified advertising notices in the Olympia Pioneer and Democrat. The ad warned all miners and prospectors to keep out of the Fraser River district unless they were prepared to "pay a fee of twenty-two shillings a month to the British Crown."

Considering the amount and quality of the "Come to Canada" advertising that British Columbia inserts in the local news media today, it was quite a modest approach. And the average tourist must be prepared to spend considerably more than twenty-two shillings a month to the British Crown . . . or is it the the B. C. Government?

And eighty percent of the American tourists who venture into the big Canadian Province north of Seattle do so through the Seattle Gateway.

It all started on December 28, 1858, through that small notice in the *Olympia Pioneer and Democrat . . .*

And we've collected our fair share of the cumshaw since . . .

Which proves it pays to advertise.

Dr. Tolmie was operating on instructions from James Douglas, on behalf of the British Crown. In December of 1857 Douglas wrote the British Foreign Office saying, "The auriferous character of the country is becoming more extensively developed, through the exertions of the native Indian tribes, who have tasted the sweets of goldfinding, and are devoting much of their time and attention to that pursuit. The reported wealth of the mines is causing much excitement among the population of the United States territories of Washington and Oregon, and I have no doubt that a great number of people from those territories will be attracted thither, with the return of fine weather this spring."

And a good thing the Bay Company had been making out of the goldfinding of the Indians. With the aborigines the company pegged the price of gold at the price of lead.

Governor Douglas had a neat plan for enriching the monopoly which he had served so long and so well. He would franchise the Pacific Mail Steamship Company to haul prospectors up the river and collect two bucks a head for Hudson's Bay in the process. But the Foreign Office, aware that Douglas was attempting to expand the operation of his company, informed him that he only had a license to deal with Indians . . . and on Vancouver Island. The British Government itself, would take care of collecting money from the prospectors. So the new province of British Columbia was created. Great Britain liked his approach to things so much that it offered him governorship of the new province . . . and he liked the idea so well that he accepted it.

In the meantime, the weekly ads continued.

In March, 1858, Charles Prosch, who had established the *Puget Sound Herald* in Steilacoom, informed his readers that miners on the Fraser were reaping twenty-five to fifty dollars a day in gold . . . and that squaws were hauling in ten to twelve dollars a day. The implication was that if squaws could do it, anybody could. Copies of the Herald were sent to San Francisco where at first they sold for a buck apiece . . . and then five bucks apiece . . . and then galley proofs sold for five bucks apiece.

On April 25, 1858, the *San Francisco Herald* picked up the cry, stating that the "Fraser River excitement" in the Atlantic states equalled that which had stimulated the "rush" to California nearly a decade earlier.

And the Fraser River goldrush was on.

By mid-May, steamers from California were landing hundreds of passengers in the Pacific Northwest. On May 20, the steamer *Panama* landed 500 prospectors in Bellingham Bay. A month later, 1,800 were landed at the same place within three days, and during the same period 1,000 were landed in Victoria. By July 1, Bellingham Bay was a town with eleven general stores, two butcher shops, three bakeries and two restaurants.

The population was considerably larger than Seattle's 182.

Bellingham Bay had 10,000 people.

Among them was Ezra Meeker of the Puyallup valley who had figured out a way of hauling cows there on a scow and selling milk at a dollar a quart. In his memoirs on the subject, Meeker leaves us with a priceless piece of Seattle's heritage. There were, of course, the usual camp followers attendant to a gold rush. Referring to the many boats in the bay, Meeker writes: "There were but a few women in this crowd, but ashore, quite too many, a large majority of whom (those on the ground will remember), were too much like their arch representative, 'Old Mother Damnable,' well and truly named. But I draw the veil."

Within the next six months, 100,000 prospectors "rushed" the Fraser . . . through Victoria . . . through Bellingham Bay . . . up the Columbia . . . over Naches Pass and over Snoqualmie Pass.

A lot of them starved to death.

The mills on Puget Sound closed as their crews joined the rush. Ships in the bays were abandoned by their crews. Soldiers at Fort Steilacoom deserted. The population of Seattle emptied out like water in an overturned bucket.

"Let's go!" Charlie Terry said.

Doc Maynard had been through a gold rush before and had failed to be stampeded. He pointed to a small notice that had been issued by a beleaguered Canadian government. Thousands of the prospectors were starving to death. The government listed the supplies that were needed for ten men for six months. The bill came to $1,800.

"Mine the miners, not the mines," Doc Maynard counselled.

The potential take for outfitting miners was $18,000,000.

All we had do was get our fair share.

The following year, Seattle businessmen lobbied through the

legislature a bill calling for the construction of a road from our town to Bellingham Bay. Charlie Terry, Dexter Horton, Charles Plummer and Joseph Williamson outfitted pack trains that went over Snoqualmie Pass to the diggings.

Within six months, the population on Bellingham Bay would drop from 10,000 to ten. But during the next ten years, 250,000 miners would produce about $50,000,000 in gold from what came to be known as the "Golden Caribou."

Thomas Prosch would write later that: "Seattle shared in the excitements, and her people received their full share of the financial benefits resulting therefrom, the place being locally prominent as an outfitting point."

The Fraser River was the first of Seattle's important gold rushes.

The second came in 1864, when the miners rushed to Boise, Idaho.

The following year there were reports of gold strikes on the upper Columbia and in the Coeur d'Alene mountains. In 1878, there was a minor rush to diggings on the Sultan River. A year later came news that gold had been found on the Skagit. By that time, Seattle merchants had developed a keen sense of the importance of gold rushes to our economy and subscribed a sum to finance the construction of a trail to Ruby Creek.

Part of that trail was so awful we gave the name Diablo Canyon to that section . . . and years later we would build Diablo Dam at that location. It may have been the "Devil" to travel or later build a dam on. But in 1880, four hundred miners outfitted themselves in our town. We thoughtfully kept track of how much they spent.

It came to $50,000.

Our merchants were impressed.

We were even more impressed when returning miners initiated one of Seattle's early real estate booms.

The final and most important gold rush came in 1898.

Writing about this one, J. Willis Sayre says: "It is virtually impossible to overestimate the value, to Seattle, of the sixth and last gold rush . . . Seattle, in common with the rest of the United States, had suffered severely from the hard times which began in 1893 and continued for several years.

"There was a saying, in 1895, that the location of every twenty-dollar gold piece in Seattle was known. Leading merchants carried their lunches with them to their stores to save money.

"Then the gold rush suddenly and literally began pouring millions of dollars into this city. Outfitting stores, specializing in the needs of gold seekers, centered the trade here. Working night and day, they struggled to keep up with their orders; the sidewalks were piled with goods awaiting shipment north. The town was jammed with incoming hosts and money was spent upon a scale never known here."

Wise old Doc Maynard said, "Mine the miners."

Now, let's see . . .

What was that about an Alaska pipeline?

The tale of Asemath Ann

There have been various versions of the tale of Asemath Ann in Seattle history, and finally an enterprising reporter for the *Chehalis Bee Nugget* tried a drastic new approach to the legend and published it on August 28, 1931.

What he did was get it from the mouth of the lady, herself.

The story is prefaced by the fact that on December 15, 1863, Dr. Maynard and Catherine opened Seattle's first hospital on First Avenue South between South Main and South Jackson Street. There is some disagreement among authorities on where the doctor and Catherine were living at the time. Some say that they were living in the hospital. Asemath Ann's story reveals they were living in a far more pretentious place. Knowing the doctor, I'm inclined to agree. When he was at Alki Point, which he was for a time, he lived in what would be the equivalent of a $50,000 mansion constructed at current pre-inflation prices. The doctor always succeeded in living high on the hog.

One of the employees in the doctor's hospital was eighteen-year-old Christopher Columbus Simmons, the Simmons' fifth child. Prior to his arrival in Seattle, Chris wooed and won the heart of Asemath Ann Kennedy, daughter of Franklin Kennedy, the first probate judge in Mason County.

What Chris and Asemath Ann wanted to do was get married, but both families frowned on the idea. Chris was banished to Seattle and Asemath Ann was trundled off to school in Steilacoom. Chris pined for his loved one and one night in the summer of 1864, Chris "borrowed" a rowboat from the doctor and headed for Steilacoom. Asemath Ann takes up the story from there:

"Chris stole me. Just think! I was only thirteen. He just carried me off, but I didn't make much fuss about going. And he got my brother-in-law and a brother of mine to go along to Seattle. They did most of the rowing. Chris and I were in the stern of the canoe. We rowed all night and all day to Seattle. Uncle and Aunt Maynard took us into their big new home. And gave us the wedding. Here's a picture of the house and the corner room upstairs there was Auntie's. That's the room we were married in. Rev. Daniel Bagley married us. It was the 23rd of August, 1864—almost 67 years ago. Quickly uncle took a slip of paper, wrote the number '18' on it. He made me take off my shoe and put the number in the heel of it. He says to me, 'you look so young he will likely ask you how old you are and you must say right off, 'I'm over 18.'"

Well, it worked.

They were married.

Asemath Ann continued with: "Father and mother were mad as a wet hen and so were Chris' folks, but they got over it."

So they were married in the upstairs corner room of the Maynard Mansion. One of two mansions in town at the time. The other belonged to Charles Plummer.

The money machine

Ten years ago, with information collected to that point, I wrote in *Sons of the Profits* that it was the story of how the fellas who built

Seattle made their money. Adding, "If they could have made more money by *not* building a city, then that is what they would have done."

Further research has revealed that Doc Maynard invented a money-making machine.

All they had to do was crank it.

Research on this book began with the Pioneer National Title Company records dating back to the time when the land was owned by the United States Government. I then found who got what donation claims . . . to whom they sold it . . . and what the people who bought it did with it. Subsequent research took me back even further than the U. S. Government ownership to when the land belonged to the Indians . . . and how Doc Maynard got the land, on which Seattle was built, into his hands. It was a relatively simple matter to look through the archives and find out how he used it to invent the city.

The whole thing was a game with Doc. He was like a kid with a new toy. According to actuarial statistics, he should have been long gone, and here he was with eighteen years of experience in city building in Cleveland and a shot at the greatest project of his life. He was Pygmalion to our Galatea. He was solely responsible for putting her together and breathing life into her.

His was the creative genius that made our city. He ran her, as Arthur Denny complained in his book as though he thought he "not only was monarch of all he surveyed, but what Boren and I surveyed as well."

Oh, what a Freudian slip that was!

Except for one major detail, when Denny screwed up our street system on his land and in defiance of the doctor, Maynard ruled the destiny of his town for the first seven years of her existence . . . and any competent behavioral psychologist will tell you that's long enough to bend the twig the way the tree will grow.

Denny fails to mention, for instance, that he didn't sell a single piece of property of any kind to anybody until after all of the events that have occurred so far in this book had taken place. Yet, thirty years later, when the people who could refute him were dead, he took credit for being father of Seattle.

And frankly, that kind of stuff ticks me off.

Twenty-five years after the doctor got here, the *Seattle Intelligencer*, (now the *Post Intelligencer*) put together Seattle's first directory of businesses. There were 208 of them—not counting somewhere between eighteen and fifty houses of prostitution which were thoughtfully omitted from the directory and had to be compiled from other sources.

Of the 208 businesses, *196* were in Maynardtown.

(Maynardtown's what today we call the Pioneer Square Historic District.)

These included every architect, attorney, bank, baker and confectioner, billiard parlor, blacksmith, boot and shoemaker, brewer, candy and nut store, chop house, drugstore, cigar manufacturer, Chinese laundry, butcher, commission merchant, civil engineer, dentist, restaurant, florist, whorehouse, fruit and vegetable market, gristmill, gunsmith, hotel, department store, jeweler, beer tavern, saloon, ladies wear store, marine architect and wholesale house.

Wholesale house.

That's the one that made Seattle important.

There were sixteen of them . . . five times as many as any other town on Puget Sound . . . even more wholesale houses than saloons . . . of which there were only thirteen.

But all of them were in Maynardtown.

Maynardtown was the heart of this city for the next fifty years.

The last hurrah

Doc Maynard died on March 13, 1873. Two days later, all of the shops in town were closed, and anybody who was anybody at all attended his funeral.

Presumably, that was the last hurrah for the man who invented Seattle. Fifteen years later, Arthur Denny wrote the first history of

MAYNARDTOWN
CIRCA 1859

McCAUSLAND

Seattle. He began the process of writing the doctor out of Seattle history. Following Denny's book there was a larger volume edited by Frederick James Grant, who frankly conceded in the preface that he had relied almost entirely on Denny for his information about the city's beginnings. Ninety-nine percent of the city's history has stemmed from Grant's volume.

Then, in 1906, Thomas Prosch wrote a slim monograph on David and Catherine Maynard in which he generally followed the "Party Line," but with one or two significant observations like the following:

"He was a home buyer, a protectionist, a friend to his nearest neighbors. Stepping into a shop one day he told the keeper, whom he had been patronizing for years, that he would not see him there anymore. 'Why doctor, what's the matter?' inquired his astonished friend.

"We are going to have a shop in Maynardtown, and I always stand by my own side and help my own people,' the doctor replied. The shop he was giving up was on Yesler's land, about sixty feet from Maynardtown.

"It was always this way with him. He favored the United States above all other nations; Washington Territory above all other American commonwealths; Seattle above all other towns or cities; and his own nearest neighbors above all other peoples."

When Harborview Medical Center was dedicated in 1931, a bust of the doctor was placed in the lobby. (It subsequently has been moldering away in the library.)

In 1951, when Murray Morgan's *Skidroad* appeared, his research revealed a quote from the floor at the doctor's funeral, "Without him, Seattle will never be the same. Without him, Seattle might not have been."

Now nearly thirty years later, this volume.

Is it the last hurrah?

I doubt it.

The Doctor, of course, couldn't have cared less what posterity thought of him. As far as he could tell at the time, there was nothing posterity ever had done for him. And he sure left the folks with plenty to think about—like "up your nose with a rubber hose" in his last public appearance. The doctor never minded astonishing the people of the town.

Let's face it, he enjoyed it.

Shortly before his death, an early-day shyster who made a practice of finding flaws in donation claims, discovered one in the doctor's. A question was raised over which of his wives was legally entitled to half of his donation claim. It obviously belonged to Catherine. She'd helped him develop it. And as long as the question remained with authorities in the territory, there was no problem. But when it got into the bureaucratic red tape in Washington, it became very serious indeed.

For $500 the shyster bought from Lydia whatever might be her rights to half of the Maynard donation claim. And, shortly before Maynard's death, she appeared on the scene . . .

Broke, naturally.

On the day of her arrival, Doc Maynard entered his favorite barber shop. (They were known as "shaving saloons" in those days.) "Dixon," he said, "I want you to fix me up in your best style." "What's up, doctor," the barber asked. "What are you going to do?" "I'm going to give the people here a sight they never had before and may never have again. I'm going to show them a man walking down the street with a wife on each arm." So Lydia lived with the doctor and Catherine while she was giving her depositions designed to deprive them of half their donation claim.

I can understand Lydia doing it . . .

But how in God's name did he talk Catherine into it?

And what a curve to pitch at the Sons of the Profits.

From the doctor's standpoint, he had accomplished his objective. Seattle was a vibrant, functioning city. But the Sons of the Profits had bought and paid for half of his donation claim. Would they have to pay for it again . . . At ten, maybe a hundred times the original price? As far as Doc Maynard was concerned, that was *their* problem. And, oh, yes. There was one final irony.

Madam Damnable was long gone . . . and the doctor and both wives were living in her mansion . . . on Maynard's Point . . . with a fabulous view of Mt. Rainier.

POSTSCRIPT
The Story Behind the Story

The first bound volume of any kind that treats with the history of Seattle was published by Arthur A. Denny in 1888. Entitled "Pioneer Days on Puget Sound," it came out fifteen years after David S. Maynard's death and was eighty-three pages long. It obviously was Denny's version of what happened.

Thanks entirely to Arthur Denny, who believed that anybody who took a drink was a "drunk," Doc Maynard's role in our history has been billed as that of the "town drunk." Whether or not he became the victim of what we now recognize as a disease called alcoholism in his later life is moot. He certainly was functioning with all of his faculties a month or so before his death. And it is completely evident that during the "Maynard Years," when the character of this city was formed, that disease was not at issue.

ACKNOWLEDGEMENTS, SOURCES, BIBLIOGRAPHY

The essence of this book lies in a labyrinth of hitherto untapped archival information. And particular thanks goes to the guides who provided me with conducted tours of the records.

The book is based on information provided by LEO BOYAJIAN of the Pioneer National Title Company. We traced ownership of the land from the original Donation Claims, found out who it was sold to and then determined what contribution these people made to the invention of Seattle. Most of the people who participated in the invention were left out of the early books, the first of which were not written until thirty-six years after the original stakes were driven . . . fifteen years after David S. Maynard's death.

The most astonishing piece of information revealed in this phase of research was that Arthur Denny, who always has been billed as the father of our city, didn't sell a single piece of land to anybody for the first six years . . . in other words, the period covered in this book.

I am totally indebted to NANCY PRYOR, TOM MAYER and KATHRYN HAMILTON of the Washington Room of the Washington State Library, who cheerfully unearthed archival information which I would not have believed possible. Tom uncovered the great gem of the book, which was the amount of money Doc Maynard got for the woodpile which financed the invention of Seattle. The question I put to Tom was, "How much did a cord of firewood sell for in San Francisco in 1851?" He went after the information with such aplomb that later somebody queried, "Did he ask, 'Let's see . . . was that alder, fir or cedar?' " Tom didn't ask that, but he did find out that firewood sold for forty dollars a cord in San Francisco at that time.

RUBY EL HULT provided me with in depth research in her unpublished manuscript, *Seattle: A Different Sort of Pioneering.*

I am particularly indebted to JACK and BARBARA HOLLOPETRE and my nephew, JACKIE HOLLOPETRE, who painstakingly unearthed the history of Cleveland, Ohio, for the period during which Doc Maynard functioned as physician and businessman there.

Further kudoes go to JIM McALPIN, Washington State Archivist, and to JIM MOORE who is in charge of the vast supply of archives stored at Western Washington University in Bellingham . . . to the MUSEUM OF HISTORY AND INDUSTRY of Seattle, which has some of Doc Maynard's actual surgical instruments . . . to DR. MARC SCHUCKIT of the Alcohol and Drug Abuse Program at the University of Washington whose advice has led to the conclusion that, historic legend to the contrary and notwithstanding, the disease of alcoholism played no role in the invention of Seattle.

I also wish to extend a vote of appreciation to LETA EDWARDS, director of community relations for Harborview Medical Center, for finding the bust of Doc Maynard where it had been kept from public view for fear that one of the Sons of the Profits might appropriate it for his own use.

To PAT ROBERTS, for work over and above the call of duty in keeping the proofs straight, and to BOB CRAM for the cartoons and jacket design, BOB McCAUSLAND, for the scenic illustrations and maps.

For seventy-two years the only extant picture of Doc Maynard has been a less-than-satisfactory rendition of him which appeared in Thomas Prosch's biography of the doctor in 1906. The sketches of the doctor which appear here and on the book jacket capture the spirit of the man at a glance. They were done by TED RAND, one of the Pacific Northwest's most talented artists. The Rand sketch was taken from a tintype of the doctor which Jim Hermanson of Port Townsend discovered in the files of the old Seaman's Hospital in Port Townsend, where the doctor practiced medicine occasionally in his later years.

I finally am indebted to MURRAY MORGAN who in 1951 captured the essence of Doc Maynard in his chapter in his book *Skidroad* entitled "Doc Maynard and the Indians, 1852-1873."

I am also indebted to BRUCE and RILEY GETTYS of Beaufort, South Carolina, for the interior description of Madam Damnable's handsome establishment. We visited the Gettys in the spring of 1978 and found their lovely home bore a striking resemblance to Seattle's first mansion. Through their kind permission, we took pictures of the interior and thus were able to provide the description which has been missing in all of our histories.

JIM HERMANSON of Port Townsend came up with a real find in the tintype of Dr. Maynard, from which the Ted Rand sketch on the cover of the jacket and the frontispiece were made.

Special thanks also go to newspaperman JACK LELAND, of Charleston, South Carolina, for the quote concerning the character of the people in that town and for directing us to the "Big Brick," Charleston's most famous House of Ill Repute, which functioned from 1819 to 1946 and proves that Seattle's was not the only fine establishment of its kind in the United States at the time.

Although I have not made as much use of their facilities in this book as I have in previous volumes, the Main Branch of the SEATTLE PUBLIC LIBRARY provided a comparison of the value of the dollar between 1852 and 1978 . . . and the UNIVERSITY OF WASHINGTON LIBRARY provided a copy of the letter about Dr. Maynard sent by Commander Swarthout to Governor Stevens.

Additional thanks to go MARY FLINTON of the Washington State Library who came across the story in the Lummi Indian magazine on the Point Elliott Treaty . . . and to ANNIE SWENSSON, who uncovered material on filling in of the tidelands.

SELECTED BIBLIOGRAPHY
BOOKS

(In this bibliography the presumption is made that people wishing to pursue the subjects further will have access to the normal published histories of Seattle, King County and the state of Washington. So they are not listed except in instances where direct quotes have been used.)

BAGLEY, CLARENCE B., *History of King County, History of Seattle;* BANCROFT, HUBERT HOWE, *History of Washington, Idaho and Montana, History of Oregon;* BEATON, WELFORD, *The City That Made Itself;* CANTWELL, ROBERT, *The Hidden Northwest;* COMAN, EDWIN T. Jr., and GIBBS, HELEN M., *Time, Tide and Timber;* CORNING, HOWARD M., *Dictionary of Oregon History;* COX, THOMAS R., *Mills and Markets, A History of the Pacific Coast Lumber Industry to 1900;* DENNY, ARTHUR A., *Pioneer Days on Puget Sound;* DENNY, EMILY INEZ, *Blazing the Way;* EVANS, ELWOOD, *History of the Pacific Northwest;* FEDERAL WRITERS' PROJECT, *Washington, Oregon;* GATES, CHARLES M., *The First Century of the University of Washington, Readings in Pacific Northwest History;* with DOROTHY O. JOHANSEN, *Empire of the Columbia;* GRANT, FREDERIC JAMES, *History of Seattle;* HENDRICKSON, JAMES E., *Joe Lane of Oregon;* HAZARD, JOSEPH T., *Companion of Adventure;* JOHNSON, EDWIN F., *Railroad to the Pacific, Northern Route;* KENNEDY, JAMES H., *The History of Cleveland;* LONGSWORTH, BASIL, *The Oregon Trail;* LYONS, CICELY, *Salmon, Our Heritage;* McCARTHY, RAYMOND G. and DOUGLASS, EDGAR M., *Alcohol and Social Responsibility;* MEANY, EDMOND S., *History of the State of Washington;* MEEKER, EZRA, *The Busy Life of Eighty-Five Years, Pioneer Reminiscences of Puget Sound;* MORGAN, MURRAY, *Skid Road;* MORRIS, RICHARD B., *Encyclopedia of American History;* NEWELL, GORDON, *Rogues, Buffoons & Statesmen;* PARKMAN, FRANCIS JR., *The Oregon Trail;* PROSCH, THOMAS W., *David S. Maynard and Catherine T. Maynard* and *A Chronological History of Seattle From 1850 to 1897;* ROSE, WILLIAM GANSON, *Cleveland: The Making of a City;* ROSENBERG, CHARLES E., *The Cholera Years;* SAYRE, J. WILLIS, *This City of Ours;* SNOWDEN, CLINTON A., *History of Washington;* STEVENS, HAZARD, *Life of General Isaac I. Stevens;* SWAN, JAMES G., *The Northwest Coast.*

GENERAL

BEGINNINGS, PROGRESS AND ACHIEVEMENTS IN THE MEDICAL WORK OF KING COUNTY; C. B. BUSSELL, *Tidelands, Their Story;* HERRICK, RUTH E., *Cherry Grove;* ILLINOIS GUIDE & GAZETTEER, *Abingdon Through Zion;* AKIN, JAMES JR., *(Oregon Trail) Journal;* BEARDSLEY, ARTHUR S., *The Bench and Bar in Washington, First Fifty Years,* (unpublished manuscript No. 35, Washington State Library photocopy of restricted manuscript); BODEMER, CHARLES W., *Glory, God and Gold: Medicine Comes to the Pacific Northwest;* BUNDY, GEORGE, *Maynard Point and Its Upstart Neighbor, the Community of Seattle;* CARVER, MARGARET R. AND FRED E., *The Ancestors and Descendants of Jonathan Simmons and Mary Troutman and of Their Children;* CHEHALIS BEE

NUGGET, August 28, 1931, *A Review of Three Pioneer Lives of the Southwest;* COLLIAS, EUGENE E. and WESTLEY, RON, *Tide Heights for July 1859 at Seattle;* CONOVER, C. T., (Seattle Times, October 11, 1959), *Charles Plummer had Many Business Activities;* COWLITZ COUNTY HISTORICAL QUARTERLY, February, 1967, *The Blanchet Family;* DIMOCK, ARTHUR H., Transactions of the American Society of Civil Engineers, 1926, *Preparing the Groundwork for a City; The Regrading of Seattle, Washington;* DORRIS, JONATHAN TRUMAN, (Ye Galleon Press, Fairfield, Wash.), *The Oregon Trail;* EL HULT, RUBY, (unpublished manuscript), *Seattle: A Different Sort of Pioneering;* FARRAR, VICTOR J., *Diary of Colonel and Mrs. I. N. Ebey;* FINGER, JOHN R., *Seattle's First Sawmill, 1853-1869;* GENINI, RONALD, (Journal of the West, Vol. 11, No. 3, July, 1972), *The Fraser and Cariboo Gold Rushes and Contrasts with California;* GRIFFIN, RICHARD T., (Penthouse Magazine), *Grandma Was a Junkie;* HINES, GEORGE, (manuscript, Washington State Library), *Biography of George A. Barnes;* HOWARD-JONES, NORMAN, (Journal of the History of Medicine and Allied Sciences, Oct., 1972), *Cholera Therapy in the Nineteenth Century;* THE INTELLIGENCER, (Monday, March 17, 1873), *Death of Old Pioneer—Dr. David S. Maynard;* LENOX, EDWARD HENRY, *Overland to Oregon;* LOCKLEY, FREDERICK (Ye Galleon Press), *Recollections of Benjamin Franklin Bonney, Reminiscences of Col. Henry Ernst Dosch, Captain Sol Tethero, Wagon Train Master,* and, *To Oregon by Ox-Team in 1847;* LONGSWORTH, BASIL NELSON, *Memorandum of Thoughts, Reflections & Transactions as Transcribed on His Journey from Washington Township, Guernsey County, Ohio, to Oregon in the Summer of 1853;* KRENMAYR, JANICE, (Seattle Times, January 5, 1975), *"The Earth Is Our Mother," Who Really Said That?;* LOVETTE, LELAND P., (United States Naval Institute, 1939), *An Attempt at Mutiny;* McBRIDE, DELBERT J., (curator, State Capitol Museum), *Governor Isaac Ingalls Stevens and the Treaties with the Nisqually Indians, An Examination of the Promises Made to the Indians in December, 1854, and the Manner in Which They Were Kept;* McDONALD, LUCILLE (Seattle Times, March 28, 1954), *Washington's First Territorial Secretary;* (Seattle Times, May 25, 1958), *James Tilton, Territorial Surveyor;* MAHLBERG, BLANCHE BILLINGS (Pacific Northwest Quarterly, October, 1953), *Edward J. Allen, Pioneer and Roadbuilder;* MEANY, EDMOND S. (Washington Historical Quarterly, July, 1924), *Chief Patkanim,* (Washington Historical Quarterly, January, 1922), *The Cowlitz Convention; Inception of Washington Territory;* OREGON STATESMAN, November 8, 1853, (Story about George N. McConaha); OREGON SPECTATOR, December 4, 1850 (Prices obtained for the sale of firewood in San Francisco); PHELPS, THOMAS (Ye Galleon Press), *Reminiscences of Seattle, Washington Territory, and of the U.S. Sloop-of-War Decatur During the Indian War of 1855-1856;* RICH, JOHN M., *Chief Seattle's Unanswered Challenge;* PRATT, FLETCHER, *The Navy, A History;* SEATTLE GAZETTE, January 9, 1864, p. 3, ads for Doc Maynard's Hospital, Plummer's and Dexter Horton's stores and A. B. Rabbeson's saloon; SEATTLE TIMES, July 4, 1896, *Aged Mrs. Maynard; She Talks About Seattle;* SQUOL QUOL, Vol. 1, No. 1, 1973 (Lummi Indian magazine), *Point Elliott, 1855;* STRACHAN, MARGARET PITCAIRN (Seattle Times, Dec. 3, 1954), *Early-Day Mansions, No. 14—Plummer;* SYME, LEONARD, *Personality Characteristics and the Alcoholic;* TARBILL, V. V.,

(Harvard Business Review, July, 1930), *Mountain-Moving in Seattle;* WALKER, ANNA SLOAN, (Washington Historical Quarterly, April, 1914), *History of the Liquor Laws of the State of Washington, and, WARD, D.B., Across the Plains in 1853.*

GOVERNMENT SOURCES

BUREAU OF INDIAN AFFAIRS, U.S. DEPARTMENT OF INTERIOR, DOCKET 109, *The Duwamish Tribe of Indians, petitioner, vs The United States of America, defendant, July 6, 1959;* CONGRESSIONAL GLOBE, pp 540-542, Feb. 8, 1853; HOUSE JOURNAL, WASHINGTON TERRITORY, March 25, April 12, April 14, 1854, Prohibition legislation; JUDICIAL RECORDS, Division of Archives, State of Washington, Third Territorial District Court, 1852-1859, King County Probate Court, 1852-1891; SISLER, H. H., *Fifth Annual Report of the King County Road Engineer, 1939;* MICROCOPY OF RECORDS IN THE NATIONAL ARCHIVES, WASHINGTON SUPERINTENDENCY OF INDIAN AFFAIRS, 1853-1874, Microfilm Number 5. *Letters from Sub-Indian Agent, David S. Maynard, Fort Kitsap, to Governor Isaac Ingalls Stevens; Letter from Henry L. Yesler to Acting Governor Charles H. Mason, and Mason's Reply to Yesler;* WASHINGTON (TERRITORY) VOLUNTEER RECORDS, 1854-1858, Manuscript Number 28 at Washington State Library, *Receipt to Chief Patkanim for Indian heads and amount paid him and his tribe* and *Letter from Bishop A.M.A. Blanchet to Governor Stevens;* OREGON HISTORICAL SOCIETY, Papers of the Provisional Territorial Government of Oregon, 1841-1859.

INDEX

A NOTE ON DESIGN

The text of this book is set in 11 point Souvenir Light, chapter headings in 24 point *Souvenir Light Italic* and subheads in 14 point **Souvenir Medium.** The text is printed on Gladfelter Emerson, substance 55, and the endsheets and jacket on Whiting Crestline felt, substance 70. It was printed on a Cameron Belt Press, perfect bound and cased in Holliston Novelex binding cloth.

Doc Maynard's cover portrait is by Ted Rand. Text illustrations are by Bob Cram and terrain maps and sketches are Bob McCausland. Composition by Vashon Graphics, Vashon, Washington. Design and production are by William C. Speidel.